Dedication

This book is dedicated to both my grandfathers, Myddrin Evans and Stanley Cureton, who worked in the pits of South Wales, spending most of their working lives in Trelewis Drift and Merthyr Vale Collery, respectively. They went down the pit as young boys...emerging as men.

Acknowledgments

To all at Merthyr Writes for your constant encouragement and support. Namely: Thea Phillips, Betty Osment, Claire Jones and Val Williams. My deepest gratitude.

Thanks go to:

Graham Watkins [author of 'The Iron Masters'] and Sallyann Cole for your proofreading skills.

Special Mention

For my ancestor, William Harman, who was born in Merthyr Tydfil in 1820. He became a member of the Church of Jesus Christ of Latter-day Saints and emigrated to Utah.

Before leaving, he was offered the chance to become sole beneficiary in the will of wealthy Uncle Edmund Harman, on the proviso that he renounce his religion. Instead, he chose his faith and 'Zion', Salt Lake City in Utah.

An acknowledgement to all the brave men and women who followed The Mormon Trail, remaining true to their faith and themselves.

Early Praise for Black Diamonds

"Lynette Rees takes the reader through the many twists and unexpected turns of the story with skill so that the pace of the novel never flags, creating a page-turner. There is a great deal of warmth and emotion in the novel which reveals the true nature of the Welsh peoples. Highly recommended."

Reviewed by Gwen Madoc author of
"No Child of Mine" and
"Daughter of Shame"

"The heroine is a character with whom the reader will immediately relate to and share all her trials and tribulations. Her life becomes a roller coaster in more ways than one, with the reader becoming gripped by all her adventures, good and bad.I cannot recommend this book highly enough. It will keep you reading through the day and night, as you will be unable to put it down. I look forward to the sequel, as I keep wondering what will happen next in this enthralling saga."

Reviewed by Thea Horton author of
"The French Letter King."

Lily Jenkin, a collier's daughter in South Wales, waits forlornly at the pit head as miner's bodies are bought to the surface. There has been an explosion underground and her brothers are missing. So begins the story of a working class woman in a pit village, graphically drawn by the Rees. Black Diamonds is a novel about love, class division, maternal jealousy and forgiveness. Rees writes with passion and, I found, her attention to detail illuminated the mundane grind of daily life. As the story progresses, Lily grows in confidence and learns to deal with the complexities of marriage to a minster, the temptation of a new life and wagging tongues. What more can I say without spoiling the ending?

Reviewed by Graham Watkins author of "The Ironmasters"

Excerpt

It was no good. She was going to have to do something to attract their attention. "I am willing to pay," she continued as they stopped mid flow, "a shilling to anyone who knows where he might be."

A woman wearing a low cut red dress, showing off ample cleavage, walked towards her. "I know him!" she said, holding out her filthy palm for the shilling.

"You have to tell me what you know first," Lily told the woman.

"All right then, dearie." The woman flung back her dark locks and pursed her painted lips. "He was here not a couple of days since, in that tavern behind me. He got into a fight with a man."

"What sort of a man?"

"I don't know, do I? He looked a bit upper crust if you ask me. Think he might be one of the bosses from the iron works."

"What happened then?"

"Look darling, if you want more information than that, I'm going to want more than a bloody shilling for my time."

William Morgan stepped forward. "Mind your language, Madam, please!"

The woman shrugged and stared at Lily in expectation, whilst holding out her grubby palm, her nails caked black.

Lily took a deep breath in and nodded. Undoing the stings on her purse, she pulled out another shilling. It was money she could ill afford, but if it helped get her brother back then it would be worth every penny.

The woman smiled, flashing her teeth. If she had a good bath, combed her hair and wore the right clothing, she could pass for a beauty, but as it was, it was obvious from her very manner that she was a prostitute. How anyone could live like that was beyond Lily.

"Come with me," the woman said in a whisper, snatching the coin from Lily's hand as she led her around the corner. Mr. Morgan gave the woman a hard stare.

"It's all right, Mr. Morgan," Lily reassured, "If I don't come back within a few minutes, you are quite at liberty to follow after me..."

PART ONE

Chapter One

Lily Jenkin took the silver shilling from the old lady's outstretched, gnarled hand and handed her three shiny farthings change.

"Thank you, *cariad.*" Mrs Jones placed a loaf of bread, potatoes, carrots and a small pat of butter into her basket. "How's your first day going working here?"

Lily looked up. "Oh very good, Mrs Jones. I'm settling in here quite well. Mr. and Mrs Morgan have been ever so good to me." She slipped a strand of hair that had worked loose, under her mop cap and smiled.

The elderly woman nodded. "Glad to hear it, Lily. You take care that Mr. Morgan doesn't run you ragged my girl. Our Gwyneth worked here last year and he was always making her work extra hours. Now she has a good job mind you, working for Dr Owen, cleaning for him and his good wife." She lowered her voice to barely a whisper. "They are good employers, the Morgans, I suppose. They will always pay you on time. It's just that Mr. and Mrs Morgan like to get their money's worth. Are you understanding me?"

Lily nodded. She knew the woman had her best interests at heart, but she didn't want to hear anything bad about her new employers, especially not on her first day at the shop. All she wanted to do was to get the job done and create a good impression. She was lucky to have been offered the job in the village in the first place.

"Now, I'll bid you good day. And don't forget what I've told you."

"I won't," Lily said brightly. She breathed a sigh of relief as Mrs Jones let herself out through the shop door, the overhead bell jangling behind her.

"Lily!" Elsa Morgan's voice emanated from the back room, their living quarters.

Lily brushed down her apron and smoothed down the skirts of her dress. "Yes, Mrs Morgan?"

"Come and make a cup of tea for us, will you dear, please?"

"Yes, Mrs Morgan."

At least her employers allowed her to brew up and take short breaks. She didn't need telling twice how lucky she was to have this job and the extra money helped Mam with the housekeeping. Her elder brothers, Delwyn and Dafydd, contributed with the money they earned from the Gethin Pit, but since their father had died last year, it had been a struggle for her mother.

Mrs Morgan settled herself down at the table in the Spartan living room she shared with her husband. "The kettle has just boiled, Lily. If you can fetch the tea from the caddy in the cupboard and there's milk in the pantry."

"Yes, Mrs Morgan." Lily busied herself making the tea and handed a cup to her employer. "Will Mr. Morgan be joining us?"

"No, Lily. He's gone into Merthyr on business today. He's taken the pony and trap."

"I see," Lily said, waiting for Mrs Morgan to invite her to sit down.

When she did, Lily shyly settled herself down at the table opposite her employer, who was a large, silver-haired lady, with an ample bosom. She would have liked to have asked her what the business Mr. Morgan was getting up to in Merthyr, but that would have been too forward, rude her mother would have called it. It wasn't that she was particularly nosy; more that she had a natural curiosity.

"Sorry, Lily. I forgot to mention... there are some Welsh cakes in a tin in the cupboard as well. Would you like one?"

Lily nodded eagerly. "Oh, yes please, Mrs Morgan."

Mrs Morgan heaved her heavy frame out of the chair and returned with a plate of lovely looking, sugar-coated cakes, offering one to Lily.

"I made them myself last night. Mr. Morgan is partial to a nice Welsh cake, although his favourite cake is *Teisen Lap*," she announced proudly.

"I love all cakes myself, Mrs Morgan. Sorry, I suppose that makes me sound somewhat of a glutton."

Mrs Morgan laughed, her full cheeks rosy and blue eyes gleaming. Lily had a feeling she was going to get on well with the elderly lady.

"Now tell me, Lily. You have two brothers?"

"Yes. Delwyn and Dafydd. They're twins, a few years older than me. They're both colliers at the Gethin Pit. Hewers they both are."

"Is that where your father works too, Lily?"

Lily felt a lump rising in her throat at the mention of her father.

Taking a steadying breath, she said, "Yes, Mrs Morgan. I mean it was where he worked but…"

"What's the matter child?" Mrs Morgan's eyes were full of compassion.

"He died last year. He had consumption."

"Oh, I'm sorry to hear that. I haven't lived in Abercanaid that long you see. William and I moved here last year, so I don't know everyone in the village, only those that I see in the shop and those that come in to gossip."

"Yes, well, you would only have seen me coming here to shop, not my mother. She doesn't go out any more, see. Not since Dad passed away. She still wears black and only goes to chapel on Sunday."

Elsa Morgan nodded. "Yes. It can be hard to lose someone, believe me I know all about that. I was married myself and became widowed a few years ago. A good man he was and all. Then about a year ago I met William and we got married."

A sudden rumble shook the room and Lily watched as the crockery on the shelf rattled. She looked at Mrs Morgan in puzzlement. "Is it some kind of earth tremor?"

The elderly woman shook her head. "I'm not so sure, Lily...I'll pop outside and see if anyone knows what's going on...Stay here, *cariad*. I'll see to it. You drink your tea; you will have enough work to be getting on with later."

Lily smiled and took a sip of tea. It was nice to know she had an employer she could talk to and who seemed concerned with her welfare.

By the time she had finished her tea, she heard the shop bell jangle and hushed voices inside. Mrs Morgan returned, her face ashen and eyes wide and alert.

"I'm sorry Lily. You have to go."

"Go, Mrs Morgan. What have I done? Have I done something wrong today, please tell me."

"No dear. It's the pit. There's been an accident. Are your brothers in work today?"

Lily's legs felt boneless and her stomach flipped over as she struggled to think. Yes of course they were in work today, she had heard them getting ready early this morning. She had even heard them lighting the fire and chatting in the scullery and then closing the door behind them as their hob nail boots clattered on the cobbles outside Chapel Square.

She swallowed, her mouth now dry, like a piece of parchment paper. "Yes. What shall I do? I can't think straight Mrs Morgan. Shall I go and get my mother?"

"No, *cariad.* I'll go and see to your Mam. Mrs Jones came into see me, she'll watch the shop. You get off over to Gethin. Check that your brothers are all right." The urgency in her employer's voice chilled Lily to the bone as she slipped her woollen shawl off the hook and cradled it around her shoulders as if it would somehow protect her from the anxiety she was now experiencing.

* * *

When Lily arrived at the pit her stomach lurched with fear as she made her way through the crowd of onlookers.

"There's a young boy from Pond Row trapped in there." She heard one of the women saying. "He's only thirteen years old, recently gone into long trousers. I can't bear it."

"What happened here?" Lily asked, still in a state of shock as everything had happened so suddenly.

"There was an explosion. A lot of men and boys are trapped underground, see. It doesn't look good—" one of a group of women said, her heavily hooded eyes filling with tears as she focused on the scene before her. Acrid smoke emanated from the pit entrance. The men scurried around to help with the rescue as the women clung to one another as they worried about their loved ones.

Drawing closer to the onlookers, Lily asked, "Have any of the men got out yet?"

The lady shook her head and muttered something in Welsh under her breath.

Lily's knees buckled as she swayed, someone grabbed hold of her from behind and shouted, "Make a bit of room by there, the lady has fainted." She thought she recognised the man's voice from somewhere, but wasn't entirely sure. She felt herself being lifted and carried over to a grassy bank and a light tapping on her cheek.

"Come on now, there's a good girl." Opening her eyes, she saw the face of Evan Davies, gazing down on her. How had she ended up in his arms? She had only known him for a few weeks, he was the handsome new minister at the chapel.

"I am all right, Mr. Davies," she said breathlessly. "I'm just concerned about my two brothers. They are on duty today."

"I know them, Delwyn and Dafydd. I remember meeting them last week during the chapel service. I'll see if I can find out anything for you, Lily. Now you stay where you are, keep your head down to stop you fainting again."

Lily felt safe in Evan's hands. He was a good man. She watched as he pushed his way through the crowds, asking as he went along had anyone heard any news about the men below.

A few minutes later, Evan returned to her side. "There is not a lot of news I'm afraid. It looks as though several of the pit ponies have died in the explosion and they have to be moved before anyone can get to the men. I'm going to do what I can to help. I promise I'll come back the moment I hear anything about your brothers."

Lily nodded. She had little choice, all she could do was wait. "Thank you Mr. Davies," she said.

Evan turned around and shouted back, "Pray Lily. Everyone could do with your prayers right now. If you are feeling up to it, get everyone together to pray."

"Yes. I will." He had given her the motivation to do something that might really help. She believed in God and praying had really helped her when her father was ill and afterwards too.

Getting herself up onto her feet, she brushed down her skirt and made her way over to a crowd of women, who were becoming hysterical with fear.

"Ladies," she interrupted them, "Mr. Evan Davies, the minister has requested that we all pray for the men and boys in there. He has gone to see what he can do for them."

"What bloody use is that?" An Irish voice in the crowd shouted out fiercely, "The poor bastards in there, need more than that. How is praying going to help them?"

"Thomas Shanklin, you should be ashamed of yourself." Lily recognised the voice of Mrs Edwards, her neighbour at Chapel Square, who was now prodding the man in the arm, "Of course praying is a good thing to do, and it is what every God fearing person around here should be doing. You heathen, you!"

Tom Shanklin looked down at the ground as if he was ashamed of himself. Mrs Edwards beckoned Lily over to where she stood and all the women linked hands and started to say the Lord's Prayer in Welsh. Lily felt a roughened hand taking hers and her heart felt gladdened as she glanced sideways, realising it was Tom himself who was joining in with the group.

After the prayer was over, he looked at her and apologised, removing his Dai cap, squeezing it between both hands as if his very life depended upon it. "I didn't mean no harm, Miss. It's just I feel so helpless, see. I was laid off from the pit a month ago on account of my gammy leg. I was buried alive under a pile of coal and my leg hasn't been right since. I find the constant pain wears me down and makes me say things that maybe sometimes, I shouldn't. And especially in front of a lady, like yourself."

Lily smiled at him. "That's all right. We all react differently in unpleasant circumstances, Mr. Shanklin."

"Well, I shouldn't have. My missus says that I should count my lucky stars that I'm still alive. And of course, if I hadn't had that accident in the first place, I could well be in there with the men right now."

Lily tasted the bitterness of bile at the thought of what had gone on in there. Then she heard a voice call out her name. Thank goodness, Delwyn had appeared amongst the crowd, striding through to hug her. "I'm fine, *cariad*. I don't know about Dafydd though."

The white of his eyes and teeth shone through the black dust that covered every inch of his face. Lily wanted to hug him forever, but eventually, he pulled away. "I have to go now, I need to help bring the pit ponies out. Some of the men are still alive down there, I've heard them."

"And the others?" Lily didn't need an answer, she already knew as he shook his head and ran back in the direction of the pit.

Lily waited breathlessly as she watched the men haul out the dead ponies who had got in the way of the rescue. It was bad enough watching their lifeless bodies, never mind the men's, it just didn't bear thinking about.

Feeling a hand on her shoulder, she spun around. "Oh Mam." She hugged her mother and sobbed into the shoulder of her shawl. It must have taken a lot for her mother to have left the house.

"Now, now, Lily," her mother comforted as Mrs Morgan stood by her side. "It will be all right. One of the neighbours just told me, so I rushed down here as quick as I could. Your brothers are strong boys." A pang of guilt coursed through her for laying her fears on her mother after all the loss she had been through recently, and now not knowing if Dafydd was dead or alive, and if he was alive, if he was injured.

"Mam!" she exclaimed as soon as she could. "Delwyn is fine. I've seen him."

"You have?" her mother asked, holding her at arm's length to look into her daughter's eyes.

"Yes, he's gone to help with the rescue. There he is, see, he's been helping to move the dead pit ponies."

"Praise to the Lord." Her mother closed her eyes with thankfulness. Then, opening them again said, "I suppose there is no news of Dafydd?"

"Not yet Mam." She knew she needed to be strong for her mother. "But we've all prayed. That's about all we can do for now." Her mother said nothing, just squeezed Lily's hand.

Lily turned to see her employer stood next to her. "I've closed up the shop for time being..." she explained. "I'll think I'll go and make some tea for the men. They look as though they could do with it. Would you like to come and help me?" she asked, looking at Lily.

Of course, it was natural that Lily should want to stay until she was sure that Dafydd was safe, but it would give her something else to think about and a way of helping out, after all, she should still be on duty at the shop.

"Do you mind, Mam, if I go?"

Her mother shook her head. "I'll wait here with the other women, if I need you, I'll come to the shop."

Lily walked back to the shop with Mrs Morgan and they got down to the task of brewing up copious amounts of tea and slicing and buttering bread for everyone. "They will be there for hours yet," Mrs Morgan explained. "Believe me, Lily, I know. Where my first husband worked there was a pit accident and they were days digging out the bodies."

Lily shivered, then Mrs Morgan draped a hand around her shoulder. "Sorry Lily. I didn't mean to scare you, but we have to face the facts, there are going to be some deaths."

Lily nodded, knowing full well that Mrs Morgan was right. "Now, you take a tray with cups and the tin jug of tea, and the plate of bread to the men, and tell the women they are quite welcome to come back here for a cup of tea themselves while they are waiting for news." Lily put her shawl back on and carried the tray out of doors, wondering what she was about to face.

* * *

When she arrived back at the scene, the crowd had increased and now some of the men had been brought to the surface and laid on beds of straw. She could tell that already some were dead as Evan Davies dropped to his knees and prayed over the bodies. Pushing her way through the crowds she handed out cups of tea and wedges of bread to the grateful men, who needed to keep their strength up.

Handing a cup over to Delwyn, she was about to ask about their brother when he shook his head. "No news yet, Lily. I have seen Mam and told her the same." Lily experienced a sliver of desolation as she walked away and then, remembering Evan Davies, when she could see that he had finished praying, handed him a cup of tea.

"Thank you, Lily. That is so kind of you," he said, looking up into her eyes. Any other time and she would have been mesmerised by his kindly green eyes, but not right now. It did not feel right somehow.

"Don't thank me, Mr. Davies. It is the kindness of Mrs Morgan that is responsible for all of this, I am just the errand girl."

He smiled. "Nevertheless, you do yourself a great disservice; you have done your bit here, praying with the women and bringing us sustenance."

"It was the least I could do," she said. Then walked towards the crowd of women where her mother stood, some were now openly weeping, wiping their eyes on their pinafores or on the edge of their shawls, it was desolation of the highest order.

"Mam!" Lily took her mother to one side, "Mrs Morgan wants the women to know they are welcome to come back to the shop for a cup of tea while they are waiting for news."

"I'll inform them in a moment, but I doubt any will leave, Lily. That young lad from Pond Row, his mother is standing there waiting," she pointed to a woman, who then dropped to her knees as she sobbed uncontrollably. "She was screaming out a few minutes ago, saying he is only a baby. Too young to have gone down the pit."

Lily bit her lip. It was true, a lot of these were young lads that had no choice.

She held her breath as she heard someone in the distance start singing an old Welsh hymn and people everywhere began to join in. It was only a few days before Christmas, what sort of Christmas would any of them have now?

* * *

Lily returned to the shop with the empty cups to see Mrs Morgan bringing in the sacks of vegetables from outside, a sure sign she was closing for the day. "No one come back with you then?" Mrs Morgan looked at her in expectation as she laid down her heavy load.

Lily shook her head. "They don't want to leave, in case anyone is brought out. Here, let me help you Mrs Morgan." She laid down her own load inside, then carried both sacks into the shop for her grateful employer. Mrs Morgan locked the front door from the inside and they retired into the back room.

"I thought the women would want to stay. I'll brew up some more tea and you can take it out to them, Lily. Now will you wash up those dirty cups for me as we'll need to reuse them?"

"Of course I will, Mrs Morgan. You are such a good person."

Mrs Morgan beamed, but Lily thought she detected a sadness beneath her blue eyes.

Lily heard the back door opening and Mr. Morgan stood there with his hat in his hand.

"What on earth is going on, I can see there is some sort of commotion going on at Gethin?" he asked, looking at his wife for direction.

"Oh William..." She walked over to where he stood and hugged him. "It's the miners from the pit. There was an explosion and most of them are still trapped down there. It's awful. Lily and I have been brewing up tea the past hour or so. Get yourself over there, to see what you can do."

Although Mr. Morgan looked weary, he laid down his best hat on the kitchen table. He shook his head sadly and went in search of a shovel. "Can one of you ladies feed the horse for me when I am gone, then?" Lily nodded. "She's tired after that trip to Merthyr today."

"There are some vegetable peelings in a bucket by the back door." Mrs Morgan explained to Lily. "Take it over to the field for her and then stable her for the night."

"Yes, Mrs Morgan." Lily draped her shawl around her shoulders, the day was getting colder. She followed Mr. Morgan outside the back door, carrying a lantern Mrs Morgan had insisted she take. As she turned to go up the canal bank, Mr. Morgan pulled her to one side.

"How is my wife?" he asked. This puzzled Lily. Was something wrong?

"She's been fine Mr. Morgan. A great pillar of strength. Why are you asking?"

"It's just that is how she lost her first husband see, in a mining accident."

Lily's jaw dropped. Poor Mrs Morgan, it must have been hard on her having to relive that again. Her admiration for the lady grew even more after hearing that.

"Don't worry Mr. Morgan. I shall keep a watchful eye over her and make sure she does not wear herself out."

"You're a good girl Lily." He walked off with his shoulders held back, towards the pit. It would get dark soon and the rescue work would be that much harder for the men. As soon as she had fed the horse, she was going to go back to see if there was news about her brother and the rest of the men. The little boy from Pond Row kept going through her mind. She had often seen him in the village going on errands to various shops for his Mam. She hoped he was all right.

The horse was fine when she got to the field, just offside the bank. Once she had completed her task, she dropped the bucket in the field and went off at a fast pace towards the pit. When she arrived, her mother was sitting on the grass, shoulders wracking with what Lily presumed was grief. Dafydd, he had to be dead.

"Oh Mam," she said, falling down onto her knees. "Is Dafydd gone?"

"No, he's still alive, Lily." Evan Davies just came over to tell me, he's crushed mind you. He doesn't know how badly, but he's alive." She squeezed Lily's hand. Her mother's hand was ice-cold. There was snow on the way, Lily sensed the temperature had dropped and the sky that day had been a slate grey colour from its onset.

"They're trying to get him out now," Evan Davies said breathlessly, coming over to where Lily knelt. He put his hand on her shoulder in quiet reassurance. "He's going to be fine. I have bad news for someone though," he said thoughtfully.

"Is it anyone I might know?" Lily looked up, hoping upon hope, that it was no one she had any knowledge of—that would make things a thousand times worse.

"I'm afraid, so, Lily. Mrs Thomas from Rhydycar, standing with that group over by there, her husband is dead. I'm just going to have to break the news to her."

"Would you like me to come with you?" Lily offered.

"Yes, that would be most helpful." A look of relief passed over Evan's features. It was good to feel that she was a help in some way to him. She rose to her feet and brushed the skirt of her dress.

"Once you have told her, I will take her back to Mrs Morgan's. She is in for a terrible shock."

It was going to be an awful time for the people of Abercanaid and the surrounding areas, men came from all over to work in the pit. She knew Mrs Morgan would not mind her taking the ladies back to the shop, she would stay up all night if needs be.

Mrs Thomas trembled and then her legs gave way from beneath her when she heard the news. Someone whispered that she was pregnant. *How awful, for that poor child, who will never know its father,* Lily thought. She roused the woman by tapping her cheek and then uttered a quiet prayer over her. It was all any of them had for now.

Helping her onto her feet, Lily walked the woman over to the shop. Rapping urgently on the back door, until they were both allowed into the warmth of the back room, where Mrs Morgan had a nice fire on the go.

"You go back to the pit, Lily," Mrs Morgan advised, "I am sure there will be many more that need bringing back here tonight.

They can't go home in the dark anyway; I will let them stay here. I'll warm Mrs Thomas up with a nice hot drink."

"She's in the family way," Lily whispered under her breath.

Mrs Morgan nodded as she took on board the information she had been given. Lily was afraid that the poor woman would lose the baby after the shock she had just received.

Lily sat her down at the kitchen table. "There, there, warm yourself up now. It is not good for you and the baby to get too cold, the winter has been really cold this year."

Mrs Thomas nodded and sat herself down at the table. Mrs Morgan put a cup of tea in front of her, but it was several moments before the woman even noticed it was there as she stared into the crackling flames of the fire.

What could possibly be going through her mind right now? Lily wondered. She hated to think what it was and what would be going through the minds of others that lost loved ones too.

"Lily are you all right, *cariad*?" Mrs Morgan searched deep into her eyes.

"Yes, Mrs Morgan. They have found our Dafydd. He's still trapped, but they hope to get him out soon, he has some crush injuries. I don't know how we will get him back home though."

"Not to worry. Mr. Morgan can take him and your Mam back home with the pony and trap. It will be the best place for him to recover. Are there any signs of any doctors as yet, Lily?"

Lily shook her head and sat down opposite Mrs Thomas as finally, she sipped the strong sweet tea.

"Is there anyone you need to inform?" she asked, stretching out and touching the woman's pallid hand across the table.

She shook her head and then patted her swollen belly. Then, raising her dark-rimmed eyes to meet with Lily's, said, "Sorry, yes. My husband's mother works as a housekeeper to a family in Twynyrodyn."

"Well, if you give me the address, I'll see if I can get someone to pass a message on for you."

The woman looked up and gave a wan smile. Lily felt utterly helpless in the situation, what was she supposed to say to someone who had just lost her husband? One of the women had informed her they had only been married for one year. Mrs Thomas's life was about to change forever and Lily was very sad about that.

When Mrs Thomas had finished her cup of tea and refused a slice of cake, Mrs Morgan went upstairs to make up the spare bed for her. "She's going to need all the rest she can get, poor mite. Lily, you get off and try to find out how your brother is, you must be very anxious, *cariad*?"

"I am, yes. I'm going to see if there is any more I can do. At least I know Dafydd is still alive," she muttered under her breath, as Mrs Thomas continued to stare in the flames of the fire.

Lily didn't know how many times she had crossed the bank that day, she had almost lost count. Arriving at the pit, she saw two ladies guiding another through the crowd, who was inconsolable with grief. The woman's guttural cry sent shivers down Lily's spine.

"It's her son," one of them explained as they passed by, "only thirteen years old..."

Of course it was the young lad from Pond Row. Too young to die, what had he seen of life?

An icy wind blew in Lily's direction causing her to wrap her shawl even tighter around her shoulders.

Evan Davies was still there, attending to the men with another, older man, whom she recognised as Doctor Owen.

Groans permeated from all around her, so that it was difficult to locate where they were coming from.

"Do they know what has caused this terrible explosion yet?" she asked a man in the crowd.

"They think it was a naked flame and a build up of coal gas. Those men never stood a chance in there. Those bloody Crawshays have got a lot to answer for." Lily knew that a lot of folk despised the Crawshay family who ran the Iron Works at Cyfarthfa and owned Gethin Pit. They had a reputation locally as being hard taskmasters.

"Lily!" A man's voice called out behind her and she turned around to see her brother lying on the ground with another miner attending to him.

Retching, as she saw his skin cut open wide, and the pool of blood that had seeped out around his injured limb, she fought back the wave of nausea that swept over her.

"It's all right, Lily," Dafydd winced, "it's not as bad as it appears, I was one of the lucky ones."

Composing herself, she took a deep breath. Whatever she did, she knew she mustn't alarm Dafydd by her reaction. "Have you broken it?"

"Looks like it," interrupted the other collier, "but it seems a clean break, so it should knit back together nicely."

Those poor men, they are making light of a bad situation. How I admire their bravery, she thought.

"Where has Delwyn got to?" she asked.

"He's over there with Mam, they're helping some of the casualties."

Lily looked around and was relieved to see both her mother and Delwyn helping out two young boys, who didn't appear to be badly injured, more stunned. One, who looked not much older than ten years old, was sobbing his heart out.

As she approached, her mother said, "Thank goodness you are here, Lily. Can you please take young Richard home to his sister? His mother wants to wait to see if there is any news about their father."

Lily nodded. "Oh Mam, do not worry about Dafydd getting home, Mrs Morgan says we can use their pony and trap."

"That is such a relief..." her mother dusted herself down and pulled her shawl around her shoulders.

Lily walked young Richard back to his home in Pond Row, only a couple of doors away from the dead boy's house. She knocked at the door of the house-over-house style building, where some families lived on the top and others in the cellars below. As the door opened slowly, she noticed his sister Hannah's red-rimmed eyes.

"I've just brought your brother back."

The young girl, who could have been no more than fourteen, fell to her knees and hugged her coal-blackened brother.

"Thank you so much," she wept. Then getting back onto her feet, "Have you heard anything about our Dad?" She stood in wide-eyed anticipation.

"I am afraid not. There are still a lot of miners trapped there, but your mother is hanging on until they find him."

Hannah hunched her shoulders, suddenly looking defeated.

Lily lifted the girl's chin with her thumb and forefinger, "Now look here, Hannah Griffiths, your Mam and young Richard need you to be strong for them, whatever the outcome. Go and make your brother something hot to eat, I'm sure he could do with it and keep that fire in for your Mam, now there's a good girl." Hannah nodded and managed a smile. "And if you need me, I am not too far away, I am helping out at the Morgan's shop."

The young girl thanked her, and Lily turned back in the direction she had come from, back down alongside the canal bank and to the shop. It had been an upsetting, yet moving first day.

Chapter Two

Lily and Mr. Morgan got the pony and trap out to take Lily's brother and mother home. There was a risk of Dafydd going into shock, Doctor Owen had said, due to the loss of the blood and the freezing cold air. The doctor had made a make-shift splint to support the leg out of two pieces of wood and some bandages.

"Now Lily..." the doctor advised, when Dafydd was safely installed onto the trap and covered in some blankets loaned by Mrs Morgan, "you make sure he rests that leg and watch out for any bleeding mind you. If it looks like it's getting infected, like there is a bad smell or the loss looks a funny colour, come get me immediately. Do you hear?"

"Yes, Doctor."

"I shall be calling sometime tomorrow, obviously I am too busy right now. My priority is saving lives for the moment, as soon as any more men are brought to the surface. I am expecting some severe burns." He shook his head with a look of despair in his eyes.

Lily thanked the doctor and helped her mother into the seat alongside Mr. Morgan. "Come on, Lily, there's room for a little one back to Chapel Square," Mr. Morgan said.

"It's all right Mr. Morgan, I shall walk back. I just want to check on Mrs Thomas first."

"Right you are. Well, if you are still here then when I return I will take you most of the way back home or you can stop at our house if you like and go back home in the morning. I doubt we shall be opening the shop."

"Thank you, Mr. Morgan."

When Lily had seen them safely on their way, she returned to the shop to find the kitchen overflowing with women, word must have got around that Mrs Morgan said they could come in for sustenance. She doubted very much if she would indeed go home tonight, Mrs Morgan needed her here.

"Good news, Lily," Mrs Morgan greeted her. "Young Richard and Hannah's father has been found alive."

"Thank goodness for that!" That bit of news made Lily so happy, she knew how much it meant to the children. "Would you like me to speak to the family?"

"There's no need for that. Mr. and Mrs Griffiths have gone to tell them the good news themselves. After a quick check over by the doctor, he was told there were no bones broken, so they were able to walk home together."

"What about the other wives here?" Lily whispered in the hall way.

"No such luck, I am afraid. They are still waiting anxiously. By the way, Mr. Davies the minister, is sitting in the parlour. I let him rest in there, he has been working ever so hard. Go and ask him if he would like some more tea, will you?"

Lily shyly removed her shawl and patted down her hair, she didn't know why, but she intended looking her best in front of the young minister.

"Ah, just the lady, I needed to see," he said, a huge smile appearing on his lips. "I think I need your help."

"Oh?"

"Don't look so worried. I am going to hold a special service at the chapel tomorrow and I would like you to inform as many people as you can and maybe help me choose a couple of appropriate hymns."

"Yes, I'd like that." Lily had a deep faith in God and knew that her faith had got her through so many bad times and would continue to do so in the future.

"I thought it would help to keep up morale of those who are still waiting to hear anything and for those who have lost loved ones."

"How many have died so far, Mr. Davies?"

"The last count was ten, Lily. I am just taking a short rest and a warm here, then I am going back out in case they bring up any more."

"Is it right that the explosion was caused by a naked flame?"

Evan frowned. "It looks that way. One of the men said some had noticed a strange smell and the next thing they knew, there was a huge fire ball coming to meet them. Those were the lucky ones of course, if you can count bad burns as being lucky."

Lily gulped, remembering Doctor Owen's prophetic words.

"After you have rested over night, call to the chapel tomorrow around noon to see me about choosing some hymns. You know the people here much better than I do. I am just a new comer."

Lily smiled. "Although you are, I am sure the people here have found solace already with your words, Mr. Davies." Lily's face grew hot and she realised she was blushing. She liked Evan a lot. He was just three years older than herself, and to her knowledge, had never been married, but although she liked him, she experienced a pang of guilt for thinking that way.

"What's the matter, Lily?" Evan stood now, wrapping his muffler around his neck.

"Nothing. You would think me very strange if I told you."

He appeared as if he was about to say something to her as he looked her directly in the eyes with a gaze that sent a flutter straight to her heart, but the moment was lost as Mrs Morgan entered the room.

"I thought you were going to let me know if Mr. Davies wanted a cup of tea, Lily?" she asked, with a twinkle in her blue eyes.

"It's my fault Mrs Morgan. I kept Lily talking. I want her to help me with a special service tomorrow for the villagers. It shall serve as a vigil for the missing men and boys and to comfort those already bereaved."

Elsa Morgan smiled. "A good idea it is and all. I know this time of the year, we normally have a Christmas service, but there are not many out there that will want to celebrate the season."

Evan nodded and putting his Dai cap firmly on his head, headed for the door, before leaving, he smiled at Lily as her cheeks blazed hot. Closing the door behind him she let out a long breath. This was neither the time nor the place to have such thoughts.

* * *

The following morning, Lily returned to Chapel Square to attend to Dafydd. "How has he been, Mam?" she asked, removing her shawl and hanging it on a hook behind the door.

Her mother smiled, the frown lines Lily had seen very much in evidence yesterday, now seemed to have smoothed out a little. "Very good, to be honest, considering what he has been through. He did wake up a few times in the night mind you, mumbling something under his breath; I think he was having a nightmare. He seems to be in a lot more pain today though."

"I'll fetch the Doctor if it gets any worse, now you go rest, Mam."

Her mother sat down in the wooden chair by the fire, closing her eyes for a moment and opening them again. She gazed directly into Lily's eyes. "It looks as though it is you that needs to rest, our Lily."

Lily forced a smile. "Me? I'm fine. I managed to have a couple of hours sleep afterwards last night." This was totally untrue, she hated lying to her mother, but did not want to tell her she had been awake worrying until the early hours at the plight of those poor men and boys. "Most of the women have gone now, some back to the pit to wait, others who have had bad news have gone home. A miner called Selah Thomas, said that he rushed away after hearing an explosion and a collier running alongside him suddenly stopped and said, *"I must go back for the boy",* but when he went back, he met his own death." She bit her lip to fight back the tears that were threatening to spill down her cheeks.

"That's so sad, *cariad.* There are lot of fathers, sons and brothers working alongside one another in that pit. I heard about the young lad from Pond Row and I thought of Delwyn and Dafydd at that age. They couldn't have been much older when they followed your father underground. I wish there was some other way for them, but there is mostly the mine or the iron works in these parts and believe me, there seem to be far more accidents working for the Cyfarthfa Iron Works than there has been underground. Unless, a man is well educated, or has a lot of money, what other choice does he have other than to work in the pit or ironworks?"

Lily swallowed hard and then nodded. "Not many have escaped Merthyr, Mam. Not many want to leave in any case. At least there is work in this valley, people come near and far to work here, so we should be glad of that."

Her mother frowned. "Yes, but at what cost? And look at the way there is overcrowding and sewage on the street in some areas. That is not good for everyone's health. That outbreak of cholera some time ago claimed many lives."

Her mother was right of course, but unless you were one of the landed gentry, what else could a Merthyr man or woman hope for? Each person had to live as best as they could and very often that involved living in houses that were overcrowded and uninhabitable.

Lily climbed the winding stone steps to Delwyn and Dafydd's bedroom. "How on earth did you manage to get up here last night?" She smiled at her brother in his bed.

"Oh, Mr. Morgan knocked on next door for John Evans to help lift me up the stairs, so I didn't need to bend my leg, see."

"Are you in any pain now?"

He bit his lip, beads of perspiration forming on his forehead. "No."

"Don't lie to me, Dafydd. I can see that you are." She walked over to his side and sat on the bed next to him.

"Yes, but I don't want to make a fuss, see. Don't want to worry our Mam." He shook his head.

"All right, I can appreciate that, but at least let me take a look at your dressing." Dafydd winced as Lily unwrapped the bandages. "It looks clean enough to me, no infection. But let me get the doctor to give you something for the pain. Will you?"

Reluctantly, he nodded. "If it gets any worse, then yes, you can. But the doctor will probably have been up all night. Have you heard any more?"

"Mrs Morgan said that now sixteen bodies have been recovered, but some of the men are still missing."

Dafydd closed his eyes. He was probably counting his lucky stars he was still here at all.

She carefully replaced his bandages and tidied his bed. "I'll fetch you a cup of tea."

His eyes flicked open again. "Thanks, Lily. I don't know what I am going to do. I hate not working."

"Oh, you will manage. I don't think they'll be reopening the pit for a while with it being Christmas and in such an unsafe condition too."

"You're probably right."

"I'll fetch you some books to read. I'm meeting with Evan Davies at noon today. I'll ask him if he has any to loan you."

Dafydd lifted his eyebrows. "Evan Davies, eh? He is quite a catch for any young lady in these parts."

"Stop it. It is not like that," she said rather too quickly. "I am helping him to choose some hymns for a special service he's putting on for the villagers."

"If you say so, Sis. I thought I caught him looking at you in chapel last week, but thought I must have been imagining things, but now I am not so sure."

Lily face grew hot with embarrassment. "Well, would it be so bad if he did take an interest in me?" She gazed intently at her brother to see if she could see what his reaction to the new minister might be.

"Not at all. It's just I never imagined you being a minister's wife." He laughed and then grabbed hold of his leg as if in pain.

"Don't over excite yourself, dear brother. I think you are getting ahead of yourself, I only said I would help out. In any case, we should not be making light at a time like this."

Dafydd's face coloured up and he looked down at the bed clothes as if ashamed of himself. "You are right, Lily. I am sorry."

"Now let me get you that cup of tea, and later when I have been to the chapel, I shall call on the doctor to see if he will come out to see you. If he can spare the time."

Dafydd took hold of Lily's hand. "Thanks. I am so fortunate to have a sister like you."

Lily bent over to kiss the top of her brother's head, thinking how lucky she was to still have brothers like Delwyn and Dafydd after yesterday's tragedy.

Lily's mother was making a big pot of cawl when she returned to the kitchen.

"Need a hand, Mam?"

"Yes, please. I've put the neck of lamb on to boil, can you chop up some onions and carrots, *cariad*?"

Lily nodded. "Of course. You're feeding him up are you?"

"Yes, he needs all his strength if he wants to go back to work sometime in the future."

"Do you think he would be better off though, getting a different job? After all, there have been two pit explosions at Gethin in the past three years."

"Well it would be nice of course, if he can find work elsewhere. Perhaps he can get something on the canal, on the barges."

"Yes, that might be a good idea, although it would mean him working away a lot."

"I'd rather that than…" Oh no, now she had upset her mother, who was dabbing her eyes with the end of her pinafore.

Lily held her mother. "It's a silly old fool I am. The onions are making my eyes water." But Lily knew it was more than that, a lot more. She knew her mother couldn't believe that her sons were the lucky ones, when so many of the women she knew from the village had lost husbands and sons in the explosion, and of course, there were some that knew nothing at all as yet.

Lily released her mother and looking directly into her watery eyes, with both hands firmly on her mother's shoulders, said, "We're so fortunate, Mam. Evan Davies wants to put on a special service for everyone, so I will be picking out some hymns with him at mid day today."

"That's a nice idea, Lily," her mother said sniffing. "It will help keep up the morale of the village and offer some comfort for the bereaved."

It just didn't seem right somehow, they should have been celebrating the run up to Christmas right now, not burying the dead men and boys.

After helping her mother, Lily could bear Dafydd's cries of pain no longer and so decided to fetch Doctor Owen. It was some time before she located him, he was having a well-earned beverage in the Llwyn-Yr-Eos public house on the canal bank. As she pushed her way through the crowd of men, she heard them talking about yesterday's sad affair. There would hardly be a person in the village who was not touched in some form or another by this tragedy.

She finally stood in front of Doctor Owen, who was sitting at the back of the pub, in amongst a group of miners. They had probably all been working throughout the night.

The doctor rubbed his eyes as she approached, the dark rings beneath them, informing her that he had not slept at all.

"Ah, Lily. How is that brother of yours?"

"He's not so good now, Doctor. He's in a lot of pain. Can you please give him something for it?"

He nodded. "What about the wound? Have you attended to it as I have asked?"

She nodded. "Yes. It looks clean."

"Good girl. Keep an eye on it for me. I shall give you a bottle of tincture of Laudanum. Don't give him too much, mind you, it may make him hallucinate."

Lily knew all about such things. When her father had been ill, he had been in so much pain that he had picked up the bottle and drank almost a half of it. The family had been really worried as he became aggressive thrashing around and calling out names, unknown to them all. It was the opium that was responsible, her mother had told her. It was such a powerful drug.

Doctor Owen opened up his black leather bag and handed her a small brown bottle. "I can't spare any more than that, I am afraid. I need it for the men. I had to perform an amputation last night and those poor souls who got burnt, if they survive at all, would be better off dead."

Lily's stomach somersaulted, bringing the situation home to her, those poor men and their families. She remembered the last Gethin Pit accident three years previously, then the explosion had occurred in the Lower pit in the four feet seam killing 47 men and boys. Naked lights had been in general use with safety lamps issued to men working in stalls where gas had been found. Her brothers hadn't been working on that particular shift and so were lucky then as well. Should they return to work, would they be fortunate to survive another accident in the future? If she had anything to do with it, she was going to ensure that they got jobs elsewhere that did not involve working in either the pit or the iron works. They were no jobs for men, yet alone young children. She would ask Mr. Morgan if he had any ideas later on.

Thanking the doctor she made her way back to Chapel Square and let herself in through the back door. As soon as she entered the kitchen she heard her brother cry out in pain, "Oh, hell it is, pure hell!"

If there was one thing she knew, it was that Dafydd must be in severe pain to cry out like that, for one thing he would not want to upset their mother, and for another, he was the type of man who bore any injury with dignity. He was really suffering, poor dab.

"I'm coming, Dafydd!" She made her way up the stairs with the medicine bottle and a spoon.

He grabbed the bottle from her hand, trembling as he attempted to loosen the cork with his teeth. "Oh, no you don't!" Lily warned. "Remember what happened to our Dad when he took this medicine, it made him go really queer it did. Doctor Owen says you are to have a spoonful every few hours."

Dafydd grimaced, but must have known he was beat as he relaxed back onto the pillow and allowed his sister to pour out a spoonful and take it to his lips. When she had finished, she handed the bottle to her mother who had been standing close by. "Keep this safe, Mam. And be very strict with it."

Her mother nodded and Dafydd closed his eyes, within moments he was drifting off to sleep.

"Sleep is the best thing for him right now."

"Yes, you are right, Mam." Then in a whisper, Lily said, "Doctor Owen has had a bad night, he has had to perform an amputation and some of the men are badly burned."

"Oh, dear dear! How awful, Lily. Are they all up from the pit now?"

"No, there are still some missing. I am going to have to go shortly to see the minister."

"Come and have a bowl of cawl before you do then, you need to keep your strength up. Your brother and I have already had ours."

Lily followed her mother down the stone stairs and removing her hat and shawl, sat down at the table to eat the nourishing soup.

* * *

The meeting with Evan Davies at the chapel went very well, Lily chose two hymns that she thought would be appropriate: *Ar Hyd Y Nos* [All through the night] and *Guide Us O Thou Great Jehovah.*

Evan had chosen a reading from Psalm 23.

As they chatted over a cup of tea, a group of people entered, heads bowed low. One elderly man who had removed his cap, said, "We thought we would like to come here, Mr. Davies, it seems appropriate somehow. Do you mind?"

"Not at all, my good man. Sit down all of you. Would you like me to pray with you?" Evan reassured them. The small group muttered their thanks.

"I'll go and make some more tea, shall I Mr. Davies?" Lily asked, really wanting to do something to help the situation.

"Thank you, Lily. That would be a big help." Then taking her to one side, Evan whispered, "These poor people don't know what to do with themselves whilst they are waiting for news of their loved ones."

Lily busied herself in the small kitchen belonging to the chapel. She had been coming to this very same building since she was a small child, three times on a Sunday, so it felt like home. She hadn't been so keen on the last minister, mind you, he was full of fire and brimstone and quite an unforgiving character, so it was nice to have someone young, with new ideas like Evan Davies taking over the chapel. The congregation had really taken to him.

When the small group had prayed and been given a hot cup of tea, Lily put her shawl back on and made to leave for home as well.

"Hang on a moment there," Evan said, as he slipped on his overcoat, "I will walk you back to your house, it will be dark soon." She hadn't been expecting him to accompany her, after all, she had walked it alone so many times in the past.

They made their way along the canal bank, and in the distance, the orange yellow glow from the Cyfarthfa Iron Works shone forth like a beacon, illuminating the inky darkness of the sky.

They fell into step as they walked along. "I really appreciate your help today, Lily. I was going to ask you a favour."

"Go ahead and ask then?"

"I notice that you are very good with people and I was wondering if you would help to run the Sunday school for me?"

"Oh."

"You sound surprised."

"I am. I had not even considered it before. I should have to give it some thought." It wasn't that she didn't want to help at the chapel, it's just that she had never thought of herself teaching a class before.

"It would be a big help to me if you could, as Mrs Williams says she is too old. She has enjoyed taking the class all these years, but now she feels it is time for someone much younger to step into her shoes. In fact, it was she, who suggested you." He stopped walking and looked at her for a moment under the lamp light.

That was flattering to know that Mrs Williams who had once taught her in the very same Sunday school, thought so much of her to put her name forward. "I'm not sure," she replied honestly.

"Take all the time you like. She will not leave until someone takes over. She said she didn't want to let me or the chapel down. How is Dafydd by the way?"

"Oh, he's all right Mr. Davies. He was in a lot of pain earlier, so I got something from the doctor for him, but when I think of the alternative, it could have been a damn sight worse. Sorry. I shouldn't have sworn like that."

Evan stopped and looked at her, even in the semi-darkness, she could see he bore a bemused expression on his face. "It's only natural that you should have strong feelings, you were very worried about both of your brothers."

They fell into step once more.

"Yes. Delwyn is still helping to look for the men. I would like to see my brothers leave this dirty old job and find some new employment elsewhere, it's just too dangerous."

Evan cleared his throat. "Yes, I know all about that. I was a miner myself once."

"You were?" That fact surprised her.

He laughed. "Don't you believe me, Lily Jenkin?"

"I don't know, you just seem too..."

"Posh, were you about to say?"

"No, I mean you look too refined. I cannot imagine you coming home covered in coal dust and your mother scrubbing your back in an old tin bath!"

"Ah, but I was. In fact, if you invite me into your home, I will show you my blue blood."

"Blue blood?"

"Yes, most colliers get blue blood at some time or another when they have worked down the pit for long enough, they're our battle scars. If we get injured and coal dust gets into our veins we get blue marks."

"Yes, of course, my father had them. And my brothers too. So you were a miner then. How did you become a minister, if you don't mind me asking you?"

He let out a breath. "Not at all. My grandfather was a minister and it was always expected that I would follow his footsteps, but I insisted on seeing a bit of life beforehand. Then I became a minister."

"I see."

"Yes. I went to Bible College in Cardiff and I have not regretted it one bit, the only thing that is missing from my life is a wife." He was about to say something else when two colliers passed them, heading for the pub, distracting him from what he had been about to say. Instead he said, "I expect they want to drown their sorrows and I can't say that I blame them right now."

The spell was broken and she wondered what else he had been about to say about getting himself a wife.

When she got home, she welcomed Evan inside and was pleased to hear that Dafydd was feeling much better. So the medicine had helped then. Delwyn was seated by the table spooning the chunky cawl into his mouth.

"Would you like some, Mr. Davies?" Lily's mother asked.

"My, it smells wonderful, Mrs Jenkin, but I think I need to get back to the pit to check on everyone."

Mrs Jenkin frowned and folded her arms. "Now, it will do you good to sit down and eat something warm for a few moments. Seat yourself down." Lily's mother was not going to take no for an answer. She nodded at Lily.

Delwyn's lip curled into a knowing smile. "You just as well do as you're told, Mr. Davies, the women in this house like to be listened to."

Evan laughed. "I can see that. Thank you very much, Mrs Jenkin. I have to confess I am rather hungry." He rubbed his stomach and Lily went off to fetch him some cawl.

"There's a good man he is," Lily's mother said, as she followed her into the kitchen, "seeing you home like that. You could do a lot worse you know."

"Mam!" Lily's face blazed red hot. It was so embarrassing the way her family were behaving in front of the minister, in any case she had no idea if he liked her in that way or not. She hadn't wanted to behave in a forward manner in front of him. For all she knew he might well have a sweetheart that she knew nothing about.

"Now you take that soup in while it's still hot, my girl. Ask him if he would like a slice of bread to go with it."

As Lily placed the bowl down in front of Evan, her hand tingled at the thought of being so close to him. "Mam asked if you would like some bread to go with it, Evan?"

"Yes, I would, thank you. This cawl smells lovely. Are you eating yourself, Lily?"

"No, I had some earlier on. I will eat later." In any case, she couldn't eat a thing right now, she had lost her appetite, just being in the same room as Evan made her feel as though she had butterflies dancing around in her tummy.

As she observed him eating, she watched as he dipped his head over the bowl to eat and noted the way his dark hair fell into little curls along the neckline of his shirt. She knew she shouldn't think that way, but she had to admit she was falling for the handsome minister.

Warming her hands in front of the open fire for a moment, she asked Delwyn how their brother was.

"He seems fine. It's just as well you brought him that medicine, it has knocked him out good and proper. The sleep is just the cure he needs. I'm fortunate I got off without so much as a scratch myself."

"Until the next time," Lily uttered, beneath her breath.

"Pardon?" Delwyn's eyebrows shot up in surprise to hear Lily come back at him.

She cleared her throat. "I mean, I hope you and Dafydd will not be returning to the pit in the future."

Delwyn thumped his fist on the table, taking his sister and everyone else by surprise at the vehemence in his tone of voice. "What choice do we have? It's either there or the iron works."

"You could move out of Merthyr to find work," Lily suggested hopefully.

"I suppose we could, but we don't want to."

"So you're answering for Dafydd as well now are you?"

Lily's heart beat quickened.

"Lovely soup," Evan said, trying to change the subject and then as if he noticed a bad atmosphere between them that could not be ignored, set down his spoon and said, "Look, these sorts of accidents bring out the worst in people. Give it time to die down. Then talk about what you want to do, everyone's emotions are all over the place right now."

"There's right you are, Mr. Davies." Mrs Jenkin had joined them by the fireside. "I would like my boys to find different jobs if possible, but I know our Delwyn has his heart set on staying underground like his father."

"And a lot of good that did him as well!" Lily shouted, standing up and leaving the room, surprising herself at the passion within her own voice. Evan was right. Her emotions were all over the place right now. She was so angry that she didn't quite know who or what it was she was angry with.

She lit a candle and climbed the stairs to check on Dafydd, otherwise she might just say something she might later regret. Holding up the candle in his room, she noticed he was still sleeping, unsure whether to wake him or not, she tiptoed over to check his dressing, it still looked clean, it didn't appear as if any blood had seeped through, so that was a good sign. Then as she was about to leave, her brother stirred.

Groaning he asked, "Where am I?"

"You're at home, Dafydd. Don't you remember?" Lily said softly, feeling guilty that she and Delwyn might have woken him with the sound of their raised voices downstairs.

He sat up and rubbed his eyes. "Yes, of course. I was having some silly dream about working on a canal barge for a moment there."

She returned to his bed and sat down next to him, still holding the candle. "Would that be so bad?"

"No, I suppose it wouldn't, in view of what has happened at the pit. You know, I doubt that Delwyn would ever leave his work underground though, don't you?"

"I've just found that out."

He smiled. "Yes, he's as stubborn as a mule. Got a lot of pride that one. You can tell he was born before me!"

"Well only by twenty minutes, Mam says."

He laughed. "But that still makes him the eldest and I have always followed after his lead…"

"But not this time?"

"No," he answered firmly. "Working on the barges is what I have always wanted to do ever since I was a little boy as I watched them pass on the Glamorganshire Canal transporting goods to Cardiff. It always seemed an exciting life to me."

"Well, I expect it would be. Although, we would have to get used to not having you around so much."

"Yes, but that won't be for some time, that is if I can get a job and my leg has to fully heal first. We can't afford for me to be out of work for too long now, can we?"

Lily shook her head. "Suppose not. Although, I think we are more fortunate than some in Abercanaid, we have two wages coming in regularly, and of course, now I have a little job as well."

Dafydd hugged her. "I'm proud of you our Lily."

It surprised her to hear her brother saying those words, not so long ago he had been pulling her pig tails and making her cry. Now she was close to tears again, but for an entirely different reason.

"You daft thing, you are making me weep," she sniffed. "In any case, it is me who should be saying how proud I am of you and our Delwyn, you are men now, not the young boys you were only a couple of years back."

Hearing voices downstairs, she realised she was being rude by leaving the minister alone with her mother and brother, not that they would have minded, they seemed to be really taken with him.

She set the candle down in the holder on the small bedside table. "I'll come back to see you later. Oh, I forgot, Evan, I mean Mr. Davies, has given me a couple of books to give to you, a Charles Dickens and a Daniel Defoe."

Dafydd's eyes lit up. "So it's Evan now is it? My, my, but you two are getting friendly."

She picked up a pillow and threw it at him. "Dafydd Jenkin if you were not in your sick bed I would slap your face right now!"

It was good to hear his laughter as she descended the stairs to find Evan standing at the bottom putting his coat and muffler back on.

"Is Dafydd all right?" he asked, his eyes full of concern.

"Yes, well he's laughing up there right now and not crying out in pain, so that is something I suppose. Although I suspect the medicine will wear off shortly, so I'll have to give him another dose soon."

Evan made for the front door. "I'll come over to see him in a day or so."

"He says to say thank you for the books, by the way."

"The pleasure is all mine," he replied, pulling on his cap.

Lily followed him outside to the doorstep.

"I'll see you in chapel tomorrow then, Lily." She was about to say something, but as she opened her mouth he dipped his head and kissed her on the cheek. Lily's heart fluttered frantically and for a short while she thought she might pass out on the doorstep, then taking hold of her hand he said, "When all of this business is over, we need to talk."

She nodded. It was neither the time nor the place right now to discuss matters of the heart, but that was what he was referring to, she just knew it.

Lily watched him stride off down the street until he was out of sight and then, she touched the side of her face where he had kissed her, leaning back against the door, her family inside oblivious to what had just gone on. If she was not surrounded by such tragedy right now she would be over the moon with delight, but for now, she and Evan had to put their feelings on hold.

* * *

The mining disaster was reported in *The Cardiff and Merthyr Guardian* on Friday the 22nd of December.

Mr. Morgan placed his newspaper down on the kitchen table, "It says here," he said, addressing his wife and Lily, "that six men burnt to death and maybe as many as twenty suffocated."

"Oh, you are sending shivers down my spine, William." Mrs Morgan grimaced. "Those poor men."

"Not to forget the boys too," he said, peering over his glasses. "Christmas won't be the same again for the people of Abercanaid."

"Are you both coming to the chapel service this evening?" Lily addressed the couple.

"Yes, we'll both be there, we are going to shut up the shop early. I expect the place will be packed to the rafters." Mrs Morgan placed her hand on Lily's shoulder.

It was a dark time indeed for the people of Abercanaid and the surrounding areas; men and boys had died from: Rhydycar, Cyfarthfa, Georgetown, Brecon Road and Heolgerrig. The youngest thought to have died, just barely eleven years old and the eldest, seventy five. What their families must be going through right now was barely worth thinking about.

The shop still maintained a decent trade following the disaster as people still needed to eat and most did not want to venture out of the village. In any case, it seemed to bring a comfort, a meeting point for people to discuss their feelings whilst they were buying a loaf of bread or a few potatoes. And if Mrs Morgan could see that someone was becoming upset, she instructed Lily to take care of the shop while she took that person out to the backroom for a chat and a cup of tea.

* * *

When Lily turned up early for the evening service to help Evan, she was surprised to see that the chapel was already packed out, there was hardly an available seat anywhere. More often than not, there would be quite a few spare seats in the upstairs pews, but now even they were hard to come by as people squeezed in tightly to make room for others. It was so full, that she and Evan went out to the church hall and brought in as many spare chairs and benches as they could to place down the front of the chapel, beneath the pulpit. They also opened the side doors, so people could stand to hear the service outside if they couldn't get into the overcrowded chapel.

Everyone appeared as a sea of black, in mourning for the village. There was hardly a dry eye in the house as Evan Davies spoke so passionately about the tragedy. Despite the people being full of grief, they sang the hymns with all their hearts.

Lily scanned the chapel for her mother and Delwyn, whom she found seated at the back, hugging one another. It had been a close call for both her brothers and she was thankful they had not been too seriously injured.

When the service finished, the crowds took a long time to disperse as some stayed behind talking and comforting one another, but finally when the last person had left, Evan locked the doors and sat Lily down in a pew.

"You know that thing I mentioned last night, when I said it was neither the time nor the place?"

She nodded, and he took both of her hands into his larger, rather warmer ones, "Well, I think I am going to ask you now anyway."

Lily held her breath, then bit on her lower lip as she watched him fall to his knees, "Lily, if your father was still alive, I would go to see him now this very instant, but seeing as he is no longer with us, I will ask you this…Lily Jenkin, would you please become my wife?"

Lily almost burst from the very pleasure of being asked the question by Evan. For a moment she was silent as she savoured the moment, then she jumped to her feet, "Oh yes. Yes, I would love to marry you Evan."

Evan beamed, his eyes shining with delight. "I know it seems wrong asking you right now, but this accident has made me realise how short life is, and even though I believe one day we shall both join one another in heaven, I think life is too short to waste."

"I so agree with you, Evan."

"But we shall keep it quiet for now, shall we, as it doesn't seem appropriate in the present circumstances?"

"Yes. I think that would be for the best. What about telling Mam and my brothers?" For a split second, Lily wondered if they might disapprove, but then she dispelled her fears.

Evan rubbed his chin in quiet contemplation. "I think we should tell them after Christmas. I want to ensure they are happy about it all."

A multitude of thoughts flittered through Lily's mind as she picked up the discarded hymn books and put them away in the cupboard. She, Lily Jenkin, was going to become a minister's wife. They would have to live in the house next door to the chapel, where Evan was now already living with an elderly housekeeper, whom he said he would let go once they were married and she moved in. It was a decent size house with three bedrooms, enough to start a family. There would be no going down the mines for their children though, she would see to that.

* * *

Christmas came and went that year in a haze of confusion for the family as a huge, black cloud of grief covered the village of Abercanaid and surrounding areas. There were many funerals to get through, several taking place on the same day which took up a lot of Evan's time. Life it felt, would never feel the same again, even though Lily had her future marriage to look forward to.

It wasn't until New Year's Eve, that Lily thought it sensible to broach the subject of her future wedding with her mother and brothers. She had invited Evan around for his tea and afterwards, they had all sat around amicably by the fire side. It had been snowing for the past couple of days and somehow that seemed to make life feel a little better in Upper Abercanaid.

"Mam," Lily broached the subject, "Evan and I would like to talk with you all."

"Well, isn't that what we are all doing right now?" Asked her mother, with a twinkle in her eye.

Evan cleared his throat. "It's like this see, Mrs Jenkin, Delwyn and Dafydd. I am very fond of your sister…"

"Fond?" Delwyn lifted his eyebrows. "Is that what you call it Mr. Davies?"

Evan cleared his throat and shifted about in his chair. "Well, no actually…" His face had deepened by two shades of pink. "It's more than that. I, that is, we are in love with one another and we would like it if you could all give us your blessing to get married."

There was a long silence and Lily worried that her family were not taking the news too well, until Dafydd let out a stifled laugh. "Mam, had a feeling you were going to ask!"

Everyone laughed, including Evan and Lily who laughed more nervously than the rest.

Delwyn got onto his feet and shook Evan's hand. "If you are to be married to my sister, then you take care of her, you hear, Evan?"

"Of course I will."

"No funny business, like getting her in the family way before you are wed, now is it?" Delwyn continued, giving his future brother-in-law a slap on the back.

"Delwyn!" his mother scolded, "Don't talk to Mr. Davies like that he is our minister after all."

"He knows I am only joking with him, Mam," Delwyn exclaimed, bigheartedly.

Their mother went out to the kitchen and returned with a bottle of homemade elder flower wine that someone had given them as a present over Christmas. "Let's all drink to celebrate the forthcoming occasion!" she said brightly. It was good to see her mother happy again following past events and now she had something to look forward to.

Evan squeezed Lily's hand in quiet reassurance. "It's to be a spring wedding then, is it?" he asked looking deep into her eyes. Spring was Lily's favourite time of the year so it seemed more than appropriate.

"Yes, I would like that very much."

"Cheers to the both of you!" Mam said, holding up her glass. As the clock struck midnight, she toasted, "Here's to the New Year 1866. A better year for us all!"

Everyone stood and raised their glasses, drank and embraced one another.

Evan took Lily aside. "Close your eyes and give me your hand."

"What is it? Please tell me?" Lily could hardly contain her excitement.

"Do as you're told."

She nodded and firmly closed her eyes and held out the palm of her hand.

"No peeping, mind you." He chuckled. She felt something cold being put into her hand. "You can open them now."

Lily gazed at the palm of her hand, to see a silver locket there. Picking it up with her other hand, she ran her thumb over the delicate engraving. "Oh, Evan, it's beautiful."

"You like it then?"

She nodded enthusiastically. "Would you put it on for me, please?"

Lily held up her hair as Evan secured the locket around her neck and she proudly showed it to her family.

"I'm never going to remove it!" Lily enthused.

"Well, I'd better be getting back home now." Evan made to put his coat on.

"No, you won't," Mrs Jenkin said firmly. "You will soon be one of the family and the snow is coming down thick and fast. You can have Delwyn's bed for the night, he can sleep down here in front of the fire." Evan looked at his future brother-in-law for confirmation, and when he nodded and smiled, Evan visibly relaxed.

"That's settled then," Mam declared. "By the way, when are we to meet your parents, Evan?"

"I am taking Lily next week on the train to Cardiff to visit them. Perhaps we can all meet up before the wedding."

"That's a nice idea." Mam straightened her dress as if she was already somehow competing with the other woman.

Lily hadn't given it too much thought before now. She knew that Evan was an only child and that his parents were quite comfortably off, but now she wondered what they would be like.

Would they be as welcoming as her own family had been to him? She reassured herself, that of course they would.

Chapter Three

Lily and Evan took the train on the Taff Vale Railway from the neighbouring village of Troedyrhiw to where Evan's parents resided in Pentyrch near Cardiff. It was a lovely fresh, but sunny day. Lily clutched her wicker basket tightly on her lap for the journey. She had packed some of her mother's baked bread, cheese, Welsh cakes, red rosy apples and some homemade lemonade for their journey. After embarking from the train they would have quite a long walk to Mr. and Mrs Davies' home.

The house stood proud at the end of the terrace. Lily let out a breath as she realised how much bigger and grander it was, than her humble home in Chapel Square. It also surprised her that Evan had to knock the door before being allowed access, it was rarely like that at her home—the door there was usually left off the latch. Lily watched in anticipation as a large, friendly woman opened the door.

"Why, you must be tired after your journey," she said kindly.

"I am rather, Mrs Davies." Lily was impressed with the woman's hospitality.

Evan cleared his throat as a lady's sharp voice from the hallway said, "I am Mrs Davies, if you don't mind—this is Daisy, my housekeeper."

Lily wanted the ground to swallow her up whole. What could have made her come to that conclusion? This was obviously not a world she was used to and she silently cursed Evan for not forewarning of the fact.

"I apologise, Mrs Davies," she said humbly, bringing her eyes to meet with those of her future mother-in-law.

Mrs Davies smiled politely, but it did not quite reach her eyes. "Daisy will take your outer garments and lead you into the drawing room where you will have tea with Mr. Davies and myself." Evan's mother held herself so erect that Lily could have sworn she had a metal poker pushed down the back of her beautiful gown. Her own mother did not possess a gown as beautiful as that. She surmised that it must have cost the woman a pretty penny.

Suddenly, she felt very small and inadequate, even though she was wearing her Sunday best, a green velvet gown and her new hat and cloak.

"Don't worry about Mother," Evan whispered. "She tends to have delusions of grandeur. Father is much more grounded."

Lily managed a weak smile, but now she wondered how she was going to get through the next couple of hours, especially as Evan was going to give them the news of their betrothal to be married.

When Lily had tidied herself up and handed her garments and basket to the housekeeper, she and Evan entered the drawing room. Immediately, a middle-aged man with a warm smile came towards them and took her hand.

"So you must be Lily?" he asked, his face full of laughter lines. He had bushy white side-burns and a long drooping moustache, Lily warmed to him immediately.

"I am. And so you are Mr. Davies?" She hoped she had got it right this time and luckily she had. Although she got the impression this man would not mind at all if she hadn't for one moment.

"I am indeed. George Davies..."

Gazing around the room breathlessly, Lily absorbed her sumptuous surroundings. The silk wallpaper was delicately woven and the heavy, thick drapes around the window, reminded her of the ones she had seen on stage at a local theatre in Merthyr. No one she knew in Abercanaid had curtains like those. Many poor people in the district could not even afford proper curtains at all, having to make do with Hessian sack cloth or old newspaper attached to their windows to keep out the cold.

"Come and sit down my dear. It is getting quite chilly outside. Now what will you have to drink?" Mr. Davies asked.

Lily seated herself on a high-backed armchair, staring in awe at the table laid out with fancy looking sandwiches. She had never seen pieces of bread sliced so thinly before, or such colourful fondant cakes.

"I should like a cup of tea, please." She looked at Evan's mother as if expecting her to pour as her own mother would have done back home. Then finding that was not the case said, "Would you like me to pour for you, Mrs Davies?"

"You most certainly will not," replied Evan's mother abruptly. "That is what I employ Daisy for." She rang a little gold bell by the side of her to catch the housekeeper's attention.

"You rang, Madam?" The housekeeper asked. Lily noticed that the poor woman's eyelid twitched from time to time and she assumed that she was afraid of her employer.

"Yes. Pour the tea, would you, Daisy." Why couldn't Mrs Davies do that herself? Lily guessed that the poor housekeeper was probably rushed off her feet. She was beginning to take a bit of a dislike to her future mother-in-law.

When the tea had been poured, Lily waited for Mrs Davies to lift her china cup from the saucer before lifting her own—she didn't want to seem too keen.

This woman was not living in the same world she inhabited, that was for sure. She had a definite plum in her mouth. How could someone as nice as Evan have been born to such a woman?

"My son tells me, you have been very helpful to him at the chapel?" Mr. Davies asked, as if to ease the tension between the two women.

"That is correct Mr. Davies. I am now also helping at the Sunday school and running the women's bible group."

Mr. Davies smiled as if he appreciated what she had been doing. Mrs Davies, on the other hand, lifted her nose in the air. "Yes, those working class, slum areas, certainly need the chapel, don't they? For handouts, especially since the pit problem."

Lily balled her hands into fists at her side. "It is not a slum area as you call it Mrs Davies. There is overcrowding in the area, but most people I know take pride in their homes."

Evan shifted about in his seat, obviously uncomfortable with the atmosphere created between the two women.

"I am sure my wife did not mean it quite like that, did you Olwen?"

Olwen Davies turned her head to the side and sniffed loudly as if that would somehow help to retain her air of authority over the small gathering, only she had not bargained on someone as spirited as Lily talking back to her. Eventually, she smiled and picked up the plate of cakes, offering it around to everyone. Lily was surprised that she didn't ring for the maid to carry out that little task for her too.

Mr. Davies visibly relaxed and then whispered under his breath, "Good for you. You keep on sticking up for yourself Lily. Otherwise she will walk all over you. Believe me I know." Then he laughed, so she wasn't really sure whether he meant what he was saying or not.

"Are you all right, Lily?" Evan asked, as he took her for a walk around the large well-kept garden at the rear of the house.

"Yes. Why are you asking?"

"It's just that my mother has a tendency to frighten people, her bark is worse than her bite you know." He laughed nervously.

"Don't you worry, Evan Davies, in my life I have had to encounter bigger dragons than your mother."

"Are you calling my mother a dragon?" He pretended to sound serious for a moment, but Lily knew when he was teasing, it illuminated his green eyes.

"No, not really. She could though, make a vulnerable person, quite upset."

"Then it's good that she's met her match in you Lily Jenkin." He held her tightly and planted a kiss on her cheek. Lily glanced across at the window at the back of the house, surprised to see Mrs Davies standing there, arms folded, pursing her lips. When she noticed Lily, she stepped back into the shadows.

"Come on, let's go back indoors. It's rude for us to stay out here much longer," Lily advised.

"Yes, the time has come for me to inform my parents we are to be married." Evan took a deep breath before taking Lily's hand and escorting her back into the house.

Evan's father took the news very well, pumping his son by the hand. Lily glanced at Olwen Davies to see if she could gauge what the woman was thinking. Her manner told her one thing, but the woman's dark beady eyes, told her another. She was not happy, not happy about it at all, even though she had welcomed Lily into the family for the sake of her son. There was no fooling Lily.

I'm not good enough for her Evan. She has expectations for him. Perhaps she has someone more suitable in mind for him, someone from a more affluent family? Thoughts she inwardly kept to herself.

It was quite amicable as Evan and Lily said their goodbyes to Evan's parents and they set off back down the road to catch the train.

"I'm famished," Lily said, unhooking her arm from Evan's to peer into the basket.

"I noticed you didn't eat much at the house," Evan said, stopping for a moment to look questioningly into her eyes.

"I just couldn't. My stomach was all a flutter. But I'm ravenous now."

"Well, what did you think of them?"

Lily held her breath and then let it out again. "Your father is quite a card, he made me laugh a lot."

"And my mother, you haven't said anything nice about her. She told us she was pleased about our engagement."

Lily bit her lip. "I am not so sure, Evan. I feel she doesn't think I am good enough for you."

"Don't be silly," he said, draping one arm around her shoulder. "She is happy for us."

Well Evan might think so, but Lily knew in her heart that the woman would be really pleased if the engagement were broken off, and other than her thinking she was not good enough for her son, what other reason could there possibly be why she obviously disliked her so?

* * *

It was biting cold by the time they arrived back in Abercanaid and although it hadn't snowed for a couple of days, there was still some slush remaining on the ground and now it was starting to ice over, so the ground was quite slippery under foot.

Evan made light of the situation by pretending to ice skate, Lily knew he was really happy about everything, but why did she feel that somehow, something or someone was about to burst her bubble?

"I think I will write to the Reverend Watkins tomorrow to ask if he will marry us in the chapel," He beamed. "He's only moved to Pontypridd, but I know he will perform the ceremony for us."

"That's a good idea, Evan. But is he still acting as a minister, now that he has left the chapel?"

"Yes, I heard from his sister that he takes the odd service as a lay preacher."

"That is good then. What date were you thinking of?"

"I think April would be a nice month. The weather will be a lot warmer then."

"April sounds lovely to me, too. I love the spring time and Dafydd will be well enough by then."

"How is he by the way?"

"He's getting up and down the stairs by himself and he's vowed never to return to the pit. Delwyn called to see a man about getting Dafydd a job on the barges. The man said that my brother can start as soon as he is well enough."

"That's good news then. And Delwyn? Will he return to the pit?"

"Yes. There is no stopping him. He says he is not afraid to go back down there. It will be the death of him if he is not careful." She shivered, involuntary.

Evan stopped for a moment. "Don't talk like that Lily. There has been a shadow of death over this village for the past couple of weeks, it's not long since people have buried their loved ones."

Lily took in a deep breath, feeling thoroughly ashamed of herself. She and her family had everything to live for. Doctor Owen had told her that the explosion had left 13 widows and 27 fatherless children. An inquest had been held not long afterwards and Selah Thomas, a collier, had given evidence that a great quantity of gas was in the pit and that a fireman, or the man whose duty it had fallen, had neglected to take serious precautions.

So it had been a simple case of negligence that had caused so many deaths.

"What are you thinking?" Evan asked, gazing intently into her eyes.

"I was just thinking that the explosion needn't have happened at all."

"Yes. It is such a shame. If only we could turn back the clock, but we can't Lily. We all have to move on."

Lily knew Evan was talking sense, but it didn't make it any the easier when she thought of those women who would now have to struggle to make ends meet, what about those? And what about the poor children, some not yet born, without their fathers?

"I think it might help if we can set up something at the chapel to help the families," Lily declared.

Evan raised a brow, then placed the wicker basket on the ground in front of him. "Like what?"

"I think we should operate a soup kitchen there a couple of times a week, and maybe talk to local shopkeepers in Merthyr Tydfil about donating food and useful items for the families."

"That's a good idea," he said, swept along by the passion in her voice. "I know we cannot solve all their problems, but it will go a long way to making things easier for them."

"That's what I love about you, Evan, you always make it sound as if I have great thoughts, you're not like some of the men around here who think that women are only good for cooking and cleaning, you treat me as though I am an intelligent person."

"And so you are, my lovely," he said, lifting the basket and taking her arm for the walk back to Chapel Square.

* * *

The following day, Mrs Morgan allowed Lily to finish her shift at the shop early so she and Evan could borrow the pony and trap to set off for Merthyr.

Most of the shopkeepers were very obliging when it came to donating food, clothing and household items toward The Gethin Pit Disaster Fund that she and Evan had set up. Some of the more affluent businesses even gave sums of money.

"When all this over, Evan," Lily said, as she carried a basketful of vegetables to the awaiting trap, "I hope we can do something special for the children who have lost their fathers, they must have had a miserable Christmas."

"Yes, *cariad*. Have you had any thoughts on what that might be?"

"Maybe to hold a special party for them at the chapel, or when the weather is warmer, take them for a picnic. Or even a trip on the train."

Evan put his hand on her shoulder, "Yes, all in good time. Our first priority is to keep the widows, colliers and children well-nourished."

Lily nodded as Evan loaded the last of the donated goods, which was warm clothing from the drapers and a half a sheep from the butcher, into the back of the trap. She would employ the help of her mother and Mrs Morgan to get the soup kitchen up and running. The soup would probably keep for several days, the weather was cold enough, and so it should not become spoiled.

Evan had already hung a large sign to advertise the free soup kitchen for anyone at all connected with the disaster. The men needed to build up their strength as well if they were to return to employment, whether they decided to go back to the pit or not. Lily guessed with such large families, that many had no choice.

It was getting dark by the time they arrived back in Abercanaid. Evan wanted to drop her off at Chapel Square, but Lily insisted on helping him to unload the food and clothing at the chapel hall first.

"We shall have to be selective as to who we give this clothing to," Lily advised, as she sorted through the clothes, pulling out woollen shirts, trousers and shawls. "I think we need to give to the neediest. Mrs Evans from Catherine Square has six children and they always look as though they are wearing their clothes out."

Evan agreed. "I think we have to be careful that we don't cause a lot of avarice between the people. I mean we can give out the soup equally, but the clothing is another matter, we don't have a lot of it."

"Perhaps, then, we should give to the neediest in the first instance and then pull names out of a hat for the distribution of the rest. Lady Charlotte Guest did a lot to help the people of Dowlais when they needed it, so why shouldn't we do the same?"

"That is such a good idea, Lily. She has done so much for the people of Dowlais already, particularly the children."

"Yes, I think we make a good team," Lily declared.

"And we shall make an even better one after we are married." Evan put down the wooden crate of food he was carrying and took her into his arms. Lily's heart hammered beneath the bodice of her dress. Marriage? It wouldn't be that long now would it? In a couple of months she would be Mrs Lilian Davies. The thought sent her heady with desire for Evan. She could hardly wait.

* * *

A letter arrived the following morning for Lily. She did not recognise the hand writing, but as soon as she tore open the envelope, and smelled the scented parchment, she realised it was from Evan's mother.

Dear Lily,

My husband and I were so happy to make your recent acquaintance, and look forward to attending your forthcoming wedding. We should like to meet with you again in the near future to discuss the event.

Yours Sincerely,

Mrs Olwen Davies.

For a rare moment, Lily bubbled up with excitement to have received the letter, but then a little voice inside her head kept telling her that the woman was merely toying with her, after all, she had not shown any pleasure at all when Evan informed her of his plans. What was she up to? She would have to tell Evan of course, would he be able to reassure her?

At least she would have plenty of support with Evan and Mr. Davies being present, Mrs Davies would not be able to get away with much if it was her intention.

"What is that letter you are reading?" Dafydd asked, as he watched her walk into the living room and place it into her pinafore pocket.

"It's nothing much."

"Now, let me be the judge of that. It's not every day we get a letter in this house with fancy handwriting."

Dafydd didn't miss a thing. He was highly observant. Eyes like a hawk, their mother often said.

"It's from Evan's mother, if you must know. She wants to meet with me again before the wedding takes place."

Dafydd frowned and then folded his arms as he sat reclining in the wooden fireside chair.

"Well, what is so wrong with that? Many a bride-to-be would be happy receiving a welcoming letter from her future mother-in-law."

Lily cleared her throat. "It is the intention behind it that is worrying me, Dafydd."

Lily was startled for a moment as their mother entered the room, carrying a bucket of small coal for the fire. "What intention?" she asked, lifting an eyebrow and then turning around to set the metal bucket down by the fire place.

"Oh, nothing, Mam. We were just talking about the intention of the men regarding going back to work," Dafydd replied.

Thank goodness he hadn't told their mother about their conversation. She'd had enough on her plate the past year or so. Lily didn't want her worrying. Mrs Davies was a world away from her own mother, like chalk and cheese the women were.

* * *

The meeting took place a fortnight later at the home of Mr. and Mrs Davies. Evan was immediately summoned out of the room by his father, which unnerved Lily somewhat. Mrs Davies was all sweetness and light, but Lily knew that somehow the woman was not being sincere.

"So, how long have you and my son known one another, my dear?" Olwen Davies asked, sitting upright in her high-backed armchair. "Surely, it cannot be for very long as he has only been living in Abercanaid for five months?"

Butterflies danced in Lily's stomach. So that was her game was it? She was trying to stall the wedding by the sound of it, to talk her out of marrying her son.

"I have known him for all of that time, Mrs Davies. And no, it is not that long, I grant you, but Evan and I are very close to one another. I help him at the chapel. I have started to teach Sunday school as well."

Mrs Davies raised an eyebrow. "So you can read and write then can you, Lily Jenkin?"

"I can, Ma'am. Did you think I am without knowledge?"

Olwen Davies lifted an eyebrow. "No, not at all. I just want the right woman to marry my son, that's all."

"That is understandable, but I see it is of little consequence, if we both love one another."

"Love!" Lily trembled as Mrs Davies suddenly rose to her feet. "Love. Don't talk to me about love." Then her voice softened and Lily thought she detected tears in the woman's eyes. "Love is about having food on the table. The world cannot go around with all hearts and flowers, you know. A couple need money to live off."

Lily wondered why the woman spoke so passionately about this issue. "Yes, I totally agree with you on that point, Mrs Davies. Evan earns a decent wage as a minister and we are fortunate to have a house to go with the chapel. I also have a small part-time job at the corner shop."

Mrs Davies smiled. Had she imagined that Lily was some sort of a gold digger?

"It's just that when George and I die, we plan to leave a large sum of money and our estate to our son. Evan is our only child. He will receive a considerable inheritance. We have to make sure he marries the right woman, or otherwise he won't receive a penny piece." She sat back down in the armchair.

Was this some kind of an idle threat?

"Well I can assure you, Mrs Davies, I have no intention of marrying Evan for money. I never even knew anything about you when he asked me to marry him. Believe me, my family has had to work hard for everything we have ever owned." Tears threatened to form and spill down her cheeks and she didn't want to break down in front of Mrs Davies. So, she took a deep breath of composure.

The door swung open and Evan walked in behind his father. "Mother?" he said with a questioning frown, "What have you been saying to Lily?"

"Nothing." The woman stiffened in her chair.

Evan's face grew crimson with anger. "Don't give me that, Mother. What have you said to her?"

His mother shook her head, avoiding everyone's gaze.

Then George Davies, looked at Lily and seeing she was close to tears said, "Lily, I am so sorry. I wish to apologise to you on behalf of my wife."

There was a long uncomfortable silence from all parties as both men looked at Evan's mother, waiting for a response. The only audible sound was the ticking of the grandfather clock in a corner of the room.

Lily's mouth fell open as she was just about to say something in reply, when Evan butted in. "Very well then, Mother, have it your own way. Father should not need to apologise for you. You have had your chance to make amends." Taking Lily by the arm, he helped her to her feet.

Then, turning, said, "May God forgive you, Mother, for treating my betrothed this way."

Lily had never seen Evan look angry before, he was such a mild mannered person normally. Then he stopped to mutter something to his father, who nodded, and all the while his mother sat in a catatonic-like state in the chair as if things were happening to someone else and not to her.

When they'd left the house, Lily finally found her voice. "Evan, if you are to become my husband, then you are not to talk over me. I am quite capable of fighting my own battles."

"I am sorry, *cariad*. But this is not the first time this kind of thing has happened to a fiancée of mine."

Lily stopped walking and turned to look at Evan. "You mean to tell me you have been engaged before?"

He hesitated before answering, "Yes, twice."

She could not believe what she was hearing. Evan engaged twice before, surely not? Did he make a habit of getting himself engaged to someone, only to have his mother destroy his happiness?

"Please say something?" He implored.

Lily trembled as she responded. "Well, the words I am thinking will not quite come to mind," she said firmly. "It just begs the question, why you have not told me of this before? Are your feelings so fickle that you will break off your engagements at the drop of a hat?"

"No, not at all," he replied, falling into step with her. "They broke the engagements off because they could not compete with Mother."

"So, is that what you expect me to do, to compete with her? Because I am telling you this, Evan Davies, I will not compete with a woman who has so little regard for me that she wants to ruin her son's happiness. My family may not be quite as wealthy as yours, but our love for one another holds no bounds." She started to walk off on her own into the cold night air.

She was surprised that he had not started to follow after her, thinking perhaps he had gone back to the house. If she did not hurry she would miss the train back home, she hesitated for a moment between retracing her steps and finding Evan or heading towards the station. Darkness was falling at an alarming rate and she wasn't quite sure of the way.

* * *

Picking up her wicker basket, she decided to carry on with her journey alone, after all, Evan only had himself to blame if he missed the train. Her mother would be worried about her if she did not arrive home on time.

Lily walked for a few minutes when she heard footsteps behind her. Thank goodness, Evan had swallowed his silly pride and come after her.

Turning, her mouth opened for her to say something, when she saw the silhouette of a large man, who was definitely not her intended. She gasped, the man was so close to her that he was invading her personal space.

"What is it you want?" she asked, trying not to sound as petrified as she inwardly felt.

The man let out a hollow laugh. "Oh, I'll show you want I want all right, Miss," he said in a Cardiff accent.

"Please take my basket. There's plenty of food left inside, here's some bread and cheese and some fruit…" but before she had a chance to continue, he had grabbed hold of her with his strong arms and pinioned her up against a wall. The street lighting was very dim and the nearest house was way in the distance, in any case, this area was heavily shielded by trees.

She let out a scream, but fear had made her voice sound weak. "Is that the best you can do, my lovely?" The man said, then he clamped his large hand over her mouth as she struggled to breathe. She knew what he wanted of her, that much was obvious, as she inhaled the smell of his beery breath and the odour of unwashed skin.

Dragging her down a small pathway, he pushed her to the ground and she felt the full weight of his heavy body on top of her. This couldn't be happening to her. No, no, no. She was a virgin and she had fully intended to keep herself that way until the night of her wedding.

She fought back furiously at the man, but he was much stronger and she knew he was going to be able to get the better of her quite easily. As he roughly hoisted her skirts above her knees, his hands trying to fumble with her under garments, she kicked out at him.

"Quite a little, fiery vixen we have here!" Then he let out a huge raucous laugh as if he was somehow enjoying the sport of seeing her frantically struggling to set herself free.

Suddenly, something scampered past them, giving Lily the opportunity to pull herself away from the man.

"What the..." he said, now confused.

In the distance Lily heard the sound of voices, heading towards them. Quick as a flash, the man got onto his feet, did up his trousers and ran off, shouting, "Dirty little whore!" at her.

Lily let out a long breath and tidying herself up, was about to stand up as a lady and gentleman came towards her.

"Are you all right, dear?" The gentleman spoke in a kindly voice. "Let's get you on to your feet."

"What happened?" asked the lady. "We were out walking our dog and he ran off in this direction."

Lily started to sob. "There…was…a…man…" she began, but she had difficulty getting her words out.

"All right, dear," the gentleman said, helping her on to her feet. "Come into our house, we live just across the way."

The dog had now returned to its owners and she knew she had him to thank for her being saved from possibly being raped that evening, or even worse. Shock was beginning to set in as for a moment, she could not even remember where she was going.

The lady put a friendly arm around her shoulder and guided her back to their warm, well-kept house, where she instructed her maid to brew up tea for all of them.

"Now then..." began the gentleman, who she could see in the light of indoors was middle-aged and reminded her a little of her father in his appearance, "you say that a man approached you?"

"Yes. He came up behind me. You see I was on my way back to the catch the train back to Merthyr, and I had lost my fiancé in the darkness. I heard footsteps and thinking it was him, turned around. Only I realised immediately it wasn't. The man dragged me off to the pathway where you found me and was about to…"

Lily started to sob again. The lady softly stroked her hair, "There, there," she comforted, "it's all over now."

"If it wasn't for your dog rushing past, disturbing him, and then you two coming along, I don't know what might have happened to me."

"It was a close call that is for sure. There have been reports of someone attacking women in this area in the past, but the last time was about a year ago, I think," the man said. "Now you are quite safe with us my dear. I am Mr. Nathaniel Pryce and this is my wife, Elizabeth."

"My name is Lily Jenkin."

The maid brought the tea in and as Lily welcomed the hot sweet drink, Elizabeth studied her. "My, my, but your clothing is in a terrible state, Lily. We need to check you haven't got any injuries, I will give you one of my own gowns to wear if you like."

"Thank you. You are both so kind. I am worried now, I think I will have missed my train home and my mother will be concerned about me."

"Don't fret, dear. We will find some way around the problem," Mrs Pryce reassured her. "Let me inform your fiancé for a start. You mentioned his parents live a couple of streets away. Perhaps Mr. Pryce and I know his family?"

"Oh no, please Mrs Pryce. I don't want him to know about this, it will only make him feel guilty."

"Very well, Lily," Mr. Pryce reassured. "Now you are quite welcome to spend the night here, or if you would like, I can walk you around to your fiancé's family home."

Lily reasoned that no matter what she felt about Olwen Davies, she should find Evan, he would be worried sick about her, that much she knew. "Yes please, Mr. Pryce. If you wouldn't mind walking me around there. It is just around the corner."

"Very well then. Take your time drinking your tea, you have had a nasty shock and I am going to see the police tomorrow about your attacker. Are you quite sure you didn't see his face?"

"I am perfectly sure." It was true, she would never recognise the man again in a month of Sundays, but she realised the importance of informing the police, so that people in the area would be on their guard in case it should happen again.

Lily bit her lip. "What's the matter?" Mrs Pryce gazed at her, eyes full of concern as Mr. Pryce left the room.

"Please will you ensure that Mr. Pryce does not pass on my name to the police? I am concerned that if my brothers find out, they will come to take their revenge on this man if they find out who he is."

"Lily, you have our word on that. Now come upstairs with me and I shall let you try on one of my gowns as yours appears to be torn."

Lily looked down at her best velvet dress, the hem all splattered in mud. The tear she could mend quite easily, but the emotional wounds she reasoned, were quite another matter.

As she undressed in Mrs Pryce's bedroom, she noticed that her arms were covered in small fresh bruises where the man had held her down. She also had a slight graze to her elbow. With any luck, Evan, nor her family need ever know about this.

Mrs Pryce parcelled up Lily's gown in some brown paper, tying it with string. The gown she had loaned Lily was beautiful. It was a dark chocolate brown, with intricate embroidery on the bodice, long puff sleeves and a high neck. If this had been some other occasion then Lily would have been over the moon to wear it, but the truth of the matter was that it only served to remind her of that awful incident, not yet even one hour ago. Evan would be in a blind panic by now. Why or why, did she have to storm off like that and maybe more importantly, why hadn't Evan followed after her?

She sighed deeply, and then, tidied up her hair. She would cope, she knew she would, but if that other awful thing had happened to her robbing her of her maidenhood, what then? It was every woman's nightmare. What man would want her then?

* * *

Evan's eyes widened as Lily stood at the door with Mr. Pryce.

"Lily, where on earth did you get to? Were you lost or something? My father came after us and I stopped for a moment to see what he wanted and the next moment you had gone. I followed after you."

It was then Lily realised she must have taken a wrong turning in the dark.

"Yes, Evan," she lied, "I did get lost and Mr. and Mrs Pryce kindly took me to their home." Mr. Pryce stood behind her, not getting involved in the conversation.

"Thank you, Mr. Pryce," Evan said, as he escorted Lily into the house. Lily smiled and waved to the man hoping he would not mention about the earlier incident.

As they stood in the well-lit hallway, Evan let out a gasp. "Why have you changed your dress?"

Lily hesitated for a moment, but she had earlier rehearsed how she would explain things to him. "I tripped over in the dark when Mr. and Mrs Pryce found me. Mrs Pryce kindly loaned me this gown, wasn't it nice of her?"

Evan's eyebrows knitted together as his eyes narrowed in disbelief, but if he thought otherwise, then he said no more about it.

"Father has instructed Daisy to make up two bedrooms for us. It's too late for the train, I thought you might have caught it without me."

Lily fiddled about with the string on her parcel. "Yes, if I hadn't had that fall and got lost, I suppose I might have made it."

"Lily, what happened to the picnic basket?"

In her blind panic at being attacked it had gone clean out of her mind. "I suppose I must have left it at the Pryce house." In reality, she realised it was far more likely that she had dropped it where she was attacked. Tears were now quite close to the surface, so she was pleased, when Evan suggested she go right up to bed without even his parents laying eyes on her.

What was she going to say to her family tomorrow, how was she going to explain why she had not caught the train home?

As she removed her clothing, she studied herself in the mirror. Was it just hours ago that she was that young, spirited woman, facing Olwen Davies head on, slaying her personal dragon? Now she just needed to retreat inwardly to lick her wounds like an injured animal. She didn't know how to feel any more.

She removed all her clothing except her petticoat, she would have to use that as a night gown. Unclipping her hair, she let it fall loose upon her shoulders. What would the Davies's think of her if they knew what had happened?

More importantly what would Evan think?

* * *

The following morning at breakfast, there was no sign of Olwen Davies. Daisy served Lily and Evan their breakfast in the drawing room and later Evan's father joined them for a morning cup of tea.

"There will be a train to Merthyr in about an hour, if you hurry you should make it this time," he smiled.

Lily swallowed hard, it was only a reminder about what had taken place last night. It was hard to believe that it had really happened to her.

On the journey back to Merthyr, Lily tried to avoid Evan's questions by changing the subject, she knew he wasn't fooled for a moment, but she couldn't help herself, she didn't want to hurt him, but he looked it just the same.

As soon as she arrived back home at Chapel Square and Evan had left to go back to his home, she fell into her mother's arms.

"Oh *cariad*," her mother said, dabbing at her watery eyes, "I've worried all night about you. Where did you get to?"

She was about to tell her mother a lie, but instead the whole sorry tale came tumbling out. "What an ordeal it was for me..." She sobbed.

"I am so sorry, Lily, for what has happened to you. Men like that brute you encountered last night, want a good old horsewhipping."

As Lily dried her eyes, feeling some relief for recounting the tale to her mother, she suddenly became anxious in case her brothers should hear of it.

Her mother caught her looking around the room and said, "What's the matter child?"

"Are Dafydd and Delwyn here?"

"No fear. Delwyn has gone to work and Dafydd has gone to Merthyr today."

Lily let out a long breath. Hopefully, there was no need for them to ever know for they would surely horsewhip the man themselves if they ever found out who he was.

"Now come and sit down by the fire and I'll brew up a nice cup of tea."

It was good being back on familiar territory, safe somehow.

"So what does Evan think about what happened to you last night and why wasn't he with you in the first place?" Her mother frowned.

"Oh Mam, please don't think ill of him. It was a misunderstanding. I walked off and I haven't had the heart to tell him what happened to me, but I am sure he suspects something."

"Then you must tell him, Lily. That is no way to start a marriage, believe me."

Lily knew in her heart that her mother was right, otherwise this awful incident would come between them and their plans for the future. Resolving to speak with him that evening as she prepared for the soup kitchen at the chapel, she knew it was the right thing to do.

* * *

Evan looked aghast as she told him, when the last of the people had left the chapel.

Taking her firmly by the shoulders he looked intently into her eyes. "Why didn't you tell me, perhaps I could have done something to help?"

"What could you have done though, Evan? The man ran off into the night and it was too dark. I am a stranger to Pentyrch, so I had no idea who he was."

He sat on a pew, shoulders hunched like a beaten man, hands covering his face in despair. "I am so sorry for what happened to you Lily."

"So is it going to change the way you think about me now? Do you see me as soiled? It did not get that far, Evan, believe me."

Allowing his hands to fall from his face, he looked at her and she saw the pain and compassion in his eyes. "No, of course not. Even if things had got much worse, I would still love you, Lily. It's just that I feel so helpless and guilty too, for not following you immediately."

Lily straightened her shoulders. "Well, do you know what this had made me think of?"

He shook his head.

"That women and young girls need to be able to protect themselves. To know of the dangers out there and maybe find ways of defending themselves."

Evan listened with interest as she told him about her plans for holding a women's defence class at the chapel. Although something like that had been unheard of in the small village, Evan could see the sense of it. The only thing he wasn't happy about was her telling everyone what had happened to her. He didn't want the villagers gossiping about her and there was one in particular with a vicious tongue.

Chapter Four

It was the first sign of spring as buds blossomed on the trees and new lambs nestled with their mothers on the lush green hillsides around the valley. There were only two weeks to go to the wedding and Lily was tremendously excited. Her mother had already made up her dress with some material she had saved up for from a drapers in Merthyr Tydfil. A seamstress from the village had embroidered the bodice and sewn on small seed pearls.

As she studied her reflection in the mirror, Lily thought how lucky she was to have met a man like Evan Davies. Dafydd's leg was on the mend, and the day after her wedding it had been arranged that he would start working on the barges. Delwyn had found a new job in a different mine called, Cwm Pit. Life seemed to be on the up and up as the awful incident at Pentyrch started to fade from her mind.

There had been no word from Olwen Davies since that fateful day and Evan had no wish to return to his family home. Life in the small village was starting to return to its usual routine following the pit disaster, but of course it would never be normal again for those who'd lost loved ones. A couple of families had to move into the workhouse at St. Tydfil's as they could no longer afford to live in their homes now that their breadwinner was deceased. In some families they had lost more than one wage.

It made Lily sad to think about it, but as Delwyn had reassured her, she had done a lot for the villagers of Abercanaid and it was all resting in God's hands now.

* * *

Lily and Evan stood in front of the pulpit under the watchful eyes of the minister, Lily's family and friends, and neighbours from the village of Abercanaid.

Lily could hardly believe her wedding day was finally here. She would have loved it of course if her father had been alive to see her wed and had accompanied her down the aisle, but instead, Delwyn, as her slightly eldest brother, had insisted on doing the deed.

One look into her new husband's eyes told her how much he loved her and that his love for her was totally unconditional.

Mrs Morgan was the first to congratulate the happy couple afterwards, throwing a handful of rice at them and promising the loan of the pony and trap for their honeymoon, which pleased Lily. It was decked out in colourful ribbons to take them to her Uncle Edmund's inn at Cefn Coed.

"Oh, my darling," Lily's mother said, as the happy couple prepared to leave the village, "I have never seen you looking as beautiful as you do right now, Lily."

Evan smiled as he took the reins, thanking Mr. and Mrs Morgan and the rest of the congregation for their wonderful send off. If he was missing his parents on their big day, then he wasn't showing it.

"This is the happiest day of my life," Lily said, as she settled herself down into her seat on the trap. "I can never imagine myself being as happy as I am at this very moment in time."

Evan brought his lips crashing down on hers and she felt a desire stirring within.

***

The few days they spent in Cefn Coed were wonderful, the weather was sunny and bright. Lily resolved to be a good wife to Evan. The only cloud on the horizon was the rift with his mother, she so wanted to heal it for him.

Evan carried his new bride over the threshold of Chapel House when they returned from honeymoon.

It was good at last to have a house of their own and now to be Mrs Evan Davies, wife of a minister of Abercanaid.

Lily was becoming worried that Delwyn no longer attended services at the chapel. He had made it plain to all who asked him that he was going to embrace the Mormon faith, he had made friends with several people who attended the Mormon meetings after hearing the word preached on the streets of Merthyr. He spoke eagerly of his plan to emigrate to the New World, America, to follow after those who had gone before him.

Lily feared losing her brother, but knew she had no powers to stop him, he had indeed changed for the better as a person since attending the church. He was no longer the headstrong brother she remembered and was impressed with the way he had matured as he regularly attended meetings at Cymreigyddion Hall, Merthyr, above the White Lion pub.

Dafydd, seemed unconcerned with the change in his brother, after all, he spent a lot of his time working on the barges now that his leg had healed, even though it had left him with a slight limp.

Mam too, seemed happy for Delwyn. It puzzled Lily that her family should feel pleased for one of their own to embrace a faith that none of them knew or understood that much about.

Evan tried to reassure her, but failed. In her heart of hearts, she eventually realised that it was not Delwyn's faith she feared, but the fact that one day she might lose him forever as he went in search of his Zion at Great Salt Lake as many had done in the 1840s before him.

* * *

A few weeks into married life, Evan received a letter from his father, telling him that he and his mother wished to visit them at their home in Abercanaid.

Evan frowned as he placed the letter on the kitchen table. Then turning to his wife, he said, "It's not that I don't wish to see them, Lily. It's just that I know things are going to be awkward between me and my mother, with the way she has spoken to you. I just will not stand for her treating my wife in that manner."

Lily understood his need to protect and had hoped and prayed they would have resolved the rift in time for his parents to attend their wedding, but it was not to be so.

Lily placed a reassuring hand on his shoulder. "They are your parents, Evan. I would hate to be estranged from my mother, and now that my father has died..." there was a catch in her voice. "How I wish that every day I could have him back here with us."

He lowered his voice to almost a whisper. "I know I should be ashamed of myself, *cariad*. But I can't help it."

"I think you should write back to your parents and tell them they are welcome to come to see us. I bear your mother no grudges." Life was just too short to be cut off from family, she thought. And the Davies's were indeed her new family.

"But what about if she is rude to you again, Lily? She is a very strong woman."

Lily smiled nervously, took in a deep breath and with hands placed squarely on her hips said, "Evan Davies, don't you think that I am a strong woman, too?"

"Of course you are my sweet." He kissed her gently on the cheek. "That is what I love most about you."

"Well then, tell them they are both welcome to come to stay for a few days. We have a spare bedroom."

Evan fiddled with the stiff collar on his shirt. "All right, I shall write that letter now this very minute!" he declared, as he went in search of a quill and paper.

Lily remained in the chapel, arranging the daffodils and irises that Mrs Morgan had brought from her own garden. The blooms looked lovely and would brighten things up. The place had taken on a new life since she'd had a hand in it, not just décor wise with the little touches here and there, but also with the groups she'd been running during the week. The women's groups seemed to be doing very well, especially the self defence one, but in later weeks the children's groups were also growing too.

It had long been at the back of her mind to start a school at the chapel, like some of those Dame Schools that had been springing up lately. A lot of the children in the village could neither read nor write. It was high time they learned. It would help to set them up for their future. She had witnessed many a collier in the area who signed his name with a cross. Men who were highly intelligent, yet lacked the intellectual knowledge to help them achieve more in life.

She needed to find some way to finance this. It would work alongside the soup kitchen at the chapel. If she only managed to get the children to learn to read and write and to perform simple arithmetic, that would be fine with her. Rose Crawshay from Cyfarthfa Castle had achieved this and she so admired women like her and Charlotte Guest for what they had done for the people of Merthyr.

* * *

It was towards the end of August, during the blistering heat, that Lily's mother first took ill, she had some sort of a fever and had not been herself for some time.

Doctor Owen was called and when he had examined Mrs Jenkin, he came downstairs and took Lily to one side. "I am not entirely sure, Lily," he whispered, "but I am suspecting an outbreak of cholera in the village. I was called to see a lady living behind you in Lewis Square, there is severe overcrowding in that small house. She has some lodgers as you know and the house is in a filthy state as the woman is ill. Does your mother have any connections with anyone living there?"

"I'm not sure Doctor Owen..." Lily frowned. "Hang on, I do remember her saying she had befriended a thirty two year old lady when I was working at the shop. I think she used to help her sometimes." Lily's heart beat fast at the thought of her poor mother. She remembered her father telling her about a severe outbreak some years ago when hundreds of Merthyr people had died. Living conditions had improved somewhat in Abercanaid and Merthyr, but there were still some houses where overcrowding and bad ventilation were breeding grounds for diseases. One such area was known as 'China'. A notorious area of the town. So called because it was said to be ruled by an 'Emperor'. A place where most decent people feared to tread after dark. The 'Emperor' himself had people working for him known as 'bullies' who in turn ran groups of pick pockets and prostitutes.

The doctor's gaze was drawn to the ceiling as he spoke of Mrs Jenkin quietly as she rested in the bedroom above. "Now dehydration is going to be a problem, so make sure she has plenty to drink, but I'm warning you mind, boil all the water you give her. There was a warning issued in the last outbreak that cold water was best, it's not so Lily. Boiling will help to kill the germs. Keep people away from the house. And we need to keep an eye on the rest of you. I would keep away from the chapel for time being. You will need to move back into your house to attend to your mother in any case. Where are your brothers?"

"They are both in work. They don't appear to be ill."

"That's good. I fear for that poor family at Lewis Square, mind you. It might just be that your mother has a bad stomach bug. Let's hope and pray it is so. I will go back to your house and inform Evan about this. He must keep away until we are certain it's not cholera revisiting the town once again."

When the doctor had gone, Lily put the large kettle on to boil on the fire. Then she poured some water into a tin jug to cool for everyone in the house to drink. She changed the bed clothing and her mother's damp nightdress as she'd been perspiring profusely. She would need to boil those too, just in case. She was going to need to warn her family to stay away from Chapel Square.

"Lily," her mother held out her fragile looking hand. Her eyes sunken and her skin seemed lifeless, pale and sallow. "What did Doctor Owen say to you?"

"He just said that I had to make sure you drink plenty of fluids and for you to rest, Mam."

But there was no fooling her mother. "He thinks it's the cholera, doesn't he?"

Lily nodded and bit her lower lip. What could she say? Pausing for a moment, she finally said, "Mam, he's very concerned about a family that have taken ill in Lewis Square. Have you been there recently?"

"No, I haven't. I used to help there a few months ago, but my back has put me in agony sometimes. No, Lily. I should be all right then, shouldn't I?"

Lily almost shrugged her shoulders as she just didn't know the answer to that, instead she said, "Of course you will, Mam. You're a strong woman."

Over the next few days, seven people died out of twelve in that one dwelling house in Lewis Square, including the thirty two year old woman Lily's mother had once befriended. Meanwhile, Mrs Jenkin was not getting any better at all. Miraculously, Delwyn and Dafydd, did not submit to the disease, nor Lily herself. She felt guilty that Evan would now have to stop his parents from visiting Abercanaid in case they picked up the disease, even if it was all for the best.

A few weeks later, when it looked as if they had turned a corner with regards to their mother's illness, Mrs Jenkin caught pneumonia and passed away. It was all Lily could bear. She finally returned home to Evan before the funeral was to take place, the service being held at the same chapel Mrs Jenkin attended every week and where she had seen her daughter baptised and married.

"Lily, I am quite worried about you," Evan said, taking his wife's hand when they left the graveyard after the burial.

Lily had tears in her eyes and said, "I know this is not the right time to tell you, but I think I am with child."

Evan smiled his eyes also filling up. He hugged her close to him. "We'll talk about it later, when we are at home," he advised. There were too many people leaving the graveyard who might hear them. For now, it was wise to keep things quiet.

Once back home he advised her to rest for a while.

"Thank you, Evan." She forced a smile, when all she felt like doing was crying for her poor Mam and her brothers. What would Delwyn and Dafydd do now? Delwyn still spoke about emigrating to America. He had told her that he could take a ship from the port of Liverpool. His faith seemed to get stronger and stronger every day.

Now it was Dafydd who concerned her, being the youngest of the twins, he had always followed after his brother's lead. What would he do if his brother went to live in Utah? There was a good chance they'd never see Delwyn again, even though they'd said they would go over to visit. It would cost a lot of money and take a long time to get there, and now the baby was coming.

Evan brought Lily a cup of tea and a Welsh cake, announcing, "Mrs Morgan kindly sent these cakes over for us today."

Lily smiled. "That was lovely of her, I must thank her. I feel awful that I had to take so much time off from work."

"That could not be helped, *cariad*. What else were you supposed to do? You could not leave your Mam to look after herself, now could you?"

"That is true. But I can't help feeling guilty."

"Don't you worry about it. Mrs Morgan understands. In any case, you will have to stay off work now for the foreseeable future with the baby on the way."

Lily had considered that. "I suppose so. I am used to working though, Evan. I have to keep myself occupied."

"So, how far do you think you are gone?" He asked, gently patting her belly.

"Around three months or so I think. I shall need to talk to Doctor Owen."

"Yes, that would be wise, especially after all the stress you have been under the past few weeks."

"Yes, though isn't it ironic that Mam survived the cholera and died of pneumonia?"

Evan nodded. "I expect her body was very weak. If she had been in her normal good health, I don't suppose the pneumonia would have taken her like that. But rest assured, she was a good Christian lady, she will have gone to the right place. If anyone deserved to go to heaven it was your mother. And of course she is with your father now."

That thought comforted Lily. "Evan, I was just thinking...we are going to have to tell your mother and father about the baby."

"Yes, I will send them a letter tomorrow. Mother seems more understanding now. I think she will look forward to spoiling her first grandchild."

Lily put down her cup of tea and laid back in the armchair, suddenly she was feeling very tired and she drifted off into a deep sleep...the past few weeks had taken a lot out of her.

* * *

Evan's parents came to pay their respects one week later following the death of Lily's mother, expressing their sincere condolences. Both seemed delighted about the imminent arrival. Maybe now things would improve, Lily thought.

"Are you sure you're resting up?" Evan's mother asked, as they took a stroll along the canal bank. The leaves on the trees were now changing to a deep shade of copper and russet. The woman seemed to have softened since she had heard of the death of Lily's mother.

"Yes, have no fear. Evan would not let me return to work right now. In fact, I am resting too much I feel."

"I should think he had better not allow you return to work in your condition, nor after the baby is born either." Olwen Davies brushed some imaginary flecks from her gown, the vibrancy of her attire looking totally out of place in Abercanaid. Still, Lily reassured herself that even though the woman was prone to thinking of herself as someone above her station, at least she had her best interests at heart and those of her unborn grandchild.

"I am so looking forward to the birth of this child," Lily enthused. In all honesty, it was the baby that was keeping her going since the death of her Mam. She hardly saw either Delwyn or Dafydd these days, it was the feeling that the family she had once known, had all but gone forever, even though she had a new family to look forward to.

Both brothers knew about the baby, but none had shown the enthusiasm she had expected, but who could blame them with the announcement coming so soon after the death of their beloved mother.

Doctor Owen had said that she would probably have the baby in early January. She must have conceived, not long after their marriage.

She knew she shouldn't have, but having little to do, had driven her mad with boredom, so she had spent the past couple of days, sorting out the spare bedroom for the baby. Evan had a made a wooden crib, which he'd even painted, and she had sewn curtains with some material Mrs Morgan had given her. It was going to look lovely.

Her mother-in-law had surprised her by asking questions about the groups she ran at the chapel, she was particularly interested in the women's defence group and had said she would like to sit in one evening.

Her father-in-law had spent his time sorting out the garden for them, they could grow their own vegetables and some flowers too, now that he had dug up all the weeds.

If only her mother was still alive to see the birth of the baby. She even had a little bump to show for it and her morning sickness had stopped, she didn't seem to be putting on much weight though.

She awoke that night with severe stomach pain, her body damp with perspiration.

"Evan!" she called out, thinking he was downstairs, but he was in the bed next to her.

He lit a candle by the side of the bed. "What's the matter, Lily?"

"Something's wrong, I'm in agony with my stomach."

He pulled back the blankets and she could see the big red stain on the sheets for herself, there was no doubt about it, she was losing the baby.

"I'm going to fetch Doctor Owen," he said with authority. "I'll wake Mother up and ask her to sit with you, all right?"

She nodded in a blind panic. She would rather die herself than lose the baby she had been carrying for the past five months.

Doctor Owen turned up within ten minutes with a grave look on his face.

"How long have you been bleeding for?" he asked.

"I only noticed just now when I woke up, Doctor." Mrs Davies stood at her side, holding her hand.

"If you can all leave the room, please, I would like to examine Lily," he requested. Evan guided his mother down the stairs.

When they had both left, Lily said, "I am going to lose the baby, aren't I Doctor?"

"Let me be the judge of that," he said, as he laid down his bag and palpated her stomach. "Have you been doing anything strenuous lately? Like lifting anything heavy for instance?"

"No, Doctor. I had been sorting out the spare bedroom for the baby's arrival, but asked Evan to move the furniture around."

"I suspect it might have something to do with all the stress placed upon your shoulders during and after your mother's illness. Now, it could be that you might just need bed rest and your body is telling you to slow down. My suggestion is that you have someone to help you at home, Lily, at least until the baby is born. You need complete bed rest, until I suggest otherwise."

"So, it is not inevitable that I shall miscarry, Doctor?"

He shook his head. "I can't say for certain, of course, but if you rest up and eat well, you will be increasing your baby's chances of survival."

Lily breathed a sigh of relief. The doctor was probably right, she had been over doing things lately and she would never forgive herself if it was the reason that she lost the baby.

When the doctor left her, she heard him talking in hushed tones to Evan and his mother down stairs, who both came up to see her once he had gone.

"It is agreed, Lily. Mother will stay here for a while, until we can sort something else out. Father will go back to Pentrych to keep an eye on the house."

Lily nodded. She was in no state to disagree.

"Now where can I find clean sheets?" Olwen Davies asked, rolling up the sleeves on her dressing gown.

"In the cupboard in the spare bedroom," Lily murmured. "Would you like me to get them for you?"

"You'll do nothing of the sort, young lady. I am going to clean you up and then change the bed. This room shall be your four walls for the foreseeable future."

* * *

Lily was surprised to find Delwyn knocking on her bedroom door the following morning.

"I passed Doctor Owen this morning, Lily. I had no idea you were unwell," he whispered, his hazel brown eyes full of concern.

"I am fine, Delwyn. I just need bed rest, that's all."

She gestured for him to sit down on the chair by her bedside. He put his head in his hands and wept. "I am so sorry, Lily. I have been so wrapped up in myself since Mam died, I have not thought of anyone else, it has been so selfish of me."

"Now, don't be silly, Delwyn. We all have our own lives to lead. Where is Dafydd?"

Delwyn's dropped his hands from his face, which had turned a deep shade of crimson. "I…I…I'm not sure," he stammered.

"Where is he? There is something you are not telling me, isn't there?" Lily detected the panic in her own voice.

"I haven't seen him for a week. He has not been in work, his boss on the barges has been looking for him. Someone in the village said they saw him drinking in the pubs in China."

"China!" Lily sat up in bed. "What on earth is he doing in *that* hell hole?"

Delwyn drew nearer to the bed and taking Lily's hand, said, "He has taken Mam's death very badly, maybe worse than we have. He just didn't see it coming and now he is drinking heavily. He has spent all his wages on beer and now his boss says he has no job to go back to. Oh Lily, if I did not have my faith to cling to, what would I have?"

"You would still have me, dear brother. It has been hard on us all. You must go and look for Dafydd as soon as you leave here. Bring him here for Evan to talk to. I don't want him to end up a vagrant living off the streets of China. We have to save him before it is too late."

"I am sorry. Perhaps I should not have told you this, in your condition, Lily."

"I am glad that you have. Now that Mam has gone, we have to look out for one another. And if you manage to get him sobered up, then we must speak with his boss to see if we can get his job back."

Delwyn nodded. It obviously hurt him to see his brother in so much pain and his sister in a different kind of pain all together.

* * *

Delwyn did not find his brother that day, nor the next, or the one after that. Lily was becoming increasingly worried as her brother walked around the area asking everyone he came into contact with if they knew Dafydd Jenkin, and not that many did. He decided to look for him in the inns and public houses. Eventually, he found him in The Star Inn, opposite St Tydfil's Parish church at the lower end of Merthyr Town.

"The place was awash with all sorts of undesirables," he explained to Lily later that day. "I had to cut my way through a thick haze of smoke, before I spotted him sitting in the corner about to pass out."

"Well, where is he now?" She was worried in case Delwyn had left him there.

"Now don't get concerned, it is bad for you and the baby. I managed to get him back here. He is sitting downstairs, taking a cup of tea with Mrs Davies."

Lily felt mortified. What would the woman think of her brother? "Where is Evan then?"

"She told me he had to slip out to see to a woman who has just lost her husband in the village." Delwyn sat looking uncomfortable squeezing his flat cap in both hands. Who knew what kind of conversation Dafydd and Mrs Davies were having downstairs? After all, the woman's own son did not touch a drop of alcohol.

"Please Delwyn," Lily implored, "would you go downstairs in a little while to check that Dafydd is all right?"

"What you mean is, you want me to ensure that Mrs Davies is able to handle our drink-sodden brother?" he asked, with a lop-sided grin.

"Yes, something like that."

He got up onto his feet and headed for the bedroom door, then turning, said, "Don't worry so much, Lily. Dafydd will be all right. This is just a temporary setback for him. He's my younger twin and if anyone should know him, it is I."

Lily managed a weak smile and laid her head back down on the pillow to rest. When she opened her eyes again the room was in darkness. She must have drifted off to sleep and now, Delwyn had probably left for home.

There was a tap at the bedroom door and Evan came in carrying a cup of tea. "I thought you might like this," he suggested.

"Oh, I would. Thank you, Evan." She took the china cup and saucer from his outstretched hand. "I hear you had to visit someone today who lost her husband?"

"Yes, I am afraid so. I had to see Mrs Jones in Nightingale Street. Her husband died in his sleep last night."

"Is she coping?"

"As well as can be expected under the circumstances. It's the best way to go though, isn't it? When you are already dreaming."

"I suppose so," Lily agreed. "Is Dafydd still downstairs?"

"No." Fear coursed through Lily's veins. What if he'd gone to another pub to get a drink, maybe this time in the village? "Delwyn told me what happened. Rest assured he is sober now. He had a sleep downstairs and now both your brothers are going to see if they can catch the barge when it stops in Troedyrhiw. He is heartbroken that he has lost his job."

Lily took a sip of her tea, then put it down. "I know. He loved that job, more than he loved it down the pit. It would be a shame if he has to go back underground."

Evan nodded. "My mother is making something for us to eat."

"Your mother?"

"Don't look so surprised. She is able to cook." It was indeed a bit of a shock to Lily after the way the woman had acted when she first visited her home. Then it had been too much trouble for her to have even poured herself a cup of tea.

"Well thank her for me will you and while you are at it, if you can please call over to Mrs Morgan's shop and tell her to come over here to see me tomorrow, if you will."

Evan kissed her softly on the forehead. It was nice resting for a change, but she didn't want to be treated like a piece of porcelain for much longer. It just wasn't her, doing nothing all day.

* * *

The following morning, Doctor Owen, called around to see her and finding the bleeding had completely stopped, allowed her to get out of bed for short periods to sit in the chair, providing she did no more than that.

It was a relief to hear him tell her that. Then after her breakfast, Mrs Morgan arrived.

"How are you feeling?" she asked, her blue eyes full of compassion.

"Better today, Mrs Morgan."

"I've brought you a couple of books to read and I thought you might like to try some embroidery."

"That's very kind of you. It's a long time since I've done anything like that though."

"You'll soon pick it back up," she said kindly. "I'll show you some of the stitches before I leave. It will give you something to occupy your mind."

"That's very thoughtful. I wish I was back at the shop now serving customers that would give me plenty to do. I expect you are rushed off your feet, Mrs Morgan?"

Mrs Morgan's face flushed bright red, then looking at the counterpane, she said, "I am afraid I have had to get a new girl in to take your place, she is minding the shop right now."

"Well of course you did, Mrs Morgan. And in any case I shall have my hands full when this little one is born." She patted her swollen belly.

Mrs Morgan sat down on the bed and touched Lily's hand. "Lily, there is something I need to tell you."

Why was she looking so serious? Had something happened? Was it something to do with Dafydd?

"What is it? You can tell me."

"I have had little sleep all night worrying about whether I should say something, but there is a lot of talk in the village and as I run the shop, I am privy to what people are saying and when they have said it Lily, I have put them straight, believe me."

The colour drained from Mrs Morgan's face, and Lily felt a nausea rise within her. "Go on, Mrs Morgan…"

"The talk is that it's not Evan's baby you are carrying, but some other man's."

Suddenly, Lily felt the sickness rise up from within and she retched and then vomited all over the bed. Mrs Morgan held her hair out of the way and when she was certain she had finished, removed the dirty counterpane, and poured water out of a jug into a bowl and gave it to Lily, so she could clean herself.

"I am all right. It is the baby." Lily explained as she dried herself with a towel. Mrs Morgan took the towel and put the bowl of water to one side. Lily knew this sickness had little to do with her pregnancy and more to do with the shock of hearing what she had just been told.

"Would you like a cup of water?" She nodded and Mrs Morgan passed it to her. "I am sorry, but I felt you had to be told. You know what this village is like for gossip."

"I think I know how that started, when I told the women in the defence group about how I was attacked in Pentyrch." Mrs Morgan nodded as if she understood all too well. "I swear to you, he did not rape me. His intentions were there, but I was lucky, I got away."

"I think you need to tell Evan about what people are saying. One or two in particular are very bad minded around here."

Lily shook her head. "I don't want Evan worrying about this."

"Look," said Mrs Morgan, firmly, "he's your husband now, Lily. You have to tell him. Remember how you felt when you kept the attack from him in the first place? You told me you felt better for telling him."

Lily knew the elderly lady was right, it was just that she didn't want to see the hurt in his eyes again.

When Mrs Morgan had departed, Evan came up to see her. "Mrs Morgan said you needed to speak with me, Lily?"

Lily nodded. "Sit down, Evan." Then she recounted the whole tale to him watching his face change from disbelief to anger.

"How dare they! You have been so good to the people of this village, Lily. You don't deserve this after all you have been through lately."

"Well according to Mrs Morgan, it is one woman in particular who is putting around the rumour."

Evan took her hand in his. "You must tell me, Lily. Who is it?"

Biting her lip, she replied, "It is Tom Shanklin's wife, Maggie."

Evan let go of her hand and jumped onto his feet. "Of course, I should have guessed right away it was her. That Irish woman has caused a lot of grief in Abercanaid with her evil tongue."

Lily knew this all too well. The woman was quite crafty in her way, she lulled folk into a false sense of security by being nice to them and then she would go in for the kill by either dropping a piece of gossip that more often than not had its foundations in hearsay at the local pub, or she would say something uncomplimentary to the person concerned, leaving them feeling that they were a bad mother or that they didn't know how to look after their husband very well.

She had even taken in a young wife who had been badly beaten by her husband in the village, just so she had plenty of fodder to feed off and relate in the shops around Abercanaid and Merthyr. Then when she'd had no further use for the woman, she sent her on her way, so that the woman fell destitute and ended up selling herself in China.

"She's not going to get away with this, Lily. Her evil tongue has flapped about in that prim and proper head of hers for far too long."

"What are you going to do, Evan?" Now Lily was worried, she had never seen her husband looking so angry. It was just as well that Dafydd and Delwyn had not heard of this either as Delwyn, in particular, would march around to the woman's house and confront her.

"Now you shouldn't be worrying, I just want her to learn the errors of her ways, that's all my sweet."

But Lily did worry and she fretted most of the day, so much so that she found it hard to concentrate on the embroidery table cloth she was working on, having to undo the stitches several times.

She hoped Evan would calm down and with it being Sunday tomorrow, she guessed that he would do nothing for a while, so may be by the following week, he would just let it go.

But she was wrong.

The Doctor had told her that as long as she just went to the one Sunday service at the chapel and then went straight back to bed, it would be all right.

So she sat with Evan's mother quietly in an upstairs pew. Evan's sermon had been most interesting—he spoke about a still tongue keeping a wise head from the book of Proverbs. The congregation joined in with the hymn, *Jerusalem* and then, he started to speak again.

Both of his hands gripped the pulpit, so much so that his knuckles appeared white, then he said:

"That was a very old proverb I spoke about in my sermon and one I feel has relevance today. There is someone in this very chapel, here this very Sunday…"

Lily gasped as she realised what he was about to say, her mother-in-law looking at her in bemusement as she had no idea what was going on.

"Someone who is slandering the name of my good wife to the villagers. This woman, knowing that my wife has not been very well and has recently lost her dear mother as well as almost losing our child, has repeatedly spoken ill of my wife. Yes, it is true that my wife was attacked in Pentrych earlier this year and I only wish that I had been there to rescue her myself, but I have with me today a lady and gentleman who kindly came to my wife's rescue that evening."

Lily looked over the balcony and for the first time saw Mr. and Mrs Pryce from Pentrych sitting down below. Evan beckoned them to come to the front of the church, where they spoke about finding Lily that night and how impressed they had been with how she had conducted herself following the assault.

"I would publicly like to thank Mr. and Mrs Pryce for taking care of Lily during a time that must have been truly terrifying to her. Lily has done a lot for this community and so to hear someone speaking ill of her, is just awful. This person knows who she is and many of you will know her as well. She will only be welcome in this chapel in the future, if she remembers as it says in the proverb: 'A still tongue keeps a wise head'."

Many members of the congregation nodded their heads in agreement and muttered to one another, several turning around to stare at Mrs Shanklin, who lowered her head in shame.

Olwen Davies patted Lily's hand and said, "My husband and I had no idea about this, Lily. You should have told us."

Lily just smiled and nodded, there was no way that she would have told her back then, she hadn't trusted the woman one inch. Now she was beginning to realise that she was warming towards her mother-in-law. The woman had a softer side to her that she hadn't seen before.

Lily, herself, sat upright and lots of people came up to her after the service to ask how she was doing. It would be a long time before Mrs Shanklin spread any gossip around the village again.

Chapter Five

The leaves on the trees started to fall and then autumn turned to winter. It was the week before Christmas, almost a year since the pit accident had claimed so many lives. Lily was now more active as her pregnancy flourished and she became excited as the new life kicked inside her.

Dafydd had been fortunate to be reinstated on the barges with the promise that he was never going to get in a state like that again, and that if something awful happened, he would talk about it instead.

Delwyn surprised Lily by staying true to his Mormon faith, even though he came across a lot of opposition from other denominations. "It's just that people don't understand that we believe in God as well," Delwyn explained one afternoon when he took tea with Lily and Evan at Chapel House. "They think it is Satan's work, but I know in my heart that this is the true faith. The Saints have been pelted on the streets as they preach in the town..." he shook his head sadly.

"So are you still going to emigrate, Delwyn?" Evan asked the question that Lily had tried so long to push to the back of her mind.

"Yes. There is a young lady that I have started to see who is a member of the Church. I am going to ask her father's permission to take her hand in marriage and then I hope for both of us to leave Wales next year."

Lily and Evan looked at one another in amazement. This was news to them, they had no idea that Delwyn had a sweetheart.

"Well, you are going to have to bring her to meet with us," Lily said, offering Delwyn a piece of *Bara Brith*.

"Yes, I would like that. She is very shy mind you." He took the slice offered to him from the plate. "Thank you."

Lily placed the plate back on the table. "So, what is your young lady's name then, Delwyn?"

"It's Rose. Rosemary Evans. She's from Heolgerrig."

Lily smiled. "And is that how you met her, at your meetings?"

Delwyn nodded, his mouth too full with the fruit bread to answer, swallowing, he answered, "Yes. I liked the look of her from the moment I first laid eyes on her. It took me a long time to pluck up the courage to speak to her, mind you. And she is such a shy girl herself, if I had not made the first move, she would never have spoken to me." *His face has flushed beetroot red. This is the one,* Lily thought to herself. *He really likes her, I can tell.*

She was really pleased for her brother, to see him settling down, but she didn't like the idea of him going so far away to live even though it was his vision, his dream for the future.

"Good. Well bring her over for her tea on Wednesday, Delwyn," Lily enthused.

"We will have to make it another day, Lily. I will be preaching on the streets with other members of the Church that day."

Her brother was beginning to surprise her more every day. "Very well. How about Friday?"

"Yes, that should be fine."

Lily was looking forward to meeting the girl who had captured her brother's heart.

* * *

The following morning, Lily called into Mrs Morgan's shop to fetch some groceries.

"There's well you are looking, *bach*," Mrs Morgan said and then gave Lily a beaming smile, "but I think you should take the weight off your feet. Mari go fetch a chair for Mrs Davies."

The young assistant obliged and Lily sat down for a moment. "I need to buy some flour to make some Welsh cakes as Delwyn is bringing his young lady for tea tomorrow afternoon."

Mrs Morgan raised a silver eyebrow. If she had any misgivings about Delwyn joining the Mormon Church, she was not about to say so, although, Lily guessed there were many in Abercanaid who would say he was doing the work of the Devil. Even though Lily did not agree with what he was doing herself, she could see how passionate he was about his faith. In fact, she felt he had a stronger dedication to his religion than many of the Welsh Baptists in the village had to theirs.

"How are you feeling, Lily?" Mrs Morgan asked.

"Oh, I'm fine. Just a little tired that's all."

"Well that's understandable, your body is preparing for the birth. How about a nice cup of tea?" Lily nodded gratefully, as Mrs Morgan sent Mari off to prepare the tea for them all.

"Any more gossip in here from Maggie Shanklin?" Lily needed to ask.

"Not a word. She has been in here, but she has been quiet. I could swear someone had cut her tongue out of her head." Mrs Morgan laughed. Lily hoped that would be the end of it. If Delwyn or Dafydd ever found out, then she dreaded to think of the consequences.

Sitting in the shop, Lily reflected on the past year. Was it only one year ago when she had started her new job here that the pit accident had happened? Such a lot had gone on since then that she felt as though she had aged by twelve years and not twelve months.

Even though the village had slowly got back to some sort of normality, Lily realised that there would be many families in Abercanaid feeling the pinch this year without their men folk. Life would never be the same again; she thanked the Lord for giving her a wonderful man such as Evan Davies. He would never be involved in a pit accident, other than to help out.

Mari brought in the tea on a tray, and taking Lily's order from her, proceeded to weigh out the flour and currants as the two women sipped their tea together.

"How is Dafydd, since that incident?" Lily knew all too well, what Mrs Morgan was referring to and preferred not to dwell on it as if by thinking about it, it could happen again, that was her real fear.

"He's quite well now, Mrs Morgan. Back working on the barges. I worry that if something else happens to upset him, he will drink like that again. It's not nice to see someone you love losing their senses, is it?"

"No, it isn't. Thank goodness he has Delwyn to keep an eye on him."

Lily bit her lip.

"What's wrong?"

"Delwyn wants to leave for America. The Mormon religion has all but consumed him, I am afraid."

Elsa Morgan frowned. "But maybe he will change his mind in time, *cariad*?"

"I don't think so. He has now taken to preaching on the streets of Merthyr around the China area."

Mrs Morgan's eyes widened. "Oh, I wish he would stay away from there. The people are dreadful. They will rob you of your last farthing good as look at you. And the stench…" The elderly lady held her nose. "It's not a place I would wish to set foot in."

"Me neither. But he feels it is his calling."

"There's not a lot you can do about it then, is there?" Mrs Morgan shrugged her shoulders.

Lily shook her head, suddenly feeling very tired. "I suppose not. And of course, when Delwyn emigrates, what will happen to Dafydd?"

"Now look here, Lily..." Mrs Morgan glanced across to see if Mari was listening, but she had just left to attend to a customer, "you need to worry about *you* at the moment, not anyone else. It's just not good for the baby."

Realising that Mrs Morgan was right as she usually was, Lily thanked her for the tea and paid her for the groceries, she was going to need a lie down before preparing to bake a couple of loaves of bread and a batch of Welsh cakes. Evan's mother had gone back to Pentyrch that very morning and Evan was out working in the community, she would have plenty of peace and quiet to rest.

When she got back to the house, there was a young girl knocking on her door. The poor little mite couldn't have been more than seven or eight years old. Her shabby well-worn clothes were tattered and torn.

When she saw Lily, she looked down at the ground as if she had been caught doing something she shouldn't.

Lily recognised her as the younger sister of Richard Griffiths from Pond Row, the young lad she had walked home from the pit explosion almost exactly a year ago.

"What's your name, *cariad*?" Lily asked, bending down so she was on the same level as the child.

"Gwenllian, Miss."

"So Gwenllian... what brings you knocking on my door?"

"Please Miss, my mam is unwell. My sister Hannah sent me to fetch you. She said you were a kind lady and that she likes you teaching her in the Sunday School."

Lily gave the child a warm smile. Even though the weather was freezing the child was not wearing enough clothing.

"Hang on a moment," she said, going inside the house and coming out with one of her old shawls to wrap around the child's shoulders, to shield her from the elements.

"Now then," she said, once she was certain the child was well-wrapped, "what is the matter with your Mam?"

"I don't know Miss. She won't keep her eyes open and Hannah has tried to waken her. My brother and father are in work."

"Take me to her, then," she advised the child, taking her hand as they passed through the streets and along the canal bank to Pond Row.

When they arrived at the house, the door was already ajar letting cold air into the sparse living room. It seemed much more poorly and shabby than it had been when she'd seen it last year, what could have happened during that time?

Hannah, who once looked well-scrubbed, stood in dirty clothing, her lovely blonde hair now matted like a bunch of rats' tails.

"Take me to your mam," she told the girl. Hannah led her to a bedroom, where her emaciated mother lay in a filthy bed on her back. There were deep hollows beneath her eyes. The woman was close to death, that much was evident. Lily gasped in horror.

"Has the doctor been?" Lily asked.

"No," Hannah answered, "I sent Gwen out to look for him earlier, but she couldn't find him. I didn't want to leave Mam." The girl started to sob profusely. As Lily took in the whole sorry situation, she too felt close to tears, but realised she needed to be strong for the girls. What if it was cholera again?

"Can you fetch your father from work?" Lily asked, as she put her hand on Hannah's shoulder.

"He's not in work, Miss." Lily was confused, hadn't Gwenllian told her that he was?

"I don't understand?"

Hannah looked around the room to ensure that Gwenllian was out of earshot. "He's gone. He drank all the money away, Mam said. That's why she's been ill see, we haven't had enough money to live on, so she's been going without to feed us."

Lily's heart went out to the woman and her family. "Now listen to me Hannah," Lily said firmly, "We are going to get your mother well again. I am going to give you some money to run down to Mrs Morgan's to buy some food and I am going to make your mother some nourishing cawl to build up her strength." Hannah nodded eagerly, "And of course, I will save some for all you children, too."

Hannah's face clouded over. "Mam was afraid that we might have to go into the workhouse, Miss."

"Not if I have anything to do with it, you won't," Lily said firmly and she watched Hannah smile for the first time. "Take your sister with you to help you carry the food."

Lily wrote a letter to Mrs Morgan on the back of the list she had earlier used when she went into the shop, explaining everything and then listed the food the family would need. She gave it to Hannah along with some money from her purse.

"God Bless you, Miss Lily," the girl said, her eyes that were earlier dead, now shining like two beacons full of hope.

Lily found some spare coal and some stick to start a small fire in the grate in the bedroom to keep Mrs Griffiths warm, being so thin she would lose a lot of heat through that thin skin of hers. Then she went to boil a kettle in the kitchen. Returning, she tried to rouse the woman.

Bending over her lifeless form, she tapped her gently on the cheek. "Mrs Griffiths, it's Lily Davies. I have sent the girls out to get some food for you all for Christmas."

The woman groaned, but did not open her eyes. Lily was beginning to wonder if she was a hopeless case, until she felt the woman squeeze her hand. She did understand, but was probably too weak to rouse herself yet.

It seemed to take an age while she waited for Hannah and Gwenllian to return. It was dark by now and she knew Evan would be worried about her, but luckily the bedroom was starting to warm up nicely. Lily tried to rouse Mrs Griffiths again, she needed to make her drink something. The woman already looked dehydrated.

She tried again and this time the woman's eyes flicked open to reveal two huge brown eyes that looked as though they were sunken back down into her skull.

"Oh thank the Lord," Lily said. "Do you know who I am?" She asked her to see if the woman was confused or not; she knew from the time her mother was dehydrated when she had cholera that it could make people confused.

"Lily," the woman said in barely a whisper, she tried to lick her lips but her tongue appeared swollen, dry and sore.

"I'll fetch you something to drink, Mrs Griffiths." Lily went to the kitchen and made the woman a cup of tea, which she allowed to cool before taking it to her lips for fear she should knock it over herself and get scalded.

Lily placed the cup down on the windowsill and helped the woman to sit up in the bed. Then helping her to hold the cup steady in her hand, she assisted her to take small sips.

"How long have you been like this for?" she asked when the woman had drunk her fill.

"I'm not sure," she replied. "Only a couple of days I think. What date is it anyway?"

"It's the twentieth of December."

The woman's mouth fell open with shock. "I thought it was only the beginning of the month, I must have been ill for a long time."

Lily nodded. "I have sent the girls out to get provisions for you."

"But I can't afford to pay for them," she protested. "My husband is not living here no more, so we only have Richard's money and his wages have been cut. He's not been paid for a month."

"It's all right, Mrs Griffiths. Call it a Christmas present if you like to see you over the season."

The woman smiled. "I had no clue that there was such benevolence left in this world." Lily drew closer and smoothed Mrs Griffiths' lank hair. She took hold of Lily's hand and wept. "What am I to do?"

"Well rest assured, I will see that you don't starve. I am thinking of starting up a school next year at the chapel and there will still be the soup kitchen going. So your children and yourself can at least have one meal a day."

"You are kindness itself, Mrs Davies."

Lily sat down on a chair next to the bed. "How about I clean you up a little before the girls return? I have boiled up some water, so I can use that."

The woman nodded eagerly, life seemed to be returning slowly to her body. Lily poured the now tepid water into a tin bowl and brought a bar of soap from the kitchen and a towel to wash Mrs Griffiths down. Then she found her a partially clean nightdress from the wardrobe and changed her into that and then combed her hair, so she looked much tidier. Then she found an old shawl to wrap around her shoulders to keep her warm.

Ten minutes later, the girls returned with huge beaming smiles. “Mrs Morgan says that she will pay for half of this food, Mrs Davies,” Hannah explained.

“She also gave us some sweeties for Christmas,” Gwenllian said, stepping from foot-to-foot in excitement, she didn’t seem to understand the seriousness of the situation like her sister did.

“Right, pass me that basket of food, Hannah. Stay with your mother while I’m cooking the food please,” Lily ordered. “Gwenllian, you can help me in the kitchen and show me where everything is.”

The little girl nodded eagerly. “Can I have some sweeties now?” she asked.

“Later, if you eat up all your food,” Lily said, patting her on the head.

It wasn’t long before she had a big pan of cawl bubbling on the stove, there would be plenty there for Richard when he finished his shift as well. He needed to keep his strength up to work under ground.

When the soup was ready, Lily poured some into a bowl for Mrs Griffiths. She made sure the meat and vegetables were well cut up in case the woman had difficulty swallowing after not eating properly for days. “If your Mam can’t manage it,” she said to Hannah, “then just give her spoonfuls of the juice to drink.”

Hannah nodded taking the bowl from Lily. Lily was surprised that Hannah’s mother not only ate the soup, but she said she wouldn’t mind a little drop more.

There would be enough food here for the family for a couple of days if they eked it out with some bread.

When Lily was satisfied that the family were well fed and warm, she bade them goodnight with a promise that she would be back to check on them the following morning. She also made a mental note to see if she could get Doctor Owen to call on them before Christmas.

* * *

"Where have you been?" Evan asked, even before she had a chance to remove her shawl. "You look perished. It can't be good for you to be out in this cold weather."

"Evan," she said, holding her hands out to warm in front of the open fire, Mrs Griffiths's youngest, Gwenllian, called here earlier this afternoon, she wanted me to see to her Mam."

Evan raised a questioning eyebrow. "Well it's time you rested up, couldn't the woman have managed on her own?"

"Mrs Grifffiths is very ill, Evan. She hasn't eaten in days."

"Oh no." Evan's face clouded over. "What happened to her husband then? He's earning money at the pit, there are two wages going into that house."

Lily shook her head. "Not any more there isn't. Young Richard has had to take a pay cut and he hasn't been paid in a month or so and Dai Griffiths drank his wages away. He's left the family in the lurch."

Evan drew near to his wife and hugged her. "That poor family. How are they managing?"

"Well, Mrs Griffiths has been going without herself to feed her family, she's very weak, but I have managed to feed them all up for the night. There should be enough food left for a couple of days."

"Listen, you need to rest. I shall call around and see if they are all right tomorrow."

"Take Doctor Owen with you, Evan."

"I will, don't worry. Now we need to feed you…"

But before he had a chance to say anymore, Lily's legs buckled beneath her, and Evan caught her before she fell to the floor.

"Lily, are you all right?"

"I'm fine." She protested.

"No you are not," he reiterated. "I am getting you up to bed. Nothing is going to happen to you or the baby."

"But I have to make Welsh cakes for tomorrow, Delwyn and his young lady are calling on us."

"Now don't worry, *cariad.* You don't have to make them, I will call to the shop tomorrow and buy some cakes from Mrs Morgan."

Satisfied that all was under control, Lily allowed her husband to lead her up to the bedroom, glad of the chance to catch up on some rest.

* * *

The following morning, Lily felt more energised, especially when Evan told her he had called on the Griffiths family and all was well.

"Doctor Owen will call in later today, he said he hadn't realised that Mrs Griffiths was in such a bad way."

"Thank you for doing that, Evan."

"What time are your brother and Rose calling in today?"

"About three o'clock. Will you be here then?"

"Yes, I should be back about that time. I have to go up to Rhydycar to see a miner and his wife. The poor woman really isn't well, it looks as if she might not see Christmas." Lily was so proud of her husband and the work he did. "Then I have to prepare my sermon for Christmas morning."

Christmas was coming a lot sooner than she expected, last year it had all happened in a whirl following the pit explosion. So much so, that she just could not feel excited about it. But this year was different, with the baby due in January, the feeling was one of expectation and hope. How she wished her parents were still here right now.

By the time Delwyn and Rose arrived just after 3 o'clock, the table was laid with the best linen, china cups, saucers and plates.

"Well, there's nice to meet you, Rose," Lily greeted the young woman warmly.

Shyly, Rose smiled and waited for an invitation to sit down.

"Sit down, Rose," Delwyn reassured, we do not stand on ceremony in this house."

Lily laughed. It was nice to see Delwyn with his young lady at last. She noticed Rose had a lovely complexion and pink cheeks, so her name suited her very well.

"So Rose," Lily began, "Delwyn tells me that you are one of the Saints too?"

"Yes, my father was converted during the time Dan Jones first came to Merthyr. He has already gone to Utah, we are going to follow him out there as soon as possible."

Lily felt a lump in her throat as she realised what was going to come next.

"Lily," Delwyn began, "Rose and I are going to be married. I asked her father's permission before he left Merthyr. I am to be baptised into the Mormon faith in January."

Tears sprung to Lily's eyes and swallowing, she said, "So we shan't be seeing you here in Merthyr for much longer?"

"No. We will wait until the time is right to travel by ship from the port of Liverpool to New York."

Lily was devastated to hear this news, even though it had always been on the cards.

"What's the matter? Aren't you pleased about the marriage?" Delwyn's forehead creased into a frown.

"It is not that. I am happy for the both of you, it is the fact that I might never see you again dear brother. And what about Dafydd?"

"Lily, don't be silly. Dafydd is a grown man, he will take a wife of his own some day. He has work to keep him busy."

"I am worried about the other thing?" she said.

"Other thing? You mean his drinking?" She nodded. "Have no fear, I feel he has learned his lesson. In any case he has you and Evan to keep a watchful eye on him."

Hearing her brother say that should have brought her some comfort, but instead, she found her anxiety increasing.

"Lily, are you all right? You have gone very pale." Delwyn blinked.

"I'm fine," she said as she went to pour the tea knowing that soon she would gain a new member of the family and just as soon she would lose yet another.

* * *

By the time Evan had returned to the house, Delwyn and Rose were on the point of departure.

Lily made a quick introduction and watched them walk away in the direction of the canal bank. Delwyn had told her that Rose's brother was waiting to escort her back home. It would not be the seemly thing to do to take a young lady into his home un-chaperoned.

"What's the matter?" Evan asked his wife.

Lily shook her head. "Delwyn and Rose are to be married shortly."

"Well that's a cause for celebration, isn't it?" Evan grinned.

Lily chewed on her bottom lip. "It's not that, it's the fact that soon he is to be baptised into the Mormon faith and then he's off to Utah."

Evan took his wife by the shoulders, looking deep into her eyes. "Well it had to happen sometime, didn't it?"

By now Lily was close to tears. "I suppose so, it's just that everything seems to be happening too quickly, Evan. Mam dying, the new baby and now all of this, I have hardly had time to catch a breath."

"It's called life, Lily. There are such bad things happening that we need to celebrate the good, so put a smile on your face and be happy for them both."

"But I'm worried I might never see my brother again," she said clasping her hands in despair.

"Don't you worry about that. There is enough money in my family to allow us to one day take a trip out to America. You'll see."

Lily wished she felt as confident about that as her husband sounded.

* * *

On Christmas Eve, Mrs Morgan called around to the house with a homemade fruit Christmas cake for Lily and Evan. "I've taken one up to the Griffiths family as well," she enthused.

Lily gratefully accepted the unexpected gift. "How are they doing? I wanted to call in to see them today, but Evan insisted that I rest up."

"They are looking very well and speaking highly of you, Lily Jenkin."

Lily beamed inwardly. "Me? I have not done a lot."

"Oh yes you have. You have given them hope when they thought there was none. The children are looking forward to attending the new school at the chapel next year."

"That is good to hear. And Mrs Griffiths, how is she?"

"She's up on her feet now. I can tell she is feeling better because she told me if she ever catches up with that drunken husband of hers she is going to flatten him with the iron."

Lily laughed. "I sent a few small presents up to their house with Evan this morning. They were only a table cloth I embroidered; remember when you brought the embroidery around for me?" Mrs

Morgan nodded. "And a new shawl each for the girls and a book of Red Indian stories for young Richard."

"I am sure they will love those," Mrs Morgan said. "How are you feeling any way?"

"Not so bad. Just a little exhausted. I never realised that a new life growing inside you could feel so draining."

"Yes. It makes you wonder why women ever go on to have more than one child, doesn't it?"

Lily nodded. "We received a Christmas card this morning from Evan's parents, they said they would be over in the New Year to see the baby. They sound really excited."

"What will you and Mr. Morgan do on Christmas day?"

"I expect it shall be a quiet time for us. We'll go to chapel in the morning of course, and then we might go out for a walk after Christmas dinner if the weather is all right."

"Why don't you and Mr. Morgan spend Christmas day over here?"

Mrs Morgan's face brightened up. The pair had no children of their own, so it would be nice for them to have some company. "I'd really like that," she beamed. "But please let me help you with the cooking, Lily."

"All right. We can both work together. I'll really look forward to it. Dafydd is coming and Delwyn is invited, but I think he and Rose will choose to spend the day with her uncle's family who are also members of the faith."

Mrs Morgan nodded as if she understood all too well.

"Well, I'll pop back home now to tell William. I shall be shutting the shop early on Christmas Eve, but after that, I will take a well-earned break for a couple of days."

"Yes, you will have deserved it the way you have served this village, Mrs Morgan."

Lily felt a twinge and winced in discomfort.

"Are you all right, Lily, my dear?" Mrs Morgan asked.

"Yes. I am fine. I have been having these strange twinges for the past couple of days, but the baby is not due until January."

"Well, he or she will make an appearance when they are ready, I've no doubt."

"No doubt," Lily said, patting her stomach.

When Mrs Morgan had left, Lily busied herself sorting out what she would make for the Christmas dinner. The goose had been ordered from the poulterer, who would be delivering it on Christmas Eve.

Lily reflected for a moment on last Christmas, her mother had cooked that particular dinner for them, she was such a wonderful cook too. But last year had been tinged with a deep sadness in Abercanaid. She so wanted this year to be different. It just had to be.

Chapter Six

Lily fretted about Dafydd on Christmas morning, she had not heard from him for a few days since he had been told the news about Delwyn's intentions to emigrate with his new bride to America.

Of course it was not unusual for Lily to not see him for that length of time as he worked on the barges, but what was unusual was that lots of villagers had told her the same thing: they thought Dafydd had gone away to work as they had not seen him in months. Had he been shutting himself away so much since their mother's death that people thought that? Or had Maggie Shanklin been up to her rumour mongering again? On this occasion, Lily hoped it was the latter.

Grief did funny things to folk, Lily was aware of that. "Evan," she said, when she had put her best fitting gown on for the Christmas day service at the chapel and sat at her dressing table brushing her hair, "if Dafydd does not turn up for this service, I will know that something is wrong. If that is the case, will you please call up to Chapel Square to ensure everything is all right? I still have a house key."

Evan came up behind her and rested the palms of his hands on her shoulders. He gazed at her reflection in the mirror and said, "Don't fret so much, *cariad*. If it pleases you, I will go and look for him right this very minute."

She turned around, "No, that will make you late for the service. You can't let the congregation down. Afterwards will be as good a time as any." In her heart she had guessed what had happened to him. Poor Dafydd, he did not have the same strength as his elder brother. If only he could meet a good woman too.

The service went very well. Evan read out the Christmas story from the Bible, Luke chapter two, he spoke about the importance of giving and receiving. Afterwards they sang the Christmas carols, O Come All Ye Faithful and Joy to the World.

As Lily was about to make her way back to Chapel House, Maggie Shanklin stood in her path. For a moment, she feared the woman would say something hurtful to her, but instead she wished her and her husband a Merry Christmas, with the kind of look in her eye she had not seen before, a glint of mischief perhaps. Then she went on her way. The woman had mentioned nothing about the baby, maybe it was her way of apologising, putting things right between them, but somehow she doubted it. In any case, Lily had far more on her mind today than to be worried about what the likes of Maggie Shanklin thought about her.

Ever more fearful now that something was wrong, she took Evan aside as the last of the congregation were leaving after they'd shook hands with him and given him little Christmas gifts and cards for the both of them.

"I don't wish to be rude," Lily whispered in his ear, "but Dafydd wasn't here, was he?"

Evan shook his head. "I will go right away to check up on him."

"All right, thank you. I'll keep a check on the dinner. Mrs Morgan is coming to help me, she has made a Christmas pudding with her special recipe." Even knowing that, couldn't cheer her up. She wouldn't rest until she knew that her brother was safe.

Pottering about in the kitchen and laying the dining room table, did little to occupy Lily's mind. Every so often, she glanced at the clock on the mantelpiece, which hardly seemed to move its hands.

Just as she was about to give up hope that Dafydd would arrive, she heard the back door opening and rushed to greet him, only it was Mrs Morgan carrying the pudding over to boil.

"Now, I've part boiled it, so it should only need one hour's steaming or so," she said brightly, but then catching sight of Lily's face, said, "Whatever is wrong, dear? Is it the baby?"

"No, it's my brother."

"Delwyn? Has he left for America already?"

"No, not him. It's Dafydd. Evan has gone to check the house to see if he can find him. He hasn't been seen for days."

"Now you sit down, *cariad.* All this worrying is no good for you or the baby. I'll make you a cup of tea, although I bet you feel like something stronger."

Lily knew that Mrs Morgan was referring to a glass of alcohol, but the mere thought of it turned her stomach. "Yes, a cup of tea would be nice."

After the drink had calmed her stomach, Lily heard the back door opening again and looked up in expectation, but could see it was Evan and he was alone.

"Did you find him?" she asked, knowing full well by the look on his face what the answer was.

"I knocked and knocked for ages, the curtains were still drawn, so I tried the key in the lock…"

"And?"

"And I am sorry to tell you the house is a right pig-sty since you left Lily. He is not looking after himself that's for sure. I have to tell you though, when Maggie Shanklin was leaving the service she had a strange gleam in her eye."

"How do you mean, Mr. Davies?" Mrs Morgan asked.

"Well, like she knows something, but is not saying so."

"I know just what you mean, Evan," Lily agreed. "I had that feeling when she wished me a Merry Christmas, like she knows something that she is not going to tell us, especially since she had that ticking off from you in the chapel in front of everyone."

"You might well be right," Evan said, rubbing his chin thoughtfully. "Would you like me to have a word with her later?"

"No, don't do that. Today is Christmas day, let's try to enjoy it even though my brother is not here with us, and Delwyn and his young lady have obviously chosen to spend it elsewhere." Lily choked back a sob. She had lost her father, mother, and now, she felt as though she had lost both brothers as well.

* * *

Lily managed to get through the rest of day as best as she could, forcing a smile when she was able. Mrs Morgan had given her a present she had crocheted for the baby, it was a delicate christening gown, shawl and bonnet. Lily gave Mrs Morgan a jewelled brooch. They were not real gems set inside the brooch, just coloured glass and paste, from Merthyr Market. It was all she could afford, but it was very pretty. For Mr. Morgan she had bought a new clay pipe and tobacco. It was her way of repaying her old employers for their kindness to her and Evan.

When the clock on the mantelpiece chimed 6 o'clock, Mrs Morgan stood and declared, "Well I think it's time we left Lily and Evan to themselves, it has been a lovely day. Thank you for your kindness in inviting us here."

"It's a pleasure," Lily said warmly.

"I think you could do with the rest now, Lily," Mrs Morgan said, as she hugged her.

"Not at all," Lily said, not to appear rude, but in all honesty she was glad to take time out to think. Her mind had been racing all day at the thought of Dafydd, where on earth could he possibly be?

When she had shown the elderly couple to the door, she turned to Evan, "I am going to see Mrs Shanklin right away. She knows something, I am sure of it."

Evan took both of her hands in his, "Sweetheart, please rest tonight and we'll both speak with her tomorrow."

"No, Evan," Lily said firmly. "I want to hear whatever that woman has got to say. If it helps me find Dafydd then it's all to the good."

Evan sighed deeply. "It's quite evident that when your mind is made up Lily, that there is no stopping you. But let me accompany you."

"No. This is something I need to do on my own. Please fetch me my new cloak and bonnet."

There was no way Lily was going to Mrs Shanklin's door dressed in her old shawl.

With a look of resignation on his face, Evan did as he was told, helping to drape the cloak around his wife's shoulders. "Now, please take care my sweet," he said, as he opened the door for her to leave.

* * *

Lily walked briskly. It was starting to get slippery underfoot as the ground frosted over. All the streets were deserted as families took what they could from Christmas. Some would have a better Christmas than others.

As she rounded the corner into Maggie Shanklin's street, she almost slipped, but saved herself in time as she clung onto a low wall. She would have to be more careful, her anger was spurring her on, and she didn't want anything to happen to the baby should she take a tumble.

Standing outside the house, she gave three short, hard raps on the heavy wooden door. There was no answer, but she thought she heard the sound of muffled voices inside and spied a candlelight in an upstairs window.

Eventually, the door was opened by a young girl of about sixteen. "Mrs Davies," the girl smiled at her as she had recognised her from chapel. "What brings you here?"

"I am looking for your mother," Lily replied anxiously, trying to look past the girl into the darkened passageway behind her.

Without saying another word, the girl retraced her steps and a few moments later, Maggie Shanklin appeared on the doorstep, wide-eyed with astonishment to see Lily there. Lily thought she could smell alcohol fumes on the woman, which surprised her as Maggie portrayed herself in the village as a paragon of virtue.

"Mrs Davies," she said with a smirk on her face. "Would you like to come inside?"

"No," Lily replied firmly. "What I have to ask you I will say to you here out on the street." The weather was biting cold, so if it were another person she was addressing she would only be too glad to be invited inside to warm up a little.

"Go ahead and ask anything you like!" Maggie threw back her head and laughed, obviously enjoying the attention she was getting from the minister's wife. "But please do bear in mind," she continued mockingly, "that I am not allowed to spread any gossip around this village."

Lily took a step backwards, then composing herself, said, "It is not gossip I am interested in Mrs Shanklin, it is the facts."

"And what facts might they be?" Maggie folded her arms.

"I have a feeling that you know something about my brother, Dafydd."

Maggie Shanklin gave a wry smile. "And why would I know anything about your brother now? 'Tis fine you coming 'ere to my home, but I have my own family to think about."

"I quite understand that." Why was the woman so evasive?

"I don't think I know anything that you need to know."

"Please let me be the best judge of that."

"What is it that you want to hear then?"

"The truth." Lily let out a breath of frustration.

"Ha, the bloody truth. Hark at me swearing and on Christmas day an' all. Well, I'll tell you the truth, your brother is nothing but a hooligan using his fists for street fighting and the like. He has taken this past few weeks to visiting the slums in China too."

Lily put her hand to her mouth in horror. "This can't be true," she said, feeling as though the ground were coming up to meet her, her legs now, boneless.

"Ah, but it is. He's not the fine upright man that you think. Your Dafydd is a drunk. He hangs around the whores up in China." Maggie Shanklin threw her head back and laughed. She was obviously enjoying relaying this piece of tittle-tattle to Lily. Relishing every moment of it.

Lily straightened. "Well, if it is true, and I'm not wholly certain it is, then I shall go and find my brother and bring him back home where he belongs."

"You won't drag him away from those whores up there. There is too much of a pull for him in that direction. Plenty of ale houses and all. Lots of ways to quench his thirst for beer and other things... When he sobers up, he makes his money with his fists and then indulges in the pleasures of *Sodom and Gomorrah*! All over again. Aye, 'tis a right old merry-go-round that he's on..."

Lily knew too well what the woman was referring to. How she was going to walk away from this encounter with a shred of dignity, she had no idea. She was just about to raise her voice and tell Maggie Shanklin what she really thought of her, when her legs started to give way. She put her hands out for Maggie to help her, but the woman just stood there laughing until finally, she felt herself falling and hitting the freezing cold floor. Then everything went black.

* * *

"She's coming around," Lily heard a female voice saying. She knew that voice from somewhere. Of course it was Mrs Morgan, what was she doing outside Maggie Shanklin's house and why did the floor suddenly feel cosy and warm?

Struggling to open her eyes, she brought them in to focus to find she was safely tucked up in a strange bedroom.

"Where am I?" she asked, blinking.

"Now, Lily, you are quite safe, you are in my house now. You had a little tumble in the street. You just rest dear," Mrs Morgan said, stretching over the bed to look at her.

"But how did I get here in the first place? I don't understand." She was totally baffled as to how one moment she was outside in the street and the next, inside Mrs Morgan's bedroom above the shop.

"It's quite simple. Evan got worried about you, so he followed after you. He heard the altercation on Maggie Shanklin's doorstep and watched you fall, but he was too far away to help. He told me that awful woman went back in her house, shut the door and left you lying in the street. Then he picked you up and carried you here."

"What time is it?" Lily asked, thankful for the loan of Mrs Morgan's bed.

"It's half past eight, *cariad.* Evan has gone to fetch the doctor, to make sure you are all right. He's been gone for a while, I expect he is having difficulty finding him. What were you doing out in the street in any case, is it something to do with your brother having gone missing?"

Lily nodded and buried her head in the pillow as the tears came fast and furiously. How foolish she had been rushing off in anger like that, she could have harmed her baby. Dafydd was a grown man, she should have left it be, but for far too long she had felt like she should take her mother's place, now she had come to the realisation that it was not her responsibility.

"That Maggie Shanklin is an old crone!" Mrs Morgan said venomously, making Lily laugh through her tears.

Lily nodded. "She was really nasty. The things she said about my brother were awful, it was a shock to hear her say things like that. She said he had been drinking and whoring up in China."

Mrs Morgan didn't comment about that. Instead, she just tidied up the bed clothes and said, "You lie back and relax, young lady. You've had quite a nasty outing this evening. Would you like something to eat?"

"No, thanks. I wouldn't mind a glass of water though."

"Very well and if you feel hungry later, I'll make you some stew to keep your strength up." Lily knew she was fortunate to have someone like Mrs Morgan in her life.

* * *

The following morning, Lily was back in her own bed after being given a clean bill of health by the doctor. He'd said it was probably the cold that had made her faint and there didn't appear to be any broken bones.

Word had got around the village about the row on the doorstep last night, and so as a consequence, Lily found herself inundated with calls from well-wishers.

"I didn't realise that people could be so kind," Lily said later as she arranged some flowers she had been given, in a glass vase.

"Yes, most folk around here are the salt of the earth..." Evan nodded. "Of course, there are always the odd bad ones. I have half a mind to go around and speak to Mrs Shanklin myself today. I want to ban her from the church all together speaking to you like that."

Lily stopped what she was doing and turned to face her husband. "No, don't do that. It wouldn't be the Christian thing to do."

Evan shrugged his shoulders. "I guess you are right." Then he planted a kiss on the top of her head and continued, "In any case, there are a fair few who are on the lookout for her. They have taken offence at what she did to you last night, not only what she said, but leaving you to fend for yourself on the ground."

"Well, I am quite all right now, Evan. I don't want to make a fuss."

"But what if you had lain there all night in the cold? You could have perished to death."

Evan was quite right of course, Lily herself would never have treated an animal like that, never mind a fellow human being.

"I expect Mrs Shanklin has problems of her own, Evan. She has a large family to look after and she reeked of alcohol when she answered the door, so maybe she wasn't in her right senses last night."

Evan snorted in disgust. "There are too many people in this town who bury their problems in the bottom of a bottle. Far too many."

Evan saying that made her think of her brother again. "Evan," she began, "Mrs Shanklin said Dafydd is spending his time in China…" If Evan was surprised, he didn't show it. There was a long uncomfortable silence. "You already knew about it, didn't you? Why didn't you tell me?"

"I didn't want to worry you in your condition."

"Worry me? This has caused me more worry hearing the news from the likes of that Irish woman."

"I'm sorry, I should have said something, I know, but I feared it would hurt you so."

She stood with hands on hips, fiercely proud. "From now on I don't want anything kept from me, understood?"

Evan nodded. She hoped he had now got the message. If it wasn't that she was so tired she would have asked Mr. Morgan to take her up to China on his pony and trap and she would hunt around until she found her brother and bring him back home where he belonged. What their poor mother would say about all of this, if she were alive, she dreaded to think, but then again, she suspected that if Mam were still around he would not have got in this mess in the first place.

* * *

The days passed fairly slowly, until at last it was New Year's Eve. 1867 was just around the corner and Lily hoped they would see better times; surely it couldn't be any worse than the past couple of years. She planned to start up the school mid March after the baby was born. She intended to take the child with her and to ask Hannah Griffiths if she would help out at the school. So as well as being taught, she could help Lily with the little ones.

One thing she had to do though, was to find her brother as soon as possible. Evan had kept a watchful eye over her for the past few days, but now he had been called away to some emergency or another, she decided to take that trip to China.

Mr. Morgan was only too happy to oblige with running her there, but his wife had other ideas.

"Lily, you cannot go traipsing off to Merthyr, especially around the China area looking for your brother, it is full of vagabonds and other undesirables. I know of a gentleman visitor and his wife, who came to the town only to become lost and end up in that hell hole. The poor pair were accosted, their clothing ripped and the woman's jewellery stolen from her very person. They were never quite the same again."

"I will be all right, Mrs Morgan. William has said he will stay near. Anyhow, with God on my side, I shall not be afraid. I am more afraid of what will happen to my brother than for myself."

Mrs Morgan shook her head. "If I did not have the shop to run, I would come with you myself. I am sure Evan will be none too pleased though when he finds out about this."

"But my husband is not going to find out about it, at least not until after I have gone. And hopefully, by the time he does find out, I shall have found Dafydd."

"Be realistic, Lily. It will be like looking for a needle in a haystack," Mrs Morgan implored. "At least wait until you have had the baby, who knows what danger might befall you there."

But Lily had already made up her mind. Even the thought of the night she was attacked in Pentrych was not enough to put her off the business in hand.

Mrs Morgan gave it one last try to dissuade her. "What about Delwyn? Perhaps he can find your brother for you?"

"Mrs Morgan, I have not heard from Delwyn since before Christmas. He could not even be bothered to come for Christmas dinner. He is more interested in his new family now," she declared bitterly, realising in her heart that she was jealous of the attention he gave the Church.

Mrs Morgan shook her head sadly. Lily knew that once she had made her mind up about something, there was no going back.

She allowed Mr. Morgan to help her onto the front of the trap, whilst Mrs Morgan brought a thick woollen blanket to wrap around her legs. "Now you hear me, *cariad*, take care in Merthyr, come back safely to Abercanaid."

"I will, Mrs Morgan." She kissed the old woman softly on the cheek, and then waved, as the horse set off at a fine trot for Merthyr.

They had left in plenty of time, so they should be back before nightfall. Lily had already left a note for Evan, who with any luck might not find it at all. Perhaps she might get back before him.

As Mr. Morgan drove the trap towards China, the first thing that hit Lily was the overpowering stench. She knew full well that the people used the streets and the river as a toilet and were used to living in filth. That's why so many in that area died in the 1840 cholera outbreak. The area was teeming with life: ragged children, and women in gaudy, dirty dresses, passed in the street. A couple of people, who were swinging overflowing tankards of ale, sang outside a tavern.

What a place this was. She asked Mr. Morgan to pull up the trap and the men looked at her wide eyed as if they had not seen someone of her sort in a long while.

Mr. Morgan disembarked first and then rushed to Lily's side to help her down. She brushed down her skirts and took a deep breath of composure. Then she walked tentatively towards the group.

"I am looking for a Mr. Dafydd Jenkin from Abercanaid," she declared. The group ignored her and carried on drinking and singing.

It was no good. She was going to have to do something to attract their attention. "I am willing to pay," she continued as they stopped mid flow, "a shilling to anyone who knows where he might be."

A woman wearing a low cut red dress, showing off ample cleavage, walked towards her. "I know him!" she said, holding out her filthy palm for the shilling.

"You have to tell me what you know first," Lily told the woman.

"All right then, dearie." The woman flung back her dark locks and pursed her painted lips. "He was here not a couple of days since, in that tavern behind me. He got into a fight with a man."

"What sort of a man?"

"I don't know, do I? He looked a bit upper crust if you ask me. Think he might be one of the bosses from the iron works."

"What happened then?"

"Look darling, if you want more information than that, I'm going to want more than a bloody shilling for my time."

William Morgan stepped forward. "Mind your language, Madam, please!"

The woman shrugged and stared at Lily in expectation, whilst holding out her grubby palm, her nails caked black.

Lily took a deep breath in and nodded. Undoing the stings on her purse, she pulled out another shilling. It was money she could ill afford, but if it helped get her brother back then it would be worth every penny.

The woman smiled, flashing her teeth. If she had a good bath, combed her hair and wore the right clothing, she could pass for a beauty, but as it was, it was obvious from her very manner that she was a prostitute. How anyone could live like that was beyond Lily.

"Come with me," the woman said in a whisper, snatching the coin from Lily's hand as she led her around the corner. Mr. Morgan gave the woman a hard stare.

"It's all right, Mr. Morgan," Lily reassured, "If I don't come back within a few minutes, you are quite at liberty to follow after me..."

Mr. Morgan nodded and stayed with the pony and trap. She could quite understand his reluctance to leave the poor animal on the streets of China. Who knew what might happen to it or the trap for that matter.

The woman led Lily onto a street and down a narrow, stinking alleyway, until she pointed at a door. "There's the place he's been going, see. It's a brothel. I used to work there, but the man who runs it gave me such a beating that I moved on. Works for someone else now I do..."

Lily could hardly believe that her brother, her beloved Dafydd, could frequent such a hovel. She thanked the woman and gave her an extra shilling for her trouble, as sympathy for her plight, overwhelmed her. Then the woman went on her way. So what was she supposed to do now? It was far too dangerous for her to go somewhere like that on her own. She would have to return later with Delwyn and Evan.

As she walked back in the direction of Mr. Morgan and his pony and trap, she gasped as a gang of young children ran past her in ragged, filthy clothes, with no shoes on their feet. Poor darlings, they looked as if they needed a hot meal inside of them. It was then she realised that her purse was missing. Surely not? Had they managed to steal it from her person without her realising? She heeded Mrs Morgan's words. Of course, she had warned her about the pick pockets in the area. What would Evan think of her? All the money he had given her for the week for food had now gone. Some of it would be drunk away by the prostitute in the tavern and the rest, who knew what the children would do with it. It was possible that they were working for an adult. Someone like herself would stand out like a sore thumb amidst the hovels of China.

Clutching her throat, she realised with horror that the beautiful silver locket Evan had given her, was missing. Could that have been stolen too? Her purse had been taken without her knowledge, but no one had come anywhere near her neck. She realised in desperation that she must have lost it somewhere in the dark recesses of that hell hole. She retraced her steps, but there was no sign of it. Too late, she knew it would have been claimed by someone as soon as it hit the floor and she wept bitter tears. It was a bad omen, she knew it.

* * *

Later when Mr. Morgan dropped her off back at Chapel House, her heart leapt when she realised that Evan was home as she noticed the oil lamp lit in the window. Now he would realise that she had been out all day. What was she going to do?

Even before she had a chance to push open the front door, he was there in front of her.

"Lily, where have you been?"

She looked down at the ground and then swallowing, decided to tell the truth. "I have been looking for Dafydd."

"Surely you haven't been to China?"

She nodded and felt close to tears. "I have yes and it was a horrible experience." She hoped he wouldn't notice the locket was missing from her neck.

He held her in his arms. "So what did you find out?"

"I paid a prostitute to tell me what she knows and she showed me the place he had been visiting."

"But how do you know she was telling the truth?"

That thought hadn't crossed her mind, she had been so intent on finding her brother that she was hanging on to every thread of hope she could possible cling to.

"I don't know. I just have to hope. Please Evan, will you come back with me tomorrow so we can ask around again and find out where he is?"

"Look Lily. The baby is due anytime now. You can't go walking the streets. I am sure Dafydd will return in his own time."

"And what if he doesn't?"

"We just have to hope he does. Now come in and have a warm by the fire. It was nearly out by the time I got home. I have been visiting a family in Troedyrhiw. They are facing real hardships since the pit disaster."

For once, Lily did not want to hear about anyone else's problems, she had enough of her own to contend with.

* * *

The following morning, Lily persuaded Evan to accompany her to China and they called on the hovel the woman had pointed out as the brothel Dafydd had visited. When they got there they were to be disappointed.

"This is not a whore house!" a disgruntled man shouted at them. "Leave us alone. This is a respectable home. Who do you think you are coming around here?"

A bedroom window opened. Lily and Evan were fortunate to dodge a pail of something wet being tipped over them through the open window, by someone who appeared to be the man's wife.

"That was a close call," Evan brushed his coat down. "Urine by the stench of it."

Lily gagged. "Ask him if he has heard of Dafydd, please Evan."

"Sir, we do not wish you any harm, but a lady told my wife yesterday that her brother, Dafydd Jenkin, has been coming around to these parts."

The old man scratched his head. "Dafydd Jenkin you say? I can't say as I have heard of him. Your wife didn't pay the lady any money did she?"

"Unfortunately, she did."

"It's the oldest trick in the book. The whores and thieves around here will tell any old tale to get their hands on your money." The old man appeared to soften when he realised they were respectable folk. "If I were you two, I would go on your way, it is too dangerous, especially with you wife being in that state of near confinement."

"Yes sir. You are right. But if you do come across my wife's brother, any information at all, we are living here." He handed the man their address written on the back of a Christmas card. "We will gladly pay you for your inconvenience."

"Aye. Well I hope you find him, for your sakes and his own. This isn't the type of place to hang around in, especially for strangers. I know the dangerous parts and people myself, but for newcomers, well, they are green as grass, see. They can be taken advantage of. A lot of bullies around here there are."

Lily felt a pang of nausea at the thought of her poor brother being accosted by a gang of vagabonds.

When they arrived back in Abercanaid, Evan made Lily go to bed to have a lie down and then later, he warned her about her behaviour.

"You cannot go on like this, my sweet. You are going to have to give this up for the sake of the baby. You can't search the whole of Merthyr Tydfil for Dafydd. In any case, for all you know he might have moved to another town by now."

Lily sank her head into the pillow as she realised the sense in Evan's words. For now she would have to let things go.

"Evan, there is something I need to tell you…"

He sat down on the bed next to her. "I knew there was something else troubling you, now what is it, *cariad*?"

"The locket. I lost it in China…" Evan held her in his arms as she wept bitterly, feeling as though she had let him down.

When she had finished sobbing, he held her at arm's length. "You have got to promise me you will never go to that dreadful place again."

She nodded and buried her head in the pillow. It was a bitter lesson she had learned.

* * *

Every day it was getting harder for Lily to get out of bed and get on with her daily tasks, she was becoming more and more out of breath. "If this baby does not come soon Evan, I am sure I will burst, look how big my belly is."

Evan patted her swollen stomach with pride. "Don't worry. It will not be long to go now. Soon we shall have new life living in this house and then your days will be filled up with looking after the baby and me."

Lily felt the blood run to her cheeks. "Not quite, Evan, I am afraid…"

Evan's mouth fell open in astonishment. "What do you mean?"

"I have not told you yet of my plans to start a school here at the chapel for the local children."

Evan frowned. "Well, you're already doing that on a Sunday."

"No, no. You have got it wrong. I mean like a Dame School. I will teach the children their alphabet. They will learn to read and write and count their sums."

"And how do you propose to do this with a new baby to look after?"

"I have thought of that. Hannah Griffiths is a good girl. She will help me at the school. In any case, the baby will sleep a lot in the beginning and when he or she is old enough, can join the school for themselves." Yes, she had it all worked out in her mind, it was quite simple really.

"Don't be so foolish, Lily. Babies don't always sleep all day, not unless you are prepared to dose ours up on sleeping medicine all day long, and believe me, I would never allow you to do that."

Lily knew there were lots of people that did that if they had to work, but she had no intention of drugging their baby and was quite upset that Evan should even think she would consider it.

"Evan, I am not a fool. I will carry my baby in a shawl when he or she is crying and Hannah and Mrs Morgan will both help me, they have said that they will."

"Oh, so Hannah and Mrs Morgan, know of your plans before me, your husband, knows anything?" The hurt in his eyes was evident.

"I had to ask them before I mentioned anything to you at all. I had to see if it could possibly work out."

"Well in my opinion, I think it is best that women do not work at all. I should be the bread winner. A wife should stay at home."

"Like your mother, you mean? I should stay at home like the 'Lady of the Manor'? Well I can assure you Evan Davies that I have plans. I am not a foolish person. I can work as good as any man can."

Evan held her firmly by the shoulders. "I have no doubt about it. But the type of wife I want is one who is there for me to come home to, not one who is busy doing things for others."

"Isn't that what you do yourself though, Evan? You spend a lot of your time and energy helping other people, so why shouldn't I do the same?"

Lily knew that she had made an impression as her husband fell silent and then he left the bedroom quietly, deep in contemplation.

Too often, she had seen women marry and then have to do their husband's bidding so that there was little left for themselves. She knew in her heart that as well as being a wife and mother, she wanted to be herself.

Chapter Seven

New Year of 1867 started off peacefully. Lily had by now given up on looking for Dafydd, at least for time being. It was hard for her to walk across the room, never mind to go search for him, with the impending birth of the baby.

Delwyn had visited to wish them both a Happy New Year. He made no mention of not having called over Christmas, neither did Lily feel like asking him why not. She was far too exhausted these days to get into an argument with anyone. She speculated that he was so wrapped up in his new life that he hadn't called.

Delwyn had been shocked at his brother's disappearance, but made no mention to go and look for him, making Lily a little annoyed. *It's that religion of his,* she thought. *It has gone to his head and now he's forgotten all about his family. All he can think about is getting away to America.* If she was being truthful, she felt abandoned by almost everyone right now, apart from Evan and Mrs Morgan.

She kept her mind occupied by planning on what she was going to need to start the school. She would need to get some slate boards and chalk, plenty of books for all ages, some toys and games, and a rocking horse would be nice.

There were plenty of tables and chairs used for the Sunday school, those would be ideal. She was so excited about this idea of hers that she had forgotten to be careful as she stood on top of a small wooden bench to pull some books down from a shelf. Losing her balance, she toppled off and fell to the floor, crying out in pain. Evan came running from a little room next door where he had been preparing his sermon.

"Are you all right?" he questioned Lily, as he found her sitting on the floor rubbing her ankle.

"I'm fine," she reassured. "I just need to put a cold compress on my ankle that's all."

"It's not your ankle I'm worried about," he said tersely, his top lip tightening with anger, she presumed.

"So you are not worried about me, your wife then, are you?" The vehemence in her voice both startled and astounded her.

"Of course I am, *cariad*," he replied in a softer tone. "It's just that's my child you are carrying in there, not just your own and in my opinion, sometimes you take too many risks."

"Please let me be the judge of that," she said, trying to stand, but failing as her swollen stomach got in the way.

Evan leaned down and heaved her onto her feet and into a chair. "You have got to take more care. That's an order."

She didn't much feel like taking orders from anyone right now, including the head of the household. "Don't fuss, Evan."

"I think it might be in all our best interests if my mother came to stay to look after you."

"No, please," she protested.

"Either that or we employ someone to help you with the baby and the household chores," Evan said thoughtfully.

"Over my dead body. I will not have another woman interfering in my affairs, thank you very much. I promise I will try to take more care."

Evan looked at her, his stare almost boring right through her. Why was she feeling there was now some distance between them? After a moment of thought, he said, "Very well. But if you disobey me, then you will have no option."

She had never heard her husband sound so forceful towards her before, only in the pulpit when he was preaching passionately had she ever heard him raise his voice like that. It sent a shiver coursing down her spine. This did not sound like the man she had married.

* * *

The following morning, she awoke in some discomfort. Turning over in bed, she stretched out to feel Evan's warm body, but his side of the bed was empty. Running her hands over the pillow and sheet, it felt cold to the touch. Had he slept there at all?

She heaved her heavy frame out of the bed and slipped into her dressing gown and carpet slippers. The room was freezing; maybe the cold had awoken her. She tiptoed down the stairs. That was odd; the fire in the grate was out. She would normally expect her husband to light it if he had got up before her. She looked out in the garden in case he was feeding the birds, but there was no sign.

As quickly as she could, she put kindling and coal on the fire and set a match to it. It was going to take some time to get going.

This definitely had to be the coldest day in a long while. The flowers and shrubs in the garden were iced with a coating of frost. She blew on her hands to warm them, put the old battered kettle on to boil on the stove and draped a large woollen throw from the chair around her shoulders. She needed a hot drink to warm herself up.

Perhaps Evan was in the chapel? Sometimes he went in there when he required solitude, to pray in peace. She didn't mind of course. It could be difficult for him when he was at home as she had a habit of talking to him when he was busy either praying or writing his sermon, without realising he was in deep contemplation.

The hot sweet tea did the job and she sliced a piece of bread from the loaf, then pierced it with the metal toasting fork, kept hanging on a hook next to the fireplace. Holding it out in front of the fire, she watched as it slowly turned a golden brown. Then she buttered it liberally and sat down to eat it by the fireside with a second cup of tea.

Maybe Evan had got called away in an emergency. Mr. Daniels who lived on the opposite side of the street had been very ill. His wife had said the doctor had told her he only had a few weeks left to live, if that.

As the day wore on, Lily became increasingly worried about her husband and wondered what to do.

"What on earth can you possibly do, dear?" Mrs Morgan asked later when she popped in to check on Lily.

Lily shrugged. "Nothing I suppose."

"Then you are going to have to sit and wait for his return. I will wait with you. You can't be left alone at a time like this. Mr. Morgan can see to the shop, on his own."

Being as heavily confined as she was, Lily realised how fortunate she was to have a friend like Mrs Morgan. Both women warmed themselves by the fire, the elderly woman attempting to lift Lily's spirits with tales from her own youth. For a while, it worked, but then Lily would glance at the mantel clock and her heart raced with fear.

Mrs Morgan made a cup of tea and found a small loaf cake in the cupboard to sustain them, and then at a half past ten that night, there was a loud rap on the front door. Lily held her hand to her chest, panic-stricken. "Don't worry, *cariad*. I'll answer it." Mrs Morgan reassured as she went to open the door.

Lily heard hushed voices in the hallway and then Mrs Morgan asking someone to come in. Her heart hammered when she realised who it was. A policeman lowered his head as he entered the room; he had to be a good five inches taller than her husband.

Lily rose to her feet to greet the unwelcome stranger.

"I'm sorry to bother you, Ma'am, it's about your husband." Lily's legs trembled as she fought to stay on her feet. Mrs Morgan guided her back to the chair, obviously not wanting a reoccurrence of Lily's fainting attack the other night outside the Irish woman's home.

"What's happened to him, constable?" She managed to say, her mouth now feeling dry.

"It's all right, Mrs Davies. Be reassured he is still alive and breathing." Lily visibly relaxed.

"Then, what is the matter, constable?"

"I'm afraid we found him wondering around, he appears to be injured, not badly, but he seems a bit mixed up."

"Mixed up?" Lily didn't understand quite what the policeman meant by this.

"We think he might have lost his memory. He knows he's from Abercanaid and mentioned the name of his house, but he doesn't seem to remember he has a wife or that you are expecting his child. Mrs Morgan filled us in on those details when she answered the door. I, myself, was surprised to hear of this."

Lily's mouth fell open. How could this be? Evan was as fit as a flea last night and how could he have sustained injury? Before she asked the question, the policeman, as if reading her mind, explained.

"You see, your husband was found on the ground, near China. It appears he was set upon by several people, robbed most probably."

Lily took in an intake of breath to steady her already frazzled nerves. "Oh!" she exclaimed, then bit into her knuckles.

"I am sorry, Ma'am. We had to bring him home. He's outside in the carriage. But as he doesn't seem to know anything about you or the expected child, I don't know if it would be wise for him to spend the night here."

Lily rose. "Let me see my husband, please." Then she started down the hall calling out his name. A strong arm restrained her from behind. The policeman had her in his embrace. "Please, Mrs Davies.

Your husband is not a pretty sight at the moment. It might not be a good idea to see him in this condition."

Mrs Morgan, who had remained silent until now, said, "Well, how about if you take him over to my house? My husband will take care of him and I can spend the night with Lily here, until we see how things are for the morning?"

The constable agreed that sounded a sensible idea for all concerned. Lily, though, was not happy with it. When the policeman had departed from the premises, she burst into tears.

"It's all my fault!" she wailed. "I should never have dragged Evan to China to look for Dafydd. That's what he must have been doing—looking for him."

Mrs Morgan draped a comforting arm around Lily's shoulder. "There, there. Don't blame yourself, Lily, it is not good for the baby. You didn't make him go, did you?"

Lily shook her head. "No, I actually decided to keep quiet about it this past couple of weeks. So I don't know what made him go there today."

"Perhaps," said Mrs Morgan, "he wanted to find your brother for you before the baby was born, as a surprise, like."

Lily pondered that thought and realised that the old woman was probably right. Evan had known how cut up about it all she was. That must have been it.

Mrs Morgan accompanied her to the bedroom and after helping her to undress, turned back the bed covers. "Now you get a good sleep, dear. I shall sleep in the spare room."

"You are so kind to me. I don't know what I would do without you. Now Mam has gone, I would have no one if it were not for you." She patted Mrs Morgan's hand.

"What about Evan's mother?"

"What about her? She would be no comfort to me. The woman is only keeping me sweet as she wants to get her hands on her only grandchild."

"Lily, how can you say such a thing?"

"It is true though. The woman would care nothing for me if it were not so. Otherwise I believe she would only allow Evan to visit her, without me."

"Then she can't be the woman I thought she was," Mrs Morgan said sadly.

"No, she's not." That was the last thing Lily remembered saying before she fell into a fitful sleep.

* * *

The next thing Lily knew, the sun was streaming in through the window, although it was still freezing cold. For a moment, she forgot about last night and looked for her husband in the bed. Then remembering what had taken place, she sat up and called out to Mrs Morgan, who came immediately.

"What's the matter, Lily? Are you all right?" The old woman stood hunched, wrapped in a shawl. She probably hadn't slept much all night. Lily experienced a pang of guilt.

"I'm fine Mrs Morgan. I just want to go and see how Evan is."

"Now, don't you be worrying. Mr. Morgan just popped over to say he's sleeping well and is still in bed. He recognises my husband and knows he is in Abercanaid, he also knows who you are but—"

"But what?"

"It appears he has lost about a year of his memory. He thinks he has only just arrived as a minister in the village."

"Oh," Lily exclaimed. "At least he will know who I am when I go over there."

"No, no," the old woman cried, "You are to stay put. After breakfast, it is arranged that Mr. Morgan will bring him over here to you."

Lily reluctantly shook her head. "Well, all right then. I would like him to get accustomed to his surroundings once more."

She washed and dressed, and after her breakfast, waited in anticipation for her husband to arrive. At half past ten, Mr. Morgan turned up at the door step with him. Lily almost wept, breaking her heart, when she saw the state of Evan. His coat was torn and muddy and he had several bruises and scrapes to his hands and face.

"Hello Evan," she greeted him tentatively.

"Hello," he replied. "It's Lily Jenkin, isn't it? How is your mother?" Evan had a glazed expression in his eyes.

Lily fought to hold the tears back as Mrs Morgan squeezed her hand as if to tell her to go along with it all.

"Yes, Mr. Davies. How are you feeling?"

"I have a bit of a sore head."

"What happened to you yesterday?"

He drew his eyebrows together in puzzlement, almost as though it were odd that someone he now thought was just a member of his congregation should ask him a question like that. But then he stared up at the ceiling and as he returned his gaze, his eyes looked blank. "Do you know, I don't even know. I can't remember. Let's have some tea shall we?"

Mrs Morgan raised her eyebrows, looked at Lily and then nodded. "I'll make it," she said, "You sit down with Mr. Davies, Lily."

The pair sat facing one another at the side of the hearth. "So," asked Evan, "you wanted to see me about something?"

"Yes, I did…" She chewed on her bottom lip. "Evan... I am your wife." She sat holding her breath, waiting for his response.

He frowned momentarily. "No? I don't understand…"

"When you went missing yesterday, I believe you might have been looking for my brother, Dafydd. It appears that you were set on by a couple of men in China, they probably robbed you. I think you have lost some of your memory. You married me last April, Evan. Don't you remember?"

He shook his head, staring into the flames of the fire. "How could I have married you and not know anything about it?"

"I don't know, but what I can tell you is that I am having your baby."

Tears welled up in her husband's eyes and he wept into his hands. "I just can't remember, what year is this?"

"It is 1867. Now don't struggle to remember, I will bring the doctor to you."

He looked up. "Doctor Owen?"

"You remember him?"

Evan nodded. "I remember helping him at the Gethin pit only last month."

"Dear Evan, it wasn't last month, it was just over a year ago." Lily swallowed a lump in her throat.

"Put him to bed," William Morgan advised. "I'll fetch the doctor for you, Lily."

Lily nodded in agreement. Whatever happened, he needed to see the doctor. What would happen now? It must feel to Evan that she were a stranger in his home. And even worse than that, even if he believed they were married to one another, would he accept the baby as his own?

* * *

The doctor said he thought it was probably temporary amnesia, brought on by a blow to the head. There was nothing any of them could do except wait for Evan's memory to return. Meanwhile, he suggested that Lily tried to prompt her husband's recall by talking about things they had done together and showing him old newspapers going back to that time, if she were able to get any.

Evan, on the other hand, showed no ill feelings towards her being in 'his' home, but of course, they could not carry on sharing the same bed, as to her husband they were not married, so he agreed he would take the bed in the spare room.

It was a difficult time for Lily as it now felt that she had no husband for support, the only support she now had coming from Mr. and Mrs Morgan.

"Don't worry. You'll see, everything will work out in time, Lily," Mrs Morgan reassured.

"It's just that it's so bad for it to have happened now, Mrs Morgan. I need my husband. I want him by my side at night. Now it feels as though we are two strangers. Conversation is very difficult between us."

"I know it is dear. Have you thought about asking his mother to stay? I know you two don't get on very well, but it might be a comfort for Evan, to have a familiar face around."

Although Mrs Morgan hadn't meant to, she had unintentionally upset Lily with her remark, not about Evan's mother coming to stay, but about her being a familiar face, while she, his own wife was not.

Taking a steadying breath, she said, "Maybe you are right. I know Mrs Davies and I don't see eye to eye, but it might be good for Evan having her to stop here with us. I shall write a letter to her to explain. Would you post it for me?"

Mrs Morgan patted Lily's shoulder. "Of course I will, sweetheart. You're going to need all the help you can get right now. Pride does not come into it."

* * *

Olwen Davies arrived with all her luggage the following week. Instead of greeting Lily by the door, she flounced past her leaving her luggage on the front step and embraced her son.

"Oh, you poor boy. What on earth has happened to you?" she asked, looking over Evan's shoulder directly at Lily.

"They tell me I got injured up in China, but I am fine now, except for some memory loss."

"China? What on earth were you doing in a flea pit like that? I didn't bring you up to go walking around hovels."

"I'm not too sure, although Lily says she thought I was looking for her brother."

"I should have known," Mrs Davies said bitterly, "that it would have something to do with *her* family."

Leaving her son go for a moment, she turned to Lily and said, "Rest assured, I am here now, and nothing like this is ever going to happen again to my son or my grandchild. Evan, bring my bags in, will you?"

Evan jumped at her request and immediately went outside to fetch his mother's luggage. Sleeping arrangements were now going to be awkward. It had been decided that Evan would sleep on the sofa downstairs and his mother to take the spare room. Although Lily would have preferred it if he had moved back into the main bedroom with her.

From the moment his mother arrived, the atmosphere slowly changed to one where Lily had to tread on egg shells both around her husband and her mother-in-law. Mrs Davies spent her time spoiling her son, making special cakes for him and generally feeding him up. While Lily herself began to feel her own power slowly slipping away. It even began to occur to her that if the woman was like this now with her own son, what would she be like once the baby arrived? She even considered moving back into her old house in Chapel Square, it would take some tidying up after the mess Dafydd had left, but at least she could do what she wanted there. Of course it would be difficult with a new baby.

Mrs Morgan tried to talk her out of it. "Look Lily, if things get that bad, you can always stay here for a while. You can't go back to upper Abercanaid. There will be no one to take care of you."

"I know you are speaking sense, Mrs Morgan, but that woman really is intolerable. Evan seems to be under her spell."

* * *

Lily awoke with pains during the night and Doctor Owen was called. It hurt her not to have her husband by her side as she went through labour even though she knew most men would not want to be present at the birth, it just was not done, but to have him come and check she was all right would have been fine by her. Instead, he kept well out of the way and only Mrs Davies came back and forth offering to boil up kettles of water and to get anything the doctor needed, at least the woman was practical, Lily reassured herself.

The labour was long and Lily kept herself going by thinking how proud her parents would have been of her and their grandchild and as she blinked back tears of frustration. Her baby daughter, Mollie, was born at a quarter past eight the following morning.

It hurt that Evan did not come anywhere near her or their child, even though his mother tried her best to persuade him; after all, it was her grandchild. Mrs Morgan sent for Delwyn, who turned up later that evening, but by then, Lily was so exhausted, it was hard to keep her eyes open. Delwyn though, was enchanted by the beautiful baby girl.

"Mollie looks so much like you, Lily." He stroked the child's soft cheek. "What does Evan think of her?"

"Nothing. He thinks nothing of his own offspring and shows no designs to see her."

Delwyn raised his eyebrows in surprise. "Why ever not? It doesn't sound like him."

Lily shook her head, sadly. "He's not the man I married. He is suffering from memory loss, he got hit about the head in China and now he doesn't remember even marrying me or that I was once his sweetheart."

"Oh Lily," Delwyn sympathised, drawing closer to his sister, "I had no idea. I should have been around more for you, but I have been so busy. I got baptised into the Mormon faith a couple of days ago and we are preaching on the streets every opportunity we possibly can."

Lily was beginning to understand how important her brother's faith was to him and that he wasn't being selfish as she first thought, but instead he was thinking about his wife-to-be and making plans to go to Utah. As the head of the family was already out there, he would be needed to help the rest of the family pack up to leave. Of course his mining skills would be much sort after by the Mormon brethren in Zion.

Lily patted his hand. "Don't fret, dear brother. I quite understand. I confess I didn't at first, but I am happy for you and your bride. We have made our peace and if we never see one another again, I know you will have followed your heart for your religion and your intended wife."

"Lily, it makes me glad to hear you say that." The tears flowed freely between the pair of them. Only one person was missing and that drove an arrow that pierced her heart. One day they would all be reunited, but she had no idea when that would be, but she was sure of it.

* * *

As the days passed, Lily found herself worrying less about her husband's lack of involvement with her and their baby, becoming more concerned about the way her mother-in-law started butting in to attend to the child at every given opportunity.

Whenever Mollie needed bathing or changing, the woman was there, constantly ready to take her grandchild away from her mother.

In normal circumstances, Lily wouldn't have minded someone wanting to help, but these weren't normal circumstances, this was just interference in her mind.

Evan, although not totally oblivious to the child, did not treat her as if she was his own offspring, more rather that she was a very special guest. Of course, he did not bond with her at all and it had felt very hurtful at first, but now, she was beyond caring. What she did care about though, was the way that everywhere she turned, Olwen Davies was there. Her only escape was when she wrapped Mollie in a shawl and took her to visit Mrs Morgan and even then, her mother-in-law was complaining about taking 'the dear child' out in the cold air.

"Nonsense," Lily had retorted. "It will do her good to get out of this house into a change of atmosphere, rather than cooped up here."

Of course, Lily had been talking more about herself than the child, and she hoped her mother-in-law had got the point, but somehow, she doubted that.

Lily was beginning to wonder if Olwen had treated her own child in the same way.

The wind mustn't breathe on the precious child.

She tried to broach the subject about her returning to Pentrych, but she would not take the hint, insisting that they all needed her there and that she would be willing to help out when Lily started teaching at the school.

Lily now had 18 children's names down on her list from the ages of 5 to 14. She was excited about her idea but wondered how she would cope; Mrs Davies probably wouldn't let young Hannah Griffiths look after the child, even though the girl was more than capable.

She recognised that the school might just be the escape she needed, and so by early summer, when Mollie was old enough to start taking some mashed up solid food, Lily prepared to leave her with Olwen Davies. Evan had not commented at all. He had returned to the pulpit with as much fervour as usual, and if the congregation were asking him awkward questions about his marriage, then he wasn't showing it.

* * *

The first day at the school, Lily stood at the door waiting to greet the pupils, dressed in a black, high-necked dress; her best brooch secured at the neck.

Hannah Griffiths arrived first with her younger sister and apologised that Richard would not be able to attend every day as he was on shift work down the mine. Lily told her not to worry as long as he came when he could. She could always set him homework to catch up with the others.

Four deprived children from Nightingale Street turned up in dirty, ragged clothing that first day.

"Heavens above!" Lily exclaimed when she saw their tattered clothing and unwashed faces. She told Hannah to take them into the house and get them washed and then dress them using a box of clothes she had set aside for a purpose. Later, she planned to wash their own clothes and repair the tears, so they could take them back home. She didn't want to do anything to upset their mother, who already had two younger children under three at home and another on the way.

By 9 o'clock that morning, all 18 children, except for two, turned up. She racked her brains to think who the absentees might be, and then remembered Rebecca and Daniel Evans from Rhydycar Cottages. They had a longer walk down the canal bank than the others, but twenty minutes later, they turned up as clean as two shiny pins, eager to start the day.

"Try to leave the house earlier tomorrow morning," Lily advised.

"Yes, Mrs Davies," they enthused. If only all children were as clean and well-presented as Rebecca and Daniel, but she understood that some of the parents were struggling to cope with domestic duties, especially since the pit disaster.

The first thing Lily did was to sit the children down in a circle on the floor and they each had to tell everyone their name, age, and where they lived. It was going along well, until it was the turn of Betty Thomas. The little five-year-old hung her head and twiddled with her plaits, refusing to speak to anyone.

She's shy, Lily thought. Allowing her another chance to answer, instead of telling her off, she decided to give the class Betty's details. Betty looked up and smiled and then lowered her head once more. Lily had never seen a child so shy in all her life.

After they had been introduced, Lily got a large map of Wales to show the children and she pinned it up on the wall, asking them if they knew any places on it. One or two knew where their home town of Merthyr Tydfil was, but most couldn't recognise any where on it at all. So Lily painstakingly wrote the names of major towns and cities in large letters on the map. Then she pointed with a cane to each town, telling the children a little about it.

She knew that only a handful of the children could read and write, so instead of asking them to write about what they had done, she gave each a slate and a piece of chalk so that they could draw a picture of anything they'd spoken about. As they'd concentrated mostly on their home town, some drew mountains, barges and coal mines. Betty's was the strangest drawing of all. She just scribbled violently on her slate, seeming to get frustrated and then threw her slate on the floor, breaking it to pieces.

Lily was just about to tell the little girl off, when the child's bottom lip quivered and she burst into tears. Taking the child aside and sitting her on her lap, she rocked her gently, until the child fell asleep in her arms.

Whatever is troubling her must be bad. She is so different to the other children, Lily thought.

They stopped for a break mid morning. Lily gave all the children a Welsh cake and a drink of water. She would have liked to have given them a mug of milk each, but she didn't have the money to do it, as it was, she had to rely on the charity of local shopkeepers in the village and in Merthyr town itself.

Betty seemed to have settled down after break and followed Lily around like a little puppy dog. She resolved to find out more about the child's background, she would ask Evan tonight if he knew anything.

The children all went home at 3 o'clock. She wondered if they all felt as worn out as she had, she was just about to talk to Hannah, who was helping her to sort out the slates and put toys and books away, when she spied Evan's mother standing in the doorway. The woman cast a beady eye over the scene in front of her and then returned to Chapel House next door. Lily wondered what had been going through the woman's mind.

When all was packed away and Lily had locked up and returned to the house, she expected to find Mollie taking her usual afternoon nap upstairs, but instead, she was nowhere to be found. Lily's heart raced, she didn't know why she was so panic-stricken, but deep down she felt as though her mother-in-law had plans for her child that did not include her.

"What's the matter?" Evan asked. Normally he would have put his arm around her shoulder or embraced her when he was concerned about her, but now, she could tell emotionally and physically, he was keeping her at a distance since the blow to his head and the memory loss.

"I just wondered where Mollie is?" She tried to keep her voice strong and composed, not intending to alarm her husband.

"It's all right. Mother has just taken her out for a walk in the perambulator."

"Oh!" Lily's eyes grew wide, she hadn't been expecting that. She knew her mother-in-law would hardly be waiting with a warm welcome and a hot cup of tea for her, but she had no idea that she would have taken the child without asking her permission.

Evan studied her face. "You look surprised?"

"I am, yes. I thought your mother would have realised that my first day at work would have been hard for me to be parted from Mollie. And that it would be hard for Mollie to be parted from me too."

Evan smiled. "Don't worry. Mollie has slept most of the day, like a baby lamb."

Lily frowned. That was odd, normally she dozed after breakfast for an hour and also again after lunch, she certainly never slept all day. She worried in case the child was sickening for something. So perhaps the fresh air would do her some good after all.

Relaxing a little, she asked Evan about Betty Thomas's background.

"Betty who?" he asked. Then she remembered he would hardly know the family as they moved to the area around the time she and Evan married and had stopped attending chapel for some time. He had met them before the accident, but as it had erased about a year of his memory, there was little chance he knew anything at all. She would have to ask Mrs Morgan instead.

She went upstairs to freshen up and change out of her work clothes. There was a lot to do. She needed to wash Mollie's clothes as well as the four children's tattered clothing from Nightingale Street. She hoped to get them dry and repaired by tomorrow afternoon, so they could take them back home. She didn't want their mother to get cross, although the poor woman had so much on her plate, it should be a blessing to her that Lily cared to help.

After the washing, she started to make the evening meal, a beef stew. It was Evan's favourite, normally he would eat it with relish, but he seemed to force down every mouthful.

"For goodness sake, Evan. You used to love this meal, what's got into you?" She said crossly.

He looked at her with a blank expression and then said, "I'm sorry, Lily. I've been keeping something from you, my sense of smell and taste is not so good these days since—" He set down his spoon and shook his head.

"Since the night you were attacked?"

He nodded and picked up his spoon again. Poor Evan, she had been so concerned with her own feelings about him not recognising her as his wife, or not bonding with the baby, that she hadn't taken his feelings into consideration. It would be awful for him not to remember. The only thing that seemed unchanged in him, was his passion for preaching on a Sunday. His congregation would never have guessed.

"I shall ask Doctor Owen about it for you," she reassured him.

Olwen Davies showed up with Mollie gone eight o'clock that evening.

Lily gritted her teeth, took a deep breath and then attempted to compose herself.

"Where have you been, Mrs Davies?" She asked, as the woman stood in the hallway.

"I've been taking my granddaughter around to see the neighbours," she said brightly.

"I haven't taken her around there to see them myself yet. If anyone should do that it should be me!"

"Well you weren't here to do it now, were you?" The middle-aged woman accused.

"Maybe not. But it would have been nice if you had asked me first."

Lily bent down and scooped her drowsy daughter from the perambulator. Mollie opened her sleepy eyes and gave a little yawn.

"Let's get you up to bed, *cariad*," she soothed the child. Then casting a scathing glance at Evan's mother, she said, "She should have been in bed ages ago."

Evan failed to intervene. Instead he went back to writing his Sunday sermon. If he was on Lily's side, he didn't show it, which hurt her all the more. Hot tears welled up and threatened to spill down her cheeks. Gently, she carried the child upstairs to her cot.

When she returned, she addressed Olwen Davies. "I think it's best if you go back to Pentrych."

Her mother-in-law stuck her chin out in defiance. "You all need me here," she declared.

"No, we do not, do we Evan?" Lily asked, looking at him for support.

Instead, he just shrugged and went back to writing.

"See, even my son disagrees with you," her mother-in-law sneered.

"I am asking you nicely, Mrs Davies. I would like you to leave this house. Obviously you can't go tonight, but there is a train you can catch home tomorrow."

Olwen Davies did not reply, instead she turned on her heel, muttering something under her breath. She wasn't sure if she had got through to the woman or not, but she could have slapped her husband across the face for his lack of support, but then again, she had to remind herself that he had no memory of their marital love for one another.

She busied herself clearing away the supper dishes and did not even offer her mother-in-law any stew as she had planned. She knew she should have thanked the woman for taking care of her daughter, but she was just so angry. She decided that tomorrow she would take Mollie in to work with her and Hannah Griffiths could help out as previously planned.

* * *

When she awoke the following morning, she was surprised to find her mother-in-law already up. Perhaps she was getting ready to go back to Pentrych? Lily hoped. But instead, she apologised for yesterday, saying it would not happen again and she would respect Lily's wishes from now on. She wanted to believe her, but when the woman smiled, it didn't quite reach her eyes, so as a consequence, she doubted her sincerity.

But it put her in a difficult position, should she trust her again or not? The answer to that particular question was made for her, when she discovered that Hannah was ill and could not come in the rest of the week, she had no one else to turn to, and so Olwen Davies was to stay, for time being, anyhow.

Every evening when Lily finished teaching, Olwen and Mollie would be at home, but it disturbed Lily, that more often than not, the child was still asleep. What concerned her even more was, instead of waking up at night as expected as she had slept all day, she slept through the night as well.

Getting up early on Saturday morning when there was no school, she quickly washed and dressed the infant and took her to see Doctor Owen.

"Yes, she does appear very drowsy, Lily," he agreed. "You say that there seems to be a pattern. She's drowsy during the week when she is being cared for by your mother-in-law, but livelier at the weekends when she is in your care?"

"That's right, Doctor." He scratched his head thoughtfully. "I have seen this sort of thing before I think. Now tell me has she any signs of a rash or upset stomach?"

"No, otherwise she seems quite well. Except I have difficulty rousing her."

The doctor looked gravely serious and said, "I think she might be medicated with something to keep her quiet."

Lily could not believe her own ears. "Are you sure Doctor?"

"No, I am not certain of it. But it might be an idea if you keep an eye on your mother-in-law. Have a little search around. Have you smelled anything strange on the child, like alcohol for instance?"

Lily shook her head. "No, nothing like that." It was all beginning to make sense, no wonder Olwen Davies didn't seem to be all that tired if she was looking after a young child who was sleeping all day.

Lily thanked the doctor and wondered what she could do. Later that day, the opportunity presented itself when Olwen Davies said she would take the train to Merthyr as she needed to buy some new clothes. She asked Lily if she would like to accompany her, but Lily suggested that Evan go instead.

As soon as they'd left the house, Lily searched the woman's bedroom and finding nothing, kicked the door with frustration. She was just about to leave, when she felt something under her foot—it was a small brass key. It looked like it might fit the woman's trunk that she had brought with her from home.

Lily turned it in the lock and it opened easily. Nothing untoward appeared to be inside: a selection of gowns and day dresses and night wear, as she rummaged through, she began to feel guilty for searching in the first place and then just as she was about to close it again, felt something slip beneath her fingers. It was a secret panel, for hiding valuables. She slid it across and found an old glass bottle. As she picked up the brown bottle containing some sort of liquid, medicine by the look of it, she wondered what it was. Most of the label had been scraped off, the only letters she could make out were S -RU- and then P_P_ _ES. Puzzled, she took off the top and inhaled. The odour reminded her of the medicine her father had been given when he was dying, and more recently, Dafydd had taken too following the pit accident. Oh no, it couldn't possibly be anything like that, could it?

Wrapping Mollie in a shawl, she took the bottle to Doctor Owen who confirmed that it was something strong. "The label," he said, "if it hadn't been scraped off, would have read: 'Syrup of Poppies'. It's a very strong medicine, an opiate. Your daughter has been given opium. This is very serious, Lily. She could get addicted to it. There have been cases of people in the town dosing their children up with this stuff, so that they can work long hours in the ironworks while their children are asleep. I don't suppose they mean any real harm, but unfortunately a few children have died."

Suddenly, Lily's breath began ebbing out of her body and a wave of nausea swept over her. She retched, but nothing came up.

"Sit down, dear. You have had a nasty shock. Now if you can't get that woman out of your house tonight, then I suggest that you and your daughter move out. I'll take a look at the child right away." He laid the child on his couch and looked at her eyes and general demeanour. "Yes, she does appear quite drowsy, though not comatose…" He handed Mollie back to her mother.

Doctor Owen left the room and came back with a cup of water. "Sip that slowly," he ordered Lily. "It's been a trying time for you with all you have had to put up with since your husband's amnesia. I can inform the police about your mother-in-law, if you like."

Lily shook her head vigorously. Whatever she thought about Olwen Davies, she was sure that the woman meant no real harm to come to the child. "I think I will have to deal with this myself."

Lily waited anxiously for Evan and his mother to return from Merthyr. Olwen Davies arrived glowing with excitement as she proudly showed off her wares as she unpacked boxes and parcels of the most exquisite clothes and hats.

Evan stared at Lily for the longest time and then taking her aside said, "For a moment then, I felt like I knew you Lily. Really knew you as if you meant something to me."

"Oh Evan. You don't know how long I have waited to hear you say that." She stepped forward to embrace him, but he took a step back.

"Lily," he said, "I am not ready for that quite yet. Please give me time. Now what is concerning you?"

"Nothing," she lied. She intended to bide her time to get Olwen Davies on her own and out of their lives forever.

Chapter Eight

Lily managed to get through the rest of the weekend even though she longed to drag the woman outside onto the street and throw her luggage out with her. Instead, she tried to concentrate on looking after her daughter and helping out at the chapel as Evan preached his sermon.

As soon as Monday morning arrived though, she had a plan. She waited to see if Hannah Griffiths was back at school and when she saw she was indeed fit and well, she asked her to take over the class by reading them a story and helping them to draw pictures about the story afterwards. That would take up at least a half hour or so she estimated.

Meanwhile, she sneaked back into the house and hid upstairs in her bedroom behind the wardrobe. She heard Olwen talking to the child and all sounded fine, she was saying something about taking her out for a walk later. She questioned herself whether she had got things wrong and perhaps if the medicine were for her mother-in law-herself and not for her child.

But then, after a few minutes she heard her climbing the stairs, still talking to the child and going into her own bedroom. Lily came out from behind the wardrobe and taking off her shoes, tiptoed along the landing until she stood outside her mother-in-law's room. The door was ajar. She watched Olwen place Mollie down on her bed and then go to pick something up from her dressing table. Lily held her breath as she saw it was the key to the trunk that her mother-in-law held in her hand. Then, taking it over to the trunk, she watched in horror as the woman unlocked it, rummaged inside and came out with the bottle of medicine.

Surely she must be mistaken? She wouldn't give it to her own granddaughter? Picking up a small spoon from the dressing table, she poured out the medicine and held it towards the child.

"Come along now, Mollie," she said, in a sickly sweet voice, "this will help you to sleep!"

Lily stood grounded to the spot, frozen with terror and shock. She had to do something quick, but felt momentarily helpless and powerless. Her strong maternal, protective instinct, took over as she heard Mollie start to cry. The child obviously didn't like to take the medicine and it was being forced upon her.

Barging out from her hiding place, Lily shouted, "Stop that at once, you evil witch!" Olwen let go of the child, so that she fell back on the bed, but was otherwise unharmed.

The woman's mouth fell open. She'd obviously not expected to get caught in the act.

"S…S…She's not well this morning," she stuttered, when she had found her voice.

"Oh yes, and what happens to be the matter with her?" Lily said, pushing past the woman almost knocking her flying to pick up her daughter.

"I heard her coughing violently."

"Now, let me tell you this, you old crone... I know what you are up to. I took that bottle over to Doctor Owen and he confirmed my suspicions. It is a dangerous medicine you are giving my child."

"Stuff and nonsense!" Olwen retorted. "It's just cough medicine."

Lily straightened. "Oh, no it's not. It's syrup of poppies."

"Yes, lots of people use it."

"Well, I am not lots of people and let me tell you another thing...the doctor says some children have died from being overdosed with that stuff."

Olwen Davies laughed nervously. "Don't be silly. I've taken it myself and it didn't harm me."

"It's a powerful drug and it can kill if it is given in too large a quantity. Not only that, but it's habit forming."

Olwen's eyes opened wide in horror. She opened her mouth and closed it again and then said, "Lily I had no idea. It will not happen again."

"Yes, it certainly will not. Now if you do not wish me to tell your son that you have been drugging his child with something that might kill her, then I suggest that you leave for home today. I will gladly put you on the next train myself."

Olwen Davies could tell when she was beat. "Please don't do that. I will do whatever you wish, but don't say anything about this to Evan." She looked at Lily in desperation.

"Now why would that be, dear mother-in-law? Would it be because Evan would find out what an awful mother he has?"

The woman's lip trembled as she wrung her hands in despair. "I will do as you ask. But please do not stop me from seeing my only grandchild. I love Mollie."

"Then tell me why you did it?" Lily tilted her chin.

"I am not that great with children to be truthful. We had a nanny when Evan was born. I can't cope with the crying."

"Did Mollie cry a lot last week when I was at work?"

Olwen nodded. "I took her around to the neighbours to ask what might be wrong with her. Maggie Shanklin said it was probably teething and she was the one who gave me the bottle of medicine."

Maggie Shanklin! She should have guessed. That woman was trouble. "Right now, listen to me. I am prepared to forgive you as I know that you wouldn't want to purposely hurt your own grandchild. But I would still like you to leave and I will write to you when I next want you to come pay us a visit."

Olwen Davies nodded gratefully. "I can't leave right this moment though," she explained. "It would look strange if I went back to Pentrych without saying goodbye to Evan." Lily had to admit that the woman was correct. Evan just would not understand and undoubtedly would be a little hurt. It was in his best interests and her own, if Olwen Davies left at the right time.

"I'll tell you what you will do," Lily said, her tone now a little softer. "You shall announce to Evan tonight that you are going back home. If he asks you why, you will say it is because you fear his father is missing you. Then, you shall leave on the first available train tomorrow."

Olwen nodded with tears in her eyes. "I am so sorry for all I have put your through."

"Well, it's just as well I discovered what you had been doing, even if you meant no harm to your granddaughter."

"It's not just that," Olwen explained, "I have been awful to you, dear Lily. You have been nothing but kindness itself to me."

"Then why did you act that way?"

The woman's head slumped. "Because I feared losing my only son."

"But can't you see that in time you might have driven him away because of your behaviour?"

Olwen lifted her head and nodded, blinking away the tears. "I feel so ashamed of myself."

"Well let's hope that we can all get off on a different footing next time you come to stay with us. Things have been difficult enough with my husband not knowing that I am his wife and now that he does know, him not remembering."

Olwen bit her lip. "And I have made things worse for you, haven't I? I should have known better as my own mother-in law-was a tyrant who made my life a misery."

"Well, I wouldn't exactly say you have been quite that bad, Mrs Davies. But you will have to understand that I shall not be able to leave Mollie with you alone in the future, not unless I am reassured of your intentions towards her."

"I understand and I promise I will tell Evan tonight of my plans to leave tomorrow."

Lily smiled, at last she had got through to the woman and could see that beneath her hard exterior there was a real human being. "Now come on, let's have a nice cup of tea. You can look after Mollie for me at the school, where I can keep a watchful eye."

* * *

Olwen Davies was as good as her word and announced to Evan that evening that she would leave the following day. He did not protest as Lily thought he might, perhaps he had picked up on the difficulties between the two women and was secretly relieved that his mother was returning home.

Lily, Mollie and Evan waved her off as she took the train back to Pentyrch, and this time, there was genuine warmth when both women embraced one another. Lily decided that she would not tell Evan about the medicine his mother had been giving Mollie, it would only hurt his feelings.

* * *

Life settled back down again and Lily took great pleasure in teaching at the school. The children were doing well too, not only with their lessons, but the frailer looking of the children were now well-nourished and glowing with health. Several had started to learn to read. They took great delight in poring over books containing colourful stories.

When the weather was nice, Lily took them on nature walks with Hannah's help, to places like Cwm Woods and along the river and canal bank. There, they spotted wild flowers and birds, drawing them on their slates when they got back to school.

Her life with her husband did not seem to improve that much, but they got on well enough, it was just that he showed no interest in her as a wife. He did, however, seem to get closer to his daughter, insisting on helping by watching her for Lily to have a break now and then. *It's just not fair,* Lily thought. *I wish he'd remember...*

* * *

Delwyn and Rose were married in early June and on the 21st of the same month, were due to sail from Liverpool to New York on the steamship, *Manhattan.* Lily, Evan and Mollie went to say goodbye to them before they left Merthyr for their journey to Liverpool.

"I shall miss my brother," Lily said, wiping away a tear as Mollie looked at her wide eyed as they set off for home.

"I know you shall, *cariad.*" It was the first time since his blow to the head that Evan had addressed her in such a manner. She stopped crying as it brought hope to her heart.

"Do you know what you called me then?" He shook his head and looked at her blankly. "Never mind, it was nothing," she muttered under her breath.

Lily said her first word two months later, "Dad". Evan was thrilled as he bounced his daughter up and down on his knee, he seemed to have accepted her as his child at long last, but there was little sign he had got his memory back.

Mrs Morgan called when Lily had put Mollie to bed for her afternoon nap and Evan had left to go on business to Merthyr.

"So how are things now, Lily?" she asked, as she took a sip from her cup of tea.

"Not so bad thank you." Lily brushed some imaginary crumbs from the table cloth.

"Come on now, this is me you are talking to. What's the matter?" There was no fooling Mrs Morgan, she had a way of sensing when something was wrong.

Lily wrung her hands in despair. "It is Evan, Mrs Morgan. I have tried for these past few months to help him to get his memory back, but it still feels as though we are polite acquaintances rather than husband and wife."

"I know, dear." She patted Lily's hand thoughtfully. "What does Doctor Owen say about it all?"

"Not a lot, just that his memory might return at any time...but on the other hand, it might not."

"My way of thinking is this…" The elderly lady hesitated as if using her words carefully.

"Go on," Lily urged.

"Well, if he was able to fall in love with you once, then he can do it again, if it is meant to be."

Lily honestly had not thought of that, but recognised that Mrs Morgan could be right.

"Mrs Morgan, do you honestly think so?"

"Yes, I do. Now what were you doing when you first met one another. What happened to make you draw close?"

"It was at the time of the pit disaster. I helped him at the chapel to pick out hymns for the memorial service, and then he asked me to help in the Sunday School. We were a team."

"Then you must try doing that again," Mrs Morgan advised.

"But what if it doesn't work?"

"Then you must keep on trying. Don't give up on him, Lily."

It was easy for Mrs Morgan to say that, but what if she had to go through the rest of her life living with someone who was never intimate with her again?

The following day, she offered her services in an attempt to get close to him once more, but he declined. If this were to carry on, she would have to move back to her family home, she could bear this no longer. She had been up to Chapel Square to clear up a couple of times after Dafydd's departure. There was still no word of him and she was beginning to think that perhaps something had happened to him.

After she had bathed Mollie and put her down to sleep for the night, she washed and was about to change into her nightgown, going across the landing to check again on her daughter, as she did so, she noticed Evan at the top of the stairs. She had forgotten to cover herself up in front of him and he gave her a long, hard stare, as if she were a scarlet woman; attired only in her corset and pantaloons. The man who had known every inch of her body was now treating her like a leper as he turned away in disgust. This was getting too much for her to bear, her shoulders wracked with grief for the husband she had lost.

She made a decision right there and then, she would ask Mr. and Mrs Morgan for their help. Tomorrow she would tell Evan she was leaving him. She and Mollie would move back into Chapel Square.

* * *

Evan had not shown much emotion when she told him, he seemed to accept that she was leaving just as he would have a guest leaving his home. The only tug of emotion that emanated from him was when he kissed Mollie goodbye. Lily had promised that he could see the infant whenever he wanted. She had closed the school down for the summer and intended to start it back up in September, so whatever happened in the future there was no real way of avoiding him.

If Mr. and Mrs Morgan were surprised that Lily was moving back to Chapel Square, they didn't show it. Mrs Morgan kindly gave Lily some provisions to help her on her way and the couple helped her to move back into the neglected family home.

"Will you both be all right, dear?" Mrs Morgan said as she and her husband were leaving later that day.

Lily nodded, fighting to hold back the tears that threatened to spill down her cheeks. "You know, there are a lot of ghosts here for me," Lily said, "but I know I have to face up to them."

Mrs Morgan put her hand on Lily's shoulder and kissed her cheek. "I understand," she said, and then giving Mollie a kiss as well, she left them alone in their new home.

Mr. Morgan had already lit the fire for them, even though it was summer, the evenings could get quite chilly. All Dafydd's belongings had been packed away in the wardrobe in what had once been the boys' bedroom.

Lily changed the bed and then, after feeding Mollie, washed her and settled her down in the bed they would both share for the night. She had thought about bringing the cot with her, but her instincts for some reason, told her to leave it where it was.

She started to clean and tidy around the place, it wasn't too bad really, it was just that she wanted to get rid of that stale, musty smell that houses had when they hadn't been lived in for some time.

Later, as she sat at the old kitchen table where they'd had many a family meal together, when her father would carve the roast and her mother would constantly reprimand the twins for their naughty behaviour, the tears flowed freely.

It just wasn't fair. She had her own family now, but for Evan it was as if she was still an acquaintance to him, practically a stranger. She wondered how he was coping tonight without her. Deep down, she had the feeling that she would hardly be missed.

Chapter Nine

It wasn't long before Lily and Mollie settled back down into her old house, in a way it was comforting seeing the same four walls again. The neighbours who knew her very well, popped in occasionally for a chat and a cup of tea, not just to see her but because they were enchanted with her beautiful daughter. That was helpful, because Lily could walk down the village for a while to buy groceries whilst Gwennie Edwards, who lived next door, kept an eye on Mollie. Gwennie, had three young children herself, who loved to play with Mollie. And it was good for the child to be in the company of other children, particularly as the school was closed for the summer.

Evan walked up from the village now and again to see his daughter and if she was passing that way, she took Mollie to see him at Chapel House, but there was still no sign that he missed Lily herself. So Lily resolved that she would just have to get on with life for now.

A few months or so after Delwyn and Rose had left for America, she received a letter from them that arrived at Chapel House and Evan passed it on to her.

Dearest Lily,

It was rather exciting on our passage over as it was the ship's maiden journey. It took just over two weeks. Our Captain, James Williams, is a fine man and it was an honour to be aboard the steamship as it took its first journey to the New World. There were many Saints aboard heading for Zion.

Rose, my poor darling, was very nauseous. We have since found out that she is with child. We are both so excited. I cannot believe that I am to be a father.

The second part of the journey to Utah, was gruelling, but worth it in the end as we arrived at our final destination, Salt Lake.

You would not believe the welcome we have received from the brethren and how my skills as a miner are valued out here.

Have you heard anything from Dafydd? I have been very troubled about our brother, I am praying for him day and night.

How is Evan keeping? And what about your beautiful daughter, Mollie? I expect she is growing more beautiful with each passing day, like her mother. Please give her a kiss from me.

Rose sends her love and we hope to hear back from you soon.
Fondest regards,
Delwyn.

Lily wiped away a tear with the back of her hand, half wishing she and Mollie could have gone with them to start a new life. What was her purpose in staying here? All her family were gone, one way or the other. She felt if it were not for her daughter, she would have no family at all.

Evan came to visit Mollie that evening and seemed very interested when she showed him the contents of the letter. "I have thought of joining them both, to start a new life…" she began, half hoping that he would tell her it was not the thing to do. If only he would take her in his arms once again as he had in the past, all her cares were comforted then in the circle of his embrace.

"Then just what is preventing you?" he asked.

She was about to say, "You. It is you, who is preventing me from leaving. I love you, Evan." But instead she just shrugged and turned back to the letter she held in her trembling hands.

Could her husband really watch the two of them leave Merthyr for a land so far away, probably never to see them again? It looked as if he could, without a fight. She couldn't have been more wounded if he had pierced her heart with an arrow.

"Come along, Mollie," he said, lifting her up in his arms. "Daddy is going to take you for a walk to see the ducks on the canal bank." The little girl had now started to pull herself up on the furniture and Lily thought it would not be long before she was walking.

She watched them both leave and then put her head in her hands and wept for what might have been. They could have been a family and should have been all together, not like this. She inwardly chastised herself for spending too much time crying lately. School would be starting up again next week and would keep her mind occupied. She had been delighted that several of her class had learned to read and there would be a couple of new pupils starting next week. Word had got around the community and now she had a waiting list from eager parents of those who wanted to join the small school.

* * *

Monday arrived and Lily was dismayed to see that young Betty had not shown up on the first day of term. She questioned the other children who seemed to know nothing about it. So she resolved to call around to the child's house after school.

Upon arrival, the house appeared dark and uninviting. She tapped the door and got no reply. The door, she noticed, was ajar. Pushing it open she called out the child's name. The overpowering stench of human waste hit her in the guts, so much so that her stomach retched and she forced herself not to vomit.

It was obvious that the family had vacated the hovel and she was just about to leave when she heard a whimper. Thinking it was a stray cat; she turned and found a child curled up in a foetal position in the corner. It wasn't until she drew close that she saw that the filthy child was Betty.

"Oh, *cariad*," she said, sweeping the child's light frame up in her arms, "what are you doing here on your own?"

The child said nothing, which wasn't unusual of course, Lily had never heard her speak, but just thought she was shy, but this was something more.

Betty hung on for dear life as Lily carried her to Mrs Morgan's shop.

"The poor mite," Mrs Morgan said. "It looks as though she hasn't eaten in days."

Mrs Morgan cut off a hunk of bread and poured a cup of milk and they both watched the child eat ravenously. She had huge, dark rings beneath her eyes. "I will clean her up and put her to bed," Mrs Morgan said kindly. "Lily, I think you should ask the neighbours what has happened to her family."

"Right you are, Mrs Morgan."

Lily went from door-to-door asking Betty's closest neighbours if they knew what had happened, but no one seemed to know anything, either that or if they did know, they weren't telling.

Breathless and exhausted with concern for the child, Lily returned to the shop, where she found Mrs Morgan sitting at the table with a cup of tea. "Any news?" she asked looking up from her cup and saucer.

"No one appears to know anything at all. It looks as if the family packed everything up and went very quickly. Why on earth would someone leave a lovely child like Betty behind?"

Elsa Morgan shrugged. "Who knows? All I can tell you is that the family were struggling for money. Perhaps they thought they were doing a kindness to the child and that someone would take her in."

"I would take her myself, but I have Mollie and the school to run. What about you Mrs Morgan?"

Mrs Morgan's mouth fell open. "Oh Lily, I would not be suitable."

"Of course you would. You told me yourself that you always wanted a child. You have plenty of living accommodation. Think about it, please."

"I don't know if I am too old to cope with a young child."

"Well, it's either that or St. Tydfil's Workhouse," Lily stated, knowing full well that really was the case. That thought sent a chill through Lily's bones, she couldn't watch the poor little child taken in there. There were some that went into workhouses as children and were so institutionalised that they never returned to normal society again.

Mrs Morgan thought all of two minutes. "You are right," she said brightly. "I am sixty five years old and I am fit as a flea. God willing that I live long enough to see the child grow up so that she can fend for herself. I shall have to speak to William, mind you."

"Of course you must," Lily said, taking Mrs Morgan's hands in her own. "You are kindness itself."

The woman beamed. Lily had the feeling that secretly she was more than happy to take on the child.

* * *

Lily watched Betty over the next few months grow fit and well. Her skin took on a rosy glow in place of her pale, milky complexion. Her hair grew long and Mrs Morgan curled it for her every night by putting it into rags. She bought her pretty dresses and pinafores and gave her good, wholesome food, something the child hadn't had for a long time by the look of it.

She seemed to take more interest in school too, even though she was still mute, she seemed to enjoy being read to and the surprising thing was that she had even learned to write.

Doctor Owen checked her over and found her to be in a healthy state. "You cleared the head lice very well, Mrs Morgan," he complimented. "It's a shame that her family saw fit to leave her, but let's just say it was probably a blessing in disguise for the child, otherwise she might have died by now."

Lily knew all too well, that the doctor's words were probably prophetic. If it had been last year, when the cholera had returned, then she surely wouldn't have been strong enough to survive it.

Lily had given up hope of her husband ever rekindling his love for her and had decided that from now on she would just concentrate on her own and her daughter's interests. Olwen Davies was arriving for a visit tomorrow. It would be the first time the woman would see her granddaughter since the drugging episode. Lily was not looking forward to it, although she bore the woman no ill will. She had half decided to move back into Chapel House as her mother-in-law had no idea that she and Evan were living apart, so it would have been for appearances' sake. But at the last moment, she decided against it. Honesty, she believed was the best policy, so she told Evan to tell his mother to visit at Chapel Square.

The following day was a Saturday and so Lily had a longer sleep and was busying herself washing and dressing when there was a knock at the door. Olwen Davies stood there with tears in her eyes, holding her arms open for Lily. She embraced her warmly and Lily invited her into her humble home, a far cry from Olwen's beautiful home in Pentrych.

"Oh Lily, I am so sorry," she apologised. "Is it all my fault that you and my son are living separate lives?"

"Please don't blame yourself," Lily said kindly. "It's no one's fault. Evan does not recognise me as his wife. I seem a stranger to him, so I have decided this is the best way."

"I don't understand..." Olwen began, "How is it he knows me as his mother then?"

"I should have explained properly to you when you last visited, he remembers nothing from about a year before the blow to his head. So of course, he knows you are his mother. He remembers growing up, but as for me, I am the stranger I always was to him." Lily looked down at the floor.

"Oh, you dear child," Olwen hugged her again. This was a complete change in the woman, was it only a few months since her mother-in-law had held her at arm's length?

Seeing her granddaughter over Lily's shoulder, her mood changed to one of exultation. "Oh my beautiful Mollie," she held out her hands to walk towards the child and Lily instinctively stepped in her way to block her path.

"Lily, you do not need have any fear from me. I have learned my lesson in more ways than one."

Lily let out the breath she had been holding and allowed her mother-in-law to pass her by and scoop little Mollie up into her arms. "Can I take her out for a stroll, please?" The woman implored, placing Lily in a difficult position of either offending her or of compromising her own values. After a moment of thought, she stood firm. "No, you cannot take her out unaccompanied, Mrs Davies."

Olwen's smile vanished, her mouth now turning down at the corners, but what did the woman expect after drugging her granddaughter?

"I would just like to take her for a few minutes up the canal bank, it's a lovely day. I will wrap her up well."

Lily straightened. "No, absolutely not."

Lily was just about to argue her case, when Olwen Davies headed for the door with the child in her arms, who wore just her nightdress. It was a moment before Lily reacted. The woman had not learned her lesson at all and was a danger to her child.

"Give my daughter back to me!" she cried out.

Her mother-in-law did not answer, but carried on walking. Lily ran after her, in bare feet into the street outside.

Lily's heart beat quickened as she tried to catch up with them.

There was no one to help her as the woman in front of her strode off with her grandchild. As they turned the corner at Quay Row a large figure blocked their path.

"What is going on here then?"

Lily wept with relief when she saw it was Dafydd. Breathless, she shouted, "Please follow that woman, she's taken my daughter!"

Dafydd might have not recognised Evan's mother as the only time he had made her acquaintance was the very time he was inebriated, when Delwyn brought him to Chapel House during Lily's confinement.

"No sooner said than done," he said, sprinting after the woman and child, blocking her way.

Lily managed to catch up with them eventually, not even caring that the stony ground hurt her bare feet.

"Hand that child back to her mother!" Dafydd ordered.

"She's my grandchild. I only want to see her. I have not been allowed to see her for months," Mrs Davies said, as if Lily was the worst mother in the world.

"Well, there are ways about doing it, see," Dafydd's large frame towered over the woman.

The woman visibly relaxed and handed Mollie back to her mother. "Now, you had better go off and visit your son instead. I am taking my sister and my niece back home."

"Dafydd?" Mrs Davies asked. He nodded. She obviously hadn't recognised him either. "But I thought you were missing?"

"I am back now, for good. So I'll bid you good day."

Olwen Davies shook her head and muttered something under her breath, turning back in the direction of the village, not even bothering to apologise. Fortunately, Mollie hadn't got upset in the process. That would have been too much for Lily to bear.

"Oh Dafydd," Lily cried, wrapping her free arm around her brother. "It's so good to have you back, but where have you been?"

"I'll tell you all about it shortly. But can I please have a hot bath and some food first?"

Lily nodded gratefully, the tears streaming down her face. He put out his finger and Mollie grabbed it in her hand, letting out a little giggle of amusement.

* * *

Dafydd looked much better now he had cleaned himself up and sat down at the table to some bacon and fried eggs. She noticed he had filled out a lot these past months and seemed to have matured.

"So, where did you get to?" she asked, as she poured out his tea.

"Well, that's a long story, but I am sure you won't rest until I've explained my absence."

"You gave us all a shock, I can tell you."

"I am sorry about that, Lily *bach*, but I went off the rails. The drink had me all but consumed, up in China. I moved into a doss house up there and weeks later when I had sobered up, I decided to get back to earning some money. I knew that I had blown any chance

I had with my old job on the barges, so I earned money another way." He dunked a crust of bread into the runny yellow of his egg.

Lily watched in expectation. "Well, go on then—" she said impatiently.

He took a ravenous bite, then swallowed his food and took a deep breath. "Street fighting."

Lily almost choked on her cup of tea.

"You? A street fighter, Dafydd Jenkin?"

"Yes, I made quite a lot of money at it as well, visiting neighbouring towns. I am proud to say that I have never been beaten as yet. People came from miles around to see me."

"Oh Dafydd, that's not how our parents brought you up. You and Delwyn are so different. And in case you're wondering why Lily and I are here…we have both moved in."

"Oh?" There was a long silent pause.

"Evan had an accident in China. A blow to the head and lost his memory. He can't even remember marrying me. It has been so hurtful, Dafydd."

He stood and embraced her. "I am so sorry Lily. I should have been here. What was a fine upstanding man like him doing somewhere like that in the first place?"

"Looking for you I think..." Her face flushed with embarrassment, but her brother had to be told the truth.

"I feel awful now…if I hadn't gone there, you and Evan would still be together as man and wife." He lowered his head in shame.

"Don't worry about it now. All that matters is that you're back safe and well. I've been lost without you and Delwyn…"

He raised his brows. "So how is my dear brother?" he asked amicably.

"You wouldn't have known, would you? He has left the country."

Dafydd frowned. "You mean he's living in England?"

Lily shook her head. "No. America."

Dafydd's mouth fell open. "America. I can't believe it, what took him there?"

"He was baptised into the Mormon faith and now has gone to the Great Salt Lake Valley in Utah, with his new wife, Rose."

Dafydd sat back down. "This is all too much for me to take in." Suddenly he looked sad and seemed to have lost his appetite as he pushed his half-eaten meal across the table. "I am so sorry that I missed so much this past year. I mean I knew that Delwyn had taken to the religion, but I didn't think he would have gone so far, nor that he would be married by now."

"Rose is expecting a baby."

"I am ashamed of my selfishness, Lily. I even missed the birth of my niece..."

"Don't be so hard on yourself." She hugged her brother to her bosom, allowing him to cry tears of regret for what might have been.

When he had finished, he looked exhausted, so she sent him upstairs to lie down while she got on with attending to her daughter and the washing up. Later, when he awoke, she sat at the side of the bed and asked, "What I don't understand is why you never contacted us, Dafydd? I know in the beginning perhaps you were steeped in alcohol, but afterwards when you were earning money as a street fighter, surely you must have kept off the drink then to keep yourself fit and well?"

Dafydd shook his head. "I am afraid it was a question of pride, knowing that I had failed everyone. The longer I stayed away, the harder it was to come back home." She nodded as if she understood.

"Well, you're back now and I hope it is for good."

"Yes. Don't worry. I will not let you down again." He rubbed his eyes.

"I hope not. Now then, you didn't eat much of your food, I have cooked some cawl, come and have some with me after you have washed your face."

"Yes, Mam," he laughed, bringing a tear to her eye. It was good to have her brother back again.

* * *

The following day, she and Dafydd took Mollie into Merthyr to visit the market, where they bought some pretty material to make some new dresses for her. "She has grown so quickly these past few months, Dafydd. I cannot believe it." Lily bent over the stall. "Look at this material here, it is ever so cheap, I could make some clothing for the poorest children in the school."

Dafydd raised his eyebrows. "What school are you talking about?"

"I haven't told you have I?" He shook his head. "I have set up a small school for the village children. It has been going really well."

Taking her breath away, he hugged her tightly. "I am so proud of you, Lily Jenkin." He coloured up. "Sorry, I mean Lily Davies."

"Don't worry about it. I feel more of a Jenkin these days the way my husband treats me."

"I am so sorry to hear that. Do you want me to have a word with him, Lily?"

"Heavens above, no," she retorted angrily. "This is my problem and mine alone."

Dafydd kept quiet for the rest of the shopping trip, just answering when he was spoken to and taking Mollie from time-to-time to look at the various toy shops and sweet shops in the town.

"It is I who should be sorry," Lily said finally when he had returned, "I should not have lost my temper with you like that. It's just that it has been so hard for me."

"I understand," he said, patting her hand.

"Dafydd, I have been thinking of something for some time now and wonder if you would be interested?"

"Please ask me."

"I am thinking of joining Delwyn and Rose in Salt Lake. Would you like to come with us?"

Dafydd shook his head vigorously. "I cannot leave Merthyr," he said sadly.

"Well what is to keep us here? Mam and Dad have gone. There are plenty of opportunities out there, particularly for miners. And I could teach out there as well. I know Delwyn would love it if we joined him and Rose."

He scratched his chin thoughtfully. "Well, even if I did agree to coming with you, what about Evan? He is your husband after all."

"In name only. I don't think he would miss me if I left."

"He might miss his daughter though." Of course Lily had considered that and did not want to prevent her husband from keeping contact with Mollie, but his visits to the child had been far and few between.

"Dafydd, I think Evan would hardly notice it at all if we left. It's a rare occasion when he calls here to see his daughter," Lily said sadly.

"That may be so, but I think you should consider this carefully."

"Think of the life we would have out there," Lily enthused. "Delwyn says Salt Lake is so beautiful and clean, not at all like dirty, old grey Merthyr Tydfil."

"Lily, Merthyr is not all that bad. We still have green fields and mountains. I think you only feel this way because your marriage is not as you expected it to be."

"I have clung on for far too long. I have given Evan every opportunity to be a husband to me. Don't you think it hurts me when my own husband will not even hold my hand or kiss me on the cheek?"

Dafydd stroked her face. "Of course, Lily love, but it sounds as if he is not a well man, you cannot abandon him right now. Have a little faith that he will get well in good time."

"I've waited long enough," she said, taking Mollie from Dafydd's strong arms. "I intend to make a decision soon." At the back of her mind was the thought that if Evan knew she was going for good that he would come to his senses and beg her to stay.

Chapter Ten

Lily decided to wait until after Christmas before she would break the news to her husband about her plan to emigrate. Meanwhile, she had to raise the money for her passage to America. Her Landlord Uncle in Cefn Coed offered to pay the sum, and while, perhaps, she should have accepted the money, pride got in the way.

The answer came in another letter from Delwyn who told her when he'd heard of her predicament that he could pay for her fare if she could pay it back when she settled in Utah. He could also arrange to find a teaching job for her in the area.

Lily had mixed up emotions from feeling the joy of getting everything sorted to experiencing the sadness of leaving what had once been, a happy marriage, behind.

Evan hadn't said much about her departure, just that he was happy for her and if it was better for her to start a new life out there instead of living in near poverty in Merthyr Tydfil, then he was pleased. He seemed to assume it was for a better life. Of course, he would miss Mollie, but he felt it in the child's best interests if she remained with her mother. He had said it all, except the words she had longed to hear: *I Love You.*

Taking a new step of resolution to put the past behind them, she handed the reins of the school over to Hannah Griffiths and Mrs Morgan, who hopefully would keep it going until a new teacher could be found.

Dafydd had decided to stay behind for now and said he was going to get a job to save up to join them as soon as he was able. At the back of Lily's mind, she wondered if that would ever transpire, but at least he would be a link to Merthyr for her and could keep her informed of how Evan was doing.

There were many in the village that gossiped about her for leaving 'that poor husband' behind. Lily guessed that Maggie Shanklin had been the one to whip up that gossip and silently cursed the woman.

Winter turned to spring. Mrs Morgan, together with Betty, were both there for Lily and Mollie's departure. Mrs Morgan, weeping into the fringes of her shawl. Betty had grown a couple of inches and filled out as well.

"I shall miss you, *cariad*." Mrs Morgan hugged Lily and Mollie.

"And I'll miss you too, Mrs Morgan. I shall write as often as I can."

"You see you do, Lily Jenkin." She said between sobs. Lily noticed the woman had used her maiden name and realised she wasn't best pleased the way Evan had chosen apathy as opposed to action at his wife's desire to emigrate to the New World.

As Lily and Mollie were about to get on to the trap with Mr. Morgan, who was taking them to catch the train to Cardiff, Lily turned and kissed Betty on top of the head.

The small child beamed. "Goodbye, Betty," Lily waved.

"Goodbye," the little girl replied.

Lily's heart somersaulted with pleasure. "Betty...So you can talk," Lily said through tears of joy, handing Mollie over to Mrs Morgan, she swept the child into her arms. "I am so pleased. This is all down to you, Mrs Morgan. Your love and devotion has healed her."

Mrs Morgan, for once, was speechless. Then after a few moments of swallowing and fighting back the tears, she said, "I really haven't done that much at all and if I have done anything, then it's with your help teaching Betty and taking care of her at the school."

Blinking back the tears, Lily placed Betty back down on the ground, and patting the child's head said, "Now you be a good girl for Mrs Morgan, won't you, *cariad*?"

Betty nodded, but said no more. Whatever happened, the child would talk again in her own good time. Lily was so pleased, excited not only at the prospect of the child talking again, but at the thought of starting a new life. In her mind there was only one cloud that was tearing her apart, but she knew she needed to leave.

The sound of hobnail boots caught her attention and she turned to see Dafydd, puffing as if out of breath.

"I thought I'd missed you, Lily," he apologised. "I would have been here earlier but I've got a new job." He took a couple of breaths, and then relaxed, as if all was well he'd managed to get to his sister before she left Abercanaid.

Lily blinked in amazement. "I am so pleased for you," she enthused. At least her brother would have something to occupy himself and to save up enough money to join them in the future. "What job is it?"

"I'm going back underground," he said firmly as though he expected some opposition from his sister.

Lily smiled warmly. "Don't worry, Dafydd. I quite understand that coal mining is in your blood and your skills will come in useful when you leave Merthyr."

He nodded as Lily kissed him softly on the cheek.

Hugging Mrs Morgan once more, she retrieved Mollie from her friend's arms. Mr. Morgan helped Lily and her child on to the trap. It would be a long journey to Liverpool and an even longer one to New York.

"Take care of Mollie, won't you!" Dafydd shouted after them as they left for the first part of their journey.

Whatever happened in the future, her daughter would be her main concern now and as they left the village, Lily gazed back one last time and hugging her daughter tightly to her breast said, "It is time to go, my little one..."

PART TWO

Chapter Eleven

Evan laid down his quill and rested his head in his hands. He was in the midst of composing his Sunday Sermon. What was wrong with him? It had been three months since Lily had taken their baby daughter to America and in all that time he hadn't received one word from her to inform him how Mollie was or even if they had arrived safely.

He'd managed to keep himself busy attending to the needs and wants of the local community and he'd secretly marvelled at the way the school was being run by Mrs Morgan and young Hannah Griffiths until a new teacher could be found. To think that Lily, his wife, had done all this made him proud to the core. But why had he never told her so? And why was it only now that his heart yearned to see her and his daughter, Mollie? Yet, at the time of their departure, he'd felt so confused he'd truly believed it was the right thing to do to let them cross an ocean to another continent. Now, he realised that it couldn't have been easy for her at all, for her to have her very own husband treat her as a stranger and then to uproot herself, moving away into the unknown. It took a brave woman to do something as bold as that. A lone tear found its way down his cheek and landed on the parchment in front of him, causing an inky stain. He blotted the paper and took a deep breath—well he could have stopped them from going and he did nothing at all. Now he was paying the price for his stupidity and apathy.

A tap at the back door brought him back to reality. He rose to answer. Standing on the garden path with a look of urgency on her face, was Mrs Morgan.

"I've brought the key to the chapel room, Mr. Davies," she said breathlessly, avoiding his eyes. "Hannah has tidied up and all the children have gone home. Now I have to get myself off home."

"Thank you, Mrs Morgan," he replied, taking the key from her outstretched hand. She was about to turn to leave. "Mrs Morgan?"

"Yes?"

"Have you heard anything from Lily as yet?"

For the first time, she looked him in the eye. What he saw there was a guarded look that he didn't much care for.

"I received a letter from her a couple of weeks back, I didn't tell you in case you didn't want to know," she said stiffly.

Was that what she really thought? That he had so little regard for his wife and child that he wanted no news at all of their welfare? It made him feel thoroughly ashamed that this was the impression he'd created.

"I would be most interested of course," he said, opening the door wide to invite her inside.

Tentatively, she walked into the kitchen and he beckoned her to sit at the table.

"Lily said it was a hard journey getting there," Mrs Morgan said seating herself, "and she found it hard crossing the ocean. She was very sea sick. Mollie, though, was fine and adapted to the situation very well. When they arrived at Great Salt Lake, Delwyn and Rose were there to greet them and for time being, they've given her a room in their home. Delwyn and some of the Mormon Brethren built the house themselves you know."

Evan nodded thoughtfully. "And is she happy? Are they settled there, Mrs Morgan?"

Mrs Morgan shrugged her shoulders. "I could not make that out from her letter. She has started teaching at the local school whilst Rose takes care of Mollie for her. She didn't say much more than that, other than to ask about everyone back home."

Evan leaned forward across the table in expectation. "And did she ask about me?"

Mrs Morgan shook her head. "What can you expect, Mr. Davies? You gave her the impression that you just didn't care. You didn't even show up to say goodbye to your wife and your own baby daughter the day they left Abercanaid for good." There was more than a note of accusation in her tone of voice.

A deep pain crushed Evan from within the core of his very being. At the time it hadn't seemed to matter, he thought he had no feelings for Lily at all. But now he wasn't so sure. Being without her just didn't feel right somehow. His days were empty. Yet, his memory still hadn't returned.

Mrs Morgan heaved herself up from the table. "Well, I'm just going to make Betty her tea and then relieve William in the shop. I'll bid you a good evening, Mr. Davies," she said curtly, as she left.

Why, if he thought he had no feelings for Lily, did it hurt him so much when he realised that she hadn't even asked after him? And why did he yearn for some contact from her? Mollie would probably be walking properly by now. He was missing her so very much.

***

The following morning, he called at Chapel Square to have a word with Lily's brother. Perhaps he would know best how to advise him.

Dafydd opened the door, unshaven, with deep, dark rings beneath his eyes. For a moment, Evan wondered if he had been at the drink again.

"Well now there's an honour!" Dafydd exclaimed with a hint of sarcasm in his voice. "The local minister finds time to visit one of his own. So what's the reason for your visit, Mr. Davies? It can't be to see my sister and your child, because they left here three months ago. But you already knew that, didn't you?"

Stepping forward, Evan said, "Yes, there is no excuse. All I can say is Dafydd, I miss them both."

Dafydd furrowed his brow. "Then why did you let them go?"

Evan heard the catch in his voice and knew the man was not far away from tears. He smelled no alcohol on his breath, which was a relief.

"I have no excuse, as I just said. All I can tell you is that my memory has not returned since I received that blow to my head up in China at the beginning of the year."

"So you are trying to blame me for that are you, Evan Davies? After all, if you had not had to go looking for me, then you would not have lost your memory, would you?"

Evan shook his head. "No, not at all. On the contrary in fact. I need your help, Dafydd."

Pausing for a moment, Dafydd opened the door fully. "Then you had better come in. I don't want my sister's private business discussed on the doorstep."

Evan followed the well-built, young man, into the house, pleasantly surprised to find it was clean and tidy. As if sensing the minister's thoughts, Dafydd said, "I've employed a housekeeper to come in here a couple of times a week. And don't fret, I'm not drinking any longer. The reason I'm looking so rough is I've just finished a night shift."

"I am sorry. I'm keeping you from your bed. I shall leave." Evan turned to go.

"No, you will not. Sit down and we shall talk."

Evan removed his cap and sat at the table and Dafydd followed suit. "I want to get my memory back," he stated flatly.

Dafydd frowned. "But what can I do to help you?"

He took a sharp breath and let it out again. "I want you to come to China with me. I wish to retrace my steps."

Dafydd shook his head vigorously. "I don't know..."

"I know it sounds a silly thing to do, but Dr Owen has told me that if I try to jolt my memory it might well return, although there are no guarantees of course."

Dafydd narrowed his eyes. "But why ask me to come with you?"

"Because you know how to handle yourself, Dafydd. You stayed there long enough and you have a reputation as a street fighter, no one would dare touch you."

Dafydd looked thoughtful for a moment. "I suppose you're right. But why do you want to do this so much?"

"Because I want things to go back to how they were with Lily. I know now, and don't ask me how, that she was once very important in my life and that I did love her. Dearly."

Dafydd's eyes grew wide as he stared at him intently. Evan feared for a moment that he would put him on his way, but instead, he nodded eagerly and extended his hand for a shake.

"Lily will be so pleased about this, Evan!" he announced.

"No, please do not write to tell her of this yet. I want to be the man I once was before I try any sort of reconciliation. Perhaps my memory will not return at all."

"Well, I suppose it's well worth a try!" Dafydd exclaimed eagerly. "When do you want me to come with you?"

"I would have suggested right now, but I know you're tired. When do you have a day off?"

"Not until the weekend I'm afraid. How about Saturday morning? I know you can't go on a Sunday, Evan."

Evan nodded gratefully. "Saturday it is then."

Both men shook hands once more and Evan sighed deeply as Dafydd closed the door behind him. He had no idea what it would be like returning to China, and indeed, he had no memory of going there in the first place, but if it was what he needed to do, then he would do it.

***

Evan was up and dressed by seven o'clock on Saturday morning. It was only now beginning to get light. He forced himself to eat a bowl of porridge and drink a cup of tea, but in reality food tasted bland now Lily was not here to cook for him.

A chill wind blew as he made his way to Chapel Square to find Dafydd already on the doorstep waiting for him, blowing on his hands and lightly stamping his feet to keep warm.

"I feared you might have forgotten," Evan said, good-naturedly.

"Not a chance. I have been thinking of nothing else these past few days. Come along. It will take us a good half hour or so to get there. We need to keep moving to keep the cold out."

Dafydd pulled the door shut and both men made their way along the canal bank in the direction of Merthyr town. They walked in companionable silence only broken by Evan's doubts about the destination and what they would both find when they got there. He felt reassured by Dafydd's bulky shape these days. It was good to see he had put on a bit of muscle since his pit accident, the shape and size suited him. Unfortunately, Evan had no memory of the pit accident in the first place, even though he'd been told he played a particularly prominent part during that time. He'd had to make do with information given to him by Mr. and Mrs Morgan, who'd filled in the gaps in his memory for him.

Mrs Morgan had made no secret of his past loving relationship with Lily and he often observed the wistful look in the woman's eyes when she spoke of her sadness at seeing the couple divided.

Well if his relationship with his wife was so good then he was going to do all in his power to resurrect it somehow.

Upon approaching Merthyr, decent housing gave way to broken down filthy cellars and sewer filled streets. China, the place he had been dreading so much. The stench was hard to bear. It was all Evan could do to stop his breakfast from ending up all over the floor. He shuddered violently.

"Are you all right?" Dafydd's eyes were full of concern as he stopped walking to check on Evan.

“I don’t know what it is. I can just sense something bad about this place.”

“If you want, we can always go home”

“No, no.” Evan protested. “I have to go through this. We need to ask anyone we come across if anyone can remember me here the day I was attacked.”

Dafydd nodded thoughtfully. “We might have to dip into our pockets though. Money talks as they say.”

Evan nodded grimly. “Yes, I am well aware of that, Dafydd. I have come fully prepared for it.”

Dafydd lowered his voice. “Just take care mind you because the folk around here will rob you blind good as look at you.”

Evan clenched his fists. “Don’t you think that I don’t realise that!” he shouted.

Dafydd lowered his gaze. “Sorry I was forgetting, someone bumped you over the head, didn’t they? And robbed you as well.”

Evan frowned. Perhaps it was a bad idea coming back here, but he had to try, didn’t he?

***

Lily stared out of the window in awe. She hadn’t been in Salt Lake for very long, but every morning was like a new gift to her. The scenery here was truly breathtaking. She slipped on her dressing gown and house slippers and tiptoed over to the wooden cot Delwyn had made for Mollie when they first arrived. Her beautiful child still slept like an angel. That was good, now she would have a chance to eat her breakfast without being disturbed. She would then have almost an hour to wake, wash and dress Mollie before leaving for work.

She so enjoyed teaching at the school, and knowing that her daughter was safe in the care of her sister-in-law, Rose, was a blessing. Lily did not experience the feeling of dread she got every time she’d left Mollie with her mother-in-law when she had started her own school back home.

Rose was great to be around. Although a little younger than herself, she was very mature and looking forward to having her own baby in the spring. By then, Lily considered it would be best if she could employ someone else to take care of Mollie, even though Rose had offered to look after the child, even after her own baby had arrived. No, it would be too much work for one that much was apparent to her.

Putting on the oatmeal to boil to make porridge, she hummed softly to herself.

"Enough there for me as well, Lily?" Delwyn asked, kissing her softly on the cheek.

"More than enough. I'm making some for Rose too."

Delwyn frowned for a moment. "I don't know if she will be up to eating it though. She has started to feel nauseous in the mornings now with the little one on the way."

Lily knew all too well what that had felt like, but she had been fortunate that her morning sickness had not lasted that long and she had found that if she ate her breakfast immediately upon rising, it soon passed off. Some women, she knew though, found it very hard. Poor Rose appeared to be one of those.

She patted her brother on the shoulder. "Take her a small bowl before she even sets a foot out of her bed. It may help to ward off the nausea. The poor dab."

Delwyn nodded and sat at the kitchen table to wait for Lily to finish making the breakfast. "And how are you feeling?" he asked, causing her to put down the wooden spoon for a moment and stop stirring the oatmeal.

"Oh me, I'm fine."

"Don't tell your fibs, Lily!" he scolded. "I know you and you have something on your mind, don't you?"

There was no fooling her brother. He was sharp as a tack. "I'm just a little home sick that's all."

Delwyn startled Lily as he raised his voice an octave. "And pray tell me exactly what you are homesick for then? A man who has deserted both you and your child?"

Pain seared into her heart at the mention of her husband even though Delwyn had not mentioned his name. The abandonment and rejection were all too much for her. Her shoulders wracked with grief as she broke down in tears.

Delwyn jumped out of his seat and removed the pan from the heat. Taking his sister into his arms he said, "I am so sorry, Lily. I should not have said anything. But there is nothing in Merthyr for you now. You have to remember your life is here with us and Mollie."

"What about our brother though?" She managed to say between sobs.

"Dafydd will be fine. In any case as soon as he has saved up enough money he will join us, I am sure of that."

Lily relaxed for a moment. "But…"

Delwyn lifted her chin with his thumb and forefinger and looked into her tear-rimmed eyes.

"I know, you miss Evan, even though he treated you badly. It is only natural, *cariad*. But you need to forget all about him now. You have a good job out here and the lifestyle is so much healthier being away from that dirty, old grey town."

Lily took a deep breath to hold back the sobs. "I know you are right, Delwyn, and in time I might just do that. But for now, I still have my grief to contend with, but I know in time it will get easier and I have been thinking…"

"What?"

"That it is just as well it happened now. Mollie will have no memory of the father who deserted her or her horrible grandmother either. So it is all for the best." Although she spoke the words, inside she hoped that one day she and Mollie would be reunited with Evan again.

***

Evan looked around in despair. Never in all of his days had he seen a place so desolate, so dirty or so lacking in hope as the place the locals dubbed as 'China'. Surely, if he had visited the hovel before, he would have remembered?

A gang of young boys pushed past him, almost knocking his feet from under him. He wondered where their manners were. Not one of the filthy youngsters said 'Sorry' to him. Their clothing hung like dirty rags on their pitiful thin bodies, their feet bare. What kind of a life was it for the people who lived here?

"Are you remembering anything yet, Evan?" Dafydd looked at him hopefully.

Evan frowned. "No. Nothing at all. I am so sure I would not have forgotten a hell hole like this one."

"I'll take you to a couple of the taverns and we'll speak to some folk. That might prompt your memory."

Evan shook his head sadly. "Whatever you think is best."

The pair spent the best part of the day walking from pub-to-pub, door-to-door, asking if anyone remembered seeing Evan visiting the area last January.

Most people were very wary of the two callers. "Why are they so resistant to our questions, Dafydd?" Evan held up his hands in despair.

"Because a lot of them are vagabonds and thieves. They probably doubt our motives. They might think we are something to do with the law."

"Oh. I had no idea."

"You have lived a different lifestyle to these people. A very sheltered one, if I might say so. Some of these folk know no better than to take to opium and alcohol. For them, this is the world they were born into and this is the world where they shall die. They know no other." It was a sorry state indeed.

"Do you wish to return home?" Dafydd placed his hand on Evan's shoulder.

Evan was about to say, yes, when his attention was drawn to a young woman wearing red, garish clothing. In other circumstances, she might have been considered quite pretty, beautiful even. But her raven-black, long hair, hung in rats' tails and her cheeks were heavily rouged.

A lady of the night. But there is something vaguely familiar about her.

"What's the matter?" Dafydd also stared in the woman's direction.

"That young lady there. I feel I have met her before."

Dafydd chuckled. "I very much doubt it, Evan. She's a common whore. You would not want to be seen dead with someone of her sort."

Perhaps Dafydd was right, but instinct told him he had encountered her before. Was she the person who had robbed him?

Before he had the chance to approach her, a large man stepped out of the shadows with a small fierce looking dog at his side.

"What are you doing here?" He took the woman roughly by the elbow and quickly escorted her down an alley way.

The young woman tried to wriggle free from his grasp, but the man, who looked better dressed than others in these parts, brought his cane down brutally on the woman's shoulders.

"Hey! Stop that at once!" Dafydd rushed over to the pair. The woman's eyes were wide with fear.

"Mind your own business!" The man growled, raising his cane again. Dafydd grabbed hold of it and grappled with the large figure.

"Be careful," Evan advised. He had never been in a fight in all his life and didn't intend to get into one now. Luckily there was no need. It became evident as the man backed away that he knew he was no match for Dafydd.

"Be off with you!" Dafydd shouted after him as the man skulked away, his dog at his heels.

Turning, Dafydd addressed the young woman who gasped for breath as she held onto a wall. "Are you all right?"

She nodded. Then when she had found her breath, she said, "It was foolish of you to do that."

Dafydd frowned. "Why do you say that?"

"Because now he will come after me again and I will get an even worse beating."

His voice softened. "Sorry. I was only trying to help."

The woman tossed back her hair in defiance. "If I was both of you, I would go home. This is not the place for either of you."

"Who is he, that man?" Evan asked.

"Believe me, you just don't want to know." She shook her head vigorously.

"But I do," Evan persisted. He felt he needed to know the identity of the brute.

She glanced around quickly in case anyone was watching, then whispered, "They call him 'Sioni' in these parts. He's responsible for girls like myself."

"You mean he makes money off you?" Evan probed.

The woman nodded. "He wanted my earnings for last night. But I didn't take very much, see. It's always the same. He takes most of it. On a good night, I hide some away, but someone told him. My secret stash will cost me dearly now." The woman trembled.

A silver gleam around the girl's throat caught Evan's eye. "That's a nice locket you have around your neck," Evan said.

The girl just blushed and put her head down. There was something about that locket that reminded him of his wife and he just couldn't put his finger on it.

"Before we go," Dafydd said, "Do you recognise Mr. Davies?"

She shook her head.

Evan remembering what Dafydd had advised about money talking, extracted a silver shilling from his pocket and placed it in the girl's outstretched, grimy hand. Her fingernails, caked with filth.

Immediately, she brightened and straightening her stance, said, "Well, now as you come to mention it. You do look kind of familiar, like. Were you here asking questions some time ago?"

"I believe I was. At least that's what I was told by the police." The girl shrank back into the shadows at the mere mention of the law. "Have no fear. You are not in any trouble. I was just looking for someone that's all."

She narrowed her gaze.

"It's right what Mr. Davies is telling you," Dafydd explained. "You see, I went missing. I had some problems and took to drinking. Someone from our village is supposed to have spotted me here, so Mr. Davies who's married to my sister, kindly came to look for me. Unfortunately, the police believe he was attacked here that night and has since lost his memory of that time."

"I see," said the girl. "I just wish that I could help you both, but I can't." She started to back away from the duo. "Look, I shouldn't be seen speaking to you, especially after what happened."

Dafydd grabbed hold of her wrist forcefully. "Look, my brother-in-law has just paid you a shilling for your time, which is probably more than you make lying on your back."

The girl's eyes widened.

"Leave her go, Dafydd," Evan advised. "We can't keep her against her will."

The girl looked at Evan and said, "It was him that did it mister."

"Who?" Evan drew closer to the girl.

"The man *he* warned off..." she pointed to Dafydd. "He was the one who hit you about the head with his cane and robbed you."

Evan's stomach threatened to spew its contents up on the ground beneath his feet. There was something in what the girl said that was triggering something off in the recesses of his mind. He took a deep, calming breath to ward off the nausea. No, he didn't remember that brute's face, but now he remembered something coming down heavily on the back of his head again and again, until he dropped to his knees and tumbled onto the ground into oblivion, until he was found by a passerby and taken to the police station.

"Evan, are you all right?" Dafydd stood in front of him.

"Yes. I think something is coming back to me. I don't remember that man, but I do remember that beating now. There is something else…"

Evan was about to tell him when they both turned and saw the girl running away, her footsteps echoing down the alley.

"I'll go after her!" Dafydd made to go, but Evan restrained him.

"No, leave her be, please. She will get into enough trouble because of us. Let's get out of this hell hole and I'll tell you what I remembered on our walk home."

Chapter Twelve

Lily and Rose were in the garden pegging out the washing in the sunshine. Lily took a step back as she admired their morning's handiwork, flapping in the breeze. She ran her hand through her hair and let out a breath as she gazed across the mountainous region of Great Salt Lake. Here, the mountains didn't enclose you in like back home. There, they were like dark beacons, tyrannical links enclosing a chain of despair. Here the mountains were lower, the valley wider. There was space, acres and acres of it. Expansive land and azure blue skies, which contrasted sharply with the slate-grey silhouettes of the Welsh valleys.

"What are you thinking?" Rose asked, as she hoisted the wooden prop to raise the washing up from the ground and into the air.

Lily folded her arms across her chest and smiled. "I was just thinking how this is God's country here..."Lily folded her arms across her chest and smiled. "I was just thinking how this is God's country here..."

"Yes, it is, Lily." Rose hooked a strand of hair that had worked loose, behind her ear, then letting out a breath said, "Delwyn was only saying last night that he wondered if you would like to take lessons in the faith?"

Lily's jaw slackened. "Me? Become a Mormon?"

Rose patted Lily's shoulder. "Yes. Why not? You've come a long way to settle with us all here. It's a sign."

Lily shook her head. "Rose, I'm a Welsh Baptist through and through. It hasn't even entered my head to enter the faith and join the Brethren. I came here to be close to you and Delwyn, my family."

Rose straightened, her chin jutting out. "But if that were the case Lily, you could just as easily have remained where you were to be close to your Merthyr family. Stayed with Evan and Dafydd."

That much was true. If she thought about it long enough, why had she chosen the pathway to Zion? And not stayed put or gone elsewhere like other emigrants to Patagonia?

"Maybe you're right, Rose. I would consider being instructed in the faith as long as it is not forced upon me. There are certain aspects I am not comfortable with like those Mormon men who take more than one wife. It is not a biblical teaching to have more than one spouse..."

"I understand that, Lily. It is not something I like myself and Delwyn is dead set against that. Most Mormon folk do not care for that particular practice."

Lily frowned. "There is one man I know who came from Merthyr and he left his wife behind. All because she would not follow him here. She converted to the faith, but would not leave the land she loves so much behind. Now there is talk that he has taken a new, much younger wife out here. She's a widowed woman and she is now pregnant with his child."

Rose stood, pursing her lips for a moment. "I know of whom you speak and he is a good man. I have sympathy for his plight. I think that is a different case of a man who just takes more than one wife to sow his seed whenever possible, Lily, to one who feels abandoned by his spouse. You of all people should understand that."

Lily's nodded. "Yes, of course I do. I need to find out more about the faith. I...I want to know more."

Rose's face lit up. "Oh Lily, your brother has been praying for this moment, I can't wait to tell him." She hugged Lily warmly.

Well for now she would find out more about it, but if she had reservations then she would not join. It was one thing to teach in the school but another to join the Church itself.

Lily drew a breath. "Yes, well, we'll see..."

"The Saints have finished building the Tabernacle Church..." Rose was glowing with pride. Her own family from Merthyr had helped with its construction and Lily knew how proud Rose was of their involvement with it.

"Yes." Lily wiped her hands on her pinafore. "It's a mighty fine building."

"And to think that not just the construction is a fine thing, but that some involved in setting it up originated from our home town. It gladdens my heart."

Lily had to admit she felt cheered at the thought. Delwyn had matured a lot since being baptised in the faith. Her mind reflected on his twin brother back home. She was so glad he had given up the street fighting, even if he had gone back down the pit. Each night she prayed he saved enough money to join them in the New World and every day she prayed that Evan would remember the love they once shared as man and wife.

***

"What is it you remember, Evan?" Dafydd asked, falling into step with his brother-in-law as they walked back to Abercanaid.

Evan stopped on the canal bank and glanced across at Dafydd. "It was that silver locket around that woman's neck."

"Yes, what of it?"

"It was the one I gave Lily as a gift one New Year after I had asked her to marry me."

Dafydd frowned. "Are you sure? I remember that locket, but to me they all look the same."

Evan nodded. "Yes, I am certain it is the same one. It was the only one like it in the shop, it has a very intricate design that was why I chose it for Lily. It set me back a pretty penny I can tell you."

Dafydd's face darkened. "Then we must get it back from that floosie..." Dafydd turned around as if expecting Evan to follow him back to China.

"No, don't you see you are missing the point here, Dafydd? In any case we might get the girl into trouble, she could be beaten to death by that brute. I would rather let things lie. What I am saying to you though, is that I remember buying it for Lily and presenting it to her. So my memory is beginning to return."

Dafydd patted Evan on the back. "I didn't think of that. So, you now remember everything about my sister?"

Evan shook his head. "Sadly no. That was all I do remember, but it's a start, isn't it?"

"Yes," Dafydd replied, enthusiastically. "So our trip to China has not been wasted."

Evan smiled. "No, not at all." He blew on his hands. It was freezing cold and he couldn't wait to return to Chapel House and sit by the fire. He had all the time in the world to think about Lily and what she meant to him.

***

Lily sat in an armchair by the fire. She was making a patchwork quilt for the bed. It had taken months so far, but she knew it would be worth it in the end. It helped to pass away the long hours when Mollie was fast asleep and Rose and Delwyn were in the sitting room spending precious time together. She didn't like to get in their way. They were newly-weds and she knew how it felt to be imposed on. That time Evan's mother had stayed at her own home had been difficult, so she well understood the need to give the couple space. Rose and Delwyn kept trying to encourage her to join them, but she made it a priority to allow them a couple of hours in the evening together.

Delwyn was using his mining skills in the community. She wasn't entirely happy about that but he swore it was only to help pass his skills on to the new Brethren and then he intended preaching full time in the Church.

She had begun taking instruction in the faith herself and was surprised at how well she was taking to learning about the prophet Joseph Smith and his findings recorded in the Book of Mormon.

Back in Merthyr, a lot of Welsh Baptists had thought the preaching and teaching as being the Devil's handiwork, and had spoken out against it in the chapels and at various meetings in the town. Some of the Saints had even got pelted with stones on the streets whilst preaching. Evan had not been so dismissive, believing himself that Mormons were Christians. That, she had loved about him. It would have been so easy for him to have denounced the Church along with fellow Baptists but he knew what it meant to Delwyn and other followers in the town.

Her mind drifted back to Evan and she wondered what he was doing right now. She imagined him writing his sermon at his desk near the window downstairs, trying to think of something interesting to preach that weekend. He might have lost his passion for her but he had never lost his passion for God. Maybe she had granted him a big favour by coming here. Now he could get on with his life without her and it might draw him even closer to his mother. Olwen Davies would be pleased at them parting, that was one thing she could be sure of. She winced slightly as she stabbed herself with the sewing needle. She should learn to concentrate more.

Hearing voices from the sitting room, she stood and dabbing the blood from her finger onto her lace handkerchief, she went to the door to find Delwyn standing there, with Rose behind him, in his shadow.

"Is everything all right?" she asked. "It's not Dafydd is it? Have you received word?"

Delwyn shook his head. "No, it's not Dafydd. It's you Lily. We need to speak to you. Please sit down..."

Lily retook her seat near the fireside and Rose and Delwyn seated themselves opposite her. By the look on their faces she dreaded what they had to say.

***

Evan entered Mrs Morgan's shop, the overhead bell jangled as he did so. Betty was stood on a stool behind the counter replacing a jar of sweets on the shelf and Mrs Morgan was just seeing an elderly customer from the premises.

"Is there anything you require, Mr. Davies?" Elsa Morgan asked, furrowing her brow. "I'm just about to close up the shop for the night."

"Yes I know that Mrs Morgan, that's why I was hoping you could spare a few moments of your time right now."

Breathlessly the elderly lady nodded. "Betty, can you please lay the table for Mr. Morgan's supper?"

The little girl descended from the stool and nodded, then ran eagerly into the backroom.

Mrs Morgan ran her gnarled fingers through her silver hair. It was scraped back in a bun as always but a few strands had worked loose. "So, what is it you want, Mr. Davies?"

Evan looked at his feet and then raised his glance to meet with hers. "It's about Lily, has there been any more word since?"

"Look, Mr. Davies..." Elsa said tiredly, "If there was, I would tell you. I have only received the one letter so far."

"It's just that I thought, had hoped even, she would have written to me by now... it has been several months since their departure."

Mrs Morgan rolled up her sleeves and started tidying up the shop, muttering to herself.

"What was that?" Evan asked.

She turned away from the counter to face him head on. "Well, what can you expect? Not just after what you did to her by not showing you wanted her to stay, but your mother's hand in all of this?"

"My mother? I don't understand. I know they did not care for one another, but mother was very helpful to Lily and Mollie."

Elsa Morgan's blue eyes flashed. "Helpful? Do you call trying to dose her own grandchild up to the hilt with Syrup of Poppies to cause her to sleep most of the day, helpful, Mr. Davies? Or trying to run off with Mollie against your wife's wishes, helpful? Or how about how she tried to drive a wedge between the pair of you? Is that enough for you? Helpful enough?"

Evan stood there in disbelief. Elsa Morgan's words cut him to the core. He drew a breath and let it out again. "I had no idea Mrs Morgan, Lily never told me of these things."

"Well maybe she didn't want to come between mother and son, but how she suffered at the hands of Olwen Davies. Now if you don't mind I have my own family to attend to. At least they know I am here for them when they need me. *Nos da*, Mr. Davies." Elsa said firmly, ushering him out of the shop and closing the door behind him.

This was all too much for Evan to digest. No wonder Lily had wanted to leave and take their daughter with them. Not only had his mother let all of them down, but he had let his wife and child down too. His mother owed them all an awful lot for her bad behaviour.

He had an idea how she could make good for the suffering she had caused. He intended catching a train to Pentyrch first thing in the morning.

Chapter Thirteen

Lily studied the pair sat in front of her. "What is it you want to say to me?" She asked, wringing her hands.

Delwyn hesitated and then looked at his wife, who nodded in reassurance. Taking a deep breath, he said, "We are concerned about you Lily and that is why we both want to say this to you. We think you should remarry..."

Lily could not believe what she was hearing, her heart beat quickened and quite suddenly she was hot and uncomfortable. She stood, moving away from the fireplace, turning to gaze out of the window for a moment. To get married to someone else? That wasn't what she was thinking of at all.

"Remarry?" She said, turning to face the pair. "What right do you both have to tell me to do that?"

"The right as your only family in this country, Lily," Delwyn said, then he looked down at his shoes, she realised she had made him uncomfortable now. He raised his head. "The reason I am telling you this, is that your marriage with Evan is dead. He didn't even try to stop you coming here; he gave up everything that he should have held precious. There is a man in the Church...a good man, a kind man. He's recently widowed. He is a lot older than you Lily...but he needs a good wife and you need a good husband."

Lily clenched both hands into fists. "Delwyn Jenkin, if you were not my brother I would wish to slap your face right now. Do you think I can so easily brush off my marriage to Evan as if it were crumbs upon a tablecloth? Do you think I can just move on to a man I do not know, just like that?"

"Please sit down, Lily," Delwyn advised. "It was not our intention to upset you. You would not have to marry him straight away, there would be a period of courtship of course, and I would be more than willing to chaperone you, dear sister."

Lily exhaled and seated herself. Tears formed at the back of her eyes and she began to sob. An arm wrapped around her, gently massaging her back. She looked up to see Rose there with Delwyn at her side.

"Please say you will think about it, Lily? You are still a young woman and neither of us wish to see you waste your life away pining for a man who does not care for you..."

For some reason those words cut her to the very core. Rose had said what was at the back of Lily's mind all that time. She wept bitterly for a minute or so and then looked up through glassy eyes, bringing her eyes to focus on the pair. "Who is this man you speak of?"

Delwyn straightened. "His name is 'Cooper Haines'. He has recently moved here, but he is a good man, a kind man, a hard worker. He would be a good provider for you and Mollie."

"Cooper Haines? That doesn't sound like a Welsh name to me."

Delwyn cleared his throat. "He's not Welsh, Lily. He's an American."

"American? Delwyn I could not envisage myself married to an American man! It would be such a culture difference. In any case, I don't think I'm ready to speak about this as yet."

Rose was chewing her lip and now looking at her husband.

Delwyn continued. "Lily… we took the liberty of inviting him to tea on Saturday afternoon. We hope you will be here to meet him."

Lily's chin jutted out in indignation. "Oh, haven't you both got it well planned out? Let's offload Lily to the first available man. You're fed up of me living here, aren't you?"

Delwyn was smiling now, his eyes too, filling with tears. "Oh our Lily...we love you so much. We would have you here always, but we want more than anything just for you to be happy, *cariad.* Come here, please..."

She stood and fell into her brother's open arms, realising without a shadow of a doubt that he meant what he said and by the look on Rose's face, she knew her sister-in-law was in agreement.

"But what if I did decide that I liked this Cooper Haines, how could we marry? I am still married to Evan."

Delwyn released her from his embrace and looked deep within her eyes. "I shall have to discuss this with one of the elders from the Church. It might be a question of divorce or it might not. You see, I'm not certain your former marriage would be recognised within our Church in any case. And the law of the land might be different here too. And don't forget, Evan deserted you really. It could be a good case for a divorce."

Divorce from Evan? She had not even questioned it. It just wasn't done was it? If you made your bed you lay in it, whether the bed was messed up or not. But Evan had practically thrown her out of the marital bed...all sorts of thoughts were now going through her head.

"I see..." she said, finally. "There has been no news from Evan even though I posted a letter to him when I first got here. I shall go ahead and meet this Cooper Haines on Saturday, but be warned, if I don't like him then I shall have no more to do with him."

Delwyn and Rose both smiled at one another.

"I think," said Rose, "now we should have a nice cup of tea and a slice of Lily's apple pie..."

Lily smiled. Saturday would be eventful that was for sure, already she felt as though a thousand butterflies were fluttering around inside her stomach. She had another two days left to meet with the man who might become her future husband.

***

Evan stepped down from the train and walked the distance to his family home. Living here had seemed a life time away. He thought back to that fateful day he had brought Lily here and how his mother hadn't really taken to his bride-to-be. How awful that must have been for Lily, yet a little voice inside told him, he had done nothing afterwards to protect his wife from his own mother. A thought just occurred to him. *I am remembering things. Because I have taken this journey, it is coming back to me.*

Excitedly he made his way to the large terraced houses and dashed up the steps, stopping when he got to the top to get his breath, before ringing the bell.

Daisy opened the door, greeted him, and showed him into the drawing room. Why was he being so formal in his old family home? He wondered.

Presently his mother appeared, dressed her in finery as usual. Her face looked pale and worn. She swept him up with her gaze, reminding him of a predatory animal.

"Evan," she said curtly. "What brings you to these parts?"

"I've come to pay you a visit, Mother. Please sit down, won't you?"

She sat down. "So? I am waiting..."

"I need to speak to you about Lily."

"Lily? And why have you not brought her and my grandchild here with you? Your father and I have not seen hide nor hair of any of you for months."

"Well do not fear, as you shan't see Lily again."

His mother's face contorted grotesquely. Then, she smiled, a sweet sickly smile. "Oh really. What has happened then?"

"She has left me and taken our Mollie with her."

Olwen Davies threw back her head and laughed manically. "I knew it! I knew that girl was no good for you. Has she run off with another man? And what has happened to my grandchild?"

"No, she has not run off with another man as you put it, Mother. She left because I was no longer loving towards her. That bump I had on my head caused me to lose some of my memory as you well know, but it's now coming back and I am not liking the things I am remembering, nor being told."

"Being told? About your wife?" His mother was sitting forward in her chair now, taking a keen interest.

"No, not about my wife, about *you*, Mother."

"Me? And what have I done, pray tell me?"

He let out a long breath. "Oh you have done plenty. How about poisoning your own grandchild? Dosing her up all day on syrup of poppies to keep her quiet while Lily worked at the school?"

His mother's face paled a faint shade of ivory. "No, no, you must not listen to idle gossip, Evan. It was only a drop, to help the child get to sleep. I shall not do it again."

"Precisely, you shall not do it again, because you shall not get another chance to."

"But I want to see my only grandchild, Evan. I am sorry. Where might I find her?"

"You will have no chance of seeing either of them again, the daughter-in-law you despised so strongly, nor your grandchild, they are both in Utah."

Olwen Davies frowned. "Utah, isn't that in America? How would they be so far away, Evan?"

Evan sighed. “Because, Lily joined the Mormon Trail. Remember, Delwyn emigrated with his new wife, Rose? Well, Lily followed not long afterwards. And I am afraid...” He put his head in both hands and wept. “I am afraid that I shall never see either of them again. It is our fault Mother. Both yours and mine. You upset my wife so much when she was already going through hell and then when you tried to take our child from her...”

“B...but I only did that for your sake, Evan. I was taking the child to see you that was all.”

“But what was your intention?”

“To bring the child back to live at Chapel House of course, with us.”

“Mother...You should hang your head in shame to take a child from her mother.”

“Well, there’s nothing either of us can do now, is there? How about a nice glass of homemade lemonade, Evan? Daisy made it. The drink really is so refreshing....” She glanced at her son and let out a breath. “At least Lily’s departure has brought you to my door, I have not seen you for months.”

Evan looked around the neat, nicely furnished drawing room, with its expensive drapes and embossed wallpaper and realised this had never been a home to him. Chapel House was though, but now the heart and soul was ripped out of it since his wife and child had departed.

He sighed deeply. “And you wonder why I don’t call to see you, Mother? Life is bleak for me at the moment without my wife and child.”

For the first time his mother showed some genuine compassion as she stood and placed the palm of her hand on his shoulder. “Well, how can I help?”

“There is a favour I would like to ask you and father, but it would involve parting with most of your life savings...”

His mother’s hand quickly recoiled from his shoulder. “I don’t know about that Evan. We have saved a long time for that money. Of course, it would all pass to you should we both die anyhow.”

He looked up at her, yearning for her to feel his heartbreak. “But I would have no use of it then. I need it now to get my wife and child back. I want to follow them to Utah.”

His mother's jaw slackened. "But that's just not possible. Your father and I will not pass over our life savings to lose you overseas to a woman, to be honest, who I think is not right for you. Lily Jenkin has no breeding, nor class..."

"See!" said Evan standing, his breathing fast and furious. "You do not even address her as my wife. She isn't deemed worthy of our family name. I should have realised this from the start and not allowed you to put a spoke between us. I shall bid you good day then..."

He made for the door, but his mother caught hold of his arm. "Please Evan, let us talk more of this, you have come all this way." She searched his eyes.

"Never, Mother. I do not wish to see you or this house in Pentyrch ever again!" He pulled away and left the house, slamming the door behind him. He knew it was bad mannered of him, but his mother made him so angry. He was going to have to find some other way to get that money.

***

Lily gazed at herself in the long mirror in her bedroom. Wearing her new, best green dress with flowered lapels, she smoothed it down, aware of the sheen and how it shimmered in the light. She felt like a queen as she patted down her recently curled hair that was tied with a matching green ribbon.

"Lily!" Rose called from the foot of the stairs. "Are you ready? I can see your brother walking up the road with Cooper Haines, they're on their way."

Lily's heart beat a steady rhythm, she took a deep breath and descended the stairs and made for the parlour room, which was neatly set out with cakes both women had baked for the occasion. There were Welsh cakes, *Teisen lap*, apple pie, small sandwiches and there would be a pot of tea on the go in a proper china tea pot with matching cups and saucers. The fine white lace table cloth really set it all off.

Lily heard voices in the hall way. "Quick Lily, take a seat," Rose commanded. Lily did as told and watched as a very tall, smartly-dressed man entered the room behind Delwyn. He removed his brown bowler hat and nodded at Lily.

"May I introduce you to my sister, Lily," Delwyn enthused.

Lily rose to her feet and the gentleman took her hand. For a moment, she thought he was about to kiss the back of it, but he looked at Delwyn and then let it go.

He wore an expensive small check brown and beige, three piece suit with a gold pocket watch and chain. He looked far smarter than most of the men she'd ever set eyes on in Merthyr.

"Why, I am very pleased to make your acquaintance, Ma'am," the man said in a Southern drawl she recognised, as there were other Saints at the church with a similar accent. "My name is Cooper Haines."

"And I am pleased to make yours, Mr. Haines," Lily said shyly. He wasn't as old as she expected, the way Delwyn had described him, she was expecting a man of about fifty or sixty years of age. But this man appeared around forty years of age or so, his bushy sideburns might have made him appear older to Delwyn, she surmised.

"Please take a seat at the table, Mr. Haines," Rose offered.

He did as told and handed his hat to Rose, who hung it on the coat stand in the hallway.

When they were all seated at the table, Rose passed around the plate of nicely cut sandwiches and everyone took one, then she poured the tea into the small china cups.

"I take it you do like tea, Mr. Haines?" Lily asked, "You being an American?"

He smiled a smile that lit up his blue eyes and looking at her said, "Why yes, I sure do. I was brought up by my Mamma to drink coffee, but since coming here and getting used to the way of the Saints and their various cultures they have brought with them, I must profess to being partial to a cup of tea also."

Lily smiled. Cooper Haines seemed a kindly sort of man so far.

"Mister Haines runs the grocery store off Main Street, our Lily," Delwyn explained. "It's a lot bigger than Mrs Morgan's store back home."

Lily laughed. "Well, I would easily have guessed that. Mrs Morgan's shop or store as you call it over here, is a small room in her house, Mr. Haines."

"I see," he said, studying her with his eyes.

She wondered what he might be thinking.

The rest of the afternoon went by in a flash and after tea they all went for a stroll, Rose and Delwyn walking with Mollie at a reasonable distance behind Lily and Cooper. Every so often, Mollie would walk then ask to be lifted into Delwyn's strong arms and he happily obliged.

"That's a mighty fine daughter you have there, Miss Lily," Cooper said, taking a backward glance at the trio.

"Yes, she's a blessing to me, Mr. Haines."

He drew a breath. "You know it must be lonely out here for you sometimes..."

Lily nodded and gulped as she felt about to cry, but instead she swallowed back her sudden pang of sadness. "It can be. But I keep myself busy with Mollie, the housework and teaching the children."

"Yes, Delwyn told me about you teaching at the local school. And he said you alone were responsible for starting a small school in the village of Abercanaid." The way he pronounced the name of the village with his heavy drawl, made her smile.

"Yes, I was. It was only a small school though."

"Nevertheless..." he said, "that showed guts and determination. You're a fine woman, Lily Jenkin."

She straightened as if for the first time since his visit, she had remembered Evan. "My surname is Davies now, Mr. Haines."

He smiled to reveal a wide expanse of good solid teeth, which would have been unusual to see back home. Evan had good teeth too, but had been brought up in an affluent household. She wondered if Cooper Haines was brought up like that too, after all he owned his own store.

"Pardon me, Ma'am," he said, nodding his head, apologetically.

She smiled. "Thank you kindly, Sir." She was growing to like this man Cooper Haines, an awful lot.

Chapter Fourteen

Evan stood on the chapel step, shaking hands with the last of the stragglers from the church that morning. He was preparing for the Harvest Service and people had kindly donated what they could and local businesses in Merthyr had been extremely kind too. He wished Lily was here to help him to distribute to the poor and needy in the area. Maggie Shanklin walked past muttering something to another woman behind the palm of her hand. She looked at him and smirked. He had not seen her at that morning's service and guessed she was speculating about his housekeeper. He had taken on a middle-aged widow woman called, Kitty Williams, to help with household chores and cook him an evening meal. He dreaded to think what was going through Maggie's mind. But it was all very innocent on his part.

He was about to close the chapel door when he noticed Dafydd stood there, cap in hand. "I thought you'd already left?" Evan smiled.

Dafydd stood there breathless twisting his cap. "No, I hung on to see you, like."

"Is there anything wrong?" Evan searched his brother-in-law's eyes as if for clues.

Dafydd shrugged. "Maybe."

"You'd better come inside the house," he said, leading him back through the chapel along a narrow, echoing corridor, into his home.

The fire was still lit in the grate, but Evan knelt down and picking up a silver pair of tongs, placed some more coal on the hearth. Then turning, said, "Please seat yourself down, Dafydd." His brother-in-law did as told. "Would you like a cup of tea?"

Dafydd shook his head. "No, thanks, Evan."

Evan sat opposite, both chairs situated either side of the fireplace. "So, what did you want to tell me?"

"It's about Lily...I don't know how to tell you this, but Delwyn has written and told me that she is planning to wed again."

Evan raised his brows. "Married again? How can that possibly be so, she is still married to me?"

Dafydd looked at the floor and then brought his gaze to meet with Evan. "I don't like it myself Evan. Apparently there is an

American man who wishes to marry her. He's a recent widower and well Lily would be a good catch for him, like. Anyhow, he is one of the Saints and our Lily is to follow after him into the faith..."

Evan took a moment to digest his brother-in-law's words. "But I don't even know if that would be legal? I know I haven't been a good husband to Lily of late but she can't do that. Unless it is something to do with their practices of polygamy but I thought that was the husbands who did that and not the wives!" His top lip tightened in anger. How dare another man try to take his wife away from him?

Dafydd drew a breath and let it out again. "Well it appears Lily would have good reason to divorce you on grounds of desertion, Evan. At least that is in the eyes of the law."

"I admit I wasn't a good husband, Dafydd, you know why though...I wasn't myself after that blow to the head, it was as if I lost a year of my life, but now my memory is coming back to me and I realise how much Lily meant to me..." his eyes began to fill with tears.

"Yes, I do understand now Evan. I admit to you I didn't at the time. My brother though thinks you have cold-heartedly deserted our sister and maybe Lily thinks you no longer want her or love her."

Evan gazed at the burning fire in the grate and shook his head. "Nothing could be further from the truth. I even went to see my mother to ask if she would loan me money to get out to Utah to see my wife and child, but she refused. How am I going to get there?"

There was a silent pause for a minute or so and all that could be heard was the ticking of the wooden clock on the mantel and the crackling kindling in the grate.

Finally, Dafydd shifted about on his chair, then said, "I can help you Evan..."

Evan narrowed his gaze. "You? But where would you have that sort of money from? In any case, I thought you were saving to get out there yourself one day to join your family?"

"Your need is greater than mine. I have saved some money from the street fighting. I made a fair penny from that, it paid better than the pit. I don't have quite enough, but if you could get the remainder from somewhere else, you might have enough money to get the ship from Liverpool."

Evan stood. "*Molwch yr Arglwydd*! Praise the Lord! Dafydd, God has answered my prayers. How will I ever be able to repay you?"

Dafydd's face coloured up as he blushed with embarrassment. "It is payment enough for me to see you reunited with your family. I have never forgotten your kindness in coming to look for me in such a dangerous area as China, and both yourself and our Lily putting up with my drunken ways. Also that day of the pit explosion, it was you Evan who kept the people of the village going with your prayers and support."

Dafydd stood and shook the minister's hand.

"Nevertheless, Dafydd, I will try my best to pay you back for your kindness."

"Like I said, Evan, I don't have all the money, so you would need to get a certain amount of it elsewhere. Could you go back and have a word with your mother?"

Evan shook his head. "No, never. I am trying to think if there is someone else to ask..."

Dafydd rubbed his chin. "How about Mrs Morgan, Evan? Surely she will help you?"

Evan bit his lip. "I am not so sure. She is not too happy with me these days, but I could ask I suppose, she can always refuse me."

"Then ask her as soon as possible as there is no time to waste. It will take about 12 days to cross to New York and then there is the arduous journey across land to Utah. There is no time to delay..."

Evan realised his brother-in-law was right. If he didn't want to lose Lily he needed to get out there as soon as possible.

***

"Such fine material, don't you think?" Rose said, casting a glance at Lily.

"Pardon? Oh yes, exquisite." Lily had been preoccupied with watching Cooper Haines at work in his store. It was a shop that sold everything from material for ladies' gowns to groceries and hardware. Mrs Morgan's shop could fit into the corner of this one.

The store was quite busy that afternoon. Several male assistants, dressed in smart matching waistcoats, trousers and bow ties, attended to the needs of well-to-do looking customers.

"I think I'll order some of that blue material," Rose said excitedly, "I could make a new dress for myself and some clothing for the new baby." She patted her ever increasing stomach.

"Yes, that sounds a good idea." Lily looked up to see Cooper walking towards them with a smile on his face.

"And what can I do for you fine looking ladies today?" he asked, gazing into Lily's eyes. Her heart fluttered as she drew a breath.

"I'm thinking of ordering some of this material, a few yards, enough to make a dress and some baby garments, Mr. Haines," Rose explained.

"As you wish, Ma'am," Cooper smiled and clicked his fingers as a young assistant appeared at his side. "This gentleman shall help you, Ma'am." He turned to Lily. "Now how about I show you around my store?"

Lily looked at Rose for confirmation, but Rose was too engrossed in discussing the material with the assistant. Cooper took Lily by the arm and walked her through the store. "Oh Lily, I know I shouldn't but I wanted to speak with you on our own without your brother and Rose watching us."

She blinked several times in surprise. "I...I don't know what to say, Mr. Haines..."

"Please call me Cooper from now on. Come with me into the back room and we shall discuss matters. Your sister-in-law is distracted for time being."

She looked behind her several times as he led her past counters, ladders and sacks of potatoes, fancy goods and displays of books. Rose was still preoccupied with the assistant, blissfully unaware that Lily was so far away from her side.

"But I don't know what to say, Cooper, should we be doing this?"

"Have no fear my sweet..." he led her behind an empty counter and out into a back room that appeared to be some sort of store cupboard filled with sacks and various packages.

His breathing became heavy and laboured and for a moment she felt threatened, it was beginning to remind her of the man in Pentyrch who had attacked her.

"Please do not harm me, Cooper," she said, looking up at him as his blue eyes widened.

He softened. “Oh no, Ma’am. It is exactly the opposite. I love you and I just wanted the opportunity to tell you that when we were alone.”

Lily let out a long breath. “Oh I see...” She didn’t know what to think, confused by his declaration. It all seemed so sudden.

“Please tell me Lily... is it true for you, too?”

Lily shivered and swallowed. “I cannot say for certain, but what I do know is that I am very fond of you. I enjoy your companionship.”

Cooper’s eyes were shining now. “Then I am a very lucky man. I will settle for that Lily and I hope one day you will become my wife, now I will get you out of here quickly before anyone notices you are missing. Maybe you had better slip out alone, as I have no wish to damage your reputation. I just wanted to tell you how I feel about you.”

He lifted her gloved hand and laid a kiss upon it. It was a long time since a man had shown her that kind of affection and she almost melted from his touch.

“Thank you so much, Cooper. I shall see you next, as arranged, at the weekend when you visit.”

He smiled at her and allowed her to slip out of the door and back into the store before taking a good time to follow her path.

By the time she’d returned, Rose was paying the assistant for the material. “Where did you get to, Lily?” Rose asked through narrowed eyes.

“I went to look at the books,” Lily lied as she experienced a pang of guilt.

“I didn’t realise there were any books here.” Rose patted her hair and went in search of them. Lily following after her, feeling slightly pleased she had an admirer who thought so much of her. She glanced across at him as he stood behind a counter attending to a customer. He was a handsome man indeed and kind and thoughtful too.

Chapter Fifteen

"I wish I could help you, *bach*. Honest I do..." Mrs Morgan was scrubbing down her front door ready to open the shop.

Evan swallowed a huge lump in his throat. Had everyone turned against him in this village since Lily's departure? "Thank you for your time, anyhow, Mrs Morgan," he said, tipping his hat and turning to leave.

"No, please wait a moment, Mr. Davies. It's not how you think it is," Elsa Morgan said forcefully as she stood wearily to face him. "Please come inside and I will explain to you..."

Evan turned and followed her into the shop, the overhead bell jangling as they set foot inside. "What's wrong, Mrs Morgan?" He asked, removing his hat.

"It's William's brother. He lost his job at the pit and well, we've been loaning him some money quietly over the past few months and Betty needs new clothes and shoes, she is growing at an alarming rate."

Evan smiled, so it was not as he first thought that she wouldn't loan him the money as she disapproved of his intentions. "Yes and your duties are to your family first and foremost Mrs Morgan," Evan said kindly.

"If I had the money I would gladly give it to you for you to be reunited with your wife and child. Dafydd has explained everything to me..."

Evan's mood darkened. "Dafydd has been in this shop discussing my private business with you, Mrs Morgan?"

"N...not exactly. He called to the shop last week when it was quiet, he explained that you needed to get to Utah, but I think his intentions were to quell the local gossips and still one tongue in particular."

Evan realised Elsa was referring to Maggie Shanklin. "Well, he has no need to fight my battles for me, Mrs Morgan..." Evan said indignantly.

"Ah, do not be too hard on your brother-in-law as I see it he wants to repay you for your kindness."

Evan let out a breath. "I suppose you are right Mrs Morgan. I shall have to find some other way to raise that money. I'll bid you good day."

As Evan walked back home he realised how futile it all was, this was no trip to Pentyrch or even London, he might just as well try getting to the moon.

***

Lily admired the string of pearls around her neck as she gazed in the mirror. Cooper Haines had delivered them to her that morning, in a pretty package, all tied up with a red ribbon. They were real pearls that much she was sure of. Delwyn had told her he was a very wealthy man and she hadn't doubted that for a moment. How could it be that someone from such a humble background as herself could end up with someone so rich, she had no clue? It all seemed to be a dream of sorts and someday soon she would wake up back in Abercanaid.

Rose walked slowly into the parlour. "Is that the gift Mr. Haines gave you, Lily?" she asked, her eyes widening.

Lily spoke to her whilst still admiring her own reflection in the over mantel mirror. "Yes, aren't they beautiful?"

Rose drew a breath. "They must have set him back a pretty penny. He must really think a lot of you, Lily."

Lily turned to face her sister-in-law, who was now heavy with child, her movements slow and laboured. "Do you think I am doing the right thing, Rose?" She studied the woman's eyes for answers.

Rose smiled. "You mean accepting his gift? It would be foolish not to. I wish some man would give me a string of expensive pearls. I know your brother would if he had the money, mind."

"No, I meant about accepting his intended proposal of marriage?"

Rose frowned. "I suppose you are still thinking of Evan back in Merthyr?"

Lily sighed. "Of course I am, Rose. He is still my husband albeit in name only."

"Lily, that is so like you to always be thinking of others. But was Evan really thinking of you and your happiness? Ask yourself that?"

It was true of course, Rose didn't need to tell her that, she already thought it for herself, but in saying so, it made it more real somehow. Lily took one last glance at herself in the mirror, fingering the delicate pearls. She deserved some happiness at last. Turning, she said to Rose, "Will you please help me to set my hair tonight to be ready when Cooper calls on me tomorrow?"

Rose nodded excitedly. It was time for her to move on.

***

The problem was Evan had now run out of people he could ask to loan him money and his stubborn pride prevented him from going back to Pentyrch. Mother had made it abundantly clear she would not loan him the money at any cost. So he found himself explaining this to Dafydd when he called at Chapel Square.

Dafydd rubbed his chin. "There is another option, Evan..." he said.

"Oh and what is that then?"

"I could loan you all of the money..."

Evan frowned. "And how do you propose doing that? You said you don't have enough?"

"No, I don't. But I can get it soon, I have thought of a way!" The excitement was shining through his eyes now.

"How though, Dafydd?" This wasn't making any sense.

"I could go back to bare knuckle fighting. There was talk in the pub last night of a big fight due on the Aberdare Mountain soon. There's one man who is the unbeaten champion and if I fought him I would be paid a pretty purse, I can tell you."

Evan shook his head. "I can't allow you to do that, Dafydd, to put your health, even your life, at risk for me and your sister."

Dafydd sniffed. "Now don't you go thinking that way. Up until now I have not lost a fight and if I were to win this one, I would be the unbeaten champion in this area."

"I can see the attraction, but aren't there new rules in force? Wouldn't it be illegal?"

"Yes, it would and all. I'm not going to lie to you, Evan. The new rules are called 'Queensbury Rules'. Fighters need to wear gloves and take breaks and all that kind of palaver. That won't stop the fight going ahead, mind you. Rules are made to be broken. I expect there'll be plenty on the lookout for the law..."

Evan pursed his lips. "I don't know, I don't like the sound of it myself..."

"Well you might as well be for me as against me as I am doing it anyhow. The title means as much to me as winning the money."

Evan chuckled. "I can tell that. What's the name of that man from Aberdare, the one who is unbeaten?"

"He's called 'The Iron Fist' by many around these parts. But that doesn't put me off, Evan. I have built my strength up and reckon I can take him on fair and square."

Evan let out a long sigh. "Well if that's the case, then who am I to stand in your way?"

***

Lily and Cooper were allowed to sit in the drawing room without being disturbed for once. Delwyn and Rose though were not far away and Lily feared in case either was eavesdropping outside the door.

"One day you shall get to share my good fortune, Lily..." Cooper was telling her.

Lily was watching the flames crackling and changing colour on the hearth. She drew her gaze away to look at him and nodded.

"What's the matter, Miss Lily? You don't look too thrilled about my proposal?"

She shook her head. "It's not that Cooper...it's just that this is all happening so quickly for me. We have only been seeing one another for barely a month."

Cooper's eyes clouded over and then brightened again. "Pardon me, Ma'am, it was not my intention to rush you. I shall take my time if that's what you want. It's just that many a lady would..." He paused for a moment as if thinking he might regret what he was about to say.

"Would have bitten your hand off to become your wife?" Lily finished the sentence for him.

He nodded slowly. "Yes, something like that, although I was not planning on speaking as directly as that."

She looked into his eyes. "Maybe I am being forthright Mr. Haines, but I am an honest woman. I will not toy with your affections, believe me."

He drew closer to her. "And that's what I love about you, Miss Lily..." Ever closer and she could feel his warm breath on her cheek and his arm wrapping around her. He pulled her to him and this time she did not resist. He swooped down and kissed her gently. She felt heady with desire. A feeling she felt she should not be feeling right now, this was a feeling she should keep for her husband, but where was he right now? Thousands of miles away, that was where. She pushed that thought to one side, allowing Cooper to kiss her passionately for a couple of minutes. This man was experienced in these matters. He was going to make a good lover. Breathlessly she pulled away.

He looked at her with such love in his eyes that she didn't doubt him anymore. "Yes, Cooper, I would be more than happy to become your wife and I don't see why we should put it off for a moment longer..."

Cooper's eyes filled with tears. "Oh Lily, you have made me one happy man today. Let's call Rose and Delwyn in and tell them the good news."

Both were delighted with the announcement. Lily knew in her heart that she wasn't in love with Cooper, but she liked and respected him and maybe given time she would grow to love him. In any case, where had love got her? She was thinking about Mollie's future right now as much as her own. Delwyn had already discussed the impending marriage with the elders of the Church and there was no opposition. Several had already left loved ones behind in Wales and remarried without question. It was seen as the right thing to do in certain circumstances.

"Oh that's wonderful news, Lily," Rose said, hugging her sister-in-law warmly. "We have something to celebrate at last."

Lily chewed on her bottom lip hoping she was doing the right thing, but the look of happiness on everyone else's faces told her not to question that. They all needed something good to focus on. It would be a fresh page of a new chapter of her life.

Chapter Sixteen

Dafydd had put his name forward to take on the champion of Aberdare, Jack [Iron Fist] Edwards, within the next fortnight. The fight was due to take place at dawn on the Aberdare Mountain. As he explained to Evan, this was because there would be less chance of the law catching them at that time of day. Rules were now being enforced that could land the men in trouble not just for defying them, but there would be a problem with illegal gambling too. It was the ruin of many a good man in the village and surrounding areas.

Every opportunity he had, he was out running through the streets of Abercanaid and on the mountain too. Sometimes he trained before going to work underground, often after completing a hard gruelling shift. It was good exercise. He knew he needed to be well prepared for Jack's iron clad fists. He also made sure he ate well as he heard that eating good meat and vegetables was good for a boxer and helped to keep his strength up.

"Are you sure you're doing the right thing?" Evan asked, at the end of his Sunday sermon when everyone had departed the chapel.

"Never more sure." Dafydd grinned.

Something that Evan noted, were the shining lights that were now back in Dafydd's eyes. He was passionate about this and it seemed to give him new purpose so maybe it was a good thing.

"Would you like to stay for dinner, Dafydd?" Evan asked. "My new house keeper, Kitty, has left me some beef stew. There is more than enough for the two of us."

Dafydd rubbed his stubbled chin. "Thank you kindly, Evan, but I'll be in training this afternoon..."

Evan lifted his brows. "Training? On the Sabbath?" That didn't sit right with him.

Dafydd twisted his cap in his hand. "I know, but I think in this circumstance for the local minister to get to see his wife, Our Lord above, will understand."

Evan managed a smile, but if he was honest with himself not only did he disapprove of Dafydd training for this bare knuckle fight on a Sunday, but also the association with gambling in the area. It went against his biblical principles. Though someone wealthy, and who preferred to remain anonymous, had put up a decent purse for this fight. So he appreciated that this wager could mean whether they both went to Utah or not. The ordinary working men could afford little of their pay to bet on this fight, it was mainly entertainment for them, but for himself and his brother-in-law, a necessity that Dafydd won the fight. Evan scratched his chin. "There's something concerning me..."

Dafydd nodded and smiled. "Yes?"

"How will you be in a fit state to fight after climbing the Aberdare Mountain first thing in the morning?"

Dafydd grinned broadly. "Oh I have thought of that, Evan. I will go there the night before and rest over night."

Evan nodded. "Yes, that sounds a good idea as long as it is not too cold nor too wet."

"Well the weather has been glorious of late and it might give me an edge over my opponent if I am fresh and he is not."

Evan shook his head. "If you've had that idea I wouldn't mind betting he is thinking along the same lines..."

Dafydd laughed. "And I thought you weren't a betting man, Evan!"

***

Lily studied herself in the mirror as Rose added the final touches to her wedding gown. It wasn't white of course as she could no longer refer to herself as a maiden. It was a beautiful, shimmering rosebud-pink, the bodice covered in dainty seed pearls with leg of mutton sleeves, edged with lace.

"Oh you are clever, Rose..." Lily enthused, "you've even managed to make me a matching purse to carry."

Rose smiled. "Just wait until Cooper Haines sees you in that dress it will soon end up on the floor!"

Lily pivoted around to face her sister-in-law. "Why Rose Jenkin, what are you implying?"

Rose quickly coloured up as Lily laughed. Rose began to see the funny side of it and soon both women were giggling.

"What's going on here?" Delwyn asked, with a bemused expression on his face.

"Oh nothing, dear brother. It's just girlish chatter about the wedding."

Rose cast Lily a glance as if to say I'm glad you didn't tell your brother. Lily liked it when Rose showed another side to herself besides being the strong upstanding Mormon wife. It made her trust Rose even more.

"Lily, you look a picture..." Delwyn said, drawing in a breath. "And you my dear wife," he turned to Rose, "have made a good job of making that dress."

"Well I did have some help," Rose explained, looking at Lily.

"Oh come on now," Lily said, "it was you Rose, who did the hardest part and I am ever so grateful to you." She hugged her sister-in-law.

"Any news about the date of the wedding?" Rose asked her husband, expectantly. Both women knew that he had to have a word with the elders about the date.

"Well, the last thing I heard is that as soon as Lily has finished taking instruction in the faith, she will be free to marry Mr. Haines in a couple of months or so."

Lily's cheeks blazed red hot and her heart raced upon hearing Cooper's name. She was excited, but if she was being honest, a little scared too. Cooper had told her when they were married she could move in with him. Delwyn had said that Cooper's house was very large, having five bedrooms and even a room that could be used as a ballroom. Her house in Abercanaid seemed very small by comparison.

She was worried in case she could not fit in with the new lavish lifestyle thrust upon her.

"What's the matter, Lily?" Delwyn gently asked.

"It's nothing, really..."

"Come now, this is your brother you are talking to. He brushed a strand of hair away from her face as he gazed into her eyes.

She chewed her bottom lip for a moment and then said, "Well, I don't know if I am fit for all this finery. It's almost like moving up a class, to a place above my station in life."

"Oh dearest Lily, do not fret so." He put a reassuring arm around her shoulder. You could fit in with a Prince or a Pauper and there are not that many who could."

She let out a breath. In that respect maybe her brother was right. "I suppose I do have that ability..."

"You can mix with the best of them, Lily, of that there is no doubt," Rose said kindly.

If they were both so sure, then why did she still have a niggling feeling in the pit of her stomach?

***

Dafydd trained so much that his legs ached and his feet blistered. Day after day he pounded the streets and pathways around Abercanaid, then, when he got home to Chapel Square, he practised his punches on an old makeshift punch bag he had suspended from the ceiling using an old sack filled with rags and newspapers. When he got the chance he sparred with locals in the village and was pleased that none could get anywhere near him. On top of his shifts at the pit, it was all starting to wear him out, but still he kept going, his muscles and sinews strengthening by the day.

Evan was making plans and enquiring about the passage from Liverpool to New York, he couldn't purchase a ticket yet as the money wasn't forthcoming, but with God's providence, soon it would be heading his way.

***

Kitty had proved to be a valuable asset at the minister's home and Evan asked if she might remain in employment whilst he went to Utah. He swore her to secrecy and arranged for another minister to fill his shoes for six months. The gentleman concerned, Myddrin Evans, was a local unmarried man and eager to do the job, it would be his first posting since Bible College and good experience for him.

Evan had his trunk packed ready to leave at a moment's notice. So the only people who knew of his plans were: Myddrin Evans, Kitty, Dafydd and Mr. and Mrs Morgan. His congregation would have a surprise to see a new minister in the pulpit on the Sunday after he left Abercanaid. He could have just written to Lily to explain what had happened to him but he felt he owed her so much more than that. He'd allowed her to leave her home believing he didn't care about her anymore. Yet, nothing could have been further from the truth once the memories returned.

Lily and Mollie were never far from his mind. How he missed his wife's kindly words and support. She had been with him through the good times and the bad and he admired her for that. It made his blood boil though at the thought of her being courted by some brash American man. In his mind he saw him as a loud man, but he was only basing his thoughts on the one American man he had met once in Pentyrch. That man was boastful and grandiose. At least the ladies liked him for it and he did his best to charm them too.

Maybe he was being unfair, but all was fair in love and war, wasn't it?

He called in to see Dafydd at his home and was shocked at how weary looking his brother-in-law was. "Are you sure you want to go ahead with this on Saturday?" he asked the brow beaten looking figure in front of him. "You look so tired?"

Dafydd grinned, his pearly white teeth shining through the black coal dust on his face. "Well aye, I am and all. I've just worked a full shift underground, you would be too, Evan."

"Yes, I know all about that, you're forgetting I once worked down the mines myself. I am concerned about you training for this fight though."

Dafydd straightened up. "Once I've had some rest, I shall be rearing to go. I'm looking forward to it. I'll meet you here tomorrow evening and we'll climb the mountain and sleep there ready for the break of dawn. May the best man win!"

Evan sensed the determination and passion in his brother-in-law's eyes. He patted his back affectionately. "That's the spirit. I will be fighting your corner too." *And so will Lily and Mollie*, he thought to himself.

Chapter Seventeen

Lily was enjoying teaching in the small Mormon school. The age ranges of the children ran from 8 to 12 years old. What a vast difference to her little Dame style school in the church hall at Abercanaid. There, the children were dressed fairly shabbily, their mothers having to make do and mend, and in the case of some poor children, Lily gave them clothing donated to the church. The children in her class were well-dressed and cleaned, their finger nails, hair and teeth, immaculate. The lifestyle here compared to back home, was far more affluent with the children having fresh air to breathe into their lungs and good food in their bellies.

She handed them out their slates and chalks and prepared a short lesson on the blackboard. These children were a joy to teach, not such a challenge as back home, wasn't that what she loved though the challenge? There was gaining little Betty's confidence and eventually the love and care of Mrs Morgan, helping her to speak once more after the trauma she had suffered. The Griffiths family and their poor Mam as well. How she missed home, her heart yearned for something that was lost forever.

Life was very structured here and highly disciplined. She sighed deeply as she wiped the chalked words from the black board and wrote the eight times table for the children to learn.

"Miss, Miss!" Tommy Hartson shouted excitedly. She was about to tell him to sit down when he piped up. "There's a gentleman by the door!"

She turned to see Cooper Haines standing there, his eyes shining as he peered in through the glass window.

She walked towards the door and spoke sharply to the class. "Now please all settle down and write your names and today's date on your easels."

The chatter died down and she opened the door to Cooper.

"Pardon me for disturbing you, Miss Lily. I was wondering if you'd care to go for a stroll with me this lunchtime…that is if you are not too busy?"

Cooper held his bowler hat in both hands and waited expectantly for her answer.

“Well...I...don’t know what to say, Mr. Haines...” She looked at the class behind her. At lunchtime the children were not her responsibility and she usually spent the time clearing up in the classroom, preparing for that afternoon’s lesson and having a bite to eat. “I don’t know if I can spare the time.”

“Please say you will?” He looked at her with such puppy dog eyes that she could hardly refuse him.

“Very well, but I can be away for no longer than three quarters of an hour. Is that understood, Mr. Haines?” She said curtly. If she was being honest, she was a bit annoyed at the disturbance when she was about her daily work.

He blinked profusely. “Thank you, Ma’am. What time shall I call back around here for you?”

“In about an hour, Mr. Haines,” she said, closing the door behind him. He just stood and waved and then disappeared down the corridor.

She let out a breath and looked at the class whose eyes were now all on her. “Please face the board, class. Now today we’re going to learn our 8 times table...” she said, taking her place beside the black board.

***

Dafydd filled a small sack with a lump of cheese, hunk of bread, some apples and a bottle of water. He was going to need some sustenance to spend the night on the Aberdare Mountain. Evan had promised to bring some food along too. It would be a long night on the mountain for both men.

The villagers had now nicknamed him, ‘The Black Diamond’. He liked that name as it really represented him. The black diamond as a lump of coal and the fact that people had said he was a diamond of a bloke.

So it would be a match between ‘The Iron Fist’ from Aberdare and ‘The Black Diamond’ from Merthyr. There had been an air of expectation all week long on the streets and in the pubs as men took bets with one another. He guessed that a lot of the money would be going on his better known, unbeaten opponent.

But although Dafydd was currently unbeaten himself, Jack Edwards had sparred with the best of them, he was a highly respected man. A tough, but worthy opponent, even once flooring ‘Mad Dog Davy’ from the Cynon Valley.

Dafydd heard a clatter on the cobbles outside and opened the door. Evan appeared breathless at the doorstep.

"What's the matter with you, man?" Dafydd asked, voice full of concern.

"There has been a lot of unrest in the village about the fight." He took in a deep breath. Dafydd was dismayed to see him looking so red in the face and worn out.

"I don't understand, Evan. Here, come inside and rest awhile."

"It's Maggie Shanklin and her cronies, they are saying it's the work of the Devil, they've all been standing and shouting obscenities outside my door!"

"But on what grounds are they doing that, Evan?"

He took a seat and then exhaled deeply. "She found out about my involvement with this fight and said that I am encouraging a den of iniquity in Abercanaid, insomuch as immoral gambling and drinking is going on in the pubs because of it."

Dafydd frowned. "But you can't be blamed for any of that, Evan...that's just not fair."

Evan shook his head. "Maggie Shanklin has had it in for me ever since I showed her up in the chapel in front of her friends and neighbours that Sunday morning after Lily's attack."

"That woman makes me want to retch, Evan!" Dafydd said forcefully.

"Please," Evan advised, "Keep your strength for the fight and your fury for your opponent, it's the only way. Believe you me."

Dafydd knew his brother-in-law was right. To waste his energies on someone like Maggie Shanklin would be foolhardy. "Well, we'll rest awhile here, for you to get your breath back and then make our way up the mountain before night fall. Did you bring some food?"

"Yes, Kitty cooked a chicken for us and I have some homemade ginger beer."

Dafydd smiled. "Then we will have more than enough with my contribution to keep us going for the night and into much of tomorrow. We are fortunate that the weather has kept good for us."

"Yes, at least someone is on our side!" Evan pointed up above.

"Come on then, let's be on our way." Dafydd lifted the small sack of food and water and slung it over his shoulder as both men left the house to make for the mountain before night fall.

***

Cooper surprised Lily by turning up with a wicker basket covered in a red and white check cloth.

"What's that Mr. Haines?" Lily asked as she closed the schoolroom door behind her. He was prompt, but she wondered what lay beneath the cloth.

He tipped his bowler hat to her and whipped back the cloth. "I've brought along a veritable feast Ma'am from my own store. Some bread, cheese, meat pies and some pretty little cakes."

She peered in the basket, he had even packed two white china plates, cutlery too and glasses.

"You seem to have thought of everything," she smiled. Inside her tummy was aflutter with nerves, if Rose and Delwyn were to find out about this about her going un-chaperoned for a picnic lunch, they might not be best pleased. But she was her own woman after all, and a strong one at that, she reminded herself.

He took her arm. The sky was sapphire blue and the heat of the day's sun shone down on them. He led her down the street and around the corner to a wooded glade near a babbling brook and there, laid down a tartan rug on the ground for her to sit, and then he unpacked the picnic lunch.

"Please eat something," he urged. "I know you don't have a lot of time."

She helped herself to a small meat pie. "This tastes really good," she said, when she had finished.

"I make those myself you know," he said proudly. "It's an old family recipe. Maybe when we are married you could help me bake them for the store?"

She nodded eagerly. "I would gladly assist you."

He poured her some lemonade into a glass. "This is also good," she said, tasting the cold, sweet refreshing drink.

"That I don't make," he laughed heartily. "I get it delivered to the store in earthenware bottles."

She laughed too.

Then his laughter stopped and his face took on a serious look.

Oh no, she shivered thinking back to the man from Pentyrch. Was she foolish to have come here alone with him? She looked this way and that, but there were no sounds of anyone around, only of the water coursing its way across the pebbled bed of the brook.

He dabbed at his forehead with his handkerchief and then reaching into his pocket, produced a small, black velvet box which he handed to her.

She let out a sigh of relief. He didn't intend to hurt her at all. "What's this Cooper?" she asked breathlessly.

"It's for you Ma'am," he said proudly. "It belonged to my mother."

She opened the box to see the most beautiful ring she had ever seen in her life. At its centre was a large ruby, surrounded by miniature diamonds that sparkled and shone as they caught the light, set into gold. It took her breath away.

"It's beautiful," she said, staring at it.

"It's yours if you want it. As you are about to become my wife..."

"You mean it's for me to wear as an engagement ring?"

He nodded wordlessly. Then taking it from the box, he slipped it on her finger and kissed her with such a passion she had never experienced in all her life, they fell down on the grass, oblivious to time and place.

***

Presently the men found a clearing in the woods not too far from the mountain top. It had been a long pull up which had taken well over an hour. Dafydd would have made it much quicker had he been on his own, but Evan seemed to find it such an effort, but as Dafydd reasoned, he was not used to physical exercise like himself.

"I'll get a fire started," Dafydd said, as he dropped his sack on the ground. "You go and seek out some old branches for kindling, Evan..." he ordered.

Evan did as told and soon Dafydd had a crackling fire alight to warm the men. It was getting nippy on the mountain. In the far distance they heard the sound of male voices and guessed it was Jack Edward's camp. They were far enough away not to cause any threat. Some of Dafydd's supporters had asked if they could join them, but he told them to wait until first light. He thought they might have been a bad influence and kept him awake if they brought any liquor with them.

When both men had eaten their fill and warmed themselves, they prepared to sleep on the ground. Evan had brought a couple of woollen blankets along. It wasn't as uncomfortable as Dafydd thought it might be. It was a cool summer evening and from the forest through the trees they could see the stars twinkling above them. Evan thought about Lily and what she might be doing right now.

***

"What time is it, Cooper?" Lily said, sitting upright.

Cooper studied his pocket watch. "It's a quarter past two o'clock..." He started to pack the food and crockery back into the basket.

Lily patted down her hair and straightened her skirts. "I'm going to be late," she said in a panic.

"Now don't you worry. A few minutes won't harm none." Cooper tried to reassure her.

He was probably right, but she didn't want to take the chance. She couldn't believe what had just happened, not only was she wearing Cooper's engagement ring, but they had got caught up in the throes of passion and now she would feel guilty about going back to the school. Would anyone guess she wondered?

Cooper gently stroked her cheek. "Maybe you had better put that ring back in its box until we tell your brother and Rose," he advised.

She nodded and twisting it off her finger, slipped it back in the box. He gave her one last passionate kiss and led her back to the school. By the time she returned, the class was in uproar, with children shouting and screaming and throwing things around the room. They immediately stopped what they were doing and became quiet as she walked in.

"Good afternoon, Class!" She greeted. "Now please sit down and get your history books out."

They did as told. Luckily the head of the school hadn't noticed the class had been left unattended for a few minutes. In all truth that often happened with the other classes at the school, but Lily liked to be punctual for her own.

For the rest of that afternoon she couldn't concentrate for thinking of Cooper, the ring, and what happened on the grassy bank. She had been unfulfilled as a woman for a long, long, time. The marriage couldn't come soon enough as far as she was concerned.

***

Dafydd awoke the following morning to the sound of Evan's voice as he stood over him. "Time to get up," he urged. "Have something light to eat and drink and then we'll head for the mountain top."

It wasn't even yet proper daylight. Dafydd rose to his feet and went to relieve himself behind a pine tree and then washed his face in a mountain stream. He was feeling good, hopeful if anything. Both men ate in silence. It was hard to know what to say. Then they made their way toward the mountain top as the sun started to rise over the Merthyr Valley.

Chapter Eighteen

There was quite a gathering assembled as Dafydd and Evan arrived at the top of the mountain.

"What kept you?" One of Jack Edward's supporters shouted.

Evan could see by the way Dafydd's top lip was set in a fine line, his hands clenched at his side, he was irritated by the crowd.

"Don't let them goad you," Evan advised. "We're not late, we are on time."

Dafydd let out a long breath. There was no sign of any of his supporters—a fine bunch—they were probably still sleeping off last night's drink. All mouth and no trousers.

Someone cut through the crowd of men and Dafydd realised by the large imposing figure casting a shadow over him, it was his opponent, Jack Edwards, The Iron Fist.

"Hello," Jack greeted. "Well, I get to meet the man who dares take me on at last!" He turned towards the baiting crowd mockingly, laughing, as they joined in.

Dafydd realised this was all to unnerve him. "It's nice to meet you, Mr. Edwards. Yes, I am the man who is willing to take you on. Unbeaten, like yourself."

Jack faced him for a moment and then, turned back to the crowd. "Can you believe this bloke? Look at the size of him! He's no match for someone like me!" A ripple of raucous laughter ensued, causing Dafydd's stomach to churn over.

Dafydd was about to say something, when Evan nudged his arm. They both looked down the mountain to see his supporters on their way singing, "Bread of Heaven" as they marched up the mountainside. Some of them carrying flame-lit torches as it would have been still dark when they set off from their homes. How that cheered his heart and spurred him on.

Another man cut through the crowd. "Hello, Mr. Jenkin," he introduced. "My name is Lewis Jones. I am here to oversee this fight. I used to do the circuit myself one time, I was known in these parts as 'The Steel Claw'"

"I remember you, mun," Dafydd said brightly. My father told me tales and said you were quite the contender."

The old man's eyes twinkled in remembrance. "Aye yes. Nowadays I keep my hand in by ensuring there is fair play at these fights."

Dafydd nodded. He noticed one or two men exchanging money. Maybe now they had seen how much smaller he was than his opponent, they thought Jack would definitely win.

Lewis Jones shouted out at the crowd. "Right lads form a circle around this pair and give them plenty of room. Get the look outs ready, we don't want no problems from the law. Now..." he said, turning to the fighters, "let's make this a clean fight. Show me both your hands." He inspected both pairs. Some men had been known to fight dirty by wearing big, gold gypsy rings, which gouged out the skin.

Satisfied they were prepared. Lewis shouted, "Right let's make this a fair fight. The fight begins and let the best man win!"

***

Lily twisted a lock of hair around her index finger, a nervous habit that came into play whenever she was concerned about something. Yesterday had been extreme foolishness on her part. Although Cooper had placed an engagement ring on her finger, she wasn't as yet married to him and she vowed it would not happen again before the marriage. She didn't intend to tarnish her reputation. Delwyn would be most angry if he knew.

She was awaiting Cooper's arrival and the intention was that after they'd partaken of tea, he would talk with her brother in the sitting room to mention their engagement and the ring. She realised of course that Delwyn was all for the impending marriage and that as the nearest to her father, it would only be courteous that Cooper should mention the engagement.

"What's the matter, Lily?" Rose said as she slowly walked into the room, stopping to rub the small of her back. The baby was due any day now and Lily didn't intend to give the woman any extra stress.

"I'm fine thank you," Lily lied. "Just a bit tired."

Rose studied her and smiled, appearing happy with the explanation. "Well, that's all right, then," she said, adjusting the flower arrangement in the middle of the table. It was all set for Cooper's arrival, laden down with sandwiches and cakes, on the best white lace table cloth.

"More to the point though," Lily said, "how are you feeling?"

Rose let out a sigh. "Oh very full," she patted her stomach and smiled. "The funny thing is I've had a lot more energy these past couple of days. I keep feeling like cleaning and tidying."

Lily smiled. She had remembered being that way too just before Mollie arrived. It usually heralded an imminent arrival.

She looked at her sleeping daughter and realised she was doing the right thing for her. She needed a father. And Lily herself needed a husband.

Lily stared out of the window and saw Cooper about to take the steps to the house, she went to the hallway to greet him and opened the door before he even had chance to knock.

He stood there smiling as he took in the scene before him. "Why Miss Lily, you look even more beautiful than you did yesterday."

It was easy for him to say that and maybe she did look that way to him, but now she felt a little shy that he should now have known her body so intimately. Something she should have kept for him until marriage. If she was back home and the villagers knew, she would surely be an outcast and that thought upset her greatly.

"Please come in, Cooper," she said. He removed his bowler hat and followed in behind her.

***

Both men danced around one another within the circle, by now Dafydd's supporters were looking on, breathless and excited with expectation. Every so often, Dafydd ducked and swerved to avoid a punch from Jack. One thing he prided himself on was being quick on his feet. Jack was no match for him in that respect, the older man whilst being experienced, was not so swift. Dafydd had been forewarned of his iron fist.

The bout had been going on for several minutes, the crowd were becoming hungry for blood for one man to throw the first punch and it came almost out of nowhere. When Dafydd through tiredness, became slightly distracted and caught a blow from Jack to his left cheek, he staggered backwards. It was not enough to floor him, he carried on moving, jabbing with his right hand. The cut was beginning to sting, but thankfully, did not feel as though he was bleeding.

He needed to concentrate for Evan and Lily's sakes.

"Come on Dafydd! Show him what you're made of!" Someone shouted from the crowd.

That spurred him on to try a punch at Jack, but to his dismay although he connected with his chin, the large brute of a man didn't seem to feel it.

Jack upper cut him with his own fist and Dafydd felt himself recoil several feet backwards into the crowd, not enough to throw him off his feet, but enough for Jack to let him know he meant business. He felt himself being pushed by a strong pair of hands back into the man made ring.

Dafydd took a deep intake of breath then danced around his opponent, the intention was to tire him out.

"Knock the bastard down!" One of Jack's supporters shouted from the crowd.

"Come on Jack, get him on his back!" Another joined in.

Then it was as if half the crowd had joined in jeering. "On his back! On his back! On his back!"

Jack threw another punch, hitting Dafydd in the mouth. He tasted the warm salty blood and hoped none of his teeth had worked loose. In a moment Evan was at his side offering him a bottle of water. Dafydd shook his head and instead, spat the bloody fluid onto the floor.

Filled with rage he went for Jack and pulled back a punch that struck him on the temple, the large man rebounded backwards as the crowd gasped.

"I've never seen anyone hit Jack like that before..." Someone muttered.

Now there was no stopping Dafydd as he rained punch after punch. Jack's forehead was now bleeding as rivulets of blood ran over his left eye and down his cheek. Dafydd realised the match wouldn't be called off until one man was lying on the ground. Men had even been killed at this sport.

He glanced across at Evan who had a concerned look on his face. But still he carried on. Jack hung on to Dafydd with tiredness, but the man was not giving up quite yet.

"You young bastard!" Jack whispered in Dafydd's ear.

Then pulling away, he punched Dafydd so hard that he saw stars as he rebounded backwards. Whatever he did he mustn't lose consciousness. He carried on dancing around Jack, the man kept turning to find him, but Dafydd was too quick off the mark for him. Jack threw a punch and Dafydd ducked as his supporters laughed at the show now Dafydd was making of the Iron fist.

The performance went on for a long time, until Dafydd threw one last punch, hitting Jack squarely on the jaw. The man staggered backwards and fell like a sack of potatoes, heavy on the ground.

There were gasps of horror amongst the crowd, then silence and then Dafydd heard one of his own supporters shout. "He's done it, lads! The Black Diamond of Merthyr has defeated The Iron Fist of Aberdare!"

There were cheers and roars abounding as men threw their Dai caps into the air and Jack's supporters dropped their heads with shame. Someone attending to Jack, who was kneeling at his side on the ground, looked up and shouted, "I think he's dead!"

Chapter Nineteen

"No, he's alive look!" One of Dafydd's supporters shouted. "I just saw his foot move."

The man kneeling beside him looked up at the crowd and nodded. "He's still breathing. That was one hell of a punch, young man."

Lewis Jones bent over Jack Edward's body and gravely said, "I've never seen him take a knock like that before. He's getting older, mind you. Might be time for him to bow out of this game. That's what I had to do..." he added with some authority.

There was a lot of muttering and sighing going on amongst Jack's supporters but presently, much to Dafydd's surprise, many came over to him and shook his hand saying how it had been a fair fight and they'd like to watch him again if he ever had another bare knuckle fight.

Dafydd though, was too concerned about Jack to enjoy his moment of glory. Eventually, he heard a groan and Jack was conscious once more and being attended to by a couple of men. The bleeding to his forehead had stopped, but he looked groggy and disorientated.

Evan offered the men the same bottle of water for Jack as he had held for Dafydd and they took it for him to swig and to clean the wounds.

Within half an hour, Jack was back on his feet and being led back over the other side of the mountain, flanked by two of his supporters. Dafydd's pockets were already bursting to the seams with money from the men.

A gentleman, representing the anonymous sponsor of the fight, handed him a small velvet bag containing several sovereigns, causing Dafydd to inhale sharply as he accepted the purse of money. The gentleman just nodded and walked off to an awaiting carriage, causing Dafydd to wonder who the mystery benefactor was. He suspected it was one of the Crawshays, who did not wish to show he was a betting man on an illegal fight. Maybe it was just as well he didn't know the person's identity as then no awkward questions could be asked of him.

"What's the matter?" Evan asked.

"Oh, I just feel bad about what happened to Jack. Maybe he'll never fight again."

Evan sighed. "Look now, that man knew what he was getting into. Do you think he'd ever feel as bad as you do right now if the shoe was on the other foot?"

Dafydd shook his head. His brother-in-law was right of course, but somehow his win was tarnished by Jack's injury and the thought the man might have died. This made him realise it was best to get out of the mountain fighting game right now, call it quits. Still now he had a pocketful of sovereigns, and with the rest of his savings, enough money to get Evan to Utah to reunite with his sister.

***

Cooper had spoken quietly with Delwyn about the engagement ring and now he was allowed to slip it onto Lily's finger. Nothing was mentioned of course about the time he'd taken her for the picnic, so both had to act as though this was for the first time. It sat a little uncomfortably with Lily that she had to lie now to her brother and sister-in-law.

"What a beautiful ring!" Rose admired as Lily held out her hand.

Another thing Lily felt guilty about was that Delwyn would never in a month of Sundays be able to afford a ring like that for Rose.

She watched Cooper's obvious delight as she showed off the ring. He was happy at least and that gave her some comfort.

After eating they all went for a walk in the warm afternoon sunshine and this time it was Cooper who held Mollie's hand and lifted her into his arms when she tired.

"Do you know I've wanted a child I could call my own for such a long time, Lily..." he said gazing at Mollie in his arms.

"How long were you married for?" Lily asked, hoping she wasn't probing too much.

"Twenty years and then some..."

"Your wife couldn't?"

He shook his head sadly. "We tried of course except she was barren. But then..."

"But then what?" Lily noticed a dark cloud sweep over his face.

"Then finally she did get with child, but she was an older pregnant woman by then, it was dangerous for her. I blame myself. I should have known..."

"You mean that's how she died?" Lily asked, realising the full horror of the situation.

He nodded and she noticed his eyes mist over.

"You must forgive me Miss Lily it was only a few months ago. Yes, she died in confinement with our child, so I lost them both."

Lily took his free hand and gave it a reassuring squeeze, realising he would not want Delwyn or Rose to know that he was crying.

They walked along for a few minutes in silence and then she said gently, "Well, although we have Mollie, we might also one day have a child of our own..." She watched as the light went back on in his tear-filled eyes. It must have been awful for him to have lost both his wife and child at the same time. It made her feel such compassion for him.

As they carried on walking, Lily turned to look behind for Delwyn and Rose, but they were nowhere to be seen. "Something's wrong!" She looked at Cooper.

He handed Mollie back to her and said, "I'll run back and retrace our steps, now don't fret, Miss Lily."

She watched as he raced back down the dirt track. She had been so caught up in what Cooper was telling her about his recent loss that she hadn't noticed the pair was no longer behind them. Taking Mollie by the hand, they started to follow after Cooper.

***

A few weeks later, Evan was preparing for his Sunday morning sermon when there was a knock on the back door, he noticed Mrs Morgan standing there, not yet dressed for chapel.

"Is anything the matter, Mrs Morgan?" he asked.

Her eyes told him that something was very much the matter.

She slipped her hand into her pinafore pocket and handed him a letter.

"Please don't stay on the doorstep, come inside," he advised.

They both seated themselves at the kitchen table. "It's from Lily," she said. "It came yesterday morning...I haven't seen you around since you were involved in that mountain fight with Dafydd.

I hear that he won the purse of money? The men in the village are proud, but Maggie Shanklin is stirring up trouble with her talk of hell fire and brimstone..."

Evan nodded. "Yes. Dafydd took a fair beating himself, Mrs Morgan. But I was proud of him, especially as..."

"As what? Mr. Davies?" Elsa Morgan straightened in her chair.

"As he is loaning me the money to get out to Utah."

"Oh I see," she said stiffly. "Well read what that letter has to say and then you might decide to get out there as soon as possible..." She took the letter from him and unfolded it as if deciding the sooner he heard it the better.

"My dearest Elsa,

I hope yourself, William and Betty, are all well. I often think about you all back in Wales.

The sun is shining here in Great Salt Lake as I write this and soon I am off to work at the village school. I am now betrothed to an American man by the name of Cooper Haines, who owns his own store. Delwyn has discussed this with the elders at the Church, and as I was abandoned by my husband and I have now decided to take up the faith, it will be deemed acceptable for me to marry another Saint.

I hope Evan will find someone new to spend his life with. Although I don't know if the laws back in Wales will allow him to remarry unless he divorces me first. So you might like to advise him of that.

By the time you receive another letter from me, I should be married. I am so excited. Mr. Haines has presented me with a beautiful engagement ring that once belonged to his mother. He is more than happy to take on Mollie as his own child.

Delwyn and Rose's child, Meirion, was born in the early hours of this morning. We were all taking a walk when Rose took unwell and my brother managed to get her back to the house and send for the doctor. By the time I got back home the baby was on his way. Poor Rose had a long labour but Meirion is bonny and bright. I am going to be looking after her for a couple of weeks as I will be arranging for someone to take over my class.

One day maybe we shall all meet again, God willing.

Lily.

Evan felt himself grow angry. How could Lily dismiss him like this? Then anger gave way to sadness as he broke down and wept pitifully in front of Mrs Morgan. Elsa said nothing for a while just patted his back and then she went to make him a cup of tea.

Presently she said, "I am sorry to have been the bearer of bad news, Evan. But I thought it better coming from me than someone else in the village. These things have a way of getting around."

Evan nodded and gratefully accepted the cup of tea from Elsa's outstretched hand. "Do you think I should still go to Utah as planned?" He sniffed.

Elsa nodded. "Most definitely. I think you need to go now more than ever and fight for what's yours..." she said firmly.

Evan felt as though he had been fighting on the mountain himself after reading that letter, all the stuffing knocked out of him. "Yes, you are right of course. May I keep the letter to show it to Dafydd?"

"Yes, of course. As long as I might have it returned to me."

"Yes, I shall keep it safe."

They both sat for the remainder of the time together sipping their tea in silence. Then Elsa got up to go and gave him a reassuring pat on the shoulder. How was he going to preach his Sunday morning service after this? Not only hearing that news for himself but some of the women in the village, led by Maggie Shanklin, were baying for blood, that of his own, they hadn't attended the chapel in weeks as a way of showing their disapproval.

***

Lily handed Rose a clean gown to put on. She looked so tired after the birth, it had been almost a month and Lily was distressed to see how much weight she had lost.

"Rose, you really need to eat something..."

Rose looked at her with doleful eyes. Something was wrong Lily was sure of it. Rose seemed disinterested in the baby, preferring for Lily to attend to his needs instead. Meirion had a fair pair of lungs on him. He cried a lot and breast fed often, all of this was wearing poor Rose out.

Delwyn had quite understood at first, but now he seemed to despair of the loss of the vibrant wife he once knew.

Once Rose was clean and dressed and sitting in the chair in the bedroom she shared with her husband, Lily went downstairs to make some porridge for all of them and to see to the baby. When she arrived in the kitchen, Delwyn was already there, his eyes flashing.

"What's the matter? Lily asked.

"I'll tell you what the matter is Lily, you are doing too much for my wife and now she is like some sort of invalid!"

Lily recoiled in horror, she had never seen her brother so angry before and now she felt like returning the favour. "Now hang on Delwyn Jenkin..." she said forcefully. "There is something seriously wrong with Rose which is nothing to do with me. For days I've been asking you to get the doctor out, but you have just insisted on praying, saying soon she will return to normal."

He looked at her as if about to say something but then she carried on. "This I believe is to do with her confinement. I have heard about women who experience some sort of severe sadness after giving birth. Rose did not intend to be like this. It is something to do with the birth. I know it."

"Oh a doctor now are you, our Lily?" Delwyn said, his nostrils flaring.

"No, not at all. But you and the elders are saying it might be the work of the devil when it is plainly not to me. Go and get the doctor at once!"

She surprised herself with the tone of her own voice. Delwyn appeared about to defy her, but realising she meant business and that she was not prepared to back down at any cost, left the kitchen. She heard the front door slam behind him.

Relief flooded through Lily's entire body. At least maybe someone would believe her. Meirion was fast asleep which was just as well as he had kept the whole household awake the previous night, which might account for her brother's bad mood. She set about making the porridge. Quickly eating some herself, and then taking a bowlful to Rose. The woman didn't eat all of it, but at least took a couple of mouthfuls.

"You're going to have to build yourself up, Rose," Lily advised, as she adjusted the patchwork quilt on the bed. "My brother has just gone to fetch the doctor to see you." Rose looked at her expressionless, and then burst into tears. "This can't go on Rose. The doctor will be here to see you shortly then everything will be well again," Lily reassured.

She wished she could believe her own words but somehow she wasn't so sure.

***

Somehow Evan managed to get through the Sunday service under the watchful eyes of Maggie Shanklin and her cronies, who had decided to show up to the chapel en masse. Afterwards he called Dafydd to one side to show him the letter from Lily. Dafydd's left eye was still troubling him after the fight, so Evan read the letter out to him in his sitting room.

"I can't believe Delwyn is going along with this engagement nonsense when our sister is married to you, Evan!" he said angrily. "Don't get me wrong, I am pleased he and Rose have a healthy baby, but why is he being like this?"

Evan shook his head. "I don't know. Maybe he thinks as Lily does that I abandoned her. Don't be too hard on him. We don't know what all the circumstances are as yet."

Dafydd let out a long breath. "Well, you're a better man than I am I can tell you..."

Evan feared that Dafydd would knock his twin brother's block off if he were here right now, so was thankful in that respect that the men were thousands of miles apart.

"I'm not that great...at least not according to Maggie Shanklin..." Evan smiled.

"Don't take notice of that old witch, Evan...Rumour has it she was born in Salem..." He chuckled.

Evan tried to prevent himself from laughing, but couldn't suppress his mirth, both men laughed heartedly. At least someone was fighting his corner, he reassured himself.

There was a tap on the back door, and Evan, thinking it was Mrs Morgan again, was surprised to see his father stood there.

"Father, what are you doing here?" he asked.

His father smiled. "I have some good news for you, Evan. Now aren't you going to ask me in?"

Chapter Twenty

Within a quarter of an hour, Delwyn had arrived back home, breathless, with the doctor. The man who introduced himself as Doctor Burton was shown up to the bedroom and asked to be left alone with Rose. After a half hour behind the closed door, he emerged and took tea with Delwyn and Lily in the sitting room.

"It's a severe case of melancholia," he explained.

A look of concern swept over Delwyn's features. "Then what do you propose we do, Doctor? So Rose just feels a bit sad?"

"It's more than just sadness, I'm afraid," the doctor continued. "I've seen this several times before. Most of the women get better with the right care. Rose needs first and foremost to be able to talk about how she's feeling. She needs good food, plenty of rest, some daily fresh air. I will also prepare a tonic for her."

"What happened to the other ladies you knew of, Doctor Burton?" Lily asked, handing the doctor a cup of tea.

"Most got well eventually with good care, but a couple of them had what I refer to as 'Insanity of Pregnancy'. Those ladies were a danger to themselves and the baby. Unfortunately, they needed to go to special asylum for their care. There is no sign of this in Rose as yet."

Lily shook her head, realising the doctor was referring to what she knew of as a 'lunatic asylum' and that scared her.

"No, at least I don't think so Doctor. She doesn't seem to be very interested in her own child though."

Delwyn shot her a glance as if she shouldn't have said that, but Lily intended being honest with the doctor. He was here to help them.

"Then if that is the case you need to encourage her to bond with the infant. Ensure that she holds the child several times a day, not only when she is breast feeding, but at other times too. I have some ointment as she told me she is sore in that area. That might be part of her melancholia because she is finding feeding her own child so painful."

In all honesty, that hadn't occurred to Lily as she had not had that problem herself when feeding Mollie. Not to that extent at least.

"I see." She passed Delwyn his cup of tea.

The trio chatted a while longer, then the doctor picked up his black bag and put on his hat and left.

When he had gone, Lily half expected a tongue lashing from her brother, but instead he hung his head. "How can I not have realised this?" he asked his sister.

"You were not to know, Delwyn. You have been busy with work. But from now on we are going to do our best for our Rose. She is not going to end up in one of those asylums if I have anything to do with it."

"Nor me. We will take care of her."

Lily smiled and nodded. "Don't forget to drink your cup of tea."

***

Evan and Dafydd gazed at the man before them.

"So, what is this good news, Father?" Evan asked.

"May I sit first?" His father asked, with a big grin on his face.

"Yes, sorry. Where are my manners?" Evan drew a kitchen chair out for his father and all three sat at the table.

George Davies put his hand into his pocket and extracted an envelope and slid it across the table. "This is for you, Evan..."

Evan scratched his head. "What is it?"

"It's the money you wanted to go to Utah to bring Lily and Mollie home," his father said proudly.

"But how? Mother positively refused me when I asked."

"Well, she's not refusing any longer and I wholeheartedly agree with her. She doesn't want to lose you Evan, nor her grandchild. Pride was stopping her from coming here today."

"I don't know how to tell you this, Father..." Evan bit his lip, then looked at Dafydd.

"Go on..." George was sitting upright, now in expectation.

"I already have the money. I have no need of your money anymore."

His father quirked a silver brow. "But how can that be?"

"Dafydd won it from a mountain fight. I now have enough money with his savings to borrow enough from him to go to Utah."

George Davies gave the matter serious thought for a moment and said, "Well, I think I have a good idea. Why doesn't Dafydd keep the money? I shall give you this, not as a loan, but as a gift mind, and then you can both go to Utah. If that is what you want, young man?" He looked across at Dafydd who was now beaming with excitement.

Dafydd threw his cap in the air. "If you were a lady, I would kiss you, Sir!" He whooped with delight.

Evan was smiling too and shaking his father's hand, this was the answer to all of their prayers.

***

Both men travelled to Liverpool the following day and booked their passage to New York. It would take a good twelve days of travelling the sea and then overland. There was talk of the Transcontinental Railway being built across America, but it wouldn't be ready for them, their journey across land would be more gruelling.

They stopped a couple of nights before travelling, at an inn near the sea port, before their journey. The place was crowded with other passengers and revellers. There was a jovial atmosphere as someone played the accordion and they all joined in singing sea shanties and other melodies.

One young lady got up and beautifully sang, 'The Rose of Tralee'. She had travelled with her family from Ireland and Evan could tell at a glance that Dafydd was besotted with her. Her family were going to join the Saints at Utah.

"You like that young lady, Dafydd?" Evan asked, as they supped their beer from pewter tankards.

Dafydd's face turned a deep shade of crimson. "Yes. I do." He carried on supping his beer and then, wiping the beery foam from his lips with the back of his hand, said, "And I intend to marry her!"

Evan's jaw dropped; in all the time he had known Dafydd Jenkin he had never known him to court a young lady, let alone think of marriage. He had wondered of course that time he took off for China if Dafydd had become intimate with one or two ladies of the night, but marriage? Until now, he thought Dafydd would wish to remain a bachelor all of his days.

"Have you spoken to her yet?" Evan whispered in his ear.

Dafydd shook his head. "No, but I overheard her saying they were headed for Salt Lake, and I can see the way she looks at me, she likes me. Her father is keeping a watchful eye though. Maybe I can get to talk to her on the crossing. She's sailing on our ship."

It gladdened Evan's heart that Dafydd was thinking of settling down. Of course, this young lady might or might not be the right one for him, but the intention was there. She was a fine looking lass, dressed in a green velvet dress, tied with a black ribbon and edged with black lace. Her auburn hair cascaded in waves on her shoulders. Her eyes were the most intense emerald green Evan had ever seen. No wonder Dafydd was falling so easily for her.

***

The crossing over the sea was arduous, conditions were not good. Dafydd's stomach had felt unsettled and many passengers were sea sick as they either lay down on deck to try to quell the motion sickness, or ran to expel the contents of their stomachs overboard. By the fourth day, Dafydd felt well enough to wander around the ship and spotted his 'Rose of Tralee' wearing a hooded black cape over her velvet gown. She was alone on deck, looking out to sea.

"Hello," he said, sidling up beside her.

She looked at him and blushed. "Hello, Sir," she said, turning away.

The sea spray hit his face as he spoke and he tasted its saltiness in his mouth. He took a deep, steadying breath. "Please forgive me for being a little forward as you are un-chaperoned, but I would like to introduce myself to you. My name is Dafydd Jenkin and I'm a collier from Merthyr Tydfil in South Wales. I'm on the way to Great Salt Lake to find my sister who has been out there for several months."

She turned to look at him and blinking said, "Pleased to meet you, Dafydd. My name is Kathleen O'Connell. I'm from Donegal in southern Ireland. I, too, am headed for Salt Lake. We are going to join the Saints."

Dafydd nodded, already knowing full well from listening to her earlier conversation that she was headed in the same direction. "Tell me," he asked, "do you already have a young man?"

She shook her head. "No, there was a young man who courted me back home but we decided to part a few months ago as his family would not allow him to join the Saints."

He thought he detected a tone of sadness for a few moments, but then she looked at him and smiled. "I have heard of that boom town called Merthyr Tydfil. Several people from my town went there to work in the iron works. They say the skies at Cyfarthfa are lit up at night as though it were day. Is that true?"

Dafydd nodded. "Yes, it is. I know people who have worked there and got badly injured though. The Crawshays, who own the foundries, are hard taskmasters. They care neither for adults nor children and work both like pit ponies. I would not work there if they paid me."

Kathleen laughed and then Dafydd, realising what he had said, threw back his head and laughed too.

As the days wore on, Dafydd and Kathleen continued to meet on deck for little conversations. He realised that he was falling in love with her, though what her father might say about that he had yet to discover.

***

With Lily's care and Doctor Burton's advice, Rose soon started to pick up and now she was bonding with the baby. "I think," said Doctor Burton, when he had called on one of his visits, "Rose might have been suffering with anaemia. That might account for her lowered mood and pallor. She lost an excessive amount of blood at the birth. But now she is progressing nicely. I also think Lily, it would be a good idea if you encouraged her to sit in the garden in the sun in the afternoons or went for a walk to exercise and absorb the rays of the sun."

Lily nodded. "As you wish, Doctor." She bit her lip for a moment, about to ask the doctor something, but then deciding against it said, "Would you like a cup of tea before you leave?"

He shook his head. "That's very kind of you to ask Lily, but I have several more house calls to make. There's a baby due in the opposite street, and Mr. Morris's wife has been suffering from chills. So I shall bid you good day." He placed his top hat on his head and lifting his black leather bag, left the house.

Lily let out a long breath. She had been feeling tired and queasy herself the past few days and didn't need the doctor to tell her what she already knew, she was pregnant. The wedding was booked and it couldn't come any sooner for her liking. Hopefully, when the baby was born, she could pretend that he or she had arrived a little earlier than expected. She deliberated about telling Cooper of her news but decided to keep it her little secret for time being. He would be over the moon of course.

It saddened her deeply that she'd never see Evan again and wandered what he was doing right now.

***

As the ship sailed into New York Harbour, Evan stood on deck in amongst the cheering and excited throng. So this was the New World that everyone spoke about, he had to admit that he was starting to feel excited himself.

He turned to look at Dafydd, who patted him on the shoulder. "Well Evan, here we are at last...we have arrived and soon you shall set foot on the same soil as our Lily..."

Evan looked at his brother-in-law and smiled, unable to speak for a few moments, being choked up with tears.

Chapter Twenty One

Evan and Dafydd arrived at Great Salt Lake, tired and exhausted. It had taken them longer to arrive than they expected. The journey taken, gruelling across land with the other Saints. Dafydd was disappointed at not encountering Kathleen on his way, thinking she had taken a different route or maybe her family had decided to stay in New York for a while and travel on to Utah later.

Evan looked at him as they walked along the dusty track towards the hotel, "What's the matter?" he asked.

Dafydd dug his hands in his pockets. "Oh it's nothing really..."

"No, go on I can tell something's up? Aren't you happy now we've made it here?"

"Yes, of course I am Evan, but Great Salt Lake is not was what I was expecting at all!"

Evan threw back his head and laughed. "I expect you are one of those who expected the streets to be paved with gold."

Dafydd nodded sheepishly. "Aye something like that. I think I expected it to look more like a city than this, this looks like something from cowboy country."

Evan lifted his brows. "And how would you know what that looks like?"

"I've read enough books and seen enough pictures over the years."

Evan nodded. "I suppose it does look a little like that compared to back home. The hills and mountains here give us more space and there's plenty of fresh air. I'm not complaining."

"Oh no, don't get me wrong, Evan. I wasn't moaning at all. I suppose I had a vision in my mind that there would be lots of grand buildings and such like. It's tiredness I think. The journey here has been long and hard."

"Well, we'll get some rest in this hotel and then we'll see if we can find Lily at Delwyn and Rose's home tomorrow."

Dafydd swallowed. "That's if she's not already..."

Evan looked at his brother-in-law and Dafydd saw the deep sadness within. "Married?" he said soberly, completing Dafydd's sentence for him. Both men entered the swing half double doors of the hotel and walked inside.

***

It was the morning of the day before Lily's wedding to Cooper Haines. The day had already been postponed as Cooper had taken ill with influenza. He was now fit and well once again, but they were now to wed later than expected. Lily realised that people might speculate that the baby was conceived out of wedlock, when he or she arrived. Though as yet, no one knew about her pregnancy. Thankfully, her bump was still small and the gown Rose had made, still fitted well and concealed her sinful tryst with Cooper Haines.

Lily had no more reservations about leaving her brother's home because now Rose was well and seemed to be coping with both baby and household tasks. It was a joy to see Rose speak softly to Meirion and listen to her sing him lullabies to sleep. He was no longer the fractious young infant he had been who kept the household awake at night. Lily now wondered if it was his mother's illness he had picked up upon.

Lily watched Rose rock the infant to sleep in the garden with Mollie at her side. Rose was still taking the afternoon sunshine, as Doctor Burton had prescribed, and it seemed to be doing her the power of good. Lily cleared away the cups and saucers from the kitchen table and was about to sit down for a moment, when there was a knock at the door, mumbling to herself she gasped as she opened it, to see Evan and Dafydd stood there, caps in hand.

"Oh goodness gracious!" Her legs felt quite boneless, and then, a pair of strong arms supported her and helped her inside the house. "Oh Dafydd," she wept in his embrace and then he helped her to sit down.

"Oh, I'm sorry, our Lily," he explained. "Maybe we should not have surprised you like this, but we have been travelling for a long, long time. We both could not wait to see you."

For the first time she realised that Evan was by his side with a concerned look on his face, she thought she had imagined him a moment earlier as he appeared so thin and gaunt. "Evan?" she said softly.

"Yes, Lily..." he said as he knelt at her side and wept bitterly as she cradled his head on her lap.

After a few moments, Dafydd spoke gruffly. "And where is Delwyn might I ask?"

Lily swallowed, suddenly realising that Delwyn might not be best pleased if he saw both men in his home under the circumstances. "He's out on business and won't be back for some time..." She stood and looked out of the back window to see that Rose was still singing to the baby, oblivious of what was going on inside.

"Lily," Dafydd said forcefully. "We have come to take you and Mollie back home with us. We cannot allow you to marry that man, Cooper Haines."

Lily's bottom lip trembled. "But it's all set for tomorrow...there is nothing I can do now."

Evan took her hand. "Look Lily, in the eyes of our Lord, you are still married to me. And I know I let you down but..."

"No, you didn't let her down," Dafydd interrupted. "You forgot you married her after that blow to your head..."

Lily glanced from Evan to Dafydd and back again. She didn't know what to think any more. What to believe about Evan, herself or her heart. It had been such a long time.

Lily's hand flew to her temple. She was beginning to feel disorientated and confused.

"Look," Dafydd said gently, "Evan has come all this way and I think you both need to speak with one another without any interference. Go for a walk or something. See how you feel. It's not too late to call off the wedding. Evan needs the chance to speak with you, you owe him that much."

Lily nodded, her emotions flitting this way and that.

"Evan, I will see you back at the hotel," Dafydd said, turning to leave.

"Thank you." Evan gazed at Lily and for the first time she could see the love and compassion behind his eyes, something she had not seen for a long, long time.

"I'll tell Rose that I have to nip out to the store," she advised. "It'll not be safe for us to be seen walking together, so meet me at the back of the bakery store just across the street. There's a quiet little walk way there where we should not be disturbed."

Evan took her hand and planted a kiss upon it. "Thank you for giving me a second chance, Lily," he said, his eyes brimming with tears.

"Now go quickly and wait for me," she whispered, "before Rose sees you..."

Lily caught sight of Evan watching his daughter through the glass window pane as if deliberating whether to go outside to see her. Her heart went out to him. Then he turned, nodded and walked away.

He departed quietly, leaving Lily feeling breathless, her heart hammering away as she put on her cloak and bonnet, lifted her wicker basket and then stepped outside in the garden to tell Rose she was off to the grocery store. She asked her to keep an eye on Mollie, who was now sat beside her on a wooden bench.

Soon she realised she must make up her mind, one way or the other.

***

Evan waited with expectation for Lily to arrive. Now that he had seen her again, he realised more than ever that he loved her. How he wished he could turn back the hands on the clock for surely he would have begged her not to have gone in the first place.

Now he was out here, he quite liked the look of Great Salt Lake. The wide open spaces, the friendliness of the people, all was light and bright here, not like the dark clouds that often loomed overhead in the valley back home.

He inhaled deeply as he watched Lily walk towards him, swinging her wicker basket.

"Lily," he said softly. "We are alone at last. Please tell me it is for you as it is for me, the love we have is still there?"

He held his breath as he awaited her answer. "Yes, it is still there, it never went away for me, Evan. But you have to understand that I thought I might never lay eyes on you again. There is something that I need to tell you first and when I have, then I don't know if you shall feel the same way about me again."

He blinked. What could she mean? "Well, whatever it is we shall get through it together..."

She stepped forward. "There's an old felled tree trunk we can sit on over there..." she said, pointing in the direction of the brook. "It's nice and peaceful and I go there to think sometimes."

He took her basket from her in one hand, and with his other took her gloved hand, as they walked towards the water. Lily brushed her skirts down as they seated themselves on the tree trunk.

"What is it you wish to tell me?" Evan said, searching her eyes for answers. He could see they were filling with tears, so he handed her a handkerchief to dab at her eyes.

"Oh Evan, I don't know how you will feel about me when I tell you," she sniffed. "It is a secret that I have not shared with a soul."

"Then what is it, *cariad*?"

She looked at him through glazed eyes. "I am with child...I have kept it a secret for it has only been a matter of weeks."

His mood darkened and his lips tightened, white with anger, but then he tried to look at the situation from her point of view. She thought she had lost him forever. She must have thought this new man of hers would be the answer to her problem.

He softened momentarily, then let out a breath. "Well, at least you haven't told anyone of this predicament. What about your intended though, does he know of the situation?"

She shook her head. "He does not know of this. But he is a good, kind man, Evan. I should marry him because this is his child I am carrying...I don't know what to do."

"Now look here, Lily. Part of this is my fault for abandoning you. In any case, in the eyes of the Lord you would be entering a bigamous marriage with that man. Can't you see that?"

She nodded, her head lowered and he hugged her to him. "Yes, I can see that, Evan. But what can I do?"

He drew in a breath and let it back out again. "Well, in light of this, I think if you wish to be with me that you must break your engagement to him tonight and not mention anything of this pregnancy. Then in a few weeks when I am rested and all is resolved, I wish to take both you and Mollie back to Wales with me. I have enough money now."

She frowned momentarily, "But how is that?"

"My parents gave it to me."

Evan noticed the look of astonishment on Lily's face and taking his own handkerchief from her hand wiped away the remainder of her tears. "Now, you need cry no more because when we get back to Wales, no one there will know that the child you are carrying is not my own."

Lily nodded. "I don't know how I will cope with speaking to Cooper Haines. He was widowed earlier this year and lost both his wife and child..."

Evan squeezed her hand. "You must not fret about that. The man has not known you as well as I have and when you think of it, I am in his position too. I could lose my wife and child. Well I did, almost. And please do not worry for you shall not tell him alone, we shall go together. He shall find a new bride soon enough, I know it. There are many widowed and single women travelling here. I met some on the journey. It shall all work out for the best, you shall see..."

She smiled at him. "And Delwyn and Rose?"

"We shall face those together too. We shall have to because we have to stay here for a while longer yet, so that I am fit for all that gruelling travel once again and for me to become reacquainted with my daughter."

Evan hugged her to him and planted a kiss on top of her head. "What about Dafydd?" she asked.

Evan sighed. "I think Dafydd has ideas of his own. He met a young Irish lass on the ship, on the passage over, and is besotted with her. He won't rest until he finds her. He's speaking of looking for work. In any case, we shall be around a few more weeks yet, so you shall have plenty of time to see him and find out what his plans are before we head back home."

Holding out his hand for her to take as they both stood to return to face the music, she dropped her basket as Evan leaned over and kissed her passionately. Lily felt safe at last in his embrace, knowing that all would be well, because her home wasn't a house, it wasn't even any country in particular, it was anywhere with the man she truly loved...

Printed in Great Britain
by Amazon

Poverty and Political Culture

Poverty and Political Culture

The Rhetoric of Social Welfare in the Netherlands and France, 1815-1854

Frances Gouda
Foreword by Arjo Klamer

AMSTERDAM UNIVERSITY PRESS

Printed in the United States of America

The paper used in this publication meets the minimum requirements of American National Standard for Information Sciences—Permanence of Paper for Printed Library Materials, ANSI Z39.48–1964.

ISBN 90 5356 158 7 (Paperback)
ISBN 90 5356 159 5 (Hardbound)

For Gary

Contents

List of Figures and Abbreviations

Figures:

Abbreviations:

AN, Paris: *Archives nationales*, Paris.
ARA, The Hague: *Algemeen Rijksarchief*, The Hague, 2nd Division.

Foreword

by
Arjo Klamer
Erasmus University and The George Washington University

Poverty is relative in many ways. It is relative to the society's standard of living, for example. Those who are considered poor in rich countries would be well-off in poor countries. Poverty is also relative in that its existence depends on the alertness of those living within it. Only after reading John Steinbeck's *Grapes of Wrath* were Americans willing to face up to the poverty that the Great Depression had brought about. Later, in the sixties, they needed Michael Harrington and his book *The Other America* to realize that not all Americans were enjoying the Great Society.

Furthermore, the seriousness with which people consider poverty, and the urgency with which they want to act upon it, depends on how they see the poor. And that, in turn, depends on their self-perception as well as their worldview. An ascetic seeks poverty as the condition of an enlightened existence, whereas the puritan may see poverty as a sign of God's disapproval. For rugged individualists poverty signifies lack of will and effort, whereas social democrats see the signs of injustice. Pursue the topic, and it becomes apparent that nothing is more revealing about a society and its people than its conceptualization of and talk about poverty.

Take my American students. They rarely seem to have clearly articulated opinions about their society. When it comes to economics, my subject, they usually plead ignorance. Whether markets work on their own or require government intervention, they confess not to know. Yet they act as if they know. They have to. To show that, I like to ask for their reaction toward a homeless person begging them for money just after they have had a good dinner in a restaurant. The reactions tend to be of three kinds. One is that of anger. "Why don't these people get a job and stop bothering me?" is a typical response in this category. Another reaction is that of guilt and bad feelings: Poverty as the embarrassment of riches. Many of the students who react this way have the inclination to give some money themselves but prefer to see more and better government programs. A third reaction is also one of anger but now the outrage is directed at a system that makes this situation possible. "It is a God-awful mess," is a typical expression. I must admit that this reaction is rare, at least among Americans. A fundamentalist Christian, for example, may recite the Bible and there are people who refuse to say what they think, or pretend to be flustered by the question. But those are the exceptions. Conventions rule.

I then point out the economic perspective that is implicit in their response. Believing that the poor can pull themselves up by their own bootstraps—the first reaction—is believing that the system works for people who want to work. In the American system that means that markets work. (Probe a little further and people whose reaction falls in this category will invariably express serious misgivings about government programs). The second reaction is typical of the Keynesian perspective in the sense that it assumes imperfections in the market system that call for government intervention. In such a perspective the poor tend to be seen as victims of discrimination or people with bad luck. Either way, they should be protected and supported. The third reaction, namely anger at the system as a whole, implies a fundamental critique of existing institutions with the poor as their victims. Only a revolution in the mode and relationships of production will prevent the disgrace of one person having a nice dinner while another has to beg for a sandwich. So you see, our economics is tied up with the way we see the world, including the poor therein.

The dependency of poverty on the way we think and talk matters to what we do about it. As Frances Gouda shows in the following study of nineteenth-century Holland and France, the contrasting social and economic perspectives of the Dutch and French produced contrasting perceptions of poverty and led to radically different approaches to alleviating poverty. Where both people had to cope with the encroachment of the capitalist mode of production with its reliance on the refereeing role of markets and the institution of private property, the Protestant Dutch did so with a personal sense of responsibility to those who could not keep up, whereas the French translated their new sense of solidarity into a centralized approach to a problem that they had not envisaged in their post-Revolutionary world.

The theme of contrasts transfers to current times. It shows up in the industrialized world during the past four decades. The attitudes of the well-to-do toward poverty appear to go through cycles with the lesson that good times are more generous for the poor, whereas bad times seem to make people tough. President Lyndon Johnson declared the War during a long upswing of the American economy in the sixties; President Ronald Reagan gave up the fight after the American economy had lost steam and the American people became preoccupied with their own economic fate. At the height of the War on Poverty the poor were portrayed as the unfortunate ones who got stuck for no reason of their own doing. Reagan replaced that with the image of the Cadillac queen buying groceries with food stamps. Generosity had made way for suspicion. "Why work hard and pay taxes when the money goes to people who live off welfare checks and do not want to work?" became the standard question. The election of the Democrat Bill Clinton appears to signify a swing back toward greater generosity and care, that is, toward a "kinder and gentler nation."

No matter how generous the American society will become, it will continue to seem harsh and inhumane to visitors from the northern European welfare states. Northern Europeans see things differently, especially when they encounter American society for the first time. While most Americans hardly notice the numerous requests for a quarter on their streets, northern Europeans tend to come away shocked from the sight of beggars next to limousines. The contrast is too much for them and they wonder how a rich nation can be so ruthless. Ask the Dutch what percentage of Americans is poor, as I often do, and they'll answer 36 percent, on average. The exaggeration (the official estimate is more like 13 percent) betrays the bias with which they see the American society in comparison to their own. The Dutch do not think much of the poverty in their own society so the sight of poor people in the rich United States startles them. That's also why Dutch journalists who report on the United States are expected to write about poor Americans, leaving the impression that their number is larger than it actually is.

The Northern Europeans, however, are being forced to rethink their own attitude toward economic misfortune and disadvantage and reconsider their welfare states. One reason is the staggering unemployment rate, but the paramount reason is the movement toward a unified Europe. A major obstacle proved to be the Social Chapter of the Treaty of Maastricht. Opinions on social issues among the nations that make up the European Union are too far apart to make agreements feasible. As a matter of fact, this book made me realize why agreement will be especially problematic because of the distinctive histories, traditions, languages, and identities within the European Union. Gouda's assiduous research has brought out how difficult the conception and construction of social policies in nineteenth-century Holland and France were, with the endless debates, controversies, and soul-searching. The Dutch and the French ended up shaping their anti-poverty programs after their own image, and because these images diverged, they ended up with very different programs. There is no reason to assume that today, given their current cultural differences, the Dutch and the French have an easier time agreeing on a common social policy than their ancestors did among themselves. Traditions go far back in Europe and the historical consciousness of the Europeans tends to be strong (how else to account for the bloodshed in the former Yugoslavia?). Also important is the fact that Europeans do not share the same language. Speak Italian and you tend to think Italian history and identity. That does not make it easy to do things the Dutch or the German way.

A related problem is the globalization of our economies. Today we are easily shocked by the tragedy of the gross inequality that characterized Western societies in the eighteenth and nineteenth centuries. The novels of Charles Dickens and Emile Zola easily engender shame for a situation that once was and should not have been. A friend declared himself a socialist after reading Zola's *Germinal* which portrays the stark contrast between the dark abodes of the mine workers and their miserable work in the shafts with the easy, relatively carefree, and joyful life of the Grégoires who live off their share in the mine. Citizens of the welfare states as well as the Americans and the British appear to be agreed that this is something of the past. Yet, it is not. If they would only extend their horizon and recognize there is a world beyond their national boundaries, they would see that they are living like the Grégoires while the majority of the people are living in poverty. As it is, the rich tend to their own, that is, to those who have the fortune of carrying the same passport while throwing a few pennies around to the masses who are really in need. In this sense the current attitude toward poverty resembles most closely the attitude that the Dutch realized in the nineteenth century: the care and generosity stay within their own circle.

Gouda's study of charity in nineteenth-century France and the Netherlands is a study of contrasts. Her approach is historical, of course, as well as rhetorical. I am not a historian and came away from my reading with a deep admiration for the richness and complexity of her account and the seriousness with which she treats the sources. Economists would never have been able to do as much justice to the process by which the Dutch and the French came to shape social policies because of their reliance on the idiom of mathematics and statistics. Her wonderful writing does not hurt. Being a rhetorician, however, I deeply sympathize with her rhetorical approach which shows in the focus on the way in which the Dutch and the French articulated their ideas about poverty and social welfare. This is an unusual position for an economist to take, so allow me to explain.

The discipline of economics pretends to focus on the hard facts of economic life, that is on costs, prices, the amount of labor, and the amount of capital. To make it all seem even more scientific, economists like to represent the world in the form of mathematical models. The idea is that by reducing complex realities to logic and facts, ideological and personal biases are eliminated. Thanks to Donald McCloskey, among others, we now understand that economists do more than speak the language of logic and fact.[1] Like everybody else, economists practice a form of rhetoric that includes specific metaphors and analogies as well as appeals to authorities and narratives. Neoclassical economists speak *as if* the economy is a system of markets and people are agents that solve constrained-maximization problems. Of course, no economist in his or her right mind believes that such representations are literally correct; they are a manner of speaking, and that makes them rhetorical.

Recently McCloskey and I have turned our attention to the rhetorical practices that make up markets. Conventional economic models presume that the economic transactions take place in complete silence. There is no talk in them. The economy is one big machine that operates in silence. Forget the shouting that traders do on the market floor. Forget the endless talking in the workplace and in the living room. Forget the endless debates and horse trades in the political arena. Forget also the fact that the way people talk about what they do is dramatically different from the silent calculations that they are alleged to do in economic models. Conventional wisdom among economists has it that all that talk does not matter. Yet what if it does? What if all that talk among stockbrokers has an economic reason? What if people need to talk to make up their minds about what they want and about what restrains them from getting all that they want? If it does, we need the skills of a rhetorician to interpret all that talk. Of course, this idea is not original. All we do is join an already thick discourse among colleagues in other disciplines with well-known names such as Foucault, Habermas, Rorty, Gadamer, and Geertz.

Gouda's study participates in this discourse, too. It is another confirmation that talk, liberally interpreted to include all forms of communication, matters. It mattered to the Dutch and the French in their deliberations about and experimenting with the best policy toward the poor in their society. It is through talk, liberally interpreted, that they came to understand themselves and their society and it is that talk that generated divergent approaches to charity.

If I have a qualm with the following study, it is the modesty with which Gouda presents her results. Presuming that it is the ethos of historians that prescribes such modesty, I take the opportunity so generously given to me to forewarn the reader that what follows is not only a rich account of the rhetoric about poverty, charity, and the Social Question in the Netherlands and France in the nineteenth century, but also a story about our own struggle with poverty. It contains crucial insights we can ignore only to our own detriment.

The account alerts us, for example, to watch for changes in the character of rich societies. It tells us to look for such a change in rhetorical shifts, that is, in the ways in which people in particular societies talk and write. A significant transformation appears to be the increasing popularity of the language of the market. In the Dutch case this language compromises the characterization of Dutch society as a family. In a traditional family, after all, members presumably take care of each other as a matter of course, whereas in a market situation, infused with the idea of a Darwinian struggle for survival, care giving seems exceptional and unnatural. In the French case, the language of a free-floating market conflicts with the image of a society that is run from the center. In both cases the adoption of a rhetoric of the capitalist market could therefore upset firmly established traditions. This historical account forces the Dutch and the French to face up to their traditions and ask themselves whether they are willing and ready to change the essential character of their society.

This book has lessons for others besides the Dutch and the French as well. It raises, for example, the question of how societies—whether the Dutch or the French or any other national community—define the rights and obligations of citizenship. It raises, too, how particular communities view the poor who receive assistance from others who are better off. Even though they are down-and-out, are such poor people nonetheless defined as full-fledged members of the very same community that extends a helping hand? Thus, the question to the reader is how modern societies will maintain their sense of community when the discourses about profit-maximizing individuals, unrestrained markets, and the global economy are becoming more dominant. The argument furthermore reinforces doubts about the possibility of a unified social policy in the European Union. It makes one wonder how a minimal consensus can be achieved with such a variety of traditions and characters?

For all these reasons this is a book to be taken seriously by anyone who is interested in the welfare of contemporary societies.

Note

1. See, for example, Donald McCloskey, *The Rhetoric of Economics* (Madison: University of Wisconsin Press, 1993), and his *If You're So Smart: The Narrative of Economic Expertise* (Chicago: University of Chicago Press, 1990). I developed a similar perspective in my *Conversations with Economists* (Totowa, N.J.: Rowman and Allanheld, 1983).

Acknowledgments

David Pinkney prompted me to formulate some initial questions in a University of Washington graduate seminar on the social history of the Restoration and the July Monarchy in France. His "Pinkney Law" also inspired me to embark on this comparative adventure. In 1958 he had urged American historians to pose broadly construed questions about European history. Rather than being an intellectual hindrance, the great Atlantic divide between American historians and European archives should compel us to ponder "big" issues; because we are far from the trees, he argued, we should at all times concentrate on the forest. While I have occasionally feared that this particular comparison was perhaps too big a bone to chew, I remember David Pinkney's infinite kindness, subtle humor, and discriminating scholarly advice with enormous pleasure and gratitude.

A Fellowship and subsequent Write-Up Award from the Social Science Research Council funded the dissertation research on which this book is indirectly based. Wellesley College granted me a year of early leave, enabling me to complete the library and archival work in the Netherlands and France; the Wellesley College Committee on Faculty Research also provided a generous subsidy for the preparation of camera-ready graphs.

Joel Krieger, Marco van Leeuwen, Jan Lucassen, Charles Maier, Leo Noordegraaf, Frans van Poppel, and Richard Unger commented on parts or all of an earlier draft of the manuscript and offered worthwhile advice and criticism. Olwen Hufton and Simon Schama served as both scholarly examples and supportive readers. Jan de Vries's counsel was judicious and valuable. Arjo Klamer and Jonathan Sisk rescued this project from a dusty drawer; for their generous encouragement I am profoundly grateful. David Turcotte rendered useful research assistance during a year at the Woodrow Wilson Center in Washington, D.C., and Gary Wingo's and John Brophy's wizardry with Harvard Graphics produced the graphs.

Joyce Walworth, Owen Flanagan, Ellen Fitzpatrick, Alice Kelikian,

Seth Koven, Laura Frader, Deborah Valenze, Stephen Bornstein, and many other friends provided support, diversion, and good cheer. Mott Greene's intellectual companionship was there from beginning to end. Rebecca Boehling and Sonya Michel have stuck with me, and this book, in various incarnations and locations; their unwavering friendship has been a mainstay. My mother and older sisters in the Netherlands, Els Brocades Zaalberg-Gouda and Ria Schenk-Gouda, have furnished both a warm family welcome and musical *divertissement* during my many research trips, while Louky Worrall-Gouda has cheered me on from Vancouver, Canada. Having earned a *doctoraal* in history from the University of Leiden at the age of 60, my father—and fellow historian—sadly did not live to see the result of many years of labor in the salt-mines of historical scholarship.

At the end, when this project had become more of a burden than a source of intellectual excitement because my scholarly interests had long since migrated to the colonial history of the Dutch East Indies, Gary Price nurtured its final completion by brightening and changing my life. With affection and gratitude, this book is dedicated to him.

Introduction

This book is an indirect outgrowth of research I completed about a dozen years ago. The original project was based on extensive qualitative and quantitative material I had gathered in several municipal and provincial archives as well as in the *Algemeen Rijksarchief* in the Netherlands and in the *Archives nationales* and the *Archives de l'assistance publique* in Paris. Since then, various historians in the Netherlands, France, and in the English-speaking scholarly world have published extremely valuable books and articles with arguments that confirm with clarity and eloquence my findings. In this book, as a result, I have taken a giant step back from the nitty-gritty details of the archival information I collected about twelve years ago. Instead, I explore more generally the rhetoric that nineteenth-century intellectuals and political actors used to represent and transcribe the existential realities of poor people in two distinct political and cultural milieus.

I make the assumption that nineteenth-century French and Dutch narratives about the tough, painful lives of destitute people tell us more about the biases or inclinations of elites than about the illiterate poor themselves. After all, robust factory laborers or simple peasants, pregnant domestic servants or impoverished widows with a residue of gentility, resided on the other side of an enormous economic divide. Poverty-stricken people occupied a social terrain that was "exotic" and unfamiliar to the literate commentators who influenced the public imagination about the ominous Social Question. The opaque worlds of poverty and their inhabitants, whether they were disorderly urban slums or backward rural communities, could be inscribed with a variety of meanings.

Often nineteenth-century chronicles about poverty revealed more about the cultural predilections, political fears, or personal idiosyncrasies of their educated authors than about the social realities they claimed to analyze and portray. However, these official stories also camouflaged the "hidden transcripts" that recorded poor people's Herculean efforts not only to survive but also to subvert, invert, challenge, or ridicule the "public transcript" that encoded the relations of command and subordination between rich and poor.[1] Indigent men, women, and children lived according to their own norms and forms, in a segregated cultural universe that answered to different behavioral codes and moral values. While poverty may have been restricted to a primitive physical terrain that resembled a "foreign country" in the eyes of respectable bourgeois citizens, they were the ones to prospect and survey the murky "continent of the proletariat" in order to define its social identity.[2] After all, society's elites enacted the legislation and social policies—or determined the economic logic—that circumscribed the lives of the poor. Hence, this book focuses on the ways, both similar and different, in which middle-class policymakers or social critics in the nineteenth-century Netherlands and France engaged—or feared and suppressed—the mysterious scenarios that presumably inspired poor people's conduct.

Some clarifications of my choice of terminology are in order. In the first place, employing the term "France" to denote a nation-state in the nineteenth century for the comparative purposes at hand should not be controversial, but perhaps my use of the words "Holland" and "the Netherlands" as synonymous entities requires a quick explanation. Technically, the label Holland refers only to two of the eleven provinces that constituted the nineteenth-century Dutch nation-state after the Belgian secession. However, not only do many Dutch people use Holland and the Netherlands interchangeably to designate the entire Dutch nation, it is also a practice common in the English-speaking world. In addition, I have excluded the southern Dutch, or rather, Belgian, provinces from my analysis, even though Belgium and the northern Dutch provinces collectively constituted the Kingdom of the Netherlands until 1830, which the Congress of Vienna had created to serve as a buffer zone against a potential resurgence of French expansionism. Excluding the Belgian provinces during the period 1815–1830 made sense. One of the central questions of this book is to examine the ways in which the prevailing perceptions of poverty were embedded in two distinct cultural environments that yielded political discourses with a different resonance and a particular outcome. Including the Belgian provinces for those first fifteen years would have made the overall comparison not only too cumbersome but also ineffective.

In the second place, I use the terms social critics, intellectuals, policymakers, public officials, politicians, bureaucrats, commentators, observers, academics, and moral, Christian, or political economists throughout the text as a reference to a fluid group of people in both

French and Dutch society who collectively constituted an elite of some kind—or what André-Jean Tudesq has called *le jardin des notables*. I do not mean to imply that these elites comprised a cohesive entity or spoke with a unanimous voice. Instead, elites in both countries were fragmented and politically divided on many grounds, be it birth, education, religion, wealth, or geography. As most gardens, to belabor Tudesq's metaphor, contain a plethora of flowers, shrubs, and trees of varying colors and shapes, so did the ''garden of notables'' encompass a wide array of people with diverse economic interests, contrasting social backgrounds, and conflicting political agendas.

Nonetheless, many of them shared a particular ''pattern of meanings,'' however vaguely configured, about civil society and political culture.[3] They espoused specific notions about the rights of citizenship and the obligations of the state or the church—or of affluent individuals and the local community—toward the less fortunate members in society. These relatively prosperous people also embraced a distinctive perspective on either defenseless mothers and doleful beggars or feisty factory laborers and unruly migrants. At some point in their lives, many members of these nebulous elite groups wrote something about poverty and the Social Question, whether they were government bureaucrats, Protestant ministers or utopian socialists. Collectively they participated in a symbolic display of power that was encoded in both formal and informal discourses. In other words, elites' rhetoric—what they wished to communicate, how they framed their arguments, and which metaphors they devised to lend strength to their contentions—was grounded in a diffuse, implicit consensus.[4]

Most notables, even those who rarely ventured beyond the intellectual serenity of a library or the spiritual sanctity of a House of God, wielded political and social power, however concealed or indirect it may have been. In the French central state's attempt to extend its sphere of influence over the nation as a whole, the government in Paris during the years between 1815 and 1855 consulted the opinions and solicited the help of local elites. Members of regional elites provided counsel in a wide range of matters such as the decisions regarding train fares, the stipulation of the disciplinary rules of insane asylums, or the definition of academic standards in primary schools for boys.

It was true that a colorful panorama of regional diversities in social and cultural traditions and linguistic peculiarities characterized France until the later decades of the Third Republic, especially in *pays* on the periphery of the French nation. In several regions perched on the edge of Paris-dominated political culture, the boundaries of French national identity continued to be contested, politicized, or renegotiated well into the twentieth century.[5] Nonetheless, the first half of the nineteenth century was the era of the state's "conquest of the national space," as David Pinkney has summarized it.[6] Thanks to the growing efficiency of the nation's communications network, whether via railroads or telegraph wires, the central state could enforce its dictates and execute its policy decisions more efficiently than ever before.

Moreover, the creation of an assortment of official advisory bodies—the ubiquitous *conseils supérieures* for public instruction, agriculture, commerce and industry, fine arts, public assistance, and many others—enabled local *grands notables*, who served on the *conseils*, to act as enlightened intermediaries between the state in Paris and civil society in more rural departments. In the miscellany of smaller villages scattered throughout provincial France, *petits notables* such as mayors, priests, or schoolmasters functioned, too, as middlemen between the burgeoning coherence of national culture and the boisterous carnival of differences at the regional level.[7] The state, in other words, shrewdly hitched the nation's local constituencies to the executive power of the central government and gradually displaced the preeminence of *politiques du clocher*—or the kinds of petty power struggles shaped by local loyalties, animosities, and kinship patterns—at the grass-roots level.[8]

A decree of October 31, 1821, for example, raised the idea of resuscitating local *conseils de charité* and charging them with the supervision of hospitals and poorhouses. The ordinance went so far as to stipulate that members should be chosen on the basis of their social stature within the community: the archbishop or the bishop, the president and *procureur* of the *cour d'appèl* or the *tribunal*, the president and vice president of the chamber of commerce, the rector of the academy, the oldest priest or the most senior justice of the peace.[9]

About twenty years later the government of the July Monarchy requested local elites' advice in trying to decide whether it should revive the moribund *dépôts de mendicité*—the ancien régime shelters which Napoleon had used so effectively to incarcerate beggars and vagabonds. On August 6, 1840, the Minister of the Interior dispensed instructions to the nation's *conseils supérieures*, via the departmental prefects, to contemplate the benefits and drawbacks of these institutions. A new name, however, would presumably bestow upon these archaic institutions a new social purpose. They might be called *maisons de réfuge* or *dépôts de bienfaisance* instead, since they would no longer serve as organisms of "repression for convicted beggars" but rather would function as "protective asylums and workhouses for the poor." The minister also asked the members of *conseils* to consider the feasibility of an "agricultural colony for indigents in their department" and requested them to "evaluate the expenses it might entail."[10] In short, by yoking the political influence of regional elites to its own agenda, the central state in Paris astutely drafted them into the process of governing the French nation.

The nineteenth-century Netherlands revealed, too, that municipal elites, despite internal tensions as well as distinct differences between the civic cultures of various cities, nonetheless participated in a joint discussion about poverty and charity. In traditionally independent cities such as Amsterdam, Haarlem, and Gouda, the friction within the groups of local notables entailed both political and economic components. Church affiliations played an important role, and affluent urban burghers were firmly ensconced as church deacons who exerted control over the charitable agencies of particular denominations (*diaconiëen*). But they also functioned as overseers of municipal poor relief institutions, which empowered upper-crust urban residents to assert their influence in both realms.

In the arena of national politics, divisions revolved around judgments about the primacy of private and religious charity versus public poor relief under the tutelage of secular authorities, which might broaden the power of the central state in The Hague. Besides, internal rivalries were also grounded in a diversity of economic opinions regarding the traditional significance of commerce, on the one hand, and an emphasis on the development of manufacture, on the other. But despite the stubborn persistence of conflict and enmity, Dutch elites lived in the same "world of thought" and they shared an array of cultural assumptions.[11] As Marco van Leeuwen has recently argued with regard to Amsterdam during the first half of the nineteenth century, the predominant characteristic of the city's wealthier citizens was "consensus rather than discord" about the kinds of social policies to be implemented, since their collective interest in an effective system of poor relief overshadowed their internal dissention.[12]

Thus, the national discussion about poverty and the nature of elites' philanthropic disposition transcended local differences and internal strife. In fact, during the first half of the nineteenth century the interests of Dutch economic elites gradually became dislodged from local preoccupations and were aligned, more and more, with economic policies crafted at the national level. Protestant ministers, government officials, city magistrates, or liberal economists may have disagreed vociferously about both the wellspring and the desired focus of the charitable impulse. They also wrangled over the moral duties of secular authorities vis-à-vis the poor, or disputed the appropriate role of the church in the allocation of poor relief. But prosperous burghers in each city shared the same language and formulated their contentious arguments within a set of rhetorical conventions that both fashioned and delineated the parameters of the debate. The discourses about poverty, in other words, inhabited a space "half way between social consensus and moral style."[13]

The intellectual questions that inspired me to do the initial research for this book issued from a variety of personal experiences and memories, molded further by an intellectual journey in an American graduate school thousands of miles away from a small town near Haarlem in the Netherlands, where I was born and raised. I learned about the requirements of adulthood at the tail end of the turbulent 1960s, an era of political questioning that convinced me that the world continued to be as tough and inequitable a place, albeit in a very different way, as it had been for the eighteenth-century French peasant women Olwen Hufton had described so eloquently and poignantly.

To some extent Hufton's *The Poor of Eighteenth-Century France* has served as an intellectual model.[14] A book full of thick description and local knowledge, published several years before Clifford Geertz became a household name among historians, Hufton's work persuaded me that this was social history as it should be written. By painting a trenchant picture of the complex realities, both gruesome and heartwarming, of ordinary people's daily struggles for survival in a harsh and unforgiving world, she forced her readers to care about the throngs of desperately poor mothers and their abandoned babies, hungry day laborers, and wily smugglers in ancien régime France. These were innocent poor folks who toiled from sunrise to sunset, but whose voices historians had not really listened to or recorded before.

Hufton's book confirmed my belief that the act of describing the social realities of an unjust world might hold political importance. Because I had lived half my life in the sophisticated welfare state of the Netherlands, however, I was fully aware that certain European societies softened social inequalities in ways that were very different from the United States, where I had moved permanently in 1972 and ended up studying French rather than Dutch history. This comparative study thus combines a series of personal queries and observations with intellectual questions forged in the American academy.

The 1970s proved to be an exciting decade to be a history student. Georges Lefebvre and fellow travelers in the United States began to advise historians to count their facts: *il faut compter*. The "new" social history of the 1970s encouraged many of us to learn statistics in order to quantify and analyze our data more rigorously. Every historical judgment, Lefebvre and his colleagues intimated, involved a never-ending process of weighing both analogies and contrasts, whether over time or synchronically; comparative work, they proclaimed, was at the core of the historian's craft. An emphasis on the distinctive aspects of a particular historical moment, event, or set of attitudes invariably assumed a different array of conditions in either another place or another time. Accordingly, writing about poverty and the Social Question, or, in the sociologist's idiom, about the origins of the welfare state, it seemed to me, cried out for comparison.

At the same time, Michel Foucault's towering intellectual presence on both sides of the Atlantic Ocean inspired historians to construct "social control" arguments. Foucault's emphasis on discipline and punishment inspired a portrayal of charity as a straightforward mechanism of surveillance which bourgeois elites, through their indomitable "will to power," imposed upon indigent—and residually volatile—working-class citizens.[15] The predominant motif of social control, so obtrusive in the writing of many social historians during the 1970s and beyond, reduced nineteenth-century intellectuals who thought with sensitivity about the Social Question—or charitable administrators who tried to alleviate poverty with sincere compassion—to a position of diabolical hypocrisy. Some historians have depicted earnest social thinkers or political actors as the eager running dogs of bourgeois capitalist hegemony; others endowed well-meaning philanthropists with a feeble impotence that resembled the helplessness of doomed "salmon in a polluted stream."[16]

But in the decade of the 1980s, social historians gradually shifted their orientation again by becoming more preoccupied with the human agency and *mentalités* of the poor or the *mission civilisatrice* of their benefactors, often using analytical techniques borrowed from anthropologists in a more self-conscious fashion than Hufton had done. There was, of course, an unequivocal logic to these new questions: if poor relief was nothing but a sinister plan on the part of elites to manipulate and silence the poor in order to entrench bourgeois supremacy, why did the "charitable impulse" and "humanitarian sensibility" endure?[17] Or, to invoke the language of Thomas Lacqueur, how can we explain the persistence of a "particular cluster of humanitarian narratives" that fostered "sympathetic passions and bridged the gulf between facts, compassion, and action?"[18] Besides, if the argument about poor relief as a ruthless system of social control was correct, why did the historical record leave such a pandemonium of "hidden transcripts" of destitute workers' rebellions, subversive actions, and spirited resistance?

In the process, a next wave of historical scholarship has produced a keen understanding of the gritty behavior and imaginative survival strategies which poverty-stricken people used in a variety of urban contexts in Europe. No longer represented as passive victims of an essentially evil capitalist structure that immured and imperiled their painful lives, indigent men, women, and children emerged, instead, as inventive operators in what could be called, with a certain amount of irony, "the charitable marketplace." In recent scholarship on European urban history, poor relief recipients have been depicted as clever agents who molded not only their personal destiny but, in the process, influenced patterns of middle-class generosity as well as the social welfare policies formulated by the state.[19] This new scholarly inflection has also yielded a more nuanced characterization of the agency of middle-class philanthropists as merely one of many components of a complicated "civilizing process" rather than a singular, blatant expression of bourgeois surveillance.[20]

In the decade of the 1990s, yet another shift in theoretical focus has taken place through the blossoming influence of the innovative academic discipline of cultural studies. Also, the "linguistic turn," or the tilt toward reflexivity, in the humanities and the social sciences—what Jean and John Comaroff have sardonically diagnosed as the current crisis of "epistemological hypochondria" or what Robert Hughes has branded a "culture of complaint" with narcissistic overtones—has nudged historians once again in another direction.[21] Many among us have started to think about discursive practices or rhetorical strategies. This new orientation is based on the recognition that the government documents, police files, institutional records of charitable agencies, memoirs of private benefactors, or statistical data we used to analyze a particular existential reality in the past were themselves both socially and culturally constructed. Such a novel theoretical twist in the road of historical scholarship has made us more aware, it seems, of the need to disentangle, as much as is feasible, the knotty problems of representation and the ways in which knowledge about the social world was inferred, contrived, and articulated.

This book has been long in the making, and as a result, I have tried to accommodate the ebb and flow of these intellectual fashions and scholarly trends to some extent. Hence, I have formulated a set of questions that address the different cultural and political constructions of poverty in two European nations in the half-century after the French Revolution. I pay attention, too, to the ways in which judgments about "genuine" poverty or "real" suffering engendered distinctive human responses in most prosperous French and Dutch citizens. Middle-class charitable projects or legislative agendas were not purely malevolent or vicarious attempts at exerting social control, even if they were constrained by mundane political realities. After all, a sense of "compassion" for the sorrow of impoverished compatriots combined with a general "fellow-feeling," as Adam Smith labeled it in his *Theory of Moral Sentiments*, that all human beings naturally harbor for each other.[22] Moreover, the manner in which elites in both France and Holland selectively codified social customs from the early modern period and revived or reinvented certain traditional practices played a role, too. Rather than focusing on the details of charitable practices and social responses in two specific urban settings, however, I have decided to concentrate on France and the Netherlands as a whole in an attempt, as Karel Davids and Leo Noordegraaf have recently rephrased Theda Skocpol's well-known exhortation, "to bring [national] politics back in."[23]

The analytical focus of this book thus lies somewhere between the rich empiricism and vibrant local color of much contemporary urban historiography on public or private philanthropy and its linkages to the behavior of the poor, and more sociologically inspired comparative work such as Abram de Swaan's recent *In Care of the State*.[24] De Swaan's remarkable book examines the "sociogenesis of the welfare state" and covers the development of a broad range of institutions in five countries in the course of half a millennium. Here, I merely want to account for the different cultural contexts and social sensibilities that rationalized and enveloped embryonic forms of social welfare in France and the Netherlands during the decades following the French Revolution and Napoleon.

I also hope to illustrate that explanations of poor relief as a mechanism of "social control" acquire greater analytical gravity in a comparative exercise. If we do not approach elites' desire to dominate or neutralize their indigent fellow citizens as a universal feature inherent in capitalist class relations but as shaped, instead, by particular historical experiences in specific political contexts, "social control" emerges as a contingent phenomenon. And as far as the scholarly efforts to show that the poor were much more than docile and malleable recipients of charity are concerned, I will keep in mind that it is difficult to establish the exact causal connections between indigents' actual behavior and philanthropists' personal responses, middle-class charitable practices, or the nature of public policy.

Notes

1. James C. Scott, *Domination and the Arts of Resistance. Hidden Transcripts* (New Haven: Yale University Press, 1990).

2. David Lowenthal, *The Past Is a Foreign Country* (Cambridge/New York: Cambridge University Press, 1985), and Jean-Baptiste Martin, *La fin des mauvais pauvres. De l'assistance à l'assurance* (Paris: Champ Vallon, 1983), p. 47.

3. Clifford Geertz, *The Interpretation of Cultures* (New York: Basic Books, 1973), p. 89.

4. John S. Nelson, Allan Megill, and Donald McCloskey, *The Rhetoric of Human Inquiry* (Madison: University of Wisconsin Press, 1987), p. 16.

5. For an insightful analysis see Caroline Ford, *Creating the Nation in Provincial France. Religion and Political Identity in Brittany* (Princeton: Princeton University Press, 1993), pp. 2–10.

6. See the chapter ''Centralization Made Real,'' in David H. Pinkney, *Decisive Years in France, 1840–1847* (Princeton: Princeton University Press, 1986), pp. 50–69.

7. Barnett Singer, *Village Notables in Nineteenth-Century France. Mayors, Priests, Schoolmasters* (Albany: State University of New York Press, 1983).

8. Ford, *Creating the Nation in Provincial France*, p. 5.

9. Albin le Rat de Magninot, *De l'assistance et de l'extinction de la mendicité* (Paris: Firmin Didot, 1856), p. 218. See also André-Jean Tudesq, *Les conseillers généraux en France au temps de Guizot* (Paris: Armand Colin, 1967).

10. ''Circulaire sur la paupérisme et la charité,'' August 6, 1840, in A. de Watteville, *Législation charitable où receuil des lois, arrêtés, decrets, ordonnances royales, avis du conseils d'état, circulaires, décisions et instructions des ministres de l'Intérieur et des Finances, arrêtés de la Cour de comptes etc. etc. qui régissent les établissements de bienfaisance, mise en ordre et annotés*, 2 vols. (Paris: A. Héois, 1843), 1, p. 42.

11. Benjamin I. Schwartz, *The World of Thought in Ancient China* (Cambridge: Harvard University Press, 1983).

12. Marco H.D. van Leeuwen, *Bijstand in Amsterdam, ca. 1800–1850. Armenzorg als beheersings- en overlevingsstrategie* (Zwolle: Waanders, 1992), p. 162.

13. Clifford Geertz, ''Local Knowledge: Fact and Law in Comparative Perspective,'' in *Local Knowledge. Further Essays in Interpretive Anthropology* (New York: Basic Books, 1983), p. 185.

14. Olwen Hufton, *The Poor of Eighteenth-Century France* (Oxford: Clarendon Press of Oxford University Press, 1974).

15. For a lucid discussion of Michel Foucault's and Jacques Derrida's influence on the writing of history, see Joyce Appleby, Lynn Hunt, and Margaret Jacob, *Telling the Truth about History* (New York: W.W. Norton, 1994), pp. 202–17.

16. Robert Hughes, *The Culture of Complaint. The Fraying of America* (New York: Oxford University Press, 1993), p. 71.

17. Thomas Haskell, ''Capitalism and the Origins of the Humanitarian Sensibility,'' Part 1, *American Historical Review*, 90, No. 2 (April 1985), pp. 339–61, and ibid., Part 2, *American Historical Review*, 90, No. 3 (June 1985), pp. 547–66.

18. Thomas W. Lacqueur, ''Bodies, Details, and the Humanitarian Narrative,'' in Lynn Hunt, ed., *The New Cultural History* (Berkeley: University of California Press, 1989), p. 179.

19. Important examples are the essays in Peter Mandler, ed., *The Uses of Charity: The Poor on Relief in the Nineteenth-Century Metropolis* (Philadelphia: University of Pennsylvania Press, 1990).

20. In the scholarly circles of figurational sociologists in the contemporary Netherlands, the work of Norbert Elias on the ''civilizing process'' has become central; for a clear discussion of the strengths and weaknesses of Elias's arguments, see Don Kalb, ''On Class, the Logic of Solidarity, and the Civilizing Process: Workers, Priests, and Alcohol in Dutch Shoemaking Communities, 1900–1920,'' *Social Science History*, 18, No. 1 (Spring 1994), pp. 127–52.

21. John F. Toews, ''Intellectual History after the Linguistic Turn: The Autonomy of Meaning and the Irreducibility of Experience,'' *American Historical Review*, 92, No. 3 (October 1987), pp. 879–907; Jean and John Comaroff, *Of Revelation and Revolution. Christianity, Colonialism, and Consciousness in South Africa*, 2 vols. (Chicago: University of Chicago Press, 1991), 1, p. xiii; and Hughes, *The Culture of Complaint*, passim.

22. Quoted by Gertrude Himmelfarb, *Poverty and Compassion. The Moral Imagination of the Late Victorians* (New York: Alfred A. Knopf, 1991), p. 3.

23. Karel Davids and Leo Noordegraaf, ''Introduction,'' *Economic and Social History in the Netherlands*, 4 (Amsterdam: NEHA, 1993), p. 3; Theda Skocpol, ''Bringing the State Back In: Strategies of Analysis in Current Research,'' in Peter B. Evans, Dietrich Rueschmayer, and Theda Skocpol, eds., *Bringing the State Back In* (Cambridge/New York: Cambridge University Press, 1985), p. 22. For a recent exploration of the theoretical literature on the origins of the welfare state by historians, see Seth Koven and Sonya Michel, ''Womanly Duties: Maternalist Politics and the Origins of the Welfare State in France, Germany, Great Britain, and the United States, 1880–1920,'' *American Historical Review*, 95, No. 4 (1990), pp. 1076–108, and James T. Kloppenberg, ''Who's Afraid of the Welfare State?'' *Reviews in American History*, No. 18 (1990), pp. 395–405.

24. Abram de Swaan, *In Care of the State. Healthcare, Education, and Welfare in Europe and the USA in the Modern Era* (Oxford: Basil Blackwell/Polity Press, 1988).

CHAPTER ONE

Similarity and Difference: The Debates about Poor Relief and the Logic of Comparative History

In France the state is the grand *aumônier*, whereas in the Netherlands the state does not interfere in matters of poor relief unless religious and municipal charities do not fulfill their obligations. Heaven forbid us from changing our practice of state responsibility brought about by the Revolution of 1789, because we regard it as excellent and in many aspects superior to all other systems. However, it is useful to compare an opposite organization of poor relief with the French situation for the purpose of examining the moral premises of our society.[1]

—Alphonse Esquiros, *La Néerlande et la vie Hollandaise*, 1851

Nothing great, nothing monumental has ever been done in France, and I shall add, in the world, except by the state. How could it be otherwise, since the government is the nation in action.[2]

—Alphonse de Lamartine in the *Chambre des Députés*, 1938

The purpose of . . . the state is to imagine a grand national community, ordered jointly by all its members. The state wants to be in a complete sense what municipal and provincial governments must be to a more limited extent, that is, communal self-government, resting on its members' shared capacity to rule.[3]

—Johan Rudolf Thorbecke, *Over het hedendaagsche staatsburgerschap*, 1844

This book compares the ways in which political and cultural elites in the Netherlands and France during the first half of the nineteenth century talked and wrote about poverty, poor relief, and the Social Question. I explore the interaction between definitions of the actual problem of poverty and the social policies both countries implemented to soothe the plight of poor people. I also examine the rhetorical strategies which policymakers and intellectuals pursued in order to advocate a particular resolution to questions of social inequity in two different societies during the half-century following the French Revolution and Napoleon.

My purpose is a deceptively simple one: to understand how two modern European nations not only framed different questions about the issue of poverty and material inequality, but also forged disparate responses. I hope to clarify what was distinctive about Dutch perceptions and formulations by casting a comparative glance at rhetorical strategies and social measures in France. My chronological focus is on the half-century that constituted the melancholy afterglow of the ideological fireworks of the French Revolution. This was an era of early, incipient industrial capitalism—to be sure, more imagined than real—which prompted many contemporary politicians and social critics to try to disentangle the relationship between an emerging industrial economy and the apparent pauperization of large sectors of the Dutch and French populations.

I probe the ideological underpinnings of the rhetoric about pauperism and income inequality and the ways in which subtle cultural factors may have influenced the day-to-day formulation and implementation of policy. Equally important is a comparison of the elaborate calculations and measurements of the number of citizens in each society who relied on public assistance, what Gertrude Himmelfarb has called ''the arithmetic of woe.''[4] I pay some attention, too, to the ways in which indigent citizens responded to their plight and tried to survive during hard times—for example, what kinds of desperate ''economies of makeshift'' they engaged in, to use Olwen Hufton's apt characterization.[5]

Thorny questions such as the friction between religious charity and secular social welfare, or the relationship between the central state and the local administration of poor relief, figure prominently. As Alphonse Esquiros and especially Alphonse de Lamartine proclaimed with great fanfare, the central state played a pivotal role—both administratively and symbolically—in French society. The state was a solitary actor on the French political stage, the flamboyant Lamartine avowed, because the central state epitomized the fraternal cohesion and embodied the unified purpose of the nation. In contrast, the prominent Dutch politician Johan Rudolf Thorbecke registered a diametrically opposed conception of the central state. In Thorbecke's vision the primary role of the central state was ''to imagine a grand, national community'' (*ver-*

beeldt een groote nationale gemeente): a genuine "imagined community" that was embedded in the citizens' collective capacity to rule but was, at the same time, circumscribed by municipal and provincial autonomy.

This book is about the history of social policy but, above all, about the history of political culture. Policymakers did not formulate their opinions and social remedies in a vacuum. The power and institutional projects of national elites shaped the propositions designed to aid the poor or to contain their volatility. Legislation tended to reflect elite interests, while most intellectuals who were educated and sophisticated enough to write about pauperism and the Social Question hailed from reasonably prosperous families who shared elite sensibilities. Obviously, poor people themselves did not live in a social void either. Instead, their lives were both marked and restrained by the legal regulations and moral proscriptions which their social superiors inflicted upon them. The behavior of the working classes, Louis Chevalier has noted, was partly conditioned by contemporary judgment. They were where they were wished to be: on the periphery or in the dark underworld of Parisian civil society, ostracized by "a moral condemnation" which isolated the poor and transformed them into the dangerous classes, a designation "they appropriated for themselves."[6]

But patterns of causality also flowed the other way. The number of indigent people who received outdoor relief, whether temporarily or more permanently, affected both the perceptions and the forbearance of politicians; so did the actual number of people who were institutionalized in poorhouses. Besides, the self-preserving behavior of the poor embraced an infinite variety of cunning practices, which hinged on the economic options and social opportunities available to them. The consequences or side effects of poverty, which ranged from finding more work and earning higher wages to begging, stealing, or rioting, molded the political and intellectual elites' attitudes, too, and inflected their ideological predispositions. Clearly, public policy was not exclusively defined by the holders of political power. Instead, the conduct of needy people who were the objects of bureaucrats' and politicians' concerns—those whom they tried "to persuade, subdue, cajole, or repress"—also affected policy strategies, either positively or negatively.[7] How politicians talked about the plight of the poor or the moral imperatives and social obligations of the community in which they lived, or how intellectuals invented and agreed on the ground rules for the discussion about poverty, defined, to a great extent, the content of the debate.

In the classical rhetorical tradition of Aristotle, the process of identifying the acceptable premises that functioned as the basic parameters of a discussion was called *inventio*. The linguistic practices employed in a debate, or the participants' choice of tropes and metaphors, not only described actual analogies between diverse aspects of the real world but also conjured up and created new ones. Rhetorical conventions both delineated and embodied the collective knowledge of a particular community, however ambiguous and indeterminate it may have been. By invoking certain kinds of figures of speech to express ideas about poor people, policymakers either echoed or helped to construct "the style in which the community [was] imagined."[8]

In the nineteenth century, poverty was a favorite *topos* among politicians and intellectuals; the manner in which they designated and outlined the problem relied on the identification of a series of common denominators that articulated the general assumptions of the community as a whole.[9] But a literal and uncontested correspondence between actual social reality and its narrative representation did not exist. However frightened, resigned, wily, or enraged nineteenth-century poor people may have been, their existential realities could be depicted only in the metaphors and stories which their social superiors chose to invoke.

Genuine "situated reality," Bryan Green has argued, became a "textual construction."[10] The composition of any text about the reality of poor people involved intricate mechanisms—constituting a premeditated as well as a subliminal process—of inclusion and exclusion or of "showing-hiding," as Jean-François Lyotard has called it succinctly.[11] The concrete behavior, the specific numbers, or the residential patterns of destitute people in society influenced the measures implemented to help and console them, or to pacify and suppress them. In turn, the language in which social superiors selected to talk about destitute people, or the idiom elites used to describe the moral culpabilities or social entitlements of the poor, constituted a matter of similar importance.

In both the Netherlands and France, middle-of-the-road government bureaucrats, conservative intellectuals, and utopian socialists collectively served as "custodians" of a particular discourse about poverty, despite their dramatically different analyses of nineteenth-century social conditions or their incongruous fantasies or fears about the future.[12] Every participant in the debate converted the "raw evidence" of the "true" existence of the poor into a linguistic artifact that mirrored its author's status or illuminated a certain political ideology. The particular cultural milieu that enveloped authors who composed serious reports about working-class unemployment—or others who dashed off sentimental stories about sorrow and human triumphs over adversity—

inscribed such narratives with a distinct national style. Hence, nineteenth-century French and Dutch social texts revealed much about the unique preoccupations of their cultural environment, although they may have conveyed little about the "domain of the real."[13]

But these written narratives, composed either in series of words or lists of numbers, are the most tangible historical records that have survived. They constitute what James Scott has called the "public transcript," representing a documentary "parade" of power that palpably demonstrated the grandeur or cultural refinement of the elite, who could thus lord their superior moral discipline and literary talents over the disenfranchised.[14] Whether historians realize they are chasing shadows or acknowledge they are tilting at windmills, or whether they claim to register nothing but the whole historical "Truth," they are "language animals" both by necessity and by inclination.[15] As a result, historians have few other options but to decipher the cultural grammar implicit in the nineteenth-century public rhetoric about poverty in order to uncover the "hidden transcripts" which it concealed. Historians, in other words, must read between the lines in order to approximate the "truth" about the sensibilities of the poor. Only by decoding the social vocabulary of the elite can we grasp the reasons why indigent people engendered in their social superiors either empathy and caring, on the one hand, or disdain and angst, on the other.

It is obvious that the "textual constructions" of poverty not only differed between two countries such as the Netherlands and France at a specific historical juncture; the rhetorical meaning of poverty had experienced a dramatic change over time as well. In the medieval imagination poverty had often been envisioned as a blessed state. Influenced, in part, by Franciscan traditions, observers in medieval society frequently portrayed destitution as a human stance toward the world that rejected material possessions in order to embrace the holiness of poverty. In the course of the early modern period, poverty began to acquire novel and shifting meanings, and was more often represented as a manifestation of God's judgment. This perception contained implicit policy advice: if elites imagined the presence of poor people on earth as flowing from divine intervention in this world, it was not, then, the proper role of men to alter God's will.

If the poor of the ancien régime seemed unworthy of God's benevolence, it was equally doubtful they deserved the generosity of their fellow citizens. But the eighteenth century also produced a greater confidence in the ability of "enlightened" rulers to change the substantive social world; toward the nineteenth century a concern with social reform yielded the conviction that civil society could be altered and improved through assertive political action. Thus, in the period after 1815 a positive commitment to try, at least, to alleviate the distress of the poor emerged alongside the reinvented early modern focus on social control and incarceration—what Sydney and Beatrice Webb called ''relief of the poor within the framework of repression.''[16] How these various discourses and definitions either overlapped or competed with each other in two distinct political environments is one of the underlying themes of this study.

It was undoubtedly true that when private or public support was not forthcoming, the poor tried to secure means of survival in any way possible, despite the many risks of arrest, subjugation, or confinement. All impoverished human beings, regardless of historical place or time, need sustenance and they consciously search for clothing and shelter. If certain people were too poor to afford something that was not legally prohibited, such as a simple loaf of bread, Isaiah Berlin has noted in his classic essay on positive and negative conceptions of liberty, they were as ''little free to have [a loaf of bread] as they would be if it were forbidden by law''; this, he argued, constituted a violation of people's negative freedom.[17] The acerbic Louis Blanc, a member of the nineteenth-century French chorus of utopian socialists, made a similar point: the freedom of movement, he intoned, is an absolutely useless right to those who can't walk because they were born as paralytics![18]

Wretched poverty, though, also represents an infraction of people's positive liberty. Being destitute and hungry limits human beings' free agency and coerces them into occupying a vulnerable position, into venturing into dangerous territory, or into disobeying the law.[19] As a result, impoverished citizens in both countries, in cities and in the countryside, resorted to a mind-boggling array of ''economies of makeshift'': they panhandled, stole, pillaged, or migrated in search of work in other cities or different countries. Many poor women, meanwhile, if no other options were available, abandoned their children or sold their bodies as commodities in the sexual marketplace.

As the French utopian socialist Victor Considérant declared with great urgency in 1848: poverty in our society, today, ''hatches out with its impure breath'' a veritable battalion of ''rascals, harlots, vagabonds, beggars, convicts, pickpockets, and bandits.'' Considérant then raised a predictable question: did fate or heredity predestine all of them to become such people? Were they ''born as bandits?'' Were they ''pickpockets, beggars, and harlots by inheritance or by necessity''?[20] His ideological fellow traveler Louis Blanc articulated a similar idea. In the annals of prostitution, privation and human misery "figured as the principal and primary cause of debauchery." Libertinage, Blanc exclaimed, functioned as a means of drowning the sense of physical suffering and emotional pain; "penury engenders concubinage, and concubinage [fosters] infanticide."[21]

Clearly, the often unjust structural realities of daily life matter. Throughout history almost all nations, even those within the theoretically classless society of the now crumbled Soviet Union, have always confronted differences between citizens who are rich and those who are poor, or in more careful language, people who are relatively better or worse off. As a result, the question of how societies have treated their less fortunate citizens over time is a topic of perpetual significance in social and economic history.[22]

On the one hand, the economic and social conditions of any nation determined, to a great extent, who was indigent and how poor he or she may have been. Employment opportunities, wage rates, and the price of food, rents, and fuel had an indelible impact on the extent of suffering, as did environmental factors such as climate or the incidence of epidemics. On the other hand, individual biography and blind fate or simply dumb luck also determined the level of poverty people experienced; illness, the particular phase in the life cycle, and illiteracy each played its part, too.[23] The particular ways in which rich citizens, through taxes or private donations, helped to alleviate the plight of their poverty-stricken fellow citizens, influenced not only the degree of poverty but also the economic and social structure of their society, at least on the margin. Besides, the chronological "age" of well-entrenched patterns of poor relief—in other words, how long ago they had been woven into the social fabric—mattered, too.[24] Accordingly, it is possible to identify at least four significant if separate issues that infused the discourses about poverty and poor relief in both countries. Even if these questions constituted points of serious disagreement, some or all of them—which David Ellwood has labeled the "Helping Conundrums," since they are problems admitting to no satisfactory solution—inflected the rhetoric of intellectuals and political officials in both the Netherlands and France.[25]

The first issue was that of equalization, or the idea that poor relief represented a means of mutual insurance or an institutional shield that mediated between individual and collective misfortune. Examples of collective bad luck in nineteenth-century Europe abounded. They constituted such phenomena as a dismal harvest in a particular year in a specific region of a nation due to flood or drought. Another example was a disruption of the market environment or a downturn in the commercial fortunes of a specific sector of society as a result of international economic pressures or war and foreign occupation. Individual adversity might include the unlucky circumstances which widows and orphans faced upon the death of their spouses or parents. People born with physical handicaps confronted desperately unfortunate circumstances through no fault of their own. In these instances, poor relief, as part of an implicit mutual insurance arrangement concluded before the fateful event, channeled resources from one sector or region of society to another, or from one group of relatively affluent citizens to another less well-endowed segment of the population. Inherent in this arrangement was the understanding that at some later stage economically comfortable members of society might themselves become the unlucky ones, and the roles of benefactor and pauper would then be reversed. In this rhetorical construction, all forms of poor relief contain an element of mutual insurance.

A second issue that imbued many proposed remedies to poverty and inequality was a recognition that giving charity entailed certain social liabilities or moral hazards. Both policymakers and intellectuals in the nineteenth century believed that poor relief could function as a disincentive to industriousness and law-abiding, ethical behavior.[26] Most societies, whether in the past or in our contemporary world, prefer not to nurture impoverished people whose suffering stems from purely personal mistakes or from laziness and character flaws. Accordingly, in nineteenth-century Holland and France public officials and private donors tried to separate the wheat from the chaff and wished to assist only those who were poor and hungry through no fault of their own—*pauvres honteux* or, as the Dutch called them, the *fatsoenlijke armen*: the appropriately shamefaced, morally respectable, and above all, deserving poor. Nineteenth-century observers feared that unless poor relief was confined only to the unlucky, it would encourage nothing but sloth, drunkenness, and depravity in its recipients and would produce a parasitic reliance on the charity of others.

This concern was hardly unique to the Netherlands and France in the post-French Revolutionary era. In the mid-eighteenth century, for example, Montesquieu wrote in Book Six of his *De l'esprit des lois* that he had noticed that when a town maintained a *hôpital général*, the carefree poor ignored the need to plan for the future with the nonchalant words ''*j'irai à l'hospice*.''[27] Such apprehensions have been the cornerstone of social welfare policies from Augustus's Rome to mayor Rudolph Giuliani's New York City or ''Thatcherite'' politicians in contemporary Europe, who have always posed the same question: how can we separate the truly unlucky person from swindlers, welfare cheats, and free riders?

A third element informing the discourses about poor relief was the notion of pacification, or the perception of poor relief as a means of suppressing petty thievery, avoiding insurrection, or preventing social disorder. The working class incarnated a potential danger to both the social elites or even very modest but self-supporting folks, because impoverished workers could band together and use their collective strength to commandeer the possessions, threaten the profits, and sabotage the psychological equanimity of society's wealthier citizens. In this construction, charity functioned as a manipulative hand, disguised as an empathetic gesture which the rich extended to the poor. Or, in more cynical language, it fostered a representation of poor relief as a few crumbs thrown to needy workers to ensure that their discontent did not spill over into an open revolt against the status quo.

With a richer gastronomical imagination, Karl Marx crafted a comparable trope in his description of Napoleon III, who, as a true demagogue and political opportunist, understood better than most that human beings might be seduced into submission because they could not withstand "certain higher powers." First and foremost among these irresistible forces, Marx wrote, were "cigars and champagne, cold poultry and garlic sausage."[28] Viewed in this mode, poor relief could be approached as a cost-effective form of social blackmail and as a preferred alternative to an expensive military campaign or police effort necessary to suppress rebellions or revolutions.[29] Later in the nineteenth century, Chancellor Otto von Bismarck invoked the same logic when he introduced rudimentary forms of health care, accident insurance, and old age pensions in Imperial Germany. These "defensive" welfare measures could function as diversionary tactics, Bismarck hoped, because they might either offset or negate the popular appeal of the German Socialist Party.[30]

A fourth consideration could be labelled the profitability principle, which entailed a perception of poor relief as a way to assure that a sufficient number of able-bodied workers could produce a steady economic output. A concern with the profitability of charitable practices focused on the need to cultivate the health and vigor of workers in order to maximize profits and guarantee the income of the well-to-do. Poor relief, especially temporary assistance, often served the interests of the rich even when they had no specific reason to fear social chaos or political rebellion. Most elites understood that widespread mortality among workers might eventually cause wages to rise and thus reduce profits.

They also grasped that undernourished and frail children would most likely grow into adults who were unproductive workers and feeble soldiers. Similarly, landlords knew that peasants lacking physical fitness and stamina might be unable to pay rent. In other words, elites understood the benefits of supporting destitute workers in extreme need, even if some prosperous citizens may have tried to avoid bearing the financial burden of assisting the poor out of fear of creating an indolent work force.

The fear of pouring charitable resources down the drain was another aspect of the anxiety about profitability: naive philanthropists or misguided public officials might sustain worthless, if sly, people who were beyond the pale as potential workers. Thus, in considering the profitability principle, a free rider problem arose once again, not only among the beneficiaries of charity but also among benefactors. Some rich but devious citizens could easily manipulate others into shouldering the financial burden of charity while getting off scot free themselves. To avoid an unequal distribution of the charitable obligations toward fellow citizens who were impoverished, state authorities, at the local and national level, often wished to "collectivize" poor relief by imposing taxes or poor rates rather than relying on private charity or voluntary donations. While charity was a quintessential form of altruistic behavior, it was also an indivisible good that bestowed free benefits even upon those who did not personally contribute: it was "a form of action that profited not only the receivers, but also the collectivity of possessors as a whole."[31] Thus, public officials' desire to convert poor relief into a universal responsibility, borne across the board by citizens substantial enough to pay taxes, was a rhetorical theme that reverberated throughout the nineteenth century, only to be officially acknowledged in the twentieth century.[32]

All of these topics surfaced in the written oratory of policymakers in both the Netherlands and France, albeit in different ways. To unravel these issues while trying to link them to elites' depictions of "actual" structures of poverty and charity, however, is not without pitfalls. But higher levels of generalization and comparative history can illuminate actual processes of social change with greater analytical clarity, even if some of the empirical richness and vivid details must be sacrificed. A search for critically different variables in otherwise similar situations can account for disparate outcomes—an approach John Stuart Mill classified as the "method of difference."[33] By bringing together a range of social phenomena under some common rubric, we can identify relationships that would otherwise remain obscure. Through an analysis of the attempted resolutions of parallel social problems in two different cultural contexts, we can learn a lot about the particular nature of those cultural environments and their role in shaping outcomes.

Hence, a dissection of the rhetorical strategies with regard to poverty and the realities of poor relief in the nineteenth-century Netherlands and France can reveal both difference and similarity. Ideally it will also provide some intellectual depth to popular, if often complicated, notions of national identity or the ''relative generosity of spirit,'' since policy outcomes do not correspond neatly to definitions of ''national character''—a somewhat archaic notion that is both problematic and ambiguous.[34]

To comprehend the differences between the French and the Dutch treatment of poverty, though, we must also appreciate the basis for comparing the two nations. Geographically and demographically, the two countries revealed striking differences. Nineteenth-century France ranked as one of the largest nations on the European continent, with a population of over 30 million in 1821. The Netherlands constituted one of the smallest, with inhabitants totaling a mere 2.6 million during the same decade.[35] France continued to have a relatively strong nobility whose economic base depended on land ownership and agriculture, whereas the upper stratum of Dutch society consisted of a wealthy commercial bourgeoisie.[36] In 1851, city dwellers in France still comprised a small minority; the overwhelming majority of French citizens subsisted in small towns and rural villages scattered throughout the countryside. Miserable peasants' quiet existence of suffering and hardship was often hidden from the scrutiny of bureaucrats in Paris. In Holland, which was one of the most densely urban societies of Western Europe, the largest proportion of impoverished citizens lived in cities, and had done so since the early modern era.[37]

Beginning in the seventeenth century the French political system had become increasingly centralized. The political culture of the ancien régime had cultivated both the idea and the reality of undivided sovereignty—of power and decision-making authority firmly ensconced in Versailles or, after 1789, in Paris. The Revolution and Napoleon, and since 1815, the Restoration and the July Monarchy, all reinforced a pattern of concentrating executive power in Paris as the political fulcrum of the nation. Louis Blanc derided this concentric pattern of confining real power only to one pivotal entity as the creation of a ''government of clerks'' which enforced ''a barren tyranny of [bureaucratic] red tape.''[38] Even though Blanc fortuitously ignored the fact that his own utopian socialist solutions also idealized a strong central state that would carefully plan the economy and distribute profits equitably among all citizens, he identified a process that was solidified further as the nineteenth century came to a close.

While countries with a different political culture, such as the Netherlands or England, fostered a respect for liberty through a gradual reconfiguration of corporate privileges, the French Revolution had made a universal "equality of rights" its reigning passion. Equality became the rationale for encroaching upon the inherited privileges that had characterized the estate society of the ancien régime. A universal *égalité* of rights and individual *liberté* would vouch for every citizen's ability, regardless of birth or social status, to mold his (not her) own destiny. This did not always entail an embrace of a superimposed de facto equality, however, because it would not allow "superior minds" to rise to the top. Instead, it implied the exaltation of "acquired distinctions" above inherited ones.[39]

The French infatuation with *égalité* and a form of political sovereignty that was indivisible and undiluted proved to be a fertile soil for seeds that contained the potential to propagate two diametrically opposed outcomes. Equality, after all, could either nurture the "plebiscitarian caesarism" of a Bonapartist variety or sprout the kind of egalitarian radicalism that ran amok during the Terror or the Commune. *Liberté*, meanwhile, assumed that all human beings were born with equal endowments, in terms of physical health or intelligence. Hence, French observers frequently attributed the glaring inequalities of existence that persisted in French society once Napoleon had finally been banished to faraway St. Helena to the moral failure and voluntary laziness of the poor.

The essence of Dutch political culture, in contrast, resided in the local community. Notions of sovereignty were layered, sequential, and fragmented, but never concentrated in one institution or locale at the center of the nation. The Kingdom of the Netherlands in the nineteenth century was compelled to acknowledge many of the sacrosanct municipal privileges and provincial freedoms associated with the early modern Dutch Republic.[40] Government administrators in The Hague were guided "from below" on many matters, and historically power ascended upward from independent towns to provincial estates and, ultimately, to the central state.[41] In addition, a tradition of cooperation with the private sector and church organizations was deeply entrenched in Dutch definitions of the appropriate role of the central state.

The Netherlands was different, too, in its religious structure. The French nation was nearly unified in its Catholicism, whereas the Dutch population was more or less evenly divided between Protestants and Catholics. Between 1815 and 1859, members of the Dutch Reformed Church comprised approximately 55 percent of the total population.[42] Members of the Dutch Reformed Church dominated the nation, both politically and culturally, and the cacophony of imperious voices of Dutch Reformed ministers or Protestant politicians eclipsed either Catholic or other dissenting ones, even if the central state did not become a monolithic Protestant entity.

The architect of the innovative and ''modern'' Dutch Constitution of 1848, the liberal Johan Rudolf Thorbecke, noted in 1844 that the power of the central state should merely be a supplement to private incentives, or an auxiliary to political initiative at the municipal or provincial level.[43] In short, Holland was a nation in which private interests and stubbornly independent municipalities and Dutch Reformed Church congregations overshadowed the independent agency of the central state in The Hague—where in times of peace the state presumably ''disaggregated'' and only an anemic bureaucracy functioned at the national level.[44] Political scientists have tended to describe the nineteenth-century Dutch state as a relatively ''weak'' one, not unlike its counterpart in England. But perhaps the ability of the government in The Hague to collaborate with both provincial and local authorities, with both religious charities (*diaconiëen*) and private organizations, constitutes evidence, too, of an ingenious capacity to orchestrate alliances between competing sources of political power in order to maintain the nation's equilibrium.[45]

Given these discrepancies, how can we engage in a successful comparison? It would be easy to argue that these two nineteenth-century nations represented the proverbial apples and oranges—entities that revealed such fundamental contrasts that comparing them is an impossible and, above all, a futile exercise. France, with its regional diversity in levels of literacy and political incorporation into the nation, its mostly rural population and agricultural economy, and its gigantic geographical dimensions, should not be compared with little Holland which was compact, commercially oriented, politically integrated with relatively high literacy rates, and intensely urbanized since the early modern period.

But an opposite argument is just as plausible. Aside from differences in size and patterns of administration, one could pose that France and the Netherlands, with their close proximity within the European metropole and their shared history of contention for political and economic power in the early modern period, were in fact quite similar. France and the Netherlands both displayed a pattern of seemingly slow economic growth in the nineteenth century, especially when compared with the sensational industrial developments across the Channel that were in the process of redesigning the English economic landscape. The public sector in both nations, at the national as well as the local level, regarded indigence as a serious problem and engaged in interminable debates about the best way to remedy the plight of the poor. Besides, a tradition of religious charity was deeply entrenched in both countries. Intellectuals and policymakers in the two countries were occasionally in touch with one another—Dutchmen, for instance, were familiar with the flurry of books on *paupérisme* written in French whereas many French *philanthropes* investigated and applauded Dutch social and economic experiments such as the agricultural colonies of the *Maatschappij van Weldadigheid* (Benevolent Society)—which nurtured a cross-fertilization of both ideas and policy proposals.

In sum, cross-national comparison is critical for the very reason that such contradictory arguments have been made about France and Holland as appropriate units of comparison. An exploration of the relative influence of such factors as the tendency to incarcerate the poor, the impact of political cultures that favored either centralization or pluralism, or the public worries about the evils of industrial capitalism can yield interesting insights. A comparison of the different constructions of historical memory and contrasting narratives about the ''true'' nature of Dutch or French society is enlightening, too. Moreover, an analysis of the role of unified Catholicism in France versus the bifurcated religious structure of the Netherlands, or the differential popularity of liberal economic ideas allows each country to shed light on the history of the other.

Notes

1. Alphonse Esquiros, *Nederland en het leven in Nederland*, (Amsterdam: Gebroeders Binger, 1851), p. 204, also published as *La Néerlande et la vie hollandaise* (Paris: Michel Lévy Frères, 1956).

2. Alphonse de Lamartine, in a speech to the Chamber of Deputies, May 10, 1838, cited by Shepard Clough, *France: A History of National Economics, 1789–1939* (New York: Scribner's, 1939), p. 147. See also Yann Fauchois, ''Centralization,'' in François Furet and Mona Ozouf, eds., *A Critical Dictionary of the French Revolution*, (Cambridge: Harvard University Press, 1989), p. 636.

3. Johan Rudolf Thorbecke, ''Over het hedendaagsche staatsburgerschap,''

1844, in C.H.E. de Wit, *Thorbecke en de wording van de Nederlandse natie. Thorbecke historische schetsen* (Nijmegen: SUN, 1980), Sunschrift 153, p. 270. For an interesting discussion of the Dutch ''imagined community,'' see Annemarie Galema, Barbara Henkes, and Henk te Velde, eds., *Images of the Nation: Different Meanings of Dutchness, 1870–1940*, Amsterdam studies on cultural identity, No. 2 (Amsterdam/Atlanta: Rodopi, 1993).

4. Gertrude Himmelfarb, *Poverty and Compassion. The Moral Imagination of the Late Victorians* (New York: Alfred A. Knopf, 1991), p. 19.

5. Olwen Hufton, *The Poor of Eighteenth-Century France* (Oxford: Clarendon Press of Oxford University Press, 1976).

6. Louis Chevalier, *Laboring Classes and Dangerous Classes in Paris during the First Half of the Nineteenth Century* (1958; repr. Princeton: Princeton University Press, 1973), p. 111.

7. Michael Ignatieff, ''State, Civil Society, and Total Institutions: A Critique of Recent Social Histories of Punishment,'' in Stanley Cohen and Andrew Scull, eds., *Social Control and the State: Historical and Comparative Essays* (Oxford: Basil Blackwell, 1983), p. 86. Ali de Regt, in *Arbeidersgezinnen en beschavingsarbeid. Ontwikkelingen in Nederland, 1870–1940* (Amsterdam: Boom/Meppel, 1984), also criticizes social control theorists for overemphasizing the desire for domination on the part of social welfare agents and for presuming that their goals are inherently in opposition to the interests of the poor and the working class. She notes further that theories of social control ''pay too little attention to the distinction between strategies of control and the actual effects of their implementation'' (p. 244). For an insightful discussion of some of the strengths and weaknesses of social control arguments, see Katherine A. Lynch, *Family, Class, and Ideology in Early Industrial France* (Madison: University of Wisconsin Press, 1988), pp. 21–26.

8. Benedict Anderson, *Imagined Communities. Reflections on the Origin and Spread of Nationalism*, 2nd ed. (London/New York: Verso, 1991), especially the new chapter on ''Memory and Forgetting'' and the new Epilogue, ''The Biography of Nations,'' pp. 187–206.

9. Radboud Engbersen and Thijs Jansen, *Armoede in de maatschappelijke verbeelding, 1945–1990. Een retorische studie* (Leiden/Antwerpen: Stenfert Kroese, 1991), pp. 12–18.

10. Bryan S.R. Green, *Knowing the Poor. A Case-Study in Textual Reality Construction* (London: Routledge & Kegan Paul, 1983), especially the Introduction and Chapter 1, pp. 1–53.

11. Geoffrey Bennington, *Lyotard. Writing the Event* (New York: Columbia University Press, 1988), p. 90.

12. Terry Eagleton, *Literary Theory* (Oxford: Basil Blackwell, 1983), p. 201.

13. Roland Barthes, ''The Discourse of History,'' in Derek Attridge, Geoffrey Bennington, and Robert Young, eds., *Post-Structuralism and the Question of History* (Cambridge/New York: Cambridge University Press, 1987), p. 3.

14. James C. Scott, *Domination and the Arts of Resistance. Hidden Transcripts* (New Haven: Yale University Press, 1990), p. 45.

15. The term ''language animals'' is Collingwood's; see Keith Jenkins, *Re-Thinking History?* (London: Routledge, 1991), pp. 43–44.

16. Sydney and Beatrice Webb, *The Problems of Modern Industry* (New York: Longman & Green, 1889), p. 157.

17. Isaiah Berlin, *Four Essays on Liberty* (Oxford: Oxford University Press, 1969), p. 92.

18. Quoted by Ozouf, ''Fraternity,'' in Furet and Ozouf, eds., *A Critical Dictionary of the French Revolution*, p. 701.

19. Amartya Sen, ''Individual Freedom as a Social Commitment,'' *New York Review of Books*, 37, No. 10 (June 1990), p. 50.

20. Victor Considérant, *Destinée sociale* (Paris: 1848), quoted by Louis Chevalier, *Laboring Classes and Dangerous Classes*, p. 458.

21. Louis Blanc, *The History of Ten Years, 1830–1840*, 2 vols. (1845; repr. Philadelphia: Augustus M. Kelley, 1969), 1, p. 546.

22. Recent scholarship on the history and origins of the welfare state in Europe and the United States includes Stein Ringen, *The Possibility of Politics: A Study in the Political Economy of the Welfare State* (Oxford: Clarendon Press of Oxford University Press, 1987); Abram de Swaan, *In Care of the State: Health Care, Education, and Welfare in Europe and the USA in the Modern Era* (Oxford: Polity Press/Basil Blackwell, 1988); Francis G. Castles, ed., *The Comparative History of Public Policy* (New York: Oxford University Press, 1989); Amy Gutman, ed., *Democracy and the Welfare State* (Princeton: Princeton University Press, 1988); Steve Fraser and Gary Gerstle, eds., *The Rise and Fall of the New Deal Order* (Princeton: Princeton University Press, 1989); and Margaret Weir, Ann Shola Orloff, and Theda Skocpol, eds., *The Politics of Social Policy in the United States* (Princeton: Princeton University Press, 1988).

23. L. Frank van Loo, *Armelui. Armoede en bedeling te Alkmaar, 1850–1914* (Bergen, N-H: Octavo, 1986), p. 13; see also Marco H.D. van Leeuwen, ''Surviving with a little help: the importance of charity to the poor of Amsterdam 1800–1850, in a comparative perspective,'' *Social History*, 18 (October 1993), pp. 319–38 and the related articles by Giovanni Gozzini, Barry Stapleton, and J.S. Craig on poverty and the life cycle in the same issue of *Social History*.

24. Harold L. Wilensky, in *The Welfare State and Equality. Structural and Ideological Roots of Public Expenditures* (Berkeley: University of California Press, 1975), has argued that the ''age of a social security system'' is the most significant variable in determining welfare spending in the modern era (pp. 9, 46–49).

25. David T. Ellwood, *Poor Support. Poverty in the American Family* (New York: Basic Books, 1990), pp. 14–44.

26. For an analysis of the issue of moral hazard, see Mary MacKinnon, *Moral Hazard and the Poor Law* (Oxford University, Dissertation, 1983), and *idem.*, ''The Use and Misuse of Poor Law Statistics: 1857–1912,'' *Historical Methods*, 21, No. 1 (Winter 1988), pp. 5–19; see also Norman McCord, ''Poor

Law and Philanthropy,'' in Derek Frazer, ed., *The New Poor Law in the Nineteenth Century* (London: Macmillan, 1976), pp. 87–110.

27. Olwen H. Hufton, *Women & the Limits of Citizenship in the French Revolution* (Buffalo: University of Toronto Press, 1991), pp. 52–3.

28. C.P. Dutt, ed., Karl Marx, *The Eighteenth Brumaire of Louis Bonaparte* (New York: International Publishers, 1972), p. 77.

29. Seth Koven and Sonya Michel, ''Womanly Duties: Maternalist Politics and the Origins of Welfare States in France, Germany, Great Britain, and the United States, 1880–1920,'' *American Historical Review*, 95, No. 4 (October 1990). Compare this position with neo-Marxist analyses of the welfare state which argue that poor relief is a ''kind of bribe intended to co-opt the legitimate conflictual political aspirations of the working class'' (p. 1081).

30. For recent statements, see George Steinmetz, *Regulating the Social. The Welfare State and Local Politics in Imperial Germany* (Princeton: Princeton University Press, 1993), and Christoph Sachsse, ''Social Mothers: The Bourgeois Women's Movement and German Welfare State Formation,'' in Seth Koven and Sonya Michel, eds., *Mothers of the New World. Maternalist Politics and the Origins of the Welfare State* (New York: Routledge, 1993), pp. 136–58.

31. De Swaan, *In Care of the State*, p. 23.

32. In some form, Marco H.D. van Leeuwen refers to all of these motifs in his recent *Bijstand in Amsterdam, ca. 1800–1850. Armenzorg als beheersingsen overlevingsstrategie* (Zwolle: Waanders, 1992), pp. 16–26, 119–35.

33. John Stuart Mill, ''Two Methods of Comparison,'' excerpt from *A System of Logic* (London: Longman & Green, 1888), in Amatai Etzioni and Frederic L. Du Bow, eds., *Comparative Perspectives: Theories and Methods* (Boston: Little Brown, 1970), p. 206. For a general analysis of the method and logic of comparative research, see Sylvia Thrupp, ''The Role of Comparison in the Development of Economic History,'' *Journal of Economic History*, 17, No. 1 (1957), pp. 554–70; William H. Sewell Jr., ''Marc Bloch and the Logic of Comparative History,'' *History and Theory*, 6, No. 2 (1967), pp. 208–18; Theda Skocpol and Margaret Summers, ''Uses of Comparative History in Macrosocial Inquiry,'' *Comparative Studies in Society and History*, 22 (1980), pp. 174–97; John R. Hall, ''Where History and Sociology Meet: Forms of Discourse and Sociohistorical Inquiry,'' *Sociological Theory*, 10, No. 2 (Fall 1992), pp. 164–93; and Andrew J. Nathan, ''Is Chinese Culture Distinctive?—A Review Article,'' *Journal of Asian Studies*, 52, No. 4 (1993), pp. 923–36.

34. James T. Kloppenberg, ''Who's Afraid of the Welfare State?'' *Reviews in American History*, No. 18 (1990), p. 396.

35. The specific figure of 2.6 million is for 1829. See Brian R. Mitchell, *European Historical Statistics 1750–1970* (New York: Columbia University Press, 1978), pp. 4–6.

36. Regarding the economic proclivities of the French nobility, see David H. Pinkney, *The Decisive Years in France, 1840–1847* (Princeton: Princeton University Press, 1986), p. 19. For a general exposition, see David Higgs, *No-*

bles in Nineteenth-Century France. The Practice of Inegalitarianism (Baltimore: Johns Hopkins University Press, 1989). I.J. Brugmans, *Paardenkracht en mensenmacht. Sociaal economische geschiedenis van Nederland, 1795–1940* (The Hague: Martinus Nijhoff, 1976), pp. 190–98, discusses the role of the Dutch middle class.

37. Around the year 1500, already 44 percent of the Dutch population lived in towns of more than 2,500 residents; by the period 1650–1680 this proportion had grown to 60 percent, only to decline to about 40 percent in 1800, thus revealing a process of moderate ''deurbanization'' that continued during the first half of the nineteenth century. See A.M. van der Woude, *Nederland over de schouder gekeken* (Utrecht: HES, 1986), p. 26. In 1800, about 20 percent of the total French population lived in towns of more than 2,000 residents, a figure that had grown to 25 percent in 1851; see William H. Sewell Jr., *Work and Revolution in France. The Language of Labor from the Old Regime to 1848* (Cambridge/New York: Cambridge University Press, 1983), p. 150.

38. Louis Blanc, *The History of Ten Years*, 2, pp. 390–91. For an elaboration, see Clive H. Church, *Revolution and Red Tape: The French Ministerial Bureaucracy, 1770–1850* (Oxford: Clarendon Press of Oxford University Press, 1981); and Michel Crozier, ''French Bureaucracy as a Cultural Phenomenon,'' in Mattei Dogan and Richard Rose, eds., *European Politics* (Boston: Beacon Press, 1971), pp. 489–500.

39. Ozouf, ''Equality'' and ''Liberty,'' in Furet and Ozouf, eds., *A Critical Dictionary*, pp. 669–83, 617–27. For a lucid analysis of French political culture and the recent historiography of the French Revolution, see Edward Berenson, ''The Social Interpretation of the French Revolution,'' *Contention. Debates in Society, Culture, and Science*, 3, No. 2 (Winter 1994), pp. 55–81.

40. For important insights into the weakness of the central state in the seventeenth-century Dutch Republic, see Marjolein 't Hart, ''Staatsvorming, sociale relaties en oorlogsfinanciering in de Nederlandse Republiek,'' *Tijdschrift voor Sociale Geschiedenis*, 16, No. 1 (1990), pp. 61–85. For a classic statement about ''consociational democracy,'' see Hans Daalder, ''Building Consociational Nations,'' in S. N. Eisenstadt and Stein Rokkan, eds., *Building States and Nations*, 2 vols. (Beverly Hills, California: Sage Publications, 1973), 2, pp. 14–31, and *idem.*, ''Moderne politieke wetenschap en het nut van de geschiedenis,'' *Bijdragen en Mededelingen betreffende de Geschiedenis der Nederlanden*, 90 (1975). See also Arend Lijphart, *The Politics of Accommodation: Pluralism and Democracy in the Netherlands* (Berkeley: University of California Press, 1968); Siep Stuurman, *Verzuiling, kapitalisme en patriarchaat. Aspecten van de ontwikkeling van de moderne staat in Nederland* (Nijmegen: SUN, 1983); Auke van der Woud, *Het lege land. De ruimtelijke ordening van Nederland, 1798–1848* (Amsterdam: Meulenhoff, 1987); and Henk te Velde, *Gemeenschapszin en plichtsbesef. Liberalisme en nationalisme in Nederland, 1870–1918* (The Hague: SDU, 1992).

41. Simon Schama, ''Municipal Government and the Burden of the Poor in

South Holland during the Napoleonic Wars,'' in *Britain and the Netherlands*, No. 6, A.C. Duke and C.A. Tamse, eds., *War and Society* (The Hague: Martinus Nijhoff, 1976), p. 133. See also Karel Davids, Jan Lucassen, and Jan Luiten van Zanden, *Nederlandse geschiedenis als afwijking van het algemeen menselijk patroon* (Amsterdam: Internationaal Instituut voor Sociale Geschiedenis, 1988).

42. Michael Wintle, *Pillars of Piety. Religion in the Netherlands in the Nineteenth Century, 1813–1901* (Hull: Hull University Press, 1987), p. 3.

43. Thorbecke, ''Over het hedendaagse staatsburgerschap'' (1844), p. 270.

44. Charles Tilly, ''History, Sociology, and Dutch Collective Action,'' *Tijdschrift voor Sociale Geschiedenis*, 15, No. 2 (1989), p. 151.

45. For a recent theoretical rethinking of the categories ''weak'' and ''strong,'' see Koven and Michel, ''Introduction: Mother Worlds,'' pp. 25–29, and Pat Thane, ''Women in the British Labour Party and the Construction of Social Welfare, 1906–1939,'' in Koven and Michel, eds., *Mothers of the New World*, pp. 343–77.

CHAPTER TWO

Rhetorical Practices and Political Cultures: Situating the Poor in the "Modern," Post-Revolutionary World

> Several tumultuous movements broke out in the marketplace of Saint-Laurent. Fortunately, the National Guard detachment from Macon had placed itself at the disposal of the mayor of Saint-Laurent, and thus the riot could be easily suppressed. It was notable that the participants in this movement were only women and children of the lowest possible classes. In the meantime, we have attempted to discover where the instigators behind these disorders were, who, under the pretext of being outraged about inflated grain prices, sought to arouse the least enlightened classes of the population only to express their hatred toward the existing order of society.[1]
>
> —Prefect of Police in the Department of Ain to the Minister of the Interior, September 15, 1830

> With the expansion of wealth, prosperity, and civility in a society, the social distinctions between those who benefit and those who suffer as a result of economic development become more palpable. In previous centuries, everyone was equally rich, or rather, equally poor. As times went on, a few rich people were capable of enjoying the fruits of the earth while the majority of the population was still caught in the chains of poverty. This group of poor people tends to acquire visibility as the gap between rich and poor grows wider and, in this way, a heterogeneous sector of society receives a single descriptive name: paupers. The more attention the poor receive, the more vivid the contrast between rich and poor becomes, and when public compassion and generosity expand, the greater the worries about the consequences of the stark distinctions between rich and poor will be.[2]
>
> —Simon Vissering, "Politische vertooghen," 1847

Despite the undeniable differences in historical legacy, economic structure, political style, and above all, geographic size, the Netherlands and France had a distinct problem in common during the decades following the French Revolution: a level of poverty that seemed more deep-seated and oppressive than it had ever been before. In both countries, public agencies and private charities tried to alleviate the distress of poverty-stricken people through a variety of social welfare measures intended to aid the sick, sustain the elderly and the disabled, or support temporarily unemployed workers.

The rhetoric about poverty and charity, whether conducted in Dutch or French, touched upon all the pressing issues that confronted the modern world in the aftermath of the French Revolution. An anguished public debate about the Social Question in both countries tried to steer a middle passage between the legitimate human suffering of the "deserving poor" and a genuine fear of the revolutionary propensity of the working class. While acknowledging the traditional Christian injunction to be charitable toward fellow citizens who were less fortunate because "the meek shall inherit the earth," public officials negotiated, as best they could, their compassion for the poor vis-à-vis the state's need to monitor and contain them—what the French called the enclosure of the poor (*l'enfermement des pauvres*).

As the letter from the Prefect of Police in the department of Ain to the Minister of the Interior indicated, being poor could serve merely as a pretext for revolting against the existing political order. In this particular incident, though, humble women and children of the most downtrodden classes of French society had presumably been incited to riot by shady characters who deluded gullible poor people for their own subversive political purposes. The Prefect of Police immediately transcribed the suffering of hungry women and children, who were outraged about the high price of grain in the local marketplace, into an episode that was essentially political in nature and thus might threaten the sovereignty of the state.

In contrast, Simon Vissering provided a profoundly different reading. To Vissering, who was a liberal economist, poverty under its ominous new designation, pauperism, was a creation of modern industrial society. He raised the issue of public perception and the labeling of social groups; he noted that when societies became preoccupied with the question of poverty, the allegedly "objective" research of contemporaries caused both the material conditions and the moral temperament of the poor to lapse in the popular imagination.

In a certain way Vissering identified what was called the Hawthorne effect in the sociological literature of the 1950s. The tendentious facts uncovered by the first generation of positivist social scientists, Vissering argued, who collected data after visiting working-class slums in Paris, Lille, Amsterdam, or Middelburg, helped to invent a new meaning of poverty.[3] ''Pauperism distinguishes itself from poverty only insofar as human suffering is viewed in connection with the afflictions and injustices of society at large,'' three Dutch authors wrote in 1852, thereby constructing their uniquely Dutch vision of the relative dimensions implicit in the new concept of pauperism.[4]

Many intellectuals and policymakers in nineteenth-century France and the Netherlands became increasingly aware of the inequality of income and material existence; it seemed as if the needs of the indigent population imposed pressures on public resources neither society had faced in the past. Yet other observers also sensed, with either paralyzing fear or vague discomfort—or, in the case of people on the political left, with excited anticipation—that such social and material injustices were more prominent and noticeable in daily life during the decades after 1815 than ever before.

Some recurrent questions troubled most people who thought and wrote about the Social Question, regardless of their ideological stance: did the unprecedented visibility of poverty during the first half of the nineteenth century signify a radical departure from the situation prior to the Revolution? Did the material suffering they witnessed in the post-Napoleonic era represent a genuine increase in the absolute number of poor citizens? Or were the concentration of a growing number of people in urban centers and changes in the social and economic organization of modern society responsible for the conspicuous new problem of indigence? If so, did the perceptible growth in poverty constitute the tangible evidence of the kind of proletarian emiseration Karl Marx and other utopian socialists in France had begun to identify in the 1840s? From all these ruminations emerged a corollary question concerning the formulation of policy: How could the French and Dutch governments implement social policies that would ensure a reasonable material existence for a greater number of citizens without producing an intolerable drain on the nation's treasury—and, perhaps more importantly, without creating a ''madding crowd'' of loiterers, wastrels, and parasites?

In France a ''new and sadly energetic name'' for poverty—*paupérisme*—had entered public discourses after 1815, which, in the mind's eye of French observers, conjured up fear of chaos and disorder rather than the idea of relative deprivation.[5] In a French political lexicon, the new word *paupérisme* no longer signified a poignant human condition that invited compassion on the part of society's more fortunate members. Instead, the recurrent use of the word pauperism in the French narrative about poverty epitomized a social plague—a stealthy contagious disease in the process of undermining the health and vigor of the body politic—that manifested a quintessential characteristic of the modern nineteenth-century world.[6]

Pauperism conjured up a social universe filled with overcrowded cities dependent on factory production and inundated with unemployed and unruly workers forever threatening to overthrow the status quo. The most exaggerated estimates of the total number of paupers in the French nation—including the marginally poor—reached the excessive number of six million, while another sensationalist calculation of the size of the beggar population alone went as high as four million.[7] These inflated numbers, unrelated to any statistics compiled in more reliable sources, registered the consternation and fright of bourgeois France. A veritable, deep-seated "neurosis," Louis Chevalier has suggested, afflicted middle-class observers, who indulged in a prurient obsession with pauperized men and women and the interlocking "criminal underworld."[8]

The word pauperism stressed the "exotic" otherness of the poor who inhabited the opposite extreme of the social abyss. Poverty might be something that happened to a hard-drinking cousin or a distant uncle who was addicted to gambling, such as the many embarrassing "poor relations" populating the pages of Honoré de Balzac's *Comédie humaine*. These disgraced relatives might fall on hard times, which forced them to drop out of fashionable social circles as a result. Whether such a downward slide from genteel propriety on the part of a family's black sheep was a temporary or permanent one, it was a descent into poverty with which the average middle-class French person could empathize. But French notables could not conceive of pauperism as having anything to do with their own tasteful and straitlaced lives. The concept *paupérisme* dissociated being poor from the kind of personal misconduct or financial miscalculation that was familiar and understandable. Instead, they converted pauperism into a horror story about terrifying, alien creatures who lived beyond the horizon of bourgeois sensibilities—as if the destitute masses constituted a herd of frightening beasts who resembled humans but were, in fact, a different species that had gotten stuck at a lower level on the evolutionary scale.

Paupérisme emblematized a curious paradox in nineteenth-century French society. In the political vocabulary of policymakers in Paris in the aftermath of the French Revolution, being miserable and hungry insinuated a moral flaw or a personal failure to exercise one's rights as a fully entitled *citoyen.* The Revolution's Declaration of the Rights of Man and Citizen, after all, had bestowed upon every Frenchman, regardless of birth or social position, equality of rights and the liberty to compete as a putative equal in the political and economic marketplace. However, the Revolution's political ideals, whether *liberté*, *égalité*, or *fraternité*, proved scant consolation to indigent working men and all women—since women were formally excluded from full-fledged citizenship—forcing them to try to survive by any means possible.

The Revolution had bequeathed a dubious legacy upon the nineteenth century: the abolition of the paternalistic protection of the poor, so crucial to their survival during times of dearth prior to 1789, was presumably offset by the greater economic and political freedoms granted to all men as individual citizens. But even if the French poor had never received much from the voluntary poor relief of the ancien régime, in the nineteenth century they encountered a closure of soup kitchens, confronted the state's attempt to manipulate the charitable labors of the Catholic Church, and heard nothing from the central government in Paris but idealistic slogans that proved to be hollow promises.[9]

The new word *paupérisme* symbolized not only the ambivalence of French policymakers toward their miserable compatriots but revealed, too, the contradictions inherent in nineteenth-century political doctrine. Held personally responsible for their indigence due to individual moral defects, the overwhelming presence of poor people in French society nonetheless represented an unsettling social problem that required the government's watchful eye. Despite the Chapelier law's abrogation of all guilds and trade corporations—and the Revolution's eventual embrace of the government's noninterference in economic and social life and a celebration of unrestrained competition—public officials in the decades after 1815 confronted a menacing crowd of miserable workers who required political surveillance and careful control. As Eugène Buret, the caustic editor of the *Courier Français*, argued in 1839:

> The word pauperism originates in England. It is this country that deserves to give such a sad condition its name, because popular misery is greater in England than anywhere else. The word pauperism does not signify anything more than misery; it is only a more generalized state of affairs. Misery applies to individuals rather than to classes. It makes us think of private suffering, while the word pauperism embraces all the phenomena of poverty: this English word reveals to us the sense of misery as a scourge, of public misery.[10]

In sum, the term pauperism, supposedly borrowed from English usage, elicited an aura of covert danger that surrounded the material suffering of paupers on a large scale. It was a word that underscored the equivocal attitudes of bourgeois France toward the nation's hungry and poor.

In the Netherlands officials employed a different language and concocted a contrasting narrative. They often used the phrase *behoeftigen*, the needy, which acknowledged individual misery without immediately assigning moral guilt or attributing personal failure. The word *behoeftig* imbricated poor people's material wants with the collective resources of Dutch society and embedded the poor in the community as a whole. Both wealth and poverty issued from the cumulative capacity of all members of society to generate, "through their collective labor power, a surplus above and beyond the requirements of subsistence"; it was the "internal distribution of this surplus," Johannes van den Bosch insisted in 1818, that determined the relative affluence and deprivation of each individual.[11]

But some people simply could not find work, however eagerly they tried, and thus their distressing need also affected others who were gainfully employed. Yearning for work, food, and shelter, or wishing for human affection and physical warmth, intimated a direct relationship with those who were well-to-do. Even self-satisfied and comfortable Dutch burghers, after all, could either remember or, at least, fathom being cold and hungry. Prosperous people could also recall, or identify with, the experience of longing for security and a full stomach. The simple term *behoeftig* thus substantiated the "common bond" between those who suffered and those who might help; it symbolized a culturally constructed discourse through which the causal linkages between a social "evil," a needy "victim," and an empathetic "benefactor" were fashioned.[12]

Another term that surfaced routinely was the neutral Dutch word *armenwezen* or *armwezen*, meaning the condition of being poor or the existential world of poverty, which again emphasized the ecumenical experience of human suffering and linked it to both individual and collective hardship without necessarily ascribing blame. *Armenwezen* sounded a bit like *handelswezen* or *bankwezen*, which referred to trading conditions and the commercial arena or the world of banking. It tended to remove the stigma from being poor by modifying it into a more neutral social circumstance, less loaded with haunting social meanings. The word *armenwezen* seemed to suggest that poverty was a particular station in life allotted to unfortunate people through little fault of their own.

Officials and intellectuals in the Netherlands appropriated the French slogan *paupérisme* into Dutch, too, but they used it less often than their neighbors to the south. They invoked the word pauperism when they wished to emphasize the social responsibilities and financial burdens associated with the presence of enormous numbers of poor people in their midst. A lively theoretical debate ensued among liberal economists, for example, about the lack of profitability of "pauper factories" and of the many Dutch work institutes that tried to link poor relief to the inculcation of an appropriate work ethic and greater industrial skills. Dutchmen also used the term pauperism as a figure of speech denoting the degradations and inequities inherent in the modern world—not as a succinct metaphor for the fear of social revolution. But the more frequently used phrases were "needy" and the "condition of being poor," which did not inspire the same kind of anxiety about political chaos and imminent disaster as it did in France. Instead, it was a story that focused primarily on the manner in which the poor could be supported without disturbing or violating the organic unity of Dutch society and, above all, without depleting its collective resources.

The discourses about poor people in the Netherlands reflected certain myths about the social harmony of the golden age of the Dutch Republic, which lingered on in the nineteenth century. To some extent the institutionalized cultural grammar of the early modern Dutch Republic defined the ideological parameters of the debate about the social entitlements of poor people in the era following the French Revolution; it also continued to shape the ground rules regulating the business of "modern" politics. Aside from the Republic's concrete structural legacy, though, more elusive factors, such as the construction of historical memory and nostalgia, played a role, too. The manner in which nineteenth-century politicians and intellectuals recalled the solidity and valor of the early modern Republic or its "dignity and enlightened calculation"—in the words of the French *philosophe* Denis Diderot, governed as it was by "bourgeois ants" rather than "aristocratic crickets"—affected modern discourses about charity and welfare.[13]

What Johan Huizinga has called *geestelijk heimwee*—a spiritual homesickness—for the "imagined community" of the Dutch Republic, inclined the visions of social justice in an era "when De Lairesse had replaced Rembrandt" as the nation's most prominent cultural icon, or when the prevailing "poverty in the streets" seemed to reflect an even more pervasive sense of the impoverishment of Dutch society's "spiritual civilization."[14] Nostalgia—or the tendency to look upon the past through a romantic haze as a lost world of cultural resplendence or "charming simplicity"—informed the proposed solutions for the problems of inequality in the nineteenth century.[15]

In 1820, a Dutchman argued that ''under the laws of our ancestors we not only made wealth, but wealth so widely distributed that it could really be called prosperity.''[16] About thirty years later, another Dutch political economist, Jeronimo de Bosch Kemper, proclaimed that Dutch grandeur and national pride did not reside in magnificent public monuments or in an ostentatious display of power. Instead, a time-honored and well-entrenched system of poor relief was Dutch society's most outstanding accomplishment because ''well-endowed orphanages and poorhouses bring a country more glory and dignity than costly triumphal arches and mausoleums.''[17]

The implication of these statements is simple and forthright: genuine prosperity could flourish only when the affluence of some was shared with others who were less fortunate. This emblematic narrative about Dutch history, which originated in the early modern period, was deeply ingrained in the popular imagination and political culture of the nation. It informed the combative and presumably ''modern'' debates about private charity versus public welfare during the first half of the nineteenth century. It is a narrative that still serves as one of the guiding principles of the contemporary Dutch welfare state.[18]

Indeed, the social architecture of nineteenth-century Dutch society revealed few, if any, grandiose funerary statues or ostentatious monuments. Instead, the most precious architectural artifacts of the social geography of the Dutch nation existed on a less opulent, and a more intimate and private, scale. They consisted of unpretentious patrician houses with elegantly gabled rooftops or of unadorned churches, which had been stripped of their most brazen religious iconography. But it was literally and figuratively in the municipal nooks and crannies, in between those hallmark monuments of Dutch culture, where one could supposedly find the true source of Dutch ''glory and dignity'': in the many *hofjes* (old age homes) and outdoor relief agencies that dotted the landscape of Dutch towns and cities. Amid the urban hustle and bustle, in between the understated solidity of a burgher's residence and the ubiquitous presence of the House of God, one could find the physical evidence of a solidly constructed bureaucratic structure of ''efficient poor relief'' that had evolved, over time, into a mechanism of social patronage for the elite as well as a ''crucial strategy of survival for the poor,'' as Marco van Leeuwen has characterized it.[19]

Obviously one of the key factors in van Leeuwen's formulation is the notion of evolution over time. Nineteenth-century notables in the city of Amsterdam or elites in other Dutch towns did not construct an ornate and complex administrative edifice of poor relief in a hasty and slapdash fashion—or as a kind of preemptive strike—in the face of what appeared to be unprecedented levels of poverty and human suffering in the decades after the French Revolution. Nor did nineteenth-century municipal residents or church officials expand or renovate the administrative monuments of public or private charity because they were suddenly imbued with a new and agitated awareness of the blatant discrepancy between rich and poor.

The novel preoccupation with issues of social inequality has so often been represented as a quintessential nineteenth-century phenomenon, and thus, as a radically "modern" sensibility. In the Kingdom of the Netherlands, however, the preoccupation with poverty was not necessarily a typically modern fixation; rather, poor relief practices in the nineteenth century were molded and shaped by the intricate, if deeply rooted, social architecture which the Republic had bestowed upon the modern era. Although not without political conflict, the practice of soothing the plight of poverty-stricken compatriots—of helping a little here and there, as long as the recipients were regarded as worthy, of assisting fellow citizens who were permanently frail and infirm, or of aiding others who were temporarily unemployed and therefore needy only in the short run—was embedded in the cultural and institutional legacy of the seventeenth-century Republic.

As a matter of fact, the clamorous public discourses about the relative merits of private and religious charity versus secular public welfare, especially during the years between 1800 and 1854, were grounded in a rhetorical tradition that had been self-consciously fashioned during the gilded era of the Dutch Republic. Thus myths about the Republic both animated and forged the modern idiom of personal entitlements or civic responsibilities. In fact, nineteenth-century politicians and social critics walked an intellectual tightrope between poignant memories of an intrepid and proud Republican past, on the one hand, and visions of the newfangled economic requirements of the nineteenth-century world, on the other. The latter entailed a particular understanding of the distinct nature of "modernity," which prompted other European countries to take cautious and gradual steps toward a conception of social welfare as an exclusively public, and collective, responsibility. In the Dutch case, however, the journey resembled, ironically, a Catholic procession, as if it was necessary in 1854 to take several steps back in order to find refuge, once again, in the realm of private charity and Christian philanthropy.

The problem of *inventio*, of specifying and demarcating the outlines of the problem of poverty, was a contested issue; moreover, the task of selecting the kinds of social measures to be implemented was as perplexing a dilemma during the first half of the nineteenth century as it is today. Definitions as to what constituted genuine indigence, what caused it, and how it could be remedied was, as a Russian radical might have called it, one of "the burning questions of the day." Jeronimo de Bosch Kemper, the perspicacious nineteenth-century interpreter of social conditions in the Netherlands, remarked in 1851, for instance, that the word poverty had no absolute significance in itself—that poverty was merely a term that signified the most extreme contrast to the word wealth. He observed that only prosperous countries could afford to pay for public assistance, and he asserted that poorer and less advanced nations could not even consider granting relief because the financial resources were simply not available. This paradox, he wrote, could be taken to extremes: "The superficial statistics on indigence would have us believe that because of a lack of wealth, a poor country that is parsimonious [in its allocation of poor relief] ought to be called rich." He elaborated further that "poverty is an exceedingly relative concept that always stands in direct relationship to the overall wealth of a society. If society's aggregate wealth increases by X degrees, then our concept of poverty has to be modified by the same X degrees."[20] As a contemporary noted, people are called poor only "when, compared with others who possess more, they appear less well endowed."[21]

In a review of the available data on the number of poor relief recipients in the Dutch nation during the first half of the nineteenth century, Simon Vissering noted at mid-century, not without a trace of exasperation: "If it is true that one in seven Dutchmen is impoverished, how, then, should we interpret the figures of one out of six in England, one out of twenty-five in Italy, or one out of forty in Turkey?"[22] These commentaries reveal with great clarity a Dutch awareness that both poverty and charity were situationally constructed. Poverty, De Bosch Kemper and Vissering maintained, was a relative condition that did not have a universal meaning. Instead, the significance of poverty as a Social Question was directly linked to a society's overall wealth and its internal distribution of income. Its meaning was associated, too, with the relative degree of urbanization and the employment opportunities available, or with the national elite's sense of obligation vis-à-vis their fellow citizens in distress.

De Bosch Kemper implied that an elaborate system of poor relief was a nation's most dignified form of conspicuous consumption. Some societies allocated surplus income to fancy public shrines that rejoiced in a nation's military prowess and manifested its political importance.

Others, such as Holland, directed their resources toward their needy compatriots who suffered because they were out of work or out of luck. Vissering's query tried to decipher the often muddled, one might even say inverted, interpretations of poor relief statistics: if only 4 percent of the Italian population, or 2.5 percent of the inhabitants of Turkey, were officially designated as indigent and therefore entitled to relief—whereas the corresponding figure for England was as high as 19 percent or had reached 16 or 17 percent in the Netherlands—did that really suggest that the problem of poverty in Italy and Turkey was of a lesser magnitude?[23]

Vissering also diagnosed one of the curious puzzles implicit in any definition of poverty and charity: the more a society formally acknowledged the presence of poor people in its midst and tried to alleviate their distress, the greater the officially categorized poor population would be. In language that echoed the insights of his famous colleague in France, Alexis de Tocqueville, Vissering argued that in the past, in simple rural societies where everyone had tilled the soil side by side and was equally poor—or equally rich—no such thing as poverty had existed, except when the presence of a lord in a nearby manor house made peasants aware of social distinctions in birth, status, and wealth.

Poverty as a general phenomenon, Vissering maintained, only emerged with the development of factory production in modern urban society, which concentrated rich and poor into a shared physical and social space. Big cities exposed the glaring inequalities of income between working-class men and women, who engaged in backbreaking labor without being able to secure a reasonable existence, and the overbearing middle-class employers who hired them and paid them paltry wages for working from sunrise to sunset and beyond. Vissering crafted his discussion about poverty and poor relief in the quintessentially modern idiom of social justice and the bitter emotional awareness of the enormous divisions between rich and poor. For him the essence of poverty resided not only in the concrete social inequalities that permeated nineteenth-century society; its equally important meaning derived from more psychological, but just as real, perceptions of social distinctions and relative deprivation.

In the setting of the very different political culture of the French capital, the Prefect of Police in Paris, Louis Debelleyme, addressed more or less the same question that De Bosch Kemper and Vissering had raised. Debelleyme produced a proposal for a bond issue in 1828 to raise funds for a more effective prosecution of beggary and vagabondage in the city. The *Moniteur* reprinted the text of Debelleyme's proposal on November 27, 1828, which unveiled a poignant picture of the contradictory reality of poverty amid affluence. Not known for his empathy for destitute Parisian workers, and probably eager to expand his personal power and the political influence of his police force, Debelleyme's proposition undoubtedly arose from a desire for greater law enforcement resources rather than from a genuine humanitarian concern with pitiable beggars. Nonetheless, the image that flared up most vividly in his text was one of dramatic contrasts, of shabby and aggressive vagabonds who violated the day-to-day equanimity of the Parisian bourgeoisie and subverted the majestic enterprise and stately decorum of the city:

> Beggary [*mendicité*] has reared its ugly head in Paris and her neighboring communities with all that is hideous and distressing. Beggars pursue passersby in the streets and they harass them in the portals of churches; they hold merchants ransom and they display a painful spectacle of infirmities, both real and feigned. Everywhere they present a shocking picture of abject misery amid wealth and abundance, of drunkenness and idleness amid active industry in the most perfect civilization. Because the law prohibits beggary, it is incumbent upon humanity to provide shelter for those who have to reduce themselves to begging only because they are deprived of material resources. It is exactly those shelters that we are lacking. A task so noble is worthy of the attention of the residents of Paris and its surrounding areas, and this appeal to the time-proven habits of generosity of our citizens is made with the confidence that it will not be in vain.[24]

The police chief's proposal was a remarkable document. It portrayed in graphic detail the prevailing French ambivalence about pauperism and physical want, which often implied spiritual weakness as well. By appealing directly to the potential social chaos and imminent danger that hordes of ragged and deceitful beggars in the city embodied, Debelleyme tried to galvanize the Parisian bourgeoisie into action by digging deep into their pockets in order to raise money for the needed "shelters." But by shelters he meant lockups and jails, which would enable the police to incarcerate vagrants and remove them from the pristine urban stage of bourgeois civility. Middle-class residents of Paris should acknowledge their personal duty to the city and to the nation, but they should also recognize their own self-interest: they ought to provide the funds necessary to enforce the laws. Bourgeois Parisians, who presumably had achieved their station in life because they personified "active industry in the most perfect civilization," should protect their civil domain from the hideous presence of pathetic, but above all, menacing, vagabonds.

Leaving aside, of course, whether affluent Parisians had simply been born into prominent families and had inherited their money and social positions or whether they had truly earned it, Prefect of Police Debelleyme stroked their vanity while nurturing their fears of urban chaos. The vagrants were lazy and dishonest creatures, he announced, since many of them feigned their horrible ailments and they accosted respectable Parisians in the streets; on sundays they even heckled faithful Catholics upon entering church for mass. But Debelleyme's invocation of the ethos of *liberté* and individual responsibility went both ways. A lack of material resources forced these sleazy vagrants to lower themselves to their wretched station in society. He hinted at the possibility that the beggars were given no option other than to be the annoying creatures they had become.

Although he conceded the possibility that society's material inequality was implicated in the problem of vagrancy, Debelleyme undoubtedly remembered the political legacy of the Revolution, which had stipulated that no citizen, whether rich or poor, should be given special treatment. Social circumstances may have contributed to the Parisian vagrants' descent into their ghastly existence, but the moral responsibility to emerge from their horrible lives was their own. If the wealthy citizens of Paris fulfilled their political duties to society and kept their part of the bargain by paying taxes and their dues to the city, then the Prefecture of Police would do its part, which was to act on the behalf of society and reduce the number of beggars by simply locking them up.

Debelleyme painted a picture of poverty that was particularly shocking because of the glaring contrasts between abject misery and Parisian ostentation, between beggary and unequaled wealth. It was a portrait of intense social contrasts and economic tensions, and he invoked a series of clichés about desperate beggars as dangerous and truculent—ready to undermine the social peace at any moment. But his startling portrayal aligned the solution to pauperism in the city straightforwardly with the incarceration of large numbers of impoverished beggars and a more efficient structure of social surveillance. The enclosure of the poor—*l'enfermement des pauvres*—would enable Parisian notables to live their elegant existence in peace without being challenged, on a daily basis, by threatening "others" who should be contained to the opposite side of a fundamental social divide.

In the same year, 1828, police chief Debelleyme formulated another plan in which he established a blunt and direct linkage between poor relief and law enforcement, or between charitable institutions and prisons. He proposed the establishment of workhouses at various locations in the city to which all poverty-stricken citizens, especially beggars officially adjudicated in court, would be admitted. But he argued with great aplomb that the *conseil spécial des prisons* should control and supervise these new workhouses ''because of the similar nature of its assignments and duties; hence, this council would present the strongest guarantee of a wise and enlightened administration.''[25]

Debelleyme's shrill and imperious voice was not an uncontested one. In the course of the next decades, a flourishing côterie of French utopian socialists began to construct an eloquent and powerful counter discourse, especially during the 1840s. The rhetoric of critics on the left divorced poverty from personal failure or character deficiencies and placed the burden of guilt squarely on the shoulders of French society's inequitable distribution of income and its unjust class structure. Not only Karl Marx lived a shifty, nervous life in Paris for part of the 1840s, constantly shadowed and harassed by the Parisian police; he shared the oppositional political stage with a retinue of native-born utopian socialists. French social commentators on the political left collectively showered the nation with a deluge of innovative ideas and applied a distinctly ''marxist'' analysis before Marx. When Marx himself wrote in *The Communist Manifesto* in 1848 that a ''specter is haunting Europe—the specter of communism,'' he was paying a theoretical debt as well as an intellectual tribute to Etienne Cabet, who had founded the first working-class communist ''party'' in Europe.[26]

But the state, or more pertinently, Prefect of Police Debelleyme and his subordinates or successors, forcefully suppressed the idealistic authors of such subversive social critiques. The French elite, meanwhile, whose interests were more or less subsumed in the political establishment of the nation, studiously ignored this alternative vision of poverty and social justice. Hence, a louder chorus of officials and intellectuals echoed Debelleyme's views. The director of the *dépôts de mendicité*—the ancien régime institutions that were nominally abolished but which the July monarchy tried to revive, albeit under a different name—had asserted ten years before in similar language that ''poverty and mendicity are the inevitable results of sloth and idleness. They are first steps on a road that will ultimately lead to the scaffold.'' He warned that if destitute and unemployed people did not receive what they demanded, ''they will end up taking what they desire, they will end up murdering.'' His ultimate admonition was simple and straightforward: ''A vigilant government, therefore, must do everything in its might to repress mendicity and eliminate vagabondage.''[27] In 1840, the conservative social critic M. A. Frégier invoked a similar fear. ''The poor and the vicious classes,'' he wrote, ''have always been and will always be the most productive breeding ground for evildoers of all sorts. Even when vice is not accompanied by perversity, the very fact that it allies itself with poverty in the same person makes him a proper object of fear to society: he is dangerous.''[28]

On the whole, the two contrasting transcriptions of the meaning of poverty, one written in French and the other in Dutch, generated a profoundly different political resonance. In the narrative of Debelleyme and his soulmates, bourgeois residents of Paris, and ergo, the French ''garden of notables'' in general, should share the financial burden associated with maintaining the public peace. Rather than donating money to high-minded philanthropic agencies or workhouses which could nurture the poor, create employment, or teach them new skills and convert them into industrious citizens, Debelleyme urged law-abiding Parisians to allocate their financial resources to a more efficacious prosecution of beggary and vagrancy. After all, the Criminal and Civil Codes, drafted during the Napoleonic era, defined *mendicité* and *vagabondage* as illegal. In his vision, bourgeois generosity should not be mobilized for poor relief as a form of mutual insurance or a means of equalization, but simply to neutralize or pacify filthy vagrants by putting them in jail and thus remove them from the civilized spectacle of middle-class life.

Even though the French civil and criminal codes were introduced in the Netherlands during the Napoleonic era, too, the stories De Bosch Kemper and Vissering told did not highlight the more lurid features of poverty and beggary. Instead, they accentuated the obligations of the Dutch ''community'' to provide a reasonable existence to impoverished people and to bridge the great moral and psychological gap between rich and poor. Implicit in their narrative was a deep-seated anxiety about profitability and the need to provide free-market employment to idle workers. Both of them worried about the moral hazards associated with unconditional charity since it might foster a parasitic reliance among the poor on the generosity of their social superiors. As liberal economists they questioned the wisdom of creating workhouses in which municipal governments would subsidize the manufacturing activities of the poor and thus interfere in the open competition, or tamper with the free forces, of the capitalist marketplace. Nonetheless, the suggestion that Dutch burghers should direct their financial resources toward a more efficient police apparatus, in order to remove poor people from the streets and sequester them in lockups and jails as despised criminals, did not enter their imagination as often.

The commentaries of De Bosch Kemper and Vissering, on the one hand, and Debelleyme's remarkable proposals, on the other, exhibited major differences in political substance as well as tone. What comes across, however, albeit in different ways, was their shared understanding of indigence as a fluid social condition. Poverty, most early nineteenth-century observers intimated, comprised a plastic analytical construct that obtained its meaning from the particularity of the economic arrangements and class relations in which it was embedded. Many other politicians and intellectuals, in both countries, also recognized this truth, even if they concocted a variety of theories about poverty that did not necessarily conform to the insights of these two Dutch economists or the Parisian police chief. Every narrative, though, attributed essentialist meanings to the word poverty that reflected the authors' personal political predilections and culturally determined biases, both their particular class locations and the unique perspectives of a given historical moment.

These "textual constructions" of the situational realities and meanings of poverty were inevitably translated into a series of laws, decrees, and statutes as well. As a result, national perceptions of pauperism and social entitlements can be deduced from the different policies formulated by either Dutch or French political elites. It is reasonable, although not unproblematic, to examine the connection between the stated intent of policies and their social outcomes. However, traveling the road from an intellectual understanding of a political initiative regarding a particular social problem to the actual implementation of policy, or vice versa, is a complicated journey.[29] As a French official remarked astringently in the mid-1840s, "too often a public administrator, having written and sent a letter, thinks his task is completed: an action ordered is an action accomplished."[30] The difficulty derives, on the one hand, from the enormous social distance between society's poverty-stricken folk and the politicians and bureaucrats who actually shaped and enacted policy. On the other hand, local particularities continued to impede a direct, linear relationship between the assessment of a social problem and the kinds of policy response it might yield, even if the central state actively canvassed the opinions of local elites about various social issues in order to yoke their interests to a national political agenda.[31]

However, the valuable preoccupation with social and economic history at the grass-roots level in particular urban settings has occasionally led to a relative indifference to important developments in the national political arenas. Hence, the crucial local insights of the ''new'' social history should be combined with questions that examine the influence of governments and policymaking at the national level. The central state, although shaped by the particular ways in which centralized power was constituted and refracted within civil society, has been a significant actor in the social and political evolution of most European nation-states since early modern times. Prevailing ideas about ''the nature and locus of political power,'' or reigning notions about what can be attained in national politics and at what costs, inflected elite attitudes. Indirectly, they also affected the social options available to citizens who were frail and powerless. A distinct political culture enveloped politicians who passed legislation; it also biased government officials who inscribed civil society with regulations and statutory mandates. Hence, the state can be reintroduced to center stage by exploring the manner in which public officials constructed social taxonomies that encoded—or blurred, for that matter—economic inequalities.[32]

The state, after all, both as a political agent and as a bureaucratic phenomenon, was at the center of partisan political passions and ideological debates in the early nineteenth century, in both France and the Netherlands, although in a different manner. Often, however, the history of the state has converged with an analysis of its inexorable growth, as if the heart of the matter was the method through which a central state extended the degree, form, and domain of its intervention in civil society. But the state was much more than merely an administrative mechanism that inventoried and superintended civil society. The state did more than merely entrench the interests of the political elites who controlled its bureaucratic apparatus at a specific historical juncture. The state was also a venerated abstract entity which, in theory, embodied principles of popular sovereignty and articulated in unique ways ''the history of facts, the history of ideas, and the history of social representations.'' Pierre Rosanvallon has recently called for an ''*intelligibilité comparative*'' as far as analyses of the state are concerned: ''we must account for the specificity of national contexts,'' he has argued, ''and at the same time challenge our lingering perceptions of a homogeneous modern state.''[33]

Clearly, a lack of cohesion or homogeneity distinguished the government in The Hague more than the French state during the early nineteenth century. As a result, the political resolution of poverty engaged the central state in Holland in a unique fashion. The time-honored tradition of political and administrative decentralization in the Netherlands implied that Dutch burghers interpreted social welfare as a local obligation. Moreover, the extraordinary wealth that seventeenth-century merchants and regents in Dutch towns had accumulated during the golden age of the Dutch Republic had spawned a culture that inspired the average prosperous merchant to represent himself ''as the steward rather than the owner of riches, by giving some of it to the poor.'' The particular civic structure inherited from the early modern period sustained thousands of poor relief agencies that forged an unbreakable ''chain of charity'' and inextricably linked affluent citizens to others who were down-and-out, Simon Schama has argued. The religious exhortation ''Give, for one day you may be needy as it pleaseth the Almighty'' intertwined the rich with the poor ''for the quiet of their souls.''[34] Rather than England being ''the exemplar of social welfare,'' as Gertrude Himmelfarb claimed in *The Idea of Poverty*, Schama assigns an exemplary role to Holland since charity as a private vocation and moral calling—and poor relief as an immanent social practice—was already engraved in Dutch culture since early modern times.[35]

Holland, moreover, had been a religiously divided nation since the sixteenth century, albeit dominated by the Dutch Reformed Church. Even several hundred years later poor relief was still viewed as a method of preventing a loss of faith among a congregation's most downtrodden members. Perhaps poor relief functioned, too, in a more subtle fashion, as a means of proselytizing, or as a way of securing spiritual authority and attracting new members into the realm of a particular congregation. The *diaconiëen*, the charitable agencies of the various churches in every Dutch town, extended a helping hand to their congregations' poverty-stricken members. Municipal organizations took care of those needy citizens who either did not belong to an identifiable religious parish or were physically fragile, elderly, or handicapped. The nineteenth-century Dutch state in The Hague, meanwhile, tried with its limited political leverage to streamline and bring some form of coherence to the chaotic system of poor relief—full of wasteful duplication—at the municipal level, but with little success.

Dutch authorities and social observers in the post-1815 era interpreted indigence as a tangible symptom of the fading ingenuity of early modern Dutch commerce. To them, the large number of indigents supplied poignant evidence of a variety of deep-seated social problems associated with modernity and Holland's apparent inability to adjust. The new level and intensity of poverty revealed flaws in the structure of society and its economic organization. This novel kind of poverty endangered not only the well-being of individual citizens but also affected the collective welfare of the nation as a whole. It required governmental "vigilance"—as mandated specifically by article 195 of the new Kingdom's Constitution—as well as moral exhortation, Christian generosity, and vocational discipline.

Dutch officials, however, were less overwhelmed by ambivalent memories of the kind of turbulent Revolutionary experience that had heralded in France a brave new world of liberty and equality on a national scale; neither were they hampered by a large and burgeoning central bureaucracy eager to extend the domain of its influence. A view of the role of the state as no more prominent than that of mediator, schoolteacher, or auxiliary paymaster persevered throughout the nineteenth century and beyond. As A. J. Nieuwenhuis summarized the situation in pithy fashion in 1852, "the protective hand of the government shall never be an intrusive one."[36]

The controversy over the autonomy of the *diaconieën*, though, was more than a single-minded defense of the unfettered practice of Christian charity against state intrusion. Inevitably proponents of orthodox Protestantism wanted to shield the free agency and financial flexibility of their well-entrenched charitable organizations from secular control, but above all, they wished to strengthen the autonomous social position and internal cohesion of their religious congregations. Municipal elites, too, struggled to safeguard their independent political patronage. It is true that the *zuilen* (pillars)—the distinct political factions in Dutch politics which aimed to transcend class alliances but were based, instead, on religious solidarity and vertical patterns of social and cultural identification—did not emerge as full-blown, formal political parties until the very end of the nineteenth century.[37] But the vitriolic arguments over the various Poor Law proposals between 1800 and 1854 anticipated the verbal boxing match among politicians that erupted toward the end of the century, when the state's co-equal funding of public and religious educational institutions was at issue.

The habits of pragmatism in Dutch politics, however, in the period 1815–1854 and later—as Arend Lijphart has aptly pointed out, referred to in Holland as the "business" rather than the "game" of politics—yielded an accommodation in which the preeminence of Christian charity and the *diaconieën* was acknowledged, while municipal authorities and the state would provide subsidiary support, but only in the very last resort.[38] Yet another compromise was forged, later in the century, when representatives from the Catholic and Protestant camps agreed with politicians on the left and in the liberal center that religious schools would receive state funding on a par with public schools. However deeply divided they might be in matters of religion, ideas about material inequality, or in their attitudes toward industry or commerce, Dutch politicians and intellectuals managed to bridge enormous gaps by focusing on the humdrum requirements of the social world, as if "political and intellectual life was not autonomous and never cut off from the practical exigencies of daily life."[39]

In France the central government exercised, as best as it could, a discernible degree of surveillance over relief measures at the local level. In general the French state tried to wield legislative control over institutional responses to the social and political problems brought about by material hardship in the country as a whole. Many Frenchmen in the middle or on the left of the political spectrum equated local autonomy with reactionary politics and the persistence of antiquated, feudal pursuits. They appealed to the power of the central state as the most effective means to undermine or co-opt the political and social grip of conservative notables on local culture.[40] The early years of the French Revolution had inaugurated a pattern of formulating poor relief policy through national legislation, by decrees issued in Paris and implemented, whether equitably or not, throughout the country. Municipal authorities and Catholic charities or private philanthropists were not expected to have a voice in the molding of policy: theirs was to be a purely administrative role. All political decisions about the form and direction of social policy, "in the sacred name of *égalité*," had to be formulated and adopted in Paris and could not embroil "local people in Privas or Perpignan."[41]

Unfortunately the Revolution's *Comité de mendicité* and later the *Comité de secours public*, critical of the ancien régime's unevenly distributed system of Catholic poor relief, had been more successful in temporarily challenging the foundation of old charitable practices than it was in creating a new structure of public assistance. Following the Thermidorian reaction in the mid-1790s and throughout the nineteenth century, people who were suffering from hunger and need were, in reality, thrown back upon the "mercies of communal and private charity" and upon traditional institutions carried over from the ancien régime but reinvented in a supposedly modern guise.[42] In 1869, for instance, 1,224 out of a total of 1,557 functioning *hospices* and *hôpitaux* in France had been established before 1790.[43]

But the Revolutionary legacy of relying on national legislation and the formal authority of the central state was perpetuated during the Napoleonic era and lingered palpably during the Restoration, only to be revived more deliberately during the July Monarchy. As a result poor relief continued to display a haphazard and spasmodic quality, since the government's concern with the poor became anxiously palpable, it seemed, only during periods of economic crisis. In normal times, the state in Paris conferred the actual responsibility for helping the poor upon altruistic nuns and other pious Catholics who labored, for the glory of God rather than the state, in poorhouses, hospitals, or private philanthropic associations in the local community. This erratic situation prompted the pioneering woman economist in America, Emily Greene Balch, to use adjectives such as "meager," "arbitrary," and "inconsistent" in her 1893 analysis of the French poor relief system.[44]

Until mid-century, a sequence of Ministers of the Interior exhibited the mercurial nature of French commitments to aid the suffering poor. On occasion they used a compassionate vocabulary that expressed humane concerns, especially during serious subsistence crises. However, the emphasis on the transitory nature of poor relief as a "prudent" emergency measure exposed the limitations of bureaucrats' vision. Temporary threats to the public peace could be defused through equally temporary social welfare measures. Besides, relief should be coupled with the creation of public works projects, since incidental employment during times of hardship "inspires salutary habits and contains the fateful effects of desperation on the population."[45]

The same ad hoc response applied to epidemic disease. When cholera broke out in the early 1830s, the Ministry of Commerce and Public Works in Paris issued a nervous *circulaire* on April 23, 1832: the "invasion of *cholera moribus* threatens to attack different regions of the kingdom." This, the decree predicted, "will temporarily require extraordinary expenses"; it urged the state to adopt immediate measures and grant charitable administrations' requests for supplementary funding "in a manner that will reconcile the need for emergency services with the rules of public accountability."[46]

While the national government in Paris officially "played a dominant role in social welfare," this centralization did not necessarily benefit the hundreds of thousands of poor people trying to survive on a day-to-day basis, either in cities or in the countryside.[47] It might also be true that France represented a model of centralized government other European nations wished to emulate, but its institutional response to indigence and the Social Question was rife with ambivalence and incongruities. Contrary to the claim of some welfare state theorists, the comparison between France and the Netherlands suggests that a higher degree of political centralization with regard to the formulation of social policy does not always produce a higher level of actual "welfare."[48]

The comparison does suggest, though, that relatively "strong" states such as the French—in other words, those nations with well-entrenched bureaucracies and a long history of state intervention in domestic policy—formally tolerated less private initiative and pluralism at the local level. Even if a bewildering array of local charitable institutions both defined and dominated the lives of the poor, official French political culture reconfigured such pluralistic arrangements into a coherent national policy. In contrast, relatively "weak" states such as the Dutch—merely a "thin superstructure by the mid-nineteenth century"—allowed local interests and resolutions a greater amount of political "space."[49] Ironically, though, this delicate Dutch state displayed a remarkable strength in its ability to modulate the competing interests of the diverse constituencies that populated the Dutch political landscape, without appearing to violate their sense of autonomy. However feeble it may have been, the Dutch government in The Hague managed to secure a sound political harmony in the nation thanks to its ability to coordinate, like the gifted conductor of a symphony orchestra, the different interest groups of Dutch society.

But the story in both Holland and France was more paradoxical. In the French case, since politicians and social scientists in the nineteenth century could not reconcile the theoretical language and political legacy of the Revolution with the pauperism that prevailed in modern society, the institutional immobility in matters of social welfare resulted from a deep-seated intellectual quandary rather than mere indifference. While the nineteenth-century central state extended its social influence in a variety of arenas, it failed to construct institutions capable of easing the plight of the poor in a systematic fashion. In defiance of the many ponderous *enquêtes* that studied the problem of working-class indigence, and despite the clamorous scholarly debates about the origins of pauperism as a social fact, many officials clung to a notion that indigence was the product of private conduct for which the individual must be held accountable. They sensed a contradiction between poverty as a menacing social force and the Revolutionary conception of each man as a free and autonomous human being responsible for his own destiny and the fruits of his labor. Pauperism, however, existed also among throngs of French men and women who toiled all day long but who earned so little that they were nonetheless penniless and hungry.

The issue of poverty thus posed a formidable task: how to reconcile the Revolutionary dictate of individual freedom and responsibility or the *Comité de mendicité*'s mandate to rectify the inequalities of human existence with the needs for a stable social order? During the Restoration and the July Monarchy this impasse was resolved through an "imperfect, anarchic, and reactionary" solution; in the words of Rosanvallon, this outcome constituted an "antimodernist consensus."[50] Not being able to translate the Revolution's program of liberty, equality, and social justice into a viable reality, officials during the Restoration and the July Monarchy did nothing but regulate and supervise institutions inherited from the ancien régime and tried to contain the dangers that lurked behind pauperism as a social problem.

Variations in the number, composition, and behavior of the poor modulated the differences in the premises and outlooks of elites in both countries. Clashing interpretations of the nature of modern, free-market capitalism or the proper role of the church in civil society further calibrated these differences. French poor relief officials relied on outdoor relief to a lesser degree than did their Dutch counterparts; instead, French charitable practices, in relative terms, emphasized to a greater extent the enclosure of indigents in *hospices* and *hôpitaux.*

Perhaps with a bit of rhetorical overkill, Michel Foucault attributed to the French bourgeoisie a deliberate strategy of trying to "corset" the entire social body in a "carceral continuum of justice, prison, and police."[51] The emerging nineteenth-century anatomy of surveillance and discipline, Foucault argued, was embodied in the punitive mechanisms of army barracks, classrooms, monasteries, hospitals, and poorhouses. In the process, he downplayed the scores of "hidden transcripts" of popular insurrections, subversive organizations, or secret Republican societies that characterized the history of France during the first half of the nineteenth century. His imagery also shrouded the profusion of private philanthropic associations that preserved a sense of independent agency and were grounded in genuine compassion and honest fellow-feeling. Besides, Catholic religious orders' humanitarian routines within the sanctity of hospitals and poorhouses, despite the state's valiant efforts, remained somewhat impervious to overly invasive meddling from the outside.

Foucault may have embellished his vision of a cunning and calculating bourgeoisie that manipulated the factory and the army base to establish its own hegemony. Nevertheless, when contrasted with Dutch charitable habits, French social welfare policies suggest that the French political bureaucracy was more preoccupied with surveillance. To engage Foucault's notions about bourgeois discipline and punishment in nineteenth-century France we do not have to become white knights in shining armor who valiantly defend historical "exactitude" and lionize "little true facts" in order to protect them from "*vague grandes idées*"—as Foucault himself has mocked his critics. By comparing the preoccupations of French elites with similar concerns in the Netherlands, we can preserve both the "cloud" of grand ideas and the "dust" of detailed facts and still say something about the relative importance of "social control" in France.[52]

Thus, a more palpable concern with "pacification" and with neutralizing the social danger inherent in pauperism shaped French poor relief practices. It was true that throughout the nineteenth century agriculture continued to be the actual mainstay of the French economy, while an earthy peasantry and the simplicity of rural life endured as the symbolic representation of France's "true" national identity.[53] In addition, the overwhelming majority of poverty-stricken French women and men lived in the countryside. But it was the volatility of the urban poor that was at the forefront of officials' minds, despite France's colorful history of rural *entraves* and *taxations populaires*. The potent and disturbing memories of explosive political outbursts in large cities such as Paris and Lyons in 1792–1795, 1830, 1834, and 1848 prompted government officials to view public assistance more as an urban mechanism of political containment. French officials were acutely aware of the "moral hazards" associated with public assistance, and they attempted at all times to restrict relief to those who were truly unlucky and deserving, and to do so in a profitable manner. In this sense they did not differ much from their Dutch colleagues, but added a uniquely French twist. Commentators in France worried that charity would entail special treatment for a particular segment of society. Group-specific legislation would violate the sacrosanct political dictate of *liberté* or equality of rights, and thus encumber the individualist duties of citizenship.

Relative to France, the "equalization" aspect of poor relief was a more dominant element in discussions about poverty and the practices of social welfare in the Netherlands. A staggering number of private and public poor relief agencies in every town and city in the country sought to cushion and regulate the realities of an unpredictable labor market and to soften the social consequences of accidents of nature. To be sure, Dutch elites were not simply more magnanimous, or less callous, than their peers in France, nor did the Dutch political establishment feel a burning desire to reduce the gap between rich and poor for its own sake. In the God-given order of Dutch society in the early nineteenth century everyone should know his or her proper place, whereas the government's economic policies favored the interests of the well-to-do (*gegoede stand*).[54]

But the preoccupation with the collective prosperity and welfare of the nation or the awareness of its steady downward slide since early modern times, created a sense that poverty affected every citizen, both rich and poor and those in between; the burden of alleviating extreme human hardship therefore ought to be shouldered by the community as a whole, whether religious congregations or an urban community (*gemeente*). The Dutch, more open to ideas of liberal economics, were also deeply concerned with "profitability." Poor relief officials tried to allocate relief in an economically constructive manner. As much as possible, they hoped to inculcate a proper work ethic in the poor in order to convert them into productive citizens. This, many argued, would be the best return on their charitable investments. Nineteenth-century Dutchmen anticipated, perhaps, Cecil Rhodes's platitude that philanthropy was a great thing, but philanthropy plus five percent was even better!

One could argue that the two systems of poor relief were "appropriate" to each society, but neither was sufficient to achieve its own objectives; perhaps we could even say that the structure of assistance tended to reinforce certain pathologies unique to each country. In fact, Simon Vissering conjured up the imagery of illness, too, when he tried to capture the diversity of emotions, opinions, and proposals regarding charity. Using a metaphor from the world of medicine, he noted that "poverty and poor relief in our society are a disease that must be cured, but it is an affliction that requires gentle nursing. Many in our midst hold forth on the symptoms of the disease, its causes, the methods of therapy to be used or the kinds of medication to be administered. One so-called doctor refers to poverty as a consumptive ailment, the next one calls it a cancer, and according to a third it is like the plague." Proceeding to mix his metaphors, Vissering appealed to the archetypal Dutch fear of maritime disaster: "The problem of pauperism has been compared to a country that is flooded." He then switched to yet another figure of speech: poor relief resembled "a clock that ticks irregularly," which presumably disturbed Dutch notions of punctuality and order. Returning to the familiar world of navigation and the sea, he continued: "yet another image has been invoked when poverty and charity are compared to a ship: bailing can no longer save the decrepit vessel. Rather, it needs to be returned to the shipyard and only after it is completely repaired and newly equipped can it return to sea." And finally, he asked the predictable rhetorical question: "But why should not we discard the old barge and build a sparkling new ship in its stead?"[55]

Whether the "ship" of social welfare should be patched up, entirely overhauled, or simply abandoned for a brand-new vessel was a key question. Intellectuals and policymakers in both France and the Netherlands contemplated and debated this question ad nauseam during the first half of the nineteenth century. Although Frenchmen were less likely than their Dutch colleagues to summon aquatic metaphors, the medical imagery of pauperism as a chronic contagion that stalked the French urban landscape, or as a "hideous leprosy" that disfigured the nation's social physique and weakened its resilience, was a familiar one to them.[56] Hence, the rhetorical practices and statutory proposals of officials in both countries reflected an array of common structural conditions, but they also echoed diverse cultural legacies and historical memories.

Notes

1. Prefect of Police, Department of Ain, to the Minister of the Interior, September 15, 1830, Premier Bureau, Division des affaires criminelles et des grâces, Ministère de la Justice. F7 6690, AN, Paris.

2. Simon Vissering, "Politische vertooghen," in *Herinneringen* (Collection of essays and memoirs written between 1840 and 1860), 3 vols. (Amsterdam: P.N. van Kampen, 1863), 2, p. 21.

3. Of the many French social investigators writing in the period 1815–1848, Louis-René Villermé was the best known in the Netherlands, whereas Baron Joseph-Marie de Gérando—as well as the Scottish Presbyterian minister Thomas Chalmers—inspired Dutch notions of middle-class patronage. In Holland itself the work of Samuel Senior Coronel, who was politically much less conservative, was inspired by methods similar to his French colleagues. See, among many other writings, *Gezondheidsleer toegepast op de fabrieksnijverheid* (Haarlem: De Erven Loosjes, 1861), and *idem*, "De diamantwerkers te Amsterdam," in *De economist* (1865), Bijblad, pp. 89–120. For a more recent examination of Coronel's contributions, see A.H. Bergink, *Samuel Senior Coronel en zijn betekenis voor de sociale geneeskunde in Nederland* (Assen: Van Gorcum, 1960).

4. H.W. Tydeman, J. Heemskerk, and Mr. J.W. Tydeman, *Het ontwerp van wet op het armbestuur* (Amsterdam: Gebroeders Kraay, 1852), p. 10. See also their *Denkbeelden omtrent een wettelijke regeling van het armwezen in Nederland* (Amsterdam: Gebroeders Willems, 1850).

5. Jean-Paul Alban de Villeneuve-Bargemont, *Economie politique chrétienne ou recherches sur la nature et les causes du paupérisme en France et en Europe et sur les moyens de les soulager et prévenir*, 3 vols. (Paris: Paulin, 1834), 1, p. 28. For a biography that exaggerates his social Catholic sentiments, see Mary Ignatius Ring, *Villeneuve-Bargemont, Precursor of Modern Social Catholicism* (Milwaukee: Bruce, 1935).

6. Jean-Paul Alban de Villeneuve-Bargemont, *Discours prononcé à la Chambre des Députés dans la discussion du projet de loi sur le travail des enfants dans les manufactures* (Metz: Colignon, 1841), p. 2.

7. The socialist Pierre Leroux attributed the number of four million beggars to government statistics, while Louis Moreau-Christophe concocted the number of six million poor people in 1851; see Gordon Wright, *Between THE Guillotine & Liberty. Two Centuries of the Crime Problem in France* (New York: Oxford University Press, 1983), pp. 49, 157.

8. See, for example, the section on ''Bourgeois Opinion'' in Louis Chevalier, *Laboring Classes and Dangerous Class in Paris During the First Half of the Nineteenth Century* (1958; repr. Princeton: Princeton University Press, 1973), pp. 359–72.

9. Olwen Hufton, Review of J.K.J. Thompson, *Clèrmont de Lodève, 1633–1789: Fluctuations in the Prosperity of a Languedoc Clothmaking Town* (1982), and Colin Jones, *Charity and Bienfaisance: The Treatment of the Poor in the Montpellier Region, 1774–1815* (1982), *European Studies Review*, 13, No. 4 (1983), p. 489.

10. Eugène Buret, *De la misère des classes laborieuses en Angleterre et France. De la nature de la misère, de son existence, de ses effets, de ses causes, et de l'insuffisance des remèdes qu'on lui a opposés jusqu'ici avec l'indication des moyens propres à affranchir les sociétés*, 2 vols. (Paris: Paulin, 1840), 1, p. 108.

11. According to J.A. Berger, in *Van armenzorg tot werkelozenzorg* (Amsterdam: Arbeiderspers, 1936), Van den Bosch was the first analyst in the Netherlands to use the term ''unemployment,'' p. 25.

12. Thomas Lacqueur, ''Bodies, Details, and the Humanitarian Narrative,'' in Lynn Hunt, ed., *The New Cultural History* (Berkeley: University of California Press, 1989), p. 177.

13. Denis Diderot, *Voyage en Hollande* (1780; repr. Paris: Maspéro, 1982), quoted by Dennis Porter, *Haunted Journeys. Desire and Transgression in European Travel Writing* (Princeton: Princeton University Press, 1991), pp. 84–85.

14. See Johan Huizinga's chapter on ''De betekenis van 1813 voor Nederland's geestelijke beschaving,'' in his *De Nederlandse natie. Vijf opstellen* (Haarlem: Tjeenk Willink, 1960), pp. 103, 108.

15. Christopher Lash, *The True and Only Heaven. Progress and Its Critics* (New York: Norton, 1992), pp. 82–119. See also the discussion about nostalgia in Selma Leydesdorff, *Wij hebben als mens geleefd. Het joodse proletariaat van Amsterdam, 1900–1940* (Amsterdam: Meulenhoff, 1987), pp. 45–47.

16. D.F. van Alphen, ''Iets over armoede en het gebrek aan arbeid in betrekking tot de staatshuishoudkunde and staatkunde,'' in H.W. Tydeman, ed., *Magazijn voor het armwezen in het Koninkrijk der Nederlanden* (Leiden: 1820), pp. 3–4.

17. Jeronimo de Bosch Kemper, *Geschiedkundig onderzoek naar de armoede in ons vaderland, hare oorzaken en de middelen die tot hare vermindering zouden kunnen worden aangewend* (Haarlem: De Erven Loosjes, 1851), p. 195.

18. Jeroen Sprenger, who is the current spokesperson for the Dutch Federation of Trade Unions, repeated the same story in almost identical language in an interview in the *Washington Post* on April 12, 1993: ''[Holland is] still a prosperous country, we do not have the levels of poverty that you see in other countries like the United States. Let's be proud of that, let's see it as a kind of decency, a level of civilization we have reached in [our] country.''

19. Marco H.D. van Leeuwen, *Bijstand in Amsterdam, ca. 1800–1950. Armenzorg als beheersings- en overlevingsstrategie* (Zwolle: Waanders, 1992), p. 289.

20. De Bosch Kemper, *Geschiedkuding onderzoek naar de armoede*, pp. 4, 13.

21. Elise van Calcar, *Tabitha. Armoede en Weldadigheid*, 2 vols. (Amsterdam: W.H. Kirberger, 1856), 1, p. 7.

22. Vissering, ''Politische vertooghen,'' 2, p. 197.

23. Vissering, ''Politische vertooghen,'' 2, p. 195. These statistics, which had entered both the French and Dutch discourses about poverty, achieved a metaphorical status and were used as ammunition for diametrically opposed rhetorical purposes. See Chapter 6 for a very different French reading.

24. *Le Moniteur*, November 27, 1828, Fosseyeux, liasse 711–2, Archives de l'assistance publique, Paris. For biographical information about the prefect of police, see M. Bertin, *Biographie de Mr. de Belleyme* (Paris: Durand, 1865).

25. *L'établissement des maisons de travail dans la ville de Paris*, 7 November, 1828, Fosseyeux, liasse 711–2, Archives de l'Assistance publique, Paris.

26. David Pinkney, *Decisive Years in France, 1840–1847* (Princeton: Princeton University Press, 1986), pp. 94–97, and Christopher Johnson, *Utopian Communism in France. Cabet and the Icarians, 1839–1851* (Ithaca: Cornell University Press, 1974), p. 66.

27. The director of the *dépôts de mendicité* to the Minister of the Interior, July 25, 1816. F16 531, AN, Paris.

28. M.A. Frégier, *Des classes dangereuses de la population dans les grandes villes, et des moyens de les rendre meilleures* (Paris: 1840), quoted by Chevalier, *Laboring Classes and Dangerous Classes in Paris*, p. 141.

29. Katherine A. Lynch, *Family, Class, and Ideology in Early Industrial France* (Madison: University of Wisconsin Press, 1988), pp. 22–30. See also Brigitte and Peter L. Berger, *The War over the Family: Capturing the Middle Ground* (Garden City, N.Y: Anchor Press, 1983).

30. René Vivien, *Etudes administratives* (Paris: 1845), quoted by Pierre Rosanvallon, *l'Etat en France de 1789 à nos jours* (Paris: Editions du Seuil, 1990), p. 126.

31. Lynch, *Family, Class, and Ideology*, pp. 22–30. Charles Tilly, in *Coercion, Capital, and European States, A.D. 990–1990* (Oxford: Basil Blackwell, 1990), argues that the legacy of political change implemented between 1789 and 1793 ''constituted a dramatic, rapid substitution of uniform, centralized, direct rule for a system of government mediated by local and regional notables'' (p. 111).

32. Theda Skocpol, ''Bringing the State Back in: Strategies of Analysis in Current Research,'' in Peter B. Evans, Dietrich Rueschmayer, and Theda Skocpol, eds., *Bringing the State Back In* (Cambridge/New York: Cambridge University Press, 1985), p. 22.

33. Rosanvallon, *l'Etat en France*, p. 13.

34. Simon Schama, *The Embarrassment of Riches. An Interpretation of Dutch Culture in the Golden Age* (New York: Alfred A. Knopf, 1987), pp. 575, 579.

35. Gertrude Himmelfarb, *The Idea of Poverty. England in the Early Industrial Age* (New York: Alfred A. Knopf, 1984), p. 5.

36. A.J. Nieuwenhuis, *Het wetsontwerp op het armbestuur* (Amsterdam: J.H. Gebhard, 1852), p. 12.

37. An extensive literature on ''pillarization'' exists. See, among others, P. van Gorkum and J.J. Gielen et al., eds., *Pacificatie en de zuilen* (Meppel: Boom, 1965); Arend Lijphart, *The Politics of Accommodation: Pluralism and Democracy in the Netherlands* (Berkeley: University of California Press, 1968); Hans Daalder, ''Politicologen, sociologen, historici en de verzuiling,'' *Bijdragen en Mededelingen betreffende de Geschiedenis der Nederlanden*, 100, No. 1 (1985), pp. 52–64; Siep Stuurman, *Verzuiling, kapitalisme en patriarchaat. Aspecten van de ontwikkeling van de moderne staat in Nederland* (Nijmegen: SUN Uitgeverij, 1983); Luc Huyse, *De verzuiling voorbij* (Leuven: Kritak, 1987); Harry Post, *Pillarization: An Analysis of Dutch and Belgian Society* (Aldershot: Avebury, 1989); Goran Therborn, ''Pillarization and Popular Movements. Two Variants of Welfare State Capitalism: the Netherlands and Sweden,'' in Francis G. Casles, ed., *The Comparative History of Public Policy* (New York: Oxford University Press, 1989), pp. 182–222; and Frans Groot, ''Verzuilingstendensen in Holland, 1850–1925,'' *Historisch Tijdschrift Holland*, 25, No. 2 (April 1993), pp. 91–115.

38. Lijphart, *The Politics of Accommodation*, p. 207.

39. F.H. Fischer, *Studiën over het individualisme in Nederland in de negentiende eeuw* (Bergen op Zoom: Stoomdruk P. Harte, 1910), p. 138.

40. Peter A. Gourevitch, *Paris and the Provinces. The Politics of Local Reform in France* (Berkeley: University of California Press, 1980), p. 9.

41. Alan Forrest, *The French Revolution and the Poor* (New York: St. Martin's Press, 1981), p. 173.

42. Roger Price, ''Poor Relief and Social Crisis in Mid-Nineteenth-Century France,'' *European Studies Review*, 13, No. 4 (1983), p. 423.

43. Léon Lallemand, *Etude sur la nomination des commissions administratives et des établissements de bienfaisance* (Paris: Picard, 1887), Preface, n.p.

44. Emily Greene Balch, ''Public Assistance of the Poor in France,'' in *Publications of the American Economic Association* (Baltimore: Guggenheim and Weil, 1893), No. 8, pp. 448–51.

45. Minister of the Interior to the King, November 25, 1818, *Rapport au Roi sur la situation des hospices, des enfants trouvés, des aliénés, de la mendicité, et des prisons* (Paris: Imprimerie Royale, 1818), p. 18. F11 445, AN, Paris.

46. Circulaires, 1832–1839. Ministère de Commerce et Travaux Publics, Premier Division, April 23, 1832. F15 190, AN, Paris.

47. Rachel Fuchs, *Abandoned Children. Foundlings and Child Welfare in Nineteenth-Century France* (Albany: SUNY Press, 1984), p. 33.

48. Tilly, *Coercion, Capital, and European States*, p. 107. See also Hugh Heclo, *Modern Social Politics in Britain and Sweden* (New Haven: Yale University Press, 1974), and Michael Shalev, ''The Social Democratic Paradigm and Beyond: Two Generations of Comparative Research on the Welfare State,'' *Comparative Social Research*, 6, (1983), pp. 315–51.

49. For a general analysis of ''strong'' and ''weak'' states, see John Brewer, *The Sinews of Power: War, Money, and the English State, 1688–1783* (New York: Alfred A. Knopf, 1989); Wim Blockmans, ''Beheersen en overtuigen. Reflecties bij nieuwe visies op staatsvorming,'' *Tijdschrift voor Sociale Geschiedenis*, 16, No. 1 (1990), pp. 19–29; and Therborn, ''Pillarization and Popular Movements,'' p. 203.

50. Maurice Rochaix uses the terms ''anarchic, imperfect, and reactionary,'' in *Essai sur l'évolution des questions hospitalières de la fin de l'ancien regime à nos jours* ((Paris: Fédération Hospitalière de France, 1959), p. 145; see also Rosanvallon, *l'Etat en France*, pp. 162–66.

51. Michel Foucault, *Discipline and Punish: The Birth of the Prison* (1975; repr. New York: Random House, 1979). See also *l'Impossible prison. Recherches sur le système pénitentiaire au XIXième siècle réunies par Michelle Perrot: débat avec Michel Foucault* (Paris: Editions du Seuil, 1980), especially Jacques Léonard's essay, ''L'historien et le philosophe. A propos de: *Surveiller et punir: naissance de la prison*,'' pp. 15–16, and the description in David Macey, *The Lives of Michel Foucault* (New York: Pantheon, 1993), pp. 330–335.

52. Foucault, ''La poussière et le nuage,'' in Perrot, ed., *L'impossible prison*, p. 29.

53. For a discussion of French national identity, see Herman Lebovics, *True France. The Wars Over Cultural Identity, 1900–1945* (Ithaca: Cornell University Press, 1992), passim.

54. Auke van der Woud, *Het lege land. De ruimtelijke ordening van Nederland, 1798–1848* (Amsterdam: Meulenhoff, 1987), p. 534. For a later period, see Henk te Velde, *Gemeenschapszin en plichtsbesef. Liberalisme en nationalisme in Nederland, 1870–1918* (The Hague: SDU, 1992).

55. Simon Vissering, ''Politische vertooghen,'' p. 195.

56. M.A. de Bourgoing, *Mémoire en faveur des travailleurs et des indigents de la class agricole* (Nevers: chez l'auteur, n.d.), Preface, n.p.

CHAPTER THREE

"Real" Poor People in a Harsh and Unforgiving World: Some Images, Facts, and Figures about Poverty in the Nineteenth Century

> *La petite Loisy*, a servant in the household of a lady in Décize, had become pregnant. Her mistress, having detected her condition, sent her away. Sadness, desperation, misery, and shame overwhelmed the girl, and after giving birth to a male child she crushed his skull and buried him in a field.[1]
>
> —*Union libérale de Nevers*, December 8, 1847

> On October 21, 1836 . . . a body was found of a recently born child, entirely naked, but not displaying any traces of external violence except that the umbilical cord was roughly torn off; soon enough it emerged that Jacoba Maria Keijm, then working as a domestic servant in the household of bricklayer Ary Schijf, had given birth to the child the previous morning, and had abandoned it during the evening of that same day in the place where it was found. According to the judicial inquest, which took place on 21 October, the local police issued a conclusion which made it impossible for the judiciary to prove that this was a case of infanticide, although the police did not doubt that the child was carried to term, was born alive, and died, to say it most mildly, as a result of unforgivable negligence on the part of the mother.[2]
>
> —L. de Wind, official of the court of Middelburg, Zeeland, to the High Court of Justice in The Hague, August 10, 1837

In popular discourses, both in the Netherlands and France, pregnant domestic servants were often depicted as the women most prone to commit infanticide. Their fear of being detected—*la petite Loisy* was one of many poor servants whose employers fired them when they became pregnant—prompted expecting domestics to hide their pregnancies and to deliver their babies under the most excruciating of circumstances. Given the anxieties about possibly losing their jobs, the effort to abandon their babies after birth in a nearby *hospice*, nunnery, or municipal orphanage may have entailed too many risks. Hence, infanticide appeared the only gruesome option available to terrified and defenseless women with no economic resources whatsoever.

For judges and prosecutors the suspicion of the crime of infanticide yielded a genuine challenge, since the legal evidence for a conviction was often lacking. Either benign or malicious neglect could easily cause an infant's death, but it was difficult for authorities to prove guilt beyond a reasonable doubt. Years of food shortage and economic depression exacerbated suffering among adults as well as children, and a greater number of infants may have been intentionally neglected because a newborn baby represented too much of a burden to a mother, who could work harder, migrate, or feed her other children better without the responsibility for a tiny infant. The police and legal officials, for their part, often found it impossible to establish with plausible certainty whether such negligence was intentional or accidental. In the case of *la petite Loisy*, a French court sentenced her to twenty years of forced labor. In this particular instance, the court apparently did not harbor any misgivings about her guilt.

Jacoba Maria Keijm's case revealed a slightly different picture. The court officer, charged with the original investigation in the town of Middelburg in the province of Zeeland, reviewed her personal testimony, in which she had set forth the poignant details of her condition and actions. She had confessed that:

> In the early morning of October 20, 1836, while she was alone in the kitchen of her boss, she gave birth to a baby that seemed to fall [almost spontaneously] from her body into her hands; she did not know whether this caused the umbilical cord to be ripped off, since there was not enough light. Neither did she hear the child cry nor could she detect other signs of life. She acknowledged, though, that shame prevented her from carefully looking at the baby and she did not even know whether it was a boy or a girl. She then wrapped the child in an apron and placed it in a laundry basket that was disguised and hidden; she passed the placenta in secret, and did check once more into the well-being of the baby although she could not detect life . . . Afterward she abandoned it outside.[3]

Following a scrupulous examination of the evidence in the case, the prosecutor could not marshal sufficient legal reasons to charge Jacoba, who was twenty-two years old, with the crime of infanticide. He had not been able to locate conclusive evidence suggesting a violent death; nonetheless, the court found her guilty of the lesser charge of negligent homicide and, as a result, she was imprisoned. Because infanticide had been a capital offense under Dutch law since early modern times, legal authorities examined each allegation of infanticide with meticulous care. However, the legal distinction between negligent abandonment and actual infanticide was difficult to establish, a problem exemplified by the fate of Jacoba Maria Keijm.

Her legal situation came to the judiciary's attention once again a year later. This time it was the High Court of Justice in The Hague that considered her case in August of 1837, when Jacoba's elderly mother petitioned the Court to grant her daughter Jacoba a pardon and release her from the remainder of her prison term. L. de Wind, an officer of the municipal court in Middelburg, drafted the documents that accompanied the petition. The High Court decided, however, it could not invoke any mitigating circumstances that might justify a pardon for Jacoba Maria Keijm, "because the helplessness of her elderly mother is no more sad than the fate of needy children whose parents are incarcerated—it is no reason to leave a crime unpunished."[4]

A few years later, similar heartrending dramas unfolded in France. In Nevers, the local newspaper reported that on the evening of December 6, 1841,

> Marie Rollot, a servant in the Commaille household and butcher shop, disappeared one evening in cold and rainy weather. When she returned after fifteen minutes, she looked ghastly pale . . . she was forced to confess that in the shed next to the house, which was used to store the remains of slaughtered animals, she had given birth to a stillborn child, and that she had then gone to the canal nearby, to throw the baby into the water. . . .[5]

Marie Rollot was sentenced to five years in prison. The prefect of the department of Côte-d'Ôr told yet another macabre tale about a mother and daughter team in Lignerolles, who had been arrested for infanticide. In a letter to the Minister of Justice he wrote that "on November 22, 1845, the *gendarme* had discovered the body of a recently born child as well as the skeleton of another child, both buried in the oven" of the house where they worked.[6]

These painful stories about hopelessly poor women, impotent in their confrontation with employers who may have raped them or with lovers who abandoned them in their hour of need, constituted narratives that could be multiplied endlessly, albeit in different settings and with different protagonists, in both the Netherlands and France. Whether women innocently believed their pre-nuptial lovemaking would lead to marriage or whether men brutally violated their honor, a solitary pregnant girl possessed few options. As Elise van Calcar, a proper Dutch lady commented in the 1850s, such a girl might augment "the number of infanticides," she might drown in the murky morass of "sexual wantonness," or she could come to a miserable end in "a prison or a poorhouse."[7]

But out-of-wedlock pregnancy was more than a distressing condition that befell impoverished women in particular; it represented, too, a discursive symbol which conveyed middle-class anxieties about the unruliness and disarray of working-class life in general.[8] As a deterrent against the "growing vice and immorality among the urban poor, due to their declining religiousness," for instance, officials in the Dutch city of Utrecht in the early nineteenth century decided that unmarried mothers could only receive help under extreme circumstances.[9]

These tragic narratives chronicled in graphic detail the human drama that being poor entailed. They were tales of unadulterated sorrow, and pregnant women's attempts to navigate the troubled waters of unmarried motherhood characterized one of a wide range of strategies poor people pursued to survive in a Hobbesian world that rendered their existence nasty, brutish, and short. Regardless of the particular locale in which they lived, people who were desperate or exploited committed legal acts of moral courage to help themselves and their families. If necessary, they also engaged in illegal schemes or pulled off sly tricks and artful deceptions. In the face of great odds, they were forced into vulnerable positions and ventured into dangerous territory, and cheating, stealing, or selling their bodies for the sexual use of the highest bidder were part of the economies of makeshift that defined the essence of the lives of the poor. Whenever the "going got tough"—which was, of course, most of the time—the poor always displayed "a knack for life in their everyday tactics of survival," as Nancy Scheper-Hughes has testified.[10] Whether impoverished people hunkered down in ghastly working-class neighborhoods of nineteenth-century Paris and Amsterdam, or whether they scraped by in frightful urban slums in Brazil, an indomitable courage kept them afloat and a Protean ingenuity ennobled the spirit of many.

These poignant personal dimensions of poverty can best be explored, of course, in the dusty halls of municipal archives, in the plentiful arrest records of cities' police departments, or in the chaotic poor relief rolls of local charitable agencies. A study at a lower level of analysis, such as an exploration of the existential realities of poverty and the distinctive arguments about private versus public charity in Amsterdam vis-à-vis those in Paris, for instance, could yield an abundance of trenchant insights into the turbulent lives of poor people.

Examples abound of the enormous intellectual value of a local approach to poverty in a variety of unique urban environments. Many historians have excavated municipal archives and analyzed statistical data in order to unearth all the engrossing details of poor peoples' resourceful methods of survival. With fastidious care, resembling the painstaking labor of dedicated archaeologists, "new" social historians have answered the clarion call "to dig and discover, to classify, reproduce, and describe, to copy and decipher, and to cherish and conserve" the bleak, if tumultuous, existence of the poor in the past, which had been silently buried in the poor relief records of municipal town halls and private charitable organizations.[11]

The novel focus on local knowledge and thick description has yielded a rich scholarly harvest in the past decade or so. In fact, historians have painted a sophisticated portrait of the urban poor: they have created veritable *tableaux vivants* of the ways in which indigent urban residents solicited, negotiated, and accumulated the charitable support that might be at their disposal, not only with a crystal-clear sense of their own self-interest but also with crafty economic judgment. Poor people in nineteenth-century metropolitan centers accepted aid whenever and wherever it was offered. If possible, they either dodged or manipulated the moral strings that bourgeois donors or public officials habitually attached to charitable gifts. Middle-class benefactors judged impoverished widows and mothers as most worthy and regarded them as sufficiently contrite or shamefaced, and women proved extremely inventive in stretching their household budgets by complementing the collective resources of their families with income cleverly derived from a variety of charitable agencies.

A surfeit of recent research on France has generated a wealth of cumulative insights. By linking the fate of the poor either to the political culture of empathetic local elites or to the compassionate engagement of the lower Catholic clergy in various French regions or towns, historians have shed a subtle light on both the gendered social tactics and fragmented political identities of the poor.[12] In a similar fashion, Dutch historians have produced a profusion of articles and books about poverty, charity, and the functioning of the labor market in a variety of nineteenth-century Dutch cities. In fact, patterns of poor relief and their impact on either industrial development or wages levels have inspired a lively debate among Dutch historians, a controversy Joel Mokyr provoked, in part, with his outspoken *Industrialization in the Low Countries*.[13] Recent quantitative reevaluations of the Dutch economic performance have played a similarly important role. These studies have generated fascinating conclusions about the essentially preindustrial nature of the Dutch economy in the early nineteenth century, in which poor relief functioned as a kind of institutional buffer, or as a homespun and flexible mechanism of survival, for marginally employed urban workers.[14]

All this valuable new research has clearly demonstrated that we can learn a tremendous amount about poverty and social welfare by immersing ourselves in the nitty-gritty details of a particular locality. But municipal archives were culturally constructed and socially biased, too. Local notables—the city magistrates, notaries, doctors, ministers, textile merchants, or master *bierbrouwers*—inscribed the historical record of any given town with their distinctive political styles and economic predilections. The lives of local elites were deeply enmeshed in the social fabric of their community. Employers' constantly shifting demand for the labor power of the city's poor, or elites' particular interpretations of the injunction to be charitable towards fellow human beings, forged unique local outcomes.

Obviously, in an effort to expand upon Pierre Rosanvallon's call for a "comparative comprehensibility" of political cultures and the social implications of policy at a national level, we have to walk several intellectual tightropes. We are wedged, it seems to me, between local rhetoric about poverty and charity and discourses in the national arena. We are also caught in between the "real" poor people who endured genuine hardship and subsisted in a world that was cutthroat and competitive—or, depending on one's perspective, unfair and unjust—and the local elites who either inflicted more pain or tried to help with clemency.

But regardless of their unique personal agendas, local notables increasingly shared the "pattern of meanings" of the nation at large, whether in the Netherlands or France. The project of transcribing the "true" meaning of "bona fide" poverty in a specific urban context mandated that local elites translate the cultural assumptions of society as a whole into a distinctive inventory of urban artifacts and texts. These tangible sources consisted of local poor relief statistics, municipal statutes, police regulations, religious sermons about human compassion, incendiary pamphlets, or erudite social-scientific publications. But even in a more intimate local context, the people who composed these social transcripts or compiled statistical tabulations were physically removed, or psychologically alienated, from the "real" tragedy of hunger and destitution. Hence, social superiors constructed the urban archival record that conveyed the "essential" reality of poor people's lives. In small-scale urban settings, too, rhetorical conventions inflected the ruling definitions of poverty and influenced social realities, either in the nineteenth century or today.

In fact, among some sociologists today, it is fashionable to claim that there is "no such thing as true poverty," whether in our contemporary world or in the past.[15] The assertion that any analysis of poverty has always depended on the conceptual apparatus or the tools of measurement it employs has some validity. Be that as it may, we should not forget that poverty as a social condition or a human state was inevitably bound by a set of definable biological limits and physical criteria. The hunger and suffering of poor people was not infinitely elastic or flexible. Poverty, when wrested from its relative social definitions or delivered from its rhetorical constructions, was also a particular circumstance in which human survival was jeopardized because it fell below some physiological minimum of nutrition, clothing, and housing. Consistently high death rates and an overall pattern of short life expectancy reflected deep-seated and enduring deprivation of this kind. The people who died young may have lacked "exchange entitlements" because they did not possess the means to obtain the work and shelter, or to secure the food, that must have been available, since many other citizens lived long and healthy lives.[16] As Amartya Sen has remarked brusquely, much about poverty is straightforward enough, and we do not need to exult in "elaborate criteria, cunning measurement, or probing analysis" in order to recognize heartbreaking and human misery.[17]

So I will not try to establish a poverty line for nineteenth-century Dutch and French society, nor will I attempt to quantify exchange entitlements or the buying power of household income in order to establish a conception of a bare minimum of existence in quantitative terms. Aggregate mortality rates will serve as one form of evidence that designates a bottom line. After all, Sen has counseled, too, that to draw a comprehensive picture of poverty as both a human condition and as a social construction it is necessary to go well beyond a mere identification the poor.[18]

In chronicling the nature and extent of indigence and its alleviation in France and the Netherlands, we can only depend on statistics at the national level. The problematic character and often unreliable nature of poor relief or criminal statistics in the nineteenth century, however, do not permit a meticulous quantitative analysis. These basically flawed data—imperfections deriving from incomplete collection techniques or crude methods of tabulation and recording—allow only for a description based on a comparison of the available data for each society. However defective these data may be, they reveal a great deal about general trends within and between the two societies; these data also illuminate the distinctive interpretations of such patterns. It is quite conceivable that enumerators in nineteenth-century France undercounted the number of people drawn into the system of social welfare by a factor of two; their Dutch statistical colleagues may have overcounted or doubled numbers by the same factor. Still, the resulting four to one ratio in the number of poor people drawn into the realm of either private charitable agencies or assistance from public sources in the Netherlands versus France, even if they only received minimal amounts of relief, constituted a meaningful difference that deserves scrutiny.

Moreover, the exact nature of the data which public officials in either Holland or France collected on a yearly basis discloses a further comparative insight. Statistical series constituted both a social document—albeit a transcript composed in columns, numbers, or percentages—and a routinized public habit that reflected the political preoccupations of a particular society. As such, the annual custom of gathering certain kinds of statistical data served as a mirror that not only divulged nineteenth-century political anxieties but also highlighted a particular nation's source of political pride. Quite predictably, the proclivity of impoverished workers in France to plunder and rebel during periods of depression—combined with a distinct revolutionary tradition in French politics—often led to a public identification of poverty with criminality, an association that at the official level inspired the systematic collection of criminal statistics in the *Compte général de l'administration de la justice criminelle* (General Report on the Administration of Criminal Justice), published annually after 1825.[19] This general report, in turn, emerged in the French public imagination as the illustrious evidence of its bureaucratic efficiency and its sophisticated, ''scientific'' approach to the management of criminal justice.

This elaborate statistical magnum opus, which appeared annually throughout the nineteenth century, provided detailed documentation of the number of individuals accused of crimes against persons and property as well as the defendants' gender, literacy, age, occupational background, and place of birth. The first edition of the *Compte général* expressed great expectations about the utility of publishing annual criminal statistics, proclaiming that "an exploration of the facts and figures of crime, when traced over time, will produce insights into the factors and circumstances that influence the growth and decline of criminal activity."[20] The yearly summary conjured up the optimistic dreams of social science par excellence. An analysis of the annual statistics on crime would enable the French government to design more effective policies, thus enhancing authorities' ability to neutralize the subversion of the social order that criminality would inevitably bring in its wake.

The statistician André-Michel Guerry, for example, noted in 1833 in his award-winning *Essai sur la statistique morale de la France* that the most challenging task for a statistician was to enumerate and classify all human activities in order to exert some kind of influence upon "isolated individuals as well as upon the conditions of the society in which they live."[21] But statistical categories could not produce any useful results unless they were "deduced from a long series of observations." Those lists of numerical statements should not only be lengthy, he wrote, but statisticians should also repeat and test them in circumstances that varied in both space and time. Above all, they must subject their data to statistical methods that rendered these systematic observations comparable. With regard to the *Compte général* he added that "never before, with no other people, had such a major task been executed in such a complete fashion."[22] Guerry celebrated the imperious, almost jubilant, claims of the science of criminology of this era, without recognizing any of the errors in logic and method contained in the *Compte général*. The annual crime statistics, after all, did not even make a simple analytical distinction between criminal allegations and actual convictions.[23]

The august intellectual presence among nineteenth-century statisticians, Adolphe Quetelet, was a lonely voice in recognizing some of the logical pitfalls inherent in the statistical analyses supplied by the *Compte général*.[24] He cautioned in 1835 that one of the greatest defects of existing statistical theories was that they displayed all the collected numbers "indiscriminately," as if they carried the same weight of significance. Statisticians, he warned, did not pay sufficient attention to the "relative importance or probable values" of their numbers. Quetelet went on to say that it was not enough to recognize that a particular effect depended on several causes; instead, statisticians should assess and "allocate the proper degree of influence to each of these causes."[25] But the *Compte général* would not heed this advice until much later in the nineteenth century, and the annual report on crime, at least until 1870 or so, was essentially the "brainchild" of an age of positivist social science and "statistical enthusiasm."[26]

As a historical artifact created and reproduced on a yearly basis by the bureaucracy of the French state, however, the annual *Compte général* suggests that the French bureaucracy in the post-Napoleonic era was more troubled by questions of criminal justice than it was concerned with issues of human hardship. It was true that episodic reports from the Minister of the Interior to the king discussed the statutes designed to limit beggary, compiled statistics on the number of people institutionalized in poor houses, or analyzed the frequency of child abandonment and its relationship to fluctuations in the annual rates of infanticide. But few reports compiled statistics on a regular basis about the number of poverty-stricken citizens in the nation or about the nature of poverty per se.

Dutch public officials, whether in a local or national arena, were less worried about the connection between poverty and criminality than their French colleagues. The Dutch nation did not create a massive policing apparatus at the center. Dutch national police archives, in fact, are slender folders in comparison with the corpulent dossiers in France, which provides eloquent testimony to the municipal primacy that remained at the heart of the Dutch policing system in the nineteenth century.[27] The central government in The Hague, instead, began to gather in 1815 intricate statistics on the number of indigent citizens who received support from both municipal agencies and private charitable institutions, which were published as the *Verslag omtrent de armoede en het armwezen in het Koninkrijk der Nederlanden* (Report on Poverty and Poor Relief in the Kingdom of the Netherlands). The report appeared annually since then, and became more detailed and complex over time, even though the actual title of the annual report varied from year to year.[28]

The annual statistical collection of the *Verslag omtrent de armoede* reflected a growing popular awareness of the grim and hopeless existence of the poor, because the first decades of the nineteenth century were especially gloomy times. Reports of unprecedented destitution and suffering came from almost every corner of the country. During 1808, for instance, the city of Amsterdam maintained approximately one-third of its population of 200,000 citizens on winter relief, although a substantial proportion of these eager recipients may have flocked to the city from outlying regions, despite city administrators' vigilance to ward off "alien" needy.[29]

Elsewhere in the country a similarly bleak picture obtained. In the city of Leiden in 1811, for example, 20 to 25 percent of the population were dependent on the dole, and by 1816–1817, which were years of subsistence crisis throughout Europe, this number may have risen to 50 percent. In Schiedam, a reduction in the number of gin distilleries from 240 in 1790 to 200 several decades later had eliminated numerous jobs and intensified destitution. In the thriving fishing village of Katwijk aan Zee, the number of active fishing boats had diminished from 80 to 30, while the trade in cured fish dried up altogether. As a result, the demand for fishing nets—knitting fishing nets being one of the "make-work" schemes for the poor during the cold winter months—declined precipitously. Farming families in rural areas, who traditionally grew and spun flax, lost their source of livelihood in the wake of the French prohibition on exports. Throughout the Netherlands, but particularly in the densely populated western provinces, economic conditions provoked pessimistic evaluations, and the official inquiry into poverty and poor relief of 1811 revealed that at least 10.5 percent of the Dutch population relied, either part-time or more permanently, on philanthropy and charitable resources.[30]

Social conditions did not dramatically improve once the French departed and diplomats at the Congress of Vienna had created the Kingdom of the Netherlands. More or less until mid-century, approximately one-third of Amsterdam's marginal population, especially those people who earned a precarious livelihood as irregular day laborers, stevedores, piece-rate workers, or servants, lived more or less consistently below the poverty line—meaning, in some definitions, that they had to spend more than 44 percent of their income on basic subsistence.[31]

The annual compilation of the Report on Poverty, it appeared, both reflected and communicated a growing consciousness of dismal social conditions, even if the statistical accuracy of the *Verslag omtrent de armoede* was just as dubious as the yearly report about criminal justice in France. The central state in The Hague could not coerce private and religious charitable organizations into supplying data, and many such institutions may have withheld information because they feared fiscal ramifications. Moreover, a single family was sometimes enumerated two or three times, and in any given year the balance sheet of the actual number of poor people was both garbled and misleading because the annual Report on Poverty counted groups of citizens previously excluded. In fact, contemporary analysts already recognized the statistical foibles of the yearly *Verslag*. "Let us examine the situation of a single, indigent family," proposed the political economist Simon Vissering in discussing the statistics gathered on the poor in the 1830s and 1840s:

> It could be that one or two religious charities and one municipal poor council supported this one family. At one point or another the wife may

> have given birth, therefore receiving extraordinary aid from a special source. Some of the members of the family may have fallen ill, therefore requiring hospitalization, while the children may have attended one or more schools for the poor. During the harsh winter months the husband may have been recruited for work in a pauper factory or workhouse. In this manner, a family of six or seven members could occupy as many as twenty-five slots in the annual poor relief statistics. To some extent this should not come as a surprise, because people who are genuinely poor will accept whatever is offered to them, but, given these observations, how can we speak with any kind of certainty about the actual size of the poor population?[32]

Even though it was not a reliable indicator whatsoever of the exact numerical level of poverty and poor relief in the Netherlands, the *Verslag omtrent de armoede* nevertheless confirmed a significant differential, each year, between the number of Dutch and French recipients of poor relief, with the Dutch outnumbering the French by a ratio of about four to one. The sheer magnitude of the bureaucratic effort required to compile the annual Report on Poverty showed the extent to which the Dutch nation, early in the nineteenth century, was conscious of the material suffering of poor people and their reliance on a ''little help'' from religious and municipal sources for survival.[33]

In addition, the *Verslag*'s tabulations, columns, lists, and percentages were incorporated into the combative discourses about poverty and poor relief. Anyone who took part in the polemical debates on this topic appropriated and distorted the *Verslag*'s statistical findings to support their particular views. L. Ph. C. van den Bergh, for example, wrote in 1845:

> If we consider the number of people who received some form of financial or material assistance during the period 1830–1840, then we will discover that in 1830 there were 439,953 people who were given support, while this number grew to 561,162 in 1840, which amounts to more than one-sixth of the entire population in 1840. In 1842, the number of paupers had again increased. In the entire country one could find 6,385 charitable institutions . . . 635,290 people received assistance, excluding those who merely accepted fuel and food during the cold winter months. The total number of indigents was 21.5 percent of the Dutch population, and the expenditures required to sustain them rose to 20,102,680 guilders, that is, the interest on the capital of more than 400 million guilders. If we assume that our annual national income is 2,400 million guilders it means that one-sixth is devoured by poor relief each year.[34]

Van den Bergh's numbers were glaringly inflated. The curiously precise figure of 635,290 poor relief recipients in 1842, for example, was much larger than the actual numbers recorded in any of the official statistics. He also included or excluded the data from the province of Limburg whenever it suited his purposes. His assumption of a gross national product of 2,400 million guilders could only be mere speculation or fantasy, since no reliable calculations of gross domestic product were available until much later. Clearly, van den Bergh pulled these exaggerated numbers out of his oratorical hat to make a forceful rhetorical point: poor relief in the Netherlands will bleed the nation dry! Jeronimo de Bosch Kemper, who was notoriously sloppy and scatterbrained in his interpretation of statistics, doctored his numbers, too, so they might support the categorical arguments about poor relief he offered in 1851.[35]

Notwithstanding all of their shortcomings, the overall picture that emerges from some of these numbers and statistics is one of similarities between France and Holland but also of intriguing contrasts. Both countries underwent a period of population growth during the first half of the nineteenth century. After two decades of relative decline between 1795 and 1815, the Dutch population increased steadily at a rate of one percent per annum during the subsequent forty years. Dutch birthrates rose abruptly after 1815 and stabilized at a relatively high level until mid-century, even though they fluctuated from year to year.[36] Death rates in the Netherlands were high, consistently higher than the annual figures on mortality in France during this period, but they tended to remain below the birthrate. Thus, the high birthrates in relation to the somewhat lower yearly mortality figures in the Netherlands jointly produced an annual increase in the national population.

France's population also grew during the first half of the nineteenth century, but it displayed "a slower heartbeat" and conformed more closely to eighteenth-century patterns.[37] The number of births, especially in the more prosperous *départements*, were surprisingly restrained, although a public concern with low population growth in France, which produced the remarkable pro-natalist policies of the early twentieth century, had not yet emerged during the first half of the nineteenth century.[38] A decline in mortality rates during this period nurtured a pattern of steady, if slow, growth of the population. Dutch and French population patterns were thus roughly similar during the first half of the nineteenth century, and so were the fluctuations in certain key economic indicators such as agricultural output, bread prices, industrial development, and to some extent, wages.

These demographic pressures and other economic trends, however, affected the patterns of poor relief in different ways. Foremost was a substantial difference in the percentage of indigent citizens who received some form of support in the two countries. According to Figure 3-1, the number of people in France receiving *secours à domicile* (outdoor relief) between 1833 and 1853 ranged from about 700,000 to about 1.2 million.[39] When those who received institutional assistance in *hospices* and *hôpitaux* are added, the range was between 1.2 and 1.8 million, comprising between 3.5 and 5 percent of the national population. As might be expected, the figures fluctuated somewhat, with fairly sharp peaks appearing during the crisis period of 1845–1847. This spasmodic pattern, though, makes eminent sense: the sharper the crisis of subsistence, the greater the level of poor relief. The French state was inclined to offer material support to a small percentage of the population, increasing aid especially during times of low harvest yields and rising food prices when authorities suspected that hunger and hardship might pose serious threats to the social order.

The general picture in the Netherlands was similar but with two main differences. The percentage of the population drawn into the Dutch system of social welfare, however meager their allowances may have been, greatly surpassed that in France, never dropping below 7.5 percent of the national population between 1817 and 1848 (Figure 3-2). Indeed, during the subsistence crisis of 1845–1847, the number of people receiving some kind of assistance, either the more usual temporary sustenance or the less common full-time aid from either private or public sources, rose to almost 19 percent, nearly four times the maximum figure for France during approximately the same period. In addition, financial allocations to outdoor relief were more consistent in the Netherlands than in France, reflecting the Dutch nation's attempt to protect the poor in their own homes, as much as was financially feasible, against recurrent unemployment rather than institutionalize them.

What, then, accounts for the contrasts in the percentage of people receiving various forms of poor relief in the two societies? The extent of both the supply of and the demand for assistance in France and the Netherlands depended on each society's values, its economic structure, and somewhat paradoxically, previous economic accomplishments. Greater accumulated wealth, whether in the form of government revenue or the disposable income of wealthy citizens, yielded, in general, more generous provisions for destitute fellow citizens. Attitudes regarding the causes of poverty or notions about individual culpability, definitions of the obligation of the state to cushion the destructive effects

Figure 3-1
People on Poor Relief in France
1832 - 1853

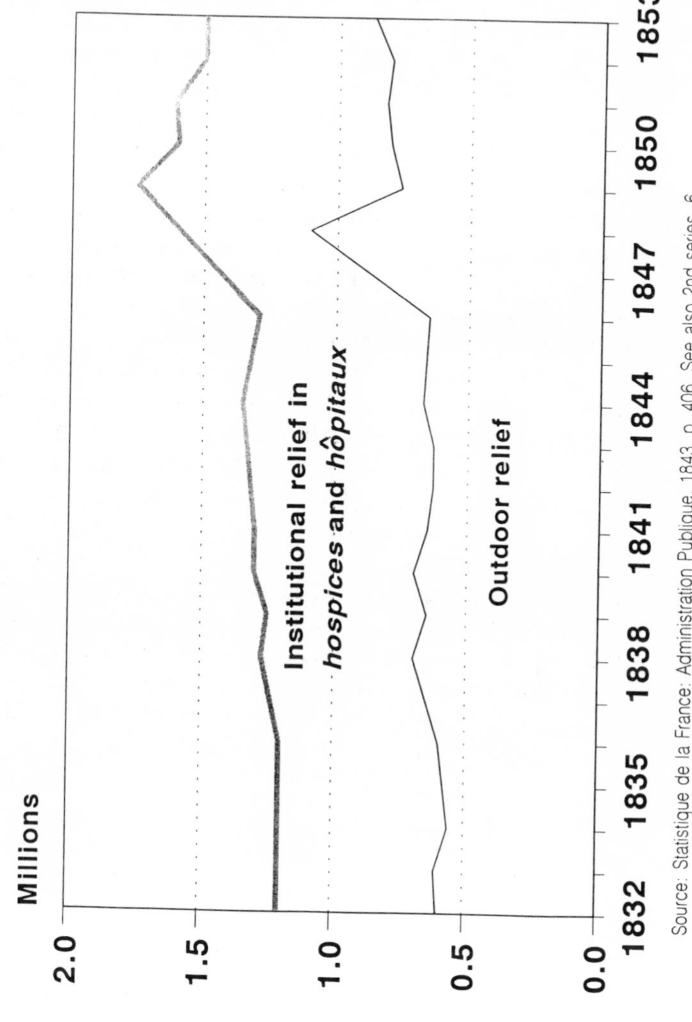

Source: Statistique de la France: Administration Publique, 1843, p. 406. See also 2nd series, 6, Statistique de l'assistance publique, 1863, p. lxiii.

of market fluctuations, and a host of other issues, whether based on myth or reality, played a large role in shaping relief programs. Once in place, policies designed to assist or control the poor may have had a tangible influence on subsequent institutional developments. Residency requirements to qualify for relief, ideas regarding a minimum or "natural" wage, tariffs to protect domestic agriculture, and a myriad of other agendas subtly pushed and tugged at workers, peasants, and notables. Collectively they affected the economic structures of France and Holland. Such structures, in turn, shaped the incentives offered and opportunities provided to poverty-stricken workers, and ultimately they influenced the need for assistance at any given time or place and molded the perceived legitimacy of assistance programs.

Thus, a kaleidoscope of cultural factors and more elusive judgments about the nature of citizenship or social justice interacted with actual economic realities. Of course, phenomena that were entirely beyond human control—the negative impact of climate on harvest yields, for instance, or the outbreak of epidemics which harmed undernourished poor people more immediately than their more robust social superiors—compounded the magnitude of need for charitable support as well as the extent to which social welfare was available.

The differences between the poor relief allocations in the two countries present a puzzle. As Figure 3-3 indicates, annual mortality rates for the Netherlands as a whole rose more sharply during the crisis periods of 1817–1818 and 1845–1847 than in France as a whole, although death rates were higher in some specific regions of France.[40] If Dutch poor relief administrations seemed more responsive to the material needs of the nation's indigent population, why were death rates in the Netherlands higher than in France during times of subsistence crisis and hardship?

There are several answers. During periods of economic depression and relatively high unemployment, the Dutch poor relief system tended to provide the increased number of indigents primarily with supplementary outdoor aid for a short period of time. Per capita expenditures on poor relief in the Netherlands were relatively constant between 1815 and 1855, suggesting that resources did not necessarily increase during times of greater need and joblessness. Hence, the minimum essential to their survival was hardly available to all needy citizens. The elaborate poor relief system of the Dutch nation, especially in its larger cities, was designed mainly to complement the functioning of the labor market rather than to provide long-term assistance. In Amsterdam during the first decades of the nineteenth century, for instance, the amount that the

Figure 3-3

Deaths Per 1,000 Of Total Population, in the Netherlands and France

1816 - 1849

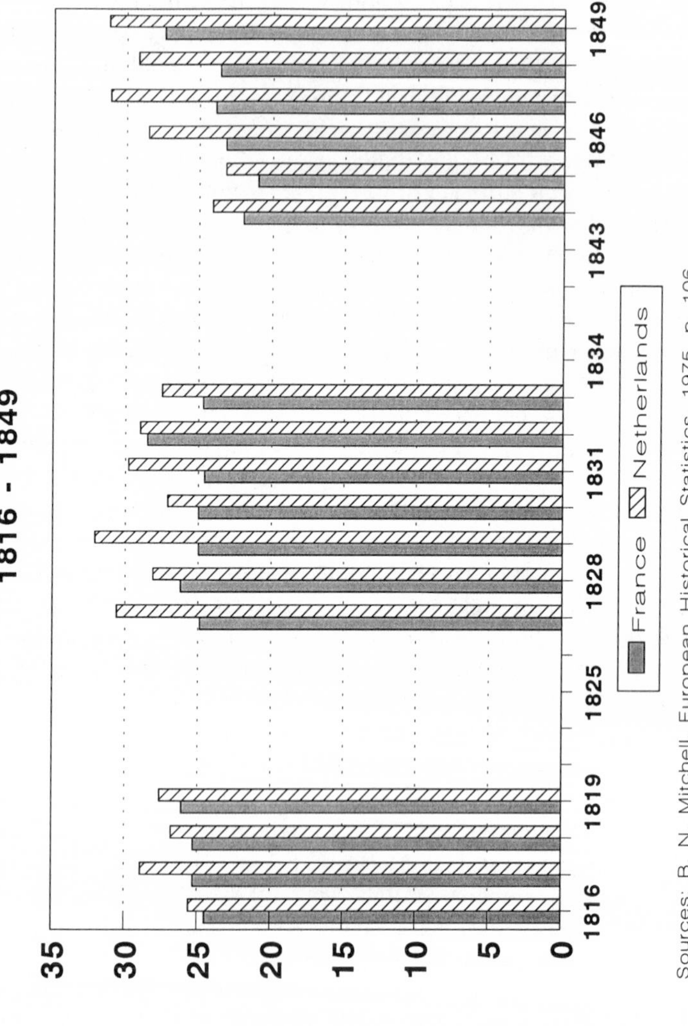

Sources: B. N. Mitchell, European Historical Statistics, 1975, p. 106
E. W. Hofstee, De Demografische ontwikkeling, 1978, p. 198

average citizen received in outdoor relief was often insufficient to sustain life for longer than two weeks.[41] And in Haarlem in 1844–1845, the percentage of poor people who received full-time aid was considerably lower than it had been fifteen years earlier, even though the total number of Haarlem citizens receiving some kind of assistance, however paltry, had risen. Thus a growing number of unemployed and needy citizens had to make do with financial resources that had remained stable.[42]

The distinctive urban character of the Dutch nation was also implicated in the higher mortality rates during times of dearth. The Dutch ecological environment and the troubling reality of contaminated water supplies, especially in the western provinces, performed a distinct role, too. Epidemic diseases such as cholera wielded a more deadly effect in the urban scramble and intense human commotion of Dutch society. A physical landscape full of polluted canals and overcrowded urban tenement buildings, Holland displayed unhygienic conditions that were rarer in the primarily rural world of France. In the Netherlands, endemic fevers such as malaria—spread by mosquitoes which thrived in the putrid canals and stagnant rivers in the western part of the country, which was submerged below sea level—were responsible for great oscillations in Dutch death rates during both normal and crisis years.[43]

Besides, infant mortality in Dutch cities was exceptionally high, ranging from one-third to one-half of all live births. In fact, the correlation between the actual physical size of a city or town and the rate of infant mortality remained positive until the 1880s.[44] A contemporary noted in 1822 that in Amsterdam, without any extraordinary causes such as epidemics or high food prices, "one out of four live-born children will be lowered into the grave before its first birthday. It is probable that this horrendous number sometimes rises to one out of three or even higher" during bad times.[45]

A physician speculated in the 1820s that one cause of death among poor children could be that "the practice of breast-feeding among the poorest of the poor is an exception rather than the rule," wondering why so many mothers were not satisfied with the "food our Creator has destined for their infants."[46] Mothers, however, were often undernourished themselves. As one poor mother wrote on a piece of paper pinned to her baby abandoned in the vicinity of the municipal orphanage in Amsterdam in 1817: "I have had to put down this little child out of the direst poverty. It is a healthy baby but it is as thin as a ghost, and I can no longer feed it." Another mother wrote sadly, "It breaks my heart, but I cannot cope any longer; I have used up all I have, and I can no longer feed my baby. Please take pity on my child, because it will otherwise die of starvation.''[47]

Religious affiliation played its part, too. Contemporary medical experts in the mid-nineteenth century pondered the differential mortality rates among poor Jews and equally pauperized gentiles in Amsterdam.[48] On the basis of careful comparative analysis, several public health authorities argued that infant mortality among Jews was lower because of the intimate bonds of the Jewish family, lower alcoholism rates, and the almost universal practice of breast-feeding among Jewish mothers. Child abandonment as an option of last resort, as a way of fostering the survival of a small child, was less prevalent among Jewish women who, regardless of hunger and hardship, had greater confidence that their breast-fed children might survive within the emotional womb of the family and extended kin. The lower incidence of illegitimate births in Amsterdam's close-knit Jewish community may also have contributed to the lower infant mortality rate.[49]

In the less urban but more predominantly Catholic southern provinces, moreover, mothers delivered many children with a shorter interval in between births; the fortifying effects of breast-feeding were thus more often withheld from newborns, while older infants ran the risk of being neglected. A gradual entrenchment of a ''shame complex'' in the more Catholic provinces further compounded high neonatal mortality rates as the nineteenth century came to a close. Women's reluctance to expose their bodies—especially to bare their breasts—prompted Catholic mothers to breast-feed their babies less frequently and for a shorter duration only.[50] In France, in contrast, a slight reduction in the infant death rate took place during the first decades of the nineteenth century; between 1840 and 1855 French neonatal mortality was considerably lower than in Holland, comprising an average of 161 deaths per 1,000 live births annually.[51]

Holland was a small country. It had achieved a relatively high level of urbanization and commercial integration by 1815; its rural sector was not focused on subsistence agriculture but was oriented, instead, toward a domestic and international market for agricultural products. Hardship in the Netherlands was spread more evenly across the entire nation, despite regional differences in such factors as ecological hazards or religious culture. The great divide between town and country, or the enormous economic differences between such thriving commercial agricultural regions as the Beauce and the marginal subsistence agriculture of ragged peasants in Brittany, existed to a lesser degree.

Compared with the Netherlands, France was a society with a highly mobile labor force, and wage earners traveled not only within their *pays* but also from one department to the next in quest of better jobs and higher earnings. Rural laborers carved makeshift paths through the jagged mountains of the Massif Central, an inhospitable region that was "a reservoir of men and human suffering," and either journeyed to Paris for a longer term or descended to the lowlands of the Nièvre and the Cher on a seasonal basis.[52] Bretons often left their dirt-poor existence of subsistence agriculture behind to migrate to Paris or other large cities in the north. Few towns within Brittany itself provided an alternative to their lives of backbreaking labor in a hostile *pays de bocage* divided into large landholdings controlled by "an intransigent aristocracy" and multitudes of scrappy peasants.[53] Many Frenchmen from *départements* near the Belgian border routinely traveled south to bring in the wheat harvests in the Beauce and the Ile de France or settled permanently in the textile manufacturing centers of the Nord. In fact, labor migration in France—Eugen Weber referred to it as an "Industry of the Poor"—actually increased between 1815 and 1914 because improvements in roads and transportation facilitated the movement of French workers.[54]

Migration was a central element in the constellation of economic strategies which poor people, living on the margin of survival, employed when high bread prices or disastrous harvests pushed them over the edge. Sons left their parents' homes in order to preserve the patrimony, while daughters departed to help earn a dowry. As peasant holdings became increasingly precarious and subdivided—since the pattern of *morcellement* intensified as a result of population growth—more members of landless or nearly landless families emigrated to earn their daily bread. Sometimes entire families and sometimes solitary young people traveled to those towns where, as they had heard through kin or village connections, they might find work and shelter.[55]

In France men were more mobile than women; men were also more likely to migrate beyond the immediate region and across departmental borders.[56] Gender-specific migration, however, varied from region to region; more young women than men, for example, left three small villages in the eastern Languedoc for the regional "metropolis" of Nîmes.[57] However, in Paris men in early adulthood outnumbered young women among the newly arrived migrant communities in the city, and a sharp decline in the female, vis-à-vis the male, population took place between 1817 and 1836, followed by a slower reduction in the proportion of women until 1851.[58]

The gender of destitute people influenced the ways in which officials perceived their worthiness; it also prejudiced the generosity of poor relief allocations in subtle ways. Officials in both countries privileged women as the deserving poor, especially if they conveyed an aura of jaded gentility. In both France and Holland poor relief officials bestowed a larger proportion of the available charitable resources upon women. But a subtle distinction between Dutch and French patterns resided in the differential attitudes to poor men. In France, bourgeois contemporaries more rapidly categorized and dismissed indigent men as free riders, whom they suspected of voluntarily choosing idleness and beggary over a fruitful existence. In the mind's eye of French elites, male migrants or wandering factory laborers in search of employment embodied covert danger: their tramping lives evoked a world filled with furtive prowlers or rowdy drifters.[59]

When men, whether rich or poor, dared to express discontent publicly, such collective displays had an immediate political resonance, whatever the actual motives were.[60] A man's solitary, if despairing, search for work raised suspicions of vagabondage and beggary, and his participation in any kind of food riot conjured up fears of political chaos or dangerous criminality.[61] French authorities approached the ''deserving poor,'' in contrast, with paternalistic concern, especially if they were women:

> Nature does not endow all human beings equally. Some are born with deformities which deny them the ability to work. Accidents, disease, and old age bring in their wake infirmities that lead to the same consequence. Women and children are naturally weak and are forced to solicit public charity because they cannot provide for their own livelihood. The government can obviously not use severe measures against this class of indigents, because they will say: if you do not come to our help, what other means of existence do we have?[62]

Regardless of its melodramatic overtones, this pronouncement indicated that public officials defined women—whose inherent nature made them physically frail and socially defenseless—as a separate social category, as maintaining a relationship to the state that diverged from men's. Inevitably this perspective endowed women with a different connection to public and private sources of charity as well.

The apparent predominance of women among the officially designated indigent population in France was a factor that influenced—and, in turn, was affected by—the perceptions of French policymakers. Poor relief administrators' view of women and children as politically harmless and socially vulnerable allowed them to assume a more compassionate posture on women's behalf. Officials tended to treat mothers, whether single heads of households or not, as economically more fragile than men and less capable of providing for their offspring without supplementary support from public authorities.

Why the difference in the perception of women in France? The Great Revolution, which shaped so many aspects of nineteenth-century French history, had erected the foundation for the differential attitudes toward men and women by bequeathing French society with legal rights and prescriptions that treated men differently from women. The Revolutionary Declaration of the Rights of Man and Citizen had ratified the principle of equality before the law, to be granted to all rightful citizens. All adult males qualified as full-fledged citizens who were free and able, in theory, to defend their own interests in civil society.[63] The Revolution, however, did not confer upon women the status of citizenship in either a legal or a political sense. The French Revolution had empowered men by bestowing them with *liberté*, *égalité*, and *fraternité*—even if it did not mean much to desperate peasants or hungry workers—but it left women in a formally disenfranchised position.

The differential treatment of women and men—or of husbands and wives—was perpetuated and ratified in the Napoleonic Code. Articles 215 and 217 in Chapter VI of the Civil Code—the chapter that regulates "the rights and respective duties of husband and wife"—established the powerlessness of wives over matters of property. Article 215 stated that "the wife can do no act in law without the authority of her husband, even when she shall be a public trader, or not in community or separate in property." Article 217 went on to stipulate that "the wife, even not in community or separate in property, cannot give, alienate, mortgage, or acquire, either gratuitously or subject to condition, without the concurrence of her husband in the act, or his consent in writing." Article 218 further articulated that "if the husband refuses to authorize his wife to proceed at law, a judge may give his authority."[64] It appeared that men, whether husbands or judges, held exclusive power over the disposition of property.

These provisions in the Napoleonic Code granted women virtually no control over their property. It was true that the Civil and Criminal Codes were drafted by bourgeois jurists, politicians, and constitutional scholars whose concerns and pronouncements regarding property revolved around middle-class definitions of ownership. The kinds of concerns with property contained in the Civil Code were a far cry from the paltry possessions owned by poverty-stricken men and women who lived on the margin of survival and engaged in migration and beggary, or bread riots and popular insurrection. But these fundamental legal injunctions affected the disadvantaged members of French society, too, because the "rights and respective duties of husband and wife" applied equally to rich and poor. There was a paradox, however. Women's official disenfranchisement may have benefited the somber lives of desperately needy mothers. Since the Revolution did not endow them with full-blown legal citizenship, women were entitled to protective legislation and deemed worthy of the state's special treatment. This "special" accommodation of women entailed, too, a departure from the ancien régime habit of incarcerating all wrongdoers, regardless of gender or age, in communal rooms stuffed to the gills with pickpockets, prostitutes, convicted murderers, and poor mothers accused, but not yet convicted, of infanticide. Nineteenth-century prisons and jails, instead, segregated women from men, or mothers from adolescent children, and secluded them in "honeycombed" units that underscored their female *différence*.[65]

This gendered definition of citizenship and the differential attitudes towards men and women had other implications as well. Women, especially if they appeared intractable or unencumbered by the exalted duties of marriage, could personify, too, a range of bourgeois phobias. In a middle-class imagination, the domesticity of family life presumably tempered women's residual wildness and imposed upon them a quiet serenity. Accordingly, nineteenth-century Frenchmen attributed a series of negative characteristics to free-floating, single women who struggled to survive as best as they could. Often single working-class women seemed to be beyond the pale of bourgeois civility and in middle-class eyes they embodied all sorts of immoral tendencies, ranging from duplicity and egotism to promiscuity and insubordination. On occasion, these fears of unruly poor women converged with bourgeois anxieties about revolution and anarchy in general.[66] The women most entitled to the special attention of charitable benefactors or public authorities, therefore, were those who displayed an appropriate mixture of genuine need and subservience: properly married women who suffered from hunger and distress but who did so with an aura of *pudeur* and contrition.

All in all the Revolution's contradictory legal legacy exerted an indelible effect on poor women who confronted material distress. When harvests failed and food shortages threatened, many husbands and sons tended to leave in order to find work elsewhere, since they should fend for themselves in the political and economic marketplace. Mothers often stayed behind and frequently became the objects of charitable empathy and local support. Robert-Jacques Turgot had already identified this process during the eighteenth century and he emphasized the role of private charity in providing for women and children. During the dire harvests of 1769, when the rye crop failed and disastrous weather had destroyed such auxiliary food crops as buckwheat and chestnuts, too, he wrote that many people could "subsist only by selling at a miserable price their articles of furniture and even their clothes. Many of the inhabitants have been obliged to disperse themselves through other provinces to seek work or to beg, leaving their wives and children to the charity of the parishes."[67]

This gendered pattern of migration in France continued beyond the ancien régime and so did the overrepresentation of women among the recipients of charity. Of those who left their departments around 1850, approximately 70 percent were men and only about 30 percent were women.[68] The figures for migration within some departments revealed a smaller differential between men and women, such as the large proportion of young women who migrated from several villages in the eastern Languedoc to the regional capital of Nîmes, but on the whole the predominance of male migration persisted until the very end of the century.

French officials, both before and after the Revolution, expressed a perennial concern about the insidious consequences of the migratory patterns of men. Commenting on the misconduct of migrant husbands and fathers, officials noticed the spread of venereal diseases, which migrants contracted in wicked big cities and transmitted to their guileless and "honest wives who soon languish and die." Government bureaucrats linked the outmigration of husbands and fathers with the decline of family stability and the abandonment of wives; in the departments of Cantal and Puy-de-Dôme in 1834 for instance, a local official reported that "the morals of men suffer from the migrations they frequently make to other parts of France."[69] The sophisticated ex-worker Martin Nadaud, who in his early years had experienced the migrant life firsthand, hit the nail on the head. In his *Mémoires* he reported that Limousin stonemasons who had migrated to Paris "are not embarrassed to abandon their wives in order to live with hussies (*coquines*)."[70]

The prefect of the department of Cantal summed it all up. In those regions of the country, especially in the area of the Massif Central, where temporary migration was an ancient and ingrained practice, it had a "deplorable effect on family life." Migration, he wrote, relaxed the "conjugal ties of husbands and wives," and it produced, too, an indifference toward their children, who were "barely educated as a result.'' Migration engendered ''the habit of intemperance and squandering money,'' unscrupulous tendencies men brought back from the city to the countryside, because it was in the cities that migrant workers absorbed the kind of ungodly values and profligate behavior that rarely affected the inhabitant of the countryside.[71]

Rural women, when left behind to care for hearth and family at a time when unemployment soared or food shortages threatened, forged their own clear-cut response. If it had not yet been sold, a mother cultivated the tiny plot of family land with the help of her young children in order to pay rent and feed her family. When conditions became desperate, women beseeched neighbors for help or they appealed to charity. But if relief was not forthcoming, women in rural France begged, stole, participated in grain riots, or engaged in popular protests by relying on their collective strength and exulting in a shared ''feminine agency.''[72] Despite this conduct, public officials did not immediately perceive these women as a political threat, unless shady characters or suspicious political agitators from the outside seemed to exploit naive women and children for their own nefarious purposes. If poor women participated in food riots, authorities may have recognized that such behavior was part of their moral calling as devoted mothers and wives. Because of their political disenfranchisement, their collective actions were often deemed worthy of special dispensation.

In addition to patterns of labor migration, several other factors influenced the balance between male and female poor relief recipients in both France and Holland. Among these were the arduous nature of work and the potential hazards posed by every kind of employment. Illness and accidents threatened the lives of workers and often left their already suffering families bereft. Articulating a version of the Rowntree life-cycle hypothesis *avant la lettre*, the French prison expert Benjamin Appert observed in 1827:

> The number of men who are ill and who reside in *hospices* has surpassed the number of females. The men are mostly between the ages of 25 and 50, because they are often subject to all sorts of accidents that endanger their lives. This is also the stage of life when most new households are being formed: it is the period of childbearing, when saving is impossible because of the funds needed to establish a new family, and the smallest mishap or illness would require expenses that would leave the household without resources.[73]

The inference is clear: when husbands became incapacitated by disease or accident, wives, especially when pregnant or burdened with small children, had to turn to charity for sustenance and survival. But the relative preponderance of adult men between the ages of 25 and 50 whom city officials cared for—or enclosed and disciplined—in *hospices*, was also part and parcel of the French conflation of indigent men and political subversion.

French historians have alluded to the predominance of women among the urban poor during the last decades of the ancien régime.[74] This trend continued in early nineteenth-century France. According to Figure 3-4, women recipients of *secours à domicile* in Paris consistently and substantially outnumbered men from 1818 to 1842.[75] Together, women and children composed approximately 76 percent of the total. This figure is considerably in excess of women's share of the total French population, and also of the proportion of women among the inhabitants of Paris.[76] It was also distinctly greater than the percentage of women in Amsterdam who received outdoor relief during the same period, which constituted 60.5 percent.[77]

Information on the internal composition of indigent households in Paris during the early 1830s, shown in Figure 3-5, confirms the preponderance of women and children among Parisian poor relief recipients, who outnumbered men by approximately three to one.[78] During the same period, the number of married and widowed heads of households receiving aid appears to be virtually identical, whereas between 1828 and 1842 the number of women who were officially listed as *femmes abandonnées* ranged between a low of 1,325 in the year 1832 to a high of 1,898 in the year 1841.[79] Deserted women, of course, were unequivocally categorized as single heads of households, although no information is available on precisely how large their households were, but the greatest number of families who received charitable support had either two or three children.[80] Regardless of the reasons for their husbands' absence, Parisian women comprised the largest percentage of recipients of charity from the mid 1820s to the mid 1840s. In 1853 in Paris, according to Armand Husson, this situation still prevailed: 25,483 women received assistance, whereas only 11,509 men collected charitable support.[81]

In the Netherlands, the annual *Verslag omtrent de armoede* throughout the first half of the nineteenth century did not specifically mention a relative predominance of women over men or vice versa. Although Marco van Leeuwen's work on Amsterdam has shown that more women than men received assistance in Amsterdam, on the whole the family unit appeared to be the focus of most relief efforts, which yielded some of the irregularities in the yearly statistics.[82] The 1850

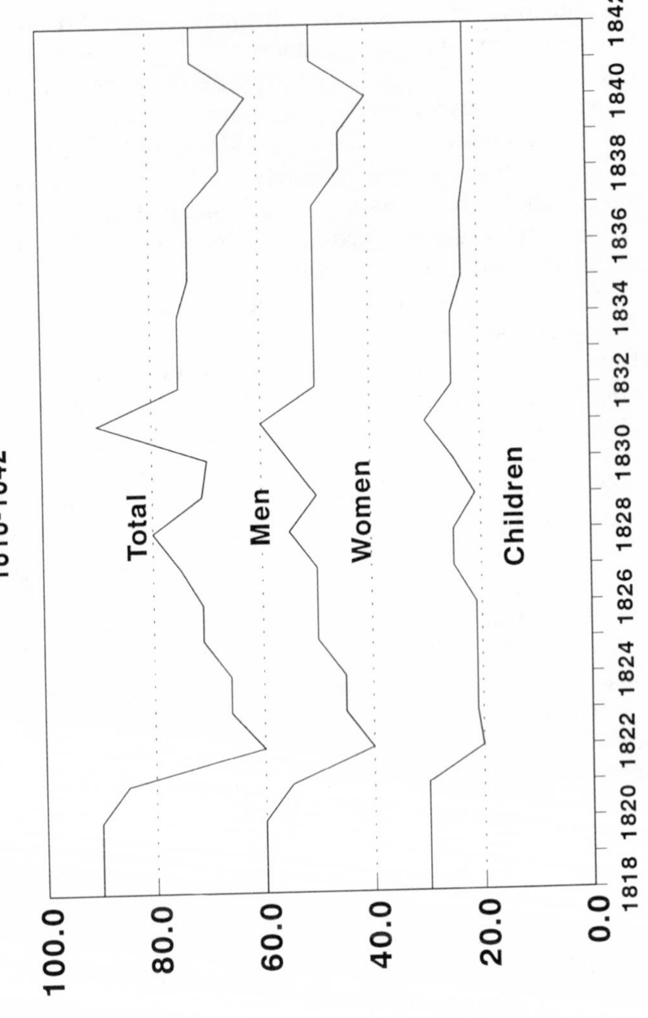

Figure 3-4
Sex and Age Distribution of Recipients of Outdoor Relief in Paris
1818-1842

Source: Statistique de la France: Administration publique, 1843, p. 404.

Figure 3-5
Composition of Indigent Households in Paris
1829 - 1835

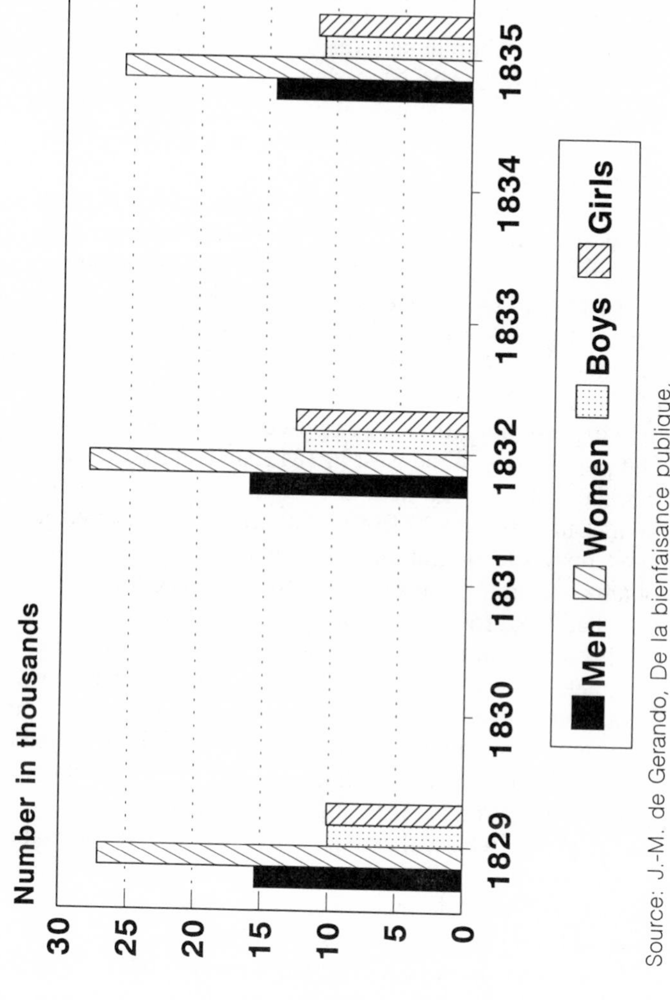

Source: J.-M. de Gerando, De la bienfaisance publique, 1839, pp. 116-117.

Report on Poverty mentioned that "a sudden shift from counting families in 1842 to listing individuals as the recipients of outdoor relief in 1843 caused the aggregate poor relief figures to augment by 44,700 in only one year."[83] Aside from these statistical confusions, the lingering tradition of enumerating family units reinforces the notion that, in a society with less internal labor mobility than France, women per se did not eclipse men in the poor relief rolls to the same degree.

The more elaborate patterns of labor migration in nineteenth-century France relative to the Netherlands can also shed light on the reasons why aggregate annual mortality rates for the French nation as a whole were lower than in Holland, where the option of migration was not as readily embraced. During times of catastrophic food shortages in a particular French region, the long-standing cultural habit of labor mobility enabled French residents to escape from suffering and death by migrating elsewhere. To be sure, migration into the western provinces of the Netherlands was considerable. Jan Lucassen has established that since early modern times, the provinces along the North Sea attracted migrant workers from elsewhere, even if the level of migration tapered off in the early nineteenth century. He has observed, for instance, that arriving migrant workers composed one percent or more of the provincial populations in the west in 1811, and a large share of these itinerant workers hailed from Hessia, Westphalia, or other German regions beyond Dutch borders.[84] But a Dutch law promulgated in 1818 discouraged domestic migration by stipulating that indigent residents could obtain poor relief only in their place of birth or in the town in which they had lived for at least four years.

This law reconfirmed the consensus, articulated as early as during the seventeenth-century Dutch Republic, that however down-and-out, the poor were full-fledged members of the community and that "such people remained understood as burghers."[85] Inevitably, the law produced a reluctance among able-bodied workers to uproot themselves. During times of high food prices and few employment opportunities, staying on in towns where they knew exactly which charitable institutions might be willing to supplement their income, even if it was only a trifling little bit, made more sense than departing for an unknown place and venturing toward an uncertain future.[86]

In the Netherlands, misery and hunger neither sparked the same explosion of collective actions nor provoked a comparable increase in criminal activity as the French *Compte général de l'administration de la justice criminelle* had tried to record so compulsively since 1825. As a Dutch official noted in 1846, with a sigh of relief: "The poor are starving in their hovels, but each of us walks unmolested along the dikes and sleeps undisturbed in his house.''[87] Of course poor people in Holland, when they were wretchedly hungry and could not find employment anywhere—or when charity was wholly inadequate in relieving their suffering—also pillaged and protested, but they did so more as a last resort.

Between 1817 and 1819 a variety of collective actions took place in Holland, which involved both subsistence-related social protests as well as ''proto'' labor conflicts. Subliminal social unrest permeated the city of Amsterdam in these years and several brawls took place in which destitute people plundered potatoes and bread. During 1816, for example, the price of rye doubled while potatoes, the staple of the Dutch diet, tripled in price in the provinces of Noord-Holland and Zuid-Holland.[88] The economic conditions of the population became so shaky during these years that on June 7, 1816, the director of police in Amsterdam wrote to the Provincial Governor:

> Last month I already mentioned the high costs of food, especially of potatoes, and I took the liberty to suggest that governmental measures were absolutely necessary. Today I regard such measures to be even more urgently needed, because members of the lower classes as well as more well-to-do citizens are banding together and they speak openly of gaining violent entry to potato ships, warehouses, and cellars in order to take the goods that might fulfill their wants. When one takes into consideration that the price of potatoes has currently risen to 1 guilder per quarter-measure—a quantity that hardly suffices to replenish the empty bellies of a husband, his wife, and their four or five children—then I do not regard it necessary to provide further justification for my request.[89]

The Amsterdam police chief's missive sent a message that differed dramatically from the entreaties that his Parisian counterpart, Louis Debelleyme, would issue twelve years later. The director of police in Amsterdam did not call for more funds for lockups and jails; instead, he requested the provincial governor's assistance in making more food available at a lower cost. Indeed, in the wake of his appeal, the municipal council of Amsterdam did decide to buy five hundred units of rye in the Baltic and sell it at a reduced rate. City magistrates also bought a large quantity of potatoes with municipal funds and sold it at subsidized prices. The Amsterdam council further encouraged the city's bakers to create a cheap, low-quality bread made from a combination of rye flour and the husks of grain that were commonly used as animal fodder during ordinary times. In fact, after checking this low-priced concoction, a member of the municipal medical commission remarked wryly that "at least it is not harmful to people's health."[90] Nevertheless, despite city magistrates' best efforts, whether in Amsterdam or elsewhere, social confrontations did take place. In Rotterdam, for instance, a hunger-related riot produced so much chaos and consternation that it required an extra cavalry detachment to disperse the plunderers.[91]

The mid-1840s revealed a similar picture. Between 1845 and 1847 a deadly fungus struck Dutch potato crops, a harvest failure further exacerbated by an extraordinarily rainy summer in 1845 and an extremely frigid winter to follow. Because of the potato's importance in the Dutch diet, the potato blight seriously undermined the marginal existence of the poor. In 1846, the harvest failed again, even in regions with fertile clay soils which, in normal times, were renowned for their bountiful crops.[92] The rye harvest, too, was a disappointment:

> While the year 1845 was a disaster, the year 1846 provided equally good reasons for great anxiety, because aside from the low potato yield the rye harvest suffered a setback also. Since the poor rye harvest of 1830, there has never been such a lamentable crop as in 1846. Its primary cause was the *roest*, a disease that affected rye production everywhere, not only in Holland but all over western Europe. In combination with the scarcity of potatoes, we are confronted with a general shortage of food which has caused prices to rise so high that even the greatest financial sacrifices cannot fulfill human needs.[93]

In the Report on Poverty for the year 1845, the statistical appendices that listed the number of people who received outdoor relief (*huiszittende armen*) were, in the case of most provinces, supplied with a footnote designed to explain the substantial increase in numbers that year: "The augmentation of the number of recipients must be attributed to the harsh winter of 1844–45 and to the failure of the potato harvest."[94] Accordingly, as figure 3-6 indicates, the growth in the number of *huiszittende armen* during the four years from 1844 through 1847 was striking. The data reveal not only that the number of people on relief increased dramatically, but also that recipients were spread fairly evenly among the various provinces; this was linked to the fact that the economy of the Netherlands as a whole was a fairly integrated one. The data further indicate that the growth was sharpest in the most heavily urban regions in the western part of the nation, thus giving support to the argument that cities represented bottlenecks for the distribution of food and supplies.

However assiduously many private and public poor relief institutions

Figure 3 - 6

Recipients of Outdoor Relief in the Netherlands 1844-1847

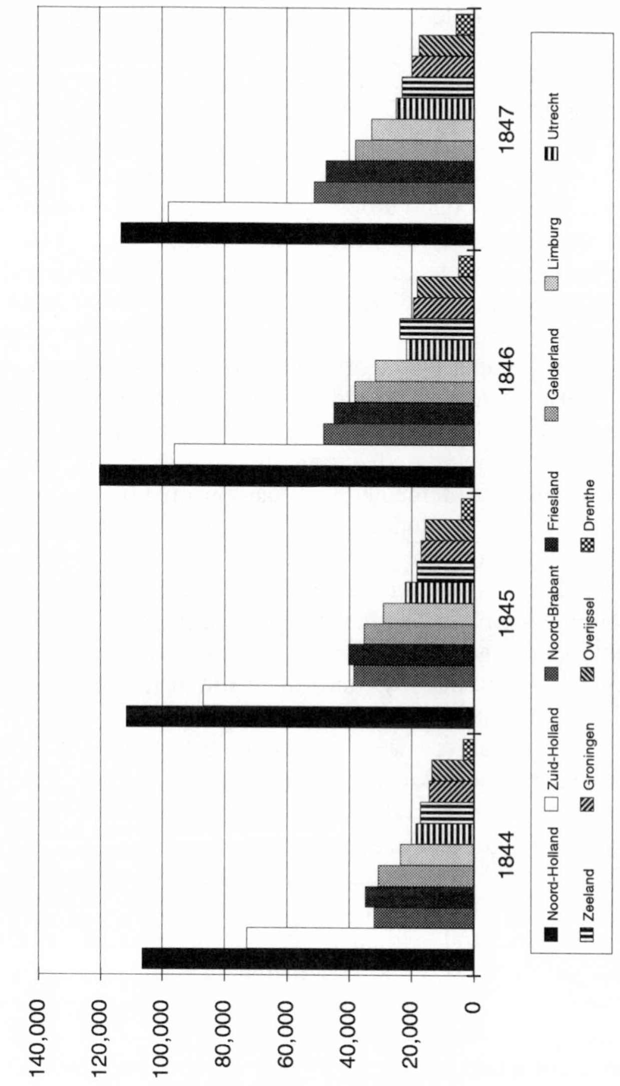

Source: Verslag omtrent de armoede dienstjaar 1848.

may have tried to care for and feed the poor during this time of food shortage and intense material deprivation, some popular protests none-theless occurred, although on a more moderate scale than in France during the same period. In some cities in the western provinces, poor and hungry people broke grocers' windows, and they forced a number of shopkeepers to rescind price hikes, but in general the outbursts were reasonably restrained. In Delft, however, the uprising had to be re-garded as serious: hungry people went on a rampage and looted grocery stores, but in the end only eight people were punished severely.[95] In the summer of 1847, after accumulated hardship due to two consecutive years of failed potato crops and very mediocre rye harvests, social un-rest erupted again, this time in the northern part of the country. In the town of Harlingen, for example, poor workers, especially longshore-men, revolted against the export of potatoes and meat to England, and they seized and ransacked a recently loaded ship.[96]

It was true that Dutch officials also remarked upon a causal relation-ship between destitution and criminal activity. Several provincial gover-nors in the Netherlands reported that delinquency, especially petty theft of food, had increased during the subsistence crisis of 1845–1847. Some officials commented that many people had been reduced to hun-ger and penury, including those who in normal times had earned a rea-sonable livelihood for themselves and their families. In general, though, Dutch discussions did not impart the same resonance of dread and panic about the incipient criminal behavior of the poor as reverberated in the stentorian language of French officials. "If we follow the lessons of economics," wrote J.A. van Roijen somewhat blithely in 1846, crimi-nality would automatically be reduced: by nurturing the overall material welfare of society, "we can cultivate a fertile soil that will propagate superior morals and manners" and impeccable law-abiding behavior.[97]

While Dutch officials expected property crimes to increase during times of hunger and dearth, they acknowledged, too, that poor people deliberately provoked authorities into arresting them for beggary and vagabondage. Their goal was to be sheltered in prisons or to be fed in the agricultural settlements of the *Maatschappij van Weldadigheid* (Benevolent Society), which maintained elaborate rural colonies for urban paupers in the eastern part of the country. During the crisis years 1845–47, for instance, when the level of need overwhelmed the re-sources of charitable institutions in Amsterdam, the Governor of Over-ijssel reported that many people began to panhandle in the city of Zwolle or harass proper burghers in the street in the most blatant of fashions.[98] The district attorney in Zwolle, a city located near the colonies of the *Maatschappij*, complained about the legal stipulation that indigents could voluntarily surrender themselves to the *Maatschappij* colonies. Many people came as far as Zwolle, he claimed, only to discover that they had run out of money and therefore could not make the final trek to the colonies. ''Once stranded in our city, they start to engage in beggary on purpose in order to be sent to the colony in Ommerschans. This is not a matter of normal begging. It is instead a special device employed solely to gain access to the colonies.'' The same legal official in Zwolle accused city officials in Amsterdam of providing travel money to its paupers, so they might sail on a barge across the Zuiderzee to reach the colonies near Zwolle. But the mayor of Amsterdam adamantly denied the charge and countered that his city ''has actually refused indigents' requests to be sent directly to the colonies, because they could have been absorbed in workhouses and pauper factories in the city of Amsterdam itself.''[99]

Despite the difficulties in determining the exact dimensions of the poor population, most of the time, whether in Amsterdam or in other Dutch cities, people suffering from want and deprivation could count on some form of supplementary income during times of hardship, as if the ubiquitous infrastructure of poor relief served as a protective shield between true desperation and material survival. Notwithstanding the evidence of hunger-induced uprisings in various cities in the Netherlands, when adjusted demographically, they were fewer and farther between than in France. This relative restraint underscores J.A. Faber's assertion that food riots in the Netherlands did not inevitably go hand in hand with periods of scarcity and high food prices.[100] The labyrinth of lakes, rivers, and canals that punctuated the Dutch landscape expedited the distribution of food and, if necessary, also facilitated the quick transit of troops to quell social unrest and ''collective bargaining by riot.''[101] In any case, inchoate notions of belonging to the same community or perhaps a residual sense of shared citizenship rendered the poor less belligerent, more quiescent, and willing to rely on the ''transfer'' payments the community as a whole might be able to muster during times of adversity.

The majority of poor people received temporary aid, though, and a reasonably strong association existed between the number of Dutch indigents receiving temporary relief and short-run fluctuations in the price of basic subsistence and other economic indicators, a finding that should come as no surprise. All in all, if we compare Dutch patterns of charity with French practices of poor relief in the same period, the political priorities in the Netherlands appeared to differ. The Dutch seemed more convinced that oscillations in the demand for poor relief were linked to inherent flaws in the functioning of a market economy. Dutch officials viewed the ebb and flow of the number of needy citizens as an epiphenomenon of an unpredictable labor market. Charity, in this context, provided supplementary income to a "reserve" labor force that, although temporarily unemployed, would be in demand again once the economic tide would turn. In contrast, French authorities trembled at the thought of an unrestrained market or an official reliance on employment in the private sector. They found it difficult to fathom charity as a humane safety net that might soften the blows which the regular rise and fall in the demand for labor inflicted upon the poor.

In Holland, however boisterously or modestly the poor expressed their requests, their plea for help rarely encountered indifference, even if the level and scale of support were painfully limited. Often charitable institutions' annual incomes were woefully insufficient to fulfill the overwhelming need, even though in most cities the *Hervormde diaconie* (Dutch Reformed poor relief board) provided assistance alongside, for example, the Catholic, Lutheran, Remonstrant, Israelite, and other religious charitable agencies. At the same time, municipal governments supported organizations allocating outdoor relief and they funded hospitals, poorhouses, and other public institutions for orphans, the handicapped, the elderly, and those who had no formal religious affiliation. The majority of Dutch cities thus presented a bewildering array of organizations dedicated to helping indigent citizens.

Because of the imposing panoply of poor relief institutions, though, the habit of giving and receiving charity, preeminently within the spiritual brotherhood and sisterhood of religious congregations, seemed deeply ingrained in the cultural landscape of Dutch society. Wealthier members of a particular church, in executing their Christian obligation to be charitable, transferred resources to their poorer fellow believers as best as they could. As a result, questions of material inequality and social justice were intimately linked to membership in a community of believers, which, in turn, yielded a fierce protectiveness of the autonomy of the *diaconiëen.*

During the Napoleonic era, the French *intendant-général* for the Ministry of the Interior in the Netherlands, Baron F. J. B. d'Alphonse, observed in 1811 that no other country in Europe had as many charitable institutions as Holland did. But he also noted that nowhere in Europe was the administration of poor relief as defective and misguided. Although he recognized that "the art of philanthropy is the most difficult of all," he castigated the Dutch for the organizational mayhem and confusion, even anarchy, of their poor relief efforts, and he criticized the stubborn Dutch refusal to implement a more efficient bureaucracy or to adopt more innovative techniques.[102] D'Alphonse's critique revealed his impatience with the bureaucratic muddle of Dutch charitable practices. He cited as an example the competition between municipal agencies, not only with each other but also with church *diaconiëen*, all of whom replicated one another's services: it was the complete absence of central guidance and direction, he implied, that caused this deplorable situation. A society should not only envision poorhouses ''with an eye to pity'' and compassion, he wrote, they also must be perceived through the eyes of administrators, and an organization that is ''most simple and most economical will always be superior.'' This, he said with self-satisfaction, the French did better.[103]

Toward mid-century, despite all the ink that had been spilled and all the voices that had become hoarse from arguing about the structure of poor relief, the situation had not changed much. ''Some communities emphasize the provision of work in winter time, even if it is unnecessary and unproductive work,'' noted three authors with liberal economic inclinations in 1850:

> Elsewhere in the country, alongside these new efforts, we can still find ancient institutions such as independent and denominational poorhouses, hospitals, orphanages, and old age homes . . . municipal poor relief agencies are the chief providers in the provinces of Noord-Brabant, Limburg, and part of Zeeland, whereas in other provinces the municipal agencies help only those who are not sheltered by religious charities. Some *diaconiëen* will soothe the plight of members of other religious denominations if they receive a subvention from the municipal treasury . . . and in Friesland, the levy of a municipal poor tax to support the poverty-stricken members of the community has already been a customary practice for a long time.[104]

In other words, despite the passage of time, the primordial friction between local particularism and coherent national policies, so emblematic of the politics of the seventeenth-century Dutch Republic, persisted. Despite the concerted efforts of King William I and his ministers to endow the nation's structure of poor relief with an organizational coherence that would enhance its overall ''public'' and collective benefits, early nineteenth-century discourses about private charity versus public welfare did not move beyond the tangible institutional inheritance or rhetorical practices of the Republic. Indeed, at mid-century, almost atavistically, the ancient patterns of private charity triumphed unequivocally, and social welfare, once again, was firmly ensconced in the hands of private benefactors and church deacons.[105]

Notes

1. Quoted by Pierre Guiral and Guy Thuillier, *La vie quotidienne des domestiques en France au XIXième siècle* (Paris: Hachette, 1978), pp. 141–42. Marcus-Henri-Casimir Mittre, in *Des domestiques en France dans leur rapports avec l'économie sociale, le bonheur domestique, et les lois civiles, criminelle, et de police* (Versailles: Ange, 1837) opened his study with the assertion that "female domestics supply the largest number of children rescued by poor-houses and they are the ones who commit the largest number of infanticides" (pp. vi–vii).

2. Archief van het Hooggerechtshof, 1813–1870, No. 659, Gratiën. Request for a pardon submitted on August 10, 1837, ARA, The Hague. See also Jolie Ermers, "Medeas or fallen angels? The prosecution of infanticide and stereotypes of child murderesses in the Netherlands in the nineteenth century"; and Sjoerd Faber, "Infanticide and criminal justice in the Netherlands," in International Commission of Historical Demography, ed., *The Role of the State and Public Opinion in Sexual Attitudes and Demographic Behaviour* (Madrid: n.p., 1990); and M. Grever, "Hetzelve in het privaat werpen," in Margret Brugmann, ed., *Vrouwen in opspraak. Vrouwenstudies als cultuurkritiek* (Nijmegen: SUN Uitgeverij, 1987).

3. Archief van het Hooggerechtshof, 1813–1870, No. 659, Gratiën.

4. Archief van het Hooggerechtshof, 1813–1870, No. 659, Gratiën.

5. *Association de Nevers*, February 20, 1842, quoted by Guiral and Thuillier, *La vie quotidienne des domestiques*, pp. 141–42.

6. Premier bureau, Division des affaires criminelles et des grâces, Ministere de la Justice, November 22, 1845. F7 12243, AN, Paris.

7. Elise van Calcar, *Tabitha. Armoede en weldadigheid*, 2 vols. (Amsterdam: J.H. Kirberger, 1856), 1, p. 205.

8. Regina Kunzel, *Fallen Women, Problem Girls: Unmarried Mothers and the Professionalization of Social Work, 1890–1945* (New Haven: Yale University Press, 1994). For a general discussion of the plight of poor pregnant women in Paris, see Rachel G. Fuchs, *Poor and Pregnant in Paris: Strategies of Survival in the Nineteenth Century* (New Brunswick: Rutgers University Press, 1992).

9. Pieter Dirk 't Hart, "Waren de armen in Nederland omstreeks 1800 zorgeloze klaplopers?" *Spieghel Historiael*, 17, No. 2 (February 1982), p. 68, and *idem.*, "Berustten de armen in Nederland omstreeks 1800 eerbiedig in hun lot?" *Spieghel Historiael*, 17, No. 3 (March 1982), p. 151.

10. Nancy Scheper-Hughes, *Death Without Weeping. The Violence of Everyday Life in Brazil* (Berkeley: University of California Press, 1992), p. 446.

11. The language is India's Viceroy George Curzon (1898–1905), but Benedict Anderson notes that Michel Foucault "could not have said it better" in *Imagined Communities. Reflections on the Origin and Spread of Nationalism* (1983; repr. London/New York: Verso, 1991), p. 179.

12. See, among others, Kathryn Norberg, *Rich and Poor in Grenoble, 1600–1814* (Berkeley: University of California Press, 1985); Jean-Pierre Gutton, *La société et les pauvres: l'exemple de la généralité de Lyon, 1534–1789* (Paris: Presses Universitaires de France, 1970); Olwen Hufton, *Bayeux in the Late Eighteenth Century: A Social Study* (Oxford: Clarendon Press of Oxford University Press, 1967), and *idem., The Poor of Eighteenth-Century France* (Oxford: Clarendon Press of Oxford University Press, 1976); Cissie C. Fairchilds, *Poverty and Charity in Aix-en-Provence* (Baltimore: Johns Hopkins University Press, 1976); Rachel G. Fuchs, "Preserving the Future of France: Aid to the Poor and Pregnant in Nineteenth-Century Paris," pp. 92–122, and Nancy L. Green, "To Give and to Receive: Philanthropy and Collective Responsibility among Jews in Paris, 1880–1914," pp. 197–226, in Peter Mandler, ed., *The Uses of Charity. The Poor on Relief in the Nineteenth-Century Metropolis* (Philadelphia: University of Pennsylvania Press, 1990); and Caroline Ford, *Creating the Nation in Provincial France. Religion and Political Identity in Brittany* (Princeton: Princeton University Press, 1993).

13. Joel Mokyr, *Industrialization in the Low Countries, 1795–1850* (New Haven: Yale University Press, 1977).

14. See, among others, Catarina Lis and Hugo Soly, " 'Total Institutions' and the Survival Strategies of the Laboring Poor in Antwerp, 1770–1860," in Mandler, ed., *The Uses of Charity*, pp. 38–67, and *idem, Social Change and the Labouring Poor: Antwerp, 1170–1860* (New Haven: Yale University Press, 1986); J.L. van Zanden, "Lonen en arbeidsmarkt in Amsterdam, 1800–1865," *Tijdschrift voor Sociale Geschiedenis*, 9, No. 1 (1983), pp. 3–27; Marco H.D. van Leeuwen en Frans Smits, "Bedeling en arbeidsmarkt in Amsterdam in de eerste helft van de negentiende eeuw," *Tijdschrift voor Sociale Geschiedenis*, 13, No. 4, (1987), pp. 431–457; Marco H.D. van Leeuwen, *Bijstand in Amsterdam, ca. 1800–1850. Armenzorg als beheersings-en overlevingsstrategie* (Zwolle: Waanders, 1992); Martien Arends, Nico Siffels, and Willem van Spijker, *Wegens verregaande brutaliteit. Haarlemse paupers in de eerste helft van de negentiende eeuw* (University of Amsterdam: M.A. thesis, 1983); Nico Siffels and Willem van Spijker, "Haarlemse paupers. Arbeidsmarkt, armoede en armenzorg in Haarlem in de eerste helft van de negentiende eeuw," *Tijdschrift voor Sociale Geschiedenis*, 13, No. 4 (1987), pp. 458–494; L. Frank van Loo, *Armelui. Armoede en bedeling te Alkmaar, 1850–1914* (Bergen, N-H: Octavo, 1986); and Herman Kaptein, *Armenzorg in de aanslag. Armoede en bedeling in De Rijp* (Bergen, N-H: Octavo, 1984).

15. Stein Ringen, *The Possibility of Politics. A Study in the Political Economy of the Welfare State* (Oxford: Clarendon Press of Oxford University Press, 1987), p. 154.

16. Amartya Sen, ''Individual Freedom as a Social Commitment,'' *New York Review of Books*, 37, No. 10 (June 1990), p. 49.

17. Amartya Sen, *Poverty and Famines: An Essay on Entitlement and Deprivation* (Oxford: Clarendon Press of Oxford University Press, 1981), p. vi.

18. Sen, *Poverty and Famines*, p. vi.

19. Michel Foucault, in *Surveiller et punir: naissance de la prison* (Paris: Gallimard, 1975), referred to reports such as the *Compte général* as ''a mass of unknown documents that constitute the effective discourse of political action'' (p. 305).

20. *Compte général de l'administration de la justice criminelle*, 1825, compiled by the Minister of Justice (Paris: Imprimerie Royale, 1827).

21. André-Michel Guerry [du Champneuf], *Essai statistique morale de la France* (Paris: Crochard, 1833), p. 2.

22. Guerry, *Essai statistique morale*, p. 3.

23. Michelle Perrot, ''Delinquencey and the Penitentiary System in Nineteenth-Century France,'' in Robert M. Forster and Orest Ranum, eds., *Deviants and the Abandoned in French Society. Selections from Annales, Economies, Societies, and Civilizations* (Baltimore: Johns Hopkins Press, 1978), No. 4, p. 228.

24. Frank H. Hankins, *Adolphe Quetelet as Statistician* (New York: Columbia University Press, 1908), pp. 83–105.

25. Adolphe Quetelet, *Sur l'homme et le développement de ses facultés ou Essai de physique sociale*, 2 vols. (Paris: Bachelier, 1935), 2, pp. 295–96. See also Stephen M. Stigler, *The History of Statistics. The Measurement of Uncertainty before 1900* (Cambridge: Harvard University Press, 1986), pp. 172–74.

26. Michelle Perrot, ''Delinquency and the Penitentiary System,'' p. 229. See also Harald Westergaard, *Contributions to the History of Statistics* (1932; repr. The Hague: Mouton, 1969).

27. Homme Wedman, ''Popular Collective Action in Groningen, 1870–1900,'' *Tijdschrift voor Sociale Geschiedenis*, 15, No. 2 (1989), p. 175. See also Charles Tilly's comments in the same issue, ''History, Sociology, and Dutch Collective Action,'' p. 153.

28. The exact titles of the Annual Report on Poverty varied between 1815 and mid-century. It occasionally included a section on the education of poor children, and was then called *Verslag omtrent het armwezen en de opvoeding der armenkinderen in het Koninkrijk der Nederlanden*. Similar to the Dutch government, the New York State Legislature directed Secretary of State John Yates to prepare a report on the state's poor relief situation in 1822. Beginning in 1830, the Secretary of State prepared an *Annual Report on Statistics of the Poor*, which contained data on relief expenditure and the number of relief recipients in each county. See Joan Underhill Hannon, ''The Generosity of Antebellum Poor Relief,'' *Journal of Economic History*, 44, No. 3 (1984), pp. 813, 816.

29. Simon Schama, ''Municipal Government and the Burden of the Poor in South Holland during the Napoleonic Wars,'' in A.C. Duke and C.A. Tamse,

eds., *Britain and the Netherlands. Papers Delivered to the Sixth Anglo-Dutch Historical Conference* (The Hague: Martinus Nijhoff, 1976), No. 4, *War and Society*, p. 120.

30. L. Noordgraaf, ''Sociale verhoudingen en structuren in de noordelijke Nederlanden, 1770–1813,'' in *Algemene Geschiedenis der Nederlanden*, 15 vols. (Haarlem: Fibula van Dishoeck, 1973), 10, pp. 373–376, and ''Armoede en bedeling. Enkele numerieke aspecten van de armenzorg in het zuidelijke deel van Holland in de Bataafse en Franse tijd,'' *Tijdschrift Holland*, 9 (1977), pp. 1–24.

31. W.P. Blockmans and W. Prevenier, ''Armoede in de Nederlanden van de 14e tot het midden van de 16e eeuw: bronnen en problemen,'' *Tijdschrift voor Geschiedenis*, 88 (1975), pp. 501–38, and Van Leeuwen, *Bijstand in Amsterdam*, pp. 61–63.

32. Simon Vissering, ''Politische vertooghen,'' in *Herinneringen*, 3 vols. (Amsterdam, P.N. van Kampen, 1863) 2, p. 206.

33. Marco H.D. van Leeuwen, ''Surviving with a little help: the importance of charity to the poor of Amsterdam, 1800–1850, in a comparative perspective,'' *Social History*, 18 (October 1993), pp. 319–338.

34. L.Ph.C. van den Bergh, *Gedachten over de armoede, overbevolking, en kolonisatie* (Leiden: S. en J. Luchtmans, 1845), pp. 18–19.

35. Van Leeuwen, *Bijstand in Amsterdam*, p. 44.

36. E.W. Hofstee, *De demografische ontwikkeling van Nederland in de eerste helft van de negentiende eeuw. Een historisch-demografische en sociologische studie* (Deventer: Van Loghem Slatherus, 1978), p. 19. See also Frans van Poppel, *Trouwen in Nederland. Een historisch-demografische studie van de 19e en vroeg 20e eeuw* (Wageningen: Landbouwuniversiteit, A.A.G. Bijdragen, 33, 1992), and O.W.A. Boonstra and A.M. van der Woude, *A statistical analysis of regional differences in the level and development of the birthrate and fertility, 1850–1890* (Utrecht: HES, 1984).

37. Charles Pouthas, ''La population française pendant la première moitié du XIXième siècle, *Travaux et Documents*, No. 25, *Institut nationale d'étude démographique* (Paris: Presses Universitaires de France, 1956), p. 22. See also André Armengaud, *Population au XIXième siècle* (Paris: Presses Universitaires de France, 1971), pp. 73–75, and Paul Hohenberg, ''Migrations et fluctuations démographiques dans la France rurale, 1836–1901,'' *Annales. Economies, Sociétés, Civilisations*, 29 (1974), p. 474.

38. Etienne van de Walle, ''Alone in Europe: The French Fertility Decline until 1850,'' in Charles Tilly, ed., *Historical Studies of Changing Fertility* (Princeton: Princeton University Press, 1978), pp. 286–87. For a recent analysis of pro-natalist policies during the Third Republic, see Alisa Klaus, ''Depopulation and Race Suicide: Maternalism and Pronatalist Ideologies in France and the United States,'' in Seth Koven and Sonya Michel, eds., *Mothers of the New World. Maternalist Politics and the Origins of Welfare States* (New York: Routledge, 1993), pp. 188–212.

39. *Statistique de la France: Administration publique* (Paris: Imprimerie Nationale, 1843), p. 406.

40. Roger Schofield, David S. Reher, and Alain Bideau, eds., *The Decline of Mortality in Europe* (New York: Oxford University Press, 1991); see also John Walter and Roger Schofield, eds., *Famine, Disease, and the Social Order in Early Modern Society. Essays in Honor of Andrew B. Appleby* (Cambridge: Cambridge University Press, 1989), and Jacques Dupâquier, *Histoire de la population française*, 4 vols. (Paris: Presses Universitaires de France, 1988), 3, *De 1789 à 1914*.

41. Van Leeuwen and Smits, ''Bedeling en arbeidsmarkt in Amsterdam,'' p. 442.

42. Arends et al., *Wegens verregaande brutaliteit*, p. 183.

43. Auke van der Woud, *Het lege land. De ruimtelijke orde van Nederland, 1798–1848* (Amsterdam: Meulenhoff, 1987), pp. 392–93. J.M.M. de Meere, in *Economische ontwikkeling en levensstandaard in Nederland gedurende de eerste helft van de negentiende eeuw* (The Hague: Martinus Nijhoff, 1982), notes that endemic malaria occurred yearly, but that during years of extraordinary warm summers such as 1808, 1826, and 1846, ''malaria acquired epidemic proportions'' (pp. 84–87).

44. William Petersen, ''The Demographic Transition in the Netherlands,'' *American Sociological Review*, 25, No. 1 (1960), p. 340.

45. C. van Nieuwenhuis, *Geneeskundige plaatsbeschrijving van Amsterdam*, 3 vols. (Amsterdam: n.p., 1822), 2, pp. 243–244.

46. November 19, 1823, Archives of the Aalmoezeniersweeshuis in Amsterdam, quoted by Peter C. Jansen in *Geschiedenis van het aalmoezeniersweeshuis te Amsterdam, 1813–1828. De zorg voor vondelingen en verlaten kinderen in het begin van de 19e eeuw* (University of Amsterdam: M.A. thesis, 1969), p. 11.

47. Jansen, *Geschiedenis van het aalmoezeniersweeshuis*, p. 11.

48. See Samuel Senior Coronel, ''Iets over het verschil in de levenshoudingen tussen Joden en Christenen,'' *Schat der gezondheid*, (1864), pp. 372–392, and H. Pinkhof, ''Onderzoek naar de kindersterfte onder de geneeskundig-bedeelden in Amsterdam,'' *Nederlands Tijdschrift voor Geneeskunde* (1907), pp. 1174–1180. See also J.A. Verdoorn, *Het gezondheidswezen te Amsterdam in de 19e eeuw* (1965; repr. Nijmegen: SUN, 1981), pp. 62–68. This trend continued in the twentieth century; see Emanuel Boekman, *Demografie van de joden in Nederland* (Amsterdam: M. Hertzberger, 1936), and Frans van Poppel, ''Religion and Health: Catholicism and Regional Mortality Differences in Nineteenth-Century Netherlands,'' *Society for the Social History of Medicine*, 5, No. 2 (1992), pp. 245.

49. Verdoorn, *Het gezondheidswezen*, pp. 67–68.

50. P. Meurkens, *Sociale verandering in het oude Kempenland; demografie, economie, en cultuur van een pre-industriele samenleving* (Nijmegen: SUN, 1984), quoted by van Poppel, ''Religion and Health,'' pp. 250–51.

51. Brian R. Mitchell, *European Historical Statistics, 1750–1970* (New York: Columbia University Press, 1978), p. 36–37. See also Yves Blayo, ''La mortalité en France de 1740 à 1829,'' *Population*, No. spécial (November 1975), pp. 123–42; Catherine Rollet, *La politique à l'égard de la petite enfance sous la IIIième République* (Paris: INED-Presses Universitaires de France, 1990); and Patrice Bourdelais, *La population française du XVIIIième siècle à nos jours: histoire du vieillissement* (Paris: Odile Jacob, 1992).

52. Olwen Hufton, *The Poor of Eighteenth-Century France* (Oxford: Clarendon Press of Oxford University Press, 1974), p. 72.

53. Pierre Merlin, *Exode rural* (Paris: Presses Universitaires de France, 1971), passim, and Caroline Ford, *Creating the Nation in Provincial France. Religion and Political Identity in Brittany* (Princeton: Princeton University Press, 1993), p. 29.

54. Eugen Weber, *From Peasants into Frenchmen. The Modernization of the French Countryside* (Stanford: Stanford University Press, 1976), pp. 278–91.

55. Leslie Page Moch, ''The Family and Migration: News from the French,'' *Journal of Family History*, 11, No. 2, (1986), pp. 193–203. Yves Lequin, *Les ouvriers de la région Lyonnaise, 1848–1914* (Lyon: Presses Universitaires de Lyon, 1977), p. 270. Catharina Lis, Hugo Soly, and Dirk van Damme, *Op vrije voeten? Sociale politiek in West Europa (1450–1914)* (Leuven: Kritak, 1985), have noted that ''seasonal and short-distance migration were the dominant patterns far into the nineteenth century, and permanent migration remained a more limited phenomenon'' (p. 134).

56. Etienne van de Walle, *The Female Population of France in the Nineteenth Century* (Princeton: Princeton University Press, 1974), p. 200; Jan Lucassen has made a similar point regarding in-migration to the North Sea area in *Naar de kusten van de Noordzee. Trekarbeid in Europees perspektief, 1600–1900* (Gouda: Druk Vonk/Zeist, 1984), p. 118.

57. Leslie Page Moch, *Paths to the City. Regional Migration in Nineteenth-Century France* (Beverly Hills: Sage Publications, 1983), pp. 143–47.

58. Alain Corbin, *Women for Hire. Prostitution and Sexuality in France after 1850* (1978; repr. Cambridge: Harvard University Press, 1990), p. 187.

59. The director of the *Dépôts de mendicité* to the Minister of the Interior, July 25, 1816. F16 531, AN, Paris.

60. For a similar observation regarding the last years of the ancien régime, see Cynthia A. Bouton, ''Gendered Behavior in Subsistence Riots: The French Flour War of 1775,'' *Journal of Social History*, 29, No. 4 (1990), p. 149.

61. Gordon Wright speaks of an ''obsessive'' preoccupation with vagrancy and vagabondage in *Between THE Guillotine & Liberty. Two Centuries of the Crime Problem in France* (New York: Oxford University Press, 1983), pp. 154–55.

62. The director of the *Dépôts de mendicité* to the Minister of the Interior, September 11, 1816. F16 531, AN, Paris.

63. See the classic statements by T.H. Marshall, *Class, Citizenship, and So-*

cial Development (Garden City, N.Y.: Anchor Press/Doubleday 1964), pp. 71–72, and Reinhard Bendix, *Nation Building and Citizenship* (Berkeley: University of California Press, 1969), p. 94. For recent feminist analyses, see Joan Landes, *Women and the Public Sphere in the Age of the French Revolution* (Ithaca: Cornell University Press, 1988); Harriet B. Applewhite and Darline G. Levy, eds., *Women and Politics in the Age of the Democratic Revolution* (Ann Arbor: University of Michigan Press, 1990); and Sara E. Melzer and Leslie W. Rabine, eds., *Rebel Daughters: Women and the French Revolution* (New York: Oxford University Press, 1992).

64. Reproduced in Susan G. Bell and Karen M. Offen, eds., *Women, The Family, and Freedom: The Debate in Documents*, 2 vols. (Stanford: Stanford University Press, 1984), 1, pp. 88–92.

65. Patricia O'Brien, *The Promise of Punishment. Prisons in Nineteenth-Century France* (Princeton: Princeton University Press, 1982), p. 18.

66. For a fascinating analysis of the conflation between unruly women and working-class anarchy, see Doris Y. Kadish, *Politicizing Gender. Narrative Strategies in the Aftermath of the French Revolution* (New Brunswick: Rutgers University Press, 1991), passim.

67. W.W. Stephens, ed., *The Life and Writings of Turgot* (London: Longman & Green, 1895), p. 50.

68. Abel Chatelain, *Les migrants temporaires en France de 1800 à 1914*, 2 vols. (Lille: Presses Universitaires de Lille, 1976), 2, p. 43; and Moch, *Paths to the City*, pp. 143–47.

69. Quoted by Chatelain, *Les migrants temporaires en France*, 2, p. 1068.

70. Maurice Agulhon, ed., *Martin Nadaud: Mémoires de Leonard, ancien garçon maçon* (Paris: Hachette, 1976), p. 102.

71. Quoted by Chatelain, *Les Migrants temporaires en France*, 2, pp. 1069–70.

72. See M.E. Avalle's story about the family of a *porteur d'eau* (water carrier) in Paris, in Frédéric Le Play, ed., *Ouvriers des deux mondes* (1858; repr. Thomery: l'Arbre Verdoyant/Armand Colin, 1983), which describes "the mother in the Auvergne who, during her husband's many absences, continued to cultivate the family's modest plot, already burdened with numerous mortgages" (p. 154–55). See also Louise A. Tilly, "The Foodriot in France," *Journal of Interdisciplinary History*, 1, No. 2 (1971), p. 56. Ruth L. Smith and Deborah Valenze analyze the unique female patterns of shared agency in "Mutuality and Marginality: Liberal Moral Theory and Working-Class Women in Nineteenth-Century England," *Signs. Journal of Women in Culture and Society*, 13, No. 2 (1988), pp. 278–99; see also Rudolf Dekker, "Women in Revolt. Popular Protest and its Social Basis in Holland in the Seventeenth and Eighteenth Centuries," *Theory and Society*, 16 (1987), pp. 352–56.

73. Benjamin Appert, *Journal des prisons, hospices, écoles primaires et établissements philantropiques, 1825–1833*, 9 vols. (Paris: Baudoin Frères, 1825–33), 2, p. 63.

74. Gutton, *La société et les pauvres*, pp. 55–7. Observers in Hamburg, Germany, identified the same phenomenon in their city at the end of the eighteenth century: ''Six-sevenths of our poor being women and children, they should be set to work spinning flax in their homes.'' See Karl de Schweinitz, *England's Road to Social Security: From the Statute of Laborers in 1349 to the Beveridge Report of 1942* (Philadelphia: n.p., 1942), pp. 91–4.

75. *Statistique de la France*, pp. 403–406; See also *Etat numérique de la population indigente de Paris, et renseignements statistiques sur cette population pour l'année 1841*, Fosseyeux, liasse 127, Archives de l'assistance publique, Paris, which contains retroactive data to the 1820s.

76. Van de Walle, in *The Female Population of France*, calculated a gender ratio of 103 women to 100 men for the city of Paris as a whole, p. 51. Chevalier, in *Laboring Classes and Dangerous Classes*, has established that the poorest *arrondissements* of the city, which housed the largest number of recent immigrants, revealed a remarkable surplus of men over women, pp. 244–52.

77. Van Leeuwen, *Bijstand in Amsterdam*, Appendix F, p. 331.

78. *Etat numérique de la population indigente de Paris*. See also Joseph-Marie de Gérando, *De la bienfaisance publique*, 4 vols. (Paris: Jules Renouard, 1839), 1, pp. 116–17.

79. *Etat numérique de la population indigente de Paris.* J.C. Toutain, in ''La population de la France de 1700 à 1959,'' *Cahiers de l'Institut de Science Economique Appliquée*, Series AF, 3 (Paris: 1963), 1, p. 24, has noted that average life expectancy around the year 1825 was assessed at 40.0 for men and 43.8 for women. During the course of the nineteenth century average life expectancy did not change significantly: around 1880 it was estimated at 40.4 for men and 42.3 for women; the widowed heads of households receiving assistance were more likely to have been women.

80. De Gérando, *De la bienfaisance publique*, pp. 116–17, and *Etat numérique de la population indigente de Paris*.

81. Armand Husson, *Les consommations de Paris* (Paris: Guillaumin, 1858), p. 33.

82. For the occasion of the anniversary of the *Maatschappij tot Nut van het Algemeen* (Society for Public Utility) in 1828, Herman Joh. Roijaards, in *Redevoering over den invloed der Nederlandse vrouw op de handhaving en wijziging van het volkskarakter* (Utrecht: J. de Kruijff, 1828), wrote that ''women, gentler in emotions and more fragile in physical constitution, belong in the family as their husbands' faithful companions, while men's destiny, because of their strength and enterprising spirit, is to stand squarely in the midst of public society'' (pp. 17–19).

83. Collectie Tets van Goudriaan, No. 23, *Verslag omtrent den staat van het armwezen over het jaar 1850*, issued by a special commission of the Second Chamber of the Estates-General, October 14, 1852, ARA, The Hague.

84. Lucassen, *Naar de kusten van de Noordzee*, pp. 174–176, and Appendix, No. 19, p. 331.

85. For details about the law of 1818 see below, especially Chapter 6. Simon Schama, *The Embarrassment of Riches. Interpretation of Dutch Culture in the Golden Age* (New York: Alfred A. Knopf, 1987), p. 579.

86. For a comparable argument, see H.R.C. Wright, *Free Trade and Protection in the Netherlands, 1816–1830. A Study of the First Benelux* (Westport: Greenwood Press, 1971), p. 49.

87. Quoted by J.M.M. de Meere, ''Misoogst en hongersnood,'' *Tijdschrift voor Sociale Geschiedenis*, 5, No. 1 (1977), p. 85.

88. N.W. Posthumus, *Inquiry into the History of Prices in Holland*, 2 vols. (Leiden: E.J. Brill, 1946), 1, pp. 22–23, and *Algemeen verslag wegens den staat van de landbouw opgemaakt door Jan Kops* (The Hague: Landsdrukkerij, 1815–1850).

89. Archief van het Kabinet van de Gouverneur van Noord-Holland, No. 62–64, June 7, 1816, Rijksarchief Noord-Holland, Haarlem.

90. Quoted by de Meere, ''Misoogst en hongersnood,'' p. 93.

91. Jacques Giele, ''Arbeidersbestaan. Levenshouding en maatschappijbeeld van de arbeidende klasse in Nederland in het midden van de 19e eeuw,'' in *Jaarboek voor de geschiedenis van het socialisme en de arbeidersbeweging in Nederland 1976* (Nijmegen: SUN, 1976), p. 49.

92. *Verslag omtrent het armenwezen*, 1845.

93. *Verslag nopens de staat van de Maatschappij van Weldadigheid en dien harer kolonien over het dienstjaar 1846*, Archieven van de Maatschappij van Weldadigheid, No. 1087, Rijksarchief Drenthe, Assen.

94. M. Bergman, ''The Potatoeblight in the Netherlands,'' *International Review of Social History*, 12 (1967), p. 404.

95. Archief van het Ministerie van Binnenlandse Zaken, September 25, 1845, No. 9, ARA, The Hague.

96. Annual Report from the Governor of Friesland, quoted by Bergman, ''The Potatoeblight,'' p. 390.

97. J.A. van Roijen, *Wetgeving en armoede beschouwd in betrekking tot het misdrijf* (Zwolle: Tjeenk Willink, 1846); see also J.A. Berger, *Van armenzorg tot werkelozenzorg* (Amsterdam: Arbeiderspers, 1936), p. 21.

98. A.J.C. Ruter, ed., *Rapporten van de gouverneurs in de provinciën, 1840–1849* (Utrecht: Kemink en Zoon, 1950), 3rd series, ''Periodieke rapporten,'' 78, p. 187.

99. Archieven van het Ministerie van Justice, No. 4922, the district attorney (*officier van justitie*) in Zwolle to the Minister of Justice, October 11, 1845, and the response from the mayor of Amsterdam to the Minister of Justice following his inquiry. ARA, The Hague.

100. J.A. Faber, *Dure Tijden en hongersnood in pre-industrieel Nederland. Inaugurele Reden, Universiteit van Amsterdam* (September 1976), pp. 16–17.

101. Rudolf Dekker, in *Holland in beroering. Oproeren in de 17e en 18e eeuw* (Baarn: Ambo, 1982), observed regarding the seventeenth and eighteenth centuries that the elaborate network of canals in the Netherlands facilitated the

authorities' repression of riots because police or soldiers could arrive quickly at a place of unrest, p. 144. See also Anne Doedens, ed., *Autoriteit en strijd. Elf bijdragen tot de geschiedenis van collectief verzet in de Nederlanden, met name in de eerste helft van de negentiende eeuw* (Amsterdam: VU Uitgeverij, 1981), p. 242. The phrase "collective bargaining by riot" has been employed by Charles Tilly, most recently in *The Contentious French* (Cambridge: Harvard University Press, 1986). See also H.J.F.M. van den Eerenbeemt, "Armoede in de gedrukte optiek van de sociale bovenlaag in Nederland, 1750–1850," *Tijdschrift voor geschiedenis*, 88, No. 4 (1977), p. 482.

102. F.J.B. d'Alphonse, *Aperçu de la Holland*, in *Bijdragen tot de statistiek van Nederland*, Nieuwe Volgreeks (The Hague: Gebroeders Belinfante, 1900), 1, pp. 158, 163.

103. See the discussion in van Leeuwen, *Bijstand in Amsterdam*, p. 86.

104. H.W. Tydeman, J. Heemskerk, and Mr. J.W. Tydeman, *Denkbeelden omtrent een wettelijke regeling van het armwezen in Nederland* (Amsterdam: Gebroeders Willems, 1850), p. 26–27.

105. Van Leeuwen, in *Bijstand in Amsterdam*, notes that the Poor Law of 1854 was "not conservative, but regressive" (p. 89).

CHAPTER FOUR

Intellectuals, Public Officials, and Economic History: Different Discourses about Agriculture, Factories, and Capitalism

> I recognize that mechanical power, in developing the resources of industry, leads to violent rendings in the social order. Steam power, like the cannon, blows holes in the masses.[1]
>
> —Léon Faucher in the *Chambres des Députés*, 1848

> Average daily wages have risen so high in [Holland] that they are between 40 and 50 percent higher than in neighboring countries. This development has a disastrous influence on the sale of our manufactured goods, because everyone wishes to buy cheap English products. Destroy the restrictive laws and guilds which restrain intelligence, hinder industry, and hamper trade, and give the *fabriqueur* the same kind of freedom enjoyed by his brothers in England. . . .[2]
>
> —F. van der Schaft, *Vrijheid, Gelijkheid, Broederschap*, 1795

The intellectual milieu of France and the Netherlands in the first half of the nineteenth century not only influenced the discussion about poverty, it also prejudiced actual policy outcomes. In both societies intellectuals and policymakers espoused an amalgam of ideas about social reality. This mixture of opinions and beliefs did not constitute a harmonious whole but revealed, instead, a great deal of internal contestation. However, the fractious discourses about these conflicting ideological points of view were grounded in a shared world of thought, which outlined the conceptual boundaries of the debate and guided the most acceptable ways of defining and interpreting social conditions.[3]

Hence, perspectives on the problem of poverty and practical schemes designed to improve the indigents' fate were part and parcel of a wider, if often inchoate, set of social values and political ideologies. They entailed distinct notions about weighty issues such as virtue and vice, progress and decline, church and state. Definitions of personal accountability and community obligation were important elements, too. In addition, any kind of coherent vision of society incorporated specific judgments about the ambiguous merits of "modernity"—opinions that were often inversely related to an overly sentimental image of the social harmony of peasant life. Of course conclusions about the desirability of centralized political power also figured quite prominently in the outlook of both policymakers and intellectuals.

These linkages between elite sensibilities and political outcomes were hardly unique to the nineteenth century. After the French Revolution, however, they were further buffeted about by the capricious winds of change that issued from the capitalist marketplace, inserting an entirely new logic into discussions about poverty and its multiple meanings. Although industrial capitalism was not yet a dominant economic reality in either France or Holland, but rather, a powerful imaginary construct, the capitalist market began to function as a deus ex machina phenomenon. Capitalism served as a flexible intellectual entity, often misunderstood, which contemporary observers could hold responsible for all the surprising or shocking changes in the world around them. Factory production, wage labor, and urban growth became the crucibles of nineteenth-century discussions about poverty and social welfare. The manner in which national elites embraced, contested, or spurned a genuine understanding of the free forces of the capitalist marketplace modulated their rhetoric about the Social Question and affected the policies they chose to support.

In the Chamber of Deputies in the Revolutionary year 1848, Léon Faucher, through inference, decried an uninhibited entrepreneurial spirit that would lead to mechanical innovations. Modern technology, he intoned, unleashed violent cleavages in the body politic, and steam power, replicating the lethal power of cannonballs, would eviscerate the masses. The improvement of the fate of impoverished workers, Faucher implied, resided in the expansion of small-scale artisanal production and peasant agriculture through government intervention, not in the unhampered laws of supply and demand for new technological inventions.

Although writing some fifty years earlier, F. van der Schaft in Haarlem painted a very different picture. He noted that the high level of taxes imposed on food and fuel exerted upward pressure on wages. Archaic guild laws, moreover, prevented employers from using the same kind of imagination and flexibility displayed by businessmen elsewhere. However, by removing tariffs and other economic restrictions, and by releasing the spontaneous energy of the capitalist market, Dutch merchants and entrepreneurs would be able to catch up with their "brothers" in England! Van der Schaft's early fascination with the potential of unfettered capitalist development was palpable, and his positive reaction was one that a considerable number of his countrymen would echo throughout the nineteenth century.[4]

In nineteenth-century Holland and France, as elsewhere in western Europe, many government officials or politicians were also serious intellectuals, careful social observers, and prolific authors of books and articles. Most of their writings were designed to highlight a particular set of social problems or to support their personal political agendas. These public servants cum scholars grappled on a regular basis with the most salient social and economic questions of the day. Their immersion in the details of statutory regulations or the actual administration of charitable institutions enabled them to examine social conditions with a certain amount of intellectual rigor. But their personal ideological leanings inevitably affected the ways in which they talked and wrote about poverty. Thus, their denial or affirmation of the alleged evils that lurked behind modern capitalism affected the practical solutions these erudite public officials were willing to nurture.

In France, the most familiar figure was Alexis de Tocqueville, whose illustrious career spanned both serious intellectual work and a lifelong devotion to public service. But Tocqueville had many lesser-known colleagues, who labored in the field of social policy and thought seriously about questions of poverty and charity. Baron Joseph-Marie de Gérando was one of them. De Gérando was a member of the Council of State under Napoleon and continued to serve in the same function during the Restoration. King Louis-Philippe valued his political counsel even more, and in 1837 he became a member of the *Chambre des pairs*. A renowned philanthropist, De Gérando served in the 1830s as the busy administrative director of the national institute for deaf-mutes; he also acted as the president of one of the first public health councils in France. In addition, he was a founder of the Society for the Encouragement of National Industry and remained an active member of the Society of Moral Christianity. Toward the end of his life he traveled to Germany and Switzerland to study those countries' charitable institutions. Throughout his energetic career De Gérando wrote many books and essays on poverty and charity, the best-known being a four-volume study entitled *De la bienfaisance publique* (About Public Welfare) published in 1839.[5]

Jean-Paul Alban de Villeneuve-Bargemont followed a similar career trajectory. He held official positions first in the subprefecture in Zierikzee in the Batavian Republic and thereafter in the departments of Charente, Meurthe, Loire-Inférieur, and the Nord. Villeneuve-Bargemont left the Nord after the Revolution of 1830 but later, as an arch-conservative legitimist, he was elected deputy to the Chamber of Deputies from the Var. He thought seriously about poverty and charity and paid a lengthy visit to the agricultural colonies of the Dutch *Maatschappij van Weldadigheid* (Benevolent Society) in the 1830s, to consider the feasibility of creating similar rural pauper colonies in France. He published his major scholarly work about Christian political economy in three volumes in 1834.[6]

Comparable public officials with serious scholarly inclinations populated the Dutch political landscape, but with one subtle difference. In Holland the chorus of Protestant ministers' assertive voices inflected the discourses about poverty and its remedies. Their possessive defense of the independent charitable activities of the "church"—which meant, of course, the preservation of not only the autonomy of Protestant, but also of Catholic and Jewish charities—resounded more loudly than the Catholic hierarchy's choir of sonorous chants in France.

It was true that several thinkers from within the French Catholic Church such as the Dominican Pierre Lacordaire and the prominent *abbé* de Lamennais, or lay Catholics such as Pierre-Simon Ballanche and Frédéric Ozanam, began to formulate early versions of an engaged, social Catholicism. Lacordaire, for instance, wrote already in 1824 that the Catholic Church was "the redemptress of poor people, the auxiliary to all just social reforms, and the universal instrument of salvation."[7] But neither progressive social Catholics in France, nor conservative Catholics yearning for a revival of the church's ancient centrality, achieved the same degree of prominence in defining the rhetoric about poor relief as did Dutch Reformed ministers in the Netherlands.[8]

Even though the Catholic Church continued to be the mainstay of poor relief in nineteenth-century France, despite the state's attempt at appropriating its charitable duties during the French Revolution, Catholic Church officials in France did not focus their intellectual attention on social welfare. Instead, they clamored for the right to master the "soul" of the French nation—in other words, to be able to control education. The French Catholic Church was deeply invested in regaining the moral influence in society it had lost during the Revolutionary 1790s. Hence, the Catholic hierarchy proclaimed that only religious schooling could provide the necessary ethical instruction to form the civic spirit of proper Frenchmen. Catholic schools would not only forge good Christians, they would also offer the politically correct education essential to the formation of obedient citizens: a ''religiously inspired youth, trained in Catholic schools, was crucial to the peace, tranquility, and prosperity'' of the French nation![9]

In defiance of the traumatic curtailment of its political influence in French social life in the 1790s, though, the Catholic Church ''still ruled, not, to be sure, over the heart and mind of French society, but over its habits.'' This meant, as Madame d'Agoult—alias Daniel Stern—speculated in 1848, that ''in a country in which principles are weak and passions so changeable, the command over habits is really the command over life itself.''[10] Hence, the reinvented habit of Catholic charity in nineteenth-century France in most instances simply continued ancien régime practices, albeit with one ''modern'' difference. The central state in Paris oversaw the shape and direction of the philanthropic labors of the many different female religious orders in hospitals and poorhouses. While contesting the state's educational monopoly, the French Catholic Church hierarchy conceded the role of formulating legislation regarding poor relief, without too many vociferous objections, to the secular government.

Holland's political culture and its embattled history of religious divisions since the late sixteenth century yielded a different setting. Protestant spokesmen were vocal contestants and they successfully demanded the right to influence national legislation. But alongside the scores of strident ministers, there were other Dutch public servants with intellectual aptitudes who threw their rhetorical hats in the ring. An important one was the voice of Johannes van den Bosch, a leading advocate of innovative Dutch experiments in public assistance. With a distinguished military career behind him, Van den Bosch began to ponder the intricate problems of indigence, unemployment, and class divisions, and in 1818 he wrote a thick, serious book about poverty and unemployment and the desired role of the public sector. During the same year he founded and became director of the *Maatschappij van Weldadigheid*. As the creator of the *Maatschappij*, he endowed the country with an elaborate set of agricultural colonies and other institutions that not only became vital in Dutch poor relief efforts, but also emerged as the focus of the central government's involvement in social welfare.

In the late 1820s, however, Van den Bosch was appointed as Governor General of the Dutch East Indies, with an assignment to increase economic productivity so that the colonies would better serve the needs and interests of Dutch commerce, and, above all, the state treasury. As the colonial official who initiated on the island of Java a system of compulsory cultivation of cash crops, to be sold on the international market via government monopolies, he laid the foundation for the extremely exploitative "cultivation system" in the Dutch imperial possessions in Asia. Nonetheless, Van den Bosch's name is permanently inscribed, too, in the annals of innovative social experiments during the nineteenth century.[11]

Another important Dutch public official and legal scholar was the already familiar Jeronimo de Bosch Kemper. After earning a doctorate in law in 1830, he became a lawyer in The Hague and subsequently a prosecutor in Amsterdam. He published his major treatise on the legal procedures of criminal prosecution in three volumes between 1838 and 1840, to be followed by the award-winning *Geschiedkundig onderzoek naar de armoede in ons vaderland, hare oorzaken en de middelen die tot hare vermindering zouden kunnen worden aangewend* (Historical Inquiry into Poverty in Our Fatherland, Its Causes and the Means That Can Be Employed in Its Reduction) in 1851. In the 1850s he became a professor at the Atheneum in Amsterdam, held a membership in the Council of Provincial Estates, and served as a representative to the Second Chamber of the Dutch Estates-General in the 1860s.[12]

These public servants cum intellectuals lived near the pinnacles of political power. What they thought about the idyllic nature of peasant agriculture and rural life, or how they interpreted the promises—or, conversely, the dangers—associated with the free forces of the capitalist market mattered enormously. In both France and Holland politicans with scholarly dispositions tried to settle their ideological disagreements regarding social legislation and economic policy through polemical exchanges in contemporary journals; they also submitted their work to Learned Societies in the hope of receiving either a prize or an honorable mention in essay competitions.[13] An avalanche of publications on the subject appeared around and after the year 1815. For example, the Dutch *Magazijn voor het armwezen in het Koninkrijk der Nederlanden* (Magazine for Poverty and Poor Relief in the Kingdom of the Netherlands), which the distinguished professor of economics at the University of Leiden, H.W. Tydeman, edited, provided an outlet for ideas about economics and their relationship to practical policy proposals.[14]

In France, too, especially during the July Monarchy, a group of writers—journalists, gentleman-scholars, government officials, academics, and other *philanthropes*—tried to analyze the Social Question in a more systematic fashion than had ever been done before. As precocious "social scientists," they were eager to acquire firsthand knowledge and raw data about the material conditions of the indigent working class; several among them embarked on fact-finding missions through the poorest urban neighborhoods or regions of France and other countries in an effort to gather empirical evidence for their scholarly works or semiofficial *enquêtes*.[15] In the same vein, the Academy of Moral and Political Sciences, reconstituted in 1832 to proliferate the new values of the July Monarchy, organized a series of essay competitions with thought-provoking titles such as "Charity as related to social economy" or "How can we most usefully apply the principles of private and voluntary association to the amelioration of poverty?" In 1846, the theme of the essay competition was a curt one: "The state of pauperism in France and its remedies."[16]

This generation of researchers, especially in the 1830s and 1840s, indulged in an enthusiasm for positivist social science, not unlike the bureaucrats who assiduously gathered statistics on criminal justice or poor relief. The French and the Dutch, of course, were not unique in this spirited attempt. In early Victorian Britain statistical analyses of social problems became *de rigueur*, too, and the parliamentary commissions engaged in revising the Poor Law and other social legislation consulted statistical studies and tried to take note of their conclusions.[17] The quest for a combination of empirical research and statistical analysis would ideally endow social scientists with a more sophisticated understanding of the larger forces operating in human society. They hoped that a fusion of numbers, facts, and theory would help them formulate practical policy solutions in matters such as the spread of contagious disease, the rehabilitation of convicted criminals, or a more harmonious distribution of the labor supply.[18]

The science of economics—or political economy—achieved a relatively privileged status in most discussions among politicians/scholars, in a positive as well as a negative sense. More so in France than in the Netherlands, scores of intellectuals harbored the impression that the progress of industrial capitalism singlehandedly multiplied the number of paupers and was uniquely responsible for poverty as a social problem of alarming proportions. In the "modern" world of the nineteenth century, poverty in the official imagination was no longer perceived exclusively as a reflection of God's grand design. Instead, poverty was intimately connected to the tangible consequences of human agency: factory production, wage labor, and urban growth—all sorts of enigmatic developments which the science of economics tried to represent as the immutable consequences of organic laws of nature.

Accordingly, by acknowledging the linkages between poverty and human activity, nineteenth-century observers both reimagined and reconfigured poverty as a socially constructed problem that required a carefully crafted political response. Some intellectuals, more so in Holland than in France, were fascinated with the explanary tools and alluring logic of the new science of economics, and several among them emerged as powerful advocates of liberal economic solutions to the problem of poverty. Others, especially in France, denounced political economy as the scholarly justification of an unregulated world that depended on factory production and was grounded in the laws of supply and demand. This vision of society, they cautioned, was un-French and would yield nothing but doom and disaster.

In nineteenth-century France, public officials no longer focused their political attention on the rural poor, breaking a pattern of persistent concern with peasant disturbances triggered by hunger and poverty during the ancien régime. The memory of the ''Great Fear'' of bands of beggars, who had terrorized the countryside in search of food and shelter in the late 1780s, lingered on and provoked some worries about starvation-induced peasant anarchy in some rural regions in later decades.[19] But once peasants had burned local *terriers* and feudal charters, and the nobility had made its grand gesture of renouncing all feudal privileges during their theatrical nocturnal performance—what Simon Schama has called a ''dizzy night''—on August 4, 1789, the source of the central government's anxieties about the poor migrated from country to city and shifted from peasants to urban laborers.[20] Even though the largest proportion of grievously poor people continued to live in the countryside until the twentieth century, indigence in urban areas monopolized the lion's share of ''official'' attention.

The French preoccupation with urban poverty produced both intellectual confusions and contradictions. France remained an overwhelmingly agricultural nation, in which millions of peasants worked as exploited sharecroppers, landless day laborers, or disheartened migrant workers. Nonetheless, analysts in the post-Napoleonic era redefined poverty—and invented pauperism—as a unique manifestation of urban industry. Numerous intellectuals, whether conservative, middle-of-the road, or radical, believed that throughout the country urban wage labor and factory production were expanding their nefarious sphere of influence. By holding an ever increasing number of workers in its clutches and by intensifying its diabolical economic grip on the nation, mechanized production threatened to replace the panoply of small and dispersed rural workshops, which many writers idealized as the archetypal form of French manufacture.

After all, master artisans and their journeymen assistants in every conceivable craft—even if they were no longer allowed to organize themselves in exclusive and tightly structured guilds—embodied the justifiable French pride in high-quality workmanship. A growing clarity as to what constituted stylish ''bourgeois taste'' perpetuated a preference for sophisticated arts and crafts over mechanized and mass-produced goods, which could service the discriminating consumer demands of French elites.[21] But the unfurling tentacles of impersonal factory production seemed to be in the process of strangling French artisans' artistry. Instead, a dangerous mob of savage and unskilled factory laborers, social critics feared, would supplant gifted craftsmen in their small-scale workshops and perhaps displace independent peasants from the land, too.

On the political left Philippe Michel Buonarotti, for example, envisioned overcrowded cities and urban industrialism as ''symptoms of a public malady, an infallible forerunner of civic convulsions.'' To create a more equitable society, he advocated that cities, especially those bursting at the seams with throngs of people, jam-packed together in tight and uncouth spaces, should be dissolved. By dispersing the urban workers throughout the countryside and encouraging them to live in ''healthy smiling villages,'' a more harmonious world would naturally evolve.[22] The utopian socialist Charles Fourier, too, deplored the trend toward urban industrialism and hoped that factories, instead of being clustered in cities where swarms of wretched people were huddled together, ''will be scattered over all the fields and phalanxes of the globe.''[23] And Etienne Cabet, in his description of the utopian communist community of *Icarie*, imagined that in the best of all possible worlds the majority of the inhabitants of his perfect community would engage in agriculture, albeit assisted by modern technology, ''because human nature, once understood, can only lead to one conclusion: that by going back to nature, men will go back to their own 'true' nature.''[24]

Conforming to a characteristic French tradition, and either anticipating or corroborating the ideas of Karl Marx, utopian socialists of many doctrinal stripes and ideological colors advocated the use of the central state to disperse workers throughout the pristine countryside. Only the power of the state and centralized planning of the nation's economy could eradicate the unequal distribution of private property in order to bring about a just, utopian world. Louis Blanc, for example, envisioned the state as an affectionate and solicitous big brother or as a faithful ''banker to the poor,'' who would fund and regulate cooperative workshops and divide the fruits of their labor impartially among all citizens. In Blanc's imagination, only peaceful collaboration in national workshops, under state supervision, could abolish private profits, end fierce capitalist competition, and destroy all hierarchical distinctions between workers and bosses.[25]

Anarchist radicals such as Pierre-Joseph Proudhon idealized peasant agriculture as well. He viewed the average peasant as the epitome of the individualist, a consummate free spirit who was not hampered by social constraints and lived completely liberated from political coercion. But Proudhon proposed an alternative vision of the utopian community. Independent peasants would serve as the ideal agents to smash the tangible instruments of state power; unencumbered peasants would be the ones to convert private into communal property in order to bring about anarchist freedom and equality.[26]

At the same time, many centrist and conservative intellectuals employed the exact same historical circumstance—the predominance of peasant agriculture—for opposite political ends. As far as they were concerned, the persistence of small peasant proprietorship and subsistence farming would ensure the continuation of traditional society based on private property and hierarchy. While they occasionally denounced peasants as primitive creatures, devoid of civilized manners and basic literacy, they also viewed peasant proprietors as emblematic of French ways of being and working. As Baron Bigot de Morogues said in 1834, ''the small farm, not the big factory,'' ought to be the object of political concern. First and foremost, he declared, ''we have to consolidate the bases upon which the social order rests if we want to preserve public tranquility.''[27]

The reactionary Louis-Gabriel Ambroise, Vicomte de Bonald, too, viewed the primacy of peasant agriculture as the most expedient way to avoid class conflict and to revive the old feudal order. Agricultural work is ''superior'' to industrial labor, he professed. On the land ''different classes work alongside each other at the same tasks and as a result, there is no social isolation between them.''[28] This kind of exaltation of peasant agriculture, on both the left and the right, remained a resonant political motif in French politics until World War II. The opportunist politician Jules Mélines, as late as 1905, advocated in his *Retour à la terre* the need for a prompt state intervention designed to fortify and enhance the economic viability of rural life. By preventing peasants from migrating to urban areas and by repatriating urban workers to the countryside, Mélines proposed, ''true France'' could recapture its authentic identity.[29]

Because the Revolution had abolished feudal dues and labor services, many nineteenth-century intellectuals and policymakers in the bureaucratic hustle and bustle of Paris harbored the mistaken opinion that the condition of small proprietors and rural laborers had actually improved. Shortsighted contemporary observers had convinced themselves that rural wages had risen; they tended to believe, too, that rural indigence was qualitatively less serious and quantitatively less widespread than material suffering in urban areas. Reality, alas, was very different. Demographic pressures on the land had enveloped peasants in a cycle of rising rents and land prices, increasing debts, dwindling employment opportunities owing to a mushrooming rural labor supply, and falling prices for agricultural products during periods of plentiful harvests. At mid-century peasants in most regions suffered from a ''growing pauperization'' and they continued to be illiterate, backward, and wretchedly poor.[30] The ''flowering'' of peasant agriculture would not occur until the end of the nineteenth century.[31]

But utopian socialists, political moderates, and diehard conservatives, despite their ideological differences, shared the same nostalgic and overly romantic vision of French agriculture. Almost all of them painted a sentimental pastoral portrait depicting robust peasants who inhabited ''smiling'' villages scattered throughout a lush, green countryside. Besides, they were equally repelled by an explanatory framework that relied on the unbridled functioning of a free labor market. Liberal theories of supply and demand, or arguments in favor of the spontaneous evolution of the capitalist market, horrified many among them, whether they were conservatives or radicals, because the logic of unregulated labor markets would not secure the kind of predictability they valued.

It was a quandary that caught most Frenchmen who participated in politics or business during the Restoration and the July Monarchy and beyond in a bind. As private interest in commerce and industry grew during the decades after 1815, French entrepreneurial behavior and social attitudes displayed a curious ambivalence. Although French entrepreneurs became somewhat less averse to risk and more willing to invest in industry rather than land, many of them, and government bureaucrats as well, clung to ancien régime notions of paternalism and regulation with regard to matters of labor management and the behavior of workers. Early industrialists maintained a distinct sense of hierarchy. To some extent they perceived themselves as well-intentioned schoolmasters and they treated workers as either malleable students or obstinate children.[32]

At the same time, many workers themselves, often hailing from rural regions, may have approached industrial wage labor as only a transitory activity; scores of industrial laborers hoped to save enough money in order to return to their *pays* as peasant proprietors. The "nomadism of workers" in France, to use Georges Duveau's phrase, was reflected in the attitudes of employers, who were anxious about the loyalty of their work force.[33] Hence, to assure both the continuity and acquiescence of wage labor, *patrons* tried to guarantee workers' steadfast obedience without having to raise wages, and they did so by providing housing, granting rudimentary forms of medical care, or offering free schooling to children.[34]

On the whole, French entrepreneurs were unsure of the best ways to engage workers as a commodity whose value was allegedly determined by the irrepressible flow of supply and demand. As William Reddy has posed the question: How were employers to know which components of a worker's behavior were actually "purchased" through the payment of wages? Did these elements include only a minimum compliance with employers' requests and demands, or did they imply abiding allegiance and personal devotion?[35] Even if a notion of the capitalist market may have informed their financial decisions, early nineteenth-century employers often found it difficult to accept that their decisions to hire and fire were also influenced by impersonal market forces.

The commercialization of capital and land, to use Karl Polanyi's familiar phrase, was a social and economic fact French businessmen could fathom, but the notion of "commercialized labor" summoned up a sense of foreboding and imminent chaos; it also raised the specter of unruly workers' antagonism.[36] The ubiquitous use of *livrets* (labor passports), allowing employers to ostracize defiant workers, and the creation of *Conseils des Prud'hommes*, which functioned as local councils of employers, elevated the interests of *patrons* over those of workers. While the Chapelier law had abrogated the right to form secondary associations, this prohibition seemed to apply less stringently to employers.[37]

The advocates of liberal economic theory and free trade such as the group of people surrounding Jean-Baptiste Say, who gave his lectures at the *Athénée* in Paris, appealed only to a small number of French entrepreneurs or public officials.[38] The majority, instead, favored protectionism and government intervention, and they questioned the validity of liberal economics as a rigorous system of scientific analysis. They also rejected liberalism in general as a set of "subversive" ideas and a "dangerous" doctrine as far as politics and religion were concerned.[39] In short, the theoretical agenda of liberal economists did not find favor among either policymakers or businessmen, if only because liberal political economy, in the minds of many, was still associated with the eccentric "free-thinking *idéologues*" of the late Enlightenment.[40]

In 1839, for instance, the Academy of Moral and Political Sciences organized an essay competition focusing on the topic "What does *la misère* consist of, by what signs can it be observed in various countries, and what are its causes?" The Academy's Price Selection Committee, however, ruled as inadmissable the entry of one contestant purely because it was judged to be too much of a work of "political economy"—in other words, the author was presumably too enamored with free-market imperatives.[41] The general distrust of capitalism, however, yielded an analytical puzzle. The often tendentious interpretations of the capitalist labor market's harmful effects on the lives of the average French worker produced the obsession with the urban poor, because in the eyes of many, the relationship between unbridled capitalism and pauperism in big cities was linear and close. While it was true that some capitalist manufacturing centers emerged during the early nineteenth century in towns such as Rouen, Saint-Etienne, and Toulouse, or Roubaix-Tourcoing and Mulhouse in northern France, these semi-industrialized cities were hardly symptomatic of general trends.[42]

Nonetheless, many French politicians and intellectuals—Léon Faucher's speech in the Chamber of Deputies in 1848 was one example in many—saw the progress of modern technology as a macabre development. All mechanical innovations, they feared, would displace honorable and independent artisans and transform them into machine-breaking Luddites *à la français*![43] This unexamined truism, in turn, blinded public officials and intellectuals to the fact that truly desperate poverty haunted a much greater number of peasants, whose subsistence was only minimally affected by capitalist logic, if at all. By interpreting urban pauperism as an epiphenomenon of capitalism, many social critics modified the dismal existence of poor peasants into an imaginary construct that functioned as a happy alternative to the sorry lives of paupers in sprawling cities.

Making distinctions between eager workers in search of honest labor and lazy beggars subsisting on the generosity of their fellow citizens was difficult. It was equally hard to distinguish between people who were truly pitiable and in need of help and others who voluntarily lived off hoax or intimidation. As chronicled in the previous chapter, officials often merged honest migrants and shiftless vagabonds into an identical social category, and throughout the first half of the century, a sequence of Ministers of the Interior reiterated this muddled perspective forcefully. Large parts of the population, one minister stated in 1817, were losing their taste for consistent work. Many people were in the habit of "leaving very poor regions and traveling long distances in search of areas that are more favorably endowed. This kind of disorderly movement does nothing but to augment vagabondage,'' the minister complained, ''and is a never-ending source of crimes and misdemeanors.''[44]

Whether on the political left—with the exception of Proudhon—or on the political right, French social critics proposed innovative state-controlled institutions which could monitor the mobility of workers and guarantee their placidity. If the state could steer workers to those regions with a demand for labor and thus limit workers' vulnerability to sudden drops in employment, it could minimize the risks and uncertainties in the market economy and diminish potential unrest. Aside from the recurring recommendation to replicate in France the elaborate agricultural colonies for the urban poor which the Dutch *Maatschappij van Weldadigheid* had created, other social investigators devised a vast assortment of plans for new government agencies.

The arch-conservative C. G. Chamborant, for example, suggested a kind of glorified labor exchange board with pedagogical side effects, which would bring about the desired combination of agriculture and cottage industry. This economic mixture of agriculture and handicraft industry would expand sources of livelihood for the poor, he believed, thereby reducing their need to migrate in times of scarcity.[45] Chamborant echoed the opinion of one his famous compatriots. Alexis de Tocqueville, in his ruminations about pauperism in England, had likewise pointed to the need to reduce the mobility of workers until the state could assure that their exodus from the land was rewarded with employment in the city. He had even referred to the regulation of production and consumption as a means of avoiding economic depressions and crises.[46]

But it was in their generic fear of the vagrancy and disorderly conduct of workers that French elites articulated their bifurcated vision of ''otherness.'' Bourgeois Frenchmen inscribed both peasants and wage laborers with attributes—consisting of a mixture of lewdness and illiteracy, of primeval savagery and congenital stupidity—that underscored the profound distance from their own refinement and civility. But there was one fundamental difference. Simple peasants in the verdant, unspoiled countryside reminded middle-class observers of France's prototypical agrarian nature and perhaps of their own rural origins as well. Peasants embodied a symbolic aspect of French national identity. Although they might still be uncultured and uneducated, peasants possessed the potential to evolve into civilized landed proprietors, who could thus join the ranks of respectable French citizens.

In contrast, degenerate urban workers, living in sleazy slums where unmarried men and women or parents and children slept helter-skelter in a stinking basement room, resembled alien, barbaric creatures, as if they were a subhuman species that had gotten stuck at, or atavistically reverted to, a lower evolutionary level. Factory laborers did not evoke the elites' own quintessential rural past nor did they conjure up France's august feudal history. Instead, urban workers personified a disturbing image of the ominous "modernity" that loomed on the French horizon—an impending future that would entrench factory production and reify capitalist labor relations.[47]

The veneration of peasant agriculture and French elites' inability—or reluctance—to understand that the lives of the rural poor were as harsh as those of urban paupers, were constitutive elements of the nineteenth-century reactionary, antimodernist consensus. In France this antimodernist posture was perhaps a matter of contingency, since nineteenth-century policymakers could translate neither the Revolution's progressive mandate of *égalité* nor the individualistic legacy of *liberté* into a stable social reality. Despite the "modern" political heritage which the Revolution had bestowed upon the nineteenth century, French political culture in the post-Napoleonic era produced mostly immobility and *attentisme* (fence-straddling).

The more or less comparable antimodern outcome in the Netherlands, however, was the result of a more deliberate set of choices. The early modern Dutch Republic's institutional history and cultural grammar still structured the discourses about poverty and poor relief in the nineteenth century. The wistful memories of the early modern Dutch Republic's economic brilliance endured. These nostalgic recollections tended to reinforce certain myths about the social harmony, or create half-truths about the organic unity, of the Dutch past.

The fixation on the triumphant seventeenth-century Republic of the United Provinces—resembling what Jacques le Goff has called a "fetishization" of the past—represented a "social danger," since it produced a sense of powerlessness in nineteenth-century public officials and intellectuals.[48] However novel some of the liberal economists' arguments about modern capitalism may have sounded—or despite the distinctly modern sensitivities to issues of social justice that others exhibited—the rhetorical conventions of the Republican past continued to shape the discussion. The history of the Dutch Republic functioned as an optical lens, which distorted the overall picture of the nation's social record and twisted the meaning of the historical narrative. As the anthropologist Steven Kemper has argued recently, some perspectives on the past are "more reliable as actual history," whereas other recollections of the past are more "serviceable" as ideology.[49] The luster of the pugnacious little Republic—a dwarf among neighboring giants—lingered on in the nineteenth century in the resplendent paintings of Johannes Vermeer, Rembrandt, and their dazzling colleagues; it functioned as an eminently "serviceable" iconography.

After all, the seventeenth century was an age when the Dutch nation had flaunted before a European world ruled by Absolutist monarchs, and torn by religious strife, its ability to build a civil society based on principles of local autonomy, religious tolerance, and civic freedom. The "collective heroism" of seventeenth-century Dutch burghers with their "healthy, concrete, down-to-earth attitudes," provided a striking historical iconography and functioned as a permanent source of national pride.[50] What nineteenth-century observers glossed over, in this context, was the fact that the cosmopolitan and permeable nature of Dutch society in the seventeenth century, and its splendid reputation for the tolerance of religious differences, issued from "purely practical habits" and served the Republic's economic self-interests.[51] While the Republic's esteemed civic culture was not necessarily an expression of a magnanimous national character but obliged, instead, more mundane purposes, in the nineteenth century it had nonetheless become a pivotal emblem of Dutchness. The memory of the Republic served as a prism through which nineteenth-century intellectuals and public officials observed the past and gauged the present.

Like their colleagues in France, nineteenth-century Dutch intellectuals also harked back to an illustrious past, but not to a history of feudal lords who lived in rustic country manors surrounded by obedient peasants with whom they worked side by side, in harmony with each other and with the bucolic French countryside. Rather, Dutch observers in the nineteenth century fondly remembered a history of maritime conquest, profitable financial transactions, and lucrative international commerce. In fact, in the Dutch public imagination, the agricultural sector was not at all dominated by innocent peasants who tilled the soil in gentle concord, who shied away from the evil capitalist market and were unresponsive to fluctuations in demand. Rather, the principal portrayal of the rural scene in Holland was populated by savvy farmers who specialized in the production and well-paying export of cheese and butter and responded to oscillations in the foreign demand for agricultural goods with great alacrity. Dutch farmers, in other words, behaved very much like calculating merchants in Amsterdam and other cities: they utilized their comparative advantage and earned handsome profits from international trade.

In those regions of the country where farmers engaged only in dairy farming, they usually "find a generous livelihood without having to perform much work," a contemporary reported in 1816. Since women were "in charge of making butter and cheese, all the farmer has to do is to milk his cows and bring his products to market. During the winter, his only task is to feed his livestock." This observer then tried to explain the employment of seasonal migrant labor from several German states near the Dutch border. Because Dutch farmers were not accustomed to doing much work, he claimed, "they are loathe to engage in heavy and strenuous tasks. During the few busy weeks in the summertime, when the hay needs to be cut and the rye must be harvested, there is a sudden demand for vigorous helping hands, and most farmers are very happy that muscular Germans are willing to offer their sevices in exchange for a high daily wage."[52] A hundred years later, the Marxist historian Henriette Roland Holst repeated this cliché when she announced that fat and self-satisfied farmers in the nineteenth century grew rich overnight, "during their sleep."[53]

While Dutch industry adapted slowly to changing economic conditions in the nineteenth century, Dutch agriculture remained one of the most dynamic sectors of the economy throughout the nineteenth century and could be counted among the most advanced in Europe. In 1849, agriculture was the largest single contributor to the Dutch national income, and approximately 45 percent of the Dutch population found its livelihood in agriculture and fishing.[54] Contemporaries described these areas as "the richest in Europe. We have all sorts of grains, vegetables, fruit, flax, hemp, tobacco, hops, and madder. We have large forests and timber in abundance, and many roads have been constructed, canals have been dug, our pastures are filled with cattle, horses, sheep, and pigs; rivers overflow with fish and the seas along our coast add further to our prosperity."[55]

Despite the economic resilience of Dutch agriculture, nineteenth-century politicians showed a reluctance to acknowledge the economic significance of farming and favored other economic sectors more than agriculture. In palpable contrast to their French counterparts, the urban and commercial biases of Dutch elites prompted them to view agriculture as less important than the "real" business of trade and shipping.[56] Farmers did not figure prominently in the "imagined community" of the Dutch nation; instead, its protagonists were cunning merchants and intrepid sea captains.

While agriculture flourished, the remaining sectors of the Dutch economy experienced slow economic growth between 1815 and 1855.

But Dutch commentators in the early nineteenth century were curiously confused about the status of the national economy, not knowing how to explain the relative decline in Dutch society's prosperity since early modern times. In comparative terms, the seventeenth-century Dutch Republic's economy had been the most advanced, or most thoroughly capitalist, in early modern Europe. It was a bustling society that had fostered complex commercial institutions and nurtured sophisticated enterprises.[57] Since then the powerful manufacturing sector seemed to have lost its vigor. By the early nineteenth century England dominated the international market for manufactured goods. Amsterdam no longer constituted a central staple market. The volume of Dutch trade had decreased relative to England's, and the early modern handicraft industries could not effectively compete with mechanized British industry. Overall investment in manufacturing and agriculture had also declined, and Dutch burghers became increasingly embroiled in banking and commercial ventures that assured a more risk-free return.[58]

The shift away from manufacturing was not simply the disappearance, to invoke Johan Huizinga's vivid imagery, of the "pitch and tar, the pluck and piety, the fire and imagination" that had inspired the colorful Dutch entrepreneurs who had been responsible for the flourishing economy during the seventeenth century.[59] In the course of the eighteenth century Dutch trade began to resemble "commerce by proxy" and relied more on commissions. Banking clearly provided fewer employment opportunities than commerce and manufacture, and during the early decades of the nineteenth century many towns with a venerable handicraft tradition fell prey to a level of unemployment heretofore unknown, while the overall population kept growing at a steady pace.[60]

Prosperous cities with vibrant civic cultures and long-standing manufacturing specialties—towns such as Gouda, Delft, Leiden, and Haarlem, individually famous for the production of either clay pipes or blue tiles and decorated pottery, for multicolored woolen blankets or bleached textiles—had lost their stamina by the early nineteenth century. The spectacular success of English mechanization and factory production, it seemed, had indirectly extinguished the daring spirit of local handicraft industries and smothered the ingenuity of entrepreneurs. Instead, these previously prosperous cities, once upon a time brimming with resourceful activity, had become "singularly uncreative" in the nineteenth century.[61]

As a result, certain segments of the urban Dutch elites harbored a nostalgic desire to recapture the financial and commercial centrality of the Amsterdam staple market. Affluent Dutch burghers were reluctant to shift from trade to factory production, since international commerce had furnished the wellspring from which their fabulous wealth had flowed. Some of them profoundly doubted, moreover, the benefits of an economy grounded primarily in manufacture.[62] One limiting factor was the paucity of natural resources needed for industry; the Dutch nation had no iron ore deposits and only a little coal. Thus, with an end to the French occupation and the demise of the Continental system—which had tried to prevent Dutch ships from sailing the English Channel in order to frustrate trade with England—maudlin merchants and businessmen in Holland longed for an economic revival through the recovery of its ancient commercial hegemony.[63]

After 1815, several well-meaning if misguided Dutch observers believed the former glory of the golden age would quickly return. ''As soon as the seas reopen, shipping and commerce will revive, the fishing industry will flourish, and the exports of our products will increase,'' wrote Gijsbert Karel van Hogendorp, an overly confident analyst of Dutch economic life, in 1814. ''Dutch ships shall visit our colonies before we have officially repossessed the lands, and our country will once again be the central marketplace of the entire world.''[64]

Van Hogendorp was the archetypal representative of the urban oligarchies' commercial interests. After spending time in the United States while he was an officer in the Dutch Republic's army—where Thomas Jefferson had befriended him—he became a secretary of state and a member of King Willem I's cabinet in late 1813.[65] He held firm to his conviction that a recovery of the nation's blossoming and unfettered trade would coincide with the return of prosperity for the country as a whole. ''As long as we can, we should maintain a liberal system and advocate free trade, so that our manufactures preserve the opportunity to export abroad.'' Commenting on the habit of Dutch capitalists to make lucrative investments elsewhere, he said: ''Foreign countries, for example, may need money so badly that they will offer extraordinary advantages to attract [our] capital; moreover, among the capitalists there may be those who value their own tranquility and idleness above all and therefore prefer to manage a portfolio instead of an estate (*landgoed*), a factory, or a trading firm.'' But if ''good laws'' would cultivate free enterprise afresh, then ''Dutch capital will once again be invested profitably in our own nation.''[66]

Others, such as Johannes Goldberg, who had been appointed the nation's *Agent van nationale oeconomie* (Agent of National Economics) in May of 1799, shared van Hogendorp's vision and tried to provide a rationale for it:

> When looking at the map of Europe, one comes to the conclusion that [our country] can be regarded as suitable only for commerce, and it must be equally obvious that our country is ill-equipped for industry. Because of our geographical location, Holland is destined to be a warehouse where merchants from every corner of the world send their goods. It would not be wise to sacrifice our strategic advantages with regard to commerce and trade for the uncertain and imaginary benefits of industry.[67]

To the commercial oligarchs in cities in the western provinces, free trade, as an idea and a practical policy that had been so near and dear to the heart of the early modern Dutch Republic, continued to function as a panacea. Although the theoretical justification of uninhibited trade differed from early modern explanations, if only because the economic logic of the world had changed, nineteenth-century arguments in favor of free trade reinvented early modern statements. ''The Netherlands has at all times owed its success and well-being to trade and shipping, and in the material realm things must continue to develop in that direction,'' argued P. Ph. van Bosse, the Minister of Finance, in his preliminary report on a tariff bill in 1858. ''It must more and more strive to become a staple market (*porto franco*) again for foreign manufactures, and in order to achieve this status we require freedom of trade and movement.'' With this somewhat archaic argument he legitimized a reduction in protective tariffs during the 1850s, a decade that yielded the abolition of protective legislation and the adoption of free-trade policies in other European countries, even in France, although to a more limited extent.[68]

Despite such hopeful attitudes, the revival of Dutch commercial preeminence after 1815 apppeared to be an elusive dream. Urban merchants, who remembered the commercial grandeur and achievements of their ancestors during early modern times with melancholy, had a difficult time evaluating the economic changes that were taking place around them, whether in Holland or in the world at large. Many among them viewed the palpable urban misery and widespread poverty as the principal characteristics of an economy that could not recover its previous commercial eminence and entrepreneurial energy. ''The unprecedented and unrelenting disasters'' that struck Europe during the past twenty-five years and ''victimized'' the Dutch provinces so sadly, wrote one concerned Dutch observer, ''had a fatal impact on the economic resources of our country.'' It used to be that prosperity was widespread, wrote Gerrit Luttenberg in 1841, but today ''commerce, shipping, and fishing have declined and, as a result, we are confronted with lower levels of well-being or, in some cases, a complete breakdown of industry and trade.'' This had deprived the poorer classes of the opportunity to earn their livelihood, he said, and they could no longer personally care for their often sizable families.[69] From various perspectives and with diverse political overtones, many commentators on the Dutch social situation described Holland as a sluggish and listless nation, composed of conservative tradesmen, self-satisfied, coupon-clipping *rentiers*, and a great mass of destitute people.[70]

Of course a series of structural factors, mostly beyond the control of entrepreneurs and policymakers, had an indelible impact on the evolution of the Dutch economy. But the disturbing contrasts between nineteenth-century realities and the rose-colored memories of the Republic's economic prowess yielded a curious set of misunderstandings. Many critics were baffled and mystified, as if the Dutch economy had suddenly lost its Midas touch. According to the most pessimistic rhetoric, the nature of modern life had converted the Dutch nation from a trailblazer into a follower of world-wide economic trends.

In the imagination of many, Holland had been transformed from a vigorous commercial champion into an injured little country, left out and abandoned by a heartless, novel set of economic relations which its chief rival on the other side of the English Channel had first reconfigured and then monopolized. The modest improvement of the Dutch economy during the period 1815–1850, which has become very apparent to modern-day historians, did not seem within the intellectual grasp of contemporary observers in the nineteenth century.[71] Instead, many disheartened Dutchmen heaped opprobrium upon the new, ''enlightened'' age—a new era dominated by novel forms of capitalist competition, mechanized manufacture, and more modern, rationalized business practices. In short, many ''wealthy, cultured, and nostalgic'' men harked back to an idealized world of the past; they expressed their longing for the nation's economic and spiritual *réveil* through a reawakening of commerce and trade and evangelical philanthropy.[72]

However, another discourse existed alongside this lachrymose—or involuted—rhetoric that seemed reluctant to embrace the realities of the ''modern'' world. Other social critics were more concerned with pragmatic economic questions such as the major drain that poor relief placed on public and private resources. Dutchmen with an activist bent could not fathom the alleviation of poverty through an endless process of expansion and contraction of the private sources of Christian charity. From a sober economic perspective, the presence of poverty-stricken citizens was a monumental problem that affected Dutch society as a whole, whether one was rich or poor, whether one lived in the countryside or in the city, and demanded structural solutions.

The voice of economic rationality reverberated more loudly in discussions about poverty in Holland than in France, and Dutch commentators placed less weight on personal guilt and moral failure. It was as if they had a keener understanding of the need for a collective, or a communitarian, resolution to the inequalities of human existence.[73] In the eyes of the French historian Emile Doumergue, this was a logical outgrowth of the moral sensibilities that Dutch Calvinism engendered. Good Calvinists were ''socially concerned individuals'' rather than monomaniacal ''pursuers of profit,'' and the wealth of the blessed minority should be mobilized in such a way that it enhanced the comfort of the community as a whole.[74]

In comparison to France, liberal economics found many more attentive ears in the Netherlands. Economics as an academic discipline in the Netherlands had been taught in the Law Faculty of the University of Leiden since 1812, and twenty years later at the University of Utrecht and elsewhere. Dutch academic economists at universities and at the *Atheneum* in Amsterdam, where Jeronimo de Bosch Kemper was a professor in the 1850s, focused their scholarly attention on issues of economic development as well as the solution of practical social problems, and twelve dissertations in economics had been written before 1840.[75] The ''science'' of economics or political economy, in fact, was a distinct voice in the contentious public debate about poverty and poor relief policy during the 1840s and 1850s, and entrepreneurs and bureaucrats, for their part, expressed a keen if guarded interest in the insights of the new discipline.[76]

When D. A. Portielje wrote about ''Trade in the Netherlands in 1844,'' he fulminated against any form of economic protectionism because of its insidious consequences for Dutch prosperity. He argued that economic protection was akin to the negative impact of an ''arbitrary'' medical intervention on the functioning of the human body, and he cited the writings of Adam Smith, David Ricardo, Jérôme-Adophe Blanqui, Jean-Baptiste Say, M. J. MacCulloch and many others as theoretical ammunition.[77] In his 1852 reflections on the role of the state in poor relief, A. Elink Sterk, too, quoted extensively from the writings of a wide range of economists elsewhere in Europe, including John Stuart Mill in England, C. J. Kraus in Germany, and Joseph Garnier in France. In a footnote he presumed that these ideas should be familiar to everyone, if only ''because of the Dutch translations that have already appeared.''[78]

De Bosch Kemper and Simon Vissering and their fellow liberal economists, eager to display the insights of their brave new discipline, underlined the pitfalls inherent in any effort to tamper with the free-floating energy of the capitalist market by granting poor relief.[79] "Because poor relief reduces mortality," de Bosch Kemper noted in Ricardian fashion, a society commits itself "to supporting a constantly growing number of people." After all, charity and public compassion extend the lives of poor people and thereby expand the supply of labor. As a result, he noted, "wages and real incomes will drop and, once again, create more poverty." De Bosch Kemper assumed that the considerable sums spent on charity were an irrevocable loss to the national economy. Even though he conceded that a certain portion of the alms given to the poor were brought back into circulation in the form of, for example, the prices people paid to bakers for bread or to greengrocers for potatoes, charity was nonetheless consumed without a remunerative and "fruitful contribution to the national wealth in return."[80]

In Holland a galaxy of work institutes and pauper factories, both big and small, waxed and waned alongside the steady flow of outdoor relief, not necessarily as cogs in the wheel of surveillance and enclosure but as an attempt to recoup some of the costs of charity. Economic logic and concerns with profitability and open competition, though, produced a lively and very "modern" debate among economists. Capital and labor always needed each other, wrote the prolific liberal economist W. C. Mees. The steady expansion of the population forced labor to compete for available jobs, and "the strongest and most capable workers have always won this competition." Those workers who lost out inevitably descended into the indigent classes. But the system of charitable workshops, he warned, was based on the "most dangerous fiction, since it postulates that they will reduce the number of poor people." Instead, owing to demographic pressures more and more people wanted to enter the work institutes, while increasingly large funds had to be spent on administering them, which deprived the "private sector of crucial capital."[81]

Mees was both strident and voluble in his denunciation of charitable workhouses; these institutions were "commercially backward and inefficient," he declared, because indigent workers, given their low levels of skill, would probably manufacture slipshod products of inferior quality. If the demand for factory goods would drop, the products made in the work institute would be the first to be spurned in the commercial marketplace. If, on the other hand, demand would rise, free enterprise would respond to it much more effectively. In the best of all possible worlds, pauper factories should have to compete openly and equally with private business, but since municipalities and private charities subsidized them, they exercised an unfair advantage that was rarely put to good use. A workhouse, Mees concluded, squandered all donations given with the best of intentions.[82]

The provision of employment in workshops was ''subject to greater financial and social costs than normal public assistance,'' another economist complained in 1853, because the labor productivity of the poor was insufficient to cover the much higher administrative expenditures necessary to run a work institute in comparison with a normal factory. ''In our contemporary society one no longer buries money in the ground without collecting interest,'' because most smart people invested their capital productively. The funding of a workhouse resembled the antiquated practice of hiding money in an old sock underneath a pillow, since pauper factories withheld ''working capital from private industry.''[83]

Other Dutchmen harbored doubts about liberal economists' denunciation of work institutes, however, and they believed firmly that some of the financial outlays for workhouses, even if large sums of money went down the drain, would nonetheless yield precious benefits. The combination of work and charity, of labor discipline in exchange for financial support, might transform morally deprived poor folks into solid workmen through didactic example and uplifting education. Although they understood that it would be difficult to render pauper factories economically profitable, it was always preferable to doling out unconditional relief with no strings attached whatsoever![84]

The Dutchman Alstorphius Grevelink summed up the confusing mixture of ideas about the ''natural'' forces of the marketplace, on the one hand, and the call for the synthetic creation of work, on the other, in a cheerful, if somewhat simplistic, fashion. All the government would have to do is to remove the obstacles to the growth of the economy and society's means of existence and no longer hinder commercial contacts with either foreign countries or the Dutch colonial empire, he said. If the state were to furnish education, wisdom, and, above all freedom, then ''popular happiness will be spread and private and church charities will be completely sufficient to take care of the poor.''[85]

In general, whether in France or in the Netherlands, the individual or collective understanding of the etiology of poverty, of course, was not based on interpretations of—or misconceptions about—the nature of modern capitalism alone. Economic perspectives fused with ideas about politics and the appropriate domains for state and church action; they also merged with views about the basic rights of individual citizens within the body politic or the community's sense of responsibility vis-à-vis less fortunate compatriots. In the public discourses about poverty and poor relief, the officially acknowledged political role of organized religion proved to be an area of significant difference between the French and the Dutch.

Political tensions in nineteenth-century France between the Catholic Church and the state revolved around the right to educate the "mind" and command the "soul" of the nation. Poor relief, meanwhile, had quietly been transformed into a series of contractual and bureaucratic "habits" between Catholic religious orders and the public sector. Nineteenth-century French politicians or their precursors had fought the ideological battles over the proper terrain for social action of the church or state during the Revolution and had resolved them in favor of the state, even if the Catholic Church reemerged as the pivotal provider of social welfare. But the radical revolutionaries' exaltation of centralized social policy, which would radiate from Paris to every remote nook and cranny of the nation, persisted.

Relative to little Holland, France was not burdened by a sense of political or economic weakness with regard to the outside world, and intellectual concerns with pauperism did not hinge on a perception of a growing economic or political vulnerability in a competitive European context. Rather, French ideas about poverty were part and parcel of an overall vision of modern industrialism and its nefarious effects on the natural well-being of human societies, in general, and France, in particular. The enigma of post-Revolutionary French politics almost always seemed to boil down to the same issue: how to translate the hopes and dreams of the Revolution into a manageable and stable social order. The Revolution had created auspicious visions of individual freedom and democratic equality. As Charles de Rémusat, who would be appointed as a Minister of the Interior during the July Monarchy, mused in 1826, "Sentiments of equality as well as universal justice abolish humiliation and disdain among the different classes of society. It means that individual inferiority and superiority no longer exist."[86]

But the idealistic political imagery of the Revolution and the cruel economic realities of early nineteenth-century French society were poles apart. The multitudes of indigent French men and women personified and underscored this discrepancy; as such they threatened the harmony of the social order and provoked haunting memories of the bloody havoc the *Terreur* had unleashed. Moreover, the appeal of economic and political liberalism eluded French policymakers and *patrons* because, as far as they were concerned, the unbridled forces of capitalist supply and demand would compound the possibility of social disorder rather than diminish it.

Accordingly, compared with prevailing perspectives in Holland, which seemed more preoccupied with "equalization" and especially with "profitability," the issue of "pacification" and neutralizing working-class volatility loomed larger in the minds of French policymakers. Many critics saw the new pauperism *au fond* as evidence of capitalism's competitive egotism and the destruction of the organic unity of French society. In response, they concocted a series of ideal-typical binary images that paired economic security with state regulation and coupled agriculture with national harmony—the kind of social stability that typified "true" France. At the same time, Frenchmen tended to conflate industrial capitalism with a malfunctioning of the social engine, while the "natural" vigor of the marketplace would trigger chaos and revolution. In the process, they summoned an inflexible sense of "visionary certainty as the opposite to ideological doubt."[87]

In the Netherlands, conflicts over turf and the proper division of labor between religious charity and secular poor relief continued to function as the pivotal source of friction. Almost all Dutch participants in the rhetorical skirmishes over poor relief worried about human suffering, efficacy, and profitability. But the many serious economic investigations into the most cost-efficient ways in which the largest number of impoverished citizens could be helped, and discussions about social justice or individual entitlements, were relegated to a secondary plan. The historically conditioned awareness of the primacy of economic factors in the well-being, or perhaps the survival, of the Dutch nation could not supersede the fire and brimstone rhetoric of Protestant ministers.

The relative economic decline of the Dutch Republic since the late seventeenth century had produced an ingrained anxiety about the vulnerability of the nation, which remained, after all, a narrow, flat, waterlogged stretch of land surrounded by powerful giants: a cunning David amid several lumbering Goliaths. In early modern times, the geographical and political vulnerability of the Dutch Republic vis-à-vis its towering neighbors had been offset by its economic might and commercial glory. But during the first half of the nineteenth century this was no longer the case, and Dutch intellectuals and public officials regarded the growth of poverty as tangible evidence of the decline of the economic and political stature of the Dutch nation and its thwarted attempts to compete with neighboring England.

The alarming size of the indigent population in the Netherlands, aside from placing enormous pressures on the nation's financial resources, embodied something else, too: it represented incontrovertible evidence of Holland's removal from the center stage of European political history. Not too long ago, nineteenth-century writers remembered wistfully, the Dutch Republic had performed a starring role as mediator in Europe's political theater. In the early nineteenth century, however, they could hardly pretend that the Dutch nation was still a major player in the European balance of power, and the country's widespread poverty was a poignant reminder of its newly assigned cameo role.

Nevertheless, internecine debates about the challenge to the independence of the *diaconiëen* overruled the less emotionally charged inquiries into the intricate relationship between economic growth and government intervention, on the one hand, and unemployment and destitution, on the other. However, the slow but steady growth of the nation's economy became more perceptible after mid-century, which combined with the astonishing wealth that began to fill Dutch coffers as a result of the lucrative ''cultivation system'' that Johannes van den Bosch had started in Java the 1830s. In the 1850s poverty no longer seemed as oppressive a problem as before, in both a tangible and symbolic sense, and Holland, indeed, avoided the fate of being reduced to yet another trivial little country in Europe. After all, without the possession of ''our'' Dutch East Indies, Holland would have become as insignificant in world affairs as Denmark!

Notes

1. Léon Faucher, in Joseph Garnier, ed., *Le droit au travail à l'Assemblée nationale* (Paris: Guillaumin, 1848), p. 331. See also Whitney Walton, *France at the Crystal Palace. Bourgeois Taste and Artisan Manufacture in the Nineteenth Century* (Berkeley: University of California Press, 1992), pp. 211–12.

2. Collectie Goldberg, No. 44, F. van der Schaft (Secretaris van het Comité van Algemene Welvaart te Haarlem), *Gelijkheid, Vrijheid, Broederschap: aan de Nationale Vergadering representerende het volk van Nederland*, (1795), ARA, The Hague.

3. See also Gertrude Himmelfarb, *The Idea of Poverty. England in the Early Industrial Age* (New York: Alfred A. Knopf, 1984), p. 11.

4. For a general discussion, see E.J. Fischer, *Fabriqueurs en fabrikanten. Twente, Borne, en de katoennijverheid, 1800–1930* (Utrecht: Matrijs, 1983), passim.

5. Jean-Chrétien-Ferdinand Hoefer, ed., *Nouvelle biographie générale depuis les temps plus reculés jusqu'à nos jours* (Paris: Firmin Didot Frères, 1855), 7, pp. 142–44.

6. Hoefer, ed., *Nouvelle biographie générale*, 46, p. 203. William Coleman, in *Death Is a Social Disease. Public Health and Political Economy in Early Industrial France* (Madison: University of Wisconsin Press, 1982), reports that Villeneuve-Bargemont also served in the department of the Tarn, p. 82.

7. Letter written by Lacordaire on March 15, 1824, quoted by Jacques-Théophile Foisset, *Vie de Lacordaire*, 2 vols. (Paris: Lecoffre Fils, 1870), 1, p. 59.

8. For a classic treatment of the historical origins of social Catholicism, see Jean-Baptiste Duroselle, *Les débuts du catholicisme sociale en France* (Paris: Presses Universitaires de France, 1951).

9. "Quelques idées sur l'éducation et l'instruction publique," *La Quotidienne*, December 4, 1816, quoted by Joseph N. Moody, *French Education Since Napoleon* (Syracuse: Syracuse University Press, 1978), p. 19.

10. Cited by Theodore Zeldin, *Introduction to Conflicts in French Society: Anti-Clericalism, Education and Morals in the Nineteenth Century* (Oxford: Clarendon Press of Oxford University Press, 1972), p. 10.

11. P.C. Molhuysen and J. Blok, eds., *Nederlands biographisch woordenboek* (Leiden: A.W. Sijthoff, 1912), 2, p. 220; see also J.J. Westendorp Boerma, *Een geestdriftige Nederlander: Johannes van den Bosch* (Amsterdam: Querido, 1950).

12. P.C. Molhuysen, P.J. Blok, and K.H. Kossmann, eds., *Nieuw Nederlands biographisch woordenboek* (Amsterdam: Van Oorschot, 1974), 3, p. 111; see also H.Th. Ambachtsheer, *Jhr. Mr. Jeronimo de Bosch Kemper. Een behoudend maatschappijhervormer* (Amsterdam: Querido, 1959).

13. For France, see Lucette le Van-Lemesle, "La Promotion de l'économie politique en France au XIXième siècle jusqu'à son introduction dans les facultés (1815–1881)," *Revue d'histoire moderne et contemporaine*, 27 (April/June 1980), pp. 278, 283.

14. H.W. Tydeman was professor of economics at the University of Leiden from 1812 to 1848. Affiliated with the Faculty of Law, he taught economics, statistics, and a course on trade law. His successor, Simon Vissering, who taught at the University of Leiden from 1850 until 1878, taught economics, statistics, and diplomatic history. See T.J. Boschloo, *De productiemaatschappij. Liberalisme en economische wetenschap in Nederland gedurende de negentiende eeuw* (University of Amsterdam: unpublished manuscript, Sociaal-Historisch Instituut, 1987), pp. 14–15.

15. For a detailed analysis, see Hilda Rigaudias-Weis, *Les enquêtes ouvrières en France entre 1830 et 1848* (Paris: Felix Alcan, 1939).

16. Le Van-Lemesle, in "La promotion de l'économie politique," indicates that the Academy of Moral and Political Sciences arranged for fifteen essay competitions between 1833 and 1848, p. 278.

17. See the discussion in M.J. Cullen, *The Statistical Movement in Early Victorian Britain: The Foundations of Empirical Social Research* (New York: Barnes and Noble, 1975), passim.

18. William Coleman, *Death Is a Social Disease*, p. 149. See also Aaron Sheon, ''Parisian Social Statistics: Gavarni, 'Le Diable à Paris,' and Early Realism,'' *Art Journal*, 44, No. 3 (Summer 1984), pp. 139–148.

19. Georges Lefebvre, *The Great Fear of 1789* (1932; repr. New York: Vintage, 1973), pp. 210–11.

20. Simon Schama, *Citizens. A Chronicle of the French Revolution* (New York: Alfred A. Knopf, 1989), p. 519.

21. For a lucid discussion, see Walton, *France at the Crystal Palace*, passim.

22. Quoted by J.L. Talmon, *The Origins of Totalitarian Democracy* (New York: Praeger, 1965), p. 244.

23. Charles Fourier, *Selections of the Works from Fourier*, (London: Swan Sonnenstein, 1901), p. 119.

24. Etienne Cabet, *Voyage en Icarie* (Paris: 1846), quoted by Georg Lichtheim, *The Origins of Socialism* (New York: Praeger, 1969), p. 29; see also Christopher H. Johnson, *Utopian Communism in France. Cabet and the Icarians, 1839–1851* (Ithaca: Cornell University Press, 1974), passim.

25. See the analysis in Heinz Strang, *Erscheinungsformen der Sozialhilfebedürftigkeit. Beitrag zur Geschichte, Theorie und empirischen Analyse der Armut* (Stuttgart: Ferdinand Enke Verlag, 1970), pp. 30–31.

26. George Woodcock, ''Introduction'' to Pierre-Joseph Proudhon, *What Is Property? An Inquiry into the Principle of Right and of Government* (New York: Dover, 1970), p. 7.

27. Pierre-Marie Bigot de Morogues, *Du paupérisme, de la mendicité et des moyens d'en prévenir les funestes effets* (Paris: Prosper Dondey-Dupré, 1834), Preface, n.p.; see also William M. Reddy, *The Rise of Market Culture: The Textile Trade and French Society*, 1750–1914 (Cambridge/New York: Cambridge University Press, 1984), p. 148.

28. Y. P. Migne, ed., *M. de Bonald. Oeuvres complètes*, 3 vols. (Paris: Calman Lévy Frères, 1859), 2, p. 239.

29. Quoted by Herman Lebovics, *True France. The Wars over Cultural Identity, 1900–1945* (Ithaca: Cornell University Press, 1992), pp. 25–26.

30. See the discussion in Ted W. Margadant, *French Peasants in Revolt. The Insurrection of 1851* (Princeton: Princeton University Press, 1979), pp. 51–52.

31. George W. Grantham, ''Scale and Organization in French Farming, 1840–1880,'' in William N. Parker and Eric L. Jones, eds., *European Peasants and their Markets. Essays in Agarian Economic History* (Princeton: Princeton University Press, 1975), p. 293.

32. Peter N. Stearns, *Paths to Authority. The Middle Class and the Industrial Labor Force in France, 1820–1848* (Urbana: University of Illinois Press, 1978), pp. 173, 179.

33. Georges Duveau, *La vie ouvrière en France sous le Second Empire* (Paris: Gallimard, 1946), p. 133.

34. Henri Hatzfeld, *Du paupérisme à la sécurité sociale* (Paris: Armand Colin, 1971), pp. 108–10.

35. Reddy, *The Rise of Market Culture*, pp. 13–14.

36. Karl Polanyi, *The Great Transformation* (Boston: Beacon Press, 1963). See also Katherine A. Lynch, *Family, Class, and Ideology in Early Industrial France* (Madison: University of Wisconsin Press, 1987), pp. 48–51.

37. See the discussion in William H. Sewell Jr., *Work and Revolution in France. The Language of Labor from the Old Regime to 1848* (Cambridge/New York: Cambridge University Press, 1980), pp. 140–42.

38. The private founders of the *Athénée*, established in 1781, aimed ''to create a school of practical sciences and a conservatory of arts and crafts'' to compensate for the practical insufficiency of official instruction. See Charles Dejob, ''De l'établissements connu sous le nom de Lycée et d'Athénee et de quelques établissements analogue,'' *Revue internationale de l'Enseignement*, July 15, 1889, pp. 136–37.

39. L. Reybaud, ''Les chaires d'économie politique en France,'' *Revue des deux mondes*, December 15, 1864, p. 950.

40. Pierre Rosanvallon, *Le moment Guizot* (Paris: Gallimard, 1985), p. 269.

41. The treatise submitted to the essay competition rejected by the Committee was F.C.P. Esterno's *De la misère, de ses causes, de ses effets et de ses remèdes* (Paris: Calman Lévy Frères, 1842). The committee evaluated twenty-two essays and gave Eugène Buret the first prize. See Lynch, *Family, Class, and Ideology*, p. 49.

42. Ronald Aminzade has recently analyzed the interaction between early industrialization and working-class activism in three French towns in *Ballots and Barricades. Class Formation and Republican Politics in France, 1831–1871* (Princeton: Princeton University Press, 1993).

43. Lynch, *Family, Class, and Ideology*, p. 5. This interpretation echoes Reddy, *The Rise of Market Culture*, especially Chapter 6. See also Coleman, *Death Is a Social Disease*, pp. 65–74.

44. Ministry of the Interior, Circulaire No. 50, November 16, 1817. F2 206, AN, Paris.

45. C.G. Chamborant, *Du paupérisme ce qu'il était dans l'antiquité, ce qu'il est à nos jours, des rèmedes qui lui étaient opposés, de ceux qu'il conviendrait de lui appliquer aujourd'hui* (Paris: Guillaumin, 1842), p. 145.

46. Seymour Drescher, *Tocqueville and Beaumont on Social Reform* (Pittsburgh: University of Pittsburgh Press, 1968), p. 24.

47. Lynch, *Family, Class, and Ideology*, p. 10.

48. Jacques Le Goff, *History and Memory* (1977; repr. New York: Columbia University Press, 1992), p. 215.

49. Steven Kemper, *The Presence of the Past. Chronicles, Politics, and Culture in Sinhala Life* (Ithaca: Cornell University Press, 1991), p. 9.

50. Zbigniew Herbert, *Still Life With a Bridle. Essays and Apocryphas* (New York: Ecco Press, 1991), p. 19, and Edward Hirsh, ''The Fidelity of Things,'' *New Yorker*, December 23, 1991, p. 104.

51. Jan van Dorsten, ''Authority and Tolerance: The Dutch Experience,'' in

Lewis H. Lapham, ed., *High Technology & Human Freedom* (Washington, D.C.: Smithsonian Institution Press, 1985), p. 133.

52. R. Scherenberg, *Bedenkingen over de armoede en door welke middelen het aantal der armen in Nederland zoude kunnen worden verminderd, hunnen toestand verbeterd, en zij tot nuttige leden der maatschappij zouden kunnen worden opgeleid* (The Hague: Algemene Landsdrukkerij, 1816), p. 12.

53. Henriette Roland Holst, *Kapitaal en arbeid in Nederland*, 2 vols. (Nijmegen: SUN, 1977), 1, p. 103.

54. J.L. van Zanden, *De economische ontwikkeling van de Nederlandse landbouw in de negentiende eeuw, 1800–1914* (Utrecht: HES Studia Historica, 1985), and Niek Koning, ''Family Farms and Industrial Capitalism,'' *Sociologica Neerlandica*, 19, No. 1, (1983), p. 29.

55. G.K. van Hogendorp, *Bijdragen tot de huishouding van staat in het Koninkrijk der Nederlanden*, 9 vols. (Amsterdam: K. H. Schadd, 1825), 1, p. 94; see also Jan de Vries, ''Peasant Demand Patterns and Economic Development: Friesland, 1550–1750,'' in Parker and Jones, eds., *European Peasants and Their Markets*, pp. 234–36.

56. J.M.G. van der Poel, ''Landbouw in de noordelijke Nederlanden, 1170–1840,'' in *Algemene Geschiedenis der Nederlanden*, 15 vols. (Haarlem: Fibula van Dishoeck, 1977), 10, notes that the public attention paid to trade, shipping, and manufacture ''overshadowed'' the important agricultural sector (p. 159).

57. See Peter Wolfgang Klein, ''Dutch Capitalism and the European World Economy,'' pp. 75–91, and Bernard Hendrik Slicher van Bath, ''The Economic Situation in the Dutch Republic during the Seventeenth Century,'' pp. 23–36, in Maurice Aymard, ed., *Dutch Capitalism and World Capitalism/Capitalisme hollandais et capitalisme mondial* (Cambridge/New York: Cambridge University Press, 1982).

58. For the classic analysis, see Joh. de Vries, *De economische achteruitgang der Republiek in de achttiende eeuw* (Amsterdam: Ellerman Harms, 1959), and for a succinct argument, *idem.*, ''Het samenvattend beeld van de economische achteruitgang van de Republiek,'' in P.A.M. Geurts and F.A.M. Messing, eds., *Economische ontwikkeling en sociale emancipatie. 18 opstellen over economische en sociale geschiedenis*, 2 vols. (The Hague: Martinus Nijhoff, 1977), 1, p. 185. See also Ger van Roon, ''Long Wave Economic Trends and Economic Policies in the Netherlands in the XIXth and XXth Centuries,'' *Journal of European Economic History*, 12, No. 2 (Fall 1983), pp. 323–53; and Jan Luiten van Zanden, *Arbeid tijdens het handelskapitalisme: opkomst en neergang van de Hollandse economie* (Bergen, N-H: Octavo, 1991).

59. J.H. Huizinga, *Dutch Civilization in the Seventeenth Century and Other Essays* (New York: Harper and Row, 1968), p. 104.

60. J. Bierens de Haan, *Van Oeconomische tak tot Nederlandse maatschappij voor de nijverheid en handel, 1777–1952* (Haarlem: Tjeenk Willink, 1952), p. 19.

61. Joel Mokyr, *The Lever of Riches. Technological Creativity and Economic Progress* (New York: Oxford University Press, 1990), p. 246.

62. The primary exponent of this view was Gijsbert Karel van Hogendorp; see Otto van Rees, *Verhandeling over de verdiensten van Gijsbert Karel van Hogendorp als staatshuishoudkundige ten aanzien van Nederland* (Utrecht: C. van der Post, 1854). See also Fisher, *Van Fabriqueurs tot fabrikanten.*

63. P.W. Klein has criticized the somewhat ''simplistic'' debate among Dutch historians about the primacy of either psychological or structural factors in the explanation of the slow industrialization of the Netherlands in a review of Fischer, *Fabriqueurs en fabrikanten*, in *Tijdschrift voor Sociale Geschiedenis*, 11, Nos. 2–3 (1985), pp. 166–67.

64. Van Hogendorp, *Bijdragen tot de huishouding van staat*, 1, p. 49, and Van Rees, *Verhandeling over de verdiensten*, pp. 162–163.

65. Van Rees, *Verhandeling over de verdiensten*, pp. 1–7.

66. Van Hogendorp, *Bijdragen tot de huishouding van staat*, 2, p. 163, and 9, pp. 105–6.

67. Collectie Goldberg, No. 44, *Extract uit het verbaal van de Agent van Nationale Oeconomie der Bataafse Republiek*, 6, April 28, 1801, ARA, The Hague. See also H.F.J.M. van den Eerenbeemt, ''De Patriotse-Bataafse-Franse tijd (1780–1813),'' in J.H. van Stuijvenberg, ed., *De economische geschiedenis van Nederland* (Groningen: Wolters Noordhoff, 1977), pp. 157–200. For biographical information, see W.M. Zappeij, *De economische en politieke werkzaamheid van Johannes Goldberg* (Alphen aan de Rijn: Samson, 1967).

68. J.A. de Jonge, *De Industrialisatie in Nederland tussen 1850 en 1914* (1968; repr. Nijmegen: SUN, 1976), p. 321.

69. G. Luttenberg, *Proeve van onderzoek omtrent het armenwezen in ons Vaderland, en naar de doeltreffende middelen, die verder ter verbetering van het lot der armen zouden kunnen aangewend worden* (Zwolle: Tjeenk Willink, 1841), p. 11.

70. W.M. Zappeij en Th. van Tijn, ''De negentiende eeuw,'' in Van Stuyvenberg, ed., *De economische geschiedenis van Nederland*, p. 202.

71. See, among many others, J.L. van Zanden, ''Economische groei in Nederland in de negentiende eeuw,'' *Economisch en Sociaal-Historisch Jaarboek*, 100 (Amsterdam: NEHA, 1987), pp. 51–76, and Richard T. Griffiths and J.M.M. de Meere, ''The growth of the Dutch economy in the nineteenth century: back to basics?'' *Tijdschrift voor Geschiedenis*, 96, No. 4 (1983), pp. 563–72.

72. Michael Wintle, *Pillars of Piety. Religion in the Netherlands in the Nineteenth Century, 1813–1901* (Hull: Hull University Press, 1987), pp. 22–23.

73. See Hans Daalder, ''Building Consociational Democracies,'' in S.N. Eisenstadt and Stein Rokkan, eds., *Building States and Nations*, 2 vols. (Beverly Hills: Sage Publications 1973), 2, pp. 14–31, for an elaboration of communitarian or ''consociational'' ideas.

74. Philip Benedict, ''The Historiography of Continental Calvinism,'' in

Hartmut Lehmann and Guenther Roth, eds., *Weber's Protestant Ethic. Origins, Evidence, Contexts* (Publications of the German Historical Institute, Washington, D.C. and Cambridge/New York: Cambridge University Press, 1993), p. 311.

75. Thirty-five additional economics dissertations were written in Dutch universities between 1840 and 1870. See Boschloo, *De productiemaatschappij*, pp. 13–16.

76. Irene Hasenberg Butter, in *Academic Economics in Holland, 1800–1870* (The Hague: Martinus Nijhoff, 1969), has argued that economics served primarily as an intellectual justification for particular social policies and was only a marginal discipline in the Dutch academic establishment. Hans Boschloo, in *De productiemaatschappij*, disagrees with this assessment, pp. 14–18.

77. See the exploration in K.E. van der Mandele, *Het liberalisme in Nederland* (Arnhem: Van Loghum Slaterus, 1953), p. 83.

78. A. Elink Sterk, *Enige bedenkingen op het geschrift van J.L. de Bruyn Kops over het beginsel van armenzorg door de staat* (The Hague: W.P. van Stockum, 1852), p. 14.

79. See Hasenberg Butter, in *Academic Economics in Holland*, for a summary of the theoretical positions of economists who participated in the debate about pauperism and public assistance, pp. 72–77.

80. De Bosch Kemper, *Geschiedkundig onderzoek naar de armoede*, pp. 9–10.

81. W. C. Mees, *De Werkinrigtingen voor armen uit een staathuishoudkundig oogpunt beschouwd* (Rotterdam: J. van Balen, 1844), pp. 202–3.

82. Mees, *De Werkinrigtingen voor armen*, p. 203. See also the discussion in Abram de Swaan, *In Care of the State. Healthcare, Education, and Welfare in Europe and the USA in the Modern Era* (Oxford: Basil Blackwell/Polity Press, 1988), p. 47.

83. Anonymous, ''Het stelsel der werkhuizen voor armen,'' *Tijdschriftvoor staatshuishoudkunde en statistiek*, 8 (Zwolle: 1853), pp. 264–65.

84. See the critique in ''Het stelsel der werkhuizen voor armen,'' p. 265.

85. P.W. Alstorphius Grevelink, *Gedachten over de armenverzorging of bedenkingen op het werk van de heren H.W. en J.W. Tydeman en J. Heemskerk Az* (Assen: J.O. van Houten, 1850), pp. 109–110.

86. Charles de Rémusat, ''Des moeurs du temps,'' *Le Globe*, No. 5, August 26, 1826, p. 29. See also Rosanvallon, *Le moment Guizot*, p. 79.

87. J.W. Oerlemans, *Autoriteit en vrijheid, 1800–1914. Een cultuur-historisch onderzoek naar de weerstanden tegen de industriele maatschappij* (Assen: Van Gorcum, 1966), p. 304.

CHAPTER FIVE

"The Problems of the Pioneer Only Foreshadow the Problems of the Follower": Dutch and French Interpretations of the English Model

> I remember with triple horror those terrible [English] towns, inhabited by a population without morals, without faith, without resources, living in hordes, as serfs a thousand times more indentured and exploited than they had ever been during the Middle Ages. [Cities] where several greedy industrialists, uniquely preoccupied with finding outlets for their foolish products, abuse for the lowest possible wage the lives and strengths of an enormous mass of men, women, and children, to whom they give in exchange for their toil neither religious consolation nor security for their old age or in sickness; they do not even provide them with air to breathe in their disgusting factories.[1]
>
> —Charles de Montalembert, letter to his wife, 1839

> England provides the exemplary model of how a society can encourage the growth of industry. It used to be that English glassblowers could only blow green glass. The government proceeded to prohibit the importation of clear glass from abroad, despite many protests. The government persisted, however, and for a time people in England had to make do with green glass only. But lo and behold, soon thereafter the English glassblowers learned how to make clear glass, and today they export it to all the countries of Europe.[2]
>
> —Pieter Vreede, *Vervolg der proeve om de verheffing van het diepvervallen fabrieks-wezen te verenigen met de belangen van de koophandel, zeevaart en landbouw*, 1802

After 1815, with the Napoleonic wars in the past and the Continental System no longer sheltering the national economies on the European mainland, political economists and social investigators in France and Holland could not help but recognize the economic power that England had garnered during the previous thirty or forty years. England had solidified its imperial control in Asia, especially in India, in part by capturing new markets and displacing indigenous handicrafts.[3] Successful in finding new sources of demand for English manufactured products beyond the European continent, which Napoleon had closed off in a vain attempt to bring England to its knees, the British industrial sector emerged stronger than ever before. In the post-1815 era what seemed to be immense factories in several parts of the country provided jobs at a dismally low wage to an ever-growing proportion of English men, women, and children.

As nineteenth-century French and Dutch social theorists began to fear that the works of human creation—steam engines and trains, spinning mills and coal mines, company housing, urban squalor, and cavernous factories with thousands of exploited workers—could undermine the stability of the state and civil society, they began to compare more explicitly the conditions in their own societies with those in other countries. Because of the economic preeminence of England in nineteenth-century Europe, academics and public officials were inclined to look toward the English experience for guidance. England began to function as a symbol, a physical manifestation of what the future might bring, and social critics on the continent projected either their worst nightmares or their sweetest dreams upon the English model, which achieved a "mythical" stature.[4]

Ambivalence and equivocation permeated continental attitudes toward English industrialization. Some observers on the European mainland hailed Great Britain as an extremely efficient society, having raised its level of productivity to unequaled heights. Others praised the resilience of the English working class, which had forged autonomous self-help societies and founded an array of independent cultural institutions that conferred upon laboring families a burgeoning sense of dignity and pride. "These Mechanics Societies," said Martin Nadaud, the sophisticated son of the Limousin working class who had become a member of the Legislative Assembly in Paris in 1848, "have established the right to instruction, a right as sacred as the right to life." He praised the Mechanics Societies in stirring prose: these self-help organizations have shown that "hands accustomed to holding tools," however gnarled and calloused they might be, "can also handle a pen, maneuver a compass, or guide a paintbrush."[5]

A few Frenchmen had offered a similar opinion earlier. The French sociologist Gustave d'Eichthal, whom Auguste Comte gently chided for his "Anglophilia," also complimented the lectures delivered to a Mechanics Society in Bolton and he admired its library of one thousand volumes. As an aspiring disciple of Saint-Simonianism and an acquaintance of John Stuart Mill, d'Eichthal traveled through England in 1828 to grant himself the intellectual joy of observing a "great people" in the throes of unprecedented progress. In contrast to his famous colleague Alexis de Tocqueville, who was circumspect in his assessment of English society, d'Eichthal "liked" the English character and registered enormous admiration for the creative commotion of British industrialism.[6]

The English "make machines as we plants cabbages," Gustave d'Eichthal wrote to Auguste Comte, his mentor. They were afraid of nothing, and "raze hills, fill in valleys, and dig tunnels underneath towns" in order to improve communications. He was convinced England would never encounter a violent convulsion such as the French Revolution, because English people participated in the political process as an ingrained "practice." Working-class associations did not wish to foment revolution, but merely to invite "the lower orders into the habit of acting together."[7] Even though d'Eichthal made some invidious comparisons with France, too—living conditions among English agricultural laborers, he claimed, were "worse" than in France—he looked at Britain through brightly colored glasses.[8]

But a powerful counter discourse delivered an antidote to these enthusiastic appraisals of English society. Other Frenchmen denounced England as a frightening and aberrant national community that was engaged in a form of economic production resembling an "unnatural" act. Regardless of their explicit judgments and evaluations, though, a large number of social critics on the European continent felt compelled to arrive at some kind of coherent opinion about the nature of British industry and the reasons for its superior productivity. It was as if England began to function like a distorted mirror that either magnified or deformed in a grotesque fashion some of the troubling features of their own cultures. Commentators on economic developments on the continent elevated England to a sounding board which either confirmed or negated the illusions they harbored for the future economic development of their own societies.

The habit of comparing and contrasting the French and Dutch economies with the example of England converted British factory production into a tangible embodiment of the logic of capitalism. If in France and Holland capitalism itself was still a vaguely defined phenomenon, grimy English factories, managed by a handful of rapacious employers who exploited thousands of working men, women, and children from dawn to dusk, transformed the idea of the capitalist market into something very real. The English example suggested that the metamorphosis from a well-balanced world based on a mixture of agriculture and small, artisans' workshops to a society dominated by huge, filthy factories was inevitable. On the European mainland, this transition was still a chimera rather than an actual social reality. Nonetheless, the concentration of manufacture and factory laborers in a smattering of Dutch or French towns, and the presumable functioning of an anonymous labor market that surrendered workers to the impersonal laws of supply and demand, raised the specter of the large-scale social problems commonly associated with a mature industrial society.[9]

The United Kingdom, observers on the other side of the English Channel often thought, as the first nation to develop a full-blown capitalist economy, represented the harbinger of their own future and revealed the inexorable course of human history. Some among them were convinced that an understanding of British economic and social developments would illuminate the path their own countries would inevitably follow in the modern world. Especially in France, a number of intellectuals who contemplated the question of poverty and inequality absorbed a mechanistic vision of societal evolution. Their interpretations of English industrial capitalism hinted at a curious mixture of arguments derived from natural history or biology. On the one hand, they conjured up a vague notion of the hierarchical Great Chain of Being. On the other hand, scholars of modern capitalism alluded to innovative speculations about biological evolution, almost as if they anticipated Charles Darwin's ideas about the evolutionary stages of growth *avant la lettre*. While it is unlikely that they were aware of the work of Jean-Baptiste de Lamarck, who had written his *Philosophie zoologique* as early as 1809, many intellectuals conjectured that every society experiencing industrialization had to pass through a series of inevitable stages and undergo a preordained "societal ontogenesis."[10]

It was true that analysts suspected that the impact of growing factory production might refract differently and vary from country to country. But, at the same time, they worried about the idea of a unilinear evolution of modern industrial capitalism, which meant that the existing conditions in England presaged the social situation that either France or the Netherlands would soon face. An awareness dawned, however inchoate and ill-defined, that human beings were not really God-given creatures who possessed no free agency whatsoever. Instead, some intellectuals wondered whether economic development or technology was the result of mankind's conscious efforts to accommodate the unpredictable demands of the natural environment. Hence, the particular responses to all the different pushes and pulls encountered in the natural milieu could be held responsible for either idyllic economic progress or human misery and social regression.[11] England, therefore, could teach continental Europeans what the future might hold. As Karl Marx would state the problem succinctly in the preface to *Das Kapital*: the problems of the pioneer foreshadowed the problems of the follower, and the country that was more developed industrially only showed, to the less developed, the image of their own future!

The evolutionary perspective on the rank-ordering of cultures or social systems represented a relatively new phenomenon that was intimately linked to intellectual developments in both geology and biology in the nineteenth century.[12] With the birth of the concept of "geological time"—or Sir Charles Lyell's recognition that the formation of the multiple layers of the earth issued from a cumulative process that had taken millions of years—it was possible for social theorists to imagine the evolution of the species. Darwin would assert in 1859 that the differences between the species were not primordial and indelible but rather, "the daughter of time."[13] Emerging notions of evolution thus offered fresh intellectual possibilities to continental Europeans eager to grasp and elucidate the differences between their own economic structures and England's advanced industrialism.

While Darwin eventually registered the opinion that evolution was an inherently random process that responded to stimuli in the natural world in a serendipitous manner, Lamarck had emphasized the creative agency of evolution. He endowed the unfolding of history with a uniform pattern of progress, as if all history displayed an inherent teleology and all organisms were capable of progressive transmutation. It was true that Lamarck's ideas were largely ignored during his lifetime, even though they resurfaced with a vengeance in the neo-Lamarckianism of Ernst Haeckel and Herbert Spencer later in the nineteenth century.[14] But the mechanistic conceptions which some earlier political economists employed—and their oft-repeated belief that capitalist development could only follow one single trajectory and would yield, in the end, a monomorphic form of industrial society that eclipsed all environmental differences—foretold, perhaps, Haeckel's and Spencer's reinvented Lamarckianism. Although it was limited in its reach, a diffuse evolutionary logic prompted some social observers, especially in France, to conceptualize the unjust economic relations of English industry as a forerunner of their own inescapable future.[15]

England emerged as Europe's living prototype of modern industrialism, yet it provoked responses across the Channel that disclosed subtle differences. Charles de Montalembert, a centrist Catholic philosopher, was horrified by the human exploitation that English factory production and wage labor imposed upon its hapless victims. When he was still an energetic young man of twenty-nine years old, he traveled across England and observed firsthand the industrial life of such cities as Manchester and Birmingham. The human degradation and spiritual depravity he saw provoked in him a sense of outrage; the British working class, he wrote in a letter to his wife in 1839, were a thousand times more mistreated and indentured—*corvéable*—than French peasants had been under medieval feudalism.

As a liberal Catholic, Montalembert merely wished to reconcile the church with the nature of modern society. His stance was "liberal" only in his disagreement with the reactionary forces within the French church, which harkened back to the hierarchical estate society of the ancien régime and glorified the traditional alliance between the Bourbon Monarchy and the Catholic Church. But Montalembert did not embrace the idea of the Catholic Church's active social involvement in alleviating poverty in order to "mediate" between the rich and the poor. Nonetheless, the image of the future that the English industrial environment portended—a landscape dotted with suffocating factories which spewed forth nothing but dirty smoke, preposterous products, and human misery—was a terrifying one to him, which may have spurred his growing conservatism. At the time of working-class turmoil in Paris in 1848 he proclaimed, for instance, that the Catholic Church should teach the poor spiritual self-restraint and respect for others. The church's role, he intoned, was to instruct downtrodden workers not to "listen to those corrupting voices that repeatedly awaken the temptations of greed and envy" and to impress upon them, instead, to resign to their poverty in expectation of their "just reward and heavenly compensation."[16]

The ebullient Dutchman Pieter Vreede, in contrast, both recognized and celebrated in 1802 the comparative advantage that a growing technological sophistication could bestow upon society. Although his story about the English glassblowers who could blow only green glass was probably an apocryphal one, it serves as a striking metaphor for the ways in which a distinct faction within the Dutch community extolled the laws of supply and demand and applauded the capitalist market, which England exemplified so vividly. But his story contained a somewhat contradictory quality, too. While acclaiming the spontaneous energy of the capitalist market, which presupposed the non-intervention of the state in economic affairs, Vreede nonetheless praised the British government for interceding. By prohibiting the importation of clear glass, the state had stimulated the technological creativity of English workmen who had since then managed to corner the European market on transparent glass!

The Netherlands shared with Britain a long history of early maritime trade, commercial capitalism, and the pursuit of profit, but the economic success of the two nations had grown apart since the early eighteenth century, a divergence that became acute and problematic in the early nineteenth century. In fact, many Dutch intellectuals and public officials pondered the phenomenon of modern industrialism and tried to grasp the changes it might bring. A few amongst them repudiated it as responsible for the new and alien forms of poverty and a greater discrepancy between rich and poor. Most observers, however, tended to establish a more clearly articulated causal connection between the alleviation of poverty and the need for economic regeneration.

The attitudes of Dutch politicians or entrepreneurs toward England were no less ambivalent than those in France, but they arose from a different historical background. A publication of the Estates-General of the United Netherlands during the French Revolution noted that for many years England had been envious of Dutch prosperity, but when England began to export manufactured goods to the Dutch Republic—many of which were not subject to import duties—domestic industry was placed at a disadvantage. Owing to the growing importation of English products, displacing the demand for goods manufactured domestically, the report continued, ''many of our needy citizens have become unemployed, compelling them to appeal to poor relief agencies.'' Accordingly, ''we have deemed it our duty to implement measures to foster the interest of our fellow citizens and to encourage them to provide for themselves.'' The Estates-General then issued various orders that prohibited the import of woolen, cotton, or other cloth fabricated in either England, Scotland, or Ireland in order to prompt ''our compatriots to buy domestic cloth for their garments and other needs.'' A pattern of heavy taxes imposed on food and fuel—and a long-standing practice of paying high wages—hampered the possibility of a more flexible response to English competition; closing off the borders to English textiles appeared to be the best option.[17]

Although this protectionist impulse remained controversial, especially in a country that at various times in the past had championed uninhibited trading across borders and on the ''Open Seas,'' it was clear that during the first decades of the nineteenth century Dutch officials stood in awe of England's economic accomplishments. But they were also painfully aware of the threats that English competition posed to the profitability of Dutch shipping and commerce. Vreede's hyperbole about the benefits of state intercession in prodding English glassblowers' creativity, despite his story's exuberance, nonetheless registered a Dutch uncertainty about the wisdom of economic interventions. Vreede's anecdote, though, whether it was a fairy tale or not, expressed a starry-eyed admiration for England's spectacular growth in the production and marketing of manufactured goods.

Many Dutch observers were ambivalent about factory industry such as England's, because the unique economic talents of the Dutch were presumably confined to commerce and shipping. But paradoxically, some Dutchmen also realized that the English model deserved conscious emulation. Although the economic historian Patrick O'Brien has argued that statesmen and businessmen on the opposite side of the English Channel rarely perceived of their national economic goals as a race to keep pace with England, King William I, in his valiant efforts to unify Holland and Belgium, embarked on a "policy of catching up with England."[18] Even if the resulting executive measures lacked coherence, the example of England was uppermost in the minds of Dutch political economists and the king himself. When founding the *Nederlandse Handels Maatschappij* (Netherlands Trading Company), for instance, King William stated that he wanted to compete with England in the market for manufactured goods; aside from its philanthropic intentions, he expected the *Nederlandse Handels Maatschappij* to supply the Dutch colonial empire in the East Indies with Dutch textiles produced in Twente and thus supplant the importation of British cloth.[19]

During the very early years of the nineteenth century, Dutch economic analysts still sensed a common destiny with England, a view articulated by the first Agent of National Economy, Johannes Goldberg, in his ruminations on political economy: "Where," he wrote, "can we find other countries that have reached a similar pinnacle of prosperity and economic success as Holland and England? And which countries have made better and more famous arrangements to soothe human misery than England and Holland?"[20] The implication was clear: both countries were wealthy and therefore capable of providing for the poor, a luxury not available to nations with fewer financial resources. As the rapid growth of English industrial capitalism began to place the Netherlands at an economic disadvantage, however, causing various sectors of the Dutch economy to flounder, Dutch observers less often claimed a common destiny with England.[21] Instead, some analysts indirectly blamed England for changes in the world economy which seemed to leave the helpless Dutch nation behind. English economic triumphs, they claimed, spawned the increase in the number of Dutch people dependent on poor relief, and a number of Dutchmen continued to insist on the need to raise barriers against the importation of English manufactured goods.[22]

Dutch commentators appeared more openly jealous of British prosperity than did the French. But they trembled at the prospect of even fiercer British competition and, ironically, they looked for guidance from the English model. A few Dutch scholars were also more respectful of the manner in which England had resolved certain social problems, such as those issuing from demographic growth. When discussing the imbalance between available jobs and the labor supply in Holland, one liberal economist, full of admiration, wrote that Britain had managed to restore this asymmetry by surrendering the laboring population to the natural flow of supply and demand in the private sector, by limiting state intervention, and by dispensing an "uncompromising dictate to work and earn their daily bread."[23] Dutch analysts were cautious in their judgments about conditions in Great Britain, and few predicted an imminent eruption of class warfare or social anarchy. Simon Vissering, for instance, identified the most salient features of English developments in the nineteenth century when he noted in an essay entitled "Westminster and St. Paul," originally written in 1847 after a trip to England, that

> The very moment that London gained control over Westminster has been the beginning of the triumph of the class referred to in France as the bourgeoisie, through which the aristocracy of money replaces the aristocracy of landed wealth. This new aristocracy is no less powerful than the old, but this new elite uses its power more for the general, public well-being. In England the relationship between private and public interest is more closely linked and clearly visible . . . But this order also has its dark side. Is it not true that the chasm between rich and poor, the divide that grows wider with each passing day, originates here, that here lies the source of the struggle between capital and labor about which we hear daily?[24]

In words anticipating those of Marx, Vissering observed the emergence of bourgeois financial power and its nefarious impact on income distribution, but at the same time, in more Tocquevillean language, he pointed to the greater need for a coalescence of public and private interests. Later, he observed that

> England must expect changes in its political structure, just like other countries. In England, a need exists for new developments in social life. In England, however, more so than in other countries, this evolution will be gradual, the transition will occur without shocks . . . [My] expectations are grounded in the clear, awake, and practical spirit of the British. Above all, they rest on the English tendency to display a proper balance between appreciating the old and the new. As such the English people know how to guard with serious respect that which already exists and to welcome the new with warm diligence.[25]

Vissering's last comments were finally published when an improvement in economic conditions and a rising trend in working-class wages had placated the political disquiet of the "Hungry Forties." But his remarks differed from those of his colleagues in France, who during the period 1815–1848 and even much later still tended to project incipient anarchy and class warfare onto British conditions. There was an occasional exception, such as the former stonemason Martin Nadaud, who echoed Vissering's insights. In his intelligent *Histoire des classes ouvrières en Angleterre*, written while in exile in England during the early years of the Second Empire, Nadaud noted that "since the beginning of its [national] history, England has pursued a course diametrically opposed to France, which pays less attention to the study of facts and history than its rival, and thus loses sight of its tradition. In France, the toil of one generation never seems to benefit the work of the next generation!"[26]

The French and Dutch response to one specific English "event," the making of the new Poor Law in 1834, deserves close scrutiny. The passage of this new law heralded an official reorientation in British social policy, intended to be of profound importance to the ideology of liberal economics and to the operation of the labor market. Before the new Poor Law was passed in 1834, parliamentary debates had focused on the nature and purpose of England's system of poor relief. Because British reformers began to include, in theory, the working of market mechanisms and capitalist incentives as a means of solving the problem of poverty, the new Poor Law was symptomatic of the spirit of liberalism and Benthamite utilitarianism, and was meant to "harmonize capitalism and social hierarchy."[27]

Until the 1830s, according to the classic argument of Karl Polanyi and its many calibrations and critiques, Britain had been reluctant to commercialize labor. While land and capital had long since been subjected to the logic of the market, the treatment of labor as a commodity, restrained merely by its pricing in the marketplace, occurred only after the revision of the Poor Law. Prior to the reform of the Poor Law, the Speenhamland system had perpetuated the feudal and paternalistic tendency inherent in most early modern European societies to supervise and "protect" labor—or, to use different language, to optimize its docility and productivity; the self-regulated market began untrammeled operation only in 1834.[28]

By enunciating the principle of "less eligibility" and establishing a system of workhouses that offered nothing but a gruesome and dehumanizing existence, the English government hoped to forge a situation in which every able-bodied citizen would exercise few options other than to search for employment in private industry. The government's stance was that the lowest possible position of workers in the private sector should at all times remain preferable to the poorhouse; hence, outdoor relief was prohibited. Unemployed indigents would be institutionalized in publicly maintained poorhouses where they would be coerced into performing some kind of work, because assistance should only be conferred in exchange for labor. The new Poor Law, in the mind's eye of the commissioners, should harness the spontaneous forces of supply and demand: the free market for labor would induce each individual worker either to survive in the private sector or to endure the horrifying conditions of the poorhouse.

A curious contradiction between official ideology and political practice characterized the new Poor Law. Despite the language of liberalism, the new Poor Law, paradoxically, precipitated a dramatic expansion of the state bureaucracy and centralized political control, since the maintenance of workhouses required a greater commitment of public resources and supervisory personnel than did outdoor relief.[29] Since ad hoc and decentralized solutions to social problems were viewed as "typically English," then the new Poor Law was an "un-English" novelty, since the parliamentary commissioners who drafted the law considered the "centralizing principle as axiomatic to the working of the reformed Poor Law."[30]

The modifications of the English Poor Law in 1834 elicited a keen interest among intellectuals on the other side of the English Channel. A few liberal Dutch participants in the discourses about poverty and social welfare absorbed developments in England carefully and read the report of the Poor Law Commission with curiosity. August Philips, for example, noted in 1851 that "amid the lively debate presently taking place in the Netherlands over the drafting of legal regulations for poor relief, the example of Great Britain is ever present; it is used by one advocate as a positive example and by another as a gruesome deterrent. Britain supplies the ammunition to both sides of the controversy over the power of secular authorities in our system of poor relief.''[31]

Philips conceded that the new English Poor Law had been executed in a fragmented fashion only, and that the expected improvements in the situation of the poor had not yet fully achieved the law's intentions and ideals, but that the law had nonetheless ''yielded wholesome fruits.'' Philips concluded that ''after considering the structure of poor relief in England one conclusion must be beyond doubt: that the many positive changes England has experienced since 1834 can be attributed to the introduction of supervision by the state, and that the continuation of certain negative circumstances should not be blamed on the [new] system of poor relief but on the fact that the workhouse has been codified into law but has yet to be completely incorporated into [social] life.''[32]

Advocates of classic liberal solutions used the British example to strengthen their case, without truly acknowledging the contradiction between the rhetoric of liberalism, on the one hand, and the expansion of state intervention, on the other. J. L. de Bruyn Kops, for example, also writing in the early 1850s, asserted that the English revisions of the Poor Laws had brought about one of the weightiest changes that had occurred in the social conditions of that country in recent times. He went on to say that when Dutch social critics ''place the issue of church versus state as a central question [in controversies over charity and assistance], then we should point them to the example of England where a reform, yes, a revolution, in poor relief occurred without any reference to the respective rights and obligations of the state or the church.''[33] De Bruyn Kops favored secular control of poor relief, especially if the alternative would constitute the primacy of Church *diaconiëen*, although he thought the state should mediate only on a temporary basis because otherwise the government would misdirect society's economic resources.

Scores of economists and government officials, dismayed by the inefficiency and duplication of efforts on the part of municipal and religious charities in the Netherlands, elevated Great Britain as an effective model to emulate. When Dutch authors employed the analytical categories of classical economic theory in their discussions of poverty and welfare, they viewed English solutions in an emphatically positive light. On occasion they furnished cogent arguments in favor of industrial ''capitalism before its final triumph'' in the realm of economic policy.[34]

Jeronimo de Bosch Kemper, among others, stated his staunch belief in the new economic theories formulated by Adam Smith or Jean-Baptiste Say, which he then applied to poverty and income inequality in the Netherlands, with several praising references to England as an economic ideal Holland should imitate.

The laws of political economy, he asserted with great confidence, "are as immutable as the laws of nature. The consequences that can be predicted on the basis of certain economic conditions are almost as iron clad as those that physicists can identify." With a residue of physiocratic logic, De Bosch Kemper wrote that "the country that is in the most optimistic circumstances in terms of its national income is England. A highly evolved trade and industry, supported by capability and energy, assures England a large share of the general wealth." He proceeded to conjure up a vision of the Netherlands' future, revealing his aspiration that Holland would be drawn into the same kind of brave new world the English had constructed.

De Bosch Kemper prophesied that when Dutch engineers, traders, and skippers would achieve the same capabilities as their English counterparts, English capital would flow across the Channel and be invested in Dutch enterprise. He conceded, though, that an overall lack of capital was hardly the cause of poverty in Dutch society, nor was "a lack of raw materials generated by our soil . . . National prosperity depends on the uses made of the natural endowments of a country. In a peaceful situation the welfare and well-being of a people depend on its industrial and commercial development."[35] De Bosch Kemper curiously misjudged the resource endowment of his country: Holland possessed no iron ore deposits whatsoever and the Limburg soil contained only a mediocre amount of exploitable coal—both of which proved to be important, if not crucial, factors in economic development. Nonetheless, his firm faith in the social value of industrial capitalism as the most propitious route any society could pursue prompted him to exalt Britain as a high and mighty example Holland should copy.[36]

When the prominent politician, Johan Rudolf Thorbecke, defended his conception of secular poor relief in the hallowed chambers of the Estates-General in The Hague in 1854, he used a modern idiom in which he seemed to describe British conditions rather than the mostly preindustrial economy with small-scale workshops (*kleinbedrijf*) that still typified the Netherlands:

> In our contemporary society, the relationship between capital and labor has undergone a profound transformation. Capital rules, and numerous

small workshops have been dissolved into large enterprises; the balance between supply and demand has been distorted, and there is a constant excess of laborers who seek employment . . . If the state does not treat them correctly, it has the saddest consequences for the well-being, the morality, the independence, and the human dignity of the largest sector of its citizens.[37]

Advocates of classic liberal solutions and, from a more pragmatic perspective, a number of government officials, dismayed by the wasteful, overlapping efforts of charity in the Netherlands, advocated social policies similar to English ones but with a peculiar Dutch twist. A newly invigorated economy, some argued, would ideally end poverty by giving everyone equal access to the market. But in the short run, society must help those whose fate in life was truly heart-wrenching through no fault of their own, because poor people should not be left out in the cold while others could wallow in the warmth of their comfortable existence. Temporary outdoor relief would nurture the self-reliance of workers, who, in return, might offer their labor power to the highest bidder. The public sector should foster employment, if need be, through the creation of a system of work institutes, which could eventually revert back to private ownership. Profitability and paying one's dues were of vital significance in the Dutch world, even if work institutes caused money to be poured down the drain. However, "the state, pursuant to the social contract," should not only encourage all able-bodied people but also compel "every beggar—in other words, all idlers and laggards—to perform labor."[38]

Partisans of religious control over charity, on the other hand, looked with scorn upon the British example and stressed, instead, the transcendent values of faith and compassion that inspired all good Christians to ease the misery of poor fellow citizens within independent church congregations. Dutch society should never emulate the materialistic and ruthless character of the British, earnest advocates of the primacy of religious charity argued. The new Poor Law locked people up in appalling poorhouses and, without mercy, separated husbands from wives or isolated delicate young children from their mothers and thus deprived them of maternal love and nurture.

The internal rules of the average English workhouse were brutal and inhuman. The judgmental Protestant minister N. B. Donkersloot quoted in 1849 one of the English Workhouse Rules, No. XIX, stipulating that "the diet of the paupers shall be so regulated as in no case to exceed, in either quantity or quality of food, the ordinary diet of the able-bodied laborers living within the same district.'' He commented, however, that poorhouse food was woefully inferior to the normal diet of people on the outside and could barely sustain human life, ''which often resulted in bitter complaints.'' He also noticed that instead of providing useful activities to poorhouse residents, the forced labor imposed on them such as pushing a treadmill ''was selected merely to repulse others from asking for public assistance'' in order to render poor relief less desirable than any form of employment in the private sector.[39]

In this discourse, the new English Poor Law constituted the symbolic hallmark of the cruelty of a secular industrial nation. False ideas about economic incentives alone, or un-Christian selfishness, guided greedy industrialists in England, who shrewdly manipulated national legislation purely to satisfy their voracious appetite for money and profit. Holland, Dutch Reformed ministers proclaimed, was fundamentally different and should supplement the income of indigent citizens by relying on the principles of Christian altruism and communitarian sharing. Devout members of the Dutch Reformed Church such as the well-known Guillaume Groen van Prinsterer objected to the practice of equating the poor relief efforts of civil society with church-based charity, because a religious congregation was a union of believers which, as a genuine spiritual community, ''carries the responsibility for individual members' chosen life path (*levenswandel*).''[40]

Perspectives on the new Poor Law in Britain again revealed the same fundamental tension within Dutch culture. Fervent Protestants attempted to universalize their own conceptions of piety and morality. The example of English poorhouses, run by uncaring secular authorities, violated their conception of charity as an integral component of a community grounded in spiritual, moral values. ''What can we learn from the example of England?'' asked A. Elink Sterk rhetorically in 1852, even if he advocated a secular system of poor relief. His answer was: ''nothing other than that the situation in England has become slightly less disastrous than it was before the new legislation of 1834.'' He conceded that the burden of poor relief had become ''a bit more bearable since the imposition of a centralized administration and the coercion of the workhouse. But in those places where the severity of the workhouses was truly repulsive, free and private *caritas* reemerged and placed itself at the center again, to a great extent undermining the effectiveness of the new legislation.''[41] And H. van Loghem observed in 1845, ''as soon as one challenges the autonomy of religious charity, as soon as donors suspect that their church congregation can no longer dispense its charitable resources freely, donations will decline and the source of gifts will dry up. And as soon as the administrators of a *diaconie* shall become subservient to the authority of the state, they will lose all their independence and all their zeal.''[42]

Passionate French Catholics were just as petulant in their denunciations of the new British Poor Law, in particular, and the conditions imposed upon the working-class, in general. But an antipathy toward English Anglicanism, or an ambivalence about Protestantism at large, quaintly colored the perspectives of some. When Jean-Paul Alban de Villeneuve-Bargemont engaged the oft-repeated statistical bromide that in Italy only one in twenty-five citizens depended on charity and in Turkey this ratio was one in forty, while in England and Holland it was either one in six or one in seven, he arrived at a conclusion very different from that of his relativist Dutch colleague Simon Vissering. Villeneuve-Bargemont argued, instead, that the differential ratios resulted from ``the Protestant religion and factory industry, which augment poverty in Holland and England. In contrast, agriculture in France, Catholicism in Italy, and a positive faith in Turkey prevent poverty from spreading.''[43]

A few years later he decried the horrible misery of workers and peasants in Catholic Ireland, ``who die amidst an English landowning aristocracy living in the lap of luxury'' and whose appeals for help were ignored by ``the opulent, egotistical Anglican clergy.''[44] Only a revival of the traditional ancien régime alliance between throne and altar—when Catholic values would once again permeate ``politics, laws, institutions, and mores''—could safeguard the social order from the horrifying dangers that threatened it. Everything else, he remonstrated, ``is nothing but an illusion or a lie.''[45]

But the omnipresent Sisters of Charity and other religious orders, who labored on behalf of the poor in *hospices* and *hôpitaux* for the glory of God and the majesty of the Catholic Church, vicariously eased the conscience and charitable burden of individual parishioners. Few Catholics, whether conservative or not, challenged the authority of the secular state in Paris over national legislation regarding poorhouses and hospitals. In their daily lives, devout French Catholics worried less about protecting Christian *caritas* from state intrusion, as Dutch Reformed proponents did. Instead, they grappled with Christ's teaching to love all their brothers and sisters, even those who lived frightful lives in hideous urban slums, since poor workers were God's children, too. Many French Catholics, in other words, struggled valiantly to give a meaningful social content to their private spiritual beliefs and to the injunctions of the Catholic Church.

A serious Catholic such as Frédéric Ozanam, for instance, recalled later in life his exuberant student years in Paris during the early 1830s, when various "systems of false science" had assaulted him. Some of his fellow students had been "Materialists, others Saint-Simonians; some were Fourierists, yet others, Deists." When Catholics tried to remind their comrades of the marvels of Christianity, the latter responded with cynicism: "in the past Christianity has performed miracles, but today Christianity is dead. You, who pride yourselves in being Catholics, what do you do? Which actions reveal your faith?"[46]

Thus provoked, Ozanam and his fellow crusaders created the Society of Saint-Vincent-de-Paul, inspired by a wish to devote their free hours to soothing the spiritual and material needs of families suffering from want and despair. In the face of the skeptical response of a fellow student, who sneered that a few young people, "wishing to help the miseries that haunt a city such as Paris, will accomplish nothing, whereas we, Saint-Simonians, elaborate ideas and systems that will reform the world and eradicate misery forever," Ozanam stubbornly persisted, only to achieve great success.[47] Within a few years, the Society of Saint-Vincent-de-Paul had two thousand members, and by 1849 it was represented in fifteen different towns throughout France, only to spread to cities abroad during later decades.[48]

Social Catholicism, in the imagination of Ozanam and others, conjured up a Church in search of understanding the fundamental causes of poverty and actively engaged in rectifying social injustice.[49] Central to Ozanam's agenda was an underlying fear of the imminent class struggle between rich and poor, or the potential encounter between "the power of gold" and "the power of despair."[50] In this sense he did not differ much from conservative Catholics. Besides, this was exactly the combustible tension that presumably characterized English society, since it hardened the hearts of factory owners and landed gentry alike and caused the "maladministration of the British government."[51]

Frenchmen tended to view English capitalism as a contrived or treacherous phenomenon; owing to its "exotic" qualities, it seemed to be a morally evil one as well.[52] In the eyes of a number of French commentators, Great Britain symbolized all that was implied by the novel term pauperism, since it had created an artificial world that deviated from the "true" nature of French society, and by implication, all sensible human communities. An early critic of industrialism, Pierre Lemontey—a member of the *Académie française* who had been an active participant in the Revolution and had served as an officeholder during the First Empire—argued in 1816 that the formation of capitalist monopolies was a direct consequence of industrial expansion. Monopolies, he warned, would lead to "a monstrous inequality in the distribution of wealth . . . a shocking confusion in the subtle nuances which constitute social harmony, and an unhappy change in the moral character and public spirit of a nation."[53]

Several years later, in a letter addressed to the General Council of Manufacturers in Lille, Auguste-Rémy Mimerel repeated a similar theme: "While England has pushed industrialism to the highest levels we know today, it has given its people nothing but misery. Thus the logical consequence is that we should guard ourselves against imitating the example provided by England."[54] And in his administrative posts in the textile regions in the North of France, Villeneuve-Bargemont had acquired a keen understanding of the degradation and suffering caused by large-scale and highly specialized factory production, which informed his negative impressions of the English factory system:

> England is destined to perish owing to the causes that have engendered pauperism, or perhaps due to poverty itself. The English system rests on the concentration of capital, commerce, land, and industry. It relies on infinite production, universal competition, the replacement of human labor by machines, a reduction of wages, a perpetual pressure on physical need and on the degradation of human beings' morale.[55]

The French economy, in contrast, should be based on a "just and wise distribution of industrial products and a reasonable remuneration of labor, on agricultural development combined with manufacture applied to the products of the earth, on the religious regeneration of mankind and, finally, on the great principle of charity."[56]

In 1844, the anonymous author of *l'Aperçu sur la condition ouvrière en France et l'Angleterre* accused the British government of motives that were crudely selfish and crassly materialistic. Great Britain had used all its energy to expand industry, the author argued, and this expansion had enabled it to flood markets all over the world with frivolous products. In the process of emphasizing its industrial production, Britain had distorted the harmonious and organic balance between agriculture and manufacture and generated a skewed distribution of population. This unknown author warned that the transformation of the agricultural population into an industrial working class was a fatal course that would irrevocably lead to disaster. Because of England's emphasis on manufacture, the misery of the British poor was so desperate that the threat of anarchy was growing by leaps and bounds.[57] Since English agriculture, although yielding abundant harvests owing to ''a perfect system of cultivation,'' could not even begin to feed the nation's population, another Frenchmen commented, the expensive import of food required ''enormous sums'' which would undoubtedly lead to England's downfall.[58]

Even several decades later, in the wake of the horrifying bloodshed of the Paris Commune, some French observers clung to various misconceptions regarding their island neighbor across the Channel, intoning that ''Great Britain is perhaps more sick than we are because of the extension of large-scale industry and the infirmity of agrarian ownership. The evil is not yet apparent because of the powerful unity of the ruling classes, who have momentarily paralyzed all manifestations of social unrest. The situation in England, however, makes us think of the slopes of a volcano where, underneath a blanket of chilled sediment, torrents of explosive lava circulate: no more than one crack in the surface will bring forth devastating waves [of violence].''[59]

On the European continent, Tocqueville was a nearly solitary voice in his understanding of the contradictions in the new Poor Law. He was one of the few intellectuals who grasped the disparities between the ideological language of *laissez-faire* capitalism, unevenly assimilated into British cultural grammar by the 1830s, and the subsequent proliferation of the central state's involvement in the institutionalization of poorhouses. While French officials trembled at the thought of an unrestrained market and reliance on private sector employment, the new English Poor Law's strenghtening of the regulatory power of the central state remained, with occasional exceptions, elusive to many. Ironically, the Poor Law reforms served the rhetorical purpose of vilifying the callous nature of British economic culture rather than lending intellectual weight to arguments justifying the central role of the Paris government.[60]

Even a well-known French Inspector of Prisons, Louis Moreau-Christophe, although uniquely preoccupied with the best methods of enclosing and rehabilitating criminals and guarding society from their dangerous presence, offered the paradoxical opinion that poorhouses, especially those in England, ''nurture misery rather cure it.'' He carried his oratory even further: poorhouses ''promote, fertilize, and multiply'' human misery.[61] Moreau-Christophe discussed the incomplete manner in which the new English Poor Law was implemented because, he wrote, the law was impossible to execute. Since then the English reservoir of paupers had ''risen again to reach its highest level; all the millions spent on trying to halt the destructive ravages wrought by the sea of paupers (*la mer paupérienne*) have accomplished nothing''; the new Poor Law had only enlarged the ocean of paupers even further.[62]

Elsewhere on the political spectrum, the mercurial Eugène Buret registered his aversion to the treadmills workhouse residents had to push in order to fulfill their forced labor requirements: ''[they] are the most terrible symptoms of poverty we know: an opulent nation, powerful because of its industrial genius and its application of the miracles of mechanical production, has returned, in order to occupy its indigents, to crude instruments of barbarism and condemns its criminals as well as its poor people to be tortured like ancient slaves.''[63] Another radical on the left, the early feminist Flora Tristan, employed the same historical metaphor of slavery to register her horror at the condition of the English working class in her 1840 *London Journal*: if our French forefathers had handled ''their serfs with no more humanity than manufacturers in England treat their workers, slavery would not have endured throughout the Middle Ages.''[64]

Tocqueville noted after a visit to England that the modifications of the Poor Law may have had a positive effect because they decreased the number of indigents dependent on public resources and improved the work ethic of the average worker. But in his *Mémoire sur la Paupérisme* Tocqueville concluded that the new Poor Law of 1834 simply removed the abuses of the existing laws rather than established a new system of public assistance.[65] Overall, Tocqueville and many of his fellow Frenchmen opposed any system of *charité légale* that was based on legal entitlements because ''any permanent, regular, administrative system whose purpose it is to provide for the needs of the poor will foster more miseries than it can cure, will corrupt the population it wants to help and nurture, in due course will reduce the rich to being no more than the tenant-farmers of the poor, will deplete the sources of savings, will halt the accumulation of capital, will hamper the development of trade and deaden human industry and activity.''[66]

In French eyes England laid bare the perversions accompanying a full-blown industrial society, and the new Poor Law merely provided yet another piece of evidence in a long litany of accusations against the egotistical and implacable British character.[67] England emblematized everything the French feared and disliked about modern capitalism: ''the industrial era begins and pauperism is born. A factory is an invention designed to produce two articles: cotton textiles and paupers.''[68] Frenchmen authored poignant narratives about the human degradation and exploitation of workers in unregulated industries in England. They drafted a profusion of reports with misleading statistics and misconstrued information on working conditions, wages, nutrition, and housing. All of these social texts and statistical artifacts functioned as lethal weapons deployed by French observers bent on denouncing the hazards of modern industrialism.

In fact, the imagery used to portray English working-class conditions began to converge with depictions of specific French situations. Social investigators such as Louis-René Villermé and Jérôme-Adolphe Blanqui painted sensationalist portraits which represented poor workers in Paris, Lille, or Saint-Etienne as a separate human species, shocking in its appearance and disgusting in its private habits. But the language they used, the metaphors they invoked, and the pious fictions they created began to overlap more and more with the horror stories Frenchmen told about the ghastly cotton mills in Manchester and Birmingham or the grisly coal mines in Yorkshire or Gloucestershire.

Dutch assessments of the British example, on the other hand, were less negative and expressed a more oblique envy; they reflected, too, a greater sensitivity to the ways in which sustained economic growth might benefit poor people through steady employment and rising wage levels. Dutch economists were familiar with the texts of classical economics, and they quoted lavishly from either John Stuart Mill or M. J. MacCulloch.[69] Dutch stories about the menace of unbridled industry, or about the shadowy and dank factories of Manchester and Birmingham—even if glittering lucre flowed forth from this ''filthy sewer''—did not linger in the public imagination as a monotonous refrain.[70] Although irascible Protestant ministers vilified the new Poor Law for dislodging *caritas* from its religious roots, it made sense to *laissez-faire* proponents in Holland. Some of them prescribed a comparable bitter medicine: De Bosch Kemper even suggested that indigent citizens should be taxed more heavily than the rich because they would not save their money anyway![71]

Notes

1. Charles de Montalembert, letter to his wife, June 18, 1839, cited in R.P. Lecanuet, *Montalembert d'après son journal et sa correspondance*, 3 vols. (Paris: Ch. Pousselgue, 1895–1902), 2, (1898), p. 95.

2. Collectie Goldberg, No. 44, Pieter Vreede, *Vervolg der proeve om de verheffing van het diepvervallen fabriekswezen te verenigen met de belangen van de koophandel, zeevaart en landbouw*, (1802). ARA, The Hague. The Dutch words are *wit glas*.

3. Morris David Morris, *The Emergence of an Industrial Labor Force in*

India. A Study of the Bombay Cotton Mills, 1854–1947 (Berkeley: University of California Press, 1965), pp. 10–15.

4. Pierre Reboul, *Le mythe anglais dans la littérature française sous la Restauration* (Lille: Bibliothèque Universitaire de Lille, 1962), passim.

5. Martin Nadaud, *Histoire des classes ouvrières en Angleterre* (Paris: E. Lachaud, 1872), p. 208.

6. Barrie M. Ratcliffe and W.H. Chaloner, eds., *A French Sociologist Looks at Britain. Gustave d'Eichthal and British Society in 1828* (Manchester: Manchester University Press, 1977), "Editor's Introduction," pp. 2, 10, and d'Eichthal, *Journal*, p. 93.

7. Ratcliffe and Chaloner, "Editor's Introduction," p. 7, and d'Eichthal, *Journal*, p. 54.

8. D'Eichthal, *Journal*, p. 57.

9. Frank E. Manuel, *The Prophets of Paris* (Cambridge: Harvard University Press, 1962), p. 310.

10. Michael Hechter, review of Immanuel Wallerstein, *The Modern World System: Capitalist Agriculture and the Origins of the European World Economy in the Sixteenth Century* (New York: Basic Books, 1974), in *Contemporary Sociology*, 42, (1975), p. 217. Lamarck had written his *Philosophie zoologique ou exposition des considérations relative à l'histoire des animaux* in 1809. See Peter J. Bowler, *Evolution. The History of an Idea*, rev. ed. (Berkeley: University of California Press, 1989), pp. 85–89.

11. See the general discussion in Henrika Kuklick, *The Savage Within. The Social History of British Anthropology, 1885–1945* (Cambridge/New York: Cambridge University Press, 1991), pp. 80–89.

12. For developments in nineteenth-century geology, see Mott T. Greene, *Geology in the Nineteenth Century. Changing Views of a Changing World* (Ithaca: Cornell University Press, 1982); for the biological sciences, see Peter J. Bowler, *The Non-Darwinian Revolution. Reinterpreting a Historical Myth* (Baltimore: Johns Hopkins Press, 1988); and David Young, *The Discovery of Evolution* (Cambridge/New York: Cambridge University Press, 1993).

13. Bernard McGrane, *Beyond Anthropology. Society and the Other* (New York: Columbia University Press, 1989), p. 91.

14. Bowler, *Evolution. The History of an Idea*, pp. 82–83.

15. George W. Stocking Jr., "Lamarckianism in American Social Science," in *Race, Culture, and Evolution. Essays in the History of Anthropology* (1968; repr. Chicago: University of Chicago Press, 1982), pp. 234–69. For the Dutch context, see Piet de Rooy, "Of Monkeys, Blacks, and Proles: Ernst Haeckel's Theory of Recapitulation," in Jan Breman, ed., *Imperial Monkey Business. Racial Supremacy in Social Darwinist Theory and Colonial Practice* (Amsterdam: VU University Press, 1990), CASA Monographs 3, pp. 7–34. For France, see Tzvetan Todorov, *On Human Diversity. Nationalism, Racism, and Exoticism in French Thought* (1989; repr. Cambridge: Harvard University Press, 1993).

16. Montalembert reproached the state for having acquired a monopoly over

public assistance in the same manner as it had obtained a monopoly over education. ''It is the state,'' he said, ''because of its restrictions, because of its confiscations, and because of its costly and sterile bureaucracy, that has killed in France the public assistance that Christianity had organized . . . The worker asks for bread, but you [the state] have given him scorpions.'' At the time of the Revolution of 1848 Montalembert called for a return to the primacy of Christian charity and the moral authority of the Catholic Church in opposition to the secular spirit of the July Monarchy. See Lecanuet, *Montalembert*, 2, pp. 438–39.

17. Collectie Goldberg, No. 44, F. van der Schaft (Secretaris, Comité van algemene welvaart te Haarlem), *Gelijkheid, vrijheid, broederschap: aan de nationale vergadering representerende het volk van Nederland*, (1795). ARA, The Hague.

18. Patrick K. O'Brien, ''Do We Have a Typology for the Study of European Industrialization in the XIXth Century?'' *Journal of European Economic History*, 15, No. 3 (1986), p. 293, and Richard Westebbe, ''State Entrepreneurship, King Willem I, John Cockerill and the Seraing Engineering Works, 1815–1849,'' *Explorations in Entrepreneurial History*, 8, No. 4 (1956), p. 256.

19. Robert Demoulin, *Guillaume Ier et la transformation économique des provinces Belges, 1815–1830* (Liège: Bibliothèque de la Faculté de Philosophie et Lettres de l'Université de Liège, 1938), p. 30.

20. Collectie Goldberg, No. 58, *Staathuishoudkunde. Handschrift in drie delen samengesteld onder de staatsregeling van 1789.* (This report was not composed with the aid of the statistical information Goldberg was in the process of collecting. On the basis of existing economic literature, this report discussed the economic history of the Netherlands. Perhaps Goldberg conceived of this manuscript as a historical introduction to the official report for which he conducted a tour of the country, sent out questionnaires, and collected statistics in 1800–01.) ARA, The Hague.

21. Collectie Goldberg, No. 48, *Extract uit het verbaal van de Agent van Nationale Oeconomie der Bataafse Republiek*, April 28, 1801. Goldberg No. 44 contains many requests from *fabriqueurs* (manufacturers) submitted to the Agent of National Economy in support of laws prohibiting the import of foreign goods. ARA, The Hague.

22. R. Scherenberg, *Bedenkingen over de armoede en door welke middelen het aantal der armen in Nederland zouden kunnen worden verminderd, hunnen toestand verbeterd, en zij tot nuttige leden der maatschappij zouden kunnen worden opgeleid* (The Hague: Algemene Landsdrukkerij, 1816), p. 29.

23. W.C. Mees, *De werkinrigtingen voor armen uit een staatshuishoudkundig oogpunt beschouwd* (Rotterdam: J. van Baalen, 1844), pp. 23–25.

24. Simon Vissering, ''Studien en Schetsen,'' in *Herinneringen*, 3 vols. (Amsterdam: P.N. van Kampen, 1863), 1, p. 46.

25. Vissering, ''Studien en Schetsen,'' p. 47.

26. Nadaud, *Histoire des classes ouvrières en Angleterre*, Preface, p. xx.

27. Peter Mandler, ''Tories and Paupers: Christian Political Economy and the Making of the New Poor Law,'' *Historical Journal*, 33, No. 1 (1990), p. 84. An extensive literature on the making of the new Poor Law exists; see, among others, Peter Mandler, ''The Making of the New Poor Law *Redivivus*,'' *Past and Present*, 117 (November 1987), pp. 131–57; and Anthony Brundage, David Eastwood, and Peter Mandler, ''Debate: The Making of the New Poor Law *Redivivus*,'' *Past and Present*, 127 (February, 1990), pp. 183–201. For a general discussion, see Anthony Brundage, *The Making of the New Poor Law: The Politics of Inquiry, Enactment and Implementation, 1832–1839* (London: Allen and Unwin, 1987); Gertrude Himmelfarb, *The Idea of Poverty. England in the Early Industrial Age* (New York: Alfred A. Knopf, 1984), Part 2; Derek Fraser, ed., *The New Poor Law in the Nineteenth Century* (London: Macmillan, 1976); and J.R. Poynter, *Society and Pauperism. English Ideas on Poor Relief, 1795–1834* (London: Routledge, 1969).

28. Karl Polanyi, *The Great Transformation* (Boston: Beacon Press, 1963), p. 80.

29. Himmelfarb, *The Idea of Poverty*, p. 165.

30. Mandler, ''Tories and Paupers,'' p. 83, and Brundage, Eastwood, and Mandler, ''Debate: The Making of the New Poor Law,'' p. 191.

31. August Philips, *De Engelse armenwetten naar inhoud en werking geschetst* (Leiden/Amsterdam: J.H. Gebhard, 1851), p. 59.

32. Philips, *De Engelse armenwetten*, p. 92.

33. J.L. de Bruyn Kops, *Over het beginsel van armenverzorging door de staat* (Leiden/Amsterdam: J.H. Gebhard, 1852), pp. 39, 46. For a critical discussion of De Bruyn Kops' ideas, see A. Elink Sterk, *Enige bedenkingen op het geschrift van J.L. de Bruyn Kops over het beginsel van armenzorg door de staat* (The Hague: W.P. van Stockum, 1852).

34. See Albert O. Hirshman, *The Passions and the Interests: Political Arguments for Capitalism before Its Triumph* (Princeton: Princeton University Press, 1977), passim.

35. J. de Bosch Kemper, *Geschiedkundig onderzoek naar de armoede in ons vaderland, hare oorzaken en de middelen die tot hare vermindering zouden kunnen worden aangewend* (Haarlem: De Erven Loosjes, 1851), pp. 167–68, 284.

36. Joel Mokyr, ed., in *The Economics of the Industrial Revolution* (Totowa, N.J.: Rowman and Allanheld, 1985), has noted that geographical factors, i.e., the ''availability of mineral wealth, particularly coal and iron, has been a popular and seemingly persuasive explanation of Britain's success, as well as the failure of some tardy industrializers such as the Netherlands and Ireland'' (pp. 7–8).

37. C.H.E. de Wit, *Thorbecke en de wording van de Nederlandse natie. Thorbecke, historische schetsen. Thorbecke, staatsman en historicus* (Nijmegen: SUN, 1980), Sunschrift 153, p. 147.

38. L.G.J. Verberne, *Het sociale en economische motief in de Franse tijd*

(Tilburg: W. Bergmans, 1947), p. 21. See also J.C.W. le Jeune, *Geschiedkundige nasporingen omtrent den toestand der armen en de bedelarij* (The Hague: A.J. van Weelden, 1816), Chapter 6, ''Werkinrigtingen,'' pp. 116–28.

39. N.B. Donkersloot, *Gedachten over de armoede, hare oorzaken en voorbehoudingsmiddelen. Uitgegeven ten voordeele van de noodlijdenden op Schokland* (Tiel: J. Campagne, 1849), p. 74.

40. F.L. van Holthoon, ''De armenzorg in Nederland,'' in F.L. van Holthoon, ed., *Nederlandse samenleving sinds 1815* (Assen/Maastricht: Van Gorcum, 1985), pp. 177–78.

41. Elink Sterk, *Enige bedenkingen op het geschrift van J.L. de Bruyn Kops*, pp. 20–21.

42. H. van Loghem, *Beoordeeling van het ontwerp van de wet betrekkelijk de ondersteuning van behoeftigen* (Deventer: J. de Lange, 1845), p. 22.

43. Jean-Paul Alban de Villeneuve-Bargemont, *Economie politique chrétienne ou recherches sur la nature et les causes du paupérisme en France et en Europe et sur les moyens de les soulager et prévenir*, 2nd ed., 2 vols. (Bruxelles: Méline Cans, 1837), 2, pp. 198–99, and *Tableau récapitulatif du nombre d'indigents en Europe*, 2, pp. 200–201.

44. Villeneuve-Bargemont, *Discours prononcé à la Chambre des députés dans la discussion du projet de loi sur le travail des enfants dans les manufactures* (Metz: Colignon, 1841), p. 4.

45. Villeneuve-Bargemont, *Economie politique chrétienne*, 2nd ed., 1, Preface, p. 15.

46. M. Ampère, ed., *Oeuvres Complètes de Antoine-Frédéric Ozanam*, 3 vols. (Paris: Jacques Lecoffre, 1873), 1, ''Lettres,'' p. 79. For biographical information about Ozanam, see Kathleen O'Meara, *Frédéric Ozanam, Professor at the Sorbonne; His Life and Works* (New York: Christian Press Association, 1911); Georges Goyau, *Frédéric Ozanam* (Paris: Payot, 1925); and Thomas E. Auge, *Frédéric Ozanam and His World* (Milwaukee: Bruce, 1966).

47. Anonymous, *Les bienfaits de l'église envers la société de Saint-Vincent-de-Paul. Discours prononcé par monsieur le president du conseil central de Besançon* (Besançon: J. Jacquin, 1856), p. 4.

48. Although Henri Rollet, in *l'Action sociale des catholiques en France* (Paris: Boivin, 1947), noted that ''the conferences of Saint-Vincent-de-Paul were more preoccupied with charity than with justice and attacked [social] ills without remedying their causes'' (p. 6).

49. Quoted by Katherine A. Lynch, *Family, Class, and Ideology in Early Industrial France* (Madison: University of Wisconsin Press, 1988), p. 40.

50. Armand Dûchatellier, *Du commerce et de l'administration où coup d'oeil sur le nouveau système commercial de l'Angleterre* (Paris: de Lachevardière Fils, 1826), p. 110.

51. Anonymous, *l'Aperçu de la condition ouvrière en France et l'Angleterre* (Paris: Imprimeur le Prince D.S., 1844), p. 46.

52. For a theoretical discussion, see Maurice Meisner, ''Utopian Socialist

Themes in Maoism,'' in John Wilson Lewis, ed., *Peasant Rebellion and Communist Revolution in Asia* (Stanford: Stanford University Press, 1974), p. 217.

53. David K. Cohen, ''Lemontey, An Early Critic of Industrialism,'' *French Historical Studies*, 4, No. 3 (1966), p. 294.

54. Auguste-Rémy Mimerel, *Du paupérisme dans ses rapports avec l'industrie en France et l'Angleterre* (letter addressed to the general council of manufacturers) (Lille: Leleux, n.d.), p. 2.

55. Quoted by William Coleman, *Death Is a Social Disease. Public Health and Political Economy in Early Industrial France* (Madison: University of Wisconsin Press, 1982), p. 82.

56. Villeneuve-Bargemont, *Economic politique chrétienne*, 2nd ed., 1, Preface, p. 15.

57. Anonymous, *l'Aperçu de la condition ouvrière*, p. 47.

58. Paul Véret, *Le bien être universel par la transformation des împots ou l'extinction du paupérisme réalisé par le travail* (Paris: chez l'auteur, 1853), p. 11.

59. Anatole Hudault, *Economie sociale. Reformons: le danger, la paupérisme, l'Internationale* (Paris: Dentu, 1871), p. 12.

60. Alexis de Tocqueville, *Mémoire sur la paupérisme* (1835; repr. Paris: Microéditions Hachette, 1971; first published in *Mémoires de la société académique de Cherbourg*), passim. In addition to Tocqueville, also Pierre-Marie Bigot de Morogues, in *Du paupérisme, de la mendicité et des moyens d'en prévenir les funestes effets* (Paris: Prosper Dondey-Dupré, 1834), registered a positive understanding of the new role of the British government, pp. 144–147. For additional assessments, see Amboise Clément, *Recherches sur les causes l'indigence* (1846; repr. Paris: Microéditions Hachette, 1971), p. 433; Eugène Buret, *De la misère des classes laborieuses en Angleterre et France. De la nature de la misère, de son existence, de ses effets, de ses causes, et de l'insuffisance des remèdes qu'on lui a opposés jusqu'ici: avec l'indication des moyens propres à affranchir les sociétés*, 2 vols. (Paris: Paulin, 1840), 1, p. 68; and Anonymous, *Aperçu de la condition ouvrière*, p. 47.

61. L.-M. Moreau-Christophe, *Du problème de la misère et de sa solution chez les peuples anciens et modernes*, 3 vols. (Paris: Gauillaumin, 1851), 2, p. 244.

62. Moreau-Christophe, *Du problème de la misère*, 3, p. 192, quoted by Philips, *De Engelse armenwetten*, p. 81. For a discussion of his quixotic ideas, see Gordon Wright, *Between THE Guillotine & Liberty. Two Centuries of the Crime Problem in France* (New York: Oxford University Press, 1983), pp. 48–50.

63. Buret, *De la misère des classes laborieuses*, 1, Chapter 5, quoted by N.B. Donkersloot, *Gedachten over de armoede*, p. 74.

64. Flora Tristan, *London Journal 1840. A Survey of London Life in the 1830s* (1840; repr. London: George Prior, 1980), p. 61.

65. Tocqueville, *Mémoire sur la paupérisme*, p. 12.

66. Tocqueville, *Mémoire sur la paupérisme*, p. 11; see also the discussion

in Himmelfarb, *The Idea of Poverty*, pp. 147–151. Seymour Drescher, in *Dilemmas of Democracy: Tocqueville and Modernization* (Pittsburgh: University of Pittsburgh Press, 1968), translated Tocqueville's *Memoire sur la paupérisme*; my translation differs slightly.

67. Villeneuve-Bargemont, *Economie politique chrétienne*, 2nd ed., 1, p. 28.

68. Emile Laurent, *La paupérisme et les associations de prévoyance. Nouvelles études sur les sociétés de secours mutuelles*, 2 vols. (Paris: Guillaumin, 1865), 1, pp. 4–7.

69. Simon Vissering, for example, in justifying some of his arguments, claimed to be in agreement with both the ideas of Malthus about population growth and M.J. MacCulloch's *Principles of Political Economy*. Irene Hasenberg Butter, in *Academic Economics in Holland, 1800–1870* (The Hague: Martinus Nijhoff Press, 1969), states that the only work of MacCulloch that had been translated into Dutch was the *Essay on the Circumstances which Determine the Rate of Wages* (1826). Vissering must therefore have consulted the *Principles of Political Economy* in English, p. 76 and Appendix A.

70. J.P. Mayer, ed., *A. de Tocqueville. Journeys to England and Ireland* (London: Faber, 1958), pp. 107–8.

71. De Bosch Kemper, *Geschiedkundig onderzoek naar de armoede*, p. 244.

CHAPTER SIX

Christian Injunctions, Private Obligations, and Public Duties: The Organization and Structure of Poor Relief

All human beings have a right to subsistence. If there are miserable people, it means society is badly organized. Assisting the unfortunate classes of society is as much a duty and a public service of the state as is the payment of salaries to public servants. Most citizens, in acquitting their social duties, do not distinguish between the portion of their taxes that is used either to support the destitute, to maintain the roads, or to pay the army. On the other hand, the unfortunate members of society, when they are placed under the unique protection of the state, will escape reproach or regret on the part of those who have been expressly imposed upon to help them.[1]

—Report of the *Comité de mendicité*, 1790

The state is in charge of expanding agriculture, commerce, and industry. It must prohibit beggary, establish workhouses and pauper factories, and improve education; the state should also organize an equitable system of taxation and raise the general prosperity of our country. But the state can never alleviate poverty. As far as relief of the poor is concerned, the best institution is the church rather than the state. Because of the church's familiarity with the domestic circumstances of the poor, it can combine loving assistance with remedial instruction. The church never humiliates the indigents by providing poor relief in public. The church maintains the voluntary nature of charity and leaves room for the altruistic compassion of the giver and the warm gratitude of the receiver.[2]

—P. J. Elout, ''Iets over de armbedeeling,'' 1846

The *Comité de mendicité* during the French Revolution, under the enlightened leadership of the aristocratic crusader François-Alexandre de

La Rochefoucauld-Liancourt, had pronounced poor relief to be the sacred duty of the state and a hallowed public obligation. The impassioned committee chairman eloquently summarized the high-minded aspirations of the *Comité* in 1790: ''society must provide sustenance to all of its members who are deprived of it, and this helpful assistance must not be regarded as a gift . . . it is an inviolable and sacred debt society must pay.''[3]

The Revolution wished to inaugurate a new era by declaring that misery was ''the daughter'' of the social state (*La misère est la fille de l'état social*). In shouldering the moral and political responsibility for all the unfortunate members of society, the state would transform poor relief into a socially neutral practice—a disinterested system designed to transfer resources from the rich to the poor without eliciting such human feelings as shame, obsequiousness, or self-satisfaction. By emphasizing the need for anonymity and universality, the *Comité de mendicité* prematurely conceived of assistance to the poor as a form of entitlement, a basic human right granted to all destitute citizens, who did not have to reciprocate with gratitude or subservience to a particular benefactor. The highest form of charity, La Rochefoucauld-Liancourt and his colleagues suggested, was anonymous help from unidentifiable sources that would enable the poor to emerge as self-supporting citizens; poor relief should enhance their autonomy and forge an organic sense of equality and kinship with compatriots born into more fortunate circumstances.

The *Comité de mendicité* explicitly rejected all proposals of either a municipal poor tax or local or regional control over poor relief. Charity was to be a straightforward public service which the state owed the poor. In carrying out its sacrosanct duty, the government would play an active role in stimulating the economy in order to reduce the number of destitute and needy citizens. ''While nurturing the public interest, the government also serves private interests by helping the poor find useful employment; by encouraging the constructive investment of capital, by increasing consumption, and by multiplying productivity, the government will expand national wealth.''[4] With these words La Rochefoucauld-Liancourt and his fellow committee members proposed an all-encompassing structure of social welfare under the supervision of the state, linking poor relief to work provision and uninhibited economic development. Rather than subsidizing bread and interfering in the pricing mechanism of food—an antediluvian habit associated with the ancien régime's paternalistic fixations—the *Comité de mendicité* made an explicit assumption of free exchange and reciprocity. If the poor had the right to say "give me a way to survive," then society should be allowed to respond with the request "to give me your ability to work."

Thus, for a brief and audacious interlude, the *Comité de mendicité* envisioned a world in which personal benevolence and gratitude would no longer function as crucial components of an immutable social hierarchy that was grounded in patterns of command and subordination. The committee members maintained that the patronizing practices of private generosity and Catholic charity, offered in exchange for mandatory appreciation, would maintain a world based on inequality and exploitation, and were therefore counterrevolutionary. Instead, every citizen in the new, revolutionized social order, the committee professed, should have the right to work and to enjoy material sufficiency without having to feel indebted or humbled.

However, as many cherished daughters tend to require great financial sacrifices on the part of their protective parents, sustaining the poor as the sheltered children of the social state proved to be expensive business, too. When social conditions in Revolutionary Paris deteriorated, food supplies dwindled, and prices in the city soared to unprecedented heights, it was no longer feasible to proclaim that "free trade was the mother of abundance." Belaboring the same metaphor of procreation and the human life cycle, the ideologically pure Louis-Antoine de Saint-Just maintained that poverty might have "given birth" to the Revolution, but *misère*, he warned with a sense of foreboding, could also provoke the Revolution's demise and cause its untimely death.[5]

Saint-Just's premonition was not far off the mark. Not long after the *Comité de mendicité* had articulated its idealistic goals, the nation's social welfare needs, in combination with the astronomical costs of military campaigns, overburdened the national treasury. Hence, the National Convention planned the next logical steps: it interfered, once again, in the free forces of the market and pronounced that all private hospitals and religious charitable institutions would be the "patrimony of the poor" and the property of the nation.[6] In trying to nurture the vitality of the Revolution's righteous ideals, Saint-Just declared that the resources of the Revolution's enemies should be made available to support the poor.

The planned confiscation of the Catholic Church's charitable institutions and hospitals never took place, and the Thermidorian Reaction put an end to most of the radical visions of poor relief as a sacred responsibility of the public sector. As a representative of the people during the Directory, Deputy Délécloy, exclaimed with exasperation in 1796, "It is time to escape from the abyss into which the exaggerated philanthropy of the Constituent Assembly has pushed us.'' Since the heady years of hope and idealism, he intoned, ''the speculators in benevolence'' had taken it upon themselves to bring an evergrowing group of people under the tutelage of the national treasury. Délécloy then posed a crucial question: What was the result of this chaos of ideas? His answer was: ''a dreadful series of limitless financial obligations and sterile laws that are impossible to execute. The state cannot carry out such a vast task, because it is impossible to regulate the expenses of 40,000 communities and of 2,000 hospitals.''[7]

Many officials in the post-1795 period recognized the inability of the government of the Directory—or any government—to manage such a widely stretched administrative task in an effective manner. Thus the government of the Directory abandoned both the utopian goals and the pragmatic agenda of reform. Henceforth French citizens in need were forced to rely once more on the generosity of communal, Catholic, or private charity.[8] The central state, for its part, would merely serve as a model and a source of inspiration. ''When the plaintive voice of the poor is heard,'' said Délécloy, ''it is not only the government that should react, but all sensible souls are obliged to help, and when the government sincerely tells mankind to 'do good' they will unfailingly do so.''[9]

Despite its wish to end the Revolution's exaggerated centralized control over poor relief, though, the Directory imposed more bureaucratic demands on local hospital and poor relief administrators and exulted in a ''pettifogging obsession with form-filling.''[10] The Napoleonic regime, too, issued countless regulations and precise rules concerning the financial accountability and budgets of the country's charitable institutions. In fact, Napoleon unleashed a legislative avalanche that buried custodians of poorhouses and hospitals in mandatory requirements to obtain formal approval for administrative decisions from Paris, whether it concerned the transfer of property, the conclusion of long-term leases, the investment of capital in real estate, or the acceptance of gifts and bequests.[11] Napoleon thus constructed a more elaborate and tightly controlled national bureaucracy that would constitute the backbone of the French administration in the century to come.

Technically, the leading role of the nineteenth-century state was to preserve public order, to educate its citizens, and to supply them with the means to develop and maintain their physical existence. The only true social burden of the Paris government focused on the young, the old, and the infirm.[12] If the government would be compelled to intervene at all, it should merely function as a didactic example or clever catalyst in encouraging the poor to seek "the protection and guardianship of the well-to-do."[13] Baron Joseph-Marie de Gérando would summarize this vision in his book on "the friendly visitor" (*Le visiteur du pauvre*) in 1826, in which he extolled personal acts of compassion and tried to spur good Catholics to absorb a hortatory interest in the plight of the poor. Public authorities have to fear two dangers equally, he remarked: "they have to defend themselves against doing too much and against doing too little." The great art of governance, De Gérando claimed, was to galvanize individuals into action, to guide citizens' compassionate instincts, and to direct them toward the most worthy causes so that *le visiteur du pauvre* would become the government's "seeing eyes and acting hands."[14]

Thus, the Revolution's exaltation of the unlucky poor as the protected daughters of the state, or the beloved children of the fatherland, was short-lived. What lingered on and was increasingly emphasized was the notion of the responsibility of the public sector, even if the state did not accomplish much more than to sign an endless series of contracts with Catholic religious orders, which managed the several thousand poorhouses and hospitals throughout the country. Sisters of Charity spread loving kindness and helped multitudes of desperately poor people. A large number of individual Catholics, meanwhile, dedicated time and money to charity on a highly personal and paternalistic basis. They were reluctant, however, to translate this support into a need to address the Social Question or working-class impoverishment on a larger scale. A deep-seated ambivalence of mainstream thinkers within the French Catholic Church about the realities of the modern world compounded this reticence. As a result, the Catholic Church alienated or ostracized a large proportion of the working class, reinforcing a pattern of anticlericalism on the political left in France that would endure throughout the modern era.

For its part, the French state tried to harness the residual spiritual authority of the Catholic Church to inspire its flock of believers to engage in individual acts of compassion and charity. The Catholic Church's legendary riches lingered on in the post-Revolutionary world. During the ancien régime the French church had presumably controlled a third of the wealth of the French nation and owned a fifth of the land. In some regions it supposedly had controlled half the land; in others, three quarters, and in some areas, all.[15] Allowing for some hyperbole, it was undoubtedly true that the Catholic Church was the largest property owner of the nation during the ancien régime, while tithes and rents received from its landholdings further bolstered its overall income.

These massive resources, of course, had entailed commensurate responsibilities. When the Revolution erupted in 1789, the church administered nearly 2,200 hospitals with a budget of 30 million francs. Close to half of the nation's 35,000 nuns were *soeurs hospitalières* who looked after the sick in hospitals or at home, helped women at childbirth, received abandoned children and nurtured them as best they could, or managed homes for women reclaimed from prostitution. Their solitary reward was to secure a place in heaven at the close of their life of toil and caring.[16]

By declaring public assistance to be an exclusive obligation of the state, the Constituent Assembly had hoped to expropriate the Catholic Church's property and to eliminate its influence over charity. The Revolution, however, failed dismally to do so. As early as 1795, members of religious orders were again permitted to work in hospitals and poorhouses, and the Thermidorians restored the ancient authority of the Catholic Church in most charitable institutions. During the Napoleonic era, though, only an imperial decree could license the revival of a particular religious order, and none of them regained entirely the independence they had enjoyed under the ancien régime.

Nonetheless, as Claude Langlois has noted, the First Empire provided a favorable political "conjuncture" for the reconstitution of religious orders.[17] On December 22, 1800, Napoleon's Minister of the Interior allowed the former mother superior of the *Filles de la charité* to train novices for medical service again, a request hospital administrators submitted to the government in a frantic search for qualified personnel. The *arrêté* of October 16, 1802 authorized the *Filles de la charité* to reestablish themselves as a religious order to care for poverty-stricken patients in hospitals and poorhouses. The sisters were also permitted to wear their religious habits again, but article 3 specified they had to refrain from contact with "superiors abroad"; the state in Paris rather than the ecclesiastical hierarchy in Rome would oversee and regulate religious orders in nineteenth-century France.[18] All in all the First Empire paved the "road to success" for a revival of religious communities and enabled the reconstruction of a panoply of female religious orders—and the creation of many new ones—devoted to nursing the sick and teaching the poor.[19]

In fact, throughout the nineteenth century the central bureaucracy in Paris monitored the internal conditions and personnel decisions of *hôpitaux* and *hospices* in even the most remote places. The state forced hospital administrators to request authorization from Paris in a wide range of matters, such as a plan to conclude a contract between the poorhouse in Maurs with the *Congrégation des soeurs de la charité de Nevers* to assume responsibility for interior services.[20] Parisian bureaucrats responded to a poignant plea to grant "a retirement pension to Mademoiselle Faglin, a sister in the *Hôtel Dieu* of Chalours," who for half a century had dedicated her altruistic life's work to the poor from "March 29, 1789 until October 1, 1841."[21]

The poorhouse in Aurillac sent a detailed missive to the Ministry of Commerce and Public Works in 1831 about its myriad employees—ranging from the number of doctors and *soeurs hospitalières* to the scores of gardeners, porters, and male and female *domestiques*—and specified the particular duties each one performed. The administrative council of the *hospice* informed bureaucrats in Paris when and where it held its weekly meetings and which particular items the institution's *econôme* had to account for in his quarterly budget. The council reported, too, that on Sundays and holidays each staff member and resident of the poorhouse "must attend a religious service in the chapel and listen to an edifying sermon of half an hour."[22]

The role of members of religious orders as nurses in hospitals and poorhouses was once again as central and stable as it had been during the ancien régime. Often a lonely *médécin* and a solitary *chirurgien* watched over the medical conditions of hundreds of poor patients in hospitals, only three times a week, on fixed days, before nine o'clock in the morning.[23] Sisters of Charity or members of other religious orders were the primary caretakers. Some historians have held them responsible for the perpetuation of obsolete and unwholesome medical practices in many nineteenth-century hospitals, since the nuns resisted innovative scientific ideas that could have rendered medical institutions more salubrious and efficient.[24] While the government, as De Gérando intoned in 1826, should watch over and steer private citizens' magnanimity, it relied on the Sisters of Charity to take care of the complex, day-to-day business of charity. But the state's supervisory task was a pivotal one, which imbricated the bureaucracy in Paris with the "good works" performed by religious orders, if only to frustrate the Vatican's meddling in the internal affairs of the French Catholic Church.

The Dutchman P. J. Elout, in contrast, embraced a diametrically opposed vision. Elout might have dismissed La Rochefoucauld-Liancourt's ideas as misguided; he also might have repudiated the vicarious French reliance on the charitable labors of the Catholic Sisters of Charity as disingenuous. He probably would have disagreed with De Gérando's argument that the state should foster the sympathy or stimulate the financial munificence of the rich vis-à-vis the poor. Elout conflated public and secular poor relief with humiliating and condescending practices; publicly inspired assistance, he contended, perpetrated personal insults and caused private embarrassment. In his view, public authorities, whether at the local or national level, had no place whatsoever in any of the efforts to alleviate the suffering of the poor.

To Elout, the division of labor between church and state was simple and aboveboard. Public authorities might provide education, establish charitable workshops, and nurture economic development; they could tax the rich and enforce the laws against vagrancy and beggary. But only religious charity was capable of providing actual assistance with loving kindness, intimate knowledge, and the appropriate uplifting guidance. Only the Christian faith should elicit *caritas* and mobilize individual citizens to reach out to their less fortunate compatriots, and the private charity of real Christians alone would preserve the dignity of the poor. In Elout's incantatory rhetoric it was crucial that the church, and not the state, awaken charitable sentiments. Only the church could ensure the voluntary nature of poor relief, and nothing but religious incentives would guarantee and actualize the selfless compassion of individual donors in exchange for the grateful appreciation of the poor.

In the cosmology of devout Protestants, the poor belonged in "the womb of the church, because it is a Christian duty to alleviate the misery of the flock of believers."[25] The church, they were wholeheartedly convinced, wielded a moral leadership and furnished an ethical example far superior to any kind of moral authority secular institutions could marshal. The civic culture of the Dutch nation could only encircle its impoverished members in a gentle embrace if it was firmly grounded in, and shaped by, religious sentiments. Knowing its members intimately, the Protestant ministers' rhetoric maintained, religious charitable agencies did not grant money, clothes, or food in an uncaring and capricious manner as secular poor relief tended to do. Instead, the *diaconiëen* extended a helping hand with affection and consideration; they placated the material desires or consoled the spiritual distress of each needy individual with an integrity no secular administrator could muster.

The Bible story of the Good Samaritan figured prominently in this discourse. An exemplary Christian should display and reenact, in his or her daily life, the spontaneous altruism of the biblical Samaritan. His instinctive gesture of helping the innocent target of the robbers' violent assault epitomized the Samaritan's intrinsic goodness. No one would have known about the Samaritan's natural decency, however, if he had not encountered the wounded victim lying prostrate on the road from Jerusalem to Jericho. Hence, it was the presence of vulnerable poor people that was essential to disclosing the rectitude of good Christians.[26] Amidst the "spectacles" of benevolence and generosity that were performed in the "theater of good works," the poor were indispensable actors.[27] After all, high-minded, noble Christians could only demonstrate their spiritual virtues, replicating the biblical example of the Good Samaritan, by exhibiting compassion to others who were their helpless social inferiors!

"The church regards poverty as an inevitable element inherent in every human society," J. van Leeuwen in 1847 recited with a medieval resonance, whereas the state, whether at a local or a national level, "has a vision and a commitment that the problem of poverty can and has to be resolved." The aid that religious congregations bestowed upon the poor could not be viewed in the same light. The church was content with protecting the lives of the poor by inspiring good Christians to guard over the spiritual well-being of their miserable fellow believers; the church should encourage its fortunate members to quell poor people's hunger and to relieve their suffering. But religious institutions were reluctant to interfere in God's grand scheme for mankind and were loathe to attempt what the state wished to accomplish. "The church does not concern itself with transforming the individual pauper into a constructive member of society," because it was solely in good works and empathy for the poor that God-fearing Christians could manifest their religious purity.[28] As Elise van Calcar wrote in 1856 in a book she dedicated to Her Majesty the Queen: "of all the kinds of love that fill the human heart during this earthly existence, generosity is the highest and most beautiful . . . it is only in our love for the poor that our own selfish interests recede to the background."[29]

Thus, religiously inspired charity entailed a complex series of quid pro quos. It provided the poor with a mechanism of survival during times of dearth and unemployment; it also enabled local employers to hire and fire workers whenever it suited their profit-maximizing purposes because economic logic mandated a contraction of the labor force. Moreover, the transfer payments from the rich to the poor not only conferred social status upon members of a local elite but also granted them political opportunities. In addition, through their largess the rich earned a certain amount of moral capital in the eyes of contemporaries—or, in the sardonic phrase of a modern-day historian, they garnered "heavenly interest" (*hemelrente*)—which might placate their residual anxieties about the salvation of their souls.[30]

This conception of charity, of course, both upheld and endorsed the prevailing hierarchical differences between wealthy elites and the doleful recipients of their benevolence. The poor should know who their benefactors were, and they owed their patrons both gratitude and deference. At the same time, the *diaconiëen*'s material assistance to the poor reinforced the vertical ties between the rich and destitute members within the same religious denomination. An important mission of poor relief, in the vision of Elout and his spiritual fellow travelers, was to strengthen the internal bonds of solidarity of each religious congregation across the great gulf that separated rich from poor. The charitable impulse and the humanitarian sensibility of the relatively comfortable members of a particular denomination would forge a greater sense of communal or spiritual fellowship as well as social harmony. In sum, each individual act of clemency and goodwill would solidify the "sovereign circles" of the many different congregations. Even though this particular phrase would not become fully ingrained in daily political discourses until the early twentieth century, in the imagination of a large segment of the Dutch population, the *diaconiëen* constituted one of the structural "pillars" that sustained the ornate social and political architecture of the Dutch nation much earlier.

The perspectives of Elout, Van Leeuwen, and Van Calcar was replicated hundreds of times in the strident proclamations and passionate writings of other defenders of the autonomy of religious charity in the nineteenth-century Netherlands. Even though the Dutch central state in The Hague tried with its limited might to endow the nation's system of overlapping and duplicating poor relief agencies with greater efficiency and coherence, the partisans of the *diaconiëen*'s supremacy scored an unequivocal victory at mid-century. Clearly, the cacophony of Dutch voices, which emphasized the superiority of religious poor relief, was in striking contrast to the abiding French faith in the dominant role of the public sector, even if altruistic and devoted Catholic nuns were the principal guardian angels who hovered over the poor.

Curiously, this fundamental difference between Dutch and French resolutions emerged from roughly similar beginnings during the decade of the French Revolution, since the Dutch state, too, had embraced a "modern" public commitment to its poverty-stricken citizens in a manner comparable to the *Comité de mendicité*. The Dutch Constitution of 1798 actually employed the same romantic terminology and had also described the poor as "children of the state," if only because this trope had become symptomatic, to some extent, of a generalized northern European rethinking of the role of philanthropy at the end of the eighteenth century.[31]

During those years of political ferment in the Netherlands, the most radical proposals for reform also called for a complete dismantling of the innumerable religious and private charitable agencies in order to replace them with a nationwide system of public assistance—a recommendation that resembled the progressive ideas of La Rochefoucauld-Liancourt and his quixotic colleagues in revolutionary Paris. In the Netherlands, too, this newly envisioned system designated the role of administrators to public officials while a direct national tax would finance a national bureaucracy of poor relief. As early as July 1800, the *Uitvoerend Bewind* (Executive Regime) of the Batavian Republic proposed a comprehensive Poor Law, a task mandated by the Constitution of 1798. Ushered through by the enthusiastic heirs of the Enlightenment and members of the modern *patriotten* movement, the law favored greater central coordination, more make-work schemes, and better education; moreover, the law was implicitly critical of the organizational bedlam and inefficiency of religious and private charity.[32]

Given the abiding importance of the pluralistic institutional structure and rhetorical patterns forged during the early modern Dutch Republic, it was no surprise that this proposal provoked immediate objections. In response to the proposed Poor Law, church deacons and other custodians of religious charities stated loudly and clearly that any attempt to undermine their autonomy would be "tantamount to an attack on private property."[33] But most municipal officials objected just as vigorously; after all, the concentration of authority over poor relief in The Hague would fracture and weaken their local sovereignty as well.

The intention of the Poor Law of 1800 was to codify public assistance as an object of state control. The totality of all poor relief funds, those which *diaconiëen* dispensed as well as the support municipal administrators parceled out, would be subjected to state intervention and divided equitably among all needy citizens, whether or not they belonged to a particular religious congregation. Thus the Batavian state hoped to care for its poor offspring as a shepherd guards and protects his herd of sheep.[34] As Gijsbert Karel van Hogendorp wrote, echoing the parental language of both La Rochefoucauld-Liancourt and Saint-Just in Revolutionary Paris, "the poor should be treated as children whose guardians will guide them upon the right path and educate them to prosperity."[35] As a champion of pluralism and local autonomy, however, he envisioned the *diaconie* as the paterfamilias, not the state.

Even before the Poor Law was officially announced on July 15, 1800, however, the Batavian government already added some qualifiers to the legislation and stated emphatically that "the state would occupy itself only with those indigents who did not already receive assistance from private charity or a church *diaconie*."[36] If the *diaconiëen* wished to continue their good works on behalf of the poor, they would be allowed to do so, provided they submitted information to the state regarding their sources of income, real estate holdings, and other capital resources. The state would also compel religious poor relief agencies to submit meticulous reports that clarified how many people they assisted and how much money, services, and goods they distributed. If particular private or religious charities could not count on an adequate income to nurture their poor, state subsidies would come to their rescue.

The Executive Regime of the Batavian Republic, however, proved to be a wayward father to its bevy of children. Very soon the insurmountable disagreements between the political proponents of municipal sovereignty and self-governing church charities, on the one side, and the central government, on the other, obliged the state to abandon the proposed Poor Law. The metaphorical status of the poor as "progeny of the state" was an evanescent one and quickly forgotten. What the *diaconiëen* and municipalities immediately rebuffed, too, was the idea of public responsibility under the auspices of the central state.

The same thorny questions resurfaced thirteen years later. When Dutch public officials and jurists confronted the task of creating a constitution for the new Kingdom of the Netherlands after King William I was crowned, the issues of private charity and public welfare appeared to be ever present in their minds. Many of them thought that the central state should impose some discipline, order, and uniformity on the nation's system of poor relief by supervising the relationship between public municipal organizations and private and religious charities. Others, with Van Hogendorp as their eloquent spokesman, favored a continuation of the irregular and particularistic practices inherited from the Dutch Republic. When the drafting of the "compromise" Constitution of the new Kingdom of the Netherlands was completed in 1814, it nonetheless mandated specifically that the state occupy itself with the fate of its poverty-stricken subjects.[37]

King William himself, in fact, issued a royal decree as early as August 27, 1814, which stipulated that pending definitive poor relief legislation "it is highly necessary that we take provisional measures to avoid that the needy (*behoeftigen*) will not become the victims of antagonistic opinions."[38] The King decreed that the poor administrations of each municipality in the country should not refuse or delay support to any poverty-stricken compatriot "who can legitimately claim assistance."[39] But the relationship among the central government in The Hague, the provincial estates, the many municipal councils administering local poor relief agencies, and church charities or private organizations remained ill-defined and controversial, despite King William's valiant efforts.[40]

As a consequence, throughout the next four decades, the internal flow of authority over, and financial liability for, assistance to the poor continued to be a political lightning rod. The perpetuation of the clumsy process of "truck, barter, and higgle," as Adam Smith might say, between cities, the provincial estates, and the central state, or between *diaconiëen* and municipal councils, did not manage to resolve the matter of private charity versus public assistance. The emerging "modern" logic of administrative efficacy or bureaucratic rationalization could not rattle the institutional heritage of the early modern Republic. Albeit with only mixed success, the king and his retainers in The Hague tried to challenge the cumbersome and, above all, fragile political equilibrium that had constantly been renegotiated during the Republic. With the help of the Constitution's article 195, they tried to unmask the nation's impractical governing façade and expose it as a delicate glass house rather than the sturdy structure of political governance it pretended to be.

Article 195 of the new Constitution, which contained the stern admonition "that poverty and poor relief should be a subject of the government's continual vigilance," could imply, on the one hand, that the central state in The Hague had nothing but a regulatory function. On the other hand, article 195 could also convey an endorsement of a more activist posture. Not surprisingly, the opaque if malleable language of this constitutional clause yielded a further attempt, three years later, to clarify the role of the state.[41]

The Law of November 28, 1818 on the *domicilie van onderstand*—the stipulation of residency requirements that entitled the poor to request relief—sought to deal resolutely with a problem that had long plagued the Dutch nation: what should be done with people in need of assistance who had recently moved to a new city? Most municipal councils in the Dutch Republic since the end of the seventeenth century had demanded *Acten van Indemniteit* (affidavits of support) from all recently arrived migrants, stating that, if and when a new resident was forced to appeal to charitable support, his or her place of origin would bear financial responsibility.[42] The Law of 1818, in article 1, specified that the place of birth was the location in which a poor person could legitimately request relief. Article 3 stipulated, however, that people who had resided in a community other than their birthplace for more than four years would be entitled to receive assistance, provided they had paid all requisite taxes during those four years.[43] A similar provision applied to foreigners, although non-Dutch citizens had to live in a given community—and pay taxes—for six years before qualifying for assistance. Article 11 clarified the procedures to be followed in case of a dispute between two communities over the obligation to provide charitable support. If conflicts arose within the same province, the Council of Deputies at the provincial administrative level would resolve the matter; if the feuding communities were located in different provinces, the central government in The Hague would render judgment.[44]

The Law of 1818 did not prescribe particular regulations for private and religious institutions, nor did it define the ticklish question of *charité légale*. King William, in his royal declaration accompanying the draft law, had spoken of the poor as being *gerechtigd* (legally entitled) to request assistance, but this language was subsequently altered to *kunnen deelen in den algemeenen onderstand* (the poor can share in general assistance).[45] Neither did the law declare unequivocally that poverty and poor relief were a *staatszaak* (an object of state attention), although such a notion had been advanced in the preliminary draft. In the face of the almost instinctual opposition from preachers and church deacons who did not want to relinquish control over their congregation's impoverished souls, the final version of the law omitted a resolution of this controversial issue. Many local elites joined the fray, too, and thwarted the centralizing tendencies of the government in The Hague, albeit for different reasons.

Nevertheless, government officials in The Hague interpreted the law, tacitly and informally, as codifying poor relief as a *staatszaak*, which seemed to intimate to the king and his ministers that every Dutch citizen who was truly in need was entitled to some form of assistance. Emboldened by its reading of the law, the central state also claimed the right to supervise local poor councils and to monitor the relationship between private church charities and municipal poor relief agencies. A distinct number of government officials in The Hague even fathomed that they might play a role, too, in determining the particular form in which relief would be allocated.[46]

One consequence of the aborted Poor Law of 1800 had been the tendency to treat religious and private charitable institutions as public and corporate entities, even though technically they were not, which were responsible for relieving the misery of the members of their congregations. Municipal agencies would only soothe the plight of poverty-stricken citizens who did not belong to a particular denomination. The law of 1818 left unresolved whether church-related charitable organizations and other private agencies were truly public corporate bodies which the state could hold accountable. The municipal treasury of many cities, however, subsidized private relief activities. Moreover, the law of 1818 conferred jurisdiction over internal disagreements between the *diaconiëen* and the municipal poor administrations upon the deputies to the Provincial Estates. As a result, the 1818 law strengthened the impression that the charitable organizations of the various religious congregations were unambiguous components of a secular system of public assistance.[47]

As one thoughtful commentator emphasized, article 13 of the 1818 law on the *domicilie van onderstand* stipulated that *diaconiëen* could claim financial restitution from public funds for the assistance they had provided. He went on to say that article 13 contradicted the alleged independence of the *diaconiëen* "to dispose freely and autonomously of their possessions without any obligation to the state." By accepting subsidies from municipal treasuries to come to the rescue of the poverty-stricken members of their congregations, "the funds of the *diaconiëen* should be considered the patrimony of [all] the poor and are thus subjected to the regulations of the nation's *jus constitutum* (constitutional law)."[48]

Despite the vagueness of legal mandates, the policies of King William's administration during the 1820s and 1830s hinted at a conviction that social welfare ought to be a public resource to which all truly destitute citizens should have access without having to show profound gratitude to a particular benefactor. The King and his ministers attempted to make poor relief an object of state concern, whether or not they had an explicit legal authorization to do so. During the 1820s, government attempts to intervene in public assistance became more widespread, and the state seemed intent on linking relief policies to its earnest efforts to strengthen the Dutch economy in general. It was as if the central government tried to bring order and discipline to the kind of administrative nightmare Baron d'Alphonse, Napoleon's emissary during the French period, had already disparaged. When push came to shove, the state bailed out those charitable institutions that were long on private goodwill but woefully short on income.

Towards the early 1830s, however, it became clear that the efforts of the central state to streamline the structure and content of the nation's system of poor relief were doomed to failure. Local authorities' jealous defense of, or attempts to reclaim, some of their ancient prerogatives, and the various denominations' equally strong desire to protect their independence constituted insurmountable obstacles. These ancient restraints combined with a historically conditioned timidity on the part of the central government in The Hague to interfere in local affairs, despite the king's personal predilections. Altogether it yielded an impasse and raised such major hurdles that they were too high to overcome. The exceptions, of course, were cases of conflict over financial responsibility or when local shortages left no acceptable alternative.

But the story about the ardent protection of local autonomy and the sovereignty of the *diaconiëen* was more complicated than a mere reliance on "archaic" rhetoric or atavistic impulses.[49] The new configuration of political and economic forces in the early nineteenth century gave rise to a change in the traditional balance of power. The government in The Hague under King William I challenged cities' ancient freedom to craft an independent economic and social policy. The central state also contested the municipalities' traditional right to fashion their own relationship with the various denominations within their political jurisdiction, which had given rise to a patchwork of local styles—a disarray Johan Rudolf Thorbecke categorized in 1841 as "political anarchy."[50] By the 1840s it became apparent, too, that economic policy was formulated more independently in The Hague by politicians whose power was primarily embedded in government ministries.

By disputing the autonomous right of local notables to formulate the economic policies of individual cities, and by restraining independent municipal authority over local religious arrangements, the government in The Hague frustrated some of the sacrosanct civic freedoms of Dutch cities. It also cultivated a gradual divergence between the nation's political and economic elites. As a result, the early nineteenth century gave rise to a tangled web of three competing centers of political power. They consisted of the king and the ministerial bureaucracies in The Hague, a commercial elite whose interests converged increasingly with economic strategies devised at the national rather than the municipal level, and municipal magistrates whose independent political agency shrank more and more.[51] While the Republic's rhetorical traditions continued to exercise a solid grip on nineteenth-century policymakers and intellectuals, the nation's political and social structures were divorced imperceptibly from the tradition of municipal dominion so characteristic of the early modern Republic.

When Revolution erupted in several major cities in Europe in 1848, the Netherlands adopted a new liberal constitution in 1848 without a turbulent, revolutionary break with the past. Its chief intellectual engineer, Thorbecke, shepherded it through with great political skill. Three years later, he maneuvered through Parliament with comparable political dexterity his draft of a national Law on Municipalities (*gemeente wet*). In this law, Thorbecke protected cities' sense of autonomy by circumscribing the extent to which the central government could rightfully intrude in local affairs. Since he viewed an engaged and active local citizenship as a necessary precondition for productive membership in the "imagined community" of the nation, he carefully avoided municipal magistrates' resentment of a central state that mucked around their own backyard.

At the same time, though, Thorbecke restricted municipalities' right to levy exorbitant excise taxes, which in some cities had risen so high that they exceeded national taxes. Thorbecke thus limited the financial independence of local elites; by equating the juridical status of cities with communities in the countryside he further narrowed the self-serving leverage of urban magistrates in national politics.[52] The national Law on Municipalities mirrored the new tripartite configuration of political power that had emerged during the first half of the nineteenth century. The confusing layers, or the "different faces" and "multiple arms" of the body politic, acquired a semblance of clarity after mid-century, if only because the demarkation between municipal, provincial, and national authority was now set forth in the Constitution of 1848, the Provincial Law of 1850, and the Law on Municipalities of 1851.[53]

In an almost formulaic fashion, the new constitution—and the deluge of legislation that came in its wake—rekindled the fiery, polemical debate over poor relief. A profusion of drafts and concepts for a comprehensive Poor Law had been published, disputed, applauded, or vilified in the periodical press as well as in the chambers of Parliament before its eventual passage in 1854. The lines of battle were clearly drawn, as usual, between the proponents of the autonomy of private and church charity and those advocating a greater secular responsibility. Another explosive issue, moreover, fueled the flames of partisan political discourses. The Constitution of 1848 had granted all the nation's churches the formal right to regulate their internal organization without interference from the state, which prompted Pope Pius IX to reinstate the ecclesiastical hierarchy of the Catholic Church in the Netherlands in 1853. When the Vatican, however, referred to the insidious "weeds of Calvinism sown in the Lord's most cherished pasture" and alluded to "the sword and rage of Calvinist heresy," it loosed a popular anti-Catholic reaction among Protestants in April 1853.[54]

Not only anti-Catholic sentiment, whether of a low-key or a more virulent variety, temporarily overshadowed the perennial divisions within the Dutch Reformed Church that always percolated beneath the surface. The newly proposed Poor Law, too, momentarily obscured internal discord, since the collective disdain among devout Protestants of public intrusions into charity forged a unity of antisecular opinion. According to adherents of the evangelical *Groninger Richting*, for instance, a segment within the Dutch Reformed Church that opposed orthodox Calvinism's reliance on strict rules and dogmatic prescriptions, Christian faith emerged from the human heart, from personal longing and tender feelings engendered by the wish to follow Christ's example on earth. It was not, they argued, ''a system of strict doctrines and clearly defined theses that are imposed externally upon individual believers who have to surrender unconditionally.''[55] Because the Groningers identified religion with a highly individualized spiritual devotion, they viewed the charitable impulse as the ultimate moral expression of a vibrant faith. Not surprisingly, the Groningers judged secular society's attempts to trespass into the church's charitable practices as immoral and saw it as an infringement upon their Christian duty—or an infraction of their private conscience and personal religious freedom.[56]

The Groningers, in other words, rejoiced in a deeply personal faith; they exalted a flexible Dutch Reformed Church that could not only accommodate but also validate and nurture members' different styles and ethical principles. This view contrasted sharply with a particular brand of orthodoxy and an emphasis on predestination espoused by Guillaume Groen van Prinsterer and his faction. The latter, nonetheless, was equally forceful in his denunciation of any state involvement in assistance to the poor. As the most prominent spokesman for the primacy of a fundamentalist Dutch Protestant faith and antirevolutionary politics, he proclaimed in 1847: ''only the Gospel contains the true principles . . . of philanthropy and constructive humanitarianism.'' When charity was dislodged from its life-giving source, Groen van Prinsterer professed, many virtuous causes became nothing but hollow commitments: so many public accomplishments heralded as the achievements of political ''progress'' and intellectual ''enlightenment'' were, in reality, nothing but the tangible evidence of the everlasting ''faith and perseverance of [good] Christians.''[57]

In the political realm, the Constitution of 1848 reiterated the stipulation of article 195 of the Constitution of 1814 that poverty and poor relief were matters of national interest and governmental concern. In addition, it decreed that poor relief be regulated by law.[58] Religious charity versus public assistance was again a major source of contestation on the legislative agenda. Accordingly, Thorbecke, by then Minister of the Interior, submitted a proposal for a Poor Law in 1851 that promised "a rational organization of poor relief under the total responsibility of the state" which would also assimilate the charitable activities of the *diaconiëen*. In an explanatory memorandum, Thorbecke implied that he imagined a gradual development that would treat "the entirety of poor relief as a public service," a utopian vision that would not be realized until more than a century later.[59]

During a meeting of the Second Chamber of the Dutch Estates-General in May 1854—a spring dominated by interminable parliamentary debates over the newly proposed law—the Minister of the Interior, responding to criticism of the notion of *charité légale*, offered the view that the new Constitution of 1848 urged a legal regulation of poor relief councils. He noted that "if we accept the fact that religious and private charitable organizations cannot be the subject of statutory regulation, then there must be a different kind of poor council that *can* be defined by law."[60] In other words, the Minister of the Interior felt an urgent intellectual need to explore, in a parliamentary forum, the implications of the constitutional admonition to regulate poor relief, mainly because not all destitute citizens fell under the tutelage of either religious or private charity.

With this statement the Minister of the Interior touched upon the central policy dilemma which poverty, economic hardship, and social inequality represented in the modern world. Thorbecke and other opponents to church-dominated charity, displaying distinctly "modern" social sensibilities, perceived hypocritical implications inherent in a reliance on the cross-fertilization between personal Christian compassion and charitable activity. Rather than transcending social distinctions, they remonstrated that the charity of the *diaconiëen* hinged, instead, on capricious, self-aggrandizing, and random gestures of support. How much support desperately poor people received depended on the accidental nature of religious affiliation, the arbitrary judgment of church deacons, or dumb luck. After all, certain Protestant *diaconiëen* in particular cities were richer and thus more extravagant than others!

In the view of Thorbecke and his ideological companions, religious and private charity did nothing but foster social injustice and reify economic inequalities, since private charitable donations seemed to accentuate and ratify the superiority of those who had presumably achieved superior standing with the worldly and spiritual powers. In their eyes, private charity bolstered traditional patterns of superiority and subservience reminiscent of the estate society of the ancien régime. Although compassionate Christians claimed to donate alms to the poor "not for the love of man, but for the love of God," the personal act of giving charity validated the preeminence of rich over poor and entrenched social inequities.[61] Instead, Thorbecke argued, anonymous *charité légale* would create a greater sense of equal human dignity, regardless of wealth or poverty, thus echoing the precocious ideas of La Rochefoucauld-Liancourt and the *Comité de mendicité* more than sixty years later in the august legislative chambers of the Estates-General in The Hague.

But Protestant preachers dispersed and silenced the chorus of Dutch social critics who sang the praises of these progressive ideas. When the combative voices in the fierce ideological debates had quieted down, the two chambers of the Dutch Parliament passed a Poor Law in 1854 that relinquished all control and decision-making authority over poor relief to private and religious charities. The advocates of Christian charity had scored a resounding victory over their antagonists. The legislation specified that secular authorities were not to play any role in dispensing social welfare. Custodians of church *diaconiëen* and private charitable agencies avowed over and over again that they managed independent institutions not subject to the strictures of civil law, despite their acceptance of public subsidies. Their parliamentary triumph meant that the Poor Law of 1854 articulated as a basic principle that Dutch citizens would have no statutory right to receive material support, and religious and private poor relief agencies would control any and all allocations of charity.[62]

The law thus conformed to the evangelical exhortation issued by A. E. Mackay in 1851 that "the rights of men do not exclude anyone, and the poor have an equal claim to humanity." The poor ask for bread, labor, and money and, above all, for spiritual salvation: "they do not know about politics or popular sovereignty: they only know about hardship." Regarding them as entirely apolitical, Mackay then stated that the poor belong to their church congregation, and to its

> High, holy, and continual Christian care. The state can not observe the growing poverty with an innocent eye, but her calling is to divert the evil, to open new sources of existence, not to give relief, not to play the role of nursemaid . . . The state shall discover that love for humanity can not be evoked through legislation but instead, through faith alone . . . The gospel rather than the law will awaken *caritas*.[63]

This was to be the official regulation of public assistance in the Netherlands after the mid–1850s: religious and private charitable organizations would be the ''nursemaid'' of the poor; the state would reorganize the economy in order to stimulate employment opportunities, and, according to article 21 of the 1854 law, perform a merely subsidiary function.[64] Public authorities were expected to safeguard social order and ensure that those who were absolutely not supported by private charity would not suffer from want and deprivation and thus turn to begging, stealing, and rioting.[65] ''Public'' assistance would play only a subservient and purely auxiliary role in the nation's system of social welfare.

Since the late sixteenth century a sense of interdependence between church and society, both in terms of the political process and in definitions of social justice, permeated popular views of poverty and poor relief in the Netherlands. Although the various strands and factions within Dutch Protestantism hardly represented ''the religious community of the people as a whole,'' Dutch Reformed spokesmen managed to infuse almost all discussions about indigence, entitlements, and the obligations of civil society with a religious vocabulary.[66] Religion, it seemed, constituted an inescapable element in the woof and warp of the social fabric as well as in the maintenance of public order. It was incumbent upon mankind, many Dutchmen avowed, to submit to God's will and His plan for mankind. In a Dutch Protestant lexicon, God endowed good Christians with the gift of perseverance and impelled the ''Dutch tribe,'' to borrow J. D. J. Waardenburg's phrase, to succumb unequivocally to God's design and to follow His dictates on earth.[67] Issues of privacy, or questions of personal faith or individual conscience, were firmly ensconced in the daily discourse of the nation, and the intermingling of politics and religion did not induce the same kind of apprehensions as it might have in France, where the Catholic Church's embrace of the forces of reaction terrified centrist or Republican politicians.

Religious imagery punctuated the cultural grammar of the Dutch nation. Ethical judgments about social entitlements or economic fairness often assimilated a religious idiom rather than being restricted to an exclusive political vocabulary of personal rights and public duties. Political conflicts could not really be settled definitively—they could only be tempered or accommodated. Hence, disagreements over the improvement of the collective welfare of the poor within the nation, it seemed, could be defused through the official accommodation of everyone's personal passions and private interests, which were inextricably joined, in the public imagination, with questions of individual moral choice and religious freedom.[68] Because Holland had been a religiously fractured nation since the late sixteenth century, almost 300 years later poor relief was still deeply embroiled in discussions about religious equity. Moreover, pious Protestants may have regarded charity as a means of solidifying the social coherence of religious communities. Urban elites, too, may have viewed their jurisdiction over poor relief agencies as a patronage network that composed an important element in their independent power base vis-à-vis the central state in The Hague.

Arjo Klamer has characterized Dutch culture metaphorically as displaying a "citadel" mentality. The physical bastion of the Dutch nation, he argued recently, has always been small and fragile and highly sensitive to threats from the outside. Within the Dutch bulwark, therefore, people sustained their mutual survival through deliberation, cooperation, and family unity. Citizenship implied the reinforcement of collective solidarity through a public acknowledgment of internal differences and a calculated respect for everyone's private conscience: *Eendracht maakt Macht* (power in unity). At the same time, the intimidating existence of "the other without"—whether the menace of the North Sea, foreign aggression, or spiritual contamination from the exterior world—bolstered the composite strength and internal cohesion of the Dutch nation.[69]

Resembling a gifted political architect, the government in The Hague arranged the many separate building blocks of the Dutch national household in such a way that each distinct constituency seemed to contribute to the citadel's strength. Since a sense of belonging to a political constituency also entailed a particular church affiliation, religion, despite its polymorphic presence, constituted a crucial "pillar" of strength in the construction of national harmony. Even though King William, and later, Thorbecke and his political soulmates, had a more unitarian and secular vision of civil society, they could not push through their agenda. To assemble a stable structure of governance, the central state was forced to erect its political edifice in such a way that it incorporated all of the separate columns, which represented both Protestants and Catholics, both liberal urban elites and progressive social democrats. While the resulting monument of state—resting as it did on an eclectic colonnade of many different pillars and posts—may have acquired a baroque appearance, it proved to be the most workable political design for the Dutch nation.

Obviously the edifice of state in nineteenth-century France displayed a dramatically different look. If the Dutch political structure resembled a rococo castle, its counterpart in France looked more like a sleek pyramid. Political power in France descended from the top of the pyramid to the bottom; government decisions traveled from the center to the periphery, often capable of circumnavigating the many regional twists and local bumps in the road. Nothing memorable had ever occurred in France, Alphonse de Lamartine intoned in 1838, without state involvement, because the government embodied the country's noble aspirations.[70] In the French public imagination, the government in Paris symbolized the cohesion of the nation and actualized its unified purpose.

While selfless nuns, well-meaning bourgeois matrons, benevolent philanthropists, and local administrators of *bureaux de bienfaisance* in most French towns managed a kaleidoscope of charitable organizations, the overall political culture of the French nation promoted the firm conviction that the central state was responsible. The empathetic individuals who softened the plight of the poor in their day-to-day lives represented no more than the ''seeing eyes'' and the ''acting hands'' of the state at the grass-roots level. In the nineteenth century the role of the French state paralleled that of a ''police commissioner'' whose calling it was to preserve public peace and tranquility.[71] At the departmental level the state adopted the guise of an impertinent inspector, who pried into the internal conditions of hospitals and poorhouses and expounded on the best ways in which worthless paupers might be transformed into industrious citizens, but who harbored no real sense of responsibility for concrete improvements.[72]

The Revolution's formulation that assistance should be provided only in exchange for work continued to capture the imagination of nineteenth-century policymakers. The Revolution had proposed that all full-fledged French citizens had the right to say to society ''permit me to live,'' which granted the state the right to say ''give me your work'' in response. The make-work schemes implemented during the Revolution, however, had achieved little success and, with an occasional exception such as a charitable spinning workshop in Paris which employed only impoverished women (*Filature des indigents*), none emerged as thriving enterprises. The Revolution's elaborate national workshops, modeled on Robert-Jacques Turgot's *ateliers de charité* during the ancien régime, had, for a fleeting moment only, employed as many as 30,000 indigent Parisian workers. Similar *ateliers* had briefly seen the light of day in the provinces, too. But the monthly expenses required to sustain such make-work schemes had risen as high as 900,000 livres per month and already in 1791 the Assembly ordered their closure throughout the country.[73] Economic and social developments since then had shown that public authorities could not distinguish between innocent victims of unemployment and carefree parasites, nor could they provide institutionalized employment on a grand scale since it might raise the specter of the ''right to work.'' Relying on temporary public work projects during unstable times, for which emergency funding could be increased by means of a simple signature in a government building in Paris, would more directly serve the national interest.

The result was a government in Paris that refrained from active participation in soothing the fate of the poor, because to guarantee assistance might encourage personal sloth and insolence or invite economic lassitude in the society at large. Such assistance would be, in the language of economists, "a disincentive to saving, to wise financial accounting, and would prevent prudence within marriage."[74] Hence, the bureaucracy in Paris supervised as much as it could the many institutions whose mission it was to help the poor even if financially they had a hard time keeping their heads above water. The central state, however, only jumped into these troubled waters when working-class misery threatened to spill over into political unrest.

The ubiquitous nineteenth-century politician Adolphe Thiers articulated the government's quandary about poverty, hardship, and unemployment in an elliptical speech to the National Assembly in 1848. Thiers endorsed the government's efforts to expand employment opportunities but refused to recognize the "right to work." The state might be able to assist workers in times of unemployment, he said, but only through a multiplication of "certain public works when jobs in the private sector are less amply available." Even these public works programs, Thiers asserted, had their natural limits, since they were "merely accidental" and no one could guarantee their success: "this is the help the state can give, but nothing else. We can therefore not call it a right to work."[75] Thiers formulated the "fundamental ambiguity" of the French state: whether French citizens were poor because of moral flaws or economic forces beyond their control, the state could not give them special treatment. Protective legislation had "natural" limits and would violate the revered principles of *liberté* and *égalité*. If poor workers jeopardized the public peace, however, the state should defend society and protect the elite's peace of mind—and bourgeois property!—through active intervention.[76]

Notes

1. "Rapport du Comité de Mendicité, VIIième rapport," in Camille Bloch and Alexandre Tuety, eds., *Procès verbaux et rapports du Comité de mendicité de la Constituante, 1790–1791* (Paris: Paul Dupont, 1911), pp. 495, 545. See also Alfred de Lassence, *L'assistance dans la commune* (Bordeaux: Cadoret,

1898), p. 331, and Allan Forrest, *The French Revolution and the Poor* (New York: St. Martin's Press, 1982), pp. 24–28. For biographical information on the chairman of the *Comité de mendicité*, see Ferdinand Dreyfus, *Un philanthrope d'autrefois: La Rochefoucauld-Liancourt* (Paris: Plon, 1903).

2. P.J. Elout, "Iets over de armbedeeling," *Tijdschrift van de vereniging "de Christelijke Stemmen,"* 2 (1846), p. 161.

3. La Rochefoucauld-Liancourt, "Plan de travail du comité," January 21, 1790, in Bloch and Tuety, eds., *Procès verbaux et rapports*, p. 311. Gordon Wright, in *Between THE Guillotine & Liberty. Two Centuries of the Crime Problem in France* (New York: Oxford University Press, 1983), reports that La Rochefoucauld-Liancourt was known as "a banal patron of all the philathropies in the world" (p. 53).

4. "Rapport du Comité de mendicité," in Bloch and Tuety, eds., *Procès verbaux et rapports*, pp. 495–96.

5. Quoted by Simon Schama, *Citizens. A Chronicle of the French Revolution* (New York: Alfred A. Knopf, 1989), p. 710. See Lynn Hunt, *The Family Romance of the French Revolution* (Berkeley: University of California Press, 1992), for the prevalent use of gendered tropes and family imagery during the Revolution.

6. Gabriel Cros Mayrevielle, *Traité de l'administration hospitalière precédé d'un historique des établissements de bienfaisance* (Paris: Paul Dupont, 1886), p. 47.

7. Délécloy, *Rapport sur l'organisation générale des secours publics*, 12 Vendémiaire, An IV (1796). Quoted by Maurice Rochaix, *Essai sur l'évolution des questions hospitalières de la fin de l'ancien régime à nos jours* (Paris: Fédération hospitalière de France, 1959), p. 106.

8. Roger Price, "Poor Relief and Social Crisis in Mid Nineteenth-Century France," *European Studies Review*, 13, No. 4 (1983), p. 423.

9. Délécloy, *Rapport sur l'organisation*, in Rochaix, *Essai sur l'évolution*, p. 109.

10. Forrest, *The French Revolution and the Poor*, p. 59.

11. Jean Imbert, *Le droit hospitalier de la Révolution et de l'Empire* (Paris: Receuil Sirey, 1954), p. 162.

12. Ferdinand Dreyfus, *L'Assistance sous la IIième République* (Paris: Cornély, 1907), p. 199.

13. Ernest Labrousse, *La crise de l'économie française à la fin de l'ancien régime* (Paris: Presses Universitaires de France, 1943), p. 50.

14. Joseph-Marie de Gérando, *Le visiteur du pauvre* (Paris: J. Renouard, 1826). In 1820 the Academy of Lyons granted De Gérando an essay prize for an earlier edition of *Le visiteur du pauvre* (Paris: L. Colas, 1820), when the author submitted it as an answer to the question: "How can we recognize true indigence, and how can we make alms useful to those who give them and to those who receive them?" See also Isaac Joseph, Philippe Fritsch, and Alain Battegay, *Recherches. Discipline à domicile, l'édification de la famille* (Fontenay-sous-Bois: Recherches, 1977), p. 83.

15. Adrien Dansette, *Religious History of Modern France*, 2 vols. (Edinburgh/London: Nelson, 1961), 1, "From the Revolution to the Third Republic," p. 8.

16. Dansette, *Religious History of Modern France*, 1, pp. 8–10. See also William J. Callahan and David Higgs, *Church and Society in Catholic Europe of the Eighteenth Century* (Cambridge/New York: Cambridge University Press, 1979).

17. Claude Langlois, *Le catholicisme au féminin. Les congrégations françaises à supérieure générale au XIXième siècle* (Paris: Editions du Cerf, 1984), p. 111.

18. Langlois, *Le catholicisme au féminin*, p. 112–13.

19. In his wish to centralize and rationalize administrative tasks and to make the control of hospitals more efficient, Napoleon wrote to the *Ministre des Cultes* Portalis that he "wanted the various separate communities of the Sisters of Charity to form one single entity." Langlois views this as evidence of Napoleon's *volonté simplificatrice*; see *Le Catholicisme au féminin*, p. 125.

20. *Réglements intérieures des hospices et traités avec les congrégations religiéuses, 1823–1839*, Ministère du Commerce et Travaux Publics à hospice de Maurs, November 28, 1831. F15 192, AN, Paris.

21. *Hospices et Bureaux de bienfaisance, correspondance et comptabilité, 1832–1884*, Ministère de l'Intérieur à hospice de Chalours, May 19, 1843. F15 3865, AN, Paris.

22. "Extrait du régistre des delibérations de la commission administrative de l'hospice d'Aurillac à Ministère du Commerce et Travaux Publics," March 6, 1831, in *Réglements intérieures des hospices et traités avec les congrégations religiéuses, 1823–1839*. F15 191, AN, Paris.

23. *Service de santé, Conseil général de l'administration des hospices civils de Paris*, which contained regulations for the treatment of indigent patients in Paris hospitals, December 14, 1825. Fosseyeux, liasse 707–24, Archives de l'assistance publique, Paris.

24. Olivier Faure, *Genèse de l'hôpital moderne. Les hospices civils de Lyon de 1802 à 1845* (Lyon: Presses Universitaires de Lyon/Editions du CNRS, 1982), p. 39.

25. A.E. Mackay, *Denkbeelden omtrent een wettelijke regeling van het armenwezen in Nederland* (The Hague/Amsterdam: Gebroeders Van Cleef, 1850), p. 48.

26. See Radboud Engbersen and Thijs Jansen, *Armoede in de maatschappelijke verbeelding, 1945–1990. Een retorische studie* (Leiden/Antwerp: Stenfert Kroese, 1991), for a detailed analysis of the rhetorical use of the parable of the Good Samaritan in the post-World War II era, pp. 23–58.

27. Sonya Michel, "Theatres of Good Works: Spectacle and Female Benevolence in Nineteenth-Century America," paper presented at the annual convention of the American Historical Association (January 1994).

28. J. van Leeuwen, *De armenwet in haar ontstaan, zin, en strekking geschiedkundig toegelicht* (Leiden: P. Engels, 1847), p. 6.

29. Elise van Calcar, *Tabitha. Armoede en Weldadigheid*, 2 vols. (Amsterdam: W.H. Kirberger, 1856), 1, p. xiii.

30. Marco H.D. van Leeuwen, *Bijstand in Amsterdam, ca. 1800–1850. Armenzorg als beheersings- en overlevingsstrategie* (Zwolle: Waanders, 1992), p. 163.

31. Simon Schama, ''Municipal Government and the Burden of the Poor in South Holland during the Napoleonic Wars,'' in *Britain and the Netherlands*, No. 6, A.C. Duke and C.A. Tamse, eds., *War and Society* (The Hague: Martinus Nijhoff, 1976), p. 103.

32. Siep Stuurman, *Verzuiling, kapitalisme en patriarchaat. Aspecten van de ontwikkeling van de moderne staat in Nederland* (Nijmegen: SUN, 1983), p. 108.

33. Schama, ''Municipal Government,'' in Duke and Tamse, eds., *War and Society*, p. 101.

34. Cornelis Rogge, *De armen kinderen van den staat, of onderzoek nopens de verplichting van het gouvernement om de armen te verzorgen en ontwerp van plan daartoe strekkende* (Leiden: 1796), quoted by P.B.A. Melief, *De strijd om de armenzorg in Nederland, 1795–1854* (Groningen/Jakarta: J.B. Wolters, 1955), p. 11. See also J. Everts, *De verhouding van kerk en staat in het bijzonder ten aanzien van het armenwezen* (Utrecht: P. den Boer, 1908), pp. 121–122.

35. G.K. van Hogendorp, *Missive over het armenwezen* (Amsterdam: Wed. J. Doll op 't Rokin, 1805; originally written in 1794), p. 15.

36. J. Everts, *De verhouding van kerk en staat*, p. 128.

37. The ''compromise'' Constitution of 1814 was a hybrid of old Dutch Republican practices based on federalism and municipal primacy merged with a more centralized structure bequeathed by the Napoleonic regime. See J.A. Bornewasser, ''De zelfstandige eenheidsstaat in de noordelijke Nederlanden gegrondvest, 1813–1814,'' in *Algemene Geschiedenis der Nederlanden*, 15 vols. (Haarlem: Fibula van Dishoeck, 1983), 11, pp. 208–22.

38. Koninklijk Besluit, No. 579, August 27, 1814, Archieven Provinciaal Bestuur, 470–897, Ag. 2, Rijksarchief, Noord Holland.

39. Koninklijk Besluit, No. 579, August 27, 1814. The Dutch language was *die aanspraak op ondersteuning maken kan.*

40. Although yet another constitution was drafted and adopted in 1815, primarily to incorporate the demands of the southern ''Belgian'' provinces, in reality the 1815 Constitution did not alter the 1814 ''compromise'' Constitution in a meaningful way, and it reiterated the article regarding the state's concern about poverty and poor relief. See J.A. Bornewasser, ''Het Koninkrijk der Nederlanden, 1815–1830,'' *Algemene Geschiedenis der Nederlanden*, 11, pp. 223–78.

41. F.L. van Holthoon, ''De armenzorg in Nederland,'' in Van Holthoon, ed., *Nederlandse samenleving sinds 1815* (Assen/Maastricht: Van Gorcum, 1985), p. 176.

42. H.J. Smit, ''De armenwet van 1854 en haar voorgeschiedenis,'' in *Historische opstellen aangeboden aan J.H. Huizinga* (Haarlem: Tjeenk Willink, 1948), p. 219. See also Van Holthoon, ''De armenzorg in Nederland,'' p. 176.

43. P.B.A. Melief, *De strijd om de armenzorg in Nederland,* Appendix, p. 227.

44. Van Holthoon, ''De armenzorg in Nederland,'' p. 176. See also J. van Leeuwen, *De armenwet in haar ontstaan, zin, en strekking geschiedkundig toegelicht*, p. 14–15.

45. Melief, *Strijd om den armenzorg*, Appendix, p. 227. The language *kunnen deelen* appears in articles 1, 2, 6, and 13.

46. Van Leeuwen, *De armenwet in haar ontstaan*, pp. 16–17.

47. W. Boonacker, *De diaconiëen en soortgelijke armen administratiën als organen van de openbare onderstand onderworpen aan de armenwet van 1818 (naar aanleiding van de bestrijding van Mr. van Nierop)* (Amsterdam: M. Coster, 1851), pp. 7–9. See also J. Everts, *De verhouding van kerk en staat*, pp. 233–34. This same issue would reemerge as a matter of central importance in the debates preceding the new Poor Law of 1854. See, for example, J. van Leeuwen, *De diaconie, beschouwd in hare betrekking tot het armwezen*, and J. Royaards, *De Hervormde diaconiëen en de concept-armenwet. Kerkrechtelijke wenken* (Utrecht: Kemink, 1851).

48. Boonacker, *Diaconiëen en soortgelijke armen administratiën*, pp. 130–131.

49. C.H.E. de Wit calls it *archaiserend.* See *Thorbecke en de wording van de Nederlandse natie. Thorbeck historische schetsen. Thorbecke, staatsman en historicus* (Nijmegen: SUN, 1980), Sunschrift 153, p. 42.

50. Johan Rudolf Thorbecke, ''Simon van Slingerlandt's toeleg om den staat te hervormen'' (1841), in De Wit, *Thorbecke en de wording van de Nederlandse natie*. Thorbecke referred to the ''internal jealousies and suspicions'' between provinces and cities and the ''infinite chaos'' that characterized the legacy of the Republic: ''a lack of unanimous strength had caused the downfall of the Republic'' (pp. 255, 262–64).

51. I am indebted to Jan Lucassen for this formulation.

52. J.C. Boogman, ''De politieke ontwikkeling in Nederland, 1840–1874,'' in *Algemene Geschiedenis der Nederlanden*, 12, p. 361.

53. For a lucid discussion, see Auke van der Woud, *Het lege land. De ruimtelijke ordening van Nederland, 1748–1848* (Amsterdam: Meulenhoff, 1987), pp. 70–71.

54. Hans Righart, *De katholieke zuil in Europa. Het ontstaan van de verzuiling onder de katholieken in Oostenrijk, Zwitserland, België en Nederland* (Amsterdam: Boom/Meppel, 1986), pp. 197–198. See also Frans Groot, ''Verzuilingstendensen in Holland, 1850–1925,'' *Historisch Tijdschrift Holland*, 25, No. 2 (April 1993), pp. 93–99.

55. Armand Fiolet, *Een kerk in onrust om haar belijdenis. Een phenomenologische studie over het onstaan van de richtingstrijd in de Nederlands Her-*

vormde kerk (Nijkerk: G.F. Callenbach, 1953), pp. 42–43. See also the discussion in Michael Wintle, *Pillars of Piety. Religion in the Netherlands in the Nineteenth Century, 1813–1901* (Hull: Hull University Press, 1987), pp. 24–26.

56. Melief, *De strijd om den armenzorg*, p. 217. The Groningers were affiliated politically with a coalition of forces called the ''Great Protestant Party'' which, according to Siep Stuurman in *Verzuiling, kapitalisme en patriarchaat*, ''harked back to the past and had no consistent [political] program for the future'' (p. 121).

57. Guillaume Groen van Prinsterer, *Ongeloof en Revolutie. Eene reeks van historische voorlezingen* (Leiden: S.en J. Luchtmans, 1847), translated as *Unbelief and Revolution* (Free University, Amsterdam: Groen van Prinsterer Fund, 1975), pp. 31–32.

58. See, among others, L. Frank van Loo, ''De armenzorg in de noordelijke Nederlanden, 1770–1854,'' *Algemene Geschiedenis der Nederlanden*, 10, p. 421, and J. Fockema Andreae, *Een mensenleven in Nederland. Driekwart eeuw ontwikkeling van openbaar bestuur, onderwijs, en onderneming* (Alphen aan de Rijn: Samson, n.d.), p. 100.

59. Van Loo, ''De armenzorg in de noordelijke Nederlanden,'' *Algemene Geschiedenis der Nederlanden*, 10, p. 421.

60. Smit, ''De armenwet en haar voorgeschiedenis,'' p. 241. See also De Wit, *Thorbecke en de wording van de Nederlandse natie*, pp. 136–148.

61. Abram de Swaan, ''Workers and Claimants—The Hard-Pressed Alliance,'' paper presented to the Conference on the Political Economy of Austerity, Pescia, Italy, July 15–18, 1983

62. *Handelingen van de Tweede Kamer van de Staten Generaal voor het jaar 1854* (The Hague: Algemene Landsdrukkerij, 1854), p. 807, sheet 218/2–808/5.

63. Mackay, *Denkbeelden omtrent een wettelijke regeling*, pp. vi, 48, 49. It is unlikely that his invocation of ''faith alone''—*sola fide*—was a conscious reference to Martin Luther.

64. Herman Kaptein, *Armenzorg in de aanslag. Armoede en bedeling in De Rijp 1850–1914* (Bergen, N.H.: Octavo, 1984), p. 8.

65. Van Loo, *Armelui. Armoede en bedeling in Alkmaar, 1850–1914* (Bergen, N.H.: Octavo, 1986), p. 51.

66. A.Th. van Deursen, *Plain Lives in a Golden Age. Popular Culture, Religion, and Society in seventeenth-century Holland* (1978; repr. Cambridge/New York: Cambridge University Press, 1991), p. 62.

67. For a lucid discussion of the unique role of religion in Dutch society, see Rita Smith Kipp, *The Early Years of a Dutch Colonial Mission. The Karo Batak Field* (Ann Arbor: University of Michigan Press, 1990), pp. 17–27; see also Wintle, *Pillars of Piety*, passim, and J.D.J. Waardenburg, ''Religion and the Dutch Tribe,'' *Verhandelingen van het Koninklijk Instituut voor Land-, Taal-, en Volkenkunde*, 74 (The Hague: Martinus Nijhoff, 1975), pp. 247–78.

68. See the discussion in Ernest Zahn, *Regenten, rebellen, en reformatoren.*

Een visie op Nederland en de Nederlanders (1984; repr. Amsterdam: Contact, 1989), pp. 38–39.

69. Arjo Klamer, *Verzuilde dromen. 40 jaar SER* (Amsterdam: Contact, 1990), pp. 174–76.

70. Cited by Shepard Clough, *France: A History of National Economics, 1789–1939* (New York: Scribner's, 1939), p. 147.

71. J.H. van Zanten, *Beschouwing over de wijze waarop armenzorg behoort beschreven te worden* (Haarlem: Tjeenk Willink, 1897) p. 21.

72. Frédérique Schaller, *Un aspect du nouveau contrat sociale: de la charité aux droits économique du citoyen* (Neufchatel: la Baconnière, 1950), p. 14. See also: Gaston Rimlinger, *Welfare Policy and Industrialization in Europe, America and Russia* (New York: John Wiley, 1971), pp. 334–35.

73. Rochaix, *Essai sur l'évolution*, pp. 80–81. Pierre Rosanvallon, in *l'Etat en France de 1789 à nos jours* (Paris: Editions du Seuil, 1990), mentions that in 1790 in Paris 27,000 people were registered to work in the *ateliers*, p. 155.

74. Joseph Garnier, "Sur l'association, l'économie politique, et la misère. Position du problème de la misère ou considérations sur les moyens généraux d'élever les classes pauvres à une meilleure condition matérielle et morale," *Journal des économistes*, 58 (Paris: Guillaumin, 1846), p. 30.

75. *Le droit au travail à l'Assemblée nationale (Receuil complèt de tous les discours prononcés dans cette mémorable discussion*) (Paris: Imprimerie Nationale, 1848), p. 217.

76. Jean-Baptiste Martin, *La fin des mauvais pauvres. De l'assistance à l'assurance* (Paris: Champ Vallon, 1983), p. 28.

CHAPTER SEVEN

Edification, Employment, or Enclosure: The Content of Poor Relief Policies

> Your Majesty placed extraordinary funds at my disposal to aid the subsistence of the poor working classes during the trying conjunctural circumstances that came in the wake of the bad harvest of 1816. While these public works sustained the life of a great number of indigents, they also prompted the repair of many roads that had long been neglected. These public works contributed, too, to the improved sanitation of many cities. Considerable sums have reached this destination under urgent circumstances, and aside from providing solace to the poor it has many other advantages: public works not only restrain the open expression of desperation by the poor population, they also prompt useful public services to be rendered.[1]
>
> —Minister of the Interior, *Rapport au Roi sur la situation des hospices, des enfants trouvés,* . . . November 25, 1818

> The government, when it tries to deal with poverty, must improve the working conditions of the general ''family of indigents'' who are in essence the illiterate children of the state. They must be made eager to work by providing employment, thus preventing laziness and beggary. The natural strengths of the poor must be rekindled through good nourishment and warm clothing. The government must oblige the poor to raise their level of civilization.[2]
>
> —R. Scherenberg, *Bedenkingen over de armoede* . . . , 1816

It is not unreasonable to argue that public officials did not always accomplish what they said they would. Policymakers often harbored secret agendas or pursued clandestine objectives. Besides, legislation in many instances neither achieved the officially stated goals nor reflected political priorities. Amid the flood of social policies released in both Holland and France to relieve the suffering of the poor after 1815, some were harmful rather than helpful. The government officials who issued decrees or the city magistrates who navigated poor relief programs through the tricky waters of political decision-making, meanwhile, often cared more about protecting their own contentment than they worried about the plight of desperate poor people inundated with sorrow and hardship. The official intention of policies, in other words, did not always correspond to their actual outcomes, nor did the rhetoric politicians invoked to justify certain policy programs necessarily divulge their true purpose.

On the one hand, the policies which encoded the relations of power between rich and poor resembled a concerted effort on the part of society's notables to render the moral dilemma of the Social Question more tractable. By passing legislation, issuing ordinances, creating workshops and agricultural colonies, or handing down moral commandments, elites hoped to orchestrate the parade of power in such a way that the poor could not steal the show and challenge their leading role at the head of the political procession. On the other hand, the public transcript of poverty and charity also assimilated utopian hopes and dreams, even if they were of a regressive variety. Nineteenth-century social policies reordained and reenacted, too, certain entrenched historical practices or tried to institutionalize already familiar humanitarian sensibilities. In Maurice Halbwach's morbid but graphic imagery, every historical era resembles a "cemetery with limited space." At any given moment politicians must decide which old graves deserve to be left unscathed and which ones should be dug up in order to make room for the shiny marble of new tombstones.[3]

Thus policies and legislation regulating the interaction between the rich and poor in the nineteenth century either buried certain social conventions or unearthed other ones, which collectively comprised the public record and served as a backdrop to official rhetoric.[4] Accordingly, it is necessary to examine and compare some of the details of poor relief programs in Holland and France, in their intent, scope, and structure. The *extent* of poor relief, as measured, for instance, in both the magnitude and the regularity of budgetary outlays, can provide an empirical indication of the depth or constancy of official concern with poverty. The *form* of poor relief revealed something about elite perceptions and their ideas regarding the best means to relieve hardship or to convert feisty paupers into pliable, proper citizens. The actual shape that charitable programs acquired also divulged the ingenious ways in which elites hoped to safeguard their superior social status.

When the French Minister of the Interior dispatched his report to the king in 1818, he unwittingly betrayed his fickle, transitory concern with the human suffering of the poor themselves. Two years earlier, the massive eruption of Mount Tambora—a volcano on the island of Sumbawa in the Dutch East Indies—had hurled into the atmosphere approximately 100 cubic kilometers of debris with a force equal to that of several hydrogen bombs. The Tambora explosion occasioned the infamous ''year without summer'' in 1816 and provoked catastrophic harvest failures in France, Holland, and elsewhere in the world. In the wake of the serious subsistence crisis of 1816, the French state, quite abruptly, had dramatically increased the minister's budget for public works.

The funds' objective was to create emergency employment for indigent workers during episodes of economic depression, designed primarily to assure that economic hardship would not automatically assimilate a subversive political dimension as well. As the Interior Minister mentioned, inclement weather and bad harvests had caused a slowdown of trade and a collapse of certain branches of industry. If, as a result, the population of particular departments plunged into distress, ''humanity and prudence impose a duty upon the administration to provide aid to this population. It is then that we need to help and support them until the equilibrium between need and the available resources has been reestablished.''[5]

This kind of sudden response entailed a consideration of available food supplies, too; if and when unstable political or social circumstances warranted, the French state also prohibited the export of domestic grain abroad. Shortly before the subsistence crisis of 1816, King Louis XVIII issued an ordinance prohibiting ''all exports of grain outside the kingdom'' and dictated ''the strictest surveillance'' of France's national borders. The measure was intended to augment the food supplies of the French population and to bring about a reduction in the price of grain which would enable ''our subjects to procure grain at more moderate costs.''[6]

The incipient threat of a subsistence crisis thus yielded a momentary ad hoc public concern with indigence. The underlying theme of the minister's report, though, was the assumption that these expenditures were of a purely exceptional nature. Only ''urgent'' conditions had made them necessary; once normalcy would be restored and poor people could silently resume their precarious and bleak existence on the margins of society, the ''extraordinary'' funding of public works would be unnecessary and the state could turn its attention, once again, to more pressing matters. This constantly shifting situation prompted the inspector of charitable institutions in the department of the Gironde to throw up his hands in despair: "laws against mendicity and vagabondage are issued in every epoch, only to be rescinded or modified a few years hence." The same was true for workshops, he wrote in 1832, which supposedly enabled indigent workers to earn their own livelihood through honest labor: "such institutions are being created all the time, only to disappear a little while later."[7]

The Dutchman Scherenberg, who harbored an odd mixture of harsh Malthusian notions as well as compassionate ideas about poor people, conveyed a message that was different from the one which the French Minister of the Interior sent, even if he advocated the creation of a central supervisory commission charged with overseeing poor relief efforts in the Dutch nation. On the one hand, Scherenberg described the poor as degenerate (*diepvervallen*) or sluggish and slothful (*vadsig*), whose repugnance of honest work represented an "all-consuming cancer" that ravaged the body politic. He even asked rhetorically whether society should not simply let the poor perish rather than allow them to recreate their misery in their children.[8] On the other hand he concocted a curiously paradoxical vocabulary of family kinship between rich and poor.

Scherenberg entrusted secular authorities with the ultimate parental duty of caring for the Dutch family of indigents. Many poor people, Scherenberg wrote, were the physically weak or mentally and emotionally underdeveloped "children of the Dutch nation." A central commission should monitor all local efforts at providing the poor with steady jobs, better schools, healthy food, or warm clothing. Taking yet another tack, Scherenberg noted that unemployed indigents were often needy as a result of causes "beyond their own guilt."[9] Instead, it was the absence of employment opportunities that rendered them idle and forced them to beg. Their generally feeble constitution derived from inferior nutrition rather than a genetic predisposition, while their low level of civilization issued from a lack of education and not from their inherently inferior character.

The vulnerability of these "poor relations" mandated a vigilance on the part of a national commission of oversight that should be constant and unwavering rather than intermittent and spasmodic, as the French Minister of the Interior implied. Whereas Dutch Reformed partisans of religious charity called upon the *diaconiëen* to serve as a "womb" or a "nursemaid," Scherenberg conjured up a stern paterfamilias who should teach the poor to work and to achieve self-reliance. Indirectly he echoed, too, La Rochefoucauld-Liancourt's notions about the "social state" as an eagle-eyed mother who watched over her brood of impoverished young.

In both countries, the idealistic and romantic metaphor of the poor as the daughters or sons of the social state tended to fade during the turbulent century following the Revolution. In France this trope was transformed into either the ghoulish preoccupations expressed in the French Minister of the Interior's report in 1818 or Adolphe Thiers' cagey pronouncements in the National Assembly in 1848. The family rhetoric that did survive in France beyond its Revolutionary birth began to sound a note of alarm about the decline of family ties. In 1837, for example, a subsequent Minister of the Interior wrote to the king that "overly liberal charity destroys filial responsibility and parental love, and the spirit of the family is becoming weaker every day until it will soon disappear altogether."[10] In Holland, too, nineteenth-century discourses about the family reverberated with different overtones and nuances and focused more and more on the evils of unrestrained demographic growth. Dutch burghers grumbled about foolhardy poor people who recklessly formed households and sired too many children without worrying about the need to support their families.[11]

At any rate, at the first sign of harvest failures in the French countryside in 1816 and the exorbitantly high bread prices that came in their wake, the allocation for *travaux publiques* jumped from 9,700,000 francs to over 21 million francs in 1817.[12] A year later the Interior Minister cheerfully reported to the king that his increased budget for public works had not only generated employment and reduced the potential of social unrest, it had also produced other propitious, and more tangible, results. By forcing the poor to fix roads in disrepair, or by compelling them to dig new sewers in cities with antiquated sanitation, the money allocated to ease the plight of the poor had achieved, too, a series of useful infrastructural successes.

Approximately thirty years later the same pattern repeated itself. In 1844, the French national budget stipulated the allocation of a little more than 149 million francs for public works. By 1846, when material conditions had become shaky and insufficient for a large segment of the French population, due once again, to harvest failures, high food prices, and reduced employment opportunities, this figure had risen to over 201 million francs. But in 1850, as soon as Napoleon III and his henchmen had stifled the furor of the Revolution of 1848 and muzzled the popular outcry for the "right to work" by seducing unemployed workers with "cold poultry and garlic sausages," as Karl Marx imagined in a dream of gluttony, the sum allocated to public works dropped again to 149 million francs.[13]

The same was true as far as the Ministry of the Interior's expenditures for *secours aux établissements et institutions de bienfaisance* were concerned. The annual budgetary outlays in the late 1830s displayed enormous oscillations. In 1836, for example, this budget item comprised 643,907 francs but rose to 1,116,358 francs in 1837, only to drop to 517,802 francs in 1838. The fluctuations between 1844 and 1849 were even more impressive:[14]

1844	439,271 francs
1845	639,312 francs
1846	1,114,808 francs
1847	5,302,777 francs
1848	1,683,329 francs
1849	904,118 francs

On the whole, the curve on the graph representing French outdoor relief expenditures is distinctly erratic (Figure 7-1). Expenditures of the *bureaux de bienfaisance* for outdoor relief in addition to the cost of maintaining hospitals and poorhouses tended to follow the fluctuations in the price of grain, rising to a dramatic peak in the late 1840s and then falling off sharply.

During critical times of emergency and dearth, French public funding increased not only at the national but also at the local level. Particular towns and regions, if dismal harvests caused widespread human suffering, devised their own temporary measures, such as enlarging the grain supplies in local storage or making bread available at a lower price. Because the working poor had to apportion a greater share of their family income to filling their growling, empty stomachs—a physical craving that revealed only a limited elasticity, of course—they had few resources left over for other expenditures. As a result, their reduced purchasing power initiated a slump in artisanal production and thus escalated unemployment, conforming to the classic pattern of a Laboussian economic crisis of a preindustrial type.

Subsidizing bread prices or supervising the baking of bread from public grain supplies constituted yet another official response in local communities that replicated the provision of public works. Both practical solutions reinforced government surveillance while placating popular discontent. During the economic crisis of 1816–1818 some departments established too much "precautionary granaries" and expanded their auxiliary supplies of wheat in case the emergency conditions endured.[15] In the city of Nantes, for instance, the mayor executed an *ordonnance* on July 4, 1818, stipulating that "no bakers were allowed to

Figure 7-1

Expenditures on Outdoor Relief in France
1833 - 1853

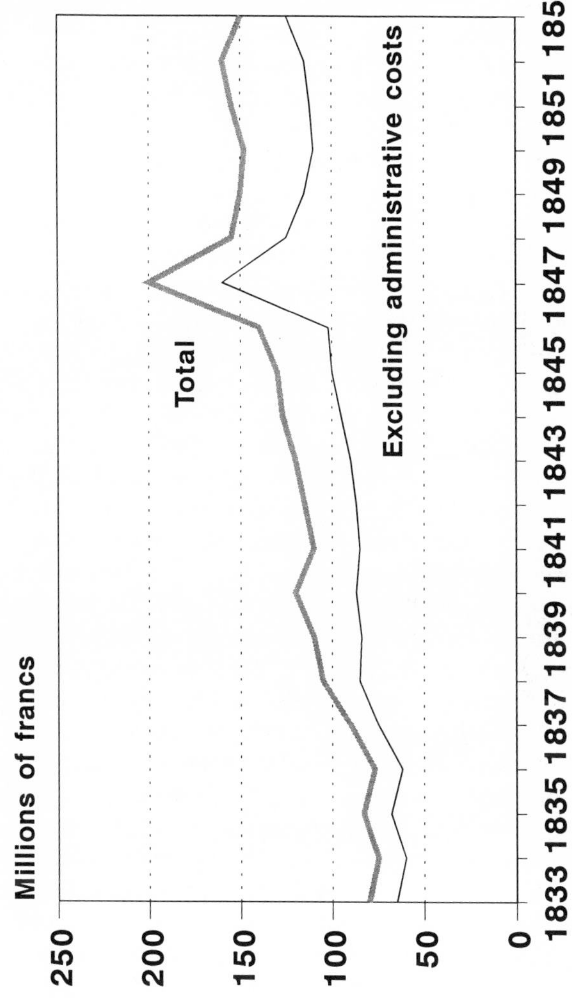

Source: Statistique de la France: Administration publique, 2nd Series, 6, Statistique de l'assistance publique, 1861, p. xxix.

refuse indigents, incapable of buying a whole loaf of bread, any smaller leftover quantities without charge.''[16]

But the response of Nantes and other French cities to episodic hardship carried a connotation different from comparable measures in Dutch cities, which, after all, also subsidized potato prices during emergencies or maintained a *gemeente broodzetting*, a municipal agency charged with stipulating local bread prices on a regular basis.[17] These French measures underscored the more cyclical nature of public concern with poverty and hunger in comparison with the Dutch case, and they persisted much longer. In the Netherlands, city magistrates began to voice doubts about the wisdom of interfering in the pricing mechanism of food in the marketplace, because all intrusive or coercive measures were ''detrimental, even deadly, to commerce.'' In the best of all possible worlds, Dutch city officials hoped, local avenues of supply and demand, ample work, and a smoothly functioning economic infrastructure would ensure the availability of food for the poor at a reasonable cost, without ever again having to tamper with prices: ''government efforts to purchase food or to prohibit food exports make things worse, because they are inefficient and disrupt the market price.''[18] Hence, the practice of municipal food subsidies in Holland became obsolete more quickly than in French cities, which clung to the old-fashioned routine of granting bread subsidies either to deflect or to co-opt potential social unrest.

Imprecise evaluations suggest that the French *bureaux de bienfaisance* during the crisis years of the late 1840s provided outdoor relief that amounted to a national average of 10.42 francs annually, increasing to 12.70 francs when administrative costs were added for each recipient.[19] These trifling amounts allowed a famished poor person to buy little more than some extra loaves of bread in the course of a year. The 1841 census indicated that nationally the *bureaux de bienfaisance* managed to donate an average of 10.60 francs per pauper yearly. In the department of the Seine this sum rose as high as 26.26 francs, and in the industrial regions of the department of the Nord it fell as low as 6.76 francs.[20] Conservative critics, though, wailed and moaned that the Parisian amount was twice as high: one of them claimed that ''unconditional'' relief had skyrocketed to no less than 50 francs per head![21]

Elsewhere in the country charitable gifts to the poor represented a mere pittance. However, few ornery conservatives displayed an inclination to exaggerate the amounts provided in rural departments; after all, orthodox solutions to pauperism in France often lionized the gentle existence of peasants in the countryside and advocated urban paupers' return to a peaceful life of tilling the soil. The minimal costs of poor relief in rural departments, it seemed, confirmed flawed reasoning: since charitable donations in rural areas were dramatically lower than in cities, there must be much less poverty in the countryside! In 1855, the minimum allocated per recipient in the different communities of the department of Côte-d'Or was a pathetic 1.27 francs per annum; in the department of Mayenne it was 1.26 francs and in the department of Doubs the smallest figure was the paltry amount of 1.40 francs.[22]

Aside from relatively low levels of *secours à domicile*, in comparison with the Dutch situation French charitable practices also placed greater emphasis on enclosing and superintending the poor in well-guarded institutions that were expensive to maintain. This fact prompted Adrien de Gasparin, the Minister of the Interior in 1837, to wonder anxiously whether "all our charitable funds are used to a maximum advantage in this day and age? The preponderance of aid provided in an institutional framework rather than at home makes our whole system more costly." The minister hit the nail of the head: institutionalized assistance not only required more personnel and more money, it also dislodged society's poor from the sheltering warmth of their families and eroded protective kinship relations. As Gasparin observed, "It is certain that the system of *hospices* has a tendency to ruin family ties. Would it not be more expedient to replace hospitals and poorhouses with a system of domestic poor relief, while reserving poorhouses for the handicapped and the aged, and hospitals for those who are ill?"[23]

A few years later, in a *circulaire* to the nation's prefects in 1840, Charles de Rémusat, a subsequent Minister of the Interior, repeated the exact same warning in almost identical language: "each new day, experience shows that the system of hospitals relaxes, if not destroys, family ties."[24] And an article in the *Journal des économistes* in 1845 proclaimed unambiguously that *secours à domicile* was a superior mode of soothing misery, a "superiority that has never been contested in theory but which is often ignored in practice." When indigents were left alone, within the affectionate embrace of their families, poor relief neither disrupted their obligations of kinship nor removed them from a well-entrenched "patronage network and employment opportunities." If the poor were allowed to stay at home, the state could be "a better judge of allocating support on the basis of genuine need. In contrast, when a multitude of hospitals and poorhouses are established in which the indigent classes will be confined, then they will stay there for once and forever."[25]

A distinct genre of implausible and, above all, fantastic stories about the luxury lavished upon lazy paupers in charitable institutions inspired cranky conservatives' fancy. French benevolent organizations presumably constituted a "coordinated whole" which cared for indigents from "cradle to grave." When following the life cycle of an individual pauper, a reactionary Frenchman wrote tendentiously in 1846, we "will see him born among foundlings. From there he graduates first to the nursery and then to an orphanage; at the age of six he goes off to primary school and later to adult schools." Hyppolyte-Ernest du Touquet continued his theatrical narrative by asserting that if his prototypical pauper could not work, he was placed on the poor relief rolls of his district, and if he fell ill, he could choose among twelve hospitals. Finally, "when this poor Parisian reaches the end of his sorry career, seven almshouses await him and often their salubrious regime will prolong his useless days well beyond those of a rich man."[26]

Despite reactionaries colorful critiques as well as the better judgment of policymakers about costs and efficacy, the proportion of French indigents receiving institutionalized relief in *hospices* and hospitals during the period between 1833 and 1852 was substantial. When compared to annual ratios in the Netherlands, poorhouses in France immured a much greater percentage of indigents relative to those who obtained outdoor relief from the *bureaux de bienfaisance* (see Figure 7-2).

Poor people receiving *secours à domicile* did outnumber paupers in institutions, but only by a factor of two to one. The proportion of people who collected outdoor relief in France rose from 923,347 in 1846 to 1,185,632 in 1847—when the impact of the harvest failures and subsistence crisis was wreaking havoc—while the number of indigents in poorhouses and hospitals increased from 593,112 to 628,937.[27] Thus, the number of outdoor relief recipients was nearly twice that of institutionalized indigents, even during periods of acute economic crisis. These figures confirm, of course, that the expenditures on *secours à domicile*, along with those on public works, were more responsive to sudden changes in economic conditions and food supplies than institutionalized aid. Given the physical and structural limits imposed upon *hospices*, which minimized their capacity to expand on an ad hoc basis during emergencies, this pattern makes eminent sense.

Policymakers in France inadvertantly disregarded, or deliberately defied, the irrefutable logic that outdoor relief was much cheaper, infinitely more efficient, and also more supportive of family cohesion. But institutional relief as opposed to *secours à domicile* sequestered the poor in specific locations that rendered them easier to count, classify, and taxonomize—a habit increasingly dear to the heart of the central state. It also utilized the well-entrenched network of poorhouses and

Figure 7-2

People Institutionalized in France

1833 - 1852

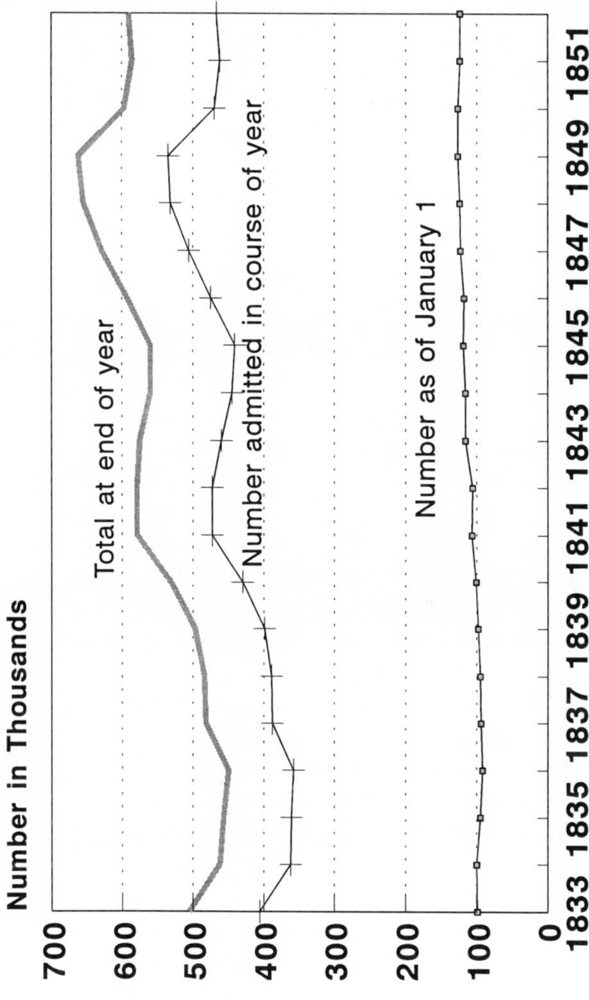

Source: Statistique de la France: Administration publique, 2nd Series, 6, Statistique de l'assistance publique, 1861, p. lxvii.

hospitals which the Catholic Church managed and supported, in part, with the financial donations collected from the faithful who attended mass on Sundays. Relying on *hospices* and *hôpitaux* enabled government officials indirectly to keep a watchful eye on indigents' behavior, whether they were able-bodied or invalids, old or young, but did not force the public sector to address the underlying issues of unemployment, labor migration, and urban concentration that comprised the crux of the problem of pauperism.

Perhaps the relative emphasis on institutional charity serves as evidence of the French state's interest in molding and shaping the conduct of poor workers in order to render it more predictable. The qualms about giving outdoor relief could also be related to French misgivings about the spontaneous flow of an unrestrained capitalist market which might push workers into startling directions and reinforce their unruly tendencies. But the nation's chaotic assortment of hospitals and poorhouses did not really operate as the backbone of a diabolical "carceral network," designed purely to solidify bourgeois hegemony.[28]

It was true that the emphasis on institutional support was part and parcel of the expanding regulatory role of a central state deeply invested in preserving the public peace. The number of civil servants actually engaged in the business of surveillance and law enforcement multiplied, too, and between 1789 and the middle of the nineteenth century the state reinvented itself as an even more palpable presence in the life of the average French citizen, whether rich or poor, whether urban or rural. On the eve of the Revolution in 1789, for instance, only 3,000 men had made up the French countryside's understaffed *maréchaussée*, a figure that soared to 15,000 during the July Monarchy.[29] In several big cities, local prefectures of police swelled in size and brandished a newly found professional zeal. Urban elites, meanwhile, eager to secure protection against what they perceived to be teeming crowds of raucous paupers, obscene vagabonds, and tawdry prostitutes, tolerated the police's growing use and abuse of their arbitrary powers.[30]

But the nation's orphanages, poorhouses, hospitals for unmarried mothers-to-be, or boardinghouses for Auvergnat chimney sweeps or teenage girls rescued from prostitution, along with police lockups, prisons, and correctional colonies for juvenile delinquents, composed a hodgepodge of local institutions. Rather than presenting a streamlined and smoothly functioning nationwide "network of surveillance," these Catholic and private philanthropic organizations, given their diversity in size, constituency, or significance, formed a highly irregular institutional landscape. French political culture, however, fostered the idea of the pivotal importance of the central state in Paris. Despite their internal diversity, the many poor relief institutions buttressed, willy-nilly and in asymmetrical fashion, the imaginary pyramid of political authority, which the state tried to monitor from its elevated perch on top.

It is no surprise, then, that almost all institutions for the needy were concentrated in cities. In 1855 a physician who cared for indigent patients registered his dismay about the lopsided geographical distribution of hospitals and poorhouses. In certain departments, he lamented, hospitals were too numerous; in others, sick poor people had to travel long distances to find a single one. *Hospices* were even more unevenly spread than *hôpitaux*, and almost none were available in rural areas. Heavily urban departments such as the Seine and the Nord provided "a joint total of 13,472 beds in poorhouses. In others, like Corsica and the Creuse, one can count only a few: a grand total of only 31 beds for the two departments combined."[31]

Charitable institutions in urban areas, of course, attended to the steady stream of rural inhabitants who had recently migrated and were at risk of drowning in the moral cesspool of a city such as Paris, unless they were rescued and supported. Paris had become a sinister place, George Sand wrote in 1846, a "hell on earth" with a rigid "caste system" that allowed the rich to live in ostentatious luxury like oriental potentates while the poor had to grovel for a chance to work and scramble for scraps of food.[32] Experience had further shown that "real" revolutions almost always erupted in cities; as a preemptive measure, urban poor relief could function as a safety valve by relieving anguish, suppressing crime, and pacifying working-class discontent. Moreover, popular wisdom held that poverty was less pervasive in the countryside, where hungry but unemployed day laborers or migrants had an immediate connection with the abundance of nature. At least they could live off fruits or chestnuts found on the side of the road, city folks claimed, eat squirrels or birds caught in fields and forests, or even consume chickens stolen from unsuspecting farmers.

As usual, political illusions overshadowed the realities of deep-seated rural poverty because peasants, after all, embodied a quintessential French identity. Besides, the quietly suffering *prolétaires des champs* generated fewer political anxieties than did the seemingly growing hordes of shiftless men and licentious women in big cities. The desolate lives of the rural poor scattered throughout the countryside, the mercurial critic Eugène Buret pointed out, were fragmented, harmless, and above all invisible. While bureaucrats in Paris confronted the troubling effects of the city's pauperism in their mundane day-to-day routines, the heart-wrenching travails of peasants in distant rural *pays* could be inscribed with any kind of meaning.[33] Hence, it made sense to channel most resources toward the urban poor, who indulged in a lifetime of sexual promiscuity in shabby quarters not far from elegant bourgeois neighborhoods: they were the ones who disrupted the elite's equanimity.

Sexual discipline and family stability, well-meaning philanthropists thought, could best be reinforced by fostering notions of proper womanhood and extending middle-class conceptions of respectable femininity to impoverished working-class wives. Accordingly, the *Société maternelle*, a venerable French organization devoted to providing charity directly to impoverished women, nourished mothers-to-be and helped them during childbirth and convalescence. Originally founded in 1788 by Madame de Fougeret, the *Société* floundered during the Revolution only to be revived in 1801. Within 30 years the Society of Maternal Charity in Paris had distributed a grand total of 1,824,020.41 francs. By showering poor mothers with "wholesome advise, guiding them with sweet exhortations, evoking sentiments of piety, and by giving them new hope, the members of the *Société* engender in the souls of these unfortunate women a greater sense of peace. Through the virtue of constancy, the rich align themselves with the poor, who forge emotional bonds with the rich by recognizing the *Société maternelle* ladies' goodwill."[34] Women were "more susceptible to tenderness," wrote Charles Dupin, an official at the *Cour des comptes*, in 1821, and did not require the same "austere" measures as men; hence, the *Société* members' kindness nurtured mothers and rescued their legitimate, but delicate, offspring and sheltered them from "abandonment."[35]

Aristocratic and bourgeois women administered and controlled the *Société*, both in Paris and elsewhere; they were upper-class wives, who were spiritually attached to the Catholic Church and dedicated to the idea of *noblesse oblige* or middle-class magnanimity. The *dames patronesses* saw their labors of love on behalf of poverty-stricken pregnant women as a natural extension of both their domestic assignment as mothers and their spiritual mission as devout Catholics.[36] The aristocratic and bourgeois women who subscribed to the *Société* thus participated in a concerted effort to solidify the working-class family and to reinforce family sentiments. They only fulfilled the needs of poor women who were properly married and had proved their impeccable moral conduct, even if they lived in "sad households" that suffered from a "timid but virtuous poverty." Rather than entering a poorhouse or hospital, an indigent pregnant wife, both before and after childbirth, would be nursed at home under the benevolent care of the well-to-do Society ladies, who ventured boldly into working-class slums to bring food, clothing, and moralizing lessons: "The *Société maternelle* assists the indigents and watches over the morals and cohesiveness of the family by soothing their pain and succoring their needs."[37]

The triumphant growth of the *Société* joined the expanding ranks of other local philanthropies specifically dedicated to the improvement of the moral conduct of female *domestiques*, young women rescued from concubinage, or impressionable waifs from the rural countryside who had recently arrived in the city.[38] But this particular Society of Maternal Charity blossomed throughout urban France. The Annual Report of 1814 submitted to the Empress-Protector and Honorary President of the *Société maternelle* announced that "the Society has undergone a rapid growth since its inception. More than fifty administrative councils are brimming with activity, reaping the benefits of an institution so precious to humanity." In 1818 many large cities in France had at least one Society of Maternal Charity and most continued to flourish throughout the nineteenth century, if only because government subsidies, as a supplement to private subscriptions, generously funded the many Societies.[39]

The Parisian *Filature des indigents*, a charitable spinning workshop which employed only poor women and girls, fit the same pattern of focusing on the moral discipline of working-class women. Although it was a financially troubled institution, the *Filature* constituted an enduring experiment in work provision. In contrast, the erratic existence of charitable workshops for indigent men revealed a constant ebb and flow, partly because they were expensive but also owing to the French ambivalence about giving men special treatment. After all, subsidized employment violated the hallowed principle of free and equal competition between full-fledged citizens, whether rich or poor. Women, because of their political disenfrachisement, were deserving of both special support and protective measures. As the workshop's annual report (*compte moral*) mentioned in 1820: "this establishment has been founded for the principal purpose of providing employment to indigent women of all ages who cannot procure work elsewhere. Because we spread so many benefits among this miserable class of women, we have to resign ourselves most willingly to the financial losses that this institution suffers annually."[40]

The *Filature des indigents*, which produced thread and linens for poorhouses and hospitals in Paris, employed 2,562 women at a pathetic daily wage of 25 centimes when it was reconstituted in 1814. During the first years administrators complained endlessly about losing money; in 1821, for instance, the *compte moral* stated that the expenditures of the *Filature* had exceeded the income by "only" 68,536 francs: "this improvement can be attributed to a more orderly system of work and to a more careful selection of raw materials. There is no doubt that this positive trend will continue. We should remember, however, that the *Filature* is not an agency of commercial speculation but, rather, a means of support for poor women who lack work. During 1821, 2,653 women have been employed for 324 days out of the year at a wage of 8 centimes per day." The report went on to declare, with an unintentional touch of irony, that it would be impossible to spread "so much goodness at a lower cost!"[41] In 1822 the annual loss had been reduced once more "because production has been wisely adjusted to the needs and demands of the buyers. We trust that the *Filature des indigents* will eventually recover its own basic expenditures and even make profits in the future."[42]

In the succeeding years, the annual *comptes moraux* began to sound an optimistic note about the economic viability of the *Filature*. In 1828 it stated that "the institution has provided work to 2,511 women, being 2,415 spinners and 96 weavers of whom 24 work in the workshop itself and 72 are employed in their homes." A competent spinner could presumably earn as much as 50 or 75 centimes per day, although the information on annual wages revealed a much lower average. The 1828 report proudly announced that the *Filature des indigents* manufactured thread of excellent quality: "The experts charged with setting the sales price are uniquely convinced that one cannot find any thread at a similar price in the commercial market that is manufactured as well and yields cloth that is as durable." Administrators also acknowledged that it might make more economic sense to set up a spinning workshop in "the countryside outside Paris, where labor is so much cheaper. But this would eliminate the employment opportunities for poor Parisian women, and thereby defy the basic purpose of the *Filature des indigents*."[43] The report for 1843 stated that whenever the spinning workshop incurred financial losses, they arose from the high cost of manual labor "at a time when commercial enterprises have substituted economical machines for this ancient practice and they achieve, as a result, a higher rate of return." The report gloated, however, that the products of the *Filature des indigents* were regarded as "infinitely superior in quality, and that more than 4,000 spinners have earned an aggregate wage of 130,000 to 150,000 francs."[44]

The number of women employed in the charitable spinning workshop varied from year to year and reached a peak in 1849, when 7,258 women labored in the *Filature*. Although the data on wages earned in the charitable spinning workshop are incomplete, they were dismally low in comparison to male wages, even if they approximated contemporaries' estimates of women's wages in the free market.[45] Given the stability of the *Filature des indigents*, which serviced the steady demand for linens of all the *hospices* and *hôpitaux* of Paris, some women may have voluntarily chosen the predictability of employment in the *Filature* over higher potential earnings elsewhere. Figure 7-3 reveals that the fluctuations in the number of women who sought employment in the *Filature des indigents* conformed to variations in the price of bread.

Similar *ateliers* exclusively for women were established in the silk industry of Lyons. Bourgeois silk merchants granted loans to purchase machinery, and nuns managed and supervised the women workers. Convents, in fact, appeared well-suited for the employment of poor women, with profitable results; the nuns disciplined their unruly female *canutes* (silk workers) with an iron fist and presumably converted them into obedient, morally upstanding, and hardworking women. The convents further provided cheap food and lodgings for their women workers, thus allowing the nuns to pay only a fraction of the average wages paid to silk weavers elsewhere.[46] Although the silk-weaving establishments in convents were technically charitable workshops, in Lyons they competed directly with freemarket industries and aroused the ire of male silk weavers, who accused the nuns of engaging in unfair competition and exploiting women like greedy, profit-maximizing employers.[47]

In the Netherlands, work institutes exclusively for women were rare; in general, they tended to employ men, women, and children as family units. Neither did the *Société maternelle* thrive to the same extent as it prospered in France.[48] After the incorporation of the Dutch provinces into the Napoleonic Empire, a lively correspondence about the *Société* ensued between Prefect de Celles of the *département du ZuyderZée* and the *sous préfet* in Haarlem. So eager was the French prefect of the Zuiderzee to build a vibrant Society of Maternal Charity in Haarlem, as he wrote to his *sous préfet* on December 18, 1812, that he had invited all the ladies who had subscribed for 500 francs or more to come to his residence for a friendly visit.[49] Despite the prefect's high-minded hopes—not acknowledging, perhaps, that his Dutch subjects may have deplored his political presence—the Society in Haarlem did not take root and blossom to the same degree as it did in Paris and other French cities, because many Dutch women declined the offer of membership.

The subprefect of Haarlem had approached most of the wives of the

Figure 7-3

Women Employed and Annual Wages

Filature des indigents, Paris, 1814 - 1850

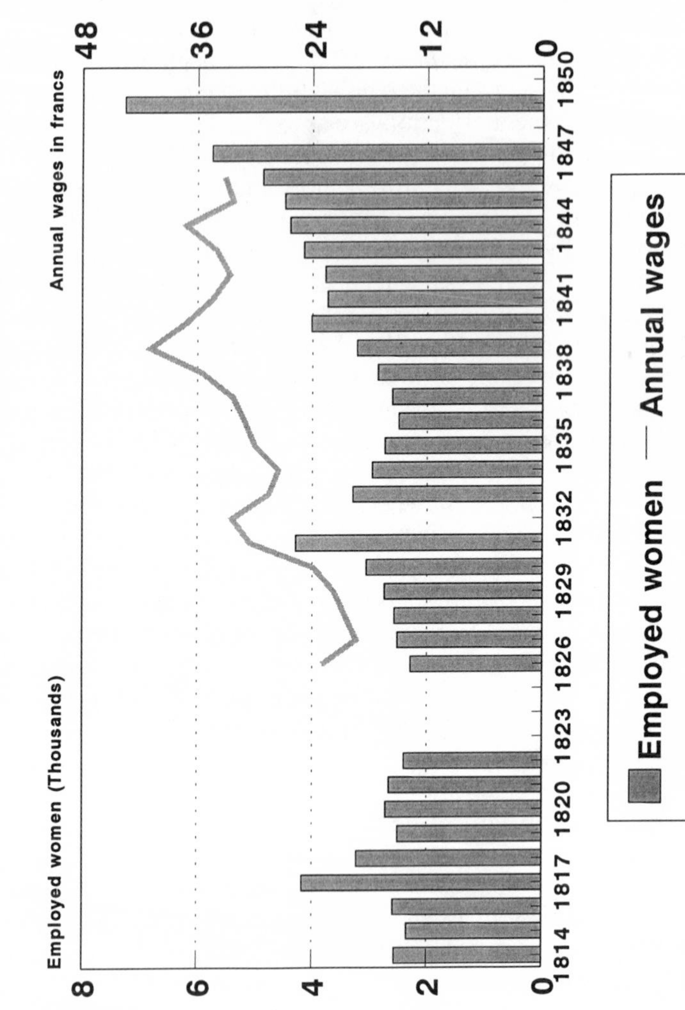

Source: Notes sur la filature des indigents.

local elite, but many among them used financial troubles as an excuse not to join. ''I cannot accept your offer owing to the considerable diminution of our fortune, even if the number of poverty-stricken people around us augments every day,'' wrote Madame H. Lewe *née* Gerlacius to the subprefect.[50] ''Being an elderly widow living off the interests and revenues of lands and possessions, the reduction in my income has placed me in a precarious position,'' claimed Madame Canter Camerling *née* Heshuyzen, whereas Mademoiselle H. J. Teding van Berkhout responded that the invitation to join the society had flattered her honor, but she, too, could not subscribe because her revenues had ''shrunk considerably'' and it was impossible to contribute to this ''pious institution.''[51]

Other wives of the Haarlem elite did have the financial resources to pay the annual 500 francs membership fee and they subscribed out of a sense of compassion: ''since the number of poor people in our environment increases daily,'' responded Madame P. P. H. Barnaart *née* Teding van Berkhout, ''I cannot deny myself the satisfaction of becoming a member of such an interesting Society that is so useful to suffering humanity.''[52] Many of the women's letters to the subprefect, though, referred to the general desperation of Haarlem's indigent residents and to the scores of charitable institutions already solidly intertwined in the social fabric of the city and actively engaged in helping the poor. It seemed as if they could not fathom the creation of yet another charitable organization, even if its focus would be exclusively on poverty-stricken mothers. As the *douairière* Wijckerslooth van Weerdesteijn *née* Ram van Schalkwijk noted in her letter of regret: ''We have a great number of people in our community who must rely on the generosity of charitable citizens. Those who suffer under our eyes appear to be most sacredly and justifiably entitled to our help, and I therefore want to continue to try to support them to the extent my [financial] holdings allow.''[53]

As soon as Napoleon's Dutch possessions were transformed into the Kingdom of the Netherlands many of the attempts to create or maintain societies of maternal charity dissipated, although the fledgling one in Haarlem survived, as did the one in Rotterdam. In Rotterdam the society lived on with the precociously feminist name of *Genootschap voor Vrouwen door Vrouwen* (Association of Women for Women). The special government Commission on Poverty and Poor Relief, which King William I convened in 1816, again considered the merits of the societies of maternal charity. The Commission noted that in areas where the number of midwives was insufficient, it was ''necessary to provide special help to poor pregnant women.'' Otherwise the commission recommended that simple outdoor relief be dispensed ''in order to relieve the costs of childbirth.''[54]

The royal Commission on Poverty and Poor Relief gave the societies only a lukewarm endorsement, and during the following decade few significant new organizations for pregnant indigent women were established. The administrator of poor relief in the Ministry of the Interior engaged in a final effort to revive the maternal societies when he wrote on March 7, 1828, to public officials at the provincial level: ''The societies of maternal charity ought to be regarded as extremely useful in providing temporary care and nourishment to poor mothers and their newborn babies. Only two such institutions exist in the northern Netherlands, in Haarlem and Rotterdam, and I have the honor to encourage you to cooperate with any municipality that might desire to institute an organization with such dignified goals.''[55]

Although he distributed an elaborate sample of regulations in June 1828, stipulating the eligibility requirements for indigent mothers-to-be, no more than a handful of municipalities created organizations of this sort in response to the official's suggestion.[56] At mid-century a women's association called *Dorcas* nurtured and visited the poor in Middelburg, while in Groningen a women's organization secured seamstress work for working-class girls on consignment.[57] Other *Arbeid Adelt* associations—meaning ''labor ennobles''—in a variety of cities commissioned needy women to stitch and embroider under the tutelage of middle-class matrons, who arranged for the sale of their fine handicrafts and distributed the profits, but on the whole, the wives of Dutch notables did not embrace feminine charity with the same devotion and enthusiasm as did affluent women in France.

In the Netherlands, church *diaconiëen* absorbed the bulk of private charitable gifts and personal efforts. It was true that various middle-class societies of ''friendly visitors'' inspired faithful Christians to become more personally involved in the *mission civilisatrice* of charity; they reached out to particular working-class families in order to go beyond the simple gesture of financial sacrifice. The stalwart liberal economist Jeronimo de Bosch Kemper, for example, founded and personally financed an organization called *De Vriend van Armen en Rijken* (Friend of the Poor and the Rich), designed to help poor people achieve self-sufficiency. In a weekly publication he offered information about savings banks, libraries, and job opportunities, as if he was trying to create an early employment bureau.[58]

Dutch propaganda in favor of direct bourgeois patronage, in fact, was borrowed directly from the ideas of colleagues in France, such as Joseph-Marie de Gérando, or from the Scottish Presbyterian minister Thomas Chalmers. It prompted the spontaneous creation of a variety of friendly visiting societies, which tried to reach out to the poor on a highly personalized basis. But the earnest advocate of middle-class patronage and the chairman of the Amsterdam Association for Assistance to the Honest and Diligent Poor, W. H. Suringar, offered the wry commentary that the poor would be annoyed at having to listen to all these individualized ''moralizing lessons'' if they received only a tiny sum of money for their patience.[59] In general, the humanitarian impulses of Dutch men and women were funneled through the nation's well-entrenched network of church *diaconieën* and ancient municipal agencies. Their long-standing and well-established rituals of benevolence and gratitude, imbricating prosperous burghers with those who were down-and-out, may have yielded the impression that additional philanthropic ventures such as the *Société maternelle* were redundant.

The financial patterns of Dutch charity exhibited a picture different from France. The data on budgetary outlays shown in Figure 7-4 reveal the regularity of the Dutch commitment to support the indigent members of society during the period 1829–1848, which contrasted with the oscillations in French poor relief efforts during this period. In Holland both private and public allocations for outdoor relief increased at a steady pace: the upward trend was constant and smooth, with only slightly exceptional disbursements in the crisis year of 1847, followed by retrenchment. The financial holdings and endowments of private charitable organizations generated approximately 30 percent of the annual funds spent on outdoor relief. Individual donors contributed a similar share, whereas municipal subsidies made up the remaining portion of about 35 percent. The national government in The Hague allocated only a marginal amount, and its share never surpassed 1 or 2 percent. Although the expenditures of the Dutch state increased somewhat during the subsistence crisis of 1845–1847, this emergency expansion did not rise as sharply as did municipal expenditures. These figures thus reveal the extent to which the *diaconieën* and municipalities carried the lion's share of caring for the poor in Holland during normal times as well as periods of extraordinary material distress.

The data on total expenditures on poor relief in the Netherlands from 1829 to 1838—including outdoor relief as well as support for the agricultural colonies of the *Maatschappij van Weldadigheid*, hospitals, poorhouses, and workhouses—indicate that public financing, almost entirely from municipalities, contributed a little more than one-fourth of

Figure 7-4
Expenditures on Outdoor Relief in the Netherlands 1829-1848

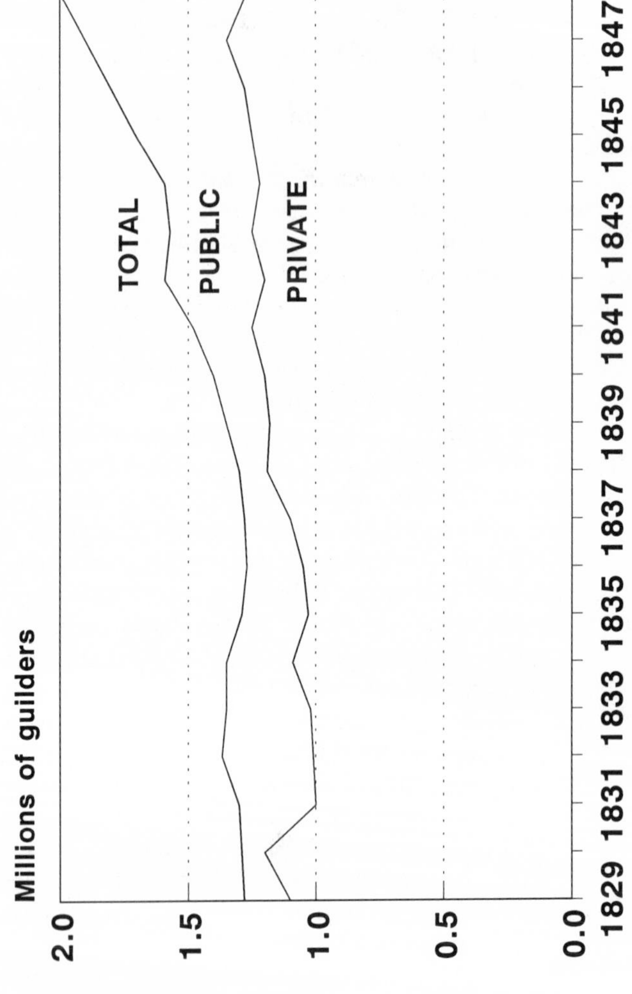

Source: J. de Bosch Kemper, Geschiedkundig onderzoek, 1851, Appendix.

the overall national budget for poor relief. The other three-fourths derived from private and religious sources. On the whole, outdoor relief constituted a much larger share than institutional relief. In Amsterdam, for instance, about 90 percent of the people on regular assistance received outdoor relief between 1829 and 1854, whereas the Dutch Reformed *diaconie* in Rotterdam in 1828 allocated 81 percent of its resources to outdoor relief.[60]

The differences in the consistency of poor relief expenditures over time in the Netherlands vis-à-vis France do not contradict the finding that the percentage of the population receiving poor relief corresponded more closely to economic fluctuations in France than in Holland. The money allocated to poor relief is a measure of policy intent, whereas the proportion of the population that actually received some form of aid is a measure of the efficacy of policy, or policy outcome. Because the Dutch poor relief system had more consistent financial support over time, it was equipped to answer the needs of a larger number of indigents temporarily affected by economic adversity, even though a greater number of poor people might have to make do with relatively stable resources (see Figure 7-5).

On a per capita basis, nationwide Dutch charitable support was more dependable, if not slightly more generous, than in France. Owing to the lack of precise statistics, any kind of measurement constitutes risky business, even if several historians have boldly ventured a guess. Joel Mokyr, in his *Industrialization in the Low Countries, 1795–1850*, estimated total Dutch expenses for poor relief in 1822 to be 5,593,000 guilders; he calculated that per capita expenditure was a mere 2.47 guilders in that year.[61] It seems doubtful that this inconsequential sum produced a situation in which Dutch workers voluntarily chose to subsist on charity because they preferred leisure over real work. Reports issued by the city of Haarlem at mid-century suggested that the aggregate annual allocation of outdoor relief per recipient was around 10 guilders; the *diaconie* of the *gereformeerde* congregation alone had provided 8.05 guilders in 1826, although its per capita allocations declined to 6.75 guilders in 1844 owing to the stability of financial resources in the face of a burgeoning number of needy people.[62] Jan de Meere has computed that the average yearly sum granted to poor residents in the province of Noord-Holland between 1832 and 1850 amounted to a measly 6.69 guilders per year, even though the average sums provided in the provinces of Zuid-Holland and Friesland were dramatically higher: 16.52 and 16.65 guilders respectively.[63] In Amsterdam, in fact, the monetary value of outdoor relief declined steadily from 16 guilders in

Figure 7-5

Recipients of Temporary or Permanent Outdoor Relief in the Netherlands

1832-1849

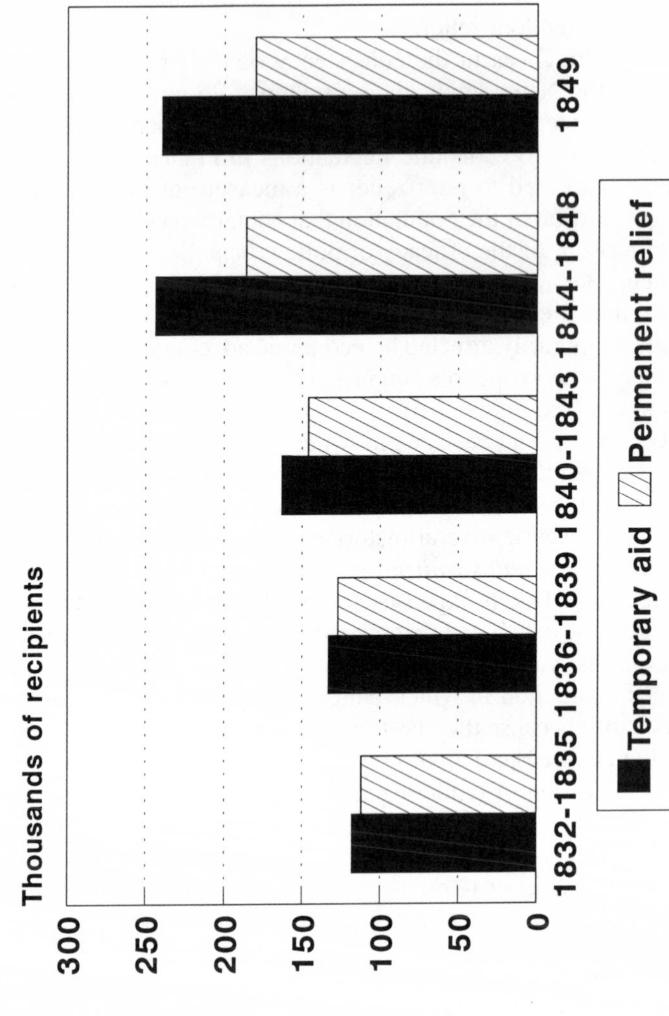

Source: Simon Vissering, Herinneringen, 1863, p. 208.

1804 to hover around the more trifling amount of 6 guilders until mid-century.[64]

In terms of national expenditures, the Frenchman Alexandre Monnier speculated about the Dutch situation in 1850 that "the total revenue and holdings of all private charitable institutions in the Netherlands generate about 6 million guilders per annum, which is the equivalent of 13 million francs."[65] But according to a special parliamentary commission of the Second Chamber of the Estates-General, appointed in October 1852, the combined level of expenditure of both private and public poor relief in 1850 amounted to 12,439,000 guilders. "This seems high for a population of 3,073,411 souls," the report noted. "Taking into account that a total of 424,514 people received outdoor relief in 1850 while 18,775 indigents are institutionalized in poorhouses, it means that between one-sixth and one-seventh of the total Dutch population is maintained at charitable expense."[66] This calculation also implied that each poor person received an average of 28.06 guilders in 1850, which seems eerily inflated.

Whether nineteenth-century observers or modern historians generated this "arithmetic" of sorrow and need, the actual numbers ranged far and wide, since hidden administrative costs, contradictory and incomplete data, or inadequate computational techniques burdened the outcomes. Nevertheless, the evidence suggests that Dutch allocations were somewhat more reliable than in France. However much Protestant ministers fulminated against any notion of *charité légale* under the auspices of secular authorities, Dutch practices still echoed the English allowance structure, which the new British Poor Law had resolutely abolished in 1833.

The Speenhamland system had "indexed" monetary relief on the basis of food prices, thereby attempting to guarantee that every poor person in England would be able to maintain a minimal physical existence.[67] The predictability of municipal and private charitable help in Dutch society tried to moderate the insecurity of existence for its poorest members in a similar fashion, even if the size of these payments was a far cry from either fulfilling daily nutritional needs or approximating the dismally low wages of unskilled workers. But the fact remains that poor relief in Holland, more so than in France, did as much as it could to sustain the unlucky members of society during their greatest hour of need. Dutch charitable efforts, by extending a helping hand to society's poorest citizens, maintained a reservoir of labor that could be mobilized again when the economic tide turned. Albeit in an extremely low-key fashion, charity served as a form of "mutual insurance" and "equalization''—as an institutional buffer for those whose survival was most precarious due to a contraction of employment opportunities.[68]

Dutch charitable agencies dispensing outdoor relief consistently outnumbered actual institutions which housed and enclosed the poor by a factor of seven or eight to one. In 1846, for example, poorhouses sheltered only 26,645 Dutch indigents—18 percent of Dutch poor relief recipients in that particular year—while 468,656 people received some form of support at home.[69] In France, during the same year, those in *hospices* numbered 593,112, or 27.2 percent of the officially designated pauper population, whereas 923,347 indigents acquired outdoor poor relief. These differences speak for themselves.

In the Netherlands, concerns about the role of the family and kinship structures among the poor also struck a different chord. Many French social critics were obsessed with the immorality of the poor or bemoaned their inherently uncouth nature. Public officials condemned the widespread French practice of labor migration as responsible for loose family ties, but closed their eyes to the unhappy circumstances that forced migrants to leave their native *pays* in search of a better life. Yet others, ironically, agitated against the insidious effects of institutionalization on the stability of the working-class family. Intellectuals and policymakers in Holland, in contrast, voiced more concerns about the size of the average indigent family rather than the decline of filial relationships and mutual obligations. Demographic expansion had outstripped the available means of existence, Dutch observers intoned, and for this the poor bore the primary responsibility.

The causal connection between demographic growth and the inexorable expansion of charity was painfully obvious to Dutch observers. They put forth a flurry of ideas to contain the dramatic growth of the population, which many of them attributed to the carefree behavior of the poor who married too young and procreated like rabbits.[70] Respectable Dutch burghers bandied about a jumble of policy ideas that might restrain further population growth or make its effects less palpable, including land reclamation, encouraging emigration overseas, or even the dubious plea that unemployed workers dependent on charity be prohibited from marrying at all.[71]

Colonization schemes focused on ''our'' Dutch East Indies, where, because of its glorious climate, ''one can cultivate the most wonderful crops such as tobacco, rice, corn, coffee, pepper, sago, nutmeg.'' Hundreds of thousands of English people depart each year for the British colonies in Asia and elsewhere. In Germany, too, in excess of ''200,000 colonists leave their fatherland every year to eat the bread of poverty and to toil in the sweltering tropical heat on the flat plains of Texas'' where they also bring Christendom and civilization, Otto Gerhard Heldring exclaimed with an evangelical call for a Dutch national *réveil.* We, however, ''are the only ones who stay [at home].''[72] Moreover, urban overpopulation could also be relieved through domestic colonization schemes, which materialized with the creation of the *Maatschappij van Weldadigheid* (Benevolent Society) in 1818.

Clearly, demographic pressures were a steady source of concern. In the *Annual Report on the Status of the Poor* for 1817, Minister of the Interior de Coninck noted matter-of-factly that ''in our country, as is the case everywhere in Europe, the growth of prosperity is inevitably accompanied by a growth of the population, especially among the lower orders.''[73] The minister echoed the unambiguously Malthusian idiom of conservatives, who routinely invoked a series of gloomy clichés borrowed from the pessimistic English cleric. ''Because animals mate and multiply without rhyme or reason, they will consume all the fruits of the earth and ultimately annihilate themselves,'' wrote C. van Vollenhoven in 1819, but rational human beings should know better. Humans were capable of knowing that the reproduction of material resources and food could not keep pace with human procreation, that a human population would double in size within twenty-five years while the production of food would inevitably lag behind. This was ''an irrevocable truth,'' he said, and a failure to recognize it was the principal cause of poverty.[74]

While few French authors took the logic of Thomas Malthus's demographic arguments too seriously, with the exception, perhaps, of Frédéric Bastiat, foreboding Malthusian warnings resonated in Holland throughout the first half of the nineteenth century and surfaced as a hackneyed refrain: ''populations have a natural propensity to exceed the expansion of a society's means of existence.''[75] Established Dutch burghers rebuked the poor for entering into marriage too often and too prematurely. Lower-class men, some self-righteous ministers exclaimed, possessed sexual appetites they could less easily bridle or suppress! Indigent men behaved like impulsive fools who failed to think about the serious business of obtaining a livelihood as a necessary precondition for marriage. Men from higher social circles would never engage in matrimony before achieving a certain status in society, which would ''give them the assurance they can support a wife and family,'' wrote the Protestant minister N. B. Donkersloot in 1849. A completely different set of circumstances existed among the destitute but irresponsible members of society. ''Without the least bit of worry about the future, without possessing a mere penny for the establishment of a household, the poor rush into marriage with abandon. Marriage thus becomes a prison of misery, and the average poor family ends up being totally dependent on poor relief.''[76]

In short, either overly generous poor relief or, paradoxically, extravagantly high working-class wages presumably prompted early marriages. Because the poor married too young, indigent women gave birth to too many children that survived infancy—a judgment that anticipated the more explicit eugenicist alarm voiced later in the century. Some critics proposed public intervention, and the introduction of the revised Civil Code in 1838 made such a gesture by raising women's minimum age at marriage.[77] Others invoked the moralizing influence of the church. Of course Dutchmen also worried about working-class concubinage and sexual debauchery, but not in the same prurient or voyeuristic way as their French counterparts. The most pressing concern was to curb the number of working-class marriages and to restrain marital fertility, a concern that entered the imagination of French social critics less often.

Holland was a densely urban society, much more so than France, and poor relief policies were naturally concerned with the misery of the indigent population in cities and towns. However, the ideological underpinnings of this urban focus seemed less political in nature than in France. Although an occasional Dutch writer considered the potentially atrocious outbursts that could erupt when the army of paupers in Dutch society swelled to ever growing proportions, pacification was not the dominant theme within Dutch officialdom.[78]

Instead, the pivotal question was how to restructure the economy in order to provide adequate employment for the poor. Equally important was the inculcation of dependable work habits and the assimilation of respectful moral values. Many Dutch burghers might have looked askance upon the French idea of impounding able-bodied but potentially volatile men in order to mollify or disarm them. This would be inefficient and, above all, would yield a bad rate of return on Dutch charitable investments. Besides, outdoor relief might spur poor people into action and prod them to find work; it would also bring some money back into circulation. Of course most observers were fully aware that it did not always work out that way. Nonetheless, payments in money or in kind, and work provision in charitable work institutes or in the colonies of the *Maatschappij van Weldadigheid*, were preferable to warehousing working-class men in *hospices*.

A spirited debate took place in the Netherlands as well as in France about the relative wisdom of providing charity in the form of either money or in kind. The officially favored mode was to distribute outdoor relief in commodities—food, clothing, or fuel—rather than monetary payments. In fact, article 25 of the new Dutch Poor Law of 1854 eventually specified that "as much as possible, assistance should not be allocated in money but should preferably consist of food, fuel, clothes, bedding, and housing."[79] Even though elementary economic analysis has shown that relief in kind is less beneficial to overall economic growth than money payments, authorities endorsed the allocation of commodities rather than money because it allowed them to impose their "preference structure" upon the poor.[80]

The desire to make payments in kind rather than in cash issued from a self-righteous and paternalistic attitude on the part of elites, who often thought that monetary relief would inevitably be wasted on self-destructive and foolish indulgences, especially alcohol. As the governor of the province of Noord-Holland reminded municipal administrators in a circular of March 23, 1826: "It is not only important to consider who receives assistance, but also how it is dispensed. Some agencies provide relief almost exclusively in money; others hardly ever give out money, but instead dole out food liberally. Without limiting themselves to primary needs, they add meat, bacon, butter, cheese, and all sorts of other luxuries. We think that both extremes ought to be avoided. Experience teaches, though, that money in the hands of the poor does not always reach the best destination, and it is sometimes even used for harmful purposes."[81]

Approximately two decades later a Dutch contemporary expressed the same opinion in somewhat blunter language. "Doling out money and alms publicly, at the doors of houses or in the open streets, is a bad habit. Such charity is not benevolent: it is a destructive activity that encourages sloth, idleness, and inebriation. However, when we give food and the necessary clothing we incur the smallest risk because, after all, we cannot allow the indigent to be personally responsible for spending his or her charitable support freely."[82]

Despite the preference for relief in kind it proved cumbersome, to say the least, for authorities to ensure a reliable supply of food, fuel, or simple items of clothing to the extent that assistance in kind could be procured and distributed whenever the poor needed them. As a result, more or less by default, outdoor relief was most often granted in the form of cash payments which indigents could spend in the marketplace as they pleased. Authorities agreed that in order to counter the fraudulent misconduct of potential free riders, relief to able-bodied adults ought to be granted only in exchange for labor rendered. Every charitable courtesy extended toward big, strong men should entail a quid pro quo of honest labor in order to instill a diligent work ethic and the appropriate moral discipline.

French officials would have agreed with these assessments and their reports echoed identical concerns: the poor who were "prevented from work because of infirmity or old age should receive bread, grain, and vegetable soup." Those who are healthy in body and mind should find their own subsistence through work in the localities where they live or elsewhere; "if they nonetheless make appeals to charity they cannot receive anything but a payment in kind in return for a day's productive work."[83]

The synthetic creation of work—in other words, the many trial-and-error experiments in Dutch pauper factories and work institutes or in French *ateliers de charité*, *dépôts de bienfaisance*, or *maisons de réfuge*—was a logical outcome of the fundamental assumption that poor relief should be given to the able-bodied only in exchange for productive labor. Questions about how these charitable workshops would function within the economic logic of society at large, however, boggled the minds of many high-minded administrators in either society. Since municipalities and private sources subsidized them, did workhouses engage in unfair competition with free enterprise? If indigent workers learned to fabricate textiles, for instance, how could workhouse officials guarantee a steady demand for the fruits of their labor? Besides, how could workshop managers encourage laborers to produce more than merely shoddy, incompetent workmanship? If overall economic conditions in society improved, would all the employees of pauper factories immediately wander away in search of higher earnings in the private sector, leaving behind ghostlike, empty charitable institutions with costly manufacturing equipment that was rendered idle? Moreover, given the uneven distribution of work institutes or *ateliers de charité*, would calculating but lazy indigent men simply appeal to less exacting sources of relief in the vicinity that did not require them to work in exchange for support? These quandaries frequently yielded a situation in which pauper factories put to work many children or elderly people rather than able-bodied men, perhaps because their behavior was more malleable and predictable.

In the Netherlands, an honorable tradition of providing employment opportunities to the poor was well entrenched by the beginning of the nineteenth century. Since the 1760s, workhouses had been founded in approximately forty communities. They provided employment to those who voluntarily asked for it, but they also functioned as a space in which obstreperous indigents could be forced to work in exchange for assistance. Many of the work institutes encompassed schools, too, and furnished vocational training as well as regular instruction in the hope of fostering basic literacy.[84]

During the very first years of the nineteenth century, when Johannes Goldberg, as the newly appointed *Agent van Nationale Economie*, set out on his fact-finding mission to study the economic conditions of the Netherlands, he encountered many enterprises with a uniquely philanthropic character. As he wrote in his journal, ''In Middelburg one can find a pauper factory where the poor spin flax and weave wall hangings, and which receives an annual municipal subsidy of 3,000 or 4,000 guilders.'' In the town of Bergen op Zoom, Goldberg was impressed by the activities of a thriving local chapter of the *Maatschappij tot Nut van het Algemeen* (Society for Public Welfare), which administered a ''work institute for the poor, with many children among them, in which they spin wool and knit stockings. The 130 children who are employed receive basic instruction in reading, writing, and arithmetic, and for the remaining time the boys comb and spin wool, while the youngest are engaged in plucking, and the girls are busily knitting stockings. Every pair of stockings yields 5 *stuivers*, and the children's labor generated profits that are reinvested in the *Instituut*.''[85]

In his travels the new Agent of National Economics discovered many other manufacturing establishments dedicated to the expansion of employment opportunities, and more often than not these establishments received some form of financial subsidy from municipal authorities in addition to private philanthropic gifts. In Zierikzee Goldberg encountered a factory, employing only children and old people, in which they spun and dyed wool. In Utrecht and Amsterdam the municipal councils similarly combined social charity with economic enterprise; a stocking factory in Amsterdam provided work to a total of 1,650 children and elderly inhabitants.[86]

A recurrent process of the optimistic creation and, then, the disappointing demise, of work institutes in the Netherlands continued beyond mid-century. The Minister of the Interior in The Hague reported in 1817 that ''the number of charitable workhouses in our Kingdom has grown. Their public utility cannot be questioned, but much careful deliberation and planning are necessary to take advantage of the economic possibilities such institutions offer.''[87] In a royal decree of February 27, 1818, King William I proclaimed: ''Considering it important to reduce the number of people being sustained by public assistance (*openbare onderstand*), we have to create employment opportunities where the indigent population can and must earn its own subsistence.''[88]

As the century progressed, the workhouses in the Netherlands, as was the case in France, produced only mixed results at best. The Annual Report on the Status of the Poor in 1825 noted that "charitable workshops are designed to provide employment for those who are able-bodied and willing. Moreover, they are intended to remove the average beggar's often-heard excuse that he begs solely because he cannot find work. In several countries, primarily in England, charitable workshops have been tested, but not with undivided positive results, because sooner or later many institutions of this nature go under. Many of our own workhouses have met the same fate, as they were more numerous twenty years ago."[89] Nonetheless, 36 pauper factories, and 8 separate workhouses for beggars, were in operation in 1825, and they provided work for almost 10,000 people. Local economic conditions determined the type of manufacture in which the work institutes engaged, although spinning, weaving, and knitting were the routine activities of most of them.

The total costs of maintaining the work institutes were 357,491 guilders in 1825; the labor productivity of the destitute workers yielded 191,852 guilders, thus defraying more than half the expenditures of all the workhouses in operation. The balance was covered to some extent by private or church contributions, but the largest share derived from municipal subsidies.[90] In 1832, 27 charitable workhouses were in existence; in 1838 the number was 32, in 1849 it had climbed to 42, and in 1850 it reached 50.[91] In 1855 their number had supposedly risen to 112 and provided work to more than 13,000 poor folks.[92]

In the city of Gouda in 1849, for instance, local notables collected voluntary contributions for the establishment of a work institute, to be housed in a building which the Municipal Council had donated, because the "number of beggars in the city had become oppressive." The workhouse opened its doors on January 2, 1850, and welcomed all indigent Gouda residents, provided "they arrive before eight o'clock in the morning and remain until seven o'clock at night and conduct themselves in an orderly fashion—to the extent that good comportment can be expected from people of such a lowly status." On the first day, 119 people reported to the work institute, a number that would climb to 220 within a week of opening its doors.[93]

In exchange for labor—men, for instance, made wooden shoes and sawed wood while women knitted socks or spun flax—the workhouse provided three nutritious meals a day; the institute's walls were covered with posters exhibiting such didactic homilies as "Poverty is not shameful, but dishonesty is," "A good name is better than money," and "Both liquor and loose women are dangerous."[94] In 1859 the work institute in Gouda celebrated its tenth anniversary and its chairman, W. J. Droogleever Fortuijn, had nothing but praise for an institution that had provided labor to poverty-stricken men and women and instilled salutory work habits at the same time. In keeping with the tendency of Dutch policymakers to judge men and women primarily as members of a family unit, though, the Gouda workhouse and similar institutes in other cities did not favor the exclusive or separate employment of women, as did the *Filature des indigents* in Paris.

Despite the well-intentioned motivations behind the creation of the Dutch work institutes, few of them became viable industrial enterprises. Competition from private industry made them precarious and vulnerable, while their life span was also intimately connected to the amount of private or public subsidy available to keep them afloat. In contrast, the textile industry in Twente thrived because the monopolistic government trading firm, *Nederlandse Handels Maatschappij* (Netherlands Trade Company), under the philanthropic inspiration of Willem de Clercq, placed its steady textile orders destined for export to the Dutch East Indies in the first instance with charitable workshops, secondarily with smaller firms, and only with large enterprises as a last resort. The support policies of the *Nederlandse Handels Maatschappij* nurtured the weaving industries in Arnhem, Tiel, Leeuwarden, and Kampen as well as the calico factory for indigents in Middelburg, thus sustaining charitable workshops that were among the most stable and enduring in the country.[95] Most other workhouses, if local economic conditions changed and a consistent flow of municipal and private funds was not forthcoming, exhibited an erratic survival rate that was comparable to the *ateliers de charité* in France.

The creation of the *Maatschappij van Weldadigheid* in 1818 provoked the central government's more complex involvement in social welfare, despite the sacrosanct principles of the autonomy of municipalities and *diaconiëen*.[96] Initially the *Maatschappij*, established by private philanthropic initiative, negotiated separate contracts with various municipal councils and *diaconiëen* to transport a specified number of people to its rural colonies, where the poor would find agricultural work and nurturance. A wide array of local subcommittees, with its greatest representation in the urban provinces in the western part of the country, composed the infrastructure of the *Maatschappij*. Pauper families in western cities could present a request to the *Maatschappij*'s local subcommittees to be placed in the agricultural colonies in the province of Drenthe in the northeastern part of the country. This procedure, the

Maatschappij founders hoped, would enable every impoverished family, provided all its members were without physical or other handicaps, "to become self-sufficient through zeal and productive labor."[97] As stated in the report of the provisional commission at the founding of the *Maatschappij van Weldadigheid* in 1818:

> The goal of this organization is, on the one hand, to ameliorate and improve the fate of hundreds of thousands of our poor fellow citizens through the most appropriate means: to bring them out of their abject misery and depraved condition and to bring them to an honest and self-sufficient existence. On the other hand, our goal is to relieve the wealthier strata of our society of the day-to-day obligation of supporting the impoverished masses around them.[98]

The simultaneous expectation was that "the uncultivated lands of our country will thus be transformed into a rich and fertile soil."

In the beginning, the bucolic colonial society evolved as a nearly self-reliant community with its own currency, consisting of copper and zinc coins and paper money, and its own school system designed to provide separate education and moral instruction to Protestant, Catholic, and Jewish colonists. The *Maatschappij* built its own stores and textile factories and cultivated its own farm lands; it also formulated its own penal code and wage system. The *Maatschappij* administration withheld from every colonist's earnings a certain percentage to cover the costs of the food and clothing it doled out, and it saved the remainder for them as an extra resource for the future. Every household received a cow, at the expense of the *Maatschappij*, and when the earnings of any individual colonial household made it feasible, the family could keep a second one.[99]

The *Maatschappij*'s policies focused on families that were morally upstanding and intact. The first report of the Supervisory Committee of the *Maatschappij* in 1818, for example, mentioned that "this organization, designed to bring indigent families to self-reliance, civilization, and morality, already serves 333 people. Although initially two-thirds of the colonists were totally unfamiliar with the ways of farming, and only 11 wives knew how to spin, after two months every family could cultivate its own plot and the remaining members have mastered the intricacies of spinning."[100] During the next year the report stated that "the number of colonists has increased fourfold, and the progress made, in agriculture as well as manufacture, has not only surpassed our expectations but goes beyond all belief."[101]

Nevertheless, administrators removed three families from the colonies for inappropriate behavior—among them "Breukels, his gross and ugly wife, and his lascivious daughters"—but new families arrived at once to replace them.[102] The Supervisory Committee of the *Maatschappij* indulged in detailed description of the unique character of each family that had settled in the colonies, and they presented each household with either a gold, silver, or bronze medal depending on the trustworthy conduct of each family member. The committee reported in 1820:

> The van der Heiden family is an ordinary household, but the husband tends to drink too much, and because of his constant inebriation they can not receive a medal. In the Westerveld family the husband has been conscientious while the wife is unreasonable and slovenly, although she is eager to work. They nonetheless received a silver medal because they paid off their entire land rent. The de Haan family, in contrast, consists of a slow and lazy husband and a wife who is alert and attentive. The Bosch family, however, is a bad household because they waste money and create disturbances.[103]

The administrators of the *Maatschappij* discussed the characteristics of many more individual households, and the quaint vignettes create an engaging picture of family life among the poor in nineteenth-century Holland. They also reveal, to some extent, the active concern of officials with the preservation of the existing family structures among the poor.

The *Maatschappij*'s annual report of 1820 again conveyed a happy tale of success: six new families had joined the colonies, while the average income of each individual household had increased by 98.39 guilders over the previous year. The *Maatschappij* now provided every family with two cows and a pig, and many colonists had succeeded in finding work in a nearby brick factory, while others dug peat: "they have reached such a level of competency that it is no longer necessary to provide vocational training."[104]

Regardless of the good intentions and formidable work of the *Maatschappij* administrators, this idyllic socioeconomic experiment confronted major financial problems soon after its inception, and the government in The Hague had to come to its rescue. On June 30, 1826, the Permanent Commission of the *Maatschappij* concluded a contract with the central government to absorb military veterans and their families in its free colonies. Aside from covering the cost of settlement, the government would pay a yearly sum of 127.50 guilders for each family. The *Maatschappij*, in return, would supply each household with housing, furniture, food and supplies as well as weekly store coupons. These veteran families could work in the *Maatschappij* fields and factories if they wanted to earn extra money. The Ministry of War supervised them, however, and the military veterans were permitted to display their special insignia in order to set themselves apart from the indigent colonists.[105]

Subsequently, a royal decree of August 27, 1827, approved a general agreement between the *Maatschappij* and the national government stipulating that foundlings, orphans, and beggars from every community in the country could find a place in the *Maatschappij* and that the government would help defray the costs. The general contract with the government preempted all the separate agreements the *Maatschappij* had negotiated with municipal poor councils or church *diaconiëen.*[106] Through the *Maatschappij* the government in The Hague became more immersed in the general administration of charity during the 1820s, when the *Maatschappij*'s assortment of agricultural colonies, factories, and beggar institutions emerged as an important prop in the baroque edifice of social welfare in the Netherlands.

The motivations behind the colonization scheme for beggars and orphans were sensible; the removal of helpless children and destitute beggars to a healthy new environment and fresh air would be good for them. With their physical strength revitalized, they could contribute their energetic labor power to the colonial project. The government in The Hague hoped to kill several birds with one stone: by sending youthful hands to work in the colonies, the orphans might contribute to the colonies' prosperity and success; at the same time the state could lighten the burden of overcrowded urban orphanages. Moreover, the beggars' transfer to the colonies might restore a more favorable balance in the ratio of labor supply to employment opportunities in both the cities and the countryside.[107]

But such solutions confronted natural obstacles. The colonies' capacity to integrate an endless stream of orphans, beggars, and destitute families had its limits. Besides, it was extremely expensive. The transportation of each family to the colonies, according to Otto Gerhard Heldring's calculations, "however large the household might be, will demand twice the amount of funds it would otherwise require to feed the same family within the city itself."[108] Placement of indigent families in the colonies raised further problems. Despite the auspicious beginnings, eventually *Maatschappij* administrators wallowed in perennial complaints about the colonists' incompetence as agricultural laborers, whose bumbling efforts "even on the best farmlands failed to convert them into self-sufficient farmers." As a caustic commentator mentioned in a review in 1859, the idealistic founders of the *Maatschappij* had believed that "the poor were poor because the cities did not supply them with adequate employment opportunities." Experience in the colonies had shown, instead, that "in reality the poor are poor because they lack the physical, intellectual, and moral capabilities to earn their own livelihood."[109]

The uncomfortable truth was that urban families, however well intentioned and hopeful they may have been, were neither physically nor psychologically equipped to perform farm labor. This gave rise to the accusation that local chapters of the *Maatschappij* used bad judgment in selecting the appropriate families to be sent to the colonies.[110] Whatever the case may have been, the lofty goals of the *Maatschappij* to "alleviate the suffering of the masses of urban poor people and simultaneously to expand society's means of existence" were not achieved. The *Maatschappij* colonies, although they did cultivate patches of sandy soil and did engage in textile manufacture, never became what Johannes van den Bosch, their founder, had envisioned: a self-sufficient micro-world, an intrepid rural utopia with ample employment opportunities and salutory living conditions where a degenerate, urban proletariat would transmute itself into a new human species that rejoiced in a life of stable and healthy agriculture.[111] Instead, the *Maatschappij* was forced, more or less by default, to function as a temporary holding station for vagabonds and orphans which imposed a military-style discipline.[112] Nonetheless, the rural settlements provided a safe haven of last resort for the poor themselves. When subsistence was precarious and life seemed bleak, the Dutch poor could seek refuge in the colonies—and enormous numbers of them did so voluntarily in the 1840s—in the knowledge that they would be fed, clothed, and sheltered (see Figure 7-6).

The French interest in the Dutch example of the *Maatschappij* colonies was keen, even if it waxed and waned over time. "Because of the polarization between rich and poor in Holland," wrote Alphonse Esquiros at mid-century, "the Dutch government began its socio-economic experiments in the first decades of this century by establishing agricultural colonies in 1818. These settlements evoked a lively interest in the rest of Europe and were praised throughout."[113] In 1832, with the Dutch model in mind, the government of King Louis-Philippe appointed a commission charged with making preparations for a system of agricultural colonies.[114] Negative information about the *Maatschappij*'s high costs and reports about urban paupers' lack of success as agricultural laborers, however, caused the government commission to die a natural death.[115]

Figure 7-6

Beggars in the Colonies of the Maatschappij van Weldadigheid 1835 - 1855

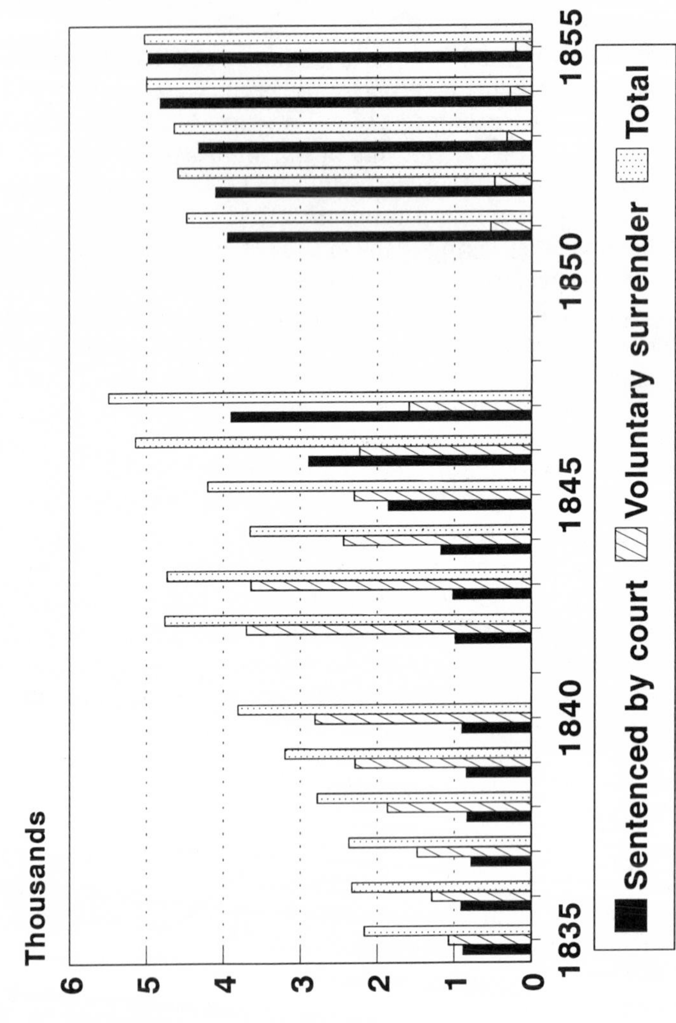

Source: Archieven van de Maatschappij van Weldadigheid.

A few years later French curiosity revived again, in part because Baron Bigot de Morogues had written about the colonies in such glowing terms, almost as if they were a panacea, in 1834.[116] In 1837 Johannes van den Bosch, the intellectual father of the *Maatschappij*, received a carefully phrased questionnaire from M. L. F. Huerne de Pommeuse, the government-appointed inspector of charitable institutions in the department of Gironde, who sought information on the administrative and organizational aspects of the Dutch colonies.[117] Soon thereafter, in 1839, an official emissary of the French government paid a visit to the establishments of the *Maatschappij* for the explicit purpose of studying the feasibility of instituting a similar organization in France.[118]

In addition, Jean-Paul Alban de Villeneuve-Bargemont, in his corpulent and widely read *Economie politique chrétienne*, described his "philanthropic pilgrimage" to the *Maatschappij* colonies. He exulted that it was difficult to express the euphoric "sense of happiness and vivid admiration" that had filled his heart in the course of his lengthy visit. He effused in elegiac prose:

> The sky above displayed a softness and beautiful serenity, and everywhere we followed magnificent roads . . . on the left and on the right, we saw new and neatly constructed farmhouses, whose simplicity did not exclude an understated elegance. Each dwelling was graced with a vegetable garden dotted with flowers . . . Behind the houses extended the five hectares of land allotted to each household: there, the healthy and varied cultivation of potatoes, wheat, rye, cabbage, beets, and vigorous and large fruit trees attested to the efforts of an active and intelligent industriousness . . . We spent the next day traversing the colonies once again and we contemplated and admired those places that offered a spectacle so dear to humanity.[119]

Appreciating the combination of thriving handicraft production and prosperous agriculture he thought he had seen in the *Maatschappij* colonies, the arch-conservative Villeneuve-Bargemont envisaged the creation of similar institutions in France in order to strengthen the economic ties—or reinvigorate the social attachments—between workers and property owners.

It was clear that the Dutch *Maatschappij* settlements captured the imagination of public officials and intellectuals in France, whether on the political left, in the center, or on the right, and acquired a somewhat metaphorical status in French minds. Holland, wrote a later commentator, a country which "we mistakenly tend to view as a nation that does not progress," had exposed the French to an enlightened example.[120] Hence the French, too, concocted a romantic fantasy of hordes of disheartened urban dwellers who, having migrated from the hectic city to the serene countryside, would transform themselves into God-fearing peasants engaged in flourishing agriculture and the cultivation of wastelands. The scope and productivity of French agriculture would thus be expanded, while the urban poor ceased to represent a revolutionary menace. However, despite the mostly rhapsodic evaluations of the *Maatschappij*, and regardless of the recurrent recommendations to reproduce its lofty goals in the French countryside, rural colonies in France were explicitly designed as Spartan correctional facilities rather than peaceful, bucolic utopias.

In early 1840, Frédéric de Metz started in Mettray an agricultural reform school for juvenile offenders—young boys convicted of crimes such as theft and arson or found guilty of status offenses such as beggary or vagrancy—on 700 hectares, which a rich landowner had donated near the city of Tours. Both small farms and large estates surrounded the colony's fertile soil.[121] Rows of pavilions, arranged around a large square with a church at its social and spiritual center, housed forty-two boys each who lived with a supervisor in a simulated "family," even though the boys dressed in uniforms and endured Draconian military training. During the day they learned handicraft skills such as woodworking in the *ateliers* and they cultivated the surrounding land, while *soeurs de la charité* tended to their moral reform at night.[122]

Michel Foucault has singled out January 22, 1840, the day of the official inauguration of Mettray, as the exact date of the "completion of the carceral system." Mettray, he argued, epitomized bourgeois France's infatuation with surveillance and installed all "the coercive technologies of behavior."[123] Other colonies followed in Mettray's wake, especially during the Second Empire. In fact, Napoleon Bonaparte—who was, after all, an alleged expert on the "extinction" of poverty—actively encouraged the creation of agricultural colonies. After mid-century, around twenty-five short-lived colonies, some run with public support and others founded by private initiative or religious congregations such as the Trappists, were established to care for troubled children, accused offenders, or orphans.[124]

Again, Foucault's assertion that the creation of Mettray signaled the definitive completion of France's network of disciplinary techniques, which incorporated all charitable institutions as essential components, reveals some hyperbole. In light of the bewildering diversity of Catholic hospitals and poorhouses and the dizzying number of private philanthropic ventures, many of which expressed a genuine humanitarian impulse, it is problematic to argue in favor of a "coordinated bourgeois regime" of working-class surveillance. In a straightforward comparison with the Dutch situation, however, it is reasonable to assert that French poor relief, relatively speaking, functioned more as a method of social control than was the case in the Netherlands. Institutions that enclosed the poor and entombed them in dark spaces, where their subversive tendencies could be kept in check, were more prevalent in France than in Holland.

We cannot disregard, of course, the caring and goodness which many of the Catholic Sisters of Charity and private philanthropists displayed. Nor should we ignore the fact that some of the workshops or rural colonies may have cultivated workers' skills and approximated the officially sanctioned notion of poor relief in exchange for labor rendered. The success and continuity of the *Filature des indigents* in Paris was not a solitary phenomenon. But relative to the Dutch situation, French institutions functioned more often as agencies of containment for able-bodied workers or beggars who belonged to a class that, in the public imagination, was routinely "a breeding ground of larcenists, arsonists, and assassins."[125]

Both the availability and the predictability of charitable support affected the behavior of indigent citizens in Holland and France during periods of economic distress. In Holland the thousands of church *diaconiëen*, work institutes, municipally sponsored agencies allocating outdoor relief, old age homes, or the agricultural colonies of the *Maatschappij* functioned as a flexible institutional shield. They collectively served as homespun mechanisms of survival that dissuaded the suffering poor from hurling themselves, *faute de mieux*, into illegal conduct or violent acts during times of hunger and destitution. French political culture endowed such institutionally sanctioned outlets with a different meaning and surrounded them with an aura of repression. If poor people in France surrendered themselves into the hands of charity, they often confronted somber institutions that wrested them away from their loved ones in the family circle, despite Catholic nuns or individual philathropists' best efforts. Hence, the poor in France often responded by making an eminently logical choice that seemed available to them: they stole, pillaged, and rioted. During periods of food shortage and inflated grain prices, many indigent folks in France, more so than the Dutch poor, with a large number of highly vocal and defiant women among them, engaged freely in a wide array of economies of makeshift.[126]

Notes

1. Minister of the Interior, November 25, 1818, *Rapport au Roi sur la situation des hospices, des enfants trouvés, des aliénés, de la mendicité, et des prisons* (Paris: Imprimerie Royale, 1818), p. 18. F11 445, AN, Paris.

2. R. Scherenberg, *Bedenkingen over de armoede en door welke middelen het aantal der armen in Nederland zoude kunnen worden verminderd, hunnen toestand verbeterd, en zij tot nuttige leden der maatschappij zouden kunnen worden opgeleid* (The Hague: 's Lands Staatsdrukkerij, 1816). pp. 16, 21.

3. Maurice Halbwachs, *La mémoire collective* (Paris: Presses Universitaires de France, 1968), p. 38.

4. Paul Connerton, in *How Societies Remember* (Cambridge: Cambridge University Press, 1989), refers to the ''social memory and commemorative ceremonies'' that are ''re-articulated'' and ''re-presented in the modern public record'' (passim). See also James Fentress and Chris Wickham, eds., *Social Memory. New Perspectives on the Past* (Oxford/Cambridge: Basil Blackwell, 1992).

5. Minister of the Interior, November 25, 1818, *Rapport au Roi*, pp. 18–19.

6. Royal decree issued on August 3, 1815. F11 206, AN, Paris.

7. M. Huerne de Pommeuse, *Des colonies agricoles et de leurs avantages. Rapport fait à la société d'encouragement de l'industrie nationale* (Paris: Hazard, 1832), p. 3.

8. Scherenberg, *Bedenkingen over de armoede*, p. 16.

9. Scherenberg, *Bedenkingen over de armoede*, p. 42.

10. Adrien Gasparin (Minister of the Interior), *Rapport au Roi sur les hôpitaux, les hospices, et les services de bienfaisance* (Paris: Imprimerie Nationale, 1837), p. 15.

11. See the discussion in Frans van Poppel, *Trouwen in Nederland. Een historisch-demografische studie van de 19e en vroeg–20e eeuw*, A.A.G. Brijdragen, No. 33 (Wageningen: Landbouwuniversiteit, 1992), pp. 63–81.

12. Charles Nicolas, *Les budgets de la France depuis le commencement du XIXième siècle (avec tableaux budgétaires)* (Paris: A. Lahure, 1882), p. 16.

13. Nicolas, *Les budgets de la France*, pp. 20–21. See Mark Traugott, *Armies of the Poor. Determinants of Working-Class Participation in the Parisian Insurrection of June 1848* (Princeton: Princeton University Press, 1985), for a discussion of Napoleon's appeal to the unemployed, if only because he had nurtured a dubious identification with socialist ideas in his *l'Exinction du paupérisme*, written during his exile in Belgium, pp. 165–74.

14. Nicolas, *Les budgets de la France*, pp. 20–21, and Annex A, No. 24, pp. 297–298, Ministry of the Interior, ''Développement rélatifs aux années 1833 à 1880, dépenses générales.''

15. Ministry of the Interior, December 18, 1817, *Bulletin de la situation générale des subsistances*. F11 445, AN, Paris.

16. Mayor of Nantes, *Ordonnance* issued on July 4, 1815, in *Bulletin de la situation générale des subsistances*. F11 445, AN, Paris.

17. J.M.M. de Meere, ''Misoogst en hongersnood. Beschouwingen naar aanleiding van een inaugurele rede,'' *Tijdschrift voor Sociale Geschiedenis*, 3, No. 1 (1977), p. 93.

18. E. van Voorthuysen, *Voorlezingen over de duurte van de levensmiddelen gehouden voor de maatschappij Felix Meritis* (Haarlem: A.C. Kruseman, 1856), pp. 16, 19–20.

19. Ad. de Watteville, *Rapport à M. le Ministre de l'Intérieur sur la situation du paupérisme et les établissements de bienfaisance en France et sur l'administration des secours à domicile par le Baron de Watteville, inspecteur général des établissements de bienfaisance* (Paris: Imprimerie Imperiale, 1855), p. 18. Emily Greene Balch, in ''Public Assistance of the Poor in France,'' in *Publications of the American Economic Association*, 8 (Baltimore: Guggenheim and Weil, 1893), p. 402, and Roger Price, in ''Poor Relief and Social Crisis in Mid Nineteenth-Century France,'' *European Studies Review*, 13, No. 4 (1983), p. 431, repeat the exact same number of 12.70 francs including administrative costs.

20. Price, ''Poor Relief and Social Crisis,'' p. 429.

21. Baron Bigot de Morogues, quoted by Louis Chevalier, *Laboring Classes and Dangerous Classes in Paris During the First Half of the Nineteenth Century* (1958; repr. Princeton: Princeton University Press, 1983), p. 137.

22. Pierre Rosanvallon quotes these numbers in *l'Etat en France de 1789 à nos jours* (Paris: Editions du Seuil, 1990), p. 146.

23. Adrien Gasparin (Minister of the Interior), *Rapport au Roi sur les hôpitaux* (1837), p. 15.

24. Quoted by Emile Laurent, *Le paupérisme et les associations de prévoyance. Nouvelles études sur les sociétés de secours mutuels*, 2 vols. (Paris: Guillaumin, 1865), 1, p. 150.

25. M. Vée, ''Du paupérisme et des secours publique dans la ville de Paris,'' *Journal des économistes*, No. 39 (1845), p. 5.

26. Hyppolyte-Ernest du Touquet, *De la condition des classes pauvres* (Paris: Guillaumin, 1846), p. 65.

27. *Statistique de la France* (Strasbourg: Berger Levrault, 1861), 2nd ed., 6, *Statistique de l'assistance publique*, p. 67.

28. Michel Foucault, *Discipline and Punish. The Birth of the Prison* (1975; repr. New York: Random House, 1979), passim.

29. Rosanvallon, *l'Etat en France,*, p. 57.

30. See Jill Harsin, *Policing Prostitution in Nineteenth-Century Paris* (Princeton: Princeton University Press, 1985), for a detailed discussion of the growing police presence in Paris.

31. Marcellin-Emile-Hubert Valleroux, *De l'assistance sociale, ce qu'elle a été, ce qu'elle est, ce qu'elle devrait être* (Paris: Masson, 1855), p. 206. See also Paul-Hubert Valleroux, *La charité avant et depuis 1789 dans les campagnes de France avec des examples tirés de l'étranger* (Paris: Guillaumin, 1890).

32. George Sand, ''Coup d'oeil général sur Paris,'' in *Le Diable à Paris*, 2 vols. (Paris: Hetzel, 1846), 1, pp. 33–40.

33. Eugène Buret, *De la misère des classes laborieuses en Angleterre et France. De la nature de la misère, de son existence, de ses effets, de ses causes, et de l'insuffisance des remèdes qu'on lui a opposés jusqu'ici: avec l'indication des moyens propres à affranchir les sociétés*, 2 vols. (Paris: Paulin, 1840), 1, p. 147.

34. *Notes historiques sur la Société maternelle et sur les resultats de ses travaux pendant 30 ans* (1831), Fosseyeux, liasse 133/13, Archives de l'assistance publique, Paris.

35. Charles Dupin, *Histoire de l'administration des secours publiques* (Paris: Alexis Eymerey, 1821), pp. 330, 388.

36. Bonnie Smith, *Ladies of the Leisure Class: The Bourgeoises of Northern France in the Nineteenth Century* (Princeton: Princeton University Press, 1981), passim, and Margaret H. Darrow, ''French Noblewomen and the New Domesticity, 1750–1850,'' *Feminist Studies*, 5, No. 1 (1979), pp. 41–65. For a recent study of maternalist policies during the Third Republic, see Alisa Klaus, *Every Child a Lion: The Origins of Maternal and Infant Health Policy in the United States and France, 1890–1920* (Ithaca: Cornell University Press, 1993).

37. Annual report presented by the administration of the *Société de charité maternelle* to the General Assembly, January 18, 1810. F15 2565, AN, Paris. See also Hyppolyte-Ernest du Touquet, *Enfants trouvés. Création de la société de Notre Dame de réfuge et de ses asiles: secourir les mères pauvres, moraliser les filles mères, diminuer le nombre des enfants trouvés* (Paris: Guillaumin, 1858), Preface.

38. Rachel G. Fuchs, ''Aid to the Poor and the Pregnant in Nineteenth-Century Paris,'' in Peter Mandler, ed., *The Uses of Charity. The Poor on Relief in the Nineteenth-Century Metropolis* (Philadelphia: University of Pennsylvania Press, 1990). p. 96.

39. Subsidies were granted annually, in proportion to the number of poor mothers supported by the *Société*. In a letter from the prefect of the department of Loire-Inférieure to the Minister of the Interior regarding the *Société maternelle* on April 2, 1819, he noted: ''I am enclosing the original of a letter I received from the president of this society which asks for prompt funding from the government. It is only too true that despite the zeal and sacrifices of the ladies who are members of this society, the available resources cannot meet the needs and I would appreciate it if you could possibly increase the allocation of funds for this society during 1819'' (F15 2565, AN, Paris).

40. *Notes sur la filature des indigents, compte moral, 1820*, Fosseyeux, No. 16, Archives de l'assistance publique, Paris. See also Lisa Dicaprio's dissertation, ''Women and Social Welfare during the French Revolution: The *Ateliers de filature*, 1790–1795,'' Rutgers University, 1994.

41. *Compte moral*, 1821.

42. *Compte moral*, 1822.

43. *Compte moral*, 1828.

44. *Compte Administrative*, 1843.

45. L. Lamothe, "Des projets de loi sur les enfants trouvés," *Journal des économistes*, No. 115 (October 1850), p. 230.

46. A female worker in one of the convent workshops wrote in *La voix des femmes* on March 27, 1948, that in light of the low daily wage she received from the nuns, "prison would give me more benefits." Quoted by Henriette Vanier, *La mode et ses métiers. Frivolités et luttes des classes, 1830–1870* (Paris: Armand Colin, 1960), p. 78.

47. Laura Strumingher, *Women and the Making of the Working Class: Lyons, 1830–1870* (Albany: SUNY Press, 1976).

48. Lily van Rijswijk-Clerkx, in *Moeders, kinderen en kinderopvang* (Nijmegen: SUN, 1981), does not mention the *Société maternelle* in her section on the early nineteenth century, pp. 116–20.

49. Gewestelijke bestuursarchieven, 1811–1814/15, No. 717, Sous prefecture de l'arrondissement de Haarlem, IIIième division, *Société maternelle*, Rijksarchief Noord-Holland, Haarlem.

50. Gewestelijke bestuursarchieven, 1811–1814/15, No. 665.

51. Gewestelijke bestuursarchieven, 1811–1814/15, No. 665.

52. Gewestelijke bestuursarchieven, 1811–1814/15, No. 665.

53. Gewestelijke bestuursarchieven, 1811–1814/15, No. 665.

54. Report of the Royal Commission on Poverty and Poor Relief, convened by King William I in 1816. See *Verslag omtrent de armoede en het armenwezen, dienstjaar 1818*, Collectie Tets van Goudriaan, No. 23, ARA, The Hague.

55. Archief van het Ministerie van Binnenlandse Zaken, No. 1771, 46H, Missive from the Minister of the Interior to the Provincial Estates, March 7, 1828. ARA, The Hague. For some inexplicable reason, the official in the Ministry of the Interior failed to mention the maternal society in Leiden which, according to the *Verslag omtrent het armenwezen* for the year 1828, claimed it aided almost four times as many poor pregnant women as the societies in Rotterdam or Haarlem.

56. The *Verslag omtrent het armenwezen, dienstjaar 1828*, provided a table with *Genootschappen van moederlijke weldadigheid* in the Kingdom of the Netherlands. In addition to Haarlem and Rotterdam, the table listed the cities (Leiden, Groningen, Hilversum, and Den Helder) which maintained a Society for Maternal Charity, the number of contributing members, the number of poor mothers supported, and the requirements imposed on them. New societies had been created in Den Bosch and Alkmaar in 1828. According to the table, the *Société de charité maternelle* in Leiden supported a grand total of 801 pregnant in women in 1828.

57. *Verslag omtrent het armenwezen, dienstjaar 1850.*

58. H.Th. Ambachtsheer, *Jhr. Mr. Jeronimo de Bosch Kemper. Een behoudend maatschappij hervormer* (Amsterdam: Querido, 1959).

59. W.H. Suringar, *Het patronaat over de armen* (Leeuwarden: G.T.N. Suringar, 1842), quoted by H.C.M. Michielse, *De burger als andragoog. Een*

geschiedenis van 125 jaar welzijnswerk (Amsterdam: Boom/Meppel, 1977), pp. 62–64. See also Ali de Regt, *Arbeidsgezinnen en beschavingsarbeid. Ontwikkelingen in Nederland, 1870–1940* (Amsterdam: Boom/Meppel, 1984).

60. Marco H.D. van Leeuwen, *Bijstand in Amsterdam, ca. 1800–1850. Armenzorg als beheersings- en overlevingsstrategie* (Zwolle: Waanders, 1992), pp. 170–171; and L.F. van Loo, ''De armenzorg in de noordelijke Nederlanden,'' *Algemene Geschiedenis der Nederlanden*, 15 vols. (Haarlem: Fibula van Dishoeck. 1978), 10, p. 425.

61. Joel Mokyr, *Industrialization in the Low Countries, 1795–1850* (New Haven: Yale University Press, 1977), p. 122.

62. Martien Arends, Nico Siffels, and Willem van Spijker, *Wegens verregaande brutaliteit Haarlemse paupers in de eerste helft van de negentiende eeuw* (University of Amsterdam: M.A. thesis, 1983), p. 201.

63. J.M.M. de Meere, *Economische Ontwikkeling en Levensstandaard in Nederland gedurende de eerste helft van de negentiende eeuw* (The Hague: Martinus Nijhoff, 1982), p. 49.

64. Van Leeuwen, *Bijstand in Amsterdam*, p. 201.

65. Alexandre Monnier, *Histoire de l'assistance publique dans les temps anciens et modernes*, 3rd ed. (Paris: Guillaumin, 1866), p. 542.

66. Collectie Test van Goudriaan, No. 23, Verslag der commissie in wier handen bij besluit van de Tweede Kamer der Staten Generaal op 14 October, 1852, het verslag omtrent den staat van het armwezen over 1850 is ingesteld. Uitgebracht in de zitting der Kamer op 28 Februari, 1853, ARA, The Hague.

67. J.R. Poynter, *Society and Pauperism. English Ideas on Poor Relief, 1795–1834* (London: Routledge, 1969), p. 77. See also Marc Blaugh, ''The Myth of the Old Poor Law and the Making of the New,'' *Journal of Economic History*, 23, No. 1 (1964), pp. 151–84; and G. R. Boyer, ''An Economic Model of the English Poor Law, ca. 1780–1834,'' in *Explorations in Economic History*, 22 (1985), pp. 129–67.

68. For a thoughtful discussion of this contentious issue, see Van Leeuwen, *Bijstand in Amsterdam*, pp. 45–46.

69. *Verslag omtrent het armenwezen, dienstjaar 1846*.

70. Gerrit Luttenberg, *Proeve van onderzoek omtrent het armenwezen in ons Vaderland en naar de doeltreffende middelen die verder ter verbetering van het lot der armen zouden kunnen aangewend worden* (Zwolle: W.E.J. Tjeenk Willink, 1841), p. 20. See also J. de Vries Jr., ''Pamfletten over het armoedeprobleem in de negentiende eeuw. Bijdrage tot de kennis van de geest der vorige eeuw,'' *Mensch en Maatschappij*, 14, No. 1 (1938), pp. 10–21. For an insightful exploration of this extensive literature, see Van Poppel, *Trouwen in Nederland*, pp. 63–81.

71. See Scherenberg's discussion in *Bedenkingen over de armoede*, who noted that ''by increasing the civilization and education of the poor, they might be convinced not to marry unless they can provide for their children. However, considering their sexual impulses (*driften*), this is a doubtful proposition, and a

government cannot force the poor to refrain from marrying without degenerating into despotism.'' He added, though, that the government ''might legitimately restrict the marital behavior of military personnel and perhaps also of poor-relief recipients'' (pp. 5–6).

72. O.G. Heldring, *Binnen- en buitenlandse kolonisatie in betrekking tot de armoede* (Amsterdam: G.J.A. Beijerinck, 1846), pp. 54, 99–100.

73. *Verslag omtrent den staat van het armenwezen, dienstjaar 1817.*

74. C. van Vollenhoven, in H.W. Tydeman, ed., *Magazijn van het Armwezen in het Koninkrijk der Nederlanden*, 2 (1819), p. 37.

75. About the ideas of Frédéric Bastiat, see William Coleman, *Death Is a Social Disease. Public Health and Political Economy in Early Industrial France* (Madison: University of Wisconsin Press, 1982), p. 81; W.C. Mees, *De Werkinrigtingen voor armen uit een staathuishoudkundig oogpunt beschouwd* (Rotterdam: J. van Balen, 1844), p. 11.

76. N.B. Donkersloot, *Gedachten over de armoede, hare oorzaken en voorbehoudingsmiddelen. Uitgegeven ten voordeele van de noodlijdenden op Schokland* (Tiel: C.J. Campagne, 1849), pp. 10–13.

77. Van Poppel, *Trouwen in Nederland*, p. 115.

78. J.A. van Royen, in *Wetgeving en armoede beschouwd in betrekking tot het misdrijf* (Zwolle: Tjeenk Willink, 1846), considered this theme.

79. L. Frank van Loo, *Armelui. Armoede en bedeling te Alkmaar, 1850–1914* (Bergen, N.H.: Octavo, 1986), p. 51.

80. See, among others, Joel Mokyr, ''Industrialization and Poverty in Ireland and the Netherlands,'' *Journal of Interdisciplinary History*, 10, No. 4 (1980), pp. 429–58; and Marc Blaugh, ''The Poor Law Reexamined,'' *Journal of Economic History*, 24, No. 2 (1964), pp. 229–41.

81. *Provinciaal blad van Noord-Holland over het jaar 1826* (Haarlem: Provinciale Drukkerij, 1826), Circulaire No. 47, March 23, 1826, p. 3.

82. F.K.W. Eijmael, *Wenken voor armenbesturen, armen-verzorgers, en allen die in de armenverzorging belang stellen* (Zwolle: Tjeenk Willink, 1849), pp. 2–3.

83. *Rapport du 2ième Division presenté à son Excellence le Sécretaire d'Etat au Ministre de l'Intérieur sur les secours aux indigents pendant l'hiver, 1815–1816*, October 26, 1816. F15 110, AN, Paris.

84. H.F.J.M. van den Eerenbeemt, *Armoede en arbeidswang. Werkinrichtingen voor onnutte Nederlanders in de Republiek, 1760–1795* (The Hague: Martinus Nijhoff, 1977), pp. 222–23.

85. Johannes Goldberg, ''Journaal der Reize van den Agent van Nationale Economie der Bataafse Republiek,'' in B.W.A.E. Sloet tot Oldhuis, ed., *Tijdschrift voor Staatshuishoudkunde en Statistiek* (Zwolle: Tjeenk Willink, 1859–1860), 2nd Series, 18 and 19, No. 7, pp. 217, 149.

86. Goldberg, ''Journaal der Reize,'' p. 149.

87. *Verslag omtrent het armbestuur en de opvoeding der armenkinderen over het jaar 1818*, in Bijlage, *Verslag der Handelingen van der Tweede Kamer*

van de Staten Generaal, Zitting 1817–1818 (The Hague: Staatsdrukkerij, 1863), p. 298.

88. Koninklijk Besluit, February 27, 1818, in *Staatsblad*, Bijvoegsel.

89. *Verslag betreffende het armwezen over het jaar 1825*, in Bijlage, *Verslag der handelingen van de tweede kamer* (Zitting 1824–1825), p. 564.

90. *Verslag betreffende het armwezen over het jaar 1825*, Bijlage, p. 565.

91. *Verslag betreffende het armwezen* for 1838, 1849, and 1850.

92. Michielse, *De burger als andragoog*, p. 58.

93. W.J. Droogleever Fortuijn, *Geschiedenis der werkinrigting tot wering van de bedelarij te Gouda. Verslag uitgebracht bij het tienjarige bestaan* (Gouda: G.B. van Goor, 1859), pp. 8–9. See also Van Loo, ''De armenzorg in de noordelijke Nederlanden,'' p. 429.

94. Droogleever Fortuijn, *Geschiedenis der werkinrigting*, pp. 10–11, 16, 22.

95. I.J. Brugmans, *Paardenkracht en mensenmacht. Sociaal-economische geschiedenis van Nederland, 1795–1940* (The Hague; Martinus Nijhoff, 1976), p. 79. See also Mokyr, *Industrialization in the Low Countries*, p. 92.

96. The most elaborate socio-demographic analysis of the free colonies of the *Maatschappij van Weldadigheid* is C.A. Kloosterhuis, *De bevolking van de vrije kolonien der Maatschappij van Weldadigheid* (Zutphen: De Walburg Pers, 1981), published posthumously. See also R. Berends, A.H. Huussen Jr., R. Mens, and R. de Windt, *Arbeid ter disciplinering en bestraffing. Veenhuizen als onvrije kolonie van de Maatschappij van Weldadigheid, 1823–1859* (Zutphen: De Walburg Pers, 1984), who concentrate on the penal aspects of the *Maatschappij* colonies.

97. F.W. Fabius, *Iets over de inrichtingen van de Maatschappij van Weldadigheid in het Koninkrijk der Nederlanden* (Amsterdam: Johannes van der Heij, 1841), pp. 1–2.

98. *Algemeen verslag van de provisionele commissie ter vergadering van de commissie van de Maatschappij van Weldadigheid* (The Hague/Amsterdam: Gebroeders van Cleef, 1818), p. 6.

99. F.W. Fabius, *De Maatschappij*, p. 2.

100. *Verslag van de Permanente Commissie van de Maatschappij van Weldadigheid over het dienstjaar 1818*, Archieven van de Maatschappij van Weldadigheid, No. 1083, Provinciaal Archief Drenthe, Assen.

101. *Verslag van de Permanente Commissie, dienstjaar 1819.*

102. *Verslag van de Permanente Commissie, dienstjaar 1819.*

103. *Verslag van de Permanente Commissie, dienstjaar 1820.*

104. *Verslag van de Permanente Commissie, dienstjaar 1820.*

105. Jan-Derk Dorgelo, *De koloniën van de Maatschappij van Weldadigheid, 1818–1859* (Assen: Van Gorcum, 1964), pp. 39–40.

106. ''De archieven van de eerste Maatschappij van Weldadigheid in de Noordelijke Nederlanden, 1818–1859,'' in *Verslag omtrent's lands Oude Archieven* (The Hague: 1915), 38, 1, p. 24.

107. Dorgelo, *De koloniën van de Maatschappij*, p. 18.

108. Heldring, *Binnen- en buitenlandse kolonisatie*, p. 11.

109. J. van Konijnenburg, *De Toestand van de vrije kolonien en het instituut te Wateren* (Meppel: H. Ten Brink, 1859), p. 20.

110. Heldring, *Binnen- en buitenlandse kolonisatie*, p. 99.

111. H.F.J.M. van den Eerenbeemt, "Armoede in de gedrukte optiek van de sociale bovenlaag in Nederland, 1750–1850," *Tijdscrift voor Geschiedenis*, 88, No. 4 (1975), p. 492.

112. Berends et al., in *Arbeid ter disciplinering en bestraffing*, point out that the *Maatschappij*'s institution for beggars in Veenhuizen resembled the architecture of a military barrack and may have served as a prototype for a military *kazerne* built in Leeuwarden a few years later (p. 46).

113. Alphonse Esquiros, *Nederland en het leven in Nederland* (Amsterdam: Gebroeders Binger, 1851), pp. 205–6.

114. F.M.L. Naville, *De la charité legale, de ses effets, de ses causes et spécialement des maisons de travail et de la proscription de la mendicité*, 2 vols. (Paris: P. Dufait, 1836), Preface.

115. Berends et al., *Arbeid ter disciplinering en bestraffing*, p. 93.

116. Pierre-Marie Bigot de Morogues, *Du paupérisme, de la mendicité, et des moyens d'en prévenir les funestes effets* (Paris: Prosper Dondey-Dupré, 1934).

117. Johannes Van den Bosch, private papers, in Collectie Johannes van den Bosch, No. 49, ARA, The Hague. M. Huerne de Pommeuse had already registered his enthusiasm about agricultural colonies in 1832 in *Des colonies agricoles et de leurs avantages*.

118. The French visitor in 1839 was M. Rollet. Collectie Johannes van den Bosch, No. 52, ARA, The Hague.

119. Jean-Paul Alban de Villeneuve-Bargemont, *Economie politique chrétienne ou recherches sur la nature et les causes du paupérisme en France et en Europe et sur les moyens de la soulager et prévenir*, 2nd ed., 2 vols. (Bruxelles: Mélines Cans, 1837), 2, appendix, p. 527.

120. Georges Berry, *Les mendiants. Colonies d'indigents* (Paris: Arnould, 1891), pp. 13, 24.

121. The owner of the land was the Vicomte Bretignières de Courteilles; see Alain Kervadid, *Bagnes de gosses. Mettray-Anianes* (Paris: La Pensée universelle, 1978). See also the melodramatic novel by E. Nyon, *Le colon de Mettray* (Tours: Pornin, 1845), which was reprinted eight times between 1845 and 1867. For a discussion of American responses to the agricultural colony at Mettray, see Barbara M. Brenzel, *Daughters of the State. A Social Portrait of the First Reform School for Girls in North America, 1856–1905* (Cambridge: MIT Press, 1983), pp. 51–56. M.M. von Baumhauer articulated a Dutch response in *De landbouwkolonie Mettray, een voorbeeld voor Nederland* (Amsterdam: Johannes van der Heij, 1847).

122. Brenzel, *Daughters of the State*, p. 55.

123. Foucault, *Discipline and Punish*, p. 293.

124. J. de Lamarque and G. Augat, *Des colonies agricoles établies en France*

en faveur des jeunes détenus, enfants trouvés, pauvres, orphelins et abandonnés. Précis historique et statistique (Paris: Rignoux, 1850). Regarding the penitentiary colony established by the Trappist order near Montagne in the department Orne, see Jean Lebrun, ''Cloîtrer et guérir: la colonie pénitentiaire de la Trappe, 1854–1880,'' in *L'impossible prison. Recherches sur le système pénitentiaire au XIXième siècle réunies par Michelle Perrot* (Paris: Seuil, 1980), pp. 236–76. See also Henri Monod, *La colonie agricole de Sainte-Foye. Discours prononcé à l'occasion du jubilé de la colonie* (Dole: Blind-Franck, 1894).

125. The director of the Dépôts de mendicité to the Minister of the Interior, July 25, 1816. F16 531, AN, Paris.

126. Frances Gouda and Peter H. Smith, ''Famine, Crime, and Gender in Nineteenth-Century France: Explorations in Time-Series Analysis,'' *Historical Methods*, 16, No. 2 (Spring 1983), pp. 59–74.

Epilogue

"With the emergence of the factory system, cottage industry disappeared and peasants deserted their solitary farms to move to cities in order to find employment in manufacture," wrote Samuel Senior Coronel, the distinguished Dutch physician and public health expert, in 1861. He invoked classic imagery: "the thundering noise of industrial machines replaced the gentle chirping of birds. Green pastures were transformed into wide streets with colossal buildings. An industrious but indigent population displaced grazing cattle, and its only goal was not to perish in the accelerated stream of progress. It was impossible to escape from this terrible maelstrom: all the [indigents] longed for was to survive and to maintain themselves."[1]

However, the onslaughts of full-scale industrial capitalism and the birth of mass culture implied more than the deafening sound of factory equipment, a wage-earning but impoverished population, and a wistful nostalgia for verdant fields with foraging cows or pristine forests with chattering birds. It also inaugurated a search in most western European societies, belatedly and in some cases, reluctantly, for legislative solutions that would define social welfare as a collective obligation. A positive social consciousness, which acknowledged the right of all members of society to a reasonable existence, slowly replaced charity based on private sentiments of generosity or personal definitions of Christian duty. As the century unfolded, intellectual discourses and political rhetoric, too, focused less often on issues of poor relief and *bienfaisance* but shifted to discussions about working-class conditions, the prevailing level of wages, and public health. Less preoccupied with the specific needs or conduct of a particular embattled sector of the population, policymakers learned to approach social welfare as merely one aspect of a trend toward the "collectivization" of all the human liabilities associated with modern industrial society.

National legislation, in the meantime, tried to spread the risks of unemployment, injury, and old age across the social spectrum. The central issue, though, was to acknowledge both entitlements and social responsibilities as a universal set of rights and obligations, regardless of personal behavior or moral flaws. Both France and the Netherlands traveled the road from private charity to universal social security between the middle of the nineteenth century and today, but their journeys differed as far as speed, trajectory, and even ultimate destination were concerned.

One of the dominant themes of the story told in the preceding pages has been the palpable tension that existed in France between a long tradition of state centralization, which formally claimed responsibility for poor relief, and the unfulfilled material needs of indigent citizens at the local level. The institutional immobility and political fence-straddling in the face of the gross inequalities of early nineteenth-century society was the direct result of a government in Paris incapable of addressing the Revolution's contradictory legacy in relation to the Social Question. The state actually intervened on behalf of its hungry and miserable citizens mostly to contain the danger implicit in pauperism, and did little more than supervise the antiquated institutions and charitable practices inherited from the ancien régime. In the process, the governments of the Restoration and the July Monarchy forged an essentially antimodernist stance. The ambiguous legacy of individualism inherited from the Revolution rendered the French state ineffectual in its confrontation with the stark realities of emerging modernity. It was a world in which scores of people, notwithstanding their backbreaking work from daybreak to nightfall, were wretchedly poor. Despite all male citizens' freedom to compete as putative equals in the marketplace, an overwhelming majority remained marginalized and unemployed through no fault of their own.

Beyond the charitable practices of Catholic institutions, the well-intentioned but erratic generosity of bourgeois patrons, or the arbitrary assistance from public authorities, the poor in France had few political options or formal institutional resources at their disposal. The French Revolution's Chapelier law, after all, had prohibited all forms of secondary associations in an attempt to eradicate guilds and trade corporations. The Chapelier law's rationale hinged on a desire to prevent secondary associations from engaging in unfair competition. Ancien régime guilds, legislators during the early stage of the Revolution claimed, had shrewdly pushed up wages through monopolistic practices. By imposing elaborate requirements and rituals upon new *compagnons*, some trade corporations had reputedly limited their membership and synthetically raised the price of the products of their labor.

After 1815 some groups of workers and artisans, at times encouraged by particular philanthropic benefactors, had founded self-help or mutual-aid societies in an attempt to steel themselves against the competitiveness of modern industrial society.[2] *Mutualités* also served as a defense against the risks of unemployment, injury, or disease, despite public fears about their corporatist and anti-individualist nature. Mutual-aid societies, members hoped, would flatten the peaks and valleys of working-class material existence; before mid-century, however, they were few and far between. Until 1850 or so *mutualités* in France were nothing but an insipid reflection of the flourishing working-class associations or mechanics societies in England.[3]

Only during the Second Empire did mutual-aid societies or a "modern" version of *compagnonnage* become a more integral element of working-class life once again. Napoleon III had intoned in his proclamation of December 2, 1851, that his mission was to "end the era of revolutions and to satisfy the legitimate needs of the population." About a decade later Emile Ollivier, in the hollow chambers of the Second Empire's quasi-Parliament defended workers' right to organize and strike. He denounced the *loi Chapelier* as "the fundamental error of the French Revolution." This law, Ollivier fulminated, was at the heart of all the "bad legislation" of the nineteenth century that had prohibited associations. The Chapelier law, he announced, caused the "excesses of centralization and prompted the exaggerations of socialist reformers." It was the Chapelier law, he said, that had inspired Grachus Babeuf, encouraged conceptions of *l'état providence*, and "provoked revolutionary despotism in all its manifestations."[4]

The repressive Second Empire, ironically, initiated a departure from the indecisive policies of the early nineteenth century. Replacing the state's passivity with active intervention in working-class life, the Empire of Napoleon III was keenly aware of the power of propaganda and exploited it in a continual effort to mollify the working class and minimize social protest. Napoleon, in his desire to curry the favor of all social classes and to temper domestic discord, allowed mutual aid societies to burgeon and eventually granted workers the right to strike in 1864, thus paving the way for the creation of a genuine labor movement. Ironically, it was the authoritarian Napoleon III who replanted the ideological seeds of corporatist solidarity that the Chapelier law of 1791 had tried to eradicate.

The Third Republic, in the wake of the divisive horror and bloodshed of the Commune, nurtured this revived notion of solidarity to full bloom by transforming it into an eclectic new ideology, *solidarisme*.[5] In the 1890s, *solidarisme* emerged as a rallying cry for social unity and articulated the wish to transcend class conflict; it also spoke in a powerful voice in favor of social legislation based on universal entitlements. *Solidaristes* viewed society as a coherent system of interaction and interdependence between all its members, both rich and poor, grounded in an elaborate set of contractual arrangements. Accordingly, advocates of *solidarisme* reconfigured the issue of poor relief as a "bilateral quasi-contract of mutual association, a reciprocal collaboration in social progress in which the benefactor and the recipient are both co-participants." They dismissed traditional charity, on the other hand, as the "unilateral moral subordination of the recipient to the benefactor."[6]

Albeit in a non-socialist and social-scientific guise, *solidarisme* conjured up an organic and idealized vision of social cooperation on behalf of "progress" and *la République*. In a certain way, this glorified image was reminiscent of the early nineteenth-century yearning, whether conservative and atavistic or radical and progressive, for the social harmony and hierarchical cooperation that French agricultural life presumably symbolized. A major difference, however, was that late nineteenth-century *solidarisme* was anchored realistically in modern Republican institutions and firmly ensconced in industrial society. Its enthusiastic supporters articulated a social policy agenda based not on group-specific legislation but on universal rights that were irrevocably divorced from individual generosity or personal culpability. Thus, in 1898, the Third Republic passed the first truly "modern" piece of social legislation: the law on industrial accidents, which granted injured but previously able-bodied workers the unequivocal right to compensation, regardless of whether they or their employers had caused the accident.[7]

This law was a crucial turning-point and partially cleared the bumpy road toward the contemporary welfare state, because the social security laws of 1928 and 1930 codified the notion of universal obligation and removed the final obstacles. The French journey had been gradual and steady, and by 1975 *l'état providence* in France allocated 22.7 percent of its gross domestic product to social expenditures.[8] Many years had elapsed since La Rochefoucauld-Liancourt and his far-sighted colleagues on the *Comité de mendicité* had proclaimed that French citizens were legitimately entitled to a humane existence and, more importantly, that it was the state's sacred duty to provide it. It took almost two hundred years before the modern welfare state would finally fulfill the precocious promise of the French Revolution.

The Netherlands, too, reached the paramount goal of providing social security, education, housing, and health care, without any form of means-testing and entirely grounded in universal entitlements. In fact, the Dutch have constructed "the world's most extensive welfare state," wrote Goran Therborn in 1989. He added, however, that this may not be a well-known fact, perhaps because it does not easily fit into "current explanatory frameworks."[9] Historians and political scientists have chronicled the arduous voyage from archaic patterns of charity to the contemporary welfare state in European countries or elsewhere in many different ways. Some have emphasized either the strength of the social democratic left or the weakness of conservative political factions; yet others have stressed more institutional factors or privileged micro-economic developments. At the journey's end, though, the most straightforward measure of an advanced welfare state is the level of the state's expenditure on behalf of social programs based on universal entitlements. As far as this criterion is concerned, the Dutch nation has clearly emerged as one of the pacesetters in our contemporary world.

Not only is the contemporary Dutch state's powerful ability to redistribute resources a little-known fact, in a certain sense it may also come as a surprise in light of the narrative of this book. Obviously, one of the story's main themes has focused on the fragmented and uncoordinated character of poor relief efforts; the triumph of private charity and the *diaconiëen* at mid-century ratified a situation that constituted the antithesis of universal entitlements. Another motif has been the residual fragility of the Dutch central state, a chronic weakness that was born in the medieval period, reinforced in the early modern era, and maintained during the nineteenth century. The Dutch state until 1854 and beyond was a mixture of decentralized, oligarchic elements and modern, bureaucratic tendencies, but attempts to solidify and streamline the authority of the central state had proved to be unsuccessful.

Hence, the pivotal role of the Dutch state in social welfare, today, is startling, to say the least. The 1854 Poor Law stipulated definitively that Dutch citizens, however desperate and poverty-stricken, had no statutory right to receive material support from public authorities. Even if religious or private charity could only "provide a penny, in other words, too little to live on," the state would remain aloof, since the fate of an individual citizen was "not the state's concern." There is no doubt that this language was stern and unsentimental, although the law, by acknowledging the requirements of civic order, conceded that public authorities, as an auxiliary source and purely as a last resort, would help the needy so "they would not die of hunger, engage in beggary, theft, and plunder, or participate in popular insurrection."[10]

The Poor Law of 1912 reaffirmed the principle that the public sector should provide only subsidiary relief. This axiom, in fact, was formally in effect until the early 1960s, even though the passage of time would prove that the financial resources of the *diaconiëen* were woefully inadequate to fulfill the needs of the poor.[11] While in 1859 only 11 percent of the 50,000 relief recipients in the city of Amsterdam received some support from municipal sources, in 1905 public assistance had surpassed private charity.[12] The city of Hertogenbosch revealed a similar trend: the public sector's share rose from 43 percent to 57 percent between 1879 and 1913.[13] But the legal stipulation that the central state should be no more than an auxiliary paymaster, who would come to the rescue of the poor and the unemployed only as a final expedient, stayed on the books until far into the twentieth century.

By the 1980s, obviously, a spectacular transformation had taken place because the Dutch state in 1975, for instance, allocated 28.3 percent of the nation's annual gross domestic product to social programs, a proportion that grew to an even more dramatic 40 percent in 1982.[14] How did the Dutch nation change so fundamentally, as Therborn has posed the question, from "Laggard to Vanguard," or, in the words of Abram de Swaan, "from its slow and niggardly beginnings" to the "late, but dramatic, expansion of social security"?[15] More specifically, how did the central state make the transition from its feeble policymaking role in the nineteenth century to commanding a political leverage that enabled the public sector to allocate as much as 40 percent of annual GDP to social programs in 1982?

Explaining this stunning metamorphosis is beyond the scope of this book, but the tale it has told can hopefully offer a few suggestions. It has shown, for example, that one of the distinctive features of the Dutch system of social welfare during the first half of the nineteenth century resided in its tangled web of parallel or competing private charities in almost every small town and large city of the country. Public authorities, for their part, acknowledged that the state harbored a "direct interest in the blossoming rather than the languishing of the *diaconiëen*."[16] This support made eminent sense: if private initiative could nurture and sustain the poor, the public sector did not have to reach out and deliver them from their misery.

The practice of offering and receiving charity, preferably within the sovereign circles of religious congregations, was embedded in Dutch political culture at the local level. Members of a particular parish who were relatively well-off perceived charity as a moral calling and as part of their Christian duty to share resources with less fortunate fellow believers. Hence, questions of material inequality were woven into the spiritual tapestry of church congregations. Municipal governments, meanwhile, supported many public institutions for orphans, the handicapped, and the elderly, and they also embraced, as much as possible, down-and-out residents who had no formal religious affiliation. As a result, issues of social justice were enmeshed, too, in the cultural fabric of the nation's urban communities, albeit in different ways depending on local economic conditions or civic styles.

Within this splintered structure of religious and municipal poor relief, however, resided the nucleus of the advanced welfare state of the future, although it required, to paraphrase De Swaan once more, "a long sizzle" before the "late bang" would be heard.[17] Actual social security legislation was slow in coming, but a radical potential smoldered in the corporatist—and internally "solidarist"—visions of organized Protestantism and Catholicism in the local community. In their passionate confrontations with the state, whether the friction derived from disagreements about the control of charity or, later, about the national treasury's co-equal funding of denominational and public schools, religious "interest groups" gradually transformed themselves into full-fledged denominational political parties. They combined in a jealous protection of their separate spiritual identities and moral cultures against the state's intrusion. The nation's religious factions firmly held to the notion of autonomy within one's own circle, and opposed public funding of social welfare for other than subsidiary purposes.

The confessional *zuilen* (pillars) favored both the idea and practice of self-sufficiency in the administration of social insurance, as their precursors in the early nineteenth century had valiantly defended the financial autonomy of the *diaconiëen*. The *zuilen* also continued to foster social generosity and they objected vehemently to the liberals' emphasis on arid economic incentives alone. Such a focus on purely materialistic motives implied that religious faith and its moral injunctions went unheeded. In addition, the religious political parties embraced the notion of a necessary and "just" wage that would be capable of sustaining a family even in times of adversity. In this conception, social welfare was increasingly linked to definitions of a reasonable level of wages rather than the alleviation of poverty. Thus the Disability Act of 1901 already paid the impressive amount of 70 percent of the applicable wage, a level of compensation that was unique in Europe at the turn of the century.[18]

The desecularization of the 1960s, however, undermined both the coherence and viability of a *Weltanschauung* based primarily on religious affiliation. Hence, the fragmented notions of community, grounded in the anxious defense of the sovereignty of each separate religious circle, gradually gave way to a burgeoning sense of collective national identity. Dutch political parties based on religious solidarity disintegrated and many of the more social-democratically oriented constituents of either the Protestant or Catholic political camp migrated and landed in the Dutch Labor Party. The reconstituted Christian Democratic forces, at the same time, embarked on a political course of shepherding through Parliament an agenda that would extend the social benefits of membership in a moral community, previously reserved for co-religionists only, to the entire community of the Dutch nation.

In sum, since the early 1960s political and cultural citizenship in the nation at large, irrespective of individuals' status or creed, began to confer the same kinds of entitlements and civic duties upon each and every citizen that used to be confined only to fellow believers within autonomous religious circles.[19] As a result, the corporatist inheritance of the confessional parties fused with the progressive social demands of the Labor Party, and their combined efforts propelled the Dutch nation with a hop, skip, and jump into one of the most elaborate welfare states of our contemporary era.

Notes

1. Samuel Senior Coronel, *De gezondheidsleer toegepast op de fabrieksnijverheid* (Haarlem: De Erven Loosjes, 1861), p. 5.

2. André Gueslin, ''l'Invention des caisses d'épargne en France: une grande utopie libérale,'' *Revue Historique*, 572 (September/December 1988), pp. 392–98.

3. Henri Hatzfeld, *Du paupérisme à la sécurité sociale* (Paris: Armand Colin, 1971), p. 321.

4. Emile Ollivier, *Commentaire sur la loi du 15 Mai 1864 sur les coalitions* (Paris: 1864), quoted by Pierre Rosanvallon, *l'Etat en France de 1789 à nos jours* (Paris: Editions du Seuil, 1990), p. 169.

5. The classic exposition of *solidarisme* is Léon Bourgeois, *La politique et la prévoyance sociale* (Paris: Charpentier, 1919). See also, among others, Celestin Bouglé, *Le solidarisme* (Paris: Giard et Brière, 1907); Jacques Donzelot, in *l'Invention du social. Essai sur le déclin des passions politiques* (Paris: Fayard, 1984), devotes a chapter entitled ''The Invention of Solidarity'' to the emergence of *solidarisme* as a political ideology, pp. 73–120. For an intellectual historian's analysis, see J.E.S. Hayward, ''Solidarity: The Social History of an Idea in Nineteenth-Century France,'' *International Review of Social History*, 2, No. 2 (1959), pp. 262–286, and ''The Official Social Philosophy of the French Third Republic: Léon Bourgeois and Solidarism,'' *International Review of Social History*, 4, No. 1 (1961), pp. 24–44.

6. Charles Brunot, ''Solidarité et charité,'' *Revue politique et parlémentaire* (June, 1901), p. 530, quoted by John H. Weiss, ''Origins of the Welfare State: Poor Relief in the Third Republic, 1871–1914,'' *French Historical Studies*, 13, No. 2 (1983), p. 59.

7. Rosanvallon, *l'Etat en France*, pp. 174–76. Although a law in 1893 had stipulated free medical care to indigents, and the law of 1905 provided for public assistance to the incurably sick, the handicapped, and the elderly, they normalized and codified public assistance policies already in force; they did not, however, establish a new positive social right.

8. Peter Flora and Arnold J. Heidenheimer, *The Development of Welfare States in Europe and America* (New Brunswick, N.J.: Transaction Books, 1981), p. 319.

9. Goran Therborn, ''Pillarization and Popular Movements. Two Variants of Welfare State Capitalism: the Netherlands and Sweden,'' in Francis G. Casles, ed., *The Comparative History of Public Policy* (New York: Oxford University Press, 1989), p. 193.

10. L. Frank van Loo, ''*Den arme gegeven...*'' *Een beschrijving van armoede, armenzorg en social zekerheid in Nederland, 1784–1965* (Amsterdam: Boom/Meppel, 1981), p. 58.

11. For a thoughtful analysis, see Loes van der Valk, *Van pauperzorg tot bestaanszekerheid. Een onderzoek naar de ontwikkeling van de armenzorg in Nederland tegen de achtergrond van de overgang naar de algemene bijstandswet, 1912–1965* (Amsterdam: Internationaal Instituut voor Sociale Gescheidenis, 1986).

12. Piet de Rooy, *Werklozenzorg en werkloosheidsbestrijding, 1917–1940. Landelijk en Amsterdams beleid* (Amsterdam: Van Gennep, 1979), p. 13.

13. Th.A. Wouters, *Van bedeling naar verheffing. Evolutie van de houding tegenover de behoeftige mens te 's Hertogenbosch, 1854–1912* (Tilburg: Stichting Zuidelijk Historisch Contact, 1968), p. 12.

14. Therborn, ''Pillarization and Popular Movements,'' pp. 192–193. See also Peter Flora, *State, Economy, and Society in Western Europe, 1815–1975*, 2 vols. (Frankfurt: Campus Verlag, 1987), 2, Appendix, National Tables. Public social expenditure as a percentage of annual gross domestic product in the Netherlands in 1980 was 40.2 percent, and 43 percent of GDP in 1982, although overall transfer payments declined to 27 percent in 1986.

15. Abram de Swaan, *In Care of the State. Health Care, Education, and Welfare in Europe and the USA in the Modern Era* (Oxford: Basil Blackwell/Polity Press, 1988), p. 210.

16. Minister of the Interior Schimmelpenninck van der Oijen to the Provincial Estates of Groningen, November 19, 1845, in A.J.C. Ruter, ed., *Rapporten van de Gouverneurs in de Provinciën, 1840–1849* (Utrecht: Kemink en Zoon, 1950), 3, ''Periodieke rapporten, 1844, 1845,'' p. 530.

17. De Swaan, *In Care of the State*, p. 210.

18. Therborn, ''Pillarization and Popular Movements,'' pp. 212–13.

19. For a recent discussion about the origins of the modern Dutch welfare state and its eventual reconfiguration, see Trudie Knijn, ''Fish without Bikes: Revision of the Dutch Welfare State and its Consequences for the (In)dependence of Single Mothers,'' *Social Politics. International Studies in Gender, State & Society*, 1, No. 1 (Spring 1994), pp. 83–105.

Index

About the Author

Frances Gouda is an independent historian living in Washington, D.C. She received her Ph.D from the University of Washington in Seattle in 1981. She has taught in the History Department of both Wellesley College and the American University, and has written a variety of articles about crime and prostitution in nineteenth-century France and the Netherlands and the Dutch colonial history of Indonesia. In recent years she has received fellowships from the Woodrow Wilson International Center for Scholars, the American Council of Learned Societies, and the Harry Frank Guggenheim Foundation to complete a book entitled *Dutchness in Diaspora: Essays on the History and Colonial Culture of the Dutch East Indies, 1900–1942*.